OLD ST. PAUL'S

ISBN 978-1-4067-9506-6

The river presented a most extraordinary scene.

     Page 568

LIBRARY OF CLASSICS

OLD ST. PAUL'S

by

W. H. AINSWORTH

CONTENTS

BOOK THE FIRST

BOOK THE SECOND

Book the First

APRIL, 1665

CHAPTER I

The Grocer of Wood-street and his Family

ONE night, at the latter end of April, 1665, the family of a citizen of London carrying on an extensive business as a grocer in Wood-street, Cheapside, were assembled, according to custom, at prayer. The grocer's name was Stephen Bloundel. His family consisted of his wife, three sons, and two daughters. He had, moreover, an apprentice; an elderly female serving as cook; her son, a young man about five-and-twenty, filling the place of porter to the shop and general assistant; and a kitchen-maid. The whole household attended; for the worthy grocer, being a strict observer of his religious duties, as well as a rigid disciplinarian in other respects, suffered no one to be absent, on any plea whatever, except indisposition, from morning and evening devotions; and these were always performed at stated times. In fact, the establishment was conducted with the regularity of clock-work, it being the aim of its master not to pass a single hour of the day unprofitably.

The ordinary prayers gone through, Stephen Bloundel offered up a long and fervent supplication to the Most High for protection against the devouring pestilence with which the city was then scourged. He acknowledged that this terrible visitation had been justly brought upon it by the wickedness of its inhabitants; that they deserved their doom, dreadful though it was; that, like the dwellers in Jerusalem before it was given up to ruin and desolation, they " had mocked the messengers of God and despised his word; " that, in the language of the prophet, " they had refused to hearken, and pulled away the shoulder, and stopped their ears that they should not hear; yea,

9

had made their heart like an adamant stone, lest they should hear the law and the words which the Lord of Hosts had sent in his spirit by the former prophets." He admitted that great sins require great chastisement, and that the sins of London were enormous; that it was filled with strifes, seditions, heresies, murders, drunkenness, revellings, and every kind of abomination; that the ordinances of God were neglected, and all manner of vice openly practised; that, despite repeated warnings and afflictions less grievous than the present, these vicious practices had been persisted in. All this he humbly acknowledged. But he implored a gracious Providence, in consideration of his few faithful servants, to spare the others yet a little longer, and give them a last chance of repentance and amendment; or, if this could not be, and their utter extirpation was inevitable, that the habitations of the devout might be exempted from the general destruction—might be places of refuge, as Zoar was to Lot. He concluded by earnestly exhorting those around him to keep constant watch upon themselves; not to murmur at God's dealings and dispensations; but so to comport themselves, that " they might be able to stand in the day of wrath, in the day of death, and in the day of judgment." The exhortation produced a powerful effect upon its hearers, and they arose, some with serious, others with terrified looks.

Before proceeding further, it may be desirable to show in what manner the dreadful pestilence referred to by the grocer commenced, and how far its ravages had already extended. Two years before, namely, in 1663, more than a third of the population of Amsterdam was carried off by a desolating plague. Hamburg was also grievously afflicted about the same time, and in the same manner. Notwithstanding every effort to cut off communication with these states, the insidious disease found its way into England by means of some bales of merchandise, as it was suspected, at the latter end of the year 1664, when two persons died suddenly, with undoubted symptoms of the distemper, in Westminster. Its next appearance was in a house in Long Acre, and its victims two Frenchmen, who had brought goods from the Levant. Smothered for a short time, like a fire upon which coals had been heaped, it broke out with fresh fury in several places.

The consternation now began. The whole city was panic-stricken; nothing was talked of but the plague— nothing planned but means of arresting its progress— one grim and ghastly idea possessed the minds of all. Like a hideous phantom stalking the streets at noon-day, and scaring all in its path, Death took its course through London, and selected its prey at pleasure. The alarm was further increased by the predictions confidently made as to the vast numbers who would be swept away by the visitation; by the prognostications of astrologers; by the prophesyings of enthusiasts; by the denunciations of preachers, and by the portents and prodigies reported to have occurred. During the long and frosty winter pre- ceding this fatal year, a comet appeared in the heavens, the sickly colour of which was supposed to forebode the judgment about to follow. Blazing stars and other meteors, of a lurid hue and strange and preternatural shape, were likewise seen. The sun was said to have set in streams of blood, and the moon to have shone without reflecting a shadow; grisly shapes appeared at night— strange clamours and groans were heard in the air— hearses, coffins, and heaps of unburied dead were dis- covered in the sky, and great cakes and clots of blood were found in the Tower moat; while a marvellous double tide occurred at London Bridge. All these prodigies were currently reported, and in most cases believed.

The severe frost, before noticed, did not break up till the end of February, and with the thaw the plague fright- fully increased in violence. From Drury-lane it spread along Holborn, eastward as far as Great Turnstile, and westward to St. Giles's Pound, and so along the Tyburn- road. St. Andrew's, Holborn, was next infected; and as this was a much more populous parish than the former, the deaths were more numerous within it. For a while, the disease was checked by Fleet Ditch; it then leaped this narrow boundary, and, ascending the opposite hill, carried fearful devastation into St. James's, Clerkenwell. At the same time, it attacked Saint Bride's; thinned the ranks of the thievish horde haunting Whitefriars, and proceeding in a westerly course, decimated Saint Clement Danes.

Hitherto, the city had escaped. The destroyer had not passed Ludgate or Newgate, but environed the walls like a besieging enemy. A few days, however, before the opening of this history, fine weather having commenced, the horrible disease began to grow more rife, and, laughing all precautions and impediments to scorn, broke out in the very heart of the stronghold—namely, in Bearbinder-lane, near Stocks' Market, where nine persons died.

At a season so awful, it may be imagined how an impressive address, like that delivered by the grocer, would be received by those who saw in the pestilence, not merely an overwhelming scourge from which few could escape, but a direct manifestation of the Divine displeasure. Not a word was said. Blaize Shotterel, the porter, and old Josyna, his mother, together with Patience, the other woman-servant, betook themselves silently, and with troubled countenances, to the kitchen. Leonard Holt, the apprentice, lingered for a moment to catch a glance from the soft blue eyes of Amabel, the grocer's eldest daughter (for even the plague was a secondary consideration with him when she was present), and failing in the attempt, he heaved a deep sigh, which was luckily laid to the account of the discourse he had just listened to by his sharp-sighted master, and proceeded to the shop, where he busied himself in arranging matters for the night.

Having just completed his twenty-first year, and his apprenticeship being within a few months of its expiration, Leonard Holt began to think of returning to his native town of Manchester, where he intended to settle, and where he had once fondly hoped the fair Amabel would accompany him, in the character of his bride. Not that he had ever ventured to declare his passion, nor that he had received sufficient encouragement to make it matter of certainty that if he did so declare himself, he should be accepted; but being both " proper and tall," and having tolerable confidence in his good looks, he had made himself, up to a short time prior to his introduction to the reader, quite easy on the point.

His present misgivings were occasioned by Amabel's altered manner towards him, and by a rival who, he had reason to fear, had completely superseded him in her good graces. Brought up together from an early age, the grocer's daughter and the young apprentice had at first regarded each other as brother and sister. By degrees, the feeling changed; Amabel became more reserved, and held little intercourse with Leonard, who, busied with his own concerns, thought little about her. But, as he grew towards manhood, he could not remain insensible to her extraordinary beauty—for extraordinary it was, and such as to attract admiration wherever she went, so that "the Grocer's Daughter" became the toast among the ruffling gallants of the town, many of whom sought to obtain speech with her. Her parents, however, were far too careful to permit any such approach. Amabel's stature was lofty; her limbs slight, but exquisitely symmetrical; her features small, and cast in the most delicate mould; her eyes of the softest blue; and her hair luxuriant, and of the finest texture and richest brown. Her other beauties must be left to the imagination; but it ought not to be omitted that she was barely eighteen, and had all the freshness, the innocence, and vivacity of that most charming period of woman's existence. No wonder she ravished every heart. No wonder in an age when love-making was more general even than now, that she was beset by admirers. No wonder her father's apprentice became desperately enamoured of her, and proportionately jealous.

And this brings us to his rival. On the 10th of April, two gallants, both richly attired, and both young and handsome, dismounted before the grocer's door, and, leaving their steeds to the care of their attendants, entered the shop. They made sundry purchases of conserves, figs, and other dried fruit, chatted familiarly with the grocer, and tarried so long that at last he began to suspect they must have some motive. All at once, however, they disagreed on some slight matter—Bloundel could not tell what, nor, perhaps, could the disputants, even if their quarrel was not preconcerted—high words arose, and in another moment, swords were drawn, and furious passes exchanged. The grocer called to his eldest son, a stout youth of nineteen, and to Leonard Holt, to separate them. The apprentice seized his cudgel—no apprentice in those days was without one—and rushed towards the combatants, but before he could interfere, the fray was ended. One of them had received a thrust through the sword arm, and his blade dropping, his antagonist declared himself satisfied, and with a grave salute walked off. The wounded man wrapped a lace handkerchief round his arm, but immediately afterwards complained of great faintness. Pitying his condition, and suspecting no harm, the grocer led him into the inner room, where restoratives were offered by Mrs. Bloundel and her daughter Amabel, both of whom had been alarmed by the noise of the conflict. In a short time, the wounded man was so far recovered as to be able to converse with his assistants, especially the younger one; and the grocer having returned to the shop, his discourse became so very animated and tender, that Mrs. Bloundel deemed it prudent to give her daughter a hint to retire. Amabel reluctantly obeyed, for the young stranger was so handsome, so richly dressed, had such a captivating manner, and so distinguished an air, that she was strongly prepossessed in his favour. A second look from her mother, however, caused her to disappear, nor did she return. After waiting with suppressed anxiety for some time, the young gallant departed, overwhelming the good dame with his thanks, and entreating permission to call again. This was peremptorily refused, but, notwithstanding the interdiction, he came on the following day. The grocer chanced to be out at the time, and the gallant, who had probably watched him go forth, deriding the remonstrances of the younger Bloundel and Leonard, marched straight to the inner room, where he found the dame and her daughter. They were much disconcerted at his appearance, and the latter instantly rose with the intention of retiring, but the gallant caught her arm and detained her.

" Do not fly me, Amabel," he cried, in an impassioned tone, " but suffer me to declare the love I have for you. I cannot live without you."

Amabel, whose neck and cheeks were crimsoned with blushes, cast down her eyes before the ardent regards of the gallant, and endeavoured to withdraw her hand.

" One word only," he continued. " and I release you. Am I wholly indifferent to you? Answer me,—yes, or no?"

" Do *not* answer him, Amabel," interposed her mother. " He is deceiving you. He loves you not. He would ruin you. This is the way with all these court butterflies. Tell him you hate him, child, and bid him begone."

" But I cannot tell him an untruth, mother," returned Amabel, artlessly, " for I do *not* hate him."

" Then you love me," cried the young man, falling on his knees, and pressing her hand to his lips. " Tell me so, and make me the happiest of men."

But Amabel had now recovered from the confusion into which she had been thrown, and, alarmed at her own indiscretion, forcibly withdrew her hand, exclaiming in a cold tone, and with much natural dignity, " Arise, sir. I will not tolerate these freedoms. My mother is right— you have some ill design."

" By my soul, no!" cried the gallant, passionately. " I love you, and would make you mine."

" No doubt," remarked Mrs. Bloundel, contemptuously, " but not by marriage."

" Yes, by marriage," rejoined the gallant, rising. " If she will consent, I will wed her forthwith."

Both Amabel and her mother looked surprised at the young man's declaration, which was uttered with a fervour that seemed to leave no doubt of its sincerity; but the latter, fearing some artifice, replied, " If what you say is true, and you really love my daughter as much as you pretend, this is not the way to win her; for though she can have no pretension to wed with one of your seeming degree, nor is it for her happiness that she should, yet, were she sought by the proudest noble in the land, she shall never, if I can help it, be lightly won. If your intentions are honourable, you must address yourself, in the first place, to her father, and if he agrees (which I much doubt) that you shall become her suitor, I can make no objection. Till this is settled, I must pray you to desist from further importunity."

" And so must I," added Amabel. " I cannot give you a hope till you have spoken to my father."

" Be it so," replied the gallant. " I will tarry here till his return." So saying, he was about to seat himself, but Mrs. Bloundel prevented him.

" I cannot permit this, sir," she cried. " Your tarrying here may, for aught I know, bring scandal upon my house;—I am sure it will be disagreeable to my husband. I am unacquainted with your name and condition. You may be a man of rank. You may be one of the profligate and profane crew who haunt the court. You may be the worst of them all, my Lord Rochester himself. He is about your age, I have heard, and though a mere boy in years, is a veteran in libertinism. But, whoever you are, and whatever your rank and station may be, unless your character will bear the strictest scrutiny, I am certain Stephen Bloundel will never consent to your union with his daughter."

" Nay, mother," observed Amabel, " you judge the gentleman unjustly. I am sure he is neither a profligate gallant himself nor a companion of such—especially of the wicked Earl of Rochester."

" I pretend to be no better than I am," replied the young man, repressing a smile that rose to his lips at Mrs. Bloundel's address; " but I shall reform when I am married. It would be impossible to be inconstant to so fair a creature as Amabel. For my rank, I have none. My condition is that of a private gentelman—my name, Maurice Wyvil."

" What you say of yourself, Mr. Maurice Wyvil, convinces me you will meet with a decided refusal from my husband," returned Mrs. Bloundel.

" I trust not," replied Wyvil, glancing tenderly at Amabel. " If I should be so fortunate as to gain *his* consent, have I *yours* ? "

"It is too soon to ask that question," she rejoined, blushing deeply. "And now, sir, you must go, indeed you must. You distress my mother."

"If I do not distress *you*, I will stay," resumed Wyvil, with an imploring look.

"You *do* distress me," she answered, averting her gaze.

"Nay, then, I must tear myself away," he rejoined. "I shall return shortly, and trust to find your father less flinty-hearted than he is represented."

He would have clasped Amabel in his arms, and perhaps snatched a kiss, if her mother had not rushed between them.

"No more familiarities, sir," she cried, angrily; "no court manners here. If you look to wed my daughter, you must conduct yourself more decorously; but I can tell you, you have no chance—none whatever."

"Time will show," replied Wyvil, audaciously. "You had better give her to me quietly, and save me the trouble of carrying her off,—for have her I will."

"Mercy on us!" cried Mrs. Bloundel, in accents of alarm; "now his wicked intentions are out."

"Fear nothing, mother," observed Amabel, coldly. "He will scarcely carry me off without my own consent; and I am not likely to sacrifice myself for one who holds me in such light esteem."

"Forgive me, Amabel," rejoined Wyvil, in a voice so penitent that it instantly effaced her displeasure; "I meant not to offend. I spoke only the language of distraction. Do not dismiss me thus, or my death will lie at your door."

"I should be sorry for that," she replied; "but inexperienced as I am, I feel this is not the language of real regard, but of furious passion."

A dark shade passed over Wyvil's handsome features, and the almost feminine beauty by which they were characterised, gave place to a fierce and forbidding expression. Controlling himself by a powerful effort, he replied, with forced calmness, "Amabel, you know not what it is to love. I will not stir hence till I have seen your father."

"We will see that, sir," exclaimed Mrs. Bloundel, angrily. "What, ho! son Stephen! Leonard Holt! I say. This gentleman *will* stay here, whether I like or not. Show him forth."

"That I will, right willingly," replied the apprentice, rushing before the younger Bloundel, and flourishing his formidable cudgel. "Out with you, sir! Out with you!"

"Not at your bidding, you saucy knave," rejoined Wyvil, laying his hand upon his sword; "and if it were not for the presence of your mistress and her lovely daughter, I would crop your ears for your insolence."

"Their presence shall not prevent me from making my cudgel and your shoulders acquainted, if you do not budge," replied the apprentice, sturdily.

Enraged by the retort, Wyvil would have drawn his sword, but a blow on the arm disabled him.

"Plague on you, fellow!" he exclaimed; "you shall rue this to the last day of your existence."

"Threaten those who heed you," replied Leonard, about to repeat the blow.

"Do him no further injury!" cried Amabel, arresting his hand, and looking with the greatest commiseration at Wyvil. "You have dealt with him far too rudely already."

"Since I have your sympathy, sweet Amabel," rejoined Wyvil, "I care not what rude treatment I experience from this churl. We shall soon meet again." And bowing to her, he strode out of the room.

Leonard followed him to the shop-door, hoping some further pretext for quarrel would arise, but he was disappointed. Wyvil took no notice of him, and proceeded at a slow pace towards Cheapside.

Half an hour afterwards, Stephen Bloundel came home. On being informed of what had occurred, he was greatly annoyed, though he concealed his vexation, and highly applauded his daughter's conduct. Without further comment, he proceeded about his business, and remained in the shop till it was closed. Wyvil did not return, and the grocer tried to persuade himself they should see nothing more of him. Before Amabel retired to rest, he imprinted a kiss on her snowy brow, and said, in a tone of the utmost kindness, " You have never yet deceived me, child, and I hope never will. Tell me truly, do you take any interest in this young gallant ? "

Amabel blushed deeply.

" I should not speak the truth, father," she rejoined, after a pause, " if I were to say I do not."

" I am sorry for it," replied Bloundel, gravely. " But you would not be happy with him. I am sure he is unprincipled and profligate :—you must forget him."

" I will try to do so," sighed Amabel. And the conversation dropped.

On the following day, Maurice Wyvil entered the grocer's shop. He was more richly attired than before, and there was a haughtiness in his manner which he had not hitherto assumed. What passed between him and Bloundel was not known, for the latter never spoke of it; but the result may be gathered from the fact that the young gallant was not allowed an interview with the grocer's daughter.

From this moment the change previously noticed took place in Amabel's demeanour towards Leonard. She seemed scarcely able to endure his presence, and sedulously avoided his regards. From being habitually gay and cheerful, she became pensive and reserved. Her mother more than once caught her in tears; and it was evident, from many other signs, that Wyvil completely engrossed her thoughts. Fully aware of this, Mrs. Bloundel said nothing of it to her husband, because the subject was painful to him; and not supposing the passion deeply rooted, she hoped it would speedily wear away. But she was mistaken—the flame was kept alive in Amabel's breast in a manner of which she was totally ignorant. Wyvil found means to deceive the vigilance of the grocer and his wife, but he could not deceive the vigilance of a jealous lover. Leonard discovered that his mistress had received a letter. He would not betray her, but he determined to watch her narrowly.

Accordingly, when she went forth one morning in company with her younger sister (a little girl of some five years old), he made an excuse to follow them, and, keeping within sight, perceived them enter St. Paul's Cathedral, the mid aisle of which was then converted into a public walk, and generally thronged with town gallants, bullies, bona-robas, cut-purses, and rogues of every description. In short, it was the haunt of the worst of characters of the metropolis. When, therefore, Amabel entered this structure, Leonard felt certain it was to meet her lover. Rushing forward he saw her take her course through the crowd, and attract general attention from her loveliness—but he nowhere discerned Maurice Wyvil.

Suddenly, however, she struck off to the right, and halted near one of the pillars, and the apprentice, advancing, detected his rival behind it. He was whispering a few words in her ear, unperceived by her sister. Maddened by the sight, Leonard hurried towards them, but before he could reach the spot Wyvil was gone, and Amabel, though greatly confused, looked at the same time so indignant, that he almost regretted his precipitation.

"You will, of course, make known to my father what you have just seen?" she said, in a low tone.

"If you will promise not to meet that gallant again without my knowledge, I will not," replied Leonard.

After a moment's reflection, Amabel gave the required promise, and they returned to Wood-street together. Satisfied she would not beak her word, the apprentice became more easy, and as a week elapsed, and nothing was said to him on the subject, he persuaded himself she would not attempt to meet her lover again.

Things were in this state at the opening of our tale, but upon the night in question, Leonard fancied he discerned some agitation in Amabel's manner towards him, and in consequence of this notion, he sought to meet her gaze, as before related, after prayers. While trying to distract his thoughts by arranging sundry firkins of butter, and putting other things in order, he heard a light footstep behind him, and turning at the sound, beheld Amabel.

"Leonard," she whispered, "I promised to tell you

when I should next meet Maurice Wyvil. He will be here to-night." And without giving him time to answer, she retired.

For awhile, Leonard remained in a state almost of stupefaction, repeating to himself, as if unwilling to believe them, the words he had just heard. He had not recovered when the grocer entered the shop, and noticing his haggard looks, kindly inquired if he felt unwell. The apprentice returned an evasive answer, and half determined to relate all he knew to his master; but the next moment he changed his intention, and, influenced by that chivalric feeling which always governs those, of whatever conditions, who love profoundly, resolved not to betray the thoughtless girl, but to trust to his own ingenuity to thwart the designs of his rival, and preserve her. Acting upon this resolution, he said he had a slight headache, and instantly resumed his occupation.

At nine o'clock the whole family assembled at supper. The board was plentifully though plainly spread, but the grocer observed, with some uneasiness, that his apprentice, who had a good appetite in ordinary, ate little or nothing. He kept his eye constantly upon him, and became convinced from his manner that something ailed him. Not having any notion of the truth, and being filled with apprehensions of the plague, his dread was that Leonard was infected by the disease. Supper was generally the pleasantest meal of the day at the grocer's house, but on this occasion it passed off cheerlessly enough, and a circumstance occurred at its close which threw all into confusion and distress. Before relating this, however, we must complete our description of the family under their present aspect.

Tall, and of a spare frame, with good features, somewhat austere in their expression, and of the cast which we are apt to term precise and puritanical, but tempered with great benevolence, Stephen Bloundel had a keen deep-seated eye, over-shadowed by thick brows, and suffered his long-flowing gray hair to descend over his shoulders. His forehead was high and ample, his chin square and well-defined, and his general appearance

exceedingly striking. In age he was about fifty. His integrity and fairness of dealing, never once called in
question for a period of thirty years, had won him the
esteem of all who knew him; while his prudence and
economy had enabled him, during that time, to amass a
tolerable fortune. His methodical habits, and strong
religious principles, have been already mentioned. His
eldest son was named after him, and resembled him
both in person and character, promising to tread in his
footsteps. The younger sons require little notice at
present. One was twelve, and the other only half that age ;
but both appeared to inherit many of their father's good
qualities. Basil, the elder, was a stout, well-grown lad,
and had never known a day's ill-health ; while Hubert, the
younger, was thin, delicate, and constantly ailing.

Mrs. Bloundel was a specimen of a city dame of the
best kind. She had a few pardonable vanities, which no
arguments could overcome—such as a little ostentation
in dress—a little pride in the neatness of her house—and
a good deal in the beauty of her children, especially in
that of Amabel—as well as in the wealth and high character of her husband, whom she regarded as the most
perfect of human beings. These slight failings allowed for,
nothing but good remained. Her conduct was exemplary
in all the relations of life. The tenderest of mothers, and
the most affectionate of wives, she had as much genuine
piety and strictness of moral principles as her husband.
Short, plump, and well-proportioned, though somewhat,
perhaps, exceeding the rules of symmetry—she had a
rich olive complexion, fine black eyes, beaming with good
nature, and an ever-laughing mouth, ornamented by a
beautiful set of teeth. To wind up all, she was a few
years younger than her husband.

Amabel has already been described. The youngest
girl, Christiana, was a pretty little, dove-eyed, flaxen
haired child, between four and five years old, and shared
the fate of most younger children, being very much
caressed, and not a little spoiled by her parents.

The foregoing description of the grocer's family would
be incomplete without some mention of his household.

Old Josyna Shotterel, the cook, who had lived with her master ever since his marriage, and had the strongest attachment for him, was a hale, stout dame, of about sixty, with few infirmities for her years, and with less asperity of temper than generally belongs to servants of her class. She was a native of Holland, and came to England early in life, where she married Blaize's father, who died soon after their union. An excellent cook in a plain way—indeed, she had no practice in any other—she would brew strong ale and mead, or mix a sack-posset with any innkeeper in the city. Moreover, she was a careful and tender nurse, if her services were ever required in that capacity. The children looked upon her as a second mother; and her affection for them, which was unbounded, deserved their regard. She was a perfect storehouse of what are termed "old women's receipts;" and there were few complaints (except the plague) for which she did did not think herself qualified to prescribe and able to cure. Her skill in the healing art was often tested by her charitable mistress, who required her to prepare remedies, as well as nourishing broths, for such of the poor of the parish as applied to her for relief at times of sickness.

Her son, Blaize, was a stout, stumpy fellow, about four feet ten, with a head somewhat too large for his body, and extremely long arms. Ever since the plague had broken out in Drury-lane, it haunted him like a spectre, and scattered the few faculties he possessed. In vain he tried to combat his alarm,—in vain his mother endeavoured to laugh him out of it. Nothing would do. He read the bills of mortality daily; ascertained the particulars of every case; dilated upon the agonies of the sufferers; watched the progress of the infection; and calculated the time it would take to reach Wood-street. He talked of the pestilence by day, and dreamed of it at night; and more than once alarmed the house by roaring for assistance, under the idea that he was suddenly attacked. By his mother's advice, he steeped rue, wormwood, and sage in his drink till it was so abominably nauseous that he could scarcely swallow it, and carried a small ball in the hollow of his hand, compounded of wax, angelica, cam-

phor, and other drugs. He likewise chewed a small piece
of Virginian snake-root, or zedoary, if he approached any
place supposed to be infected. A dried toad was suspended
round his neck, as an amulet of sovereign virtue. Every
nostrum sold by the quacks in the streets, tempted him;
and a few days before, he had expended his last crown
in the purchase of a bottle of plague-water. Being of a
superstitious nature, he placed full faith in all the predictions of the astrologers, who foretold that London
should be utterly laid waste, that grass should grow in the
streets, and that the living should not be able to bury the
dead. He quaked at the terrible denunciations of the
preachers, who exhorted their hearers to repentance,
telling them a judgment was at hand, and shuddered at the
wild and fearful prophesying of the insane enthusiasts
who roamed the streets. His nativity having been cast,
and it appearing that he would be in great danger on the
20th of June, he made up his mind that he should die of
the plague on that day. Before he was assailed by these
terrors, he had entertained a sneaking attachment for
Patience, the kitchen-maid, a young and buxom damsel,
who had no especial objection to him. But of late, his
love had given way to apprehension, and his whole
thoughts were centred in one idea, namely, self-preservation.

By this time, supper was over, and the family were
about to separate for the night, when Stephen, the grocer's
eldest son, having risen to quit the room, staggered, and
complained of a strange dizziness and headache, which
almost deprived him of sight, while his heart palpitated
frightfully. A dreadful suspicion seized his father. He
ran towards him, and assisted him to a seat. Scarcely
had the young man reached it, when a violent sickness
seized him; a greenish-coloured froth appeared at the
mouth, and he began to grow delirious. Guided by the
convulsive efforts of the sufferer, Bloundel tore off his
clothes, and, after a moment's search, perceived under the
left arm a livid pustule. He uttered a cry of anguish. His
son was plague-stricken.

CHAPTER II

The Coffin-maker

THE first shock over, the grocer bore the affliction manfully, and like one prepared for it. Exhibiting little outward emotion, though his heart was torn with anguish, and acting with the utmost calmness, he forbade his wife to approach the sufferer, and desired her instantly to retire to her own room with her daughters; and not to leave it on any consideration whatever, without his permission.

Accustomed to regard her husband's word as law, Mrs. Bloundel, for the first time in her life, disputed his authority, and, falling on her knees, besought him, with tears in her eyes, to allow her to nurse her son. But he remained inflexible, and she was forced to comply.

He next gave similar directions to old Josyna respecting his two younger sons, with this difference only, that when they were put to rest, and the door was locked upon them, she was to return to the kitchen and prepare a possetdrink of canary and spirits of sulphur, together with a poultice of mallows, lily-roots, figs, linseed, and palm-oil, for the patient.

These orders given and obeyed, with Leonard Holt's assistance,—for Blaize, who had crept into a corner, in extremity of terror, was wholly incapable of rendering any help,—he conveyed his son to an adjoining room, on the ground floor, where there was a bed, and placing him within it, heaped blankets upon him to promote profuse perspiration, while the apprentice lighted a fire.

Provided with the most efficacious remedies for the distemper, and acquainted with the mode of treating it prescribed by the College of Physicians, Bloundel was at no loss how to act, but, rubbing the part affected with a stimulating ointment, he administered at the same time doses of mithridate, Venice treacle and other potent alexipharmics.

He had soon the satisfaction of perceiving that his

son became somewhat easier; and after swallowing the
posset-drink prepared by old Josyna, who used all the
expedition she could, a moisture broke out upon the
youth's skin, and appeared to relieve him so much, that,
but for the ghastly paleness of his countenance, and the
muddy look of his eye, his father would have indulged a
hope of his recovery.

Up to this time, the grocer had acted for himself, and
felt confident he had acted rightly, but he now deemed
it expedient to call in advice, and, accordingly, commissioned his apprentice to fetch Doctor Hodges, a
physician, residing in Great Knightrider-street, Doctors'
Commons, who had recently acquired considerable reputation for his skilful treatment of those attacked by
the plague, and who (it may be incidentally mentioned)
afterwards gave to the medical world a curious account
of the ravages of the disorder, as well as of his own professional experiences during this terrible period. He
likewise told him—and he could not repress a sigh as
he did so,—to give notice to the Examiner of Health
(there were one or two officers, so designated, appointed
to every parish, at this awful season by the city authorities)
that his house was infected.

While preparing to set out, Leonard again debated
with himself whether he should acquaint his master with
Maurice Wyvil's meditated visit. But conceiving it wholly
impossible that Amabel could leave her mother's room,
even if she were disposed to do so, he determined to let
the affair take its course. On his way to the shop he
entered a small room occupied by Blaize, and found him
seated near a table, with his hands upon his knees, and
his eyes fixed upon the ground, looking the very image
of despair. The atmosphere smelt like that of an apothecary's shop, and was so overpowering, that Leonard could
scarcely breathe. The table was covered with pill-boxes
and phials, most of which were emptied, and a dim light
was afforded by a candle with a most portentous crest of
snuff.

"So you have been poisoning yourself, I perceive,"
observed Leonard, approaching him.

" Keep off ! " cried the porter, springing suddenly to his feet. " Don't touch me, I say. Poisoning myself ! I have taken three rufuses, or pestilential pills; two spoonfuls of alexiteral water; the same quantity of anti-pestilential decoction; half as much of Sir Theodore Mayerne's electuary; and a large dose of orvietan. Do you call that poisoning myself ? *I* call it taking proper precaution, and would recommend you to do the same. Besides this I have sprinkled myself with vinegar, fumi-gated my clothes, and rubbed my nose, inside and out, till it smarted so intolerably, I was obliged to desist, with balsam of sulphur."

" Well, well, if you don't escape the plague, it won't be your fault," returned Leonard, scarcely able to refrain from laughing. " But I have something to tell you before I go."

" What is the matter ? " demanded Blaize, in alarm. " Where,—where are you going ? "

" To fetch the doctor," replied Leonard.

" Is Master Stephen worse ? " rejoined the porter.

" On the contrary, I hope he is better," replied Leonard. " I shall be back, directly, but as I have to give notice to the Examiner of Health that the house is infected, I may be detained a few minutes longer than I anticipate. Keep the street-door locked; I will fasten the yard-gate, and do not for your life let any one in, except Dr. Hodges, till I return. Do you hear ?—do you understand what I say ? "

" Yes, I hear plain enough," groaned Blaize. " You say that the house is infected, and that we shall all be locked up."

" Dolt ! " exclaimed the apprentice, " I said no such thing." And he repeated his injunctions, but Blaize was too much terrified to comprehend them. At last, losing all patience, Leonard cried, in a menacing tone, " If you do not attend to me, I will cudgel you within an inch of your life, and you will find the thrashing harder to bear even than the plague itself. Rouse yourself, fool ! and follow me."

Accompanied by the porter, he hurried to the yard-

gate, saw it bolted within-side, and then returned to the
shop, where, having found his cap and cudgel, he directed
Blaize to lock the door after him, cautioning him, for the
third time, not to admit any one except the doctor. " If
I find, on my return, that you have neglected my injunctions," he concluded, " as sure as I now stand before
you, I'll break every bone in your body."

Blaize promised obedience, adding, in a supplicating
tone, " Leonard, if I were you, I would not go to the
Examiner of Health. Poor Stephen may not have the
plague, after all. It's a dreadful thing to be imprisoned
for a month, for that's the time appointed by the Lord
Mayor. Only a week ago I passed several houses in
Holborn, shut up on account of the plague, with a watchman at the door, and I never shall forget the melancholy
faces I saw at the windows. It was a dreadful spectacle,
and has haunted me ever since."

" It cannot be helped," rejoined Leonard, with a sigh.
" If we disobey the Lord Mayor's orders, and neglect
giving information, we shall all be sent to Newgate,
while poor Stephen will be taken to the pest-house. Besides, the searchers will be here before morning. They
are sure to learn what has happened from Doctor Hodges."

" True, true," replied Blaize; " I had forgotten that.
Let me go with you, dear Leonard. I dare not remain
here longer."

" What! would you leave your kind, good master, at
a time like this, when he most needs your services? "
rejoined Leonard, reproachfully. " Out, cowardly hound !
I am ashamed of you. Shake off your fears, and be a
man. You can but die once; and what matters it whether
you die of the plague or the cholic ? "

" It matters a great deal," replied Blaize. " I am
afraid of nothing but the plague. I am sure I shall be
its next victim in this house. But you are right—I cannot
desert my kind master, nor my old mother. Farewell,
Leonard. Perhaps we may never meet again. I may be
dead before you come back—I feel very ill already."

" No wonder, after all the stuff you have swallowed,"
returned Leonard; " but pluck up your courage, or you

will bring on the very thing you are anxious to avoid. As many people have died from fear as from any other cause.—One word before I go. If any one should get into the house by scaling the yard-wall, or through the window, instantly alarm our master."

" Certainly," returned Blaize, with a look of surprise. " But do you expect any one to enter the house in that way ? "

" Ask no questions, but do as I bid you," rejoined Leonard, opening the door, and about to go forth.

" Stop a moment," cried Blaize, detaining him, and drawing from his pocket a handful of simples. " Won't you take some of these with you to guard against infection ? There's wormwood, woodsorrel, masterwort, zedoary, and angelica; and, lastly, there's a little bottle of the sovereign preservative against the plague, as prepared by the great Lord Bacon, and approved by Queen Elizabeth. Won't you take *that* ?

" I have no fear," replied Leonard, shutting the door in his face. And as he lingered for a moment while it was locked, he heard Blaize say to himself, " I must go and take three more rufuses and a large dose of diascordium."

It was a bright moonlight night, and as the apprentice turned to depart, he perceived a figure hastily retreating on the other side of the way. Making sure it was Maurice Wyvil, though he could not distinguish the garb of the person—that side of the street being in shade,—and stung by jealousy, he immediately started in pursuit. The fugitive struck down Lad-lane, and ran on till he came to the end of Lawrence-lane, where, finding himself closely pressed, he suddenly halted, and pulling his hat over his brows to conceal his features, fiercely confronted his pursuer.

" Why do you follow me thus, rascal ? " he cried, drawing his sword. " Would you rob me ? Begone, or I will call the watch."

" It *is* his voice ! " cried the apprentice. " I have news for you, Mr. Maurice Wyvil. You will not see Amabel to-night. The plague is in her father's house."

" The plague ! " exclaimed Wyvil, in an altered tone,

and dropping the point of his sword. " Is she smitten by
it ? "

The apprentice answered by a bitter laugh, and without
tarrying longer to enjoy his rival's distress, set off towards
Cheapside. Before reaching the end of Lawrence-lane,
however, he half-repented his conduct, and halted to see
whether Wyvil was following him; but as he could perceive nothing of him, he continued his course.

Entering Cheapside, he observed, to his surprise, a
crowd of persons collected near the Cross, then standing
a little to the east of Wood-street. This cross, which
was of great antiquity, and had undergone many mutila-
tions and alterations since its erection in 1486, when it
boasted, amongst other embellishments, images of the
Virgin and Saint Edward the Confessor, was still not
without some pretensions to architectural beauty. In
form it was hexagonal, and composed of three tiers,
rising from one another like the divisions of a telescope,
each angle being supported by a pillar surmounted by a
statue, while the intervening niches were filled up with
sculptures, intended to represent some of the sovereigns
of England. The structure was of considerable height,
and crowned by a large gilt cross. Its base was protected by a strong wooden railing. About a hundred
yards to the east, there stood a smaller hexagonal tower,
likewise ornamented with carvings, and having a figure on
its conical summit blowing a horn. This was the Conduit.
Midway between these buildings the crowd alluded to
above was collected.

As Leonard drew near, he found the assemblage was
listening to the exhortations of an enthusiast, whom he
instantly recognised from a description he had heard of
him from Blaize. The name of this half-crazed being was
Solomon Eagle. Originally a quaker, upon the outbreak
of the plague he had abandoned his home and friends,
and roamed the streets at night, denouncing doom to the
city. He was a tall gaunt man, with long jet-black hair
hanging in disordered masses over his shoulders. His
eyes were large and black, and blazed with insane lustre,
and his looks were so wild and terrific, that it required no

great stretch of imagination to convert him into the genius of the pestilence. Entirely stripped of apparel, except that his loins were girt with a sheep-skin, in imitation of Saint John in the Wilderness, he bore upon his head a brazier of flaming coals, the lurid light of which falling upon his sable locks and tawny skin, gave him an unearthly appearance.

Impelled by curiosity, Leonard paused for a moment to listen, and heard him thunder forth the following denunciation :—" And now, therefore, as the prophet Jeremiah saith, ' I have this day declared it to you, but ye have not obeyed the voice of the Lord your God, nor anything for the which he hath sent me unto you. Now, therefore, know certainly that ye shall die by the sword, by the famine, and by the pestilence.' Again, in the words of the prophet Amos, the Lord saith unto you by my mouth, ' I have sent among you the pestilence after the manner of Egypt, yet have you not returned unto me. Therefore, will I do this unto thee, O Israel ; and because I will do this unto three, prepare to meet thy God ! ' Do you hear this, O sinners ? God will proceed against you in the day of his wrath, though he hath borne with you in the day of his patience ? O how many hundred years hath he spared this city, notwithstanding its great provocations and wickedness ! But now he will no longer show it pity, but will pour out his wrath upon it ! Plagues shall come upon it, and desolation ; and it shall be utterly burnt with fire,—for strong is the Lord who judgeth it ! "

His address concluded, the enthusiast started off at a swift pace, shrieking, in a voice that caused many persons to throw open their windows to listen to him, " Awake ! sinners, awake !—the plague is at your doors !—the grave yawns for you !—awake, and repent ! " And followed by the crowd, many of whom kept up with him, he ran on vociferating in this manner till he was out of hearing.

Hurrying forward in the opposite direction, Leonard glanced at the ancient and picturesque houses on either side of the way—now bathed in the moonlight, and apparently hushed in repose and security,—and he could not repress a shudder as he reflected that an evil angel

was, indeed, abroad, who might suddenly arouse their
slumbering inmates to despair and death. His thoughts
took another turn as he entered the precincts of Saint
Paul's and surveyed the venerable and majestic fabric
before him. His eyes rested upon its innumerable
crocketed pinnacles, its buttresses, its battlements, and
upon the magnificent rose-window terminating the choir.
The apprentice had no especial love for antiquity, but
being of an imaginative turn. the sight of this reverend
structure conjured up old recollections. and brought to
mind the noble Collegiate Church of his native town.

" Shall I ever see Manchester again ? " he sighed :—
" shall I take Amabel with me there ? Alas ! I doubt it.
If I survive the plague. she, I fear, will never be mine."

Musing thus, he scanned the roof of the cathedral. and
noticing its stunted central tower, could not help thinking
how much more striking its effect must have been, when
the lofty spire it once supported was standing. The spire.
it may be remarked, was twice destroyed by lightning:
first, in February, 1444, and subsequently in June, 1561.
when it was entirely burnt down. and never rebuilt.
Passing the Convocation House, which then stood at one
side of the southern transept, Leonard struck down
Paul's Chain, and turning to the right. speeded along
Great Knightrider-street, until he reached an old habitation at the corner of the passage leading to Doctors'
Commons.

Knocking at the door, an elderly servant presently
appeared, and in answer to his inquiries whether Doctor
Hodges was at home, stated that he had gone out, about
half an hour ago, to attend Mr. Fisher, a proctor, who
had been suddenly attacked by the plague at his residence
in Bartholomew-close, near Smithfield.

" I am come on the same errand," said Leonard, " and
must see your master instantly."

" If you choose to go to Bartholomew-close," replied
the servant, " you may possibly meet with him. Mr.
Fisher's house is the last but two, on the right. before
you come to the area in front of the church."

" I can easily find it," returned Leonard, " and will run

there as fast as I can. But if your master should pass me on the road, beseech him to go instantly to Stephen Bloundel's, the grocer, in Wood-street."

The servant assenting, Leonard hastily retraced his steps, and traversing Blow-bladder-street, and Saint Martin's-le-Grand, passed through Aldersgate. He then shaped his course through the windings of Little Britain and entered Duck-lane. He was now in a quarter fearfully assailed by the pestilence. Most of the houses had the fatal sign upon their doors—a red cross, of a foot long, with the piteous words above it, " *Lord have mercy upon us !*" in characters so legible that they could be easily distinguished by the moonlight, while a watchman, with a halbert in his hand, kept guard outside.

Involuntarily drawing in his breath, Leonard quickened his pace. But he met with an unexpected and fearful interruption. Just as he reached the narrow passage leading from Duck-lane to Bartholomew-close, he heard the ringing of a bell, followed by a hoarse voice crying, " Bring out your dead !—bring out your dead ! " He then perceived that a large, strangely-shaped cart stopped up the further end of the passage, and heard a window open, and a voice call out that all was ready. The next moment a light was seen at the door, and a coffin was brought out and placed in the cart. This done, the driver, who was smoking a pipe, cracked his whip, and put the vehicle in motion.

Shrinking into a door-way, and holding a handkerchief to his face, to avoid breathing the pestilential effluvia, Leonard saw that there were other coffins in the cart, and that it was followed by two persons in long black cloaks. The vehicle itself, fashioned like an open hearse, and of the same sombre colour, relieved by fantastical designs, painted in white, emblematic of the pestilence, was drawn by a horse of the large black Flanders breed, and decorated with funeral trappings. To Leonard's inexpressible horror, the cart again stopped opposite him, and the driver ringing his bell, repeated his doleful cry. While another coffin was brought out, and placed with the rest, a window in the next house was opened, and a

B

woman looking forth screamed, " Is Anselm Chowles, the
coffin-maker, there ? "

" Yes, here I am, Mother Malmayns," replied one of
the men in black cloaks, looking up as he spoke, and
exhibiting features so hideous, and stamped with such
a revolting expression, that Leonard's blood curdled at
the sight. " What do you want with me ? " he added.

" I want you to carry away old Mike Norborough,"
replied the woman.

" What, is the old miser gone at last ? " exclaimed
Chowles, with an atrocious laugh. " But how shall I get
paid for a coffin ? "

" You may pay yourself with what you can find in
the house," replied Mother Malmayns; " or you may
carry him to the grave without one, if you prefer it."

" No, no, that won't do," returned Chowles. " I've
other customers to attend to who *will* pay ; and, besides,
I want to get home. I expect friends at supper. Good-
night, Mother Malmayns. You know where to find me,
if you want me. Move on, Jonas, or you will never reach
Saint Sepulchre's."

The woman angrily expostulated with him, and some
further parley ensued,—Leonard did not tarry to hear
what, but rushing past them, gained Bartholomew-close.

He soon reached the proctor's house, and found it
marked with the fatal cross. Addressing a watchman at
the door, he learnt, to his great dismay, that Doctor
Hodges had been gone more than a quarter of an hour.
" He was too late," said the man. " Poor Mr. Fisher
had breathed his last before he arrived, and after giving
some directions to the family as to the precautions they
ought to observe, the doctor departed."

" How unfortunate ! " exclaimed Leonard, " I have
missed him a second time. But I will run back to his
house instantly."

" You will not find him at home," returned the watchman. " He is gone to St. Paul's, to attend a sick person."

" To St. Paul's at this hour ! " cried the apprentice.
" Why, no one is there, except the vergers or the sexton."

" He is gone to visit the sexton, who is ill of the plague," replied the watchman. " I have told you all I know about him. You can do what you think best."

Determined to make another effort before giving in, Leonard hurried back as fast as he could. While threading Duck-lane, he heard the doleful bell again, and perceived the dead-cart standing before a house, from which two small coffins were brought. Hurrying past the vehicle, he remarked that its load was fearfully increased, but that the coffin-maker and his companion had left it. Another minute had not elapsed before he reached Aldersgate, and passing through the postern, he beheld a light at the end of Saint Anne's-lane, and heard the terrible voice of Solomon Eagle, calling to the sleepers to awake and repent.

Shutting his ears to the cry, Leonard did not halt till he reached the great western door of the cathedral, against which he knocked. His first summons remaining unanswered, he repeated it, and a wicket was then opened by a gray-headed verger, with a lantern in his hand, who at first was very angry at being disturbed, but on learning whom the applicant was in search of, and that the case was one of urgent necessity, he admitted that the doctor was in the cathedral at the time.

" Or rather, I should say," he added, " he is in St. Faith's. I will conduct you to him, if you think proper. Doctor Hodges is a good man,—a charitable man,"—he continued, " and attends the poor for nothing. He is now with Matthew Malmayns, the sexton, who was taken ill of the plague yesterday, and will get nothing but thanks,—if he gets those for his fee. But, follow me, young man, follow me."

So saying, he shut the wicket, and led the way along the transept. The path was uneven, many of the flags having been removed, and the verger often paused to throw a light upon the ground, and warn his companion of a hole.

On arriving at the head of the nave, Leonard cast his eyes down it, and was surprised at the magical effect of the moonlight upon its magnificent avenue of pillars; the massive shafts on the left being completely illuminated by the silvery beams, while those on the right lay in deep shadow.

" Ay, it is a noble structure," replied the old verger, noticing his look of wonder and admiration, " and, like many a proud human being, has known better days. It has seen sad changes in my time, for I recollect it when good Queen Bess ruled the land. But come along, young man,—you have something else to think of now."

Bestowing a momentary glance upon the matchless choir, with its groined roof, its clerestory windows, its arched openings, its carved stalls, and its gorgeous rose-window, Leonard followed his conductor through a small doorway on the left of the southern transept, and descending a flight of stone steps, entered a dark and extensive vault, for such it seemed. The feeble light of the lantern fell upon ranks of short heavy pillars, support-ing a ponderous arched roof.

" You are now in Saint Faith's," observed the verger, " and above you is the choir of Saint Paul's."

Leonard took no notice of the remark, but silently crossing the nave of this beautiful subterranean church (part of which still exists), traversed its northern aisle. At length the verger stopped before the entrance of a small chapel, once dedicated to Saint John the Baptist, but now devoted to a less sacred purpose. As they advanced, Leonard observed a pile of dried skulls and bones in one corner, a stone coffin, strips of woollen shrouds, fragments of coffins, mattocks, and spades. It was evidently half a charnel,—half a receptacle for the sexton's tools.

" If you choose to open that door," said the verger, pointing to one at the lower end of the chamber, " you will find him you seek. I shall go no further."

Summoning up all his resolution, Leonard pushed open the door. A frightful scene met his gaze. At one side of a deep, low-roofed vault, the architecture of which was of great antiquity, and showed that it had been a place of burial, was stretched a miserable pallet, and upon it, covered by a single blanket, lay a wretch, whose groans and struggles proclaimed the anguish he endured.

A lamp was burning on the floor, and threw a sickly light upon the agonized countenance of the sufferer. He was a middle-aged man, with features naturally harsh, but which now, contracted by pain, had assumed a revolting expression. An old crone, who proved to be his mother, and a young man, who held him down in bed by main force, tended him. He was rambling in a frightful manner; and as his ravings turned upon the most loathly matters, it required some firmness to listen to them.

At a little distance from him, upon a bench, sat a stout, shrewd-looking, but benevolent little personage, somewhat between forty and fifty. This was Doctor Hodges. He had a lancet in his hand, with which he had just operated upon the sufferer, and he was in the act of wiping it on a cloth. As Leonard entered the vault, the doctor observed to the attendants of the sick man, " He will recover. The tumour has discharged its venom. Keep him as warm as you can, and do not let him leave his bed for two days. All depends upon that. I will send him proper medicines and some blankets shortly. If he takes cold, it will be fatal."

The young man promised to attend to the doctor's injunctions, and the old woman mumbled her thanks.

" Where is Judith Malmayns? " asked Doctor Hodges; " I am surprised not to see her. Is she afraid of the distemper? "

" Afraid of it!—not she," replied the old woman. " Since the plague has raged so dreadfully, she has gone out as a nurse to the sick, and my poor son has seen nothing of her."

Leonard then recollected that he had heard the woman, who called out of the miser's house, addressed as Mother Malmayns by the coffin-maker, and had no doubt that she was the sexton's wife. His entrance having been so noiseless that it passed unnoticed, he now stepped forward, and, addressing Doctor Hodges, acquainted him with his errand.

" What! " exclaimed the doctor, as soon as he concluded, " a son of Stephen Bloundel, the worthy grocer of Wood-street, attacked by the plague! I will go with you

instantly, young man. I have a great regard for your
master—a very great regard. There is not a better man
living. The poor lad must be saved, if possible." And
hastily repeating his instructions to the attendants of the
sick man, he left the vault with the apprentice.

They found the verger in the charnel, and before
quitting it, the doctor drew a small flask of canary from
his pocket, and applied it to his lips.

"This is my anti-pestilential drink," he remarked, with
a smile, "and it has preserved me from contagion hitherto. You must let us out of the south door, friend," he
added to the verger, "for I shall be obliged to step home
for a moment, and it will save time. Come with me, young
man, and tell me what has been done for the grocer's son."

As they traversed the gloomy aisle of Saint Faith, and
mounted to the upper structure, Leonard related all
that had taken place since poor Stephen's seizure. The
doctor strongly expressed his approval of what had been
done, and observed, "It could not be better. With
Heaven's help, I have no doubt we shall save him, and
I am truly glad of it for his father's sake."

By this time they had reached the southern door, and
the verger having unlocked it, they issued forth. It was
still bright moonlight, and Leonard, whose mind was
greatly relieved by the assurances of the physician, felt
in some degree reconciled to the delay, and kept up his
part in the conversation promoted by his companion.
The doctor, who was an extremely kind-hearted man and
appeared to have a great regard for the grocer, made
many inquiries as to his family, and spoke in terms of the
highest admiration of the beauty of his eldest daughter.
The mention of Amabel's name, while it made Leonard's
cheek burn, rekindled all his jealousy of Wyvil, and he
tried to make some excuse to get away, but his companion
would not hear of it.

"I tell you there is no hurry," said the doctor; "all
is going on as well as possible. I will make your excuses
to your master."

On reaching the doctor's house they were ushered
into a large room, surrounded with bookshelves and

cases of anatomical preparations. Hodges seated himself at a table, on which a shaded lamp was placed, and writing out a prescription, desired his servant to get it made up at a neighbouring apothecary's, and to take it, with a couple of blankets, to the sexton of St. Paul's. He then produced a bottle of medicated canary, and pouring out a large glass for the apprentice, drained another himself.

" I will answer for its virtue," he said: " it is a sure preservative against the plague."

Having furnished himself with several small packets of simples, a few pots of ointment, one or two phials, and a case of surgical instruments, he told Leonard he was ready to attend him.

" We will go round by Warwick-lane," he added. " I must call upon Chowles, the coffin-maker. It will not detain us a moment; and I have an order to give him."

The mention of this name brought to Leonard's mind the hideous attendant on the dead-cart, and he had no doubt he was the person in question. It did not become him, however, to make a remark, and they set out.

Mounting Addle-hill, and threading Ave-Maria-lane, they entered Warwick-lane, and about half-way up the latter thoroughfare, the doctor stopped before a shop, bearing on its immense projecting sign the representation of a coffin lying in state, and covered with scutcheons, underneath which was written, " ANSELM CHOWLES, COFFIN-MAKER."

" I do not think you will find Mr. Chowles at home," observed Leonard: " for I saw him with the dead-cart not half an hour ago."

" Very likely," returned the doctor; " but I shall see one of his men. The coffin-maker's business is now carried on in the night time," he added, with a sigh ; " and he drives a flourishing trade. These sad times will make his fortune."

As he spoke, he rapped with his cane at the door, which, after a little delay, was opened by a young man in a carpenter's dress, with a hammer in his hand. On seeing who he was, this person exhibited great confusion.

and would have retired; but the doctor, pushing him aside, asked for his master.

" You cannot see him just now, sir," replied the other, evidently considerably embarrassed. " He is just come home greatly fatigued, and is about to retire to rest."

" No matter," returned the doctor, entering a room, in which three or four other men were at work, hastily finishing coffins; " I *must* see him."

No further opposition being offered, Hodges, followed by the apprentice, marched towards an inner room. Just as he reached the door, a burst of loud laughter, evidently proceeding from a numerous party, arose from within, and a harsh voice was heard chanting the following strains :—

SONG OF THE PLAGUE

I

To others the Plague a foe may be,
To me 'tis a friend—not an enemy;
My coffins and coffers alike it fills,
And the richer I grow, the more it kills.
Drink the Plague! Drink the Plague!

II

For months, for years, may it spend its rage
On lusty manhood and trembling age;
Though half mankind of the scourge should die,
My coffins will sell—so what care I?
Drink the Plague! Drink the Plague!

Loud acclamations followed the song, and the doctor, who was filled with disgust and astonishment, opened the door. He absolutely recoiled at the scene presented to his gaze. In the midst of a large room, the sides of which were crowded with coffins piled to the very ceiling, sat about a dozen personages, with pipes in their mouths, and flasks and glasses before them. Their seats were coffins, and their table was a coffin set upon a bier. Perched on a pyramid of coffins, gradually diminishing in size as the pile approached its apex, Chowles was waving a glass in one hand, and a bottle in the other, when the doctor made his appearance.

A more hideous personage cannot be imagined than the coffin-maker. He was clothed in a suit of rusty black, which made his skeleton limbs look yet more lean and cadaverous. His head was perfectly bald, and its yellow skin, divested of any artificial covering, glistened like polished ivory. His throat was long and scraggy, and supported a head unrivalled for ugliness. His nose had been broken in his youth, and was almost compressed flat with his face. His few remaining teeth were yellow and discoloured, with large gaps between them. His eyes were bright, and set in deep cavernous recesses, and, now that he was more than half intoxicated, gleamed with unnatural lustre. The friends by whom he was surrounded were congenial spirits,—searchers, watchmen, buriers, apothecaries and other wretches, who, like himself, rejoiced in the pestilence, because it was a source of profit to them.

At one corner of the room, with a part-emptied glass before her, and several articles in her lap, which she hastily pocketed on the entrance of the doctor, sat the plague nurse, Mother Malmayns; and Leonard thought her, if possible, more villainous-looking than her companions. She was a rough, raw-boned woman, with sandy hair and light brows, a sallow, freckled complexion, a nose with nostrils, and a large, thick-lipped mouth. She had, moreover, a look of mingled cunning and ferocity inexpressibly revolting.

Sharply rebuking Chowles, who, in springing from his lofty seat, upset several of the topmost coffins, the doctor gave him some directions, and, turning to the nurse, informed her of her husband's condition, and ordered her to go to him immediately. Mother Malmayns arose, and glancing significantly at the coffin-maker, took her departure.

Repeating his injunctions to Chowles in a severe tone,

the doctor followed; and seeing her take the way towards Saint Paul's, proceeded at a brisk pace along Paternoster-row with the apprentice. In a few minutes they reached Wood-street, and knocking at the door, were admitted by Blaize.

" Heaven be praised, you are come at last ! " exclaimed the porter. " Our master began to think something had happened to you."

" It is all my fault," returned Doctor Hodges; " but how is the young man ? "

" Better, much better, as I understand," replied Blaize; " but I have not seen him."

" Come, that's well," rejoined Hodges.—" Lead me to his room."

" Leonard will show you the way," returned the porter, holding back.

Glancing angrily at Blaize, the apprentice conducted the doctor to the inner room, where they found the grocer, with the Bible on his knee, watching by the bedside of his son. He was delighted with their appearance, but looked inquisitively at his apprentice for some explanation of his long absence. This Hodges immediately gave; and, having examined the sufferer, he relieved the anxious father by declaring that, with due care, he had little doubt of his son's recovery.

" God be praised ! " exclaimed Bloundel, falling on his knees.

Hodges then gave minute directions to the grocer as to how he was to proceed, and told him it would be necessary for some time to keep his family separate. To this Bloundel readily agreed. The doctor's next inquiries were, whether notice had been given to the Examiner of Health, and the grocer referring to Leonard, the latter acknowledged that he had forgotten it, but undertook to repair his omission at once.

With this view, he quitted the room, and was hastening towards the shop, when he observed a figure on the back-stairs. Quickly mounting them, he overtook on the landing Maurice Wyvil.

CHAPTER III

The Gamester and the Bully

BEFORE proceeding further, it will be necessary to retrace our steps for a short time, and see what was done by Maurice Wyvil after the alarming announcement made to him by the apprentice. Of a selfish nature and ungovernable temper, and seeking only in the pursuit of the grocer's daughter the gratification of his lawless desires, he was filled, in the first instance, with furious disappointment at being robbed of the prize, at the very moment he expected it to fall into his hands. But this feeling was quickly effaced by anxiety respecting his mistress, whose charms, now that there was every probability of losing her (for Leonard's insinuation had led him to believe she was assailed by the pestilence), appeared doubly attractive to him; and scarcely under the governance of reason, he hurried towards Wood-street, resolved to force his way into the house, and see her again, at all hazards. His wild design, however, was fortunately prevented. As he passed the end of the court leading to the ancient inn (for it was ancient even at the time of this history), the Swan-with-two-Necks, in Lad-lane, a young man, as richly attired as himself, and about his own age, who had seen him approaching, suddenly darted from it, and grasping his cloak, detained him.

"I thought it must be you, Wyvil," cried this person. "Where are you running so quickly? I see neither angry father, nor jealous apprentice, at your heels. What has become of the girl? Are you tired of her already?"

"Let me go, Lydyard," returned Wyvil, trying to extricate himself from his companion's hold, who was no other than the gallant that had accompanied him on his first visit to the grocer's shop, and had played his part so adroitly in the scheme devised between them to procure an interview with Amabel,—"let me go, I say, I am in no mood for jesting."

"Why, what the plague is the matter?" rejoined
Lydyard. "Has your mistress played you false? Have
you lost your wager?"

"The plague *is* the matter," replied Wyvil, sternly.
"Amabel is attacked by it. I must see her instantly."

"The devil!" exclaimed Lydyard. "Here is a pretty
termination to the affair. But if this is really the case,
you must *not* see her. It is one thing to be run through
the arm,—which you must own I managed as dexterously
as the best master of fence could have done,—and lose
a few drops of blood for a mistress, but it is another
to brave the plague on her account."

"I care for nothing," replied Wyvil; "I *will* see her."

"This is madness! remonstrated Lydyard, still main-
taining his grasp. "What satisfaction will it afford you
to witness her sufferings—to see the frightful ravages
made upon her charms by this remorseless disease,—to
throw her whole family into consternation, and destroy
the little chance she may have of recovery, by your presence? What good will this do? No.—You must pay your
wager to Sedley, and forget her."

"I cannot forget her," replied Wyvil. "My feelings
have undergone a total change. If I *am* capable of real
love, it is for her."

"Real love!" exclaimed Lydyard, in an incredulous
tone. "If the subject were not too serious, I should
laugh in your face. No doubt you would marry her,
and abandon your design upon the rich heiress, pretty
Mistress Mallett, whom old Rowley recommended to
your attention, and whom the fair Stewart has more than
half won for you?"

"I would," replied the other, energetically.

"Nay, then, you are more insane than I thought you,"
rejoined Lydyard, relinquishing his hold; "and the
sooner you take the plague the better. It may cure your
present brain fever. I shall go back to Parravicin, and
the others. You will not require my assistance further."

"I know not," replied Wyvil, distractedly; "I have
not yet given up my intention of carrying off the girl."

"If you carry her off in this state," rejoined the other,

" it must be to the pest-house. But who told you she was attacked by the plague ? "

" Her father's apprentice," replied Wyvil.

" And you believed him ? " demanded Lydyard, with a derisive laugh.

" Undoubtedly," replied Wyvil. " Why not ? "

" Because it is evidently a mere trick to frighten you from the house," rejoined Lydyard. " I am surprised so shallow a device should succeed with *you.*"

" I wish I could persuade myself it was a trick," returned Wyvil. " But the fellow's manner convinced me he was in earnest."

" Well, I will not dispute the point, though I am sure I am right," returned Lydyard. " But be not too precipitate. Since the apprentice has seen you, some alteration may be necessary in your plans. Come with me into the house. A few minutes can make no difference."

Wyvil suffered himself to be led up the court, and passing through a door on the left, they entered a spacious room, across which ran a long table, furnished at one end with wine and refreshments, and at the other with cards and dice.

Three persons were seated at the table, the most noticeable of whom was a dissipated-looking young man, dressed in the extremity of the prevailing mode, with ruffles of the finest colbertine, three inches in depth, at his wrists; a richly-laced cravat round his throat; white silk hose, adorned with gold clocks; velvet shoes of the same colour as the hose, fastened with immense roses; a silver-hilted sword, supported by a broad embroidered silk band; and a cloak and doublet of carnation-coloured velvet, woven with gold, and decorated with innumerable glittering points and ribands. He had a flowing wig of flaxen hair, and a broad-leaved hat, looped with a diamond buckle, and placed negligently on the left side of his head. His figure was slight, but extremely well formed; and his features might have been termed handsome, but for their reckless and licentious expression. He was addressed by his companions as Sir Paul Parravicin.

The person opposite to him, whose name was Disbrowe,

and who was likewise a very handsome young man,
though his features were flushed and disturbed, partly by
the wine he had drunk, and partly by his losses at play,
was equipped in the splendid accoutrements of a captain
in the King's body-guard. His left hand convulsively
clutched an empty purse, and his eyes were fixed upon a
large sum of money, which he had just handed over to the
knight, and which the latter was carelessly transferring to
his pocket.

The last of the three, whose looks betrayed his character,—that of a sharper and a bully,—called himself
Major Pillichody, his pretensions to military rank being
grounded upon his service (so ran his own statement,
though it was never clearly substantiated) in the King's
army during the civil wars. Major Pillichody was a man
of remarkably fierce exterior. Seamed with many scars,
and destitute of the left eye, the orifice of which was
covered with a huge black patch; his face was of a deep
mulberry colour, clearly attesting his devotion to the
bottle; while his nose, which was none of the smallest,
was covered with " bubukles, and whelks, and knobs,
and flames of fire." He was of the middle size, stoutly
built, and given to corpulency, though not so much so
as to impair his activity. His attire consisted of a cloak
and doublet of scarlet cloth, very much stained and
tarnished, and edged with gold lace, likewise the worse for
wear; jack-boots, with huge funnel tops; spurs, with
enormous rowels, and a rapier of preposterous length.
He wore his own hair, which was swart and woolly, like
that of a negro; and had beard and moustaches to match.
His hat was fiercely cocked; his gestures swaggering and
insolent; and he was perpetually racking his brain to
invent new and extraordinary oaths.

" So soon returned ! " cried Parravicin, as Wyvil
appeared. " Accept my congratulations ! "

" And mine ! " cried Pillichody. " We wild fellows
have but to be seen to conquer. Sugar and spice, and
all that's nice ! " he added, smacking his lips, as he filled
a glass from a long-necked bottle on the table; " may
the grocer's daughter prove sweeter than her father's

plums, and more melting than his butter ! Is she without ? Are we to see her ? "

Wyvil made no answer, but, walking to the other end of the room, threw himself into a chair, and covering his face with his hands, appeared wrapped in thought. Lydyard took a seat beside him, and endeavoured to engage him in conversation. But, finding his efforts fruitless, he desisted.

" Something is wrong," observed Parravicin, to the major. " He has been foiled in his attempt to carry off the girl. Sedley has won his wager, and it is a heavy sum. Shall we resume our play ? " he added, to Disbrowe.

" I have nothing more to lose," observed the young man, filling a large goblet to the brim, and emptying it at a draught. " You are master of every farthing I possess."

" Hum ! " exclaimed Parravicin, taking up a pack of cards, and snapping them between his finger and thumb. " You are married, Captain Disbrowe ? "

" What if I am ? " cried the young man, becoming suddenly pale; " what if I am ? " he repeated.

" I am told your wife is beautiful," replied Parravicin.

" Beautiful ! " ejaculated Pillichody : " by the well-filled coffers of the widow of Watling-street ! she is an angel. Beautiful is not the word. Mrs. Disbrowe is divine ! "

" You have never seen her," said the young man, sternly.

" Ha !—fire and fury ! my word doubted," cried the major, fiercely. " I have seen her at the play-houses, at Mulberry-garden, at court, and at church. Not seen her ! By the one eye of a Cyclops but I have ! You shall hear my description of her, and judge of its correctness. *Imprimis*, she has a tall and majestic figure, and might be a queen for her dignity."

" Go on," said Disbrowe, by no means displeased with the commencement.

" Secondly," pursued Pillichody, " she has a clear olive complexion, bright black eyes, hair and brows to match, a small foot, a pretty turn-up nose, a dimpling

cheek, a mole upon her throat, the rosiest lips imaginable, an alluring look——"

"No more," interrupted Disbrowe. "It is plain you
have never seen her."

"Unbelieving Pagan!" exclaimed the major, clapping
his hand furiously upon his sword. "I have done more
—I have spoken with her."

"A lie!" replied Disbrowe, hurling a dice-box at his
head.

"Ha!" roared Pillichody, in a voice of thunder, and
pushing back his chair till it was stopped by the wall.
"Death and Fiends! I will make mince-meat of your
heart, and send it as a love-offering to your wife."

And, whipping out his long rapier, he would have
assaulted Disbrowe, if Sir Paul had not interposed,
and commanded him authoritatively to put up his blade.

"You shall have your revenge in a safer way," he
whispered.

"Well, Sir Paul," rejoined the bully, with affected
reluctance, "as you desire it. I will spare the young
man's life. I must wash away the insult in burgundy,
since I cannot do so in blood."

With this, he emptied the flask next him, and called to
a drawer, who was in attendance, in an imperious tone,
to bring two more bottles.

Parravicin, meanwhile, picked up the dice-box, and,
seating himself, spread a large heap of gold on the table.

"I mentioned your wife, Captain Disbrowe," he said,
addressing the young officer, who anxiously watched
his movements, "not with any intention of giving you
offence, but to show you that, although you have lost
your money, you have still a valuable stake left."

"I do not understand you, Sir Paul," returned Disbrowe, with a look of indignant surprise.

"To be plain, then," replied Parravicin, "I have won
from you two hundred pounds—all you possess. You
are a ruined man, and as such will run any hazard to
retrieve your losses. I give you a last chance. I will
stake all my winnings, nay, double the amount, against
your wife. You have a key of the house you inhabit,

by which you admit yourself at all hours; so at least the major informs me. If I win, that key shall be mine. I will take my chance for the rest. Do you understand me now ? "

" I do," replied the young man, with concentrated fury. " I understand that you are a villain. You have robbed me of my money, and would rob me of my honour."

" These are harsh words, sir," replied the knight, calmly; " but let them pass. We will play first, and fight afterwards. But you refuse my challenge ? "

" It is false ! " replied Disbrowe, fiercely; " I accept it." And producing a key, he threw it on the table. " My life is, in truth, set on the die," he added, with a desperate look,—" for if I lose, I will not survive my shame."

" You will not forget our terms," observed Parravicin. " I am to be your representative to-night. You can return home to-morrow."

" Throw, sir,—throw," cried the young man, fiercely.

" Pardon me," replied the knight; " the first cast is with you. A single main decides it."

" Be it so," returned Disbrowe, seizing the box. And as he shook the dice with a frenzied air, the major and Lydyard drew near the table, and even Wyvil roused himself to watch the result.

" Twelve ! " cried Disbrowe, as he removed the box. " My honour is saved ! My fortune retrieved—Huzza ! "

" Not so fast," returned Parravicin, shaking the box in his turn. " You are a little too hasty," he added, uncovering the dice. " I am twelve, too. We must throw again."

" This to decide," cried the young officer, again rattling the dice.—" Six ! "

Parravicin smiled, took the box, and threw ten.

" Perdition ! " ejaculated Disbrowe, striking his brow with his clenched hand. " What devil tempted me to my undoing?—My wife trusted to this profligate ! Horror !—it must not be ! "

" It is too late to retract," replied Parravicin, taking

up the key, and turning with a triumphant look to his friends.

Disbrowe noticed the smile, and stung beyond endurance, drew his sword, and called to the knight to defend himself.

In an instant, passes were exchanged. But the conflict was brief. Fortune, as before, declared herself in favour of Parravicin. He disarmed his assailant, who rushed out of the room, uttering the wildest ejaculations of rage and despair.

" I told you you should have your revenge," observed the knight to Pillichody, as soon as Disbrowe was gone. " Is his wife really as beautiful as you represent her ? "

" Words are too feeble to paint her charms," replied the major. " Shafts of Cupid ! she must be seen to be appreciated."

" Enough ! " returned Parravicin. " I have not made a bad night's work of it, so far. I'faith, Wyvil, I pity you. To lose a heavy wager is provoking enough—but to lose a pretty mistress is the devil."

" I have lost neither yet," replied Wyvil, who had completely recovered his spirits, and joined in the general merriment occasioned by the foregoing occurrence. " I have been baffled, not defeated. What say you to an exchange of mistresses ? I am so diverted with your adventure, that I am half-inclined to give you the grocer's daughter for Disbrowe's wife. She is a superb creature—languid as a Circassian, and passionate as an Andalusian."

" I can't agree to the exchange, especially after your rapturous description," returned Parravicin, " but I'll stake Mrs. Disbrowe against Amabel. The winner shall have both. A single cast shall decide, as before."

" No," replied Wyvil, " I could not resign Amabel, if I lost. And the luck is all on your side to-night."

" As you please," rejoined the knight, sweeping the glittering pile into his pocket. " Drawer, another bottle of burgundy. A health to our mistresses ! " he added, quaffing a brimmer.

" A health to the grocer's daughter ! " cried Wyvil,

with difficulty repressing a shudder, as he uttered the pledge.

" A health to the rich widow of Watling-street," cried Pillichody, draining a bumper, " and may I soon call her mine ! "

" I have no mistress to toast," said Lydyard; " and I have drunk wine enough. Do not forget, gentlemen, that the plague is abroad."

" You are the death's-head at the feast, Lydyard," rejoined Parravicin, setting down his glass. " I hate the idea of the plague. It poisons all our pleasures. We must meet at noon to-morrow, at the Smyrna, to compare notes as to our successes. Before we separate, can I be of any further service to you, Wyvil ? I came here to enjoy *your* triumph; but, egad, I have found so admirable a bubble in that hot-headed Disbrowe, whom I met at the Smyrna, and brought here to while away the time, that I must demand your congratulations upon *mine*."

" You have certainly achieved an easy victory over the husband," returned Wyvil; " and I trust your success with the wife will be commensurate. I require no further assistance. What I have to do must be done alone. Lydyard will accompany me to the house, and then I must shift for myself."

" Nay, we will all see you safe inside," returned Parravicin. " We shall pass by the grocer's shop. I know it well, having passed it a hundred times, in the vain hope of catching a glimpse of its lovely inmate."

" I am glad it *was* a vain hope," replied Wyvil. " But I must scale a wall to surprise the garrison."

" In that case, you will need the rope-ladder," replied Lydyard; " it is in readiness."

" I will carry it," said Pillichody, picking up the ladder which was lying in a corner of the room, and throwing it over his shoulder. " Bombs and batteries ! I like to be an escalader when the forts of love are stormed."

The party then set out. As they proceeded, Parravicin ascertained from the major that Disbrowe's house was situated in a small street leading out of Piccadilly, but as he could not be quite sure that he understood his in-

formant aright, he engaged him to accompany him and
point it out.

By this time they had reached Wood-street, and, keeping in the shade, reconnoitred the house. But though
Wyvil clapped his hands, blew a shrill whistle, and made
other signals, no answer was returned, nor was a light
seen at any of the upper windows. On the contrary, all
was still and silent as death.

The grocer's was a large, old-fashioned house, built
about the middle of the preceding century, or perhaps
earlier, and had four stories, each projecting over the
other, till the pile seemed completely to overhang the
street. The entire front, except the upper story, which
was protected by oaken planks, was covered with panels
of the same timber, and the projections were supported
by heavy beams, embellished with grotesque carvings.
Three deeply-embayed windows, having stout wooden
bars, filled with minute diamond panes, set in leaden
frames, were allotted to each floor: while the like number
of gables, ornamented with curiously-carved coignes, and
long-moulded leaden spouts, shooting far into the street,
finished the roof. A huge sign, with the device of Noah's
Ark, and the owner's name upon it, hung before the door.

After carefully examining the house, peeping through
the chinks in the lower shutters, and discovering the
grocer seated by the bedside of his son, though he could
not make out the object of his solicitude, Wyvil decided
upon attempting an entrance by the back-yard. To reach
it, a court and a narrow alley, leading to an open space
surrounded by high walls, had to be traversed. Arrived at
this spot, Wyvil threw one end of the rope-ladder over the
wall, which was about twelve feet high, and speedily
succeeding in securing it, mounted, and drawing it up
after him, waved his hand to his companions, and disappeared on the other side. After waiting for a moment
to listen, and hearing a window open, they concluded he
had gained admittance, and turned to depart.

" And now for Mrs. Disbrowe ! " cried Parravicin.
" We shall find a coach or a chair in Cheapside. Can I
take you westward, Lydyard ? "

But the other declined the offer, saying, " I will not desert Wyvil. I feel certain he will get into some scrape, and may need me to help him out of it. Take care of yourself, Parravicin. Beware of the plague, and of what is worse than the plague, an injured husband. Goodnight, major."

" Farewell, sir," returned Pillichody, raising his hat. " A merry watching, and a good catching, as the sentinels were wont to say, when I served King Charles the First. Sir Paul, I attend you."

CHAPTER IV

The Interview

MAURICE WYVIL, as his friends conjectured, had found his way into the house. Creeping through the window, and entering a passage, he moved noiselessly along till he reached the head of the kitchen-stairs, where, hearing voices below, and listening to what was said, he soon ascertained from the discourse of the speakers, who were no other than old Josyna and Patience, that it was not the grocer's daughter, but one of his sons, who was attacked by the plague, and that Amabel was in perfect health, though confined in her mother's bedroom.

Overjoyed at the information he had thus acquired, he retired as noiselessly as he came, and, after searching about for a short time, discovered the main staircase, and ascended it on the points of his feet. He had scarcely, however, mounted a dozen steps, when a door opened, and Blaize crawled along the passage, groaning to himself, and keeping his eyes bent on the ground. Seeing he was unnoticed, Wyvil gained the landing, and, treading softly, placed his ear at every door, until at last the musical accents of Amabel convinced him he had hit upon the right one.

His heart beat so violently, that, for a few seconds, he was unable to move. Becoming calmer, he tried the door, and finding it locked, rapped with his knuckles

against it. The grocer's wife demanded who was there.
But Wyvil, instead of returning an answer, repeated his
application. The same demand followed, and in a louder
key. Still no answer. A third summons, however, so
alarmed Mrs. Bloundel, that, forgetful of her husband's
injunctions, she opened the door and looked out; but,
as Wyvil had hastily retired into a recess, she could see
no one.

Greatly frightened and perplexed, Mrs. Bloundel
rushed to the head of the stairs, to see whether there
was any one below; and, as she did so, Wyvil slipped
into the room, and locked the door. The only object he
beheld—for he had eyes for nothing else—was Amabel,
who, seeing him, uttered a faint scream. Clasping her in
his arms, Wyvil forgot, in the delirium of the moment,
the jeopardy in which he was placed.

"Do you know what has happened?" cried Amabel,
extricating herself from his embrace.

"I know all," replied her lover; "I would risk a
thousand deaths for your sake. You must fly with me."

"Fly!" exclaimed Amabel; "at such a time as this?
—my brother dying—the whole house, perhaps, infected!
How can you ask me to fly? Why have you come hither?
You will destroy me."

"Not so, sweet Amabel," replied Wyvil, ardently. I
would bear you from the reach of this horrible disease.
I am come to save you, and will not stir without you."

"What shall I do?" cried Amabel, distractedly.
"But I am rightly punished for my disobedience and
ingratitude to my dear father. Oh! Wyvil, I did not
deserve this from you."

"Hear me, Amabel," cried her lover; "I implore your
forgiveness. What I have done has been from irresistible
passion, and from no other cause. · You promised to
meet me to-night. Nay, you half-consented to fly with
me. I have prepared all for it. I came hither burning with
impatience for the meeting. I received no signal, but
encountering your father's apprentice, was informed that
you were attacked by the plague. Imagine my horror
and distress at the intelligence. I thought it would have

killed me. I determined, however, at all risks, to see you once more—to clasp you in my arms before you died—to die with you, if need be. I accomplished my purpose. I entered the house unobserved. I overheard the servants say it was your brother who was ill, not you. I also learnt that you were in your mother's room. I found the door, and by a fortunate device, obtained admittance. Now you know all, and will you not fly with me?"

"How *can* I fly?" cried Amabel, gazing wildly round the room, as if in search of some place of refuge or escape, and, noticing her little sister Christiana, who was lying asleep in the bed—"Oh! how I envy that innocent!" she murmured.

"Think of nothing but yourself," rejoined Wyvil, seizing her hand. "If you stay here, it will be to perish of the plague. Trust to me, and I will secure your flight."

"I cannot—I dare not," cried Amabel, resisting him with all her force.

"You *must* come," cried Wyvil, dragging her along.

As he spoke, Mrs. Bloundel, who had been down to Blaize's room to ascertain what was the matter, returned. Trying the door, and finding it fastened, she became greatly alarmed, and called to Amabel to open it directly.

"It is my mother," cried Amabel. "Pity me, Heaven! I shall die with shame."

"Heed her not," replied Wyvil, in a deep whisper; "in her surprise and confusion at seeing me, she will not be able to stop us. Do not hesitate. There is not a moment to lose."

"What is the matter, child?" cried Mrs. Bloundel. "Why have you fastened the door? Is there any one in the room with you?"

"She hears us!" whispered Amabel. "What shall I do? You must not be seen."

"There is no use in further concealment," cried Wyvil. "You are mine, and twenty mothers should not bar the way."

"Hold!" cried Amabel, disengaging herself by a sudden effort. "I have gone too far—but not so far as you imagine. I am not utterly lost."

And before she could be prevented, she rushed to the
door, threw it open, and flung herself into her mother's
arms, who uttered an exclamation of terror at beholding
Wyvil. The latter, though filled with rage and confusion,
preserved an unmoved exterior, and folded his arms upon
his breast.

"And so it was you who knocked at the door!" cried
Mrs. Bloundel, regarding the gallant with a look of fury
—"it was you who contrived to delude me into opening
it! I do not ask why you have come hither like a thief in
the night, because I require no information on the subject. You are come to dishonour my child—to carry her
away from those who love her, and cherish her, and
preserve her from such mischievous serpents as you.
But, Heaven be praised! I have caught you before your
wicked design could be effected. Oh! Amabel, my
child, my child!" she added, straining her to her bosom,
"I had rather—far rather—see you stricken with the
plague, like your poor brother, though I felt there was
not a hope of your recovery, than you should fall into the
hands of this Satan!"

"I have been greatly to blame, dear mother," returned
Amabel, bursting into tears; "and I shall neither seek
to exculpate myself, nor conceal what I have done. I
have deceived you and my father. I have secretly encouraged the addresses of this gentleman. Nay, if the plague
had not broken out in our house to-night, I should have
flown from it with him."

"You shock me greatly, child," returned Mrs. Bloundel;
"but you relieve me at the same time. Make a clean
breast, and hide nothing from me."

"I have nothing more to tell, dear mother," replied
Amabel, "except that Maurice Wyvil has been in the
room ever since you left it, and might, perhaps, have
carried me off in spite of my resistance, if you had not
returned when you did."

"It was, indeed, a providential interference," rejoined
Mrs. Bloundel. "From what a snare of the Evil One—
from what a pitfall have you been preserved!"

"I feel I have had a narrow escape, dear mother,"

replied Amabel. "Pardon me. I do not deserve your forgiveness. But I will never offend you more."

"I forgive you from my heart, child, and will trust you," returned Mrs. Bloundel, in a voice broken by emotion.

"That is more than *I* would," thought Maurice Wyvil. "A woman who has once deceived those she holds dear, will not fail to do so a second time. The fairest promises are forgotten when the danger is past."

"Mr. Wyvil, if you have a particle of regard for me, you will instantly leave the house," said Amabel, turning to him.

"If I had my own way, he should leave it through the window," said Mrs. Bloundel; "and if he tarries a minute longer, I will give the alarm."

"You hear this, sir," cried Amabel:—"go, I entreat you."

"I yield to circumstance, Amabel," replied Wyvil; "but think not I resign you. Come what will, and however I may be foiled, I will not desist till I make you mine."

"I tremble to hear him," cried Mrs. Bloundel, "and could not have believed such depravity existed. Quit the house, sir, directly, or I will have you turned out of it."

"Do not remain another moment," implored Amabel. "Do not, do not!"

"Since I have no other way of proving my love, I must perforce obey," returned Wyvil, trying to snatch her hand and press it to his lips; but she withdrew it, and clung more closely to her mother. "We part," he added, significantly, "only for a time."

Quitting the room he was about to descend the stairs, when Mrs. Bloundel, who had followed to see him safely off the premises, hearing a noise below, occasioned by the return of Leonard with the doctor, cautioned him to wait. A further delay was caused by Blaize, who, stationing himself at the foot of the stairs, with a light in his hand, appeared unwilling to move. Apprehensive of a discovery, Mrs. Bloundel then directed the gallant to the back staircase, and he had got about half-way down, when he was surprised by Leonard Holt, as before related. At the very moment that Wyvil was overtaken on the landing by the apprentice, Amabel appeared at the door of her chamber with a light. The different emotions of each party at this unexpected rencontre may be imagined. Leonard Holt, with a breast boiling with jealous rage, prepared to attack his rival. He had no weapon about him, having left his cudgel in the shop, but he doubled his fists, and, nerved by passion, felt he had the force of a Hercules in his arm. Wyvil, in his turn, kept his hand upon his sword, and glanced at his mistress, as if seeking instructions how to act. At length, Mrs. Bloundel, who formed one of the group, spoke.

"Leonard Holt," she said, "show this person out at the door. Do not lose sight of him for an instant; and, as soon as he is gone, try to find out how he entered the house."

"He entered it like a robber," returned Leonard, looking fiercely at the gallant, "and if I did my strict duty, I should seize him and give him in charge to the watch. He has come here for the purpose of stealing my master's chief valuable—his daughter."

"I am aware of it," replied Mrs. Bloundel, "and nothing but consideration for my husband prevents my delivering him up to justice. As it is, he may go free. But should he return——"

"If I catch him here again," interrupted Leonard, "I will shoot him as I would a dog, though I should be hanged for the deed. Have you considered well what you are doing, madam? I would not presume beyond my station, but there are seasons when an inferior may give wholesome advice. Are you certain you are acting as your worthy husband would, in allowing this person to depart? If you have any doubt, speak. Fear nothing. Unarmed as I am, I am a match for him, and will detain him."

"Do not heed what Leonard says, dear mother," interposed Amabel. "For my sake, let Mr. Wyvil go."

"I *have* considered the matter, Leonard," returned Mrs. Bloundel, "and trust I am acting rightly. At all events, I am sure I am sparing my husband pain."

"It is a mistaken tenderness," rejoined Leonard, "and Heaven grant you may not have cause to repent it. If I had your permission, I would so deal with this audacious intruder, that he should never venture to repeat his visit."

"You know that you speak safely, fellow," rejoined Wyvil, "and you, therefore, give full licence to your scurrile tongue. But a time will come when I will chastise your insolence."

"No more of this," cried Mrs. Bloundel. "Do as I bid you, Leonard; and, as you value my regard, say nothing of what has occurred to your master."

Sullenly acquiescing, the apprentice preceded Wyvil to the shop, and opened the door.

As the other passed through it, he said, "You spoke of chastising me just now. If you have courage enough—which I doubt—to make good your words, and will wait for me for five minutes, near Saint Alban's church in this street, you shall have the opportunity."

Wyvil did not deign a reply, but wrapping his cloak around him, strode away. He had not proceeded far, when it occurred to him that, possibly, notwithstanding his interdiction, some of his companions might be waiting for him, and hurrying down the passage leading to the yard, he found Lydyard, to whom he recounted his ill-success.

"I shall not, however, abandon my design," he said. "These failures are only incentives to further exertion."

"In the meantime, you must pay your wager to Sedley," laughed Lydyard, "and as the house is really infected with the plague, it behoves you to call at the first apothecary's shop we find open, and get your apparel fumigated. You must not neglect due precautions."

"True," replied Wyvil, "and as I feel too restless to go home at present, suppose we amuse ourselves by calling on some astrologer, to see whether the stars are favourable to my pursuit of this girl."

"A good idea," replied Lydyard. "There are plenty of the 'Sons of Urania,' as they term themselves, hereabouts."

" A mere juggler will not serve my turn," returned
Wyvil.

" William Lilly, the almanack-maker, who predicted
the plague, and, if old Rowley is to be believed, has
great skill in the occult sciences, lives somewhere in Friday-
street, not a stone's throw from this place. Let us go and
find him out."

" Agreed," replied Lydyard.

CHAPTER V

The Pomander-box

ANY doubts entertained by Leonard Holt as to the
manner in which his rival entered the house, were removed
by discovering the open window in the passage, and the
rope-ladder hanging to the yard-wall. Taking the ladder
away, and making all as secure as he could, he next
seized his cudgel, and proceeded to Blaize's room, with
the intention of inflicting upon him the punishment he
had threatened; for he naturally enough attributed to
the porter's carelessness all the mischief that had just
occurred. Not meeting with him, however, and concluding he was in the kitchen, he descended thither, and
found him in such a pitiable plight, that his wrath was
instantly changed to compassion.

Stretched upon the hearth before a blazing sea-coal
fire, which seemed large enough to roast him, with his
head resting upon the lap of Patience, the pretty kitchen-
maid, and his left hand upon his heart, the porter loudly
complained of a fixed and burning pain in that region;
while his mother, who was kneeling beside him, having
just poured a basin of scalding posset-drink, down his
throat, entreated him to let her examine his side to see
whether he had any pestilential mark upon it, but he
vehemently resisted her efforts.

" Do you feel any swelling, myn lief zoon ? " asked
old Josyna, trying to remove his hand.

"Swelling!" ejaculated Blaize,—"there's a tumour as big as an egg."

"Is id possible?" exclaimed Josyna, in great alarm. "Do let me look ad id."

"No, no, leave me alone," rejoined Blaize. "Don't disturb me further. You will catch the distemper if you touch the sore."

"Dat won'd hinder me from drying to zaave you," replied his mother, affectionately. "I must see vad is de madder vid you, or I cannod cure you."

"I am past your doctoring, mother," groaned Blaize. "Leave me alone, I say. You hurt me shockingly!"

"Poor child!" cried Josyna, soothingly, "I'll be as dender as possible. I'll nod give you de leasd pain—nod de leasd bid."

"But I tell you, you *do* give me a great deal," rejoined Blaize. "I can't bear it. Your fingers are like iron nails. Keep them away."

"Bless us! did I ever hear de like of dad!" exclaimed Josyna. "Iron nails! if you think so, myn arm zoon, you musd be very ill indeed."

"I *am* very ill," groaned her son. "I am not long for this world."

"Oh! don't say so, dear Blaize," sobbed Patience, letting fall a plentiful shower of tears on his face. "Don't say so. I can't bear to part with you."

"Then don't survive me," returned Blaize. "But there's little chance of your doing so. You are certain to take the plague."

"I care not what becomes of myself, if I lose you, Blaize," responded Patience, bedewing his countenance with another shower; "but I hope you won't die yet."

"Ah! it's all over with me—all over," rejoined Blaize. "I told Leonard Holt how it would be, I said I should be the next victim. And my words are come true."

"You are as clever as a conjurer," sobbed Patience; "but I wish you hadn't been right in this instance. However, comfort yourself. I'll die with you. We'll be carried to the grave in the same plague-cart."

"That's cold comfort," returned Blaize angrily. "I

·beg you'll never mention the plague-cart again. The thought of it makes me shiver all over—oh!" And he uttered a dismal and prolonged groan.

At this juncture, Leonard thought it time to interfere.

" If you are really attacked by the plague, Blaize," he said, advancing, " you must have instant advice. Doctor Hodges is still upstairs with our master. He must see you."

" On no account," returned the porter, in the greatest alarm, and springing to his feet. " I am better—much better. I don't think I am ill at all."

" For the first time, I suspect the contrary," replied the apprentice, " since you are afraid of owning it. But this is not a matter to be trifled with. Doctor Hodges will soon settle the point." And he hurried out of the room to summon the physician.

" Oh! mother!—dear Patience!" roared Blaize, capering about in an ecstasy of terror ; " don't let the doctor come near me. Keep me out of his sight. You don't know what horrid things are done to those afflicted with any complaint. But I do—for I have informed myself on the subject. Their skins are scarified, and their sores blistered, lanced, cauterized, and sometimes burned away with a knob of red-hot iron, called ' the button.' "

" But iv id is necessary, myn goed Blaize, you musd submid," replied his mother. " Never mind de hod iron or de lance, or de blisder, iv dey make you well. Never mind de pain. It will soon be over."

" Soon over!" bellowed Blaize, sinking into a chair. " Yes, I feel it will. But not in the way you imagine. This Doctor Hodges will kill me. He is fond of trying experiments, and will make me his subject. Don't let him—for pity's sake, don't."

" But I musd, myn lief jonger," replied his mother, " I musd."

" Oh, Patience!" supplicated Blaize, " you were always fond of me. My mother has lost her natural affection. She wishes to get rid of me. Don't take part with her. My sole dependence is upon you."

" I will do all I can for you, dear Blaize," blubbered

the kitchen-maid. " But it is absolutely necessary you should see the doctor."

" Then I won't stay here another minute," vociferated Blaize. " I'll die in the street rather than under his hands."

And bursting from them, he would have made good his retreat, but for the entrance of Leonard and Hodges.

At the sight of the latter, Blaize ran back and endeavoured to screen himself behind Patience.

" Is this the sick man ? " remarked Hodges, scarcely able to refrain from laughing. " I don't think he can be in such imminent danger as you led me to suppose."

" No, I am better—much better, thank you," returned Blaize, still keeping Patience between him and the doctor. " The very sight of you has frightened away the plague."

" Indeed ! " exclaimed Hodges, smiling, " then it is the most marvellous cure I ever yet effected. But come forward, young man, and let us see what is the matter with you ? "

" You neither lance, nor cauterize an incipient tumour, do you, doctor ? " demanded Blaize, without abandoning his position.

" Eh, day ! " exclaimed Hodges, " have we one of the faculty here ? I see how it is, friend. You have been reading some silly book about the disease, and have frightened yourself into the belief that you have some of its symptoms. I hope you haven't been doctoring yourself, likewise. What have you taken ? "

" It would be difficult to say what he has *not* taken," remarked Leonard. " His stomach must be like an apothecary's shop."

" I have only used proper precautions," rejoined Blaize, testily.

" And what may those be eh ? " inquired the doctor. " I am curious to learn."

" Come from behind Patience," cried Leonard, " and don't act the fool longer, or I will see whether your disorder will not yeld to a sound application of the cudgel."

" Don't rate him thus, good Master Leonard," interposed Patience. " He is very ill,—he is, indeed."

"Then let him have a chance of getting better," returned the apprentice. "If he *is* ill, he has no business near you. Come from behind her, Blaize, I say. Now speak," he added, as the porter crept tremblingly forth, "and let us hear what nostrums you have swallowed. I know you have dosed yourself with pills, electuaries, balsams, tinctures, conserves, spirits, elixirs, decoctions, and every other remedy, real or imaginary. What else have you done?"

"What Dr. Hodges, I am sure, will approve," replied Blaize, confidently. "I have rubbed myself with vinegar, oil of sulphur, extract of tar, and spirit of turpentine."

"What next?" demanded Hodges.

"I placed saltpetre, brimstone, amber, and juniper upon a chafing-dish, to fumigate my room," replied Blaize; "but the vapour was so overpowering, I could not bear it."

"I should be surprised if you could," replied the doctor. "Indeed, it is astonishing to me, if you have taken half the remedies Leonard says you have,—and which, taken in this way, are no remedies at all, since they counteract each other,—that you are still alive. But let us see what is the matter with you. What ails you particularly?"

"Nothing," replied Blaize, trembling; "I am quite well."

"He complains of a fixed pain near de haard, docdor," interposed his mother, "and says he has a large dumour on his side. But he won'd let me examine id."

"That's a bad sign," observed Hodges, shaking his head. "I am afraid it's not all fancy, as I at first supposed. Have you felt sick of late, young man?"

"Not of late," replied Blaize, becoming as white as ashes; "but I do now."

"Another bad symptom," rejoined the doctor. "Take off your doublet and open your shirt."

"Do as the doctor bids you," said Leonard, seeing that Blaize hesitated, "or I apply the cudgel."

"Ah! bless my life! what's this?" cried Hodges,

running his hand down the left side of the porter, and meeting with a large lump. " Can it be a carbuncle ? "

" Yes, it's a terrible carbuncle," replied Blaize; " but don't cauterize it, doctor."

" Let me look at it," cried Hodges, " and I shall then know how to proceed."

And as he spoke, he tore open the porter's shirt, and a silver ball, about as large as a pigeon's egg, fell to the ground. Leonard picked it up, and found it so hot, that he could scarcely hold it.

" Here is the terrible carbuncle," he cried, with a laugh, in which all the party, except Blaize joined.

" It's my pomander-box," said the latter. " I filled it with a mixture of citron-peel, angelica-seed, zedoary, yellow saunders, aloes, benzoin, camphor, and gum-tragacanth, moistened with spirit of roses; and after placing it on the chafing-dish to heat it, hung it by a string round my neck, next my dried toad. I suppose, by some means or other, it dropped through my doublet, and found its way to my side. I felt a dreadful burning there, and that made me fancy I was attacked by the plague."

" A very satisfactory solution of the mystery," replied the doctor, laughing; " and you may think yourself well off with the blister which your box has raised. It will be easier to bear than the cataplasm I should have given you, had your apprehensions been well founded. As yet, you are free from infection, young man; but if you persist in this silly and pernicious practice of quacking yourself, you will infallibly bring on some fatal disorder —perhaps the plague itself. If your mother has any regard for you, she will put all your medicines out of your reach. There are few known remedies against this frightful disease; and what few there are, must be adopted cautiously. My own specific is sack."

" Sack ! " exclaimed Blaize in astonishment. " Henceforth, I will drink nothing else. I like the remedy amazingly."

" It must be taken in moderation," said the doctor: " otherwise, it is as dangerous as too much physic."

C

" I have a boddle or doo of de liquor you commend, docdor, in my privade cupboard," observed Josyna. " Will you dasde id ? "

" With great pleasure," replied Hodges, " and a drop of it will do your son no harm."

The wine was accordingly produced, and the doctor pronounced it excellent, desiring that a glass might a'ways be brought him when he visited the grocer's house.

" You may rely upon id, mynheer, as long as my small sdore lasds," replied Josyna.

Blaize, who, in obedience to the doctor's commands, had drained a large glass of sack, felt so much inspirited by it, that he ventured, when his mother's back was turned, to steal a kiss from Patience, and to whisper in her ear, that if he escaped the plague, he would certainly marry her—an assurance that seemed to give her no slight satisfaction. His new-born courage, however, was in some degree damped by Leonard, who observed to him, in an undertone—

" You have neglected my injunctions, sirrah, and allowed the person I warned you of to enter the house. When a fitting season arrives, I will not fail to pay off old scores."

Blaize would have remonstrated, and asked for some explanation, but the apprentice instantly left him, and set out upon his errand to the Examiner of Health. Accompanied by his mother, who would not even allow him to say good-night to Patience, the porter then proceeded to his own room, where the old woman, to his infinite regret, carried off his stores of medicine in a basket which she brought with her for that purpose, and locked the door upon him.

" This has escaped her," said Blaize, as soon as she was gone, opening a secret drawer in the cupboard. " How fortunate that I kept this reserve. I have still a tolerable supply in case of need. Let me examine my stock. First of all, there are plague-lozenges, composed of angelica, liquorice, flower of sulphur, myrrh, and oil of cinnamon. Secondly, an electuary of bole-armoniac,

hartshorn-shavings, saffron, and syrup of wood-sorrel.
I long to taste it. But then it would be running in the
doctor's teeth. Thirdly, there is a phial labelled *Aqua
Theriacalis Stillatitia*—in plain English, distilled treacle-
water. A spoonful of this couldn't hurt me. Fourthly,
a packet of powders, entitled *Manus Christi*—an excellent
mixture. Fifthly, a small pot of diatesseron, composed of
gentian, myrrh, bayberries, and round aristolochia. I
must just taste it. Never mind the doctor! He does not
know what agrees with my constitution as well as I do
myself. Physic comes as naturally to me as mother's milk.
Sixthly, there is *Aqua Epidemica*, commonly called the
Plague-Water of Matthias—delicious stuff! I will only
just sip it. What a fine bitter it has! I'm sure it must
be very wholesome. Next, for I've lost my count, comes
salt of vipers—next, powder of unicorn's horn—next. oil
of scorpions from Naples—next, dragon-water—all
admirable. Then there are cloves of garlic—sovereign
fortifiers of the stomach—and, lastly. there is a large
box of my favourite rufuses. How many pills have I
taken? Only half-a-dozen! Three more mav as well go
to keep the others company."

And hastily swallowing them, as if afraid of detection,
he carefully shut the drawer, and then crept into bed,
and, covering himself with blankets, endeavoured to
compose himself to slumber.

Doctor Hodges, meantime, returned to the grocer, and
acquainted him that it was a false alarm, and that the
porter was entirely free from infection.

" I am glad to hear it," replied Bloundel ; " but I
expected as much. Blaize is like the shepherd's boy in the
fable; he has cried ' wolf ' so often, that when the danger
really arrives, no one will heed him."

" I must now take my leave, Mr. Bloundel," said
Hodges. " I will be with you the first thing to-morrow,
and have little doubt I shall find your son going on well.
But you must not merely take care of him, but of yourself,
and your household. It will be well to set a chafing-dish
in the middle of the room, and scatter some of these perfumes occasionally upon it;" and producing several

small packets, he gave them to the grocer. " If you ever
smoke a pipe, I would advise you to do so now."

" I never smoke," replied Bloundel, " and hold it as a
filthy and mischievous habit, which nothing but necessity should induce me to practise."

" It is advisable now," returned Hodges, " and you
should neglect no precaution. Take my word for it, Mr.
Bloundel, the plague is only beginning. When the heats
of summer arrive, its ravages will be frightful. Heaven
only knows what will become of us all ! "

" If my poor son is spared, and we escape contagion,"
returned Bloundel, " I will put into execution a scheme
which has occurred to me, and which (under Providence !)
will, I trust, secure my family from further hazard."

" Ah, indeed ! what is that ? " inquired Hodges.

" We must talk of it some other time," returned
Bloundel. " Good-night, doctor, and accept my thanks
for your attention. To-morrow, at as early an hour
as you can make convenient, I shall hope to see you."
And with a friendly shake of the hand, and a reiteration
of advice and good wishes, Hodges departed.

Soon after this, the apprentice returned, and by his
master's directions, placed a chafing-dish in the middle
of the room, supplying it with the drugs and herbs left
by the doctor. About four o'clock, a loud knocking
was heard. Instantly answering the summons, Leonard
found four men at the shop-door, two of whom he knew,
by red wands they carried, were searchers; while their
companions appeared to be undertakers, from their sable
habits and long black cloaks.

Marching unceremoniously into the shop, the searchers
desired to see the sick man; and the apprentice then perceived that one of the men in black cloaks was the coffin-
maker, Chowles. He could not, however, refuse him
admittance, and led the way to the grocer's chamber. As
they entered it, Bloundel arose, and placing his finger to
his lips in token of silence, raised the blankets, and exhibited the blotch, which had greatly increased in size,
under the arm of his slumbering son. The foremost of the
searchers, who kept a phial of vinegar to his nose all the

time he remained in the room, then demanded in a low tone whether there were any other of the household infected? The grocer replied in the negative. Upon this, Chowles, whose manner showed he was more than half intoxicated, took off his hat, and bowing obsequiously to the grocer, said, " Shall I prepare you a coffin, Mr. Bloundel? You are sure to want one, and had better give the order in time, for there is a great demand for such articles just now. If you like, I will call with it to-morrow night. I have a plague-cart of my own, and bury all my customers."

" God grant I may not require your services, sir ! " replied the grocer, shuddering. " But I will give you timely notice."

" If you are in want of a nurse, I can recommend an experienced one," added Chowles. " Her last employer is just dead."

" I may need assistance," replied the grocer, after a moment's reflection. " Let her call to-morrow."

" She understands her business perfectly, and will save you a world of trouble," replied Chowles; " besides securing me the sale of another coffin," he added to himself.

He then quitted the room with the searchers, and Leonard felt inexpressibly relieved by their departure.

As soon as the party gained the street, the fourth person, who was provided with materials for the task, painted a red cross of the prescribed size—namely, a foot's length—in the middle of the door; tracing above it, in large characters, the melancholy formula—" LORD HAVE MERCY UPON US ! "

CHAPTER VI

The Libertine Punished

SIR PAUL PARRAVICIN and Major Pillichody arrived without any particular adventure at the top of the Haymarket, where the former dismissed the coach he had hired in Cheapside, and they proceeded towards Piccadilly on foot. Up to this time, the major had been in very high spirits, boasting what he would do in case they encountered Disbrowe, and offering to keep guard outside the door while the knight remained in the house. But he now began to alter his tone, and to frame excuses to get away. He had noticed with some uneasiness, that another coach stopped lower down in the Haymarket, at precisely the same time as their own; and though he could not be quite certain of the fact, he fancied he perceived a person greatly resembling Captain Disbrowe alight from it. Mentioning the circumstance to his companion, he pointed out a tall figure following them at some distance; but the other only laughed at him, and said, " It may possibly be Disbrowe—but what if it is ? He cannot get into the house without the key; and if he is inclined to measure swords with me a second time, he shall not escape so lightly as he did the first."

" Right, Sir Paul, right," returned Pillichody, " exterminate him—spare him not. By Bellerophon ! that's my way. My only apprehension is lest he should set upon us unawares. The bravest are not proof against the dagger of an assassin."

" There you wrong Disbrowe, major, I am persuaded," returned Parravicin. " He is too much a man of honour to stab a foe behind his back."

" It may be," replied Pillichody, " but jealousy will sometimes turn a man's brain. By the snakes of Tisiphone ! I have known an instance of it myself. I once made love to a tailor's wife, and the rascal coming in unawares, struck me to the ground with his goose, and well-nigh murdered me."

"After such a mischance, I am surprised you should venture to carry on so many hazardous intrigues," laughed the knight. "But you proposed just now to keep watch outside the house. If it is Disbrowe who is following us, you had better do so."

"Why, Sir Paul—you see,"—stammered the major, "I have just bethought me of an engagement."

"An engagement at this hour—impossible!" cried Parravicin.

"An assignation, I ought to say," returned Pillichody. "Couches of Cytheræa!—an affair like your own. You would not have me keep a lady waiting."

"It is strange you should not recollect it till this moment," replied Parravicin. "But be your inamorata whom she may—even the rich widow of Watling-street, of whom you prate so much—you must put her off to-night."

"But, Sir Paul——"

"I will have no denial," replied the knight, peremptorily. "If you refuse, you will find me worse to deal with than Disbrowe. You must remain at the door till I come out. And now let us lose no more time. I am impatient to behold the lady."

"Into what accursed scrape have I got myself?" thought the major, as he walked by the side of his companion, ever and anon casting wistful glances over his shoulder. "I am fairly caught on the horns of a dilemma. I instinctively feel that Disbrowe *is* dogging us. What will become of me? The moment this hare-brained coxcomb enters the house, I will see whether a light pair of heels cannot bear me out of harm's way."

By this time, they had reached a passage known as Bear-alley (all traces of which have been swept away by modern improvements), and threading it, they entered a narrow thoroughfare, called Castle-street. Just as they turned the corner, Pillichody again noticed the figure at the farther end of the alley, and, but for his fears of the knight, would have instantly scampered off.

"Are we far from the house?" inquired Parravicin.

"No," replied the major, scarcely able to conceal his trepidation "It is close at hand—and so is the lady's husband."

"So much the better," replied the knight; "it will afford you some amusement to beat him off. You may affect not to know him, and may tell him the lady's husband is just come home—her *husband*!—do you take, Pillichody?"

"I do—ha! ha! I do," replied the major, in a quavering tone.

"But you don't appear to relish the jest," rejoined Parravicin, sneeringly.

"Oh, yes, I relish it exceedingly," replied Pillichody; "her husband—ha!—ha!—and Disbrowe is the disappointed lover—capital! But here we are—and I wish we were anywhere else," he added to himself.

"Are you sure you are right?" asked Parravicin, searching for the key.

"Quite sure," returned Pillichody. "Don't you see someone behind that wall?"

"I see nothing," rejoined the knight. "You are afraid of shadows, major."

"Afraid!" ejaculated Pillichody. "Thousand thunders! I am afraid of nothing."

"In that case, I shall expect to find you have slain Disbrowe on my return," rejoined Parravicin, unlocking the door.

"The night is chilly," observed the major, "and ever since my campaigns in the Low Countries, I have been troubled with rheumatism. I should prefer keeping guard inside."

"No, no, you must remain where you are, replied the knight, shutting the door.

Pillichody was about to take to his heels, when he felt himself arrested by a powerful man. He would have roared for aid, but a voice, which he instantly recognised, commanded him to keep silence, if he valued his life.

"Is your companion in the house?" demanded Disbrowe, in a hollow tone.

"I am sorry to say he is, Captain Disbrowe," replied the bully. "I did my best to prevent him, but remonstrance was in vain."

"Liar," cried Disbrowe, striking him with his clenched hand. "Do you think to impose upon me by such a pitiful fabrication? It was you who introduced me to this heartless libertine—you who encouraged me to play with him, telling me I should easily strip him of all he possessed—you who excited his passion for my wife, by praising her beauty—and it was you who put it into his head to propose that fatal stake to me."

"There you are wrong, Captain Disbrowe," returned Pillichody, in a supplicatory tone. "On my soul, you are! I certainly praised your wife (as who would not?) but I never advised Parravicin to play for her. That was his own idea entirely."

"The excuse shall not avail you," cried Disbrowe, fiercely. "To you I owe all my misery. Draw and defend yourself."

"Be not so hasty, captain," cried Pillichody, abjectly. "I have injured you sufficiently already. I would not have your blood on my head. On the honour of a soldier, I am sorry for the wrong I have done you, and will strive to repair it."

"Repair it!" shrieked Disbrowe. "It is too late." And seizing the major's arm, he dragged him by main force into the alley.

"Help! help!" roared Pillichody. "Would you murder me?"

"I will assuredly cut your throat, if you keep up this clamour," rejoined Disbrowe, snatching the other's long rapier from his side. "Coward!" he added, striking him with the flat side of the weapon, "this will teach you to mix yourself up in such infamous affairs for the future."

And heedless of the major's entreaties and vociferations, he continued to belabour him, until compelled by fatigue to desist; when the other, contriving to extricate himself. ran off as fast as his legs could carry him. Disbrowe looked after him for a moment, as if uncertain whether to follow, and then hurrying to the house, stationed himself beneath the porch.

" I will stab him as he comes forth," he muttered, drawing his sword, and hiding it beneath his mantle.

Parravicin, meanwhile, having let himself into the house, marched boldly forward, though the passage was buried in darkness, and he was utterly unacquainted with it. Feeling against the wall, he presently discovered a door, and opening it, entered a room lighted by a small silver lamp placed on a marble slab. The room was empty, but its furniture and arrangements proclaimed it the favourite retreat of the fair mistress of the abode. Parravicin gazed curiously round, as if anxious to gather from what he saw some idea of the person he so soon expected to encounter. Everything betokened a refined and luxurious taste. A few French romances, the last plays of Etherege, Dryden, and Shadwell, a volume of Cowley, and some amorous songs, lay on the table; and not far from them were a loomask, pulvil purse, a pair of scented gloves, a richly-laced mouchoir, a manteau girdle, palatine tags, and a golden bodkin for the hair.

Examining all these things, and drawing his own conclusions as to the character of their owner, Parravicin turned to a couch on which a cittern was thrown, while beside it, on a cushion, were a pair of tiny embroidered velvet slippers. A pocket-mirror, or sprunking-glass, as it was then termed, lay on a side table, and near it stood an embossed silver chocolate-pot, and a small porcelain cup with a golden spoon inside it showing what the lady's last repast had been. On another small table, covered with an exquisitely white napkin, stood a flask of wine, a tall-stemmed glass, and a few cakes on a china dish, evidently placed there for Disbrowe's return.

As Parravicin drew near this table, a slip of paper, on which a few lines were traced, attracted his attention, and taking it up, he read as follows:—

" It is now midnight, and you promised to return early. I have felt your absence severely, and have been suffering from a violent headache, which has almost distracted me.

I have also been troubled with strange and unaccountable misgivings respecting you. I am a little easier now, but still far from well, and about to retire to rest. At what hour will this meet your eye? MARGARET."

"Charming creature!" exclaimed Parravicin, as the paper dropped from his hand; "she little dreamed, when she wrote it, who would read her billet. Disbrowe does not deserve such a treasure. I am sorry she is unwell. I hope she has not taken the plague. Pshaw! what could put such an idea into my head? Lydyard's warning, I suppose. That fellow, who is the veriest rake among us, is always preaching. Confound him. I wish he had not mentioned it. A glass of wine may exhilarate me." And pouring out a bumper, he swallowed it at a draught. "And so the fond fool is pining for her husband, and has some misgivings about him. Egad! it is well for her she does not know what has really taken place. She'll learn that soon enough. What's this?" he added, glancing at a picture on the wall. "Her miniature! It must be; for it answers exactly to Pillichody's description. A sparkling brunette, with raven hair, and eyes of night. I am on fire to behold her: but I must proceed with prudence, or I may ruin all. Is there nothing of Disbrowe's that I could put on for the nonce? 'Fore Heaven! the very thing I want!"

The exclamation was occasioned by his observing a loose silken robe lying across a chair. Wrapping it round him, and throwing down his hat, he took the lamp, and went upstairs.

Daring as he was, Parravicin felt his courage desert him, as having found the door of Mrs. Disbrowe's chamber, he cautiously opened it. A single glance showed him that the room was more exquisitely, more luxuriously furnished than that he had just quitted. Articles of feminine attire, of the richest kind, were hung against the walls, or disposed on the chairs. On one side stood the toilette-table, with its small mirror then in vogue, and all its equipage of silver flasks, filigree cassets, japan patch-boxes, scent bottles, and pomatum-pots.

As he entered the room, a faint voice issuing from behind the rich damask curtains of the bed, demanded, " Is it you, Disbrowe ? "

" It is, Margaret," replied Parravicin, setting down the lamp, and speaking with a handkerchief at his mouth, to disguise his voice and conceal his features.

" You are late—very late," she rejoined, " and I have been ill. I fancied myself dying."

" What has been the matter with you, sweet Meg ? " asked Parravicin, approaching the bed, and seating himself behind the curtains.

" I know not," she replied. " I was seized with a dreadful headache about an hour ago. It has left me; but I have a strange oppression at my chest, and breathe with difficulty."

" You alarm me, my love," rejoined Parravicin. " Were you ever attacked thus before ? "

" Never," she replied. " Oh ! Disbrowe ! if you knew how I have longed for your return, you would blame yourself for your absence. You have grown sadly neglectful of late. I suspect you love some one else, If I thought so——"

" What if you thought so, Margaret ? " demanded Parravicin.

" What ! " cried Mrs. Disbrowe, raising herself in the bed. " I would requite your perfidy,—terribly requite it ! "

" Then learn that Captain Disbrowe *is* faithless," cried Parravicin, throwing back the curtains, and disclosing himself. " Learn that he loves another, and is with her now. Learn, that he cares so little for you, that he has surrendered you to me."

" What do I hear ? " exclaimed Mrs. Disbrowe. " Who are you, and what brings you here ? "

" You may guess my errand from my presence," replied the knight. " I am called Sir Paul Parravicin, and am the most devoted of your admirers."

" My husband surrender me to a stranger ! It cannot be ! " cried the lady, distractedly.

" You see me here, and may judge of the truth of

my statement," rejoined the knight. "Your husband gave me this key, with which I introduced myself to the house."

"What motive could he have for such unheard-of baseness,—such barbarity?" cried Mrs. Disbrowe, bursting into tears.

"Shall I tell you, madam?" replied Parravicin. "He is tired of you, and has taken this means of ridding himself of you."

Mrs. Disbrowe uttered a loud scream, and fell back in the bed. Parravicin waited for a moment; but not hearing her move brought the lamp to see what was the matter. She had fainted, and was lying across the pillow, with her night-dress partly open, so as to expose her neck and shoulders.

The knight was at first ravished with her beauty; but his countenance suddenly fell, and an expression of horror and alarm took possession of it. He appeared rooted to the spot, and instead of attempting to render her any assistance, remained with his gaze fixed upon her neck.

Rousing himself at length, he rushed out of the room, hurried downstairs, and without pausing for a moment, threw open the street-door. As he issued from it, his throat was forcibly gripped, and the point of a sword was placed at his breast.

"You are now in my power, villain," cried Disbrowe, "and shall not escape my vengeance."

"You are already avenged," replied Parravicin, shaking off his assailant. "Your wife has the plague."

CHAPTER VII

The Plague Nurse

" AND so my husband has got the plague," muttered
Mother Malmayns, as she hastened towards Saint Paul's,
after the reproof she had received from Doctor Hodges.
" Well, it's a disorder that few recover from, and I don't
think he stands a better chance than his fellows. I've
been troubled with him long enough. I've borne his ill-
usage and savage temper for twenty years, vainly hoping
something would take him off; but though he tried his
constitution hard, it was too tough to yield. However,
he's likely to go now. If I find him better than I expect,
I can easily make all sure. That's one good thing about
the plague. You may get rid of a patient without any one
being the wiser. A wrong mixture—a pillow removed—
a moment's chill during the fever—a glass of cold water—
the slightest thing will do it. Matthew Malmayns, you
will die of the plague, that's certain. But I must be careful
how I proceed. That cursed doctor has his eye upon me.
As luck would have it, I've got Sibbald's ointment in my
pocket. That is sure to do its business,—and safely."

Thus ruminating, she shaped her course towards the
south-west corner of the cathedral, and passing under the
shrouds and cloisters of the Convocation House, raised
the latch of a small wooden shed fixed in the angle of a
buttress. Evidently well acquainted with the place, she
was not long in finding a lantern and materials to light it,
and inserting her fingers in a crevice of the masonry from
which the mortar had been removed, she drew forth a key.

" It has not been stirred since I left it here a month
ago," she muttered. " I must take care of this key, for
if Matthew *should* die, I may not be able to enter the vaults
of Saint Faith's without it; and as I know all their secret
places and passages, which nobody else does, except my
husband, I can make them a storehouse for the plunder
I may obtain during the pestilence. If it rages for a year,

or only half that time, and increases in violence (as God grant it may), I will fill every hole in those walls with gold."

With this, she took up the lantern, and crept along the side of the cathedral, until she came to a flight of stone steps. Descending them, she unlocked a small but strong door, cased with iron, and fastening it after her, proceeded along a narrow stone passage, which brought her to another door, opening upon the south aisle of Saint Faith's.

Pausing for a moment to listen whether any one was within the sacred structure,—for such was the dead and awful silence of the place that the slightest whisper or footfall, even at its farthest extremity, could be distinguished,—she crossed to the other side, glancing fearfully around her as she threaded the ranks of pillars, whose heavy and embrowned shafts her lantern feebly illumined, and entering a recess took a small stone out of the wall, and deposited the chief part of the contents of her pocket behind it, after which she carefully replaced the stone. This done, she hurried to the charnel, and softly opened the door of the crypt.

Greatly relieved by the operation he had undergone, the sexton had sunk into a slumber, and was, therefore, unconscious of the entrance of his wife, who, setting down the lantern, advanced towards the pallet. His mother and the young man were still in attendance, and the former, on seeing her daughter-in-law, exclaimed, in low but angry accents,—" What brings you here, Judith ? I suppose you expected to find my son dead. But he will disappoint you. Doctor Hodges said he would recover—did he not, Kerrich ? " she added, appealing to the young man, who nodded acquiescence. " He will recover, I tell you."

" Well, well," replied Judith, in the blandest tone she could assume; " I hope he will. And if the doctor says so, I have no doubt of it. I only heard of his illness a few minutes ago, and came instantly to nurse him."

" *You* nurse him ! " cried the old woman; " if you show him any affection now, it will be for the first time since your wedding-day."

" How long has he been unwell? " demanded Judith, with difficulty repressing her anger.

" He was seized the night before last," replied the old woman; " but he didn't know what was the matter with him when it began. I saw him just before he went to rest, and he complained of a slight illness, but nothing to signify. He must have passed a frightful night, for the vergers found him in the morning running about Saint Faith's like a madman, and dashing his spades and mattocks against the walls and pillars. They secured him, and brought him here, and on examination, he proved to have the plague."

" You surprise me by what you say," replied Judith. " During the last month, I have nursed more than a dozen patients, and never knew any of them so violent. I must look at his sore."

" The doctor has just dressed it," observed the old woman.

" I don't mind that," rejoined Judith, turning down the blanket, and examining her husband's shoulder. " You are right," she added, " he is doing as well as possible."

" I suppose I sha'n't be wanted any more," observed Kerrich, " now you're come back to nurse your husband, Mrs. Malmayns? I shall be glad to get home to my own bed, for I don't feel well at all."

" Don't alarm yourself," replied Judith. " There's a bottle of plague-vinegar for you. Dip a piece of linen in it, and smell at it, and it'll insure you against the pestilence."

Kerrich took the phial, and departed. But the remedy was of little avail. Before daybreak, he was seized with the distemper, and died two days afterwards.

" I hope poor Kerrich hasn't got the plague? " said the old woman, in a tremulous tone.

" I am afraid he has," replied the daughter-in-law, " but I didn't like to alarm him."

" Mercy on us! " cried the other, getting up. " What a dreadful scourge it is."

" You would say so if you had seen whole families

swept off by it, as I have," replied Judith. "But it mostly attacks old persons and children."

"Lord help us!" cried the crone, "I hope it will spare me. I thought my age secured me."

"Quite the reverse," replied Judith, desirous of exciting her mother-in-law's terrors; "quite the reverse. You must take care of yourself."

"But you don't think I'm ill, do you?" asked the other anxiously.

"Sit down, and let me look at you," returned Judith.

And the old woman tremblingly obeyed.

"Well, what do you think of me—what's the matter?" she asked, as her daughter-in-law eyed her for some minutes in silence. "What's the matter, I say?"

But Judith remained silent.

"I insist upon knowing," continued the old woman.

"Are you able to bear the truth?" returned her daughter-in-law.

"You need say no more," groaned the old woman. "I know what the truth must be, and will try to bear it. I will get home as fast as I can, and put my few affairs in order, so that if I am carried off, I may not go unprepared."

"You had better do so," replied her daughter-in-law.

"You will take care of my poor son, Judith," rejoined the old woman, shedding a flood of tears. "I would stay with him, if I thought I could do him any good; but if I really am infected, I might only be in the way. Don't neglect him—as you hope for mercy hereafter, do not."

"Make yourself easy, mother," replied Judith. "I will take every care of him."

"Have you no fears of the disorder yourself?" inquired the old woman.

"None whatever," replied Judith. "I am a safe woman."

"I do not understand you," replied her mother-in-law, in surprise.

"I have had the plague," replied Judith; "and those who have had it once, never take it a second time."

This opinion, entertained at the commencement of the pestilence, it may be incidentally remarked, was afterwards found to be entirely erroneous;—some persons being known to have the distemper three or four times.

" You never let us know you were ill," said the old woman.

" I could not do so," replied Judith, " and I don't know that I should have done if I could. I was nursing two sisters at a small house in Clerkenwell Close, and they both died in the night-time, within a few hours of each other. The next day, as I was preparing to leave the house, I was seized myself, and had scarcely strength to creep upstairs to bed. An old apothecary, named Sibbald, who had brought drugs to the house, attended me and saved my life. In less than a week, I was well again, and able to move about, and should have returned home, but the apothecary told me as I had the distemper once, I might resume my occupation with safety. I did so, and have found plenty of employment."

" No doubt,"rejoined the old woman; " and you will find plenty more—plenty more."

" I hope so," replied the other.

" Oh ! do not give utterance to such a dreadful wish Judith," rejoined her mother-in-law. " Do not let cupidity steel your heart to every better feeling."

A slight derisive smile passed over the harsh features of the plague nurse.

" You heed me not," pursued the old woman. " But a time will come when you will recollect my words."

" I am content to wait till then," rejoined Judith.

" Heaven grant you a better frame of mind ! " exclaimed the old woman. " I must take one last look of my son, for it is not likely I shall see him again."

" Not in this world," thought Judith.

" I conjure you, by all that is sacred, not to neglect him," said the old woman.

" I have already promised to do so," replied Judith, impatiently. " Good-night, mother."

" It will be a long good-night to me, I fear," returned the dame. " Doctor Hodges promised to send some blankets and medicine for poor Matthew. The doctor is a charitable man to the poor, and if he learns I am sick, he may, perhaps, call and give me advice."

" I am sure he will," replied Judith. " Should the man bring the blankets, I will tell him to acquaint his master with your condition. And now take this lantern, mother, and get home as fast as you can."

So saying, she almost pushed her out of the vault, and closed the door after her.

" At last I am rid of her," she muttered. " She would have been a spy over me. I hope I have frightened her into the plague. But if she dies of fear, it will answer my purpose as well. And now for my husband."

Taking up the lamp, and shading it with her hand, she gazed at his ghastly countenance.

" He slumbers tranquilly," she muttered, after contemplating him for some time, adding, with a chuckling laugh, " it would be a pity to waken him."

And seating herself on a stool near the pallet, she turned over in her mind in what way she could best execute her diabolical purpose.

While she was thus occupied, the messenger from Doctor Hodges arrived with a bundle of blankets and several phials and pots of ointment. The man offered to place the blankets on the pallet, but Judith would not let him.

" I can do it better myself, and without disturbing the poor sufferer," she said. " Give my dutiful thanks to your master. Tell him my husband's mother, old widow Malmayns, fancies herself attacked by the plague, and if he will be kind enough to visit her, she lodges in the upper attic of a baker's house at the sign of the Wheatsheaf, in Little Distaff-lane, hard by."

" I will not fail to deliver your message to the doctor," replied the man, as he took his departure.

Left alone with her husband a second time, Judith waited till she thought the man had got out of the cathedral, and then rising and taking the lamp, she repaired to the charnal, to make sure it was untenanted. Not content with this, she stole out into Saint Faith's, and gazing round as far as the feeble light of her lamp would permit, called out in a tone that even startled herself, " Is any one lurking there ? " but receiving no other answer than was afforded by the deep echoes of the place, she returned to the vault Just as she reached the door, a loud cry burst upon her ear, and rushing forward, she found that her husband had wakened.

" Ah ! ' roared Malmayns, raising himself in bed, as he perceived her, " are you come back again, you she-devil ? Where is my mother ? Where is Kerrich ? What have you done with them ? "

' They have both got the plague," replied his wife. " They caught it from you. But never mind them. I will watch over you as long as you live."

" And that will be for years, you accursed jade," replied the sexton ; " Dr. Hodges says I shall recover."

" You have got worse since he left you," replied Judith. " Lie down, and let me throw these blankets over you."

" Off ! " cried the sick man, furiously. " You shall not approach me. You want to smother me."

" I want to cure you," replied his wife, heaping the blankets upon the pallet. " The doctor has sent some ointment for your sore."

" Then let him apply it himself," cried Malmayns, shaking his fist at her. " You shall not touch me. I will strangle you, if you come near me."

" Matthew," replied his wife, " I have had the plague myself, and know how to treat it better than any doctor in London. I will cure you, if you will let me."

" I have no faith in you," replied Malmayns, " but I suppose I must submit. Take heed what you do to me, for if I have but five minutes to live, it will be long enough to revenge myself upon you."

" I will anoint your sore with this salve," rejoined Judith, producing a pot of dark-coloured ointment, and rubbing his shoulder with it. " It was given me by Sibbald, the apothecary of Clerkenwell. He is a friend of Chowles, the coffin-maker. You know Chowles, Matthew ? "

" I know him for as great a rascal as ever breathed,"

replied her husband, gruffly. "He has always cheated me out of my dues, and his coffins are the worst I ever put under ground."

"He is making his fortune now," said Judith.

"By the plague, eh?" replied Matthew. "I don't envy him. Money so gained won't stick to him. He will never prosper."

"I wish *you* had his money, Matthew," replied his wife in a coaxing tone.

"If the plague hadn't attacked me when it did, I should have been richer than Chowles will ever be," replied the sexton. "Nay, I am richer as it is."

"You surprise me," replied Judith, suddenly pausing in her task. "How have you obtained your wealth?"

"I have discovered a treasure," replied the sexton, with a mocking laugh;—"a secret hoard—a chest of gold—ha! ha!"

"Where—where?" demanded his wife eagerly.

"That's a secret," replied Matthew.

"I must have it from him before he dies," thought his wife. "Had we not better secure it without delay?" she added, aloud. "Some other person may find it."

"Oh, it's safe enough," replied Matthew. "It has remained undiscovered for more than a hundred years, and will continue so, for a hundred to come, unless I bring it forth."

"But you *will* bring it forth, won't you?" said Judith.

"Undoubtedly," replied Matthew, "if I get better. But not otherwise. Money would be of no use to me in the grave!"

"But it would be of use to *me*," replied his wife.

"Perhaps it might," replied the sexton; "but if I die, the knowledge of the treasure shall die with me."

"He is deceiving me," thought Judith, beginning to rub his shoulder afresh.

"I suspect you have played me false, you jade," cried Malmayns, writhing with pain. "The stuff you have applied burns like caustic, and eats into my flesh."

"It is doing its duty," replied his wife, calmly watching his agonies. "You will soon be easier."

" Perhaps I shall—in death," groaned the sufferer.
" I am parched with thirst. Give me a glass of water."
" You shall have wine, Matthew, if you prefer it. I
have a flask in my pocket," she replied. " But what of
the treasure—where is it ? "
" Peace ! " he cried. " I will baulk your avaricious
hopes. You shall never know where it is."
" I shall know as much as you do," she rejoined, in a
tone of incredulity. " I don't believe a word you tell me.
You have found no treasure."
" If this is the last word I shall ever utter, I *have*," he
returned;—" a mighty treasure. But you shall never
possess it. Never—ha ! ha ! "
" Nor shall you have the wine," she replied; " there
is water for you, she added, handing him a jug, which he
drained with frantic eagerness. " He is a dead man,"
she muttered.
" I am chilled to the heart," gasped the sexton, shivering from head to foot, while chill damps gathered on his
brow. " I have done wrong in drinking the water, and you
ought not to have given it me."
" You asked for it," she replied. " You should have
had wine but for your obstinacy. But I will save you yet,
if you will tell me where to find the treasure."
" Look for it in my grave," he returned, with a hideous
grin.
Soon after this, he fell into a sort of stupor. His wife
could now have easily put a period to his existence, but
she still hoped to wrest the secret from him. She was
assured, moreover, that his recovery was hopeless. At the
expiration of about two hours, he was aroused by the
excruciating anguish of his sore. He had again become
delirious, and raved as before about coffins, corpses,
graves, and other loathsome matters. Seeing, from his
altered looks, and the livid and gangrenous appearance
which the tumour had assumed, that his end was not far
off, Judith resolved not to lose a moment, but to try the
effect of a sudden surprise. Accordingly, she bent down
her head, and shouted in his hear, " What has become of
your treasure, Matthew ? "

The plan succeeded to a miracle. The dying man instantly raised himself.

"My treasure!" he echoed, with a yell that made the vault ring again. "Well thought on! I have not secured it. They are carrying it off. I must prevent them." And throwing off the coverings, he sprang out of bed.

"I shall have it now," thought his wife. "You are right," he added, "they are carrying it off. The vergers have discovered it. They are digging it up. We must instantly prevent them."

"We must!" shrieked Malmayns. "Bring the light! bring the light!" And bursting open the door, he rushed into the adjoining aisle.

"He will kill himself, and discover the treasure into the bargain," cried Judith, following him. "Ah! what do I see! People in the church. Curses on them! they have ruined my hopes."

CHAPTER VIII

The Mosaical Rods

In pursuance of their design of seeking out an astrologer, Maurice Wyvil and Lydyard crossed Cheapside and entered Friday-street. They had not proceeded far, when they perceived a watchman standing beneath a porch with a lantern in his hand, and thinking it an intimation that the house was attacked by the plague, they hurried to the opposite side of the street, and called to the watchman to inquire whether he knew where Mr. Lilly lived.

Ascertaining that the house they sought was only a short distance off, they repaired thither, and knocking at the door, a small wicket, protected by a grating, was opened within it, and a sharp female voice inquired their business.

"Give this to your master, sweetheart," replied Wyvil, slipping a purse through the grating; "and tell him that two gentlemen desire to consult him."

"He is engaged just now," replied the woman, in a

much softer tone; " but I will take your message to him."

" You have more money than wit," laughed Lydyard. " You should have kept back your fee till you had got the information."

" In that case I should never have received any," replied Wyvil. " I have taken the surest means of obtaining admission to the house."

As he spoke, the door was unbolted by the woman, who proved to be young and rather pretty. She had a light in her hand, and directing them to follow her. led the way to a sort of ante-room, divided, as it appeared, from a larger room by a thick black curtain. Drawing aside the drapery, their conductress ushered them into the presence of three individuals, who were seated at a table strewn with papers, most of which were covered with diagrams and astrological calculations.

One of these persons immediately rose on their appearance, and gravely but courteously saluted them. He was a tall man, somewhat advanced in life, being then about sixty-three, with an aquiline nose, dark eyes, not yet robbed of their lustre, gray hair waving over his shoulders, and a pointed beard and moustache. The general expression of his countenance was shrewd and penetrating, and yet there were certain indications of credulity about it, showing that he was as likely to be imposed upon himself as to delude others. It is scarcely necessary to say that this was Lilly.

The person on his right, whose name was John Booker, and who, like himself, was a proficient in astrology, was so buried in calculation that he did not raise his eyes from the paper on the approach of the strangers. He was a stout man, with homely but thoughtful features, and though not more than a year older than Lilly, looked considerably his senior. With the exception of a few silver curls hanging down the back of his neck, he was completely bald; but his massive and towering brow seemed to indicate the possession of no ordinary intellectual qualities. He was a native of Manchester, and was born in 1601, of a good family. " His excellent verses upon the twelve months," says Lilly, in his autobiography, " framed according to the configurations of each month, being blessed with success, according to his predictions, procured him much reputation all over England. He was a very honest man," continues the same authority, "abhorred any deceit in the art he studied; had a curious fancy in judging thefts; and was successful in resolving love-questions. He was no mean proficient in astronomy; understood much in physic, was a great admirer of the antimonial cup; and not unlearned in chemistry, which he loved well but did not practise." At the period of this history he was clerk to Sir Hugh Hammersley, alderman.

The third person—a minor-canon of Saint Paul's, named Thomas Quatremain,—was a grave, sallow-complexioned man, with a morose and repulsive physiognomy. He was habited in the cassock of a churchman of the period, and his black velvet cap lay beside him on the table. Like Booker, he was buried in calculations, and though he looked up for a moment as the others entered the room, he instantly resumed his task, without regard to their presence.

After looking earnestly at his visitors for a few moments, and appearing to study their features, Lilly motioned them to be seated. But they declined the offer.

"I am not come to take up your time, Mr. Lilly," said Wyvil, "but simply to ask your judgment in a matter in which I am much interested."

"First permit me to return you your purse, sir, since it is from you, I presume, that I received it," replied the astrologer. "No information that I can give, deserves so large a reward as this."

Wyvil would have remonstrated. But seeing the other resolute, he was fain to concede the point.

"What question do you desire to have resolved, sir?" pursued Lilly.

"Shall I be fortunate in my hopes?" rejoined Wyvil.

"You must be a little more precise," returned the astrologer. "To what do your hopes relate?—to wealth, dignity, or love?"

"To the latter," replied Wyvil.

"So I inferred from your appearance, sir," rejoined Lilly, smiling. "Venus was strong in your nativity, though well-dignified; and I should, therefore, say you were not unfrequently entangled in love affairs. Your inamorata, I presume, is young, perhaps fair,—blue-eyed, brown-haired, tall, slender, and yet perfectly proportioned."

"She is all you describe," replied Wyvil.

"Is she of your own rank?" asked Lilly.

"Scarcely so," replied Wyvil, hesitating before he answered the question.

"I will instantly erect a scheme," replied the astrologer, rapidly tracing a figure on a sheet of paper. "The question refers to the seventh house. I shall take Venus as the natural significatrix of the lady. The moon is in trine with the lord of the ascendant,—so far, good: but there is a cross aspect from Mars, who darts forth malicious rays upon them. Your suit will probably be thwarted. But what Mars bindeth, Venus dissolveth. It is not wholly hopeless. I should recommend you to persevere."

"Juggler!" exclaimed Wyvil between his teeth.

"I am no juggler!" replied Lilly, angrily; "and to prove I am not, I will tell you who you are who thus insult me, though you have not announced yourself, and are desirous of preserving your *incognito*. You are the Earl of Rochester, and your companion is Sir George Etherege."

"'Fore Heaven! we are discovered," cried the earl; "but whether by art magic, or from previous acquaintanceship with our features, I pretend not to determine."

"In either case, my lord,—for it is useless since you have avowed yourself, to address you longer as Wyvil," replied Etherege,—"you owe Mr. Lilly an apology for the insult you have offered him. It was as undeserved as uncalled for; for he described your position with Amabel exactly."

"I am sorry for what I said," replied the earl, with great frankness, "and entreat Mr. Lilly to overlook it, and impute it to its real cause,—disappointment at his judgment."

" I wish I could give you better hopes, my lord," replied Lilly; "but I readily accept your apology. Have you any further questions to ask me ? "

" Not to-night," replied the earl; "except that I would gladly learn whether it is your opinion that the plague will extend its ravages ? "

" It will extend them so far, my lord, that there shall neither be buriers for the dead, nor sound to look after the sick," replied Lilly. " You may have seen a little tract of mine, published in 1651,—some fourteen years ago, — called *Monarchy or no Monarchy in England*, in which, by an hieroglyphic, I foretold this terrible calamity."

" I heard his Majesty speak of the book no later than yesterday," replied Rochester. " He has the highest opinion of your skill, Mr. Lilly, as he cannot blind himself to the fact, that you foretold his father's death. But this is not the only visitation with which you threaten our devoted city."

" It is threatened by Heaven; not by me, my lord,' replied Lilly. " London will be devoured by plague and consumed by fire."

" In our time ? " asked Etherege.

" Before two years have passed over our heads," returned the astrologer. " The pestilence originated in the conjunction of Saturn and Jupiter in Sagittarius, on the 10th of last October, and the conjunction of Saturn and Mars, in the same sign, on the 12th of November. It was harbingered also by the terrible comet of January, which appeared in a cadent and obscure house, denoting sickness and death ; and another and yet more terrible comet, which will be found in the fiery triplicity of Aries, Leo, and Sagittarius, will be seen before the conflagration."

" My calculations are that the plague will be at its worst in August and September, and will not cease entirely till the beginning of December," observed Booker, laying aside his pen.

" And I doubt not you are right, sir," said Lilly, " for your calculations are ever most exact."

" My labour is not thrown away, Mr. Lilly," cried

Quatremain, who had finished his task at the same time. "I have discovered what I have long suspected, that treasure *is* hidden in Saint Paul's cathedral. Mercury is posited in the north angle of the fourth house: the dragon's tail is likewise within it; and as Sol is the significator, it must be gold."

"True," replied Lilly.

"Furthermore," proceeded Quatremain, "as the sign is earthy, the treasure must be buried in the vaults."

"Undoubtedly," replied Booker.

"I am all impatience to search for it," said Quatremain. "Let us go there at once, and make trial of the mosaical rods."

"With all my heart," replied Lilly. "My lord," he added to Rochester, "I must pray you to excuse me. You have heard what claims my attention?"

"I have," returned the earl, "and should like to accompany you in the quest, if you will permit me."

"You must address yourself to Mr. Quatremain," rejoined Lilly. "If he consents, I can make no objection."

The minor-canon, on being appealed to, signified his acquiescence, and after some slight preparation, Lilly produced two hazel rods, and the party set out.

A few minutes' walking brought them to the northern entrance of the cathedral, where they speedily aroused the poor verger, who began to fancy he was to have no rest that night. On learning their purpose, however, he displayed the utmost alacrity, and by Quatremain's directions went in search of his brother verger, and a mason, who, being employed at the time in making repairs in the chantries, lodged within the cathedral.

This occasioned a delay of a few minutes, during which Rochester and Etherege had an opportunity, like that enjoyed a short time before by Leonard Holt, of beholding the magnificent effect of the columned aisles by moonlight. By this time the other verger, who was a young and active man, and the mason, arrived, and mattocks, spades, and an iron bar, being procured, and a couple of torches lighted, they descended to Saint Faith's.

Nothing more picturesque can be conceived than the

effect of the torchlight on the massive pillars and low-browed roof of the subterranean church. Nor were the figures inappropriate to the scene. Lilly, with the mosaical rods in his hand, which he held at a short distance from the floor, moving first to one point then to another; now lingering within the gloomy nave, now within the gloomier aisles; the grave minor-canon, who kept close beside him, and watched his movements with the most intense anxiety; Booker, with his venerable head uncovered, and his bald brow reflecting the gleam of the torches; the two court gallants in their rich attire; and the vergers and their comrade, armed with the implements for digging;—all constituted a striking picture. And as Rochester stepped aside to gaze at it he thought he had never beheld a more singular scene.

Hitherto no success had attended the searchers. The mosaical rods had continued motionless. At length, however, Lilly reached a part of the wall where a door appeared to have been stopped up, and playing the rods near it, they turned one over the other.

" The treasure is here : " he exclaimed. " It is hidden beneath this flag."

Instantly, all were in action. Quatremain called to his assistants to bring their mattocks and the iron bar. Rochester ran up and tendered his aid; Etherege did the same; and in a few moments the flag was forced from its position.

On examination, it seemed as if the ground beneath it had been recently disturbed, though it was carefully trodden down. But without stopping to investigate the matter, the mason and the younger verger commenced digging. When they were tired, Lilly and Quatremain took their places, and in less than an hour, they had got to the depth of upwards of four feet. Still nothing had been found, and Lilly was just about to relinquish his spade to the mason, when, plunging it more deeply into the ground, it struck against some hard substance.

" It is here—we have it ! " he cried, renewing his exertions.

Seconded by Quatremain, they soon cleared off the soil,

and came upon what appeared to be a coffin or a large
chest. Both then got out of the pit to consider how they
should remove the chest; the whole party were discussing
the matter, when a tremendous crash, succeeded by a
terrific yell, was heard at the other end of the church,
and a ghastly and half-naked figure, looking like a corpse
broken from the tomb, rushed forward with lightning
swiftness, and shrieking—" My treasure !—my treasure !
—you shall not have it ! "—thrust aside the group, and
plunged into the excavation.

When the bystanders recovered sufficient courage to
drag the unfortunate sexton out of the pit, they found
him quite dead.

CHAPTER IX

The Miniature

ACCORDING to his promise, Doctor Hodges visited the
grocer's house early on the following day, and the favourable opinion he had expressed respecting Stephen Bloundel
was confirmed by the youth's appearance. The pustule
had greatly increased in size; but this the doctor looked
upon as a good sign: and after applying fresh poultices,
and administering a hot posset-drink, he covered the
patient with blankets, and recommending as much tranquillity as possible, he proceeded, at Bloundel's request,
to ascertain the state of health of the rest of the family.
Satisfied that all the household (including Blaize, who,
being a little out of order from the quantity of medicine
he had swallowed, kept his bed) were uninfected, he went
upstairs, and finding the two boys quite well, and playing
with their little sister Christiana, in the happy uncon-
sciousness of childhood, he tapped at the door of Mrs.
Bloundel's chamber, and was instantly admitted. Amabel
did not raise her eyes at his entrance, but continued the
employment on which she was engaged. Her mother,
however, overwhelmed him with inquiries as to the

sufferer, and entreated him to prevail upon her husband
to let her take his place at the sick-bed.

" I cannot accede to your request, madam," replied
Hodges, " because I think the present arrangement the
best that could be adopted."

"And am I not to see poor Stephen again?" cried
Mrs. Bloundel, bursting into tears.

" I hope you will soon see him again, and not lose sight
of him for many years to come," replied the doctor. " As
far as I can judge, the danger is over, and, aided by your
husband's care and watchfulness, I have little doubt of
bringing the youth round."

" You reconcile me to the deprivation, doctor," rejoined Mrs. Bloundel; " but can you insure my husband
against the distemper ? "

" I can insure no one against contagion," replied
Hodges; " but there is much in his favour. He has no
fear, and takes every needful precaution. You must hope
for the best. I think it right to tell you, that you will be
separated from him for a month."

" Separated from my husband for a month, doctor ! "
cried Mrs. Bloundel. " I must see him to-day. I have
something of importance to say to him."

At this point of the conversation Amabel for the first
time looked up. Her eyes were red and inflamed with
weeping, and her looks betrayed great internal suffering.

" You cannot see my father, mother," she said in a
broken and supplicatory tone.

" But she can write to him, or send a message by me,"
rejoined Hodges. " I will deliver it when I go downstairs."

" What my mother has to say cannot be confided to a
third party, sir," returned Amabel.

" Better defer it, then," said the doctor; who, as he
looked hard at her, and saw the colour mount to her
cheeks, began to suspect something of the truth. " Whatever you have to say, Mrs. Bloundel, may be very well
delayed; for the house is now closed, with a watchman
at the door, and will continue so for a month to come.
No one can quit it, except members of our profession.

searchers, nurses, and other authorized persons during
that time."

" But can no one enter it, do you think ? " asked Mrs.
Bloundel.

" No one would desire to do so, I should conceive,
except a lover," replied Hodges, with a sly look at Amabel,
who instantly averted her gaze " Where a pretty girl is
concerned, the plague itself has no terrors."

" Precisely my opinion, doctor," rejoined Mrs. Bloundel; " and as I cannot consult my husband, perhaps you
will favour me with your advice as to how I ought to act,
if such a person as you describe should get into the house."

" I seldom meddle with family matters," rejoined
Hodges; " but I feel so much interest in all that relates
to Mr. Bloundel that I am induced to depart from my
rule on the present occasion. it is evident you have lost
your heart," he added, to Amabel, whose blushes told
him he was right; " but not I hope to one of those worthless court-gallants, who, as I learn from common report,
are in the habit of toasting you daily. If it is so, you must
subdue your passion; for it cannot lead to good. Be not
dazzled by a brilliant exterior, which often conceals a
treacherous heart; but try to fix your affections on some
person of little pretension, but of solid worth. Never, I
grieve to say, was there a season when such universal pro-
fligacy prevailed as at present. Never was it so necessary
for a young maiden, possessed of beauty like yours, to act
with discretion. Never was a court so licentious as that
of our sovereign, Charles the Second, whose corrupt example is imitated by every one around him, while its
baneful influence extends to all classes. Were I to echo
the language of the preachers, I should say it was owing
to the wickedness and immorality of the times, that this
dreadful judgment of the plague has been inflicted upon us;
but I merely bring it forward as an argument to prove to
you, Amabel, that if you would escape the moral contagion by which you are threatened, you must put the
strictest guard upon your conduct.'

Amabel faintly murmured her thanks.

" You speak as my husband himself would have spoken,"

said Mrs. Bloundel. " Ah ! we little thought when we prayed that the pestilence might be averted from us, that a worse calamity was behind, and that one of the most profligate of the courtiers you have mentioned would find his way to our house."

" One of the most profligate of them ? " cried Hodges. " Who, in Heaven's name ? "

" He calls himself Maurice Wyvil," replied Mrs. Boundel.

" I never heard of such a person," rejoined the doctor. " It must be an assumed name. Have you no letter or token, that might lead to his discovery ? " he added, turning to Amabel.

" I have his portrait," she replied, drawing a small miniature from her bosom.

" I am glad I have seen this," said the doctor, slightly starting as he cast his eyes upon it. " I hope it is not too late to save you, Amabel," he added, in a severe tone. " I hope you are free from contamination ? "

" As I live, I am," she replied. " But you recognise the likeness ? "

" I do," returned Hodges. " It is the portrait of one whose vices and depravity are the town's cry, and whose name coupled with that of a woman, is sufficient to sully her reputation."

" It is the Earl of Rochester," said Mrs. Bloundel.

" You have guessed aright," replied the doctor; " it is."

Uttering an exclamation of surprise and terror, Amabel fell back in her chair.

" I thought it must be that wicked nobleman," cried Mrs. Bloundel. " Would you believe it, doctor, that he forced himself into the house—nay, into this room, last night, and would have carried off my daughter, in spite of her resistance, if I had not prevented him."

" I can believe anything of him," replied Hodges. " But your husband, of course, knows nothing of the matter ? "

" Not as yet," replied Mrs. Bloundel; " but I authorize you to tell him all."

"Mother, dear mother," cried Amabel, flinging herself on her knees before her, "I implore you not to add to my father's present distress. I might not have been able to conquer my attachment to Maurice Wyvil, but now that I find he is the Earl of Rochester, I regard him with abhorrence."

"If I could believe you sincere," said Mrs. Bloundel, "I might be induced to spare your father the pain which the knowledge of this unfortunate affair would necessarily inflict."

"I am sincere,—indeed I am," replied Amabel.

"To prove that the earl could not have had honourable intentions towards you, Amabel," said the doctor, "I may mention that he is at this moment urging his suit with Mistress Mallett,—a young heiress."

"Ah!" exclaimed Amabel.

"I was in attendance upon Mistress Stewart, the king's present favourite, the day before yesterday," continued Hodges, "and heard his Majesty entreat her to use her influence with Mistress Mallett in Rochester's behalf. After this you cannot doubt the nature of his intentions towards yourself."

"I cannot—I cannot," rejoined Amabel. "He is perfidy itself. But is Mistress Mallett very beautiful, doctor?"

"Very beautiful, and very rich," he replied, "and the earl is desperately in love with her. I heard him declare laughingly to the king, that if she would not consent to marry him, he would carry her off."

"Just what he said to me," exclaimed Amabel—"perjured and faithless that he is."

"Harp on that string, doctor," whispered Mrs. Bloundel. "You understand her feelings exactly."

"Strangely enough," pursued the doctor, how, having carefully examined the miniature, had opened the back of the case, and could not repress a smile at what he beheld—"strangely enough, this very picture will convince you of the earl's inconstancy. It was evidently designed for Mistress Mallett, and as she would not accept it, transferred to you."

"How do you know this, sir?" inquired Amabel, in a mortified tone.

"Hear what is written within it," answered Hodges, laying the open case before her, and reading as follows:—"'To the sole possessor of his heart, the fair Mistress Mallett, this portrait is offered by her devoted slave—ROCHESTER.' 'The *sole* possessor of his heart!' So you have no share in it, you perceive, Amabel. 'Her devoted slave!' Is he your slave, likewise? Ha! ha!"

"It *is* his writing," cried Amabel. "This note," she added, producing a billet, "is in the same hand. My eyes are, indeed, opened to his treachery."

"I am glad to hear it," replied Hodges, "and if I can preserve you from the snares of this noble libertine, I shall rejoice as much as in curing your brother of the plague. But can you rely upon yourself, in case the earl should make another attempt to see you?"

"I can," she averred confidently.

"In that case, there is nothing to apprehend," rejoined Hodges; "and I think it better on many accounts not to mention the subject to your father. It would only distract his mind, and prevent him from duly discharging the painful task he has undertaken. Were I in your place, Amabel, I would not only forget my present perfidious lover, but would instantly bestow my affections on some worthy person."

"It would gladden me if she would do so," said Mrs. Bloundel.

"There is your father's apprentice, Leonard Holt, a good-looking, well-grown lad," pursued the doctor; "and I much mistake if he is insensible to your attractions."

"I am sure he loves her dearly, doctor," replied Mrs. Bloundel. "He is as well-principled as well-looking. I have never had a fault to find with him since he came to live with us. It will rejoice me, and I am sure would not displease my husband, to see our child united to Leonard Holt."

"Well, what say you, Amabel?" asked Hodges. "Can you give him a hope?"

"Alas, no!" replied Amabel, "I have been deceived

once, but I will not be deceived a second time. I will
never wed."

"So every woman says after her first disappointment,"
observed Hodges; "but not one in ten adheres to the
resolution. When you become calmer, I would recommend you to think seriously of Leonard Holt."

At this moment a tap was heard at the door, and opening it, the doctor beheld the person in question.

"What is the matter?" cried Hodges. "I hope
nothing is amiss?"

"Nothing whatever," replied Leonard, "but my master
wishes to see you before you leave the house."

"I will go to him at once," replied the doctor. "Good
day, Mrs. Bloundel. Take care of your daughter, and I
hope she will take care of herself. We have been talking
about you, young man," he added, in a low tone, to the
apprentice, "and I have recommended you as a husband
to Amabel."

"There was a time, sir," rejoined Leonard, in a tone
of deep emotion, "when I hoped it might be so, but that
time is past."

"No such thing," replied the doctor. "Now is the
time to make an impression. Her heart is on the rebound.
She is satisfied of her lover's treachery. Her mother is
on your side. Do not neglect the present opportunity, for
another may not arrive." With this he pushed Leonard
into the room, and shutting the door upon him, hurried
downstairs.

"You have arrived at a seasonable juncture, Leonard,"
observed Mrs. Bloundel, noticing the apprentice's perplexity, and anxious to relieve it. "We have just discovered that the person calling himself Maurice Wyvil is
no other than the Earl of Rochester."

"Indeed!" exclaimed Leonard.

"Yes, indeed," returned Mrs. Bloundel. "But this is
not all. Amabel has promised to forget him, and I have
urged her to think of you."

"Amabel," said Leonard, advancing towards her, and
taking her hand, "I can scarcely credit what I hear.
Will you confirm your mother's words?"

"Leonard," returned Amabel, "I am not insensible to your good qualities, and no one can more truly esteem you than I do. Nay, till I unfortunately saw the Earl of Rochester, whom I knew not as such, I might have loved you. But now I cannot call my heart my own. I have not the affection you deserve, to bestow upon you. If I can obliterate this treacherous man's image from my memory—and Heaven, I trust, will give me strength to do so—I will strive to replace it with your own."

"That is all I ask," cried Leonard, dropping on his knee before her, and pressing his lips to her hand.

"Nothing would make me happier than to see you united, my children," said Mrs. Bloundel, bending affectionately over them.

"And I would do anything to make you happy, dear mother," replied Amabel, gently withdrawing her hand from that of the apprentice.

"Before I leave you," said Leonard, rising, "I must give you this note. I found it lying before your chamber door as I passed this morning. How it came there I know not, but I can give a shrewd guess as to the writer. I ought to tell you, that but for what has just occurred, I should not have delivered it to you."

"It is from Wyvil—I mean Rochester," said Amabel, taking the note with a trembling hand.

"Let me see it, child," cried Mrs. Bloundel, snatching it from her, and breaking the seal. "Insolent!" she exclaimed, as she cast her eyes over it. "I can scarcely contain my indignation. But let him cross my path again, and he shall find whether I cannot resent such shameful usage."

"What does he say, dear mother?" asked Amabel.

"You shall hear," replied Mrs. Bloundel, "though I blush to repeat his words:—'Amabel, you are mine. No one shall keep you from me. Love like mine will triumph over all obstacles!'—Love like his, forsooth!" she remarked; "let him keep such stuff as that for Mistress Mallett, or his other mistresses. But I will go on: 'I may be foiled ninety-nine times, but the hundredth will succeed. We shall soon meet again.—MAURICE WYVIL.'"

"Never!" cried Amabel. "We will never meet again. If he holds me thus cheaply, I will let him see that he is mistaken. Leonard Holt, I have told you the exact state of my feelings. I do not love you now, but I regard you as a true friend, and love may come hereafter. If in a month's time you claim my hand,—if my father consents to our union, for you are aware that my mother will not oppose it,—I am yours."

Leonard attempted to speak, but his voice was choked with emotion, and the tears started to his eyes.

"Farewell," said Amabel. "Do not let us meet till the appointed time. Rest assured I will think of you as you deserve."

"We could not meet till that time, even if you desired it," said Leonard, "for your father has forbidden any of the household, except old Josyna, to approach you till all fear of contagion is at an end, and I am now transgressing his commands. But your mother, I am sure, will acquit me of intentional disobedience."

"I do," replied Mrs. Bloundel; "it was the doctor who forced you into the room. But I am heartily glad he did so."

"Farewell, Amabel," said Leonard. "Though I shall not see you, I will watch carefully over you." And gazing at her with unutterable affection, he quitted the chamber.

"You must now choose between the heartless and depraved nobleman, who would desert you as soon as won," observed Mrs. Bloundel, "and the honest apprentice, whose life would be devoted to your happiness."

"I *have* chosen," replied her daughter.

Doctor Hodges found the grocer writing at a small table, close to the bedside of his son.

"I am happy to tell you, Mr. Bloundel," he said, in a low tone, as he entered the room, "that all your family are still free from infection, and with due care will, I hope, continue so. But I entirely approve of your resolution of keeping apart from them till the month has expired. If your son goes on as he is doing now, he will be as strong as ever in less than a fortnight. Still, as we cannot foresee what may occur, it is better to err on the cautious side."

" Pray be seated for a moment," rejoined the grocer, motioning the other to the chair. " I mentioned to you last night that in case my son recovered, I had a plan which I trusted (under Providence !) would preserve my family from the further assaults of the pestilence."

" I remember your alluding to it," replied Hodges, " and should be glad to know what it is."

" I must tell it you in confidence," rejoined Bloundel, " because I think secrecy essential to its entire accomplishment. My plan is a very simple one, and only requires firmness in its execution,—and that quality, I think, I possess. It is your opinion, I know, as it is my own, that the plague will increase in violence, and endure for months—probably, till next winter. My intention is to store my house with provisions, as a ship is victualled for a long voyage, and then to shut it up entirely till the scourge ceases."

" If your project is practicable," said Hodges, after a moment's reflection, " I have no doubt it will be attended with every good result you can desire. This house, which is large and roomy, is well adapted for your purpose. But you must consider well whether your family will submit to be imprisoned during the long period you propose."

" They shall remain close prisoners, even if the pestilence lasts for a twelvemonth," replied the grocer. " Whoever quits the house, when it is once closed, and on whatever plea, be it wife, son, or daughter, returns not. That is my fixed resolve."

" And you are right," rejoined Hodges, " for on that determination the success of your scheme entirely depends."

While they were thus conversing, Leonard entered the chamber, and informed his master that Chowles, the coffin-maker, and Mrs. Malmayns, the plague nurse, desired to see him.

" Mrs. Malmayns ! " exclaimed Hodges, in surprise.

"I heard that something very extraordinary occurred last night in Saint Faith's. With your permission, Mr. Bloundel, she shall be admitted, I want to ask her a few questions. You had better hesitate about engaging her," he observed to the grocer, as Leonard departed, "for she is a woman of very indifferent character, though she may (for aught I know) be a good and fearless nurse."

"If there is any doubt about her, I *cannot* hesitate," returned Bloundel.

As he said this, the door was opened by Leonard, and Chowles and Judith entered the room. The latter, on seeing the doctor, looked greatly embarrassed.

"I have brought you the nurse I spoke of, Mr. Bloundel," said Chowles, bowing, "and am come to inquire whether you want a coffin to-night."

"Mr. Bloundel is not likely to require a coffin at present, Chowles," returned the doctor, severely; "neither does his son stand in need of a nurse. How is your husband, Mrs. Malmayns?"

"He is dead, sir," replied Judith.

"Dead!" echoed the doctor. "When I left him, at one o'clock this morning, he was doing well. Your attendance seems to have accelerated his end."

"His death was occasioned by an accident, sir," replied Judith. "He became delirious about three o'clock, and in spite of all my efforts to detain him, started out of bed, rushed into Saint Faith's, and threw himself into a pit, which Mr. Lilly and some other persons had digged in search of treasure."

"This is a highly improbable story, Mrs. Malmayns," returned Hodges, "and I must have the matter thoroughly investigated before I lose sight of you."

"I will vouch for the truth of Mrs. Malmayns' statement," interposed Chowles.

"You!" cried Hodges, contemptuously.

"Yes, I," replied the coffin-maker. "It seems that the sexton had found a chest of treasure buried in Saint Faith's, and being haunted by the idea that some one was carrying it off, he suddenly sprang out of bed, and rushed to the church, where, sure enough, Mr. Lilly,

Mr. Quatremain, the Earl of Rochester, and Sir George Etherege, having, by the help of mosaical rods, discovered this very chest, were digging it up. Poor Matthew instantly plunged into the grave, and died of a sudden chill."

"That is not impossible," observed Hodges, after a pause. "But what has become of the treasure?"

"It is in the possession of Mr. Quatremain, who has given notice of it to the proper authorities," replied Chowles. "It consists, as I understand, of gold pieces struck in the reign of Philip and Mary, images of the same metal, crosses, pyxes, chalices, and other Popish and superstitious vessels, buried, probably, when Queen Elizabeth came to the throne, and the religion changed."

"Not unlikely," replied Hodges. "Where is your husband's body, Mrs. Malmayns?"

"It has been removed to the vault which he usually occupied," replied Judith. "Mr. Chowles has undertaken to bury it to-night."

"I must see it first," replied Hodges, "and be sure that he has not met with foul play."

"And I will accompany you," said Chowles. "So you do not want a coffin, Mr. Bloundel?"

The grocer shook his head.

"Good day, Mr. Bloundel," said Hodges. "I shall visit you to-morrow, and hope to find your son as well as I leave him. Chowles, you will be answerable for the safe custody of Mrs. Malmayns."

"I have no desire to escape, sir," replied the nurse. "You will find everything as I have represented."

"We shall see," replied the doctor. "If not, you will have to tend the sick in Newgate."

The trio then proceeded to Saint Paul's, and descended to the vaults. Hodges carefully examined the body of the unfortunate sexton, but though he entertained strong suspicions, he could not pronounce positively that he had been improperly treated; and as the statement of Mrs. Malmayns was fully borne out by the vergers and others, he did not think it necessary to pursue the investigation further. As soon as he was gone Judith accompanied the coffin-maker to his residence, where she remained till the evening, when she was suddenly summoned, in a case of urgency, by a messenger from Sibbald, the apothecary of Clerkenwell.

CHAPTER X

The Duel

AFTER Parravicin's terrible announcement, Disbrowe offered him no further violence, but flinging down his sword, burst open the door, and rushed upstairs. His wife was still insensible, but the fatal mark that had betrayed the presence of the plague to the knight manifested itself also to him. and he stood like one entranced, until Mrs. Disbrowe, recovering from her swoon, opened her eyes, and gazing at him, cried,—" You here !—Oh ! Disbrowe, I dreamed you had deserted me—had sold me to another."

" Would it were a dream," replied her husband.

" And was it not so ? " she rejoined, pressing her hand to her temples. " It is true ! Oh ! yes, I feel it is. Every circumstance rushes upon me plainly and distinctly. I see the daring libertine before me. He stood where you stand, and told me what you had done."

" What did he tell you, Margaret ? " asked Disbrowe in a hollow voice.

" He told me you were false—that you loved another, and had abandoned me."

" He lied ! " exclaimed Disbrowe, in a voice of uncontrollable fury. " It is true that, in a moment of frenzy, I was tempted to set you—yes, *you*, Margaret—against all I had lost at play, and was compelled to yield up the key of my house to the winner. But I have never been faithless to you—never."

" Faithless or not," replied his wife, bitterly, " it is plain you value me less than play, or you would not have acted thus."

"Reproach me not, Margaret," replied Disbrowe, "I would give worlds to undo what I have done."

"Who shall guard me against the recurrence of such conduct?" said Mrs. Disbrowe, coldly. "But you have not yet informed me how I was saved."

Disbrowe averted his head.

"What mean you?" she cried, seizing his arm. "What has happened? Do not keep me in suspense? Were you my preserver?"

"Your preserver was the plague," rejoined Disbrowe, in a sombre tone.

The unfortunate lady then, for the first time, perceived that she was attacked by the pestilence, and a long and dreadful pause ensued, broken only by exclamations of anguish from both.

"Disbrowe!" cried Margaret, at length, raising herself in bed, "you have deeply—irrecoverably injured me. But promise me one thing."

"I swear to do whatever you may desire," he replied.

"I know not, after what I have heard, whether you have courage for the deed," she continued. "But I would have you kill this man."

"I will do it," replied Disbrowe.

"Nothing but his blood can wipe out the wrong he has done me," she rejoined. "Challenge him to a duel—a mortal duel. If he survives, by my soul, I will give myself to him."

"Margaret!" exclaimed Disbrowe.

"I swear it," she rejoined, "and you know my passionate nature too well to doubt I will keep my word."

"But you have the plague?"

"What does that matter? I may recover."

"Not so," muttered Disbrowe. "If I fall, I will take care you do not recover. I will fight him to-morrow," he added, aloud.

He then summoned his servants, but when they found their mistress was attacked by the plague, they framed some excuse to leave the room, and instantly fled the house. Driven almost to his wits' end, Disbrowe went in search of other assistance, and was for a while unsuccess-

ful, until a coachman to whom he applied, offered, for a
suitable reward, to drive to Clerkenwell—to the shop of
an apothecary named Sibbald (with whose name the
reader is already familiar), who was noted for his treatment of plague patients, and to bring him to the other's
residence. Disbrowe immediately closed with the man,
and in less than two hours Sibbald made his appearance.
He was a singular and repulsive personage, with an immense hooked nose, dark, savage-looking eyes, a skin like
parchment, and high round shoulders, which procured
him the nickname of Æsop among his neighbours. He
was under the middle size, and of a spare figure, and in
age might be about sixty-five.

On seeing Mrs. Disbrowe, he at once boldly asserted
that he could cure her, and proceeded to apply his remedies.
Finding the servants fled, he offered to procure a nurse
for Disbrowe, and the latter, thanking him, eagerly embraced the offer. Soon after this, he departed. In the
evening, the nurse, who (as may be surmised) was no
other than Judith Malmayns, arrived, and immediately
commenced her functions.

Disbrowe had no rest that night. His wife slept occasionally for a few minutes, but apparently engrossed by one
idea, never failed when she awoke to urge him to slay
Parravicin; repeating her oath to give herself to the
knight if he came off victorious. Worn out at length,
Disbrowe gave her a terrible look, and rushed out of the
room.

He had not been alone many minutes when he was
surprised by the entrance of Judith. He eagerly inquired
whether his wife was worse, but was informed she had
dropped into a slumber.

" Hearing what has passed between you," said the nurse,
" and noticing your look when you left the room, I came
to tell you, that if you fall in this duel, your last moments
need not be embittered by any thoughts of your wife. I
will take care she does not recover."

A horrible smile lighted up Disbrowe's features.

" You are the very person I want," he said. " When I
would do evil, the fiend rises to my bidding. If I am

slain, you know what to do. How shall I requite the service ? "

" Do not concern yourself about that, captain," rejoined Judith. " I will take care of myself."

About noon, on the following day, Disbrowe without venturing to see his wife, left the house, and proceeded to the Smyrna, where, as he expected, he found Parravicin and his companions.

The knight instantly advanced towards him, and laying aside for the moment his reckless air, inquired, with a look of commiseration, after his wife.

" She is better," replied Disbrowe, fiercely. " I am come to settle accounts with you."

" I thought they were settled long ago." returned Parravicin, instantly resuming his wonted manner. " But I am glad to find you consider the debt unpaid."

Disbrowe lifted the cane he held in his hand, and struck the knight with it forcibly on the shoulder. " Be that my answer," he said.

" I will have your life first, and your wife afterwards," replied Parravicin, furiously.

" You shall have her if you slay me, but not otherwise," retorted Disbrowe. " It must be a mortal duel."

" It must," replied Parravicin. " I will not spare you this time."

" Spare him ! " cried Pillichody. " Shield of Agamemnon ! I should hope not. Spit him as you would a wild boar."

" Peace, fool ! " cried Parravicin. " Captain Disbrowe, I shall instantly proceed to the west side of Hydepark, beneath the trees. I shall expect you there. On my return, I shall call on your wife."

" I pray you do so, sir," replied Disbrowe, disdainfully.

Both then quitted the coffee-house, Parravicin attended by Rochester and Pillichody, and Disbrowe accompanied by a military friend, whom he accidentally encountered. Each party taking a coach, they soon reached the ground,—a retired spot, completely screened from observation by trees. The preliminaries were soon arranged, for neither would admit of delay. The conflict then commenced with great fury on both sides; but Parravicin, in spite of his passion, observed far more caution than his antagonist; and, taking advantage of an unguarded moment, occasioned by the other's impetuosity, passed his sword through his body.

Disbrowe fell.

" You are again successful," he groaned, " but save my wife,—save her."

" What mean you ? " cried Parravicin, leaning over him, as he wiped his sword.

But Disbrowe could make no answer. His utterance was choked by a sudden effusion of blood on the lungs, and he instantly expired. Leaving the body in care of the second, Parravicin and his friends returned to the coach, where the major rejoiced greatly at the issue of the duel; but the knight looked grave, and pondered upon the words of the dying man. After a time, however, he recovered his spirits, and dined with his friends at the Smyrna; but they observed that he drank more deeply than usual. His excesses did not, however, prevent him from playing with his usual skill, and he won a large sum from Rochester at hazard.

Flushed with success, and heated with wine, he walked up to Disbrowe's residence about an hour after midnight. As he approached the house, he observed a strangely shaped cart at the door, and halting for a moment, saw a body, wrapped in a shroud, brought out. Could it be Mrs. Disbrowe ? Rushing forward to one of the assistants in black cloaks,—and who was no other than Chowles,—he asked who he was about to inter ?

" It is a Mrs. Disbrowe," replied the coffin-maker. " She died of grief, because her husband was killed this morning in a duel; but as she had the plague it must be put down to that. We are not particular in such matters, and shall bury her and her husband together; and as there is no money left to pay for coffins, they must go to the grave without them. What, ho ! Mother Malmayns, let Jonas have the captain as soon as you have stripped him. I must be starting."

And as the body of his victim was brought forth, Parravicin fell against the wall in a state almost of stupefaction.

At this moment, Solomon Eagle, with his brazier on his head, suddenly turned the corner of the street, and stationing himself before the dead-cart, cried in a voice of thunder, " Woe to the libertine ! woe to the homicide ! for he shall perish in everlasting fire ! Woe ! woe ! "

End of the First Book

Book the Second

MAY, 1665

CHAPTER I

The Progress of the Pestilence

TOWARDS the middle of May, the bills of mortality began to swell greatly in amount, and though but few were put down to the plague, and a large number to the spotted fever (another frightful disorder raging at the period), it is well known that the bulk had died of the former disease. The rigorous measures adopted by the authorities (whether salutary or not has been questioned), in shutting up houses and confining the sick and sound within them for forty days were found so intolerable, that most persons were disposed to run any risk rather than be subjected to such a grievance, and every artifice resorted to for concealing a case when it occurred. Hence, it seldom happened, unless by accident, that a discovery was made. Quack doctors were secretly consulted, instead of the regular practitioners; the searchers were bribed to silence; and large fees were given to the undertakers and buriers to lay the deaths to the account of some other disorder. All this, however, did not blind the eyes of the officers to the real state of things. Redoubling their vigilance, they entered the houses on mere suspicion; inflicted punishments where they found their orders disobeyed or neglected; sent the sound to prison,—the sick to the pest-house; and replaced the faithless searchers by others upon whom they could place reliance. Many cases were thus detected; but in spite of every precaution, the majority escaped; and the vent was no sooner stopped in one quarter, than it broke out with additional violence in another.

By this time the alarm had become general. All whose business or pursuits permitted it, prepared to leave

London, which they regarded as a devoted city, without delay. As many houses were, therefore, closed from the absence of the inhabitants as from the presence of the plague, and this added to the forlorn appearance of the streets, which in some quarters were almost deserted. For a while, nothing was seen at the great outlets of the city, but carts, carriages, and other vehicles, filled with goods and movables, on their way to the country; and, as may be supposed, the departure of their friends did not tend to abate the dejection of those whose affairs compelled them to remain behind.

One circumstance must not be passed unnoticed, namely, the continued fineness and beauty of the weather. No rain had fallen for upwards of three weeks. The sky was bright and cloudless; the atmosphere, apparently, pure and innoxious: while the heat was as great as is generally experienced in the middle of summer. But instead of producing its usual enlivening effect on the spirits, the fine weather added to the general gloom and apprehension, inasmuch as it led to the belief (afterwards fully confirmed), that if the present warmth was so pernicious, the more sultry seasons which were near at hand, would aggravate the fury of the pestilence. Sometimes, indeed, when the deaths were less numerous, a hope began to be entertained that the distemper was abating, and confidence was for a moment restored; but these anticipations were speedily checked by the reappearance of the scourge, which seemed to baffle and deride all human skill and foresight.

London now presented a lamentable spectacle. Not a street but had a house in it marked with a red cross— some streets had many such. The bells were continually tolling for burials, and the dead-carts went their melancholy rounds at night and were constantly loaded. Fresh directions were issued by the authorities; and as domestic animals were considered to be a medium of conveying the infection, an order, which was immediately carried into effect, was given to destroy all dogs and cats. But this plan proved prejudicial rather than the reverse, as the bodies of the poor animals, most of which were

drowned in the Thames, being washed ashore, produced a
horrible and noxious effluvium, supposed to contribute
materially to the propagation of the distemper.

No precautionary measure was neglected; but it may
be doubted whether any human interference could have
averted the severity of the scourge, which, though its
progress might be checked for a few days by attention,
or increased in the same ratio by neglect, would in the
end have unquestionably fulfilled its mission. The College
of Physicians, by the king's command, issued simple and
intelligible directions in the mother tongue, for the sick.
Certain of their number, amongst whom was the reader's
acquaintance, Doctor Hodges, were appointed to attend
the infected; and two out of the Court of Aldermen were
required to see that they duly executed their dangerous
office. Public prayers and a general fast were likewise
enjoined. But Heaven seemed deaf to the supplications
of the doomed inhabitants—their prayers being followed
by a fearful increase of deaths. A vast crowd was collected
within Saint Paul's to hear a sermon preached by Doctor
Sheldon, Archbishop of Canterbury,—a prelate greatly
distinguished during the whole course of the visitation,
by his unremitting charity and attention to the sick;
and before the discourse was concluded, several fell
down within the sacred walls, and, on being conveyed to
their own homes, were found to be infected. On the
following day, too, many others who had been present
were seized with the disorder.

A fresh impulse was given to the pestilence from an
unlooked-for cause. It has been mentioned that the
shutting up of houses and seclusion of the sick was
regarded as an intolerable grievance, and though most
were compelled to submit to it, some few resisted, and
tumults and disturbances ensued. As the plague increased, these disturbances became more frequent, and
the mob always taking part against the officers, they were
frequently interrupted in the execution of their duty.

About this time a more serious affray than usual
occurred, attended with loss of life, and other unfortunate consequences, which it may be worth while to

relate, as illustrative of the peculiar state of the times. The wife of a merchant, named Barcroft, residing in Lothbury, being attacked by the plague, the husband, fearing his house would be shut up, withheld all information from the examiners and searchers. His wife died, and immediately afterwards one of his children was attacked. Still he refused to give notice. The matter, however, got wind. The searchers arrived at night, and being refused admittance, they broke into the house. Finding undoubted evidence of infection, they ordered it to be closed, stationed a watchman at the door, and marked it with the fatal sign. Barcroft remonstrated against their proceedings, but in vain. They told him he might think himself well off that he was not carried before the Lord Mayor, who would undoubtedly send him to Ludgate; and with other threats to the like effect, they departed.

The unfortunate man's wife and child were removed the following night in the dead-cart, and, driven half mad by grief and terror, he broke open the door of his dwelling, and, plunging a sword in the watchman's breast, who opposed his flight, gained the street. A party of the watch happened to be passing at the time, and the fugitive was instantly secured. He made a great clamour, however,—calling to his neighbours and the bystanders to rescue him, and in another moment the watch was beaten off, and Barcroft placed on a post whence he harangued his preservers on the severe restraints imposed upon the citizens, urging them to assist in throwing open the doors of all infected houses, and allowing free egress to their inmates.

Greedily listening to this insane counsel, the mob resolved to act upon it. Headed by the merchant, they ran down Threadneedle-street, and crossing Stocks' Market, burst open several houses in Bearbinder-lane, and drove away the watchmen. One man, more courageous than the others, tried to maintain his post, and was so severely handled by his assailants, that he died a few days afterwards of the injuries he had received. Most of those who had been imprisoned within their dwellings immediately issued forth, and joining the mob, which received fresh recruits each moment, started on the same errand.

Loud shouts were now raised of—" Open the doors ! No plague prisoners ! No plague prisoners ! " and the mob set off along the Poultry. They halted, however, before the Great Conduit, near the end of Bucklersbury, and opposite Mercers' Hall, because they perceived a company of the Train-bands advancing to meet them. A council of war was held, and many of the rabble were disposed to fly; but Barcroft again urged them to proceed, and they were unexpectedly aided by Solomon Eagle, who, bursting through their ranks, with his brazier on his head, crying, " Awake ! sleepers awake ! the plague is at your doors ! awake ! " speeded towards the Train-bands, scattering sparks of fire as he pursued his swift career. The mob instantly followed, and adding their shouts to his outcries, dashed on with such fury that the Train-bands did not dare to oppose them, and, after a slight and ineffectual resistance, were put to rout.

Barcroft, who acted as leader, informed them that there was a house in Wood-street shut up, and the crowd accompanied him thither. In a few minutes, they had reached Bloundel's shop, but finding no one on guard,— for the watchman, guessing their errand, had taken to his heels,—they smeared over the fatal cross and inscription with a pail of mud gathered from the neighbouring kennel, and then broke open the door. The grocer and his apprentice hearing the disturbance, and being greatly alarmed at it, hurried to the shop, and found it full of people.

" You are at liberty, Mr. Bloundel," cried the merchant, who was acquainted with the grocer. " We are determined no longer to let our families be imprisoned at the pleasure of the Lord Mayor and Aldermen. We mean to break open all the plague houses, and set free their inmates."

" For Heaven's sake consider what you are about, Mr. Barcroft," cried the grocer. " My house has been closed for nearly a month. Nay, as my son has entirely recovered and received his certificate of health from Doctor Hodges, it would have been opened three days hence by the officers, so that I have suffered all the inconvenience of the confinement, and can speak to it. It is no doubt very irksome, and may be almost intolerable to persons of an impatient temperament; but I firmly believe it is the only means to check the progress of contagion. Listen to me, Mr. Barcroft,—listen to me, good friends, and hesitate before you violate laws which have been made expressly to meet this terrible emergency."

Here he was checked by loud groans and upbraidings from the bystanders.

" He tells you himself that the period of his confinement is just over," cried Barcroft. " It is plain he has no interest in the matter, except that he would have others suffer as he has done. Heed him not, my friends; but proceed with the good work. Liberate the poor plague prisoners. Liberate them ! On ! on ! "

" Forbear, rash men ! " cried Bloundel, in an authoritative voice. " In the name of those you are bound to obey, I command you to desist."

" Command us ! " cried one of the bystanders, raising his staff in a menacing manner. " Is this your gratitude for the favour we have just conferred upon you ? Command us, forsooth. You had better repeat the order, and see how it will be obeyed."

" I *do* repeat it," rejoined the grocer, firmly. " In the Lord Mayor's name, I command you to desist, and return to your homes."

The man would have struck him with his staff, if he had not been himself felled to the ground by Leonard. This was the signal for greater outrage. The grocer and his apprentice were instantly assailed by several others of the mob, who, leaving them both on the floor covered with bruises, helped themselves to all they could lay hands on in the shop, and then quitted the premises.

It is scarcely necessary to track their course further; and it may be sufficient to state, that they broke open upwards of fifty houses in different streets. Many of the plague-stricken joined them and several half-naked creatures were found dead in the streets on the following morning. Two houses in Blackfriars-lane were set on fire, and the conflagration was with difficulty checked; nor was it until late on the following day that the mob could be entirely dispersed. The originator of the disturbance, Barcroft, after a desperate resistance, was shot through the head by a constable.

The result of the riot, as will be easily foreseen, was greatly to increase the pestilence; and many of those who had been most active in it perished in prison of the distemper. Far from being discouraged by the opposition offered to their decrees, the city authorities enforced them with greater rigour than ever, and doubling the number of the watch, again shut up all those houses which had been broken open during the late tumult.

Bloundel received a visit from the Lord Mayor, Sir John Lawrence, who, having been informed of his conduct, came to express his high approval of it, offering to remit the few days yet unexpired of his quarantine. The grocer, however, declined the offer, and with renewed expressions of approbation, Sir John Lawrence took his leave.

Three days afterwards, the Examiner of Health pronounced the grocer's house free from infection. The fatal mark was obliterated from the door; the shutters were unfastened; and Bloundel resumed his business as usual. Words are inadequate to describe the delight that filled the breast of every member of his family, on their first meeting after their long separation. It took place in the room adjoining the shop. Mrs. Bloundel received the joyful summons from Leonard, and on descending with her children, found her husband and her son Stephen anxiously expecting her. Scarcely able to make up her mind as to which of the two she should embrace first, Mrs. Bloundel was decided by the pale countenance of her son, and rushing towards him, she strained him to her breast, while Amabel flew to her father's arms. The grocer could not repress his tears; but they were tears of joy, and that night's happiness made him ample amends for all the anxiety he had recently undergone.

"Well, Stephen, my dear child," said his mother, as soon as the first tumult of emotion had subsided, "well, Stephen," she said, smiling at him through her tears, and almost smothering him with kisses; "you are not so much altered as I expected; and I do not think, if I had had the care of you, I could have nursed you better myself. You owe your father a second life, and we all owe him the deepest gratitude for the care he has taken of you."

"I can never be sufficiently grateful for his kindness," returned Stephen, affectionately.

"Give thanks to the beneficent Being who has preserved you from this great danger, my son, not to me," returned Bloundel. "The first moments of our reunion should be worthily employed."

So saying, he summoned the household, and for the first time for a month, the whole family party assembled, as before, at prayer. Never were thanksgivings more earnestly, more devoutly uttered. All arose with bright and cheerful countenances; and even Blaize seemed to have shaken off his habitual dread of the pestilence. As he retired with Patience, he observed to her, "Master Stephen looks quite well, though a little thinner. I must ascertain from him the exact course of treatment pursued by his father. I wonder whether Mr. Bloundel would nurse *me* if I were to be suddenly seized with the distemper?"

"If he wouldn't, I *would*," replied Patience.

"Thank you, thank you," replied Blaize. "I begin to think we shall get through it. I shall go out to-morrow and examine the Bills of Mortality, and see what progress the plague is making. I am all anxiety to know. I must get a fresh supply of medicine, too. My private store is quite gone, except three of my favourite rufuses, which I shall take before I go to bed to-night. Unluckily, my purse is as empty as my phials."

"I can lend you a little money," said Patience. "I haven't touched my last year's wages. They are quite at your service."

"You are too good," replied Blaize; "but I won't decline the offer. I heard a man crying a new anti-pestiïential elixir, as he passed the house yesterday. I must find him out, and buy a bottle. Besides, I must call on my friend Parkhurst, the apothecary.—You are a good girl, Patience, and I'll marry you as soon as the plague ceases."

" I have something else to give you," rejoined Patience. " This little bag contains a hazel-nut, from which I have picked the kernel, and filled its place with quicksilver, stopping the hole with wax. Wear it round your neck, and you will find it a certain preservative against the pestilence."

" Who told you of this remedy? " asked Blaize, taking the bag.

" Your mother," returned Patience.

" I wonder I never heard of it," said the porter.

" She wouldn't mention it to you, because the doctor advised her not to put such matters into your head," replied Patience. " But I couldn't help indulging you. Heigho ! I hope the plague will soon be over."

" It won't be over for six months," rejoined Blaize, shaking his head. " I read in a little book, published in 1593, in Queen Elizabeth's reign, and written by Simon Kelway, ' that when little children flock together, and pretend that some of their number are dead, solemnizing the burial in a mournful sort, it is a certain token that a great mortality is at hand.' This I have myself seen more than once. Again, just before the great sickness of 1625, the churchyard wall of Saint Andrew's, Holborn, fell down. I need not tell you that the same thing occurred after the frost this winter."

" I heard of it," replied Patience; " but I did not know it was a bad sign."

" It is a dreadful sign," returned Blaize, with a shudder. " The thought of it brings back my old symptoms. I must have a supper to guard against infection,—a slice of toasted bread, sprinkled with vinegar, and powdered with nutmeg."

And chattering thus, they proceeded to the kitchen.

Before supper could be served, Doctor Hodges made his appearance. He was delighted to see the family assembled together again, and expressed a hearty wish that they might never more be divided. He watched Amabel and Leonard carefully, and seemed annoyed that the former rather shunned than favoured the regards of the apprentice.

Leonard, too, looked disconcerted; and though he was in possession of his mistress's promise, he did not like to reclaim it. During the whole of the month, he had been constantly on the watch, and had scarcely slept at night, so anxious was he to prevent the possibility of any communication taking place between Rochester and his mistress. But in spite of all his caution, it was possible he might be deceived. And when on this, their first meeting, she returned his anxious gaze with averted looks, he felt all his jealous misgivings return.

Supper, meanwhile, proceeded. Doctor Hodges was in excellent spirits, and drank a bottle of old sack with great relish. Overcome by the sight of his wife and children. the grocer abandoned himself to his feelings. As to his wife, she could scarcely contain herself, but wept and laughed by turns—now embracing her husband, now her son, between whom she had placed herself. Nor did she forget Doctor Hodges; and such was the exuberance of her satisfaction, that when the repast was ended, she arose, and flinging her arms about his neck, termed him the preserver of her son.

" If any one is entitled to that appellation it is his father," replied Hodges, " and I may say, that in all my experience, I have never witnessed such generous self-devotion as Mr. Bloundel has exhibited towards his son. You must now be satisfied, madam, that no person can so well judge what is proper for the safety of his family as your husband."

" I never doubted it, sir," replied Mrs. Bloundel.

" I must apprise you, then, that he has conceived a plan by which he trusts to secure you and his children and household from any future attack," returned Hodges.

" I care not what it is, so it does not separate me from him," replied Mrs. Bloundel.

" It does not," replied the grocer. " It will knit us

more closely together than we have yet been. I mean to
shut up my house, having previously stored it with provisions for a twelvemonth, and shall suffer no member of
my family to stir forth as long as the plague endures."

"I am ready to remain within doors, if it continues
twenty years," replied his wife. "But how long do you
think it *will* last, doctor?"

"Till next December, I have no doubt," returned
Hodges.

"So long!" exclaimed Amabel.

"Ay, so long," repeated the doctor. "It is scarcely
begun now. Your father is right to adopt these precautions. It is the only way to insure the safety of his family."

"But——" cried Amabel.

"I am resolved," interrupted Bloundel, peremptorily.
"Whoever leaves the house,—if but for a moment,—
never returns."

"And when do you close it, father?" asked Amabel.

"A week hence," replied the grocer; "as soon as I
have laid in a sufficient stock of provisions."

"And am I not to leave the house for a year?" cried
Amabel, with a dissatisfied look.

"Why should you wish to leave it?" asked her father,
curiously.

"Ay, why?" repeated Leonard, in a low tone. "I shall
be here."

Amabel seemed confused, and looked from her father
to Leonard. The former, however, did not notice her
embarrassment, but observed to Hodges,—"I shall
begin to victual the house to-morrow."

"Amabel," whispered Leonard, "you told me if I
claimed your hand in a month, you would yield it to me.
I require the fulfilment of your promise."

"Give me till to-morrow," she replied, distractedly.

"She has seen Rochester," muttered the apprentice,
turning away.

CHAPTER II

In what manner the Grocer victualled his House

LEONARD HOLT was wrong in his suspicions. Amabel had neither seen nor heard from Rochester. But, if the truth must be told, he was never out of her mind, and she found, to her cost, that the heart will not be controlled. Convinced of her noble lover's perfidy, and aware she was acting wrongfully in cherishing a passion for him, after the exposure of his base designs towards herself, no reasoning of which she was capable could banish him from her thoughts, or enable her to transfer her affections to the apprentice.

This conflict of feeling produced its natural result. She became thoughtful and dejected—was often in tears—had no appetite—and could scarcely rouse herself sufficiently to undertake any sort of employment. Her mother watched her with great anxiety, and feared,—though she sought to disguise it from herself,—what was the real cause of her despondency.

Things were in this position at the end of the month, and it occasioned no surprise to Mrs. Bloundel, though it afflicted her deeply, to find that Amabel sedulously avoided the apprentice's regards on their first meeting. When Dr. Hodges was gone, and the rest of the family had retired, she remarked to her husband, " Before you shut up the house as you propose, I should wish one important matter settled."

The grocer inquired what she meant.

" I should wish to have Amabel married," was the answer.

" Married ! " exclaimed Bloundel, in astonishment, " To whom ? "

" To Leonard Holt."

Bloundel could scarcely repress his displeasure.

" It will be time enough to talk of that a year hence," he answered.

"I don't think so," returned his wife; "and now, since the proper time for the disclosure of the secret has arrived, I must tell you that the gallant who called himself Maurice Wyvil, and whom you so much dreaded, was no other than the Earl of Rochester."

"Rochester!" echoed the grocer, while an angry flush stained his cheek, "has that libertine dared to enter my house?"

"Ay, and more than once," replied Mrs. Bloundel.

"Indeed!" cried her husband, with difficulty controlling his indignation. "When was he here?—tell me quickly."

His wife then proceeded to relate all that had occurred, and he listened with profound attention to her recital. At its close, he arose and paced the chamber for some time in great agitation.

At length, he suddenly paused, and, regarding his wife with great sternness, observed, in a severe tone, "You have done very wrong in concealing this from me, Honora, —very wrong."

"If I have erred, it was to spare you uneasiness," returned Mrs. Blondel, bursting into tears. "Dr. Hodges agreed with me that it was better not to mention the subject while you had so many other anxieties pressing upon you."

"I have a stout heart, and a firm reliance on the goodness of Heaven, which will enable me to bear up against most evils," returned the grocer. "But on this point I ought, under any circumstances, to have been consulted. And I am greatly surprised that Doctor Hodges should advise the contrary."

"He was influenced, like myself, by the kindliest feelings towards you," sobbed Mrs. Bloundel.

"Well, well, I will not reproach you further," returned the grocer, somewhat moved by her tears. "I have no doubt you conceived you were acting for the best. But I must caution you against such conduct for the future." After a pause, he added, "Is it your opinion that our poor deluded child still entertains any regard for this profligate nobleman?"

"I am sure she does," replied Mrs. Bloundel; "and it is from that conviction that I so strongly urge the necessity of marrying her to Leonard Holt."

"I will never compel her to do anything to endanger her future happiness," returned the grocer. "She must not marry Leonard Holt without loving him. It is better to risk an uncertain evil, than to rush upon a certain one."

"Then I won't answer for the consequences," replied his wife.

"What !" cried Bloundel; "am I to understand you have no reliance on Amabel? Has all our care been thrown away?"

"I do not distrust her," returned Mrs. Bloundel; "but consider whom she has to deal with. She is beset by the handsomest and most fascinating man of the day— by one understood to be practised in all the arts most dangerous to our sex—and a nobleman to boot. Some allowance must be made for her."

"I will make none," rejoined Bloundel, austerely. "She has been taught to resist temptation in whatever guise it may present itself; and if the principles I have endeavoured to implant within her breast had found lodgment there, she *would* have resisted it. I am deeply grieved to find this is not the case, and that she must trust to others for protection, when she ought to be able to defend herself."

The subject was not further discussed, and the grocer and his wife shortly afterwards retired to rest.

On the following morning, Bloundel remarked to the apprentice as they stood together in the shop, "Leonard, you are aware I am about to shut up my house. Before doing so, I must make certain needful arrangements. I will not disguise from you that I should prefer your remaining with me, but at the same time I beg you distinctly to understand that I will not detain you against your will. Your articles are within two months of expiring; and, if you desire it, I will deliver them to you to-morrow, and release you from the rest of your time."

"I do not desire it, sir," replied Leonard, "I will remain as long as I can be serviceable to you."

"Take time for reflection," rejoined his master, kindly. "In all probability, it will be a long confinement, and you may repent, when too late, having subjected yourself to it."

"Last month's experience has taught me what I have to expect," remarked Leonard, with a smile. "My mind is made up. I will stay with you."

"I am glad of it," returned Bloundel, "and now I have something further to say to you. My wife has acquainted me with the daring attempt of the Earl of Rochester to carry off Amabel."

"Has my mistress, also, told you of my attachment to your daughter?" demanded Leonard, trembling, in spite of his efforts to maintain a show of calmness.

Bloundel nodded an affirmative.

"And of Amabel's promise to bestow her hand upon me, if I claimed it at the month's end?" continued the apprentice.

"No!" replied the grocer, a good deal surprised—"I heard of no such promise. Nor was I aware the matter had gone so far. But have you claimed it?"

"I have," replied Leonard; "but she declined giving an answer till to-day."

"We will have it then at once," cried Bloundel. "Come with me to her."

So saying, he led the way to the inner room, where they found Amabel and her mother. At the sight of Leonard, the former instantly cast down her eyes.

"Amabel," said her father, in a tone of greater severity than he had ever before used towards her, "all that has passed is known to me. I shall take another and more fitting opportunity to speak to you on your ill-advised conduct. I am come for a different purpose. You have given Leonard Holt a promise (I need not tell you of what nature), and he claims its fulfilment."

"If he insists upon my compliance," replied Amabel, in a tremulous voice, "I must obey. But it will make me wretched."

"Then I at once release you," replied Leonard. "I value your happiness far more than my own,"

"You deserve better treatment, Leonard," said Bloundel; "and I am sorry my daughter cannot discern what is for her good. Let us hope that time will work a change in your favour."

"No," replied the apprentice bitterly; "I will no longer delude myself with any such vain expectation."

"Amabel," observed the grocer, "as your father—as your well-wisher—I should desire to see you wedded to Leonard. But I have told your mother, and now tell you, that I will not control your inclinations, and will only attempt to direct you so far as I think likely to be conducive to your happiness. On another point, I must assume a very different tone. You can no longer plead ignorance of the designs of the depraved person who besets you. You may not be able to forget him—but you can avoid him. If you see him alone again—if but for a moment—I cast you off for ever. Yes, for ever," he repeated, with stern emphasis.

"I will never voluntarily see him again," replied Amabel, tremblingly.

"You have heard my determination," rejoined her father. "Do you still adhere to your resolution of remaining with me, Leonard?" he added, turning to the apprentice. "If what has just passed makes any alteration in your wishes, state so, frankly."

"I will stay," replied Leonard.

"There will be one advantage, which I did not foresee, in closing my house," remarked the grocer, aside to the apprentice. "It will effectually keep away this libertine earl."

"Perhaps so," replied the other. "But I have more faith in my own vigilance than in bolts and bars."

Bloundel and Leonard then returned to the shop, where the former immediately began to make preparations for storing his house; and in the prosecution of his scheme he was greatly aided by the apprentice.

The grocer's dwelling, as has been stated, was large and commodious. It was three stories high; and beneath the ground-floor there were kitchens and extensive cellars. Many of the rooms were spacious, and had curiously carved fire-places, walls panelled with fine brown oak, large presses, and cupboards.

In the yard, at the back of the house, there was a pump, from which excellent water was obtained. There were likewise three large cisterns, supplied from the New River. Not satisfied with this, and anxious to obtain water in which no infected body could have lain, or clothes have been washed, Bloundel had a large tank placed within the cellar, and connecting it by pipes with the pump, he contrived an ingenious machine, by which he could work the latter from within the house,—thus making sure of a constant supply of water, direct from the spring.

He next addressed himself to the front of the house, where he fixed a pulley, with a rope and hook attached to it, to the beam above one of the smaller bay-windows on the second story. By this means, he could let down a basket or any other article into the street, or draw up whatever he desired; and as he proposed using this outlet as the sole means of communication with the external world when his house was closed, he had a wooden shutter made in the form of a trap-door, which he could open and shut at pleasure.

Here it was his intention to station himself at certain hours of the day, and whenever he held any communication below, to flash off a pistol, so that the smoke of the powder might drive back the air, and purify any vapour that found entrance of its noxious particles.

He laid down to himself a number of regulations, which will be more easily shown and more clearly understood, on arriving at the period when his plans came to be in full operation. To give an instance, however,—if a letter should be conveyed to him by means of the pulley, he proposed to steep it in a solution of vinegar and sulphur; and when dried and otherwise fumigated, to read it at a distance by the help of strong glasses.

In regard to provisions, after a careful calculation, he bought upwards of three thousand pounds weight of hard sea-biscuits, similar to those now termed captain's biscuits, and had them stowed away in hogsheads. He next ordered twenty huge casks of the finest flour, which he had packed up with the greatest care, as if for a voyage to Barbados or Jamaica. As these were brought in through the yard an accident had well-nigh occurred which might have proved fatal to him. While superintending the labours of Leonard and Blaize, who were rolling the casks into the house,— having stowed away as many as he conveniently could in the upper part of the premises,—he descended to the cellar, and, opening a door at the foot of a flight of steps leading from the yard, called them to lower the remaining barrels with ropes below. In the hurry, Blaize rolled a cask towards the open door, and in another instant it would have fallen upon the grocer, and, perhaps, have crushed him, but for the interposition of Leonard. Bloundel made no remark at the time; but he never forgot the service rendered him by the apprentice.

To bake the bread required an oven, and he accordingly built one in the garret, laying in a large stock of wood for fuel. Neither did he neglect to provide himself with two casks of meal.

But the most important consideration was butcher's meat; and for this purpose he went to Rotherhithe, where the plague had not yet appeared, and agreed with a butcher to kill him four fat bullocks, and pickle and barrel them as if for sea-stores. He likewise directed the man to provide six large barrels of pickled pork, on the same understanding. These were landed at Queenhithe, and brought up to Wood-street, so that they passed for newly-landed grocery.

Hams and bacon forming part of his own trade, he wrote to certain farmers with whom he was in the habit of dealing, to send him up an unlimited supply of flitches and gammons; and his orders being promptly and abundantly answered, he soon found he had more bacon than he could possibly consume. He likewise laid in a good store of tongues, hung beef, and other dried meats.

As to wine, he already had a tolerable stock; but he increased it by half a hogshead of the best canary he could procure; two casks of malmsey, each containing twelve gallons; a quarter-cask of malaga sack; a runlet

E

of muscadine; two small runlets of aqua vitæ; twenty
gallons of aniseed water; and two eight-gallon runlets of
brandy. To this he added six hogsheads of strongly-
hopped Kent-ale, calculated for keeping, which he placed
in a cool cellar, together with three hogsheads of beer,
for immediate use. Furthermore, he procured a variety
of distilled waters for medicinal purposes, amongst which
he included a couple of dozen of the then fashionable and
costly preparation, denominated plague-water.

As, notwithstanding all his precautions, it was not impossible that some of his household might be attacked by
the distemper, he took care to provide proper remedies,
and to Blaize's infinite delight, furnished himself with
mithridates, Venice treacle, diascordium, the pill rufus
(oh, how the porter longed to have the key of the medicine
chest!), London treacle, turpentine, and other matters.
He likewise collected a number of herbs and simples; as
Virginian snakeweed, contrayerva, pestilence-wort, angelica, elecampane, zedoary, tormentii, valerian, lovage
devils-bit, dittany, master-wort, rue, sage, ivy-berries, and
walnuts; together with bole armoniac, terra sigillata,
bezoar-water, oil of sulphur, oil of vitriol, and other com-
pounds. His store of remedies was completed by a tun
of the best white-wine vinegar, and a dozen jars of salad
oil.

Regulating his supplies by the provisions he had laid in,
he purchased a sufficient stock of coals and fagots to last
him during the whole period of his confinement; and he
added a small barrel of gunpowder, and a like quantity
of sulphur for fumigation.

His eatables would not have been complete without
cheese; and he therefore ordered about six hundred-
weight from Derbyshire, Wiltshire, and Leicestershire,
besides a couple of large old cheeses from Rostherne, in
Cheshire,—even then noted for the best dairies in the
whole country. Several tubs of salted butter were sent
him out of Berkshire, and a few pots from Suffolk.

It being indispensable, considering the long period he
meant to close his house, to provide himself and his
family with every necessary, he procured a sufficient

stock of wearing apparel, hose, shoes, and boots. Spice, dried fruit, and other grocery articles, were not required, because he already possessed them. Candles also formed an article of his trade, and lamp oil; but he was recommended by Doctor Hodges, from a fear of the scurvy, to provide a plentiful supply of lemon and lime juice.

To guard against accident, he also doubly stocked his house with glass, earthenware, and every article liable to breakage. He destroyed all vermin, such as rats and mice, by which the house was infested; and the only live creatures he would suffer to be kept were a few poultry. He had a small hutch constructed near the street door, to be used by the watchman he meant to employ; and he had the garrets fitted up with beds, to form a hospital, if any part of the family should be seized with the distemper, so that the sick might be sequestered from the sound.

CHAPTER III

The Quack Doctors

PATIENCE, it may be remembered, had promised Blaize to give him her earnings to enable him to procure a fresh supply of medicine, and about a week after he had received the trifling amount (for he had been so constantly employed by the grocer, that he had no opportunity of getting out before) he sallied forth to visit a neighbouring apothecary, named Parkhurst, from whom he had been in the habit of purchasing drugs, and who occupied a small shop not far from the grocer's, on the opposite side of the street. Parkhurst appeared overjoyed to see him, and without giving him time to prefer his own request, inquired after his master's family—whether they were all well, especially fair Mistress Amabel,—and, further, what was the meaning of the large supplies of provision which he saw daily conveyed to the premises? Blaize shook his head at the latter question, and for some time refused to answer it. But being closely pressed by Parkhurst, he admitted that his master was about to shut up his house.

" Shut up his house! '' exclaimed Parkhurst. " I never heard of such a preposterous idea. If he does so, not one of you will come out alive. But I should hope that he will be dissuaded from his rash design."

" Dissuaded ! " echoed Blaize. " You don't know my master. He's as obstinate as a mule when he takes a thing into his head. Nothing will turn him. Besides Dr. Hodges sanctions, and even recommends the plan."

" I have no opinion of Doctor Hodges," sneered the apothecary. " He is not fit to hold a candle before a learned friend of mine, a physician. who is now in that room. The person I speak of thoroughly understands the pestilence, and never fails to cure every case that comes before him. No shutting up houses with him. He is in possession of an infallible remedy."

" Indeed ! " exclaimed Blaize. pricking up his ears. " What is his name ? "

" His name," cried Parkhurst, with a puzzled look. " How strange it should slip my memory. Ah, now, I recollect. It is Doctor Calixtus Bottesham."

" A singular name, truly," remarked Blaize ; " but it sounds like that of a clever man."

" Doctor Calixtus Bottesham is a wonderful man," returned the apothecary. " I have never met with his like. I would trumpet forth his merits through the whole city, but that it would ruin my trade. The plague is our harvest, as my friend Chowles, the coffin-maker, says, and it will not do to stop it—ha ! ha ! "

" It is too serious a subject to laugh at," returned Blaize, gravely. " But are the doctor's fees exorbitant ? "

" To the last degree," replied Parkhurst. " I am afraid to state how much he asks."

" I fear I shall not be able to consult him, then," said Blaize, turning over the coin in his pocket ; " and yet I should greatly like to do so."

" Have no fear on that score," returned the apothecary. " I have been able to render him an important

service, and he will do anything for me. He shall give
you his advice gratis."

"Thank you! thank you!" cried Blaize, transported
with delight.

"Wait here a moment, and I will ascertain whether
he will see you," replied Parkhurst.

So saying, he quitted the porter, who amused himself
during his absence by studying the labels affixed to the
jars and bottles on the shelves. He had much ado to
restrain himself from opening some of them. and tasting
their contents.

Full a quarter of an hour elapsed before the apothecary
appeared.

"I am sorry to have detained you so long," he said;
"but I had more difficulty with the doctor than I expected, and for some time he refused to see you on any
terms, because he has a violent antipathy to Doctor
Hodges, whom he regards as a mere pretender, and whose
patient he conceives you to be."

"I am not Doctor Hodges' patient," returned Blaize;
"and I regard him as a pretender myself."

"That opinion will recommend you to Doctor Bottesham," replied Parkhurst; "and since I have smoothed
the way for you, you will find him very affable and con-
descending. He has often heard me speak of your master;
and if it were not for his dislike of Doctor Hodges, whom
he might accidentally encounter, he would call upon him."

"I wish I could get my master to employ him instead
of the other," said Blaize.

"I wish so, too," cried Parkhurst, eagerly. "Do you
think it could be managed?"

"I fear not," returned Blaize.

"There would be no harm in making the trial," replied
Parkhurst. "But you shall now see the learned gentleman. I ought to apprise you that he has two friends with
him—one a young gallant, named Hawkswood, whom he
has recently cured of the distemper, and who is so much
attached to him that he never leaves him; the other, a
doctor, like himself, named Martin Furbisher, who
always accompanies him in his visits to his patients, and

prepares his mixtures for him. You must not be surprised at their appearance. And now come with me."

With this, he led the way into a small room at the back of the shop, where three personages were seated at the table, with a flask of wine and glasses before them. Blaize detected Doctor Bottesham at a glance. He was an ancient-looking man, clad in a suit of rusty black, over which was thrown a velvet robe, very much soiled and faded, but originally trimmed with fur, and lined with yellow silk. His powers of vision appeared to be feeble, for he wore a large green shade over his eyes, and a pair of spectacles of the same colour. A venerable white beard descended almost to his waist. His head was protected by a long-flowing gray wig, over which he wore a black velvet cap. His shoulders were high and round, his back bent, and he evidently required support when he moved, as a crutch-headed staff was reared against his chair. On his left was a young, handsome, and richly-attired gallant, answering to the apothecary's description of Hawkswood; and on the right sat a stout personage, precisely habited like himself except that he wore a broad-leaved hat, which completely overshadowed his features. Notwithstanding this attempt at concealment, it was easy to perceive that Doctor Furbisher's face was covered with scars, that he had a rubicund nose, studded with carbuncles, and a black patch over his left eye.

" Is this the young man who desires to consult me ? " asked Doctor Calixtus Bottesham, in the cracked and quavering voice of old age, to Parkhurst.

" It is," replied the apothecary, respectfully. " Go forward," he added, to Blaize, " and speak for yourself."

" What ails you ? " pursued Bottesham, gazing at him through his spectacles. " You look strong and hearty."

" So I am, learned sir," replied Blaize, bowing to the ground; " but understanding from Mr. Parkhurst that you have an infallible remedy against the plague, I would gladly procure it from you, as, if I should be attacked, I may not have an opportunity of consulting you."

" Why not ? " demanded Bottesham. " I will come to you if you send for me."

" Because," replied Blaize, after a moment's hesitation, " my master is about to shut up his house, and no one will be allowed to go forth, or to enter it, till the pestilence is at an end."

" Your master must be mad to think of such a thing," rejoined Bottesham. " What say you, brother Furbisher, —is that the way to keep off the plague ? "

" Gallipots of Galen ! no," returned the other ; " it is rather the way to invite its assaults."   .

" When does your master talk of putting this fatal design—for fatal it will be to him and all his household— into execution ? " demanded Bottesham.

" Very shortly, I believe," replied Blaize. " He meant to begin on the first of June, but as the pestilence is less violent that it was, Doctor Hodges has induced him to defer his purpose for a few days."

" Doctor Hodges ! " exclaimed Bottesham, contemptuously. " It was an unfortunate day for your master when he admitted that sack-drinking impostor into his house."

" I have no great opinion of his skill," replied Blaize, " but, nevertheless, it must be admitted that he cured Master Stephen in a wonderful manner."

" Pshaw ! " exclaimed Bottesham, " that was mere accident. I heard the particulars of the case from Parkhurst, and am satisfied the youth would have recovered without his aid. But what a barbarian Mr. Bloundel must be to think of imprisoning his family in this way."

" He certainly does not consult my inclinations in the matter," returned Blaize.

" Nor those of his wife and daughter, I should imagine," continued Bottesham. " How do *they* like it ? "

" I cannot exactly say," answered Blaize. " What a dreadful thing it would be if I should be attacked by the plague, and no assistance could be procured."

" It would be still more dreadful, if so angelic a creature as Bloundel's daughter is represented to be—for I have never seen her—should be so seized," observed Bottesham. " I feel so much interested about her that I would do anything to preserve her from the fate with which she is menaced."

"Were it not inconsistent with your years, learned sir, I might suspect you of a tenderer feeling towards her," observed Blaize, archly. " But, in good sooth, her charms are so extraordinary, that I should not be surprised at any effect they might produce."

"They would produce no effect on me," replied Bottesham. " I am long past such feelings. But in regard to yourself. You say you are afraid of the plague. I will give you an electuary to drive away the panic; " and he produced a small jar, and handed it to the porter. " It is composed of conserve of roses, gillyflowers, borage, candied citron, powder of *lætificans Galeni*. Roman zedoary, doronicum, and saffron. You must take about the quantity of a large nutmeg, morning and evening."

"You make me for ever your debtor, learned sir," rejoined Blaize. " What a charming mixture."

" I will also add my remedy," said Furbisher. " It is a powder compounded of crabs' eyes, burnt hartshorn, the black tops of crabs' claws, the bone from a stag's heart, unicorn's horn, and salt of vipers. You must take one or two drams,—not more,—in a glass of hot posset-drink, when you go to bed, and swallow another draught of the same potion to wash it down."

" I will carefully observe your directions." replied Blaize, thankfully receiving the powder.

" Of all things," said Bottesham, claiming the porter's attention by tapping him on the head with his cane, " take care never to be without vinegar. It is the grand specific, not merely against the plague, but against all disorders. It is food and physic, meat and medicine, drink and julep, cordial and antidote. If you formerly took it as a sauce, now take it as a remedy. To the sound it is a preservative from sickness, to the sick a restorative to health. It is like the sword which is worn, not merely for ornament, but for defence. Vinegar is my remedy against the plague. It is a simple remedy, but an effectual one. I have cured a thousand patients with it, and hope to cure a thousand more. Take vinegar with all you eat, and flavour all you drink with it. Has the plague taken away your appetite, vinegar will renew it. Is your throat ulcerated, use vinegar as a gargle. Are you disturbed with phlegmatic humours, vinegar will remove them. Is your brain laden with vapours, throw vinegar on a hot shovel, and inhale its fumes, and you will obtain instantaneous relief. Have you the headache, wet a napkin in vinegar, and apply it to your temples, and the pain will cease. In short, there is no ailment that vinegar will not cure. It is the grand panacea; and may be termed the elixir of long life."

"I wonder its virtues have not been found out before," observed Blaize, innocently.

"It is surprising how slow men are in discovering the most obvious truths," replied Bottesham. "But take my advice, and never be without it."

"I never will," returned Blaize. "Heaven be praised, my master has just ordered in three tuns. I'll tap one of them directly."

"That idea of the vinegar remedy is borrowed from Kemp's late treatise on the pestilence and its cure," muttered Furbisher. "Before you enter upon the new system, young man," he added aloud to Blaize, "let me recommend you to fortify your stomach with a glass of canary." And pouring out a bumper, he handed it to the porter, who swallowed it at a draught.

"And now," said Bottesham, "to return to this mad scheme of your master's—is there no way of preventing it?"

"I am aware of none," replied Blaize.

"Bolts and bars!" cried Furbisher, "something must be done for the fair Amabel. We owe it to society not to permit so lovely a creature to be thus immured. What say you, Hawkswood?" he added to the gallant by his side, who had not hitherto spoken.

"It would be unpardonable to permit it,—quite unpardonable," replied this person.

"Might not some plan be devised to remove her for a short time, and frighten him out of his project?" said Bottesham. "I would willingly assist in such a scheme.

I pledge you in a bumper, young man. You appear a trusty servant."

"I am so accounted, learned sir," replied Blaize, upon whose brain the wine, thus plentifully bestowed, began to operate,—"and I may add, justly so."

"You really will be doing your master a service if you can prevent him from committing this folly," rejoined Bottesham. "Let us have a bottle of burnt malmsey, with a few bruised raisins in it, Mr. Parkhurst. This poor young man requires support. Be seated, friend."

With some hesitation, Blaize complied, and while the apothecary went in search of the wine, he observed to Bottesham, "I would gladly comply with your suggestion, learned sir, if I saw any means of doing so."

"Could you not pretend to have the plague?" said Bottesham. "I could then attend you."

"I should be afraid of playing such a trick as that," replied Blaize. "Besides, I do not see what purpose it would answer."

"It would enable me to get into the house," returned Bottesham, "and then I might take measures for Amabel's deliverance."

"If you merely wish to get into the house," replied Blaize, "that can be easily managed. I will admit you this evening."

"Without your master's knowledge?" asked Bottesham, eagerly.

"Of course," returned Blaize.

"But he has an apprentice?" said the doctor.

"Oh! you mean Leonard Holt," replied Blaize. "Yes, we must take care he doesn't see you. If you come about nine o'clock, he will be engaged with my master in putting away the things in the shop."

"I will be punctual," replied Bottesham, "and will bring Doctor Furbisher with me. We will only stay a few minutes. But here comes the burnt malmsey. Fill the young man's glass, Parkhurst. I will insure you against the plague, if you will follow my advice."

"But will you insure me against my master's displeasure, if he finds me out?" said Blaize.

"I will provide you with a new one," returned Bottesham. You shall serve me if you wish to change your place."

"That would answer my purpose exactly," thought Blaize. "I need never be afraid of the plague if I live with him. I will turn over your proposal, learned sir," he added, aloud.

After priming him with another bumper of malmsey, Blaize's new friends suffered him to depart. On returning home, he proceeded to his own room, and feeling unusually drowsy, he threw himself on the bed, and almost instantly dropped asleep. When he awoke, the fumes of the liquor had, in a great degree, evaporated, and he recalled, with considerable self-reproach, the promise he had given, and would gladly have recalled it, if it had been possible. But it was now not far from the appointed hour, and he momentarily expected the arrival of the two doctors. The only thing that consoled him was the store of medicine he had obtained, and, locking it up in his cupboard, he descended to the kitchen. Fortunately, his mother was from home, so that he ran no risk from her; and, finding Patience alone, after some hesitation, he let her into the secret of his anticipated visitors. She was greatly surprised, and expressed much uneasiness lest they should be discovered; as, if they were so, it would be sure to bring them both into trouble.

"What can they want with Mistress Amabel?" she cried. "I should not wonder if Doctor Calixtus Bottesham, as you call him, turns out a lover in disguise."

"A lover!" exclaimed Blaize. "Your silly head is always running upon lovers. He's an old man,—old enough to be your grandfather, with a long white beard, reaching to his waist. He a lover! Mr. Bloundel is much more like one."

"For all that it looks suspicious," returned Patience; "and I shall have my eyes about me on their arrival."

Shortly after this, Blaize crept cautiously up to the back-yard, and opening the door, found, as he expected, Bottesham and his companion. Motioning them to follow him, he led the way to the kitchen, where they

arrived without observation. Patience eyed the new-
comers narrowly, and felt almost certain, from their
appearance and manner, that her suspicions were correct.
All doubts were removed when Bottesham, slipping a
purse into her hand, entreated her, on some plea or other,
to induce Amabel to come into the kitchen. At first, she
hesitated; but having a tender heart, inclining her to
assist rather than oppose the course of any love affair,
her scruples were soon overcome. Accordingly, she
hurried upstairs, and chancing to meet with her young
mistress, who was about to retire to her own chamber,
entreated her to come down with her for a moment in
the kitchen. Thinking it some unimportant matter, but
yet wondering why Patience should appear so urgent,
Amabel complied. She was still more perplexed when she
saw the two strangers, and would have instantly retired
if Bottesham had not detained her.

" You will pardon the liberty I have taken in sending
for you," he said, " when I explain that I have done so
to offer you counsel."

" I am as much at a loss to understand what counsel
you can have to offer, sir, as to guess why you are here,"
she replied.

" Amabel," returned Bottesham, in a low tone; but
altering his voice, and slightly raising his spectacles so
as to disclose his features. " it is I,—Maurice Wyvil."

" Ah ! " she exclaimed, in the utmost astonishment.

" I told you we should meet again," he rejoined; " and
I have kept my word."

" Think not to deceive me, my lord," she returned,
controlling her emotion by a powerful effort. " I am
aware you are not Maurice Wyvil, but the Earl of
Rochester. Your love is as false as your character.
Mistress Mallett is the real object of your regards. You
see I am acquainted with your perfidy."

" Amabel, you are deceived," replied Rochester. " On
my soul, you are. When I have an opportunity of explaining myself more fully, I will prove to you that I
was induced by the king, for an especial purpose, to pay
feigned addresses to the lady you have named. But I

never loved her. You alone are the possessor of my heart, and shall be the sharer of my title. You shall be Countess of Rochester."

" Could I believe you ? " she cried.

" You *may* believe me," he answered. " Do not blight my hopes and your own happiness a second time. Your father is about to shut up his house for a twelve-month, if the plague lasts so long. This done, we shall meet no more, for access to you will be impossible. Do not hesitate, or you will for ever rue your irresolution."

" I know not what to do," cried Amabel, distractedly.

" Then I will decide for you," replied the earl, grasping her hand. " Come ! "

While this was passing, Furbisher, or rather, as will be surmised, Pillichody, had taken Blaize aside, and engaged his attention by dilating upon the efficacy of a roasted onion filled with treacle in the expulsion of the plague. Patience stationed herself near the door, not with the view of interfering with the lovers, but rather of assisting them; and at the very moment that the earl seized his mistress's hand, and would have drawn her forward, she ran towards them, and hastily whispered, " Leonard Holt is coming downstairs."

" Ah ! I am lost ! " cried Amabel.

" Fear nothing," said the earl. " Keep near me, and I will soon dispose of him."

As he spoke, the apprentice entered the kitchen, and, greatly surprised by the appearance of the strangers, angrily demanded from Blaize who they were.

" They are two doctors come to give me advice respecting the plague," stammered the porter.

" How did they get into the house ? " inquired Leonard.

" I let them in through the back door," replied Blaize.

" Then let them out by the same way," rejoined the apprentice. " May I ask what you are doing here ? " he added, to Amabel.

" What is that to you, fellow ? " cried Rochester, in his assumed voice.

" Much, as you shall find, my lord," replied the apprentice; " for in spite of your disguise, I know you. Quit the house instantly with your companion, or I will give the alarm, and Amabel well knows what the consequences will be."

" You must go, my lord," she replied.

" I will not stir unless you accompany me," said Rochester.

" Then I have no alternative," rejoined Leonard. " You know your father's determination—I would willingly spare you, Amabel."

" Oh, goodness ! what will become of us ? " cried Patience—" if there isn't Mr. Bloundel coming downstairs."

" Amabel," said Leonard, sternly, " the next moment decides your fate. If the earl departs, I will keep your secret."

" You hear that, my lord," she cried, " I command you to leave me."

And disengaging herself from him, and hastily passing her father, who at that moment entered the kitchen, she rushed upstairs.

On hearing the alarm of the grocer's approach, Pillichody took refuge in a cupboard, the door of which stood invitingly open, so that Bloundel only perceived the earl.

" What is the matter ? " he cried, gazing around him. " Who have we here ? "

" It is a quack doctor, whom Blaize has been consulting about the plague," returned Leonard.

" See him instantly out of the house," rejoined the grocer, angrily, " and take care he never enters it again I will have no such charlatans here."

Leonard motioned Rochester to follow him, and the latter reluctantly obeyed.

As soon as Bloundel had retired, Leonard, who had meanwhile provided himself with his cudgel, descended to the kitchen, where he dragged Pillichody from his hiding-place, and conducted him to the back door. But he did not suffer him to depart without belabouring him soundly. Locking the door, he then went in search of Blaize, and administered a similar chastisement to him.

CHAPTER IV

The Two Watchmen

ON the day following the events last related, as Leonard
Holt was standing at the door of the shop,—his master
having just been called out by some important business,—
a man in the dress of a watchman, with a halbert in his
hand, approached him, and inquired if he was Mr.
Bloundel's apprentice.

Before returning an answer, Leonard looked hard at
the new-comer, and thought he had never beheld so ill-
favoured a person before. Every feature in his face was
distorted. His mouth was twisted on one side, his nose
on the other, while his right eyebrow was elevated more
than an inch above the left; added to which, he squinted
intolerably, had a long fell of straight sandy hair, a sandy
beard and moustache, and a complexion of the colour of
brick-dust.

"An ugly dog," muttered Leonard to himself, as he
finished his scrutiny; "what can he want with me?
Suppose I should be Mr. Bloundel's apprentice," he
added, aloud, "what then, friend?"

"Your master has a beautiful daughter, has he not?"
asked the ill-favoured watchman.

"I answer no idle questions," rejoined Leonard, coldly.

"As you please," returned the other, in an offended
tone. "A plan to carry her off has accidentally come
to my knowledge. But, since incivility is all I am likely
to get for my pains in coming to acquaint you with it,
e'en find it out yourself."

"Hold!" cried the apprentice, detaining him; "I
meant no offence. Step in-doors for a moment. We can
converse there more freely."

The watchman, who, notwithstanding his ill-looks
appeared to be a good-natured fellow, was easily ap-
peased. Following the apprentice into the shop, on the

promise of a handsome reward, he instantly commenced his relation.

" Last night," he said, " I was keeping watch at the door of Mr. Brackley, a saddler in Aldermanbury, whose house having been attacked by the pestilence is now shut up, when I observed two persons, rather singularly attired, pass me. Both were dressed like old men, but neither their gait nor tone of voice corresponded with their garb."

" It must have been the Earl of Rochester and his companion," remarked Leonard.

" You are right," replied the other; " for I afterwards heard one of them addressed by that title. But to proceed. I was so much struck by the strangeness of their appearance, that I left my post for a few minutes, and followed them. They halted beneath a gateway, and, as they conversed together very earnestly, and in a loud tone, I could distinctly hear what they said. One of them, the stoutest of the two, complained bitterly of the indignities he had received from Mr. Bloundel's apprentice (meaning you, of course), averring that nothing but his devotion to his companion had induced him to submit to them; and affirming, with many tremendous oaths, that he would certainly cut the young man's throat the very first opportunity."

" He shall not want it, then," replied Leonard, contemptuously; " neither shall he lack a second application of my cudgel, when we meet. But what of his companion ? What did he say ? "

" He laughed heartily at the other's complaints," returned the watchman; " and told him to make himself easy, for he should soon have his revenge. ' To-morrow night,' he said, ' we will carry off Amabel, in spite of the apprentice or her father; and, as I am equally indebted with yourself to the latter, we will pay off old scores with him.' "

" How do they intend to effect their purpose ? " demanded Leonard.

" That I cannot precisely tell," replied the watchman. " All I could hear was, that they meant to enter the house by the back-yard about midnight. And now, if you will make it worth my while. I will help you to catch them in their own trap."

" Hum!" said Leonard. " What is your name?"

" Gregory Swindlehurst," replied the other.

" To help me you must keep watch with me to-night," rejoined Leonard. " Can you do so?"

" I see nothing to hinder me, provided I am paid for my trouble," replied Gregory. " I will find someone to take my place at Mr. Brackley's. At what hour shall I come?"

" Soon after ten," said Leonard. " Be at the shop-door, and I will let you in."

" Count upon me," rejoined Gregory, a smile of satisfaction illumining his ill-favoured countenance. " Shall I bring a comrade with me? I know a trusty fellow who would like the job. If Lord Rochester should have his companions with him, assistance will be required."

" True," replied Leonard. " Is your comrade a watchman, like yourself?"

" He is an old soldier, who has been lately employed to keep guard over infected houses," replied Gregory. " We must take care his lordship does not overreach us."

" If he gets into the house without my knowledge, I will forgive him," replied the apprentice.

" He won't get into it without mine," muttered Gregory, significantly. " But do you not mean to warn Mistress Amabel of her danger?"

" I shall consider of it," replied the apprentice.

At this moment Mr. Bloundel entered the shop, and Leonard, feigning to supply his companion with a small packet of grocery, desired him, in a low tone, to be punctual to his appointment, and dismissed him. In justice to the apprentice, it must be stated, that he had no wish for concealment, but was most anxious to acquaint his master with the information he had just obtained, and was only deterred from doing so by a dread of the consequences it might produce to Amabel.

The evening passed off much as usual. The family assembled at prayer; and Blaize, whose shoulders still ached with the chastisement he had received, eyed the apprentice with sullen and revengeful looks. Patience, too, was equally angry, and her indignation was evinced in a manner so droll, that at another season it would have drawn a smile from Leonard.

Supper over, Amabel left the room. Leonard followed her, and overtook her on the landing of the stairs.

"Amabel," he said, "I have received certain intelligence that the Earl of Rochester will make another attempt to enter the house, and carry you off to-night."

"Oh! when will he cease from persecuting me?" she cried.

"When you cease to encourage him," replied the apprentice, bitterly.

"I do *not* encourage him, Leonard," she rejoined, "and to prove that I do not, I will act in any way you think proper to-night."

"If I could trust you," said Leonard, "you might be of the greatest service in convincing the earl that his efforts are fruitless."

"You *may* trust me," she rejoined.

"Well, then," returned Leonard, "when the family have retired to rest, come downstairs, and I will tell you what to do."

Hastily promising compliance, Amabel disappeared; and Leonard ran down the stairs, at the foot of which he encountered Mrs. Bloundel.

"What is the matter?" she asked.

"Nothing—nothing," replied the apprentice, evasively.

"That will not serve my turn," she rejoined. "Something, I am certain, troubles you, though you do not choose to confess it. Heaven grant your anxiety is not occasioned by aught relating to that wicked Earl of Rochester. I cannot sleep in my bed for thinking of him. I noticed that you followed Amabel out of the room. I hope you do not suspect anything?"

"Do not question me further, madam, I entreat," returned the apprentice. "Whatever I may suspect, I have taken all needful precautions. Rest easy, and sleep soundly, if you can. All will go well."

"I shall never rest easy, Leonard," rejoined Mrs.

Bloundel, "till you are wedded to my daughter. Then, indeed, I shall feel happy. My poor child, I am sure, is fully aware how indiscreet her conduct has been; and when this noble libertine desists from annoying her—or rather, when he is effectually shut out—we may hope for a return of her regard for you."

"It is a vain hope, madam," replied Leonard; "there will be no such return. I neither expect it, nor desire it."

"Have you ceased to love her?" asked Mrs. Bloundel, in surprise.

"Ceased to love her!" echoed Leonard, fiercely. "Would I had done so!—would I *could* do so! I love her too well,—too well."

And repeating the words to himself with great bitterness, he hurried away.

"His passion has disturbed his brain," sighed Mrs. Bloundel, as she proceeded to her chamber. "I must try to reason him into calmness to-morrow."

Half an hour after this, the grocer retired for the night; and Leonard, who had gone to his own room, cautiously opened the door, and repaired to the shop. On the way, he met Amabel. She looked pale as death, and trembled so violently, that she could scarcely support herself.

"I hope you do not mean to use any violence towards the earl, Leonard?" she said, in a supplicating voice.

"He will never repeat his visit," rejoined the apprentice, gloomily.

"Your looks terrify me," cried Amabel, gazing with great uneasiness at his stern and determined countenance. "I will remain by you. He will depart at my bidding."

"Did he depart at your bidding before?" demanded Leonard, sarcastically.

"He did not, I grant," she replied, more supplicatingly than before. "But do not harm him—for mercy's sake, do not—take my life sooner. I, alone, have offended you."

The apprentice made no reply, but unlocking a box, took out a brace of large horse-pistols and a sword, and thrust them into his girdle.

"You do not mean to use those murderous weapons?" cried Amabel.

" It depends on circumstances," replied Leonard. " Force must be met by force."

" Nay, then," she rejoined, " the affair assumes too serious an aspect to be trifled with. I will instantly alarm my father."

" Do so," retorted Leonard, " and he will cast you off for ever."

" Better that than be the cause of bloodshed," she returned. " But is there nothing I can do to prevent this fatal result ? "

" Yes," replied Leonard. " Make your lover understand he is unwelcome to you. Dismiss him for ever. On that condition, he shall depart unharmed and freely."

" I will do so," she rejoined.

Nothing more was then said. Amabel seated herself and kept her eyes fixed on Leonard, who, avoiding her regards, stationed himself near the door.

By-and-by, a slight tap was heard without, and the apprentice cautiously admitted Gregory Swindlehurst and his comrade. The latter was habited like the other watchman, in a blue night-rail, and was armed with a halbert. He appeared much stouter, much older, and so far as could be discovered of his features—for a large handkerchief muffled his face—much uglier (if that were possible) than his companion. He answered to the name of Bernard Boutefeu. They had no sooner entered the shop than Leonard locked the door.

" Who are these persons ? " asked Amabel, rising in great alarm.

" Two watchmen whom I have hired to guard the house," replied Leonard.

" We are come to protect you, fair mistress," said Gregory, " and, if need be, to cut the Earl of Rochester's throat."

" Oh heavens ! " exclaimed Amabel.

" Ghost of Tarquin ! " cried Boutefeu, " we'll teach him to break into the houses of quiet citizens, and attempt to carry off their daughters against their will. By the soul of Dick Whittington, Lord Mayor of London ! we'll maul and mangle him."

" Silence ! Bernard Boutefeu," interposed Gregory.
" You frighten Mistress Amabel by your strange oaths."
" I should be sorry to do that," replied Boutefeu—
" I only wish to show my zeal for her. Don't be afraid
of the Earl of Rochester, fair mistress. With all his
audacity, he won't dare to enter the house when he finds
we are here."

" Is it your pleasure that we should thrust a halbert
through his body, or lodge a bullet in his brain ? " asked
Gregory, appealing to Amabel.

" Touch him not, I beseech you," she rejoined. " Leonard, I have your promise that, if I can prevail upon him
to depart, you will not molest him."

" You have," he replied

" You hear that," she observed to the watchmen.

" We are all obedience," said Gregory.

" Bless your tender heart ! " cried Boutefeu, " we would
not pain him for the world."

" A truce to this," said Leonard. " Come to the yard,
we will wait for him there."

" I will go with you," cried Amabel. " If any harm
should befall him, I should never forgive myself."

" Remember what I told you," rejoined Leonard
sternly, " it depends upon yourself whether he leaves the
house alive."

" Heed him not," whispered Gregory. " I and my
comrade will obey no one but you."

Amabel could not repress an exclamation of surprise.

" What are you muttering, sirrah ? " demanded Leonard,
angrily.

" Only that the young lady may depend on our fidelity,"
replied Gregory. " There can be no offence in that.
Come with us," he whispered to Amabel.

The latter part of his speech escaped Leonard, but the
tone in which it was uttered was so significant, that
Amabel, who began to entertain new suspicions, hesitated.

" You *must* come," said Leonard, seizing her hand.

" The fault be his, not mine," murmured Amabel, as
she suffered herself to be drawn along.

The party then proceeded noiselessly towards the

yard. On the way, Amabel telt a slight pressure on her arm, but, afraid of alarming Leonard. she made no remark.

The back-door was opened, and the little group stood in the darkness. They had not long to wait. Before they had been in the yard five minutes, a noise was heard of footsteps and muttered voices in the entry. This was followed by a sound like that occasioned by fastening a rope-ladder against the wall, and the next moment two figures were perceived above it. After dropping the ladder into the yard, these persons, the foremost of whom the apprentice concluded was the Earl of Rochester, descended. They had no sooner touched the ground than Leonard, drawing his pistols, advanced towards them.

" You are my prisoner, my lord," he said, in a stern voice, " and shall not depart with life, unless you pledge your word never to come hither again on the same errand."

" Betrayed ! " cried the earl, laying his hand upon his sword.

" Resistance is in vain, my lord," rejoined Leonard. " I am better armed than yourself."

" Will nothing bribe you to silence, fellow ? " cried the earl. " I will give you a thousand pounds, if you will hold your tongue, and conduct me to my mistress."

" I can scarcely tell what stays my hand," returned Leonard, in a furious tone. " But I will hold no further conversation with you. Amabel is present, and will give you your final dismissal herself."

" If I receive it from her own lips," replied the earl, " I will instantly retire—but not otherwise."

" Amabel," said Leonard, in a low tone to her, " you hear what is said. Fulfil your promise."

" Do so," cried a voice, which she instantly recognised, in her ear—" I am near you."

" Ah ! " she exclaimed.

" Do you hesitate ? " cried the apprentice, sternly.

" My lord," said Amabel, in a faint voice, " I must pray you to retire. Your efforts are in vain. I will never fly with you."

"That will not suffice," whispered Leonard; "you must tell him you no longer love him."

"Hear me," pursued Amabel; "you who present yourself as Lord Rochester, I entertain no affection for you, and never wish to behold you again."

"Enough!" cried Leonard.

"Admirable!" whispered Gregory. "Nothing could be better."

"Well," cried the supposed earl, "since I no longer hold a place in your affections, it would be idle to pursue the matter further. Heaven be praised, there are other damsels quite as beautiful, though not so cruel. Farewell, for ever, Amabel."

So saying he mounted the ladder, and, followed by his companion, disappeared on the other side.

"He is gone," said Leonard, "and I hope for ever. Now let us return to the house."

"I am coming," rejoined Amabel.

"Let him go," whispered Gregory. "The ladder is still upon the wall. We will climb it."

And as the apprentice moved towards the house, he tried to drag her in that direction.

"I cannot,—will not, fly thus," she cried.

"What is the matter?" exclaimed Leonard, suddenly turning.

"Further disguise is useless," replied the supposed Gregory Swindlehurst. "I am the Earl of Rochester. The other was a counterfeit."

"Ah!" exclaimed Leonard, rushing towards them and placing a pistol against the breast of his mistress. "Have I been duped? But it is not yet too late to retrieve my error. Move a foot further, my lord,—and do you, Amabel, attempt to fly with him, and I fire."

"You cannot mean this?" cried Rochester. "Raise your hand against the woman you love?"

"Against the woman who forgets her duty, and the libertine who tempts her, the arm that is raised is that of justice," replied Leonard. "Stir another footstep, and I fire."

As he spoke his arms were suddenly seized by a powerful grasp from behind, and, striking the pistols from his hold, the earl snatched up Amabel in his arms, and, mounting the ladder, made good his retreat.

A long and desperate struggle took place between Leonard and his assailant, who was no other than Pillichody, in his assumed character of Bernard Boutefeu. But notwithstanding the superior strength of the bully, and the advantage he had taken of the apprentice, he was worsted in the end.

Leonard had no sooner extricated himself, than, drawing his sword, he would have passed it through Pillichody's body, if the latter had not stayed his hand by offering to tell him where he would find his mistress, provided his life were spared.

" Where has the earl taken her ? " cried Leonard, scarcely able to articulate from excess of passion.

" He meant to take her to Saint Paul's,—to the vaults below the cathedral, to avoid pursuit," replied Pillichody. " I have no doubt you will find her there."

" I will go there instantly and search," cried Leonard, rushing up the ladder.

CHAPTER V

The Blind Piper and his Daughter

SCARCELY knowing how he got there, Leonard Holt found himself at the great northern entrance of the cathedral. Burning with fury, he knocked at the door; but no answer being returned to the summons, though he repeated it still more loudly, he shook the heavy latch with such violence as to rouse the sullen echoes of the aisles. Driven almost to desperation, he retired a few paces, and surveyed the walls of the vast structure, in the hope of descrying some point by which he might obtain an entrance.

It was a bright moonlight night, and the reverend pile looked so beautiful, that, under any other frame of mind, Leonard must have been struck with admiration. The

ravages of time could not now be discerned, and the
architectural incongruities which, seen in the broad glare
of day, would have offended the eye of taste, were lost
in the general grand effect. On the left ran the magnificent pointed windows of the choir, divided by massive
buttresses,—the latter ornamented with crocketed pinnacles. On the right, the building had been new faced,
and its original character, in a great measure, destroyed
by the tasteless manner in which the repairs had been
executed. On this side, the lower windows were round-
headed and separated by broad pilasters, while above
them ran a range of small circular windows. At the
western angle was seen one of the towers (since imitated
by Wren), which flanked this side of the fane, together
with a part of the portico erected, about twenty-five years
previously, by Inigo Jones, and which, though beautiful in
itself, was totally out of character with the edifice, and
in fact, a blemish to it.

Insensible alike to the beauties or defects of the majestic
building, and regarding it only as the prison of his mistress,
Leonard Holt scanned it carefully on either side. But his
scrutiny was attended with no favourable result.

Before resorting to force to obtain admission, he determined to make the complete circuit of the structure,
and with this view he shaped his course towards the
east.

He found two small doors on the left of the northern
transept, but both were fastened, and the low pointed
windows beneath the choir, lighting the subterranean
church of Saint Faith's, were all barred. Running on,
he presently came to a flight of stone steps at the north-
east corner of the choir, leading to a portal opening upon
a small chapel dedicated to Saint George. But this was
secured like the others, and thinking it vain to waste
time in trying to force it, he pursued his course.

Skirting the eastern extremity of the fane—then the
most beautiful part of the structure, from its magnificent
rose-window—he speeded past the low windows which
opened on this side, as on the other upon Saint Faith's,
and did not pause till he came to the great southern

portal, the pillars and arch of which differed but slightly in character from those of the northern entrance.

Here he knocked as before, and was answered, as on the former occasion, by sullen echoes from within. When these sounds died away, he placed his ear to the huge key-hole in the wicket, but could not even catch the fall of a footstep. Neither could he perceive any light, except that afforded by the moonbeams, which flooded the transept with radiance.

Again hurrying on, he passed the cloister-walls surrounding the Convocation House; tried another door between that building and the church of Saint Gregory,— a small fane attached to the larger structure; and failing in opening it, turned the corner and approached the portico,—the principal entrance to the cathedral being then, as now, on the west.

Erected, as before mentioned, from the designs of the celebrated Inigo Jones, this magnificent colonnade was completed about 1640, at which time preparations were made for repairing the cathedral throughout, and for strengthening the tower, for enabling it to support a new spire. But this design, owing to the disorganized state of affairs, was never carried into execution.

At the time of the Commonwealth, while the interior of the sacred fabric underwent every sort of desecration and mutilation,—while stones were torn from the pavement, and monumental brasses from tombs,—while carved stalls were burnt, and statues plucked from their niches,—a similar fate attended the portico. Shops were built beneath it, and the sculptures ornamenting its majestic balustrade were thrown down.

Amongst other obstructions, it appears that there was " a high house in the north angle, which hindered the masons from repairing that part of it." The marble doorcases, the capitals, cornices, and pillars were so much injured by the fires made against them that it required months to put them in order. At the Restoration, Sir John Denham, the poet, was appointed surveyor-general of the works, and continued to hold the office at the period of this history.

As Leonard drew near the portico, he perceived to his surprise, that a large concourse of people was collected in the area in front of it; and, rushing forward, he found the assemblage listening to the denunciations of Solomon Eagle, who was standing in the midst of them with his brazier on his head. The enthusiast appeared more than usually excited. He was tossing aloft his arms in a wild and frenzied manner, and seemed to be directing his menaces against the cathedral itself.

Hoping to obtain assistance from the crowd, Leonard resolved to await a fitting period to address them. Accordingly, he joined them, and listened to the discourse of the enthusiast.

"Hear me!" cried the latter, in a voice of thunder. "I had a vision last night and will relate it to you. During my brief slumbers, I thought I was standing on this very spot, and gazing as now upon yon mighty structure. On a sudden the day became overcast, and ere long it grew pitchy dark. Then was heard a noise of rushing wings in the air, and I could just discern many strange figures hovering above the tower, uttering doleful cries and lamentations. All at once, these figures disappeared, and gave place to,—or, it may be, were chased away by others of more hideous appearance. The latter brought lighted brands, which they hurled against the sacred fabric, and, in an instant, flames burst forth from it on all sides. My brethren, it was a fearful, yet a glorious sight to see that vast pile wrapped in the devouring element! The flames were so vivid—so intense—that I could not bear to look upon them, and I covered my face with my hands. On raising my eyes again, the flames were extinguished, but the building was utterly in ruins—its columns cracked— its tower hurled from its place—its ponderous roof laid low. It was a mournful spectacle, and a terrible proof of the divine wrath and vengeance. Yes, my brethren, the temple of the Lord has been profaned, and it will be razed to the ground. It has been the scene of abomination and impiety, and must be purified by fire. Theft, murder, sacrilege, and every other crime have been committed within its walls, and its destruction will follow. The

ministers of heaven's vengeance are even now hovering
above it. Repent, therefore, ye who listen to me, and
repent speedily; for sudden death, plague, fire, and famine
are at hand. As the prophet Amos saith, ' The Lord will
send a fire, the Lord will commission a fire, the Lord
will kindle a fire; ' and the fire so commissioned and so
kindled shall consume you and your city; nor shall one
stone of those walls be left standing on another. Repent
or burn, for he cometh to judge the earth. Repent
or burn, I say ! "

As soon as he concluded, Leonard Holt ran up the
steps of the portico, and in a loud voice claimed the
attention of the crowd.

" Solomon Eagle is right," he cried; " the vengeance
of heaven will descend upon this fabric, since it continues
to be the scene of so much wickedness. Even now, it
forms the retreat of a profligate nobleman, who has
this night forcibly carried off the daughter of a citizen."

" What nobleman," cried a bystander.

" The Earl of Rochester," replied Leonard. " He has
robbed Stephen Bloundel, the grocer of Wood-street, of
his daughter, and has concealed her, to avoid pursuit, in
the vaults of the cathedral."

" I know Mr. Bloundel well," rejoined the man who
had made the inquiry, and whom Leonard recognised as
a hosier named Lamplugh, " and I know the person who
addresses us. It is his apprentice. We must restore the
damsel to her father, friends."

" Agreed," cried several voices.

" Knock at the door," cried a man, whose occupation
of a smith was proclaimed by his leathern apron, brawny
chest, and smoke-begrimed visage, as well as by the
heavy hammer which he bore upon his shoulder. " If
it is not instantly opened, we will break it down. I have
an implement here which will soon do the business."

A rush was then made to the portal, which rang with
the heavy blows against it. While this was passing,
Solomon Eagle, whose excitement was increased by the
tumult, planted himself in the centre of the colonnade
and vociferated—" I speak in the words of the prophet

Ezekiel:—' Thou hast defiled thy sanctuaries by the multitude of thine iniquities, by the iniquity of thy traffic. Therefore will I bring forth a fire from the midst of thee, and will bring thee to ashes upon the earth, in the sight of all them that behold thee ! ' ''

The crowd continued to batter the door until they were checked by Lamplugh, who declared he heard someone approaching, and the next moment, the voice of one of the vergers inquired in trembling tones who they were, and what they wanted ?

" No matter who we are," replied Leonard, " we demand admittance to search for a young female who has been taken from her home by the Earl of Rochester, and is now concealed in the vaults of the cathedral."

" If admittance is refused us, we will soon let ourselves in," vociferated Lamplugh.

" Ay, that we will," added the smith.

" You are mistaken, friends," returned the verger, timorously. " The Earl of Rochester is not here."

" We will not take your word for it," rejoined the smith. " This will show you we are not to be trifled with."

So saying, he raised his hammer, and struck such a tremendous blow against the door that the bolts started in their sockets.

" Hold ! hold ! " cried the verger, " sooner than violence shall be committed, I will risk your admission."

And he unfastened the door.

" Keep together," shouted the smith, stretching out his arms to oppose the progress of the crowd. " Keep together, I say."

" Ay, ay, keep together," added Lamplugh, seconding his efforts.

" Conduct us to the Earl of Rochester, and no harm shall befall you," cried Leonard, seizing the verger by the collar

" I tell you I know nothing about him," replied the man. " He is not here."

" It is false ! you are bribed to silence," rejoined the apprentice. " We will search till we find him."

" Search where you please," rejoined the verger; " and if you *do* find him, do what you please with me."

" Don't be afraid of that, friend," replied the smith; " we will hang you and the earl to the same pillar."

By this time the crowd had pushed aside the opposition offered by the smith and Lamplugh. Solomon Eagle darted along the nave with lightning swiftness, and mounting the steps leading to the choir, disappeared from view. Some few persons followed him, while others took their course along the aisles. But the majority kept near the apprentice.

Snatching the lamp from the grasp of the verger, Leonard Holt ran on with his companions till they came to the beautiful chapel built by Thomas Kempe, Bishop of London. The door was open, and the apprentice, holding the light forward, perceived there were persons inside. He was about to enter the chapel, when a small spaniel rushed forth, and, barking furiously, held him in check for a moment. Alarmed by the noise, an old man in a tattered garb, and a young female, who were slumbering on benches in the chapel, immediately started to their feet, and advanced towards them.

" We are mistaken," said Lampiugh, " this is only Mike Macascree, the blind piper, and his daughter Nizza. I know them well enough."

Leonard was about to proceed with his search, but a slight circumstance detained him for a few minutes; during which time he had sufficient leisure to note the extraordinary personal attractions of Nizza Macascree.

In age she appeared about seventeen, and differed in the character of her beauty, as well as in the natural gracefulness of her carriage and demeanour, from all the persons he had seen in her humble sphere of life. Her features were small, and of the utmost delicacy. She had a charmingly-formed nose—slightly *retroussé*—a small mouth, garnished with pearl-like teeth, and lips as fresh and ruddy as the dew-steeped rose. Her skin was as dark as a gipsy's, but clear and transparent, and far more attractive than the fairest complexion. Her eyes were luminous as the stars, and black as midnight; while her raven tresses, gathered beneath a spotted kerchief tied round her head, escaped in many a wanton curl down her shoulders. Her figure was slight, but exquisitely proportioned; and she had the smallest foot and ankle that ever fell to the lot of woman. Her attire was far from unbecoming, though of the coarsest material; and her fairy feet were set off by the daintiest shoes and hose. Such was the singular and captivating creature that attracted the apprentice's attention.

Her father, Mike Macascree, was upwards of sixty, but still in the full vigour of life, with features, which, though not ill-looking, bore no particular resemblance to those of his daughter. He had a good-humoured, jovial countenance, the mirthful expression of which even his sightless orbs could not destroy. Long white locks descended upon his shoulders, and a patriarchal beard adorned his chin. He was wrapped in a loose gray gown, patched with different coloured cloths, and supported himself with a staff. His pipe was suspended from his neck by a green worsted cord.

" Lie down, Bell," he cried to his dog; " what are you barking at thus? Lie down, I say."

" Something is the matter, father," replied Nizza. " The church is full of people."

" Indeed ! " exclaimed the piper.

" We are sorry to disturb you," said Leonard. " But we are in search of a nobleman who has run away with a citizen's daughter, and conveyed her to the cathedral, and we thought they might have taken refuge in this chapel."

" No one is here, except myself and daughter," replied the piper. " We are allowed this lodging by Mr. Quatremain, the minor-canon."

" All dogs are ordered to be destroyed by the Lord Mayor " cried the smith, seizing Bell by the neck. " This noisy anmal must be silenced."

" Oh no ! do not hurt her ! " cried Nizza. " My father loves poor Bell almost as well as he loves me. She is necessary to his existence. You must not—will not destroy her ! "

"Won't I?" replied the smith, gruffly;—"we'll see that."

"But we are not afraid of contagion, are we, father?" cried Nizza, appealing to the piper.

"Not in the least," replied Mike, "and we will take care the poor beast touches no one else. Do not harm her, sir,—for pity's sake, do not. I should miss her sadly."

"The Lord Mayor's commands must be obeyed," rejoined the smith, brutally.

As if conscious of the fate awaiting her, poor Bell struggled hard to get free, and uttered a piteous yell.

"You are not going to kill the dog?" interposed Leonard.

"Have you anything to say to the contrary?" rejoined the smith, in a tone calculated, as he thought, to put an end to further interference.

"Only this," replied Leonard, "that I will not allow it."

"You won't—eh!" returned the smith, derisively.

"I will not," rejoined Leonard, "so put her down and come along."

"Go your own way," replied the smith, "and leave me to mine."

Leonard answered by snatching Bell suddenly from his grasp. Thus liberated, the terrified animal instantly flew to her mistress.

"Is this the return I get for assisting you?" cried the smith, savagely. "You are bewitched by a pair of black eyes. But you will repent your folly."

"I shall never forget your kindness," replied Nizza, clasping Bell to her bosom, and looking gratefully at the apprentice. "You say you are in search of a citizen's daughter and a nobleman. About half an hour ago, or scarcely so much, I was awakened by the opening of the door of the southern transept, and peeping out, I saw three persons,—a young man in the dress of a watch-man, but evidently disguised, and a very beautiful young woman, conducted by Judith Malmayns, bearing a lantern,—pass through the doorway leading to Saint

Faith's. Perhaps they are the very persons you are in search of."

" They are," returned Leonard; " and you have re-paid me a hundred-fold for the slight service I have rendered you by the information. We will instantly repair to the vaults. Come along."

Accompanied by the whole of the assemblage, except the smith, who sulked off in the opposite direction, he passed through the low doorway on the right of the choir, and descended to Saint Faith's. The subterranean church was buried in profound darkness, and apparently wholly untenanted. On reaching the charnel, they crossed it, and tried the door of the vault formerly occupied by the sexton. It was fastened, but Leonard knocking violently against it, it was soon opened by Judith Malmayns, who appeared much surprised, and not a little alarmed, at the sight of so many persons. She was not alone, and her companion was Chowles. He was seated at a table, on which stood a flask of brandy and a couple of glasses, and seemed a good deal confused at being caught in such a situation, though he endeavoured to cover his embarrass-ment by an air of effrontery.

" Where is the Earl of Rochester—where is Amabel ? " demanded Leonard Holt.

" I know nothing about either of them," replied Judith. " Why do you put these questions to me ? "

" Because you admitted them to the cathedral," cried the apprentice, furiously; " and because you have con-cealed them. If you do not instantly guide me to their retreat, I will make you a terrible example to all such evil-doers in future."

" If you think to frighten me by your violence, you are mistaken," returned Judith, boldly. " Mr. Chowles has been here more than two hours. Ask him whether he has seen any one."

" Certainly not," replied Chowles. " There is no Amabel—no Earl of Rochester here. You must be dreaming, young man."

" The piper's daughter affirmed the contrary," replied Leonard. " She said she saw this woman admit them."

F

"She lies," replied Judith, fiercely. But suddenly altering her tone, she continued, "If I *had* admitted them, you would find them here."

Leonard looked round uneasily. He was but half convinced, and yet he scarcely knew what to think.

"If you doubt what I say to you," continued Judith, "I will take you to every chamber in the cathedral. You will then be satisfied that I speak the truth. But I will not have this mob with me. Your companions must remain here."

"Ay, stop with me and make yourselves comfortable," cried Chowles. "You are not so much used to these places as I am. I prefer a snug crypt, like this, to the best room in a tavern—ha! ha!"

Attended by Judith, Leonard Holt searched every corner of the subterranean church, except the vestry, the door of which was locked, and the key removed; but without success. They then ascended to the upper structure, and visited the choir, the transepts, and the nave but with no better result.

"If you still think they are here," said Judith, "we will mount to the summit of the tower?"

"I will never quit the cathedral without them," replied Leonard.

"Come on, then," returned Judith.

So saying, she opened a door in the wall on the left of the choir, and ascending a winding stone staircase to a considerable height, arrived at a small cell contrived within the thickness of the wall, and desired Leonard to search it. The apprentice unsuspectingly obeyed. But he had scarcely set foot inside when the door was locked behind him, and he was made aware of the treachery practised upon him by a peal of mocking laughter from his conductress.

CHAPTER VI

Old London from Old Saint Paul's

AFTER repeated, but ineffectual efforts to burst open the door, Leonard gave up the attempt in despair, and endeavoured to make his situation known by loud outcries. But his shouts, if heard, were unheeded, and he was soon compelled from exhaustion to desist. Judith having carried away the lantern, he was left in total darkness; but on searching the cell, which was about four feet wide and six deep, he discovered a narrow grated loophole. By dint of great exertion, and with the help of his sword, which snapped in twain as he used it, he managed to force off one of the rusty bars, and to squeeze himself through the aperture. All his labour, however, was thrown away. The loophole opened on the south side of the tower, near one of the large buttresses, which projected several yards beyond it on the left, and was more than twenty feet above the roof; so that it would be certain destruction to drop from so great a height.

The night was overcast, and the moon hidden behind thick clouds. Still, there was light enough to enable him to discern the perilous position in which he stood. After gazing below for some time, Leonard was about to return to the cell, when, casting his eyes upwards, he thought he perceived the end of a rope about a foot above his head, dangling from the upper part of the structure. No sooner was this discovery made, than it occurred to him that he might possibly liberate himself by this unlooked-for aid; and, regardless of the risk he ran, he sprang upwards and caught hold of the rope. It was firmly fastened above, and sustained his weight well.

Possessed of great bodily strength and activity, and nerved by desperation, Leonard Holt placed his feet against the buttress, and impelled himself towards one of the tall pointed windows lighting the interior of the tower; but though he reached the point at which he aimed, the sway of the rope dragged him back before he could obtain a secure grasp of the stone shaft; and, after another ineffectual effort, fearful of exhausting his strength, he abandoned the attempt, and began to climb up the rope with his hands and knees. Aided by the inequalities of the roughened walls, he soon gained a range of small Saxon arches ornamenting the tower immediately beneath the belfry, and succeeded in planting his right foot on the moulding of one of them; he, instantly steadied himself, and with little further effort clambered through an open window.

His first act on reaching the belfry was to drop on his knees and return thanks to Heaven for his deliverance. He then looked about for an outlet ; but though a winding staircase existed in each of the four angles of the tower, all the doors, to his infinite disappointment, were fastened on the other side. He was still, therefore, a prisoner.

Determined, however, not to yield to despair, he continued his search, and finding a small door opening upon a staircase communicating with the summit of the tower, he unfastened it (for the bolt was on his own side), and hurried up the steps. Passing through another door, bolted like the first withinside, he issued upon the roof. He was now on the highest part of the cathedral, and farther from his hopes than ever, and so agonizing were his feelings, that he almost felt tempted to fling himself headlong downwards. Beneath him lay the body of the mighty fabric, its vast roof, its crocketed pinnacles, its buttresses and battlements scarcely discernible through the gloom, but looking like some monstrous engine devised to torture him.

Wearied with gazing at it, and convinced of the futility of any further attempt at descent, Leonard Holt returned to the belfry, and throwing himself on the boarded floor sought some repose. The fatigue he had undergone was so great, that, notwithstanding his anxiety, he soon dropped asleep, and did not awake for several hours. On opening his eyes, it was just getting light, and shaking himself he again prepared for action. All the events of the night rushed upon his mind, and he thought with unutterable anguish of Amabel's situation. Glancing round the room it occurred to him that he might give the alarm by ringing the enormous bells near him; but though he set them slightly in motion, he could not agitate the immense clappers sufficiently to produce any sound.

Resolved, however, to free himself at any hazard, he once more repaired to the summit of the tower, and leaning over the balustrade, gazed below. It was a sublime spectacle, and, in spite of his distress, filled him with admiration and astonishment. He had stationed himself on the south side of the tower, and immediately beneath him lay the broad roof of the transept, stretching out to a distance of nearly two hundred feet. On the right, surrounded by a double row of cloisters, remarkable for the beauty of their architecture, stood the Convocation, or Chapter-House. This exquisite building was octagonal in form, and supported by large buttresses, ornamented on each gradation by crocketed pinnacles. Each side, moreover, had a tall pointed window, filled with stained glass, and was richly adorned with trefoils and cinquefoils. Farther on, on the same side, was the small low church dedicated to Saint Gregory, overtopped by the south-western tower of the mightier parent fane.

It was not, however, the cathedral itself, but the magnificent view it commanded, that chiefly attracted the apprentice's attention. From the elevated point on which he stood, his eye ranged over a vast tract of country bounded by the Surrey hills, and at last settled upon the river, which in some parts was obscured by a light haze, and in others tinged with the ruddy beams of the newly-risen sun. Its surface was spotted, even at this early hour, with craft, while innumerable vessels of all shapes and sizes were moored to its banks. On the left, he noted the tall houses covering London Bridge; and on the right, traced the sweeping course of the stream as it flowed from Westminster. On this hand, on the opposite bank, lay the flat marshes of Lambeth; while nearer

stood the old bull-baiting and bear-baiting establish-
ments, the flags above which could be discerned above the
tops of the surrounding habitations. A little to the left
was the borough of Southwark, even then a large and
populous district—the two most prominent features in
the scene being Winchester-house, and Saint Saviour's
old and beautiful church.

Filled with wonder at what he saw, Leonard looked
towards the east, and here an extraordinary prospect met
his gaze. The whole of the city of London was spread
out like a map before him, and presented a dense mass
of ancient houses, with twisted chimneys, gables, and
picturesque roofs—here and there over-topped by a
hall, a college, a hospital, or some other lofty structure.
This vast collection of buildings was girded in by gray
and mouldering walls, approached by seven gates, and
intersected by innumerable narrow streets. The spires
and towers of the churches shot up into the clear morning air,—for, except in a few quarters, no smoke yet
issued from the chimneys. On this side, the view of the
city was terminated by the fortifications and keep of the
Tower. Little did the apprentice think, when he looked
at the magnificent scene before him—and marvelled at the
countless buildings he beheld, that, ere fifteen months had
elapsed, the whole mass, together with the mighty fabric
on which he stood, would be swept away by a tremendous
conflagration. Unable to foresee this direful event, and
lamenting only that so fair a city should be a prey to an
exterminating pestilence, he turned towards the north,
and suffered his gaze to wander over Finsbury-fields, and
the hilly ground beyond them—over Smithfield and
Clerkenwell, and the beautiful open country adjoining
Gray's-inn-lane.

So smiling and beautiful did these districts appear, that
he could scarcely fancy they were the chief haunts of the
horrible distemper. But he could not blind himself to the
fact that in Finsbury-fields, as well as in the open country
to the north of Holborn, plague-pits had been digged and
pest-houses erected; and this consideration threw such
a gloom over the prospect, that, in order to dispel the

effect, he changed the scene by looking towards the west. Here his view embraced all the proudest mansions of the capital, and, tracing the Strand to Charing Cross, long since robbed of the beautiful structure from which it derived its name, and noticing its numerous noble habitations, his eye finally rested upon Whitehall; and he heaved a sigh as he thought that the palace of the sovereign was infected by as foul a moral taint as the hideous disease that ravaged the dwellings of his subjects.

At the time that Leonard Holt gazed upon the capital, its picturesque beauties were nearly at their close. In a little more than a year-and-a-quarter afterwards, the greater part of the old city was consumed by fire; and though it was rebuilt, and in many respects improved, its original and picturesque character was entirely destroyed.

It seems scarcely possible to conceive a finer view than can be gained from the dome of the modern cathedral at sunrise on a May morning, when the prospect is not dimmed by the smoke of a hundred thousand chimneys,—when the river is just beginning to stir with its numerous craft, or when they are sleeping on its glistening bosom,—when every individual house, court, church, square, or theatre can be discerned,—when the eye can range over the whole city on each side, and calculate its vast extent. It seems scarcely possible, we say, to suppose at any previous time it could be more striking,—and yet, at the period under consideration, it was incomparably more so. Then, every house was picturesque, and every street a collection of picturesque objects. Then, that which was objectionable in itself and contributed to the insalubrity of the city, namely, the extreme narrowness of the streets, and overhanging stories of the houses, was the main source of their beauty. Then, the huge projecting signs with their fantastical iron-work—the conduits—the crosses (where crosses remained)—the maypoles—all were picturesque; and as superior to what can now be seen, as the attire of Charles the Second's age is to the ugly and disfiguring costume of our own day.

Satiated with this glorious prospect, Leonard began to recur to his own situation, and carefully scrutinizing

every available point on the side of the tower, he thought
it possible to effect his descent by clambering down the
gradations of one of the buttresses. Still, as this experiment would be attended with the utmost danger, while,
even if he reached the roof, he would yet be far from
his object, he resolved to defer it for a short time, in the
hope that ere long some of the bell-ringers, or other
persons connected with the cathedral, might come thither
and set him free.

While thus communing with himself he heard a door
open below; and hurrying down the stairs at the sound,
he beheld to his great surprise and joy the piper's daughter,
Nizza Macascree.

" I have searched for you everywhere," she cried,
" and began to think some ill had befallen you. I overheard Judith Malmayns say she had shut you up in a
cell in the upper part of the tower. How did you escape
thence ? "

Leonard hastily explained.

" I told you I should never forget the service you
rendered me in preserving the life of poor Bell," pursued
Nizza, " and what I have done will prove I am not un-
mindful of my promise. I saw you search the cathedral
last night with Judith, and noticed that she returned from
the tower unaccompanied by you. At first, I supposed
you might have left the cathedral without my observing
you, and I was further confirmed in the idea by what I
subsequently heard."

" Indeed ! " exclaimed Leonard. " What did you hear ? "

" I followed Judith to the vaults of Saint Faith's,"
replied Nizza, " and heard her inform your companions
that you had found the grocer's daughter, and had taken
her away."

" And this false statement imposed upon them ? "
cried Leonard.

" It did," replied Nizza. " They were by this time
more than half intoxicated by the brandy given them by
Chowles, the coffin-maker, and they departed in high
dudgeon with you."

" No wonder," exclaimed Leonard.

"They had scarcely been gone many minutes," pursued Nizza, " when, having stationed myself behind one of the massive pillars in the north aisle of Saint Faith's— for I suspected something was wrong—I observed Judith and Chowles steal across the nave, and proceed towards the vestry. The former tapped at the door, and they were instantly admitted by Mr. Quatremain, the minor-canon. Hastening to the door, which was left slightly ajar, I perceived two young gallants, whom I heard addressed as the Earl of Rochester and Sir George Etherege, and a young female, whom I could not doubt was Amabel. The earl and his companion laughed heartily at the trick Judith had played you, and which the latter detailed to them; but Amabel took no part in their merriment, but, on the contrary, looked very grave, and even wept."

"Wept, did she ? " cried Leonard, in a voice of much emotion. " Then there is hope for her yet."

"You appear greatly interested in her ? " observed Nizza, pausing in her narration. " Do you love her ? "

" Can you ask it ? " cried Leonard, passionately.

" I would advise you to think no more of her, and to fix your heart elsewhere," returned Nizza.

" You know not what it is to love," replied the apprentice, " or you would not offer such a counsel."

" Perhaps not," replied Nizza; " but I am sorry you have bestowed your heart upon one who so little appreciates the boon."

And feeling she had said too much, she blushed deeply, and cast down her eyes.

Unconscious of her confusion, and entirely engrossed by the thought of his mistress, Leonard urged her to proceed.

" Tell me what has become of Amabel—where I shall find her ? " he cried.

" You will find her soon enough," replied Nizza. " She has not left the cathedral. But hear me to an end. On learning you were made a prisoner, I ran to the door leading to the tower, but found that Judith had locked it, and removed the key. Not daring to give the alarm—for I had gathered from what was said that the three vergers were in the earl's pay,—I determined to await a favourable opportunity to release you. Accordingly, I returned to the vestry-door, and again played the eaves-dropper. By this time, another person, who was addressed as Major Pillichody, and who, it appeared, had been employed in the abduction, had joined the party. He informed the earl that Mr. Bloundel was in the greatest distress at his daughter's disappearance, and advised him to lose no time in conveying her to some secure retreat. These tidings troubled Amabel exceedingly, and the earl endeavoured to pacify her by promising to espouse her at daybreak, and as soon as the ceremony was over, to introduce her in the character of his countess to her parents."

" Villain ! " cried Leonard; " but go on."

" I have little more to tell," replied Nizza, " except that she consented to the proposal, provided she was allowed to remain till six o'clock, the hour appointed for the marriage, with Judith."

" Bad as that alternative is, it is better than the other," observed Leonard. " But how did you procure the key of the winding staircase ? "

" I fortunately observed where Judith had placed it," replied Nizza, " and when she departed to the crypt, near the charnel, with Amabel, I possessed myself of it. For some time I was unable to use it, because the Earl of Rochester and Sir George Etherege kept pacing to and fro in front of the door, and their discourse convinced me that the marriage was meant to be a feigned one, for Sir George strove to dissuade his friend from the step he was about to take; but the other only laughed at his scruples. As soon as they retired, which is not more than half an hour ago, I unlocked the door, and hurried up the winding stairs. I searched every chamber and began to think you were gone, or that Judith's statement was false. But I resolved to continue my search until I was fully satisfied on this point, and accordingly ascended to the belfry. You are aware of the result."

" You have rendered me a most important service," replied Leonard; " and I hope hereafter to prove my gratitude. But let us now descend to the choir; where I will conceal myself till Amabel appears. This marriage must be prevented."

Before quitting the belfry, Leonard chanced to cast his eyes on a stout staff left there, either by one of the bell-ringers or some chance visitant, and seizing it as an unlooked-for prize, he ran down the steps, followed by the piper's daughter.

On opening the lowest door, he glanced towards the choir, and there before the high altar stood Quatremain in his surplice, with the earl and Amabel, attended by Etherege and Pillichody. The ceremony had just commenced. Not a moment was to be lost. Grasping his staff, the apprentice darted along the nave, and rushing up to the pair, exclaimed, in a loud voice, " Hold ! I forbid this marriage. It must not take place ! "

" Back, sirrah ! " cried Etherege, drawing his sword, and opposing the approach of the apprentice. " You have no authority to interrupt it. Proceed, Mr. Quatremain."

" Forbear ! " cried a voice of thunder near them—and all turning at the cry, they beheld Solomon Eagle, with his brazier on his head, issue from behind the stalls. " Forbear ! " cried the enthusiast, placing himself between the earl and Amabel, both of whom recoiled at his approach. " Heaven's altar must not be profaned with these mockeries ! And you, Thomas Quatremain, who have taken part in this unrighteous transaction, make clean your breast, and purge yourself quickly of your sins, for your hours are numbered. I read in your livid looks and red and burning eye-balls that you are smitten by the pestilence."

CHAPTER VII

Paul's Walk

IT will now be necessary to ascertain what took place at
the grocer's habitation subsequently to Amabel's abduction. Leonard Holt having departed, Pillichody was preparing to make good his retreat, when he was prevented
by Blaize, who, hearing a noise in the yard, peeped
cautiously out at the back-door, and inquired who was
there ?

" Are you Mr. Bloundel ? " rejoined Pillichody, be-
thinking him of a plan to turn the tables upon the
apprentice.

" No; I am his porter," replied the other.

" What, Blaize ! " replied Pillichody. " Thunder and
lightning ! don't you remember Bernard Boutefeu, the
watchman ! "

" I don't remember any watchman of that name, and I
cannot discern your features," rejoined Blaize. " But
your voice sounds familiar to me. What are you doing
there ? "

" I have been trying to prevent Leonard Holt from
carrying off your master's daughter, the fair Mistress
Amabel," answered Pillichody. " But he has accomplished his villainous purpose in spite of me."

" The devil he has ! " cried Blaize. " Here is a pretty
piece of news for my master. But how did you discover
him ? "

" Chancing to pass along the entry on the other side
of that wall about a quarter of an hour ago," returned
Pillichody, " I perceived a rope-ladder fastened to it,
and wishing to ascertain what was the matter, I mounted
it, and had scarcely got over into the yard, when I saw
two persons advancing. I concealed myself beneath the
shadow of the wall, and they did not notice me; but I
gathered from their discourse who they were, and what
was their design. I allowed Amabel to ascend, but just

as the apprentice was following, I laid hold of the skirt of
his doublet, and, pulling him back, desired him to come
with me to his master. He answered by drawing his
sword, and would have stabbed me, but I closed with him,
and should have secured him, if my foot had not slipped.
While I was on the ground, he dealt me a severe blow, and
ran after his mistress."

" Just like him," replied Blaize. " He took the same
cowardly advantage of me last night."

" No punishment will be too severe for him," rejoined
Pillichody, " and I hope your master will make a terrible
example of him."

" How fortunate I was not gone to bed ! " exclaimed
Blaize. " I had just taken a couple of rufuses, and was
about to put on my night cap, when, hearing a noise
without, and being ever on the alert to defend my master's
property, even at the hazard of my life, I stepped forth and
found you."

" I will bear testimony to your vigilance and courage,"
returned Pillichody; " but you had better go and alarm
your master. I will wait here."

" Instantly !—instantly ! " cried Blaize, rushing upstairs.

On the way to Mr. Bloundel's chamber, he met Patience,
and told her what he had heard. She was inclined to put
a very different construction on the story, but as she
bore the apprentice no particular good-will, she determined to keep her opinion to herself, and let affairs
take their course. The grocer was soon aroused, and
scarcely able to credit the porter's intelligence, and yet
fearing something must be wrong, he hastily attired himself, and proceeded to Amabel's room. It was empty,
and it was evident from the state in which everything
was left, that she had never retired to rest. Confounded
by the sight, Bloundel then hurried downstairs in search
of the apprentice, but he was nowhere to be found. By
this time, Mrs. Bloundel had joined him, and on hearing
Blaize's story, utterly scouted it.

" It cannot be," she cried. " Leonard could have no
motive for acting thus. He had our consent to the union,

and the sole obstacle to it was Amabel herself. Is it likely he would run away with her?"

"I am sure I do not know," replied Patience, "but he was desperately in love, that's certain; and when people are in love, I am told they do very strange and unaccountable things. Perhaps he may have carried her off against her will."

"Very likely," rejoined Blaize. "I thought I heard a scream, and should have called out at the moment, but a rufus stuck in my throat and prevented me."

"Where is the person who says he intercepted them?" asked Bloundel.

"In the yard," answered Blaize.

"Bid him come hither," rejoined his master. "Stay, I will go to him myself."

With this, the whole party, including old Josyna and Stephen—the two boys, and little Christiana not having been disturbed—proceeded to the yard, where they found Pillichody in his watchman's dress, who related his story more circumstantially than before.

"I don't believe a word of it," cried Mrs. Bloundel; "and I will stake my life it is one of the Earl of Rochester's tricks."

"Were I assured that such was the case," said the grocer, in a stern whisper, to his wife, "I would stir no further in the matter. My threat to Amabel was not an idle one."

"I may be mistaken," returned Mrs. Bloundel, almost at her wits' end with anxiety. "Don't mind what I say. Judge for yourself. Oh dear! what *will* become of her!" she mentally ejaculated.

"Lanterns and links!" cried Pillichody. "Do you mean to impeach my veracity, good mistress? I am an old soldier, and as tenacious of my honour as your husband is of his credit."

"This blustering will not serve your turn, fellow," observed the grocer, seizing him by the collar. "I begin to suspect my wife is in the right, and will at all events detain you."

"Detain me? On what ground?" asked Pillichody.

"As an accomplice in my daughter's abduction," replied Bloundel. "Here, Blaize—Stephen, hold him while I call the watch. This is a most mysterious affair, but I will soon get at the bottom of it."

By the grocer's directions, Pillichody, who very quietly entered the house, and surrendered his halbert to Blaize, was taken to the kitchen. Bloundel then set forth, leaving Stephen on guard at the yard door, while his wife remained in the shop, awaiting his return.

On reaching the kitchen with the prisoner, Blaize besought his mother, who, as well as Patience, had accompanied him thither, to fetch a bottle of sack. While she went for the wine, and the porter was stalking to and fro before the door with the halbert on his shoulder, Patience whispered to Pillichody, " I know who you are. You came here last night with the Earl of Rochester in the disguise of a quack doctor."

" Hush ! " cried Pillichody, placing his finger on his lips.

" I am not going to betray you," returned Patience, in the same tone. " But you are sure to be found out, and had better beat a retreat before Mr. Bloundel returns."

" I won't lose a moment," replied Pillichody, starting to his feet.

" What's the matter ? " cried Blaize, suddenly halting.

" I only got up to see whether the wine was coming," replied Pillichody.

" Yes, here it is," replied Blaize, as his mother reappeared; " and now you shall have a glass of such sack as you never yet tasted."

And pouring out a bumper, he offered it to Pillichody. The latter took the glass; but his hand shook so violently that he could not raise it to his lips.

" What ails you, friend ? " inquired Blaize, uneasily.

" I don't know," replied Pillichody; " but I feel extremely unwell."

" He looks to me as if he had got the plague," observed Patience to Blaize.

" The plague," exclaimed the latter, letting fall the glass, which shivered to pieces on the stone floor. " And

I have touched him. Where is the vinegar-bottle? I
must sprinkle myself directly, and rub myself from head
to foot with oil of hartshorn and spirits of sulphur.
Mother! dear mother! you have taken away my medicine
chest. If you love me, go and fetch me a little conserve of
Roman wormwood and mithridate. You will find them
in two small jars."

" Oh, yes, do," cried Patience; " or he may die with
fright."

Moved by their joint entreaties, old Josyna again
departed; and her back was no sooner turned, than
Patience said in an undertone to Pillichody,—" Now is
your time. You have not a moment to lose."

Instantly taking the hint, the other uttered a loud cry,
and springing up, caught at Blaize, who instantly dropped
the halbert, and fled into one corner of the room.

Pillichody then hurried upstairs, while Blaize shouted
after him, " Don't touch him, Master Stephen. He has
got the plague! he has got the plague! "

Alarmed by this outcry, Stephen suffered Pillichody to
pass; and the latter, darting across the yard mounted the
rope-ladder, and quickly disappeared. A few minutes
afterwards, Bloundel returned with the watch, and was
greatly enraged when he found that the prisoner had got
off. No longer doubting that he had been robbed of his
daughter by the Earl of Rochester, he could not make up
his mind to abandon her to her fate, and his conflicting
feelings occasioned him a night of indescribable anxiety.
The party of watch whom he had summoned searched the
street for him, and endeavoured to trace out the fugitives,
—but without success; and they returned before daybreak to report their failure.

About six o'clock, Mr. Bloundel, unable to restrain
himself longer, sallied forth with Blaize in search of his
daughter and Leonard. Uncertain where to bend his
steps, he trusted to chance to direct him, resolved, if he
were unsuccessful, to lay a petition for redress before the
throne. Proceeding along Cheapside, he entered Paternoster-row, and traversed it till he came to Paul's Alley,—
a narrow passage leading to the north-west corner of the

cathedral. Prompted by an unaccountable impulse, he no sooner caught sight of the reverend structure, than he hastened towards it, and knocked against the great northern door.

We shall, however, precede him, and return to the party at the altar. The awful warning of Solomon Eagle so alarmed Quatremain, that he let fall his prayer-book, and after gazing vacantly round for a few moments, staggered to one of the stalls, where, feeling a burning pain in his breast, he tore open his doublet, and found that the enthusiast had spoken the truth, and that he was really attacked by the pestilence. As to Amabel, on hearing the terrible denunciation, she uttered a loud cry, and would have fallen to the ground but for the timely assistance of the apprentice, who caught her with one arm, while with the other he defended himself against the earl and his companions.

But, in spite of his resistance they would have soon compelled him to relinquish his charge, if Solomon Eagle, who had hitherto contented himself with gazing sternly on what was passing, had not interfered; and, rushing towards the combatants, seized Rochester and Etherege, and hurled them backwards with almost super-natural force. When they arose, and menaced him with their swords, he laughed loudly and contemptuously, crying, "Advance, if ye dare! and try your strength against one armed by Heaven, and ye will find how far it will avail."

At this juncture, Leonard Holt heard a musical voice behind him, and turning, beheld Nizza Macascree. She beckoned him to follow her; and, raising Amabel in his arms, he ran towards the door leading to Saint Faith's, through which his conductress passed. All this was the work of a moment, and when Rochester and Etherege, who rushed after him, tried the door, they found it fastened withinside.

Just then a loud knocking was heard at the northern entrance of the cathedral, and a verger answering the summons, Mr. Bloundel and Blaize were admitted. On beholding the new-comers, Rochester and his com-

panions were filled with confusion. Equally astonished
at the rencounter, the grocer grasped his staff, and rushing
up to the earl, demanded, in a voice that made the other,
despite his natural audacity, quail,—" Where is my
child, my lord ? What have you done with her ? "

" I know nothing about her," replied Rochester, with
affected carelessness.—" Yes, I am wrong," he added, as
if recollecting himself; " I am told she has run away
with your apprentice."

Pillichody, who had changed his attire since his escape
from the grocer's dwelling, thought he might now venture
to address him without fear of discovery, and setting his
arms a-kimbo, and assuming a swaggering demeanour,
strutted forward and said, " Your daughter has just been
wedded to Leonard Holt, Mr. Bloundel."

" It is false," cried Bloundel, " as false as the character
you just personated, for I recognise you as the knave
who recently appeared before me as a watchman."

" I pledge you my word as a nobleman," interposed
Rochester, " that your daughter has just descended to
Saint Faith's with your apprentice."

" I can corroborate his lordship's assertion," said
Etherege.

" And I," added Pillichody. " By the holy apostle to
whom this fane is dedicated ! it is so."

" To convince you that we speak the truth, we will go
with you and assist you to search," said Rochester.

Attaching little credit to what he heard, and yet unwilling to lose a chance of recovering his daughter, the
grocer rushed to the door indicated by his informant, but
found it fastened.

" You had better go to the main entrance," said one of
the vergers. " I have the keys with me, and will admit
you."

" I will keep guard here till you return," said another
verger.

Accompanied by Rochester and Etherege, Bloundel
then proceeded to the chief door of the subterranean
church. It was situated at the south of the cathedral between two of the larger buttresses, and at the foot of a

flight of stone steps. On reaching it, the verger produced his keys, but they were of no avail, for the door was barred withinside. After many fruitless attempts to obtain admission, they were fain to give up the attempt.

" Well, if we cannot get in, no one shall get out," observed the verger. " The only key that opens this door is in my possession, so we have them safe enough."

The party then returned to the cathedral, where they found Blaize, Pillichody, and the two other vergers keeping watch at the door near the choir. No one had come forth.

Rochester then walked apart with his companions, while Bloundel, feeling secure so long as he kept the earl in view, folded his arms upon his breast, and determined to await the result.

By this time, the doors being opened, a great crowd was soon collected within the sacred structure. Saint Paul's Churchyard, as is well known, was formerly the great mart for booksellers, who have not, even in later times, deserted the neighbourhood, but still congregate in Paternoster-row, Ave Maria-lane, and the adjoining streets. At the period of this history they did not confine themselves to the precincts of the cathedral, but, as has been previously intimated, fixed their shops against the massive pillars of its nave. Besides booksellers, there were seamstresses, tobacco-merchants, vendors of fruit and provisions, and Jews—all of whom had stalls within the cathedral, and who were now making preparations for the business of the day. Shortly afterwards, numbers who came for recreation and amusement made their appearance, and before ten o'clock, Paul's Walk, as the nave was termed, was thronged, by apprentices, rufflers, porters, water-carriers, higglers, with baskets on their heads, or under their arms, fish-wives, quack-doctors, cutpurses, bonarobas, merchants, lawyers, and serving-men, who came to be hired, and who stationed themselves near an oaken block attached to one of the pillars, and which was denominated, from the use it was put to, the " serving-man's log." Some of the crowd were smoking, some laughing, others gathering round a ballad-singer,

who was chanting one of Rochester's own licentious
ditties; some were buying quack medicines and remedies
for the plague, the virtues of which the vendor loudly
extolled, while others were paying court to the dames,
many of whom were masked. Everything seemed to be
going forward within this sacred place, except devotion.
Here, a man, mounted on the carved marble of a monument, bellowed forth the news of the Dutch war, while
another, not far from him, on a bench, announced in
lugubrious accents the number of those who had died on
the previous day of the pestilence. There, at the very font,
was a usurer paying over a sum of money to a gallant—
it was Sir Paul Parravicin,—who was sealing a bond for
thrice the amount of the loan. There, a party of choristers,
attended by a troop of boys, were pursuing another
gallant, who had ventured into the cathedral booted and
spurred, and were demanding " spur-money " of him—
an exaction which they claimed as part of their perquisites.

An admirable picture of this curious scene has been
given by Bishop Earle, in his *Microcosmographia*, published in 1629. " Paul's Walk," he writes, " is the land's
epitome, or you may call it the lesser isle of Great Britain.
It is more than this—it is the whole world's map, which
you may here discern in its perfectest motion, jostling and
turning. It is a heap of stones and men, with a vast confusion of languages, and were the steeple not sanctified,
nothing could be liker Babel. The noise in it is like that
of bees, a strange humming, or buzzing, mixed of walking,
tongues, and feet: it is a kind of still roar, or loud whisper.
It is the great exchange of all discourse, and no business
whatsoever, but is here stirring and afoot. It is the synod of
all parts politic, jointed and laid together in most serious
posture, and they are not half so busy at the Parliament.
It is the market of young lecturers, whom you may
cheapen here at all rates and sizes. It is the general mint
of all famous lies, which are here, like the legends of
Popery, first coined and stamped in the church. All
inventions are emptied here, and not a few pockets. The
best sign of the Temple in it is that it is the thieves' sanctuary, who rob more safely in a crowd than a wilderness,

while every pillar is a bush to hide them. It is the other expense of the day, after plays and taverns; and men have still some oaths to swear here. The visitants are all men without exceptions; but the principal inhabitants are stale knights and captains out of service, men of long rapiers and short purses, who after all turn merchants here, and traffic for news. Some make it a preface to their dinner, and travel for an appetite; but thirstier men make it their ordinary, and board here very cheap. Of all such places it is least haunted by hobgoblins, for if a ghost would walk here, he could not."

Decker, moreover, terms Paul's Walk, or the "Mediterranean Isle," in his *Gull's Hornbook*—"the only gallery wherein the pictures of all your true fashionate and complimental gulls are, and ought to be, hung up." After giving circumstantial directions for the manner of entering the walk, he proceeds thus:—"Bend your course directly in the middle line that the whole body of the church may appear to be yours, where in view of all, you may publish your suit in what manner you affect most, either with the slide of your cloak from the one shoulder or the other." He then recommends the gull, after four or five turns in the nave, to betake himself to some of the sempsters' shops, the new tobacco office, or the booksellers' stalls, "where, if you cannot read, exercise your smoke, and inquire who has written against the divine weed." Such, or something like it, was Paul's Walk at the period of this history.

The grocer, who had not quitted his post, remained a silent and sorrowful spectator of the scene. Despite his anxiety, he could not help moralizing upon it, and it furnished him with abundant food for reflection. As to Rochester and his companions, they mingled with the crowd—though the earl kept a wary eye on the door —chatted with the prettiest damsels—listened to the newsmongers, and broke their fast at the stall of a vendor of provisions, who supplied them with tolerable viands, and a bottle of excellent Rhenish. Blaize was soon drawn away by one of the quacks, and, in spite of his master's angry looks, he could not help purchasing one of the infallible antidotes offered for sale by the charlatan. Parravicin had no sooner finished his business with the usurer than he strolled along the nave, and was equally surprised and delighted at meeting with his friends, who briefly explained to him why they were there.

" And how do you expect the adventure to terminate ? " asked Parravicin, laughing heartily at the recital.

" Heaven knows," replied the earl. " But what are you doing here ? "

" I came partly to replenish my purse, for I have had a run of ill luck of late," replied the knight, " and partly to see a most beautiful creature, whom I accidentally discovered here yesterday."

" A new beauty ! " cried Rochester. " Who is she ? "

" Before I tell you, you must engage not to interfere with me," replied Parravicin. " I have marked her for my own."

" Agreed," replied Rochester. " Now, her name ? "

" She is the daughter of a blind piper, who haunts the cathedral," returned Parravicin, " and her name is Nizza Macascree. Is it not charming ? But you shall see her."

" We must not go too far from the door of Saint Faith's," rejoined Rochester. " Can you not contrive to bring her hither ? "

" That is more easily said than done," replied Parravicin. " She is as coy as the grocer's daughter. However, I will try to oblige you."

With this, he quitted his companions, and returning shortly afterwards, said, " My mistress has likewise disappeared. I found the old piper seated at the entrance of Bishop Kempe's chapel, attended by his dog—but he missed his daughter when he awoke in the morning, and is in great trouble about her."

" Strange ! " cried Etherege. " I begin to think the place is enchanted."

" It would seem so, indeed," replied Rochester.

While they were thus conversing, Pillichody, who was leaning against a column, with his eye fixed upon the door leading to Saint Faith's, observed it open, and the apprentice issue from it accompanied by two masked females. All three attempted to dart across the transept, and gain the northern entrance, but they were intercepted. Mr. Bloundel caught hold of Leonard's arm, and Rochester seized her whom he judged by her garb to be Amabel, while Parravicin, recognizing Nizza Macascree, as he thought, by her dress, detained her.

" What is the meaning of all this, Leonard ? " demanded the grocer, angrily.

" You shall have an explanation instantly," replied the apprentice, " but think not of me—think only of your daughter."

" My father !—my father ! " cried the damsel, who had been detained by Parravicin, taking off her mask, and rushing towards the grocer.

" Who then have I got ? " cried Rochester.

" The piper's daughter, I'll be sworn," replied Etherege.

" You are right," replied Nizza, unmasking. " I changed dresses with Amabel, and hoped by so doing to accomplish her escape, but we have been baffled. However, as her father is here, it is of little consequence."

" Amabel," said the grocer, repulsing her, " before I receive you again, I must be assured that you have not been alone with the Earl of Rochester."

" She has not, sir," replied the apprentice. " Visit your displeasure on my head. I carried her off and would have wedded her."

" What motive had you for this strange conduct ? " asked Bloundel, incredulously.

Before Leonard could answer, Pillichody stepped forward, and said to the grocer—" Mr. Bloundel, you are deceived,—on the faith of a soldier you are ! "

" Peace, fool ! " said Rochester, " I will not be outdone in generosity by an apprentice. Leonard Holt speaks the truth."

" If so," replied Bloundel, " he shall never enter my house again. Send for your indentures to-night," he continued sharply, to Leonard, " but never venture to approach me more."

" Father, you are mistaken," cried Amabel. " Leonard Holt is not to blame. I alone deserve your displeasure."

" Be silent ! " whispered the apprentice; " you destroy
yourself. I care not what happens to me provided you
escape the earl."

" Come home, mistress," cried the grocer, dragging
her through the crowd which had gathered round them.

" Here is a pretty conclusion to the adventure ! "
cried Parravicin; " but where is the apprentice—and
where is the pretty Nizza Macascree ? 'Fore heaven," he
added, as he looked around for them in vain, " I should
not wonder if they have not eloped together."

" Nor I," replied Rochester. " I admire the youth's
spirit, and trust he may be more fortunate with his second
mistress than with his first."

" It shall be my business to prevent that," rejoined
Parravicin. " Help me to search for her."

CHAPTER VIII

The Amulet

As the grocer disappeared with his daughter, Nizza
Macascree, who had anxiously watched the apprentice,
observed him turn deadly pale, and stagger, and instantly
springing to his side she supported him to a neighbouring
column, against which he leaned till he had in some
degree recovered from the shock. He then accompanied
her to Bishop Kempe's beautiful chapel in the northern
aisle, where she expected to find her father. But it was
empty.

" He will be back presently," said Nizza. " He is no
doubt making the rounds of the cathedral. Bell will take
care of him. Sit down on that bench while I procure you
some refreshment. You appear much in need of it."

And without waiting for a reply, she ran off, and presently afterwards returned with a small loaf of bread,
and a bottle of beer.

" I cannot eat," said Leonard, faintly. But seeing that
his kind provider looked greatly disappointed, he swallowed a few mouthfuls, and raised the bottle to his lips.

As he did so, a sudden feeling of sickness seized him, and he set it down untasted.

"What ails you?" asked Nizza, noticing his altered looks with uneasiness.

"I know not," he replied. "I have never felt so ill before."

"I thought you were suffering from agitation," she rejoined, as a fearful foreboding crossed her.

"I shall be speedily released from further trouble," replied the apprentice. "I am sure I am attacked by the plague."

"Oh! say not so!" she rejoined. "You may be mistaken."

But though she tried to persuade herself she spoke the truth, her heart could not be deceived.

"I scarcely desire to live," replied the apprentice, in a melancholy tone, "for life has lost all charms for me. But do not remain here, or you may be infected by the distemper."

"I will never leave you," she hastily rejoined; "that is," she added, checking herself,—"till I have placed you in charge of someone who will watch over you."

"No one will watch over me," returned Leonard. "My master has dismissed me from his service, and I have no other friend left. If you will tell one of the vergers what is the matter with me, he will summon the Examiner of Health, who will bring a litter to convey me to the pest-house."

"If you go thither your fate is sealed," replied Nizza.

"I have said I do not desire to live," returned the apprentice.

"Do not indulge in these gloomy thoughts, or you are certain to bring about a fatal result," said Nizza. "Would I knew how to aid you! But I still hope you are deceived as to the nature of your attack."

"I cannot be deceived," replied Leonard, whose countenance proclaimed the anguish he endured. "Doctor Hodges, I think, is interested about me," he continued, describing the physician's residence,—"if you will inform him of my seizure, he may, perhaps, come to me."

" I will fly to him instantly," replied Nizza; and she was about to quit the chapel, when she was stopped by Parravicin and his companions.

" Let me pass," she said, trying to force her way through them.

" Not so fast, fair Nizza," rejoined Parravicin, forcing her back, " I must have a few words with you. Have I overrated her charms?" he added to Rochester. " Is she not surpassingly beautiful?"

" In good sooth she is," replied the earl, gazing at her with admiration.

" By the nut-brown skin of Cleopatra!" cried Pillichody, " she beats Mrs. Disbrowe, Sir Paul."

" I have never seen any one so lovely," said the knight, attempting to press her hand to his lips.

" Release me, sir," cried Nizza, struggling to free herself.

" Not till I have told you how much I love you," returned the knight, ardently.

" Love me!" she echoed, scornfully.

" Yes, love you," reiterated Parravicin. " It would be strange if I, who profess myself so great an admirer of beauty, did otherwise. I am passionately enamoured of you. If you will accompany me, fair Nizza, you shall change your humble garb for the richest attire that gold can purchase—shall dwell in a magnificent mansion, and have troops of servants at your command. In short, my whole fortune, together with myself, shall be placed at your disposal."

" Do not listen to him, Nizza," cried Leonard Holt, in a faint voice.

" Be assured I will not," she answered. " Your insulting proposal only heightens the disgust I at first conceived for you," she added to the knight: " I reject it with scorn, and command you to let me pass."

" Nay, if you put on these airs, sweetheart," replied Parravicin, insolently, " I must alter my tone likewise. I am not accustomed to play the humble suitor to persons of your condition."

" Perhaps not," replied Nizza; " neither am I accustomed to this unwarrantable usage. Let me go. My errand is one of life and death. Do not hinder me, or you will have a heavy crime on your soul—heavier, it may be, than any that now loads it."

"Where are you going?" asked Parravicin, struck by her earnest manner.

"To fetch assistance," she replied, "for one suddenly assailed by the pestilence."

"Ah!" exclaimed the knight, trembling, and relinquishing his grasp. "My path is ever crossed by that hideous spectre. Is it your father who is thus attacked?"

"No," she replied, pointing to Leonard, "it is that youth."

"The apprentice!" exclaimed Rochester. "I am sorry for him. Let us be gone," he added to his companions. "It may be dangerous to remain here longer."

With this they all departed except Parravicin.

"Come with us, Nizza," said the latter; "we will send assistance to the sufferer."

"I have already told you my determination," she rejoined; "I will not stir a footstep with you. And if you have any compassion in your nature, you will not detain me longer."

"I will not leave you here to certain destruction," said the knight. "You shall come with me whether you will or not."

And as he spoke, he advanced towards her, while she retreated towards Leonard, who, rising with difficulty, placed himself between her and her persecutor.

"If you advance another footstep," cried the apprentice, "I will fling myself upon you, and the contact may be fatal."

Parravicin gazed furiously at him, and half unsheathed his sword. But the next moment he returned it to the scabbard, and exclaiming, "Another time! another time!" darted after his companions.

He was scarcely gone, when Leonard reeled against the wall, and, before Nizza could catch him, fell in a state of insensibility on the floor.

After vainly attempting to raise him, Nizza flew for

assistance, and had just passed through the door of the chapel, when she met Judith Malmayns and Chowles. She instantly stopped them, and acquainting them with the apprentice's condition, implored them to take charge of him while she went in search of Doctor Hodges.

" Before you go," said Judith, " let me make sure that he is attacked by the plague. It may be some other disorder."

" I hope so, indeed," said Nizza, pausing; " but I fear the contrary."

So saying, she returned with them to the chapel. Raising the apprentice with the greatest ease, Judith tore open his doublet.

" Your suspicion is correct," she said, with a malignant smile. " Here is the fatal sign upon his breast."

" I will fetch Doctor Hodges instantly," cried Nizza.

" Do so," replied Judith; " we will convey him to the vaults in Saint Faith's where poor Mr. Quatremain has just been taken. He will be better there than in the pest-house."

" Anything is better than that," said Nizza shuddering.

As soon as she was gone, Chowles took off his long black cloak, and, throwing it over the apprentice, laid him at full length upon the bench, and, assisted by Judith, carried him towards the choir. As they proceeded, Chowles called out, " Make way for one sick of the plague ! " and the crowd instantly divided, and gave them free passage. In this way, they descended to Saint Faith's, and, shaping their course to the vault, deposited their burden on the very bed lately occupied by the unfortunate sexton.

" He has come here to die," observed Judith to her companion. " His attack is but a slight one, and he might with care recover. But I can bargain with the Earl of Rochester for his removal."

" Take heed how you make such a proposal to his lordship," returned Chowles. " From what I have seen, he is likely to revolt at it."

" Every man is glad to get rid of a rival," rejoined Judith.

"Granted," replied Chowles; "but no man will *pay* for the riddance when the plague will accomplish it for him for nothing."

"With due attention, I would answer for that youth's recovery," said Judith. "It is not an incurable case, like Mr. Quatremain's. And so Doctor Hodges, when he comes, will pronounce it."

Shortly after this, Nizza Macascree appeared with a countenance fraught with anxiety, and informed them that Doctor Hodges was from home, and would not probably return till late at night.

"That's unfortunate," said Judith. "Luckily, however, there are other doctors in London, and some who understand the treatment of the plague far better than he does—Sibbald, the apothecary of Clerkenwell, for instance."

"Do you think Sibbald would attend him?" asked Nizza, eagerly.

"To be sure he would," replied Mrs. Malmayns, "if he were paid for it. But you seem greatly interested about this youth. I have been young, and know what effect good looks and a manly deportment have upon our sex. He has won your heart! Ha! ha! You need not seek to disguise it. Your blushes answer for you."

"A truce to this," cried Nizza, whose cheeks glowed with shame and anger.

"You can answer a plain question, I suppose," returned Judith. "Is his life dear to you?"

"Dearer than my own," replied Nizza.

"I thought as much," replied Judith. "What will you give me to save him?"

"I have nothing," rejoined Nizza with a troubled look, "nothing but thanks to give you."

"Think again," said Judith. "Girls like you, if they have no money, have generally some trinket—some valuable in their possession."

"That is not my case," said Nizza, bursting into tears. "I have never received a present in my life, and never desired one till now."

" But your father must have some money ? " said
Judith, inquisitively.

" I know not," replied Nizza, " but I will ask him.
What sum will content you ? "

" Bring all you can," returned Judith, " and I will do
my best."

Nizza then departed, while Judith, with the assistance
of Chowles, covered Leonard with blankets, and proceeded to light a fire. Long before this, the sick youth
was restored to animation. But he was quite light-headed
and unconscious of his situation, and rambled about
Amabel and her father. After administering such remedies
as she thought fit, and as were at hand, Judith sat down
with the coffin-maker beside a small table, and entered
into conversation with him.

" Well," said Chowles, in an indifferent tone, as he
poured out a glass of brandy, " is it to be kill or cure ? "

" I have not decided," replied Judith, pledging him.

" I still do not see what gain there would be in shorten-
ing his career," observed Chowles.

" If there would be no gain, there would be gratification," replied Judith. " He has offended me."

" If that is the case, I have nothing further to say,"
returned Chowles. " But you promised the piper's
daughter to save him."

" We shall see what she offers," rejoined Judith; " all
will depend upon that,"

" It is extraordinary," observed Chowles, after a
pause, " that while all around us are sick or dying of the
pestilence, we should escape contagion."

" We are not afraid of it," replied Judith. " Besides,
we are part of the plague ourselves. But I *have* been
attacked, and am, therefore, safe."

" True," replied Chowles; " I had forgotten that.
Well, if I fall ill, you shan't nurse me."

" You won't be able to help yourself then," returned
Judith.

" Eh ! " exclaimed Chowles, shifting uneasily on his
seat.

" Don't be afraid," returned Judith, laughing at his

alarm. "I'll take every care of you. We are necessary to each other."

"So we are," replied Chowles; "so we are, and if nothing else could, that consideration would make us true to each other."

"Of course," assented Judith. "Let us reap as rich a harvest as we can, and when the scourge is over, we can enjoy ourselves upon the spoils."

"Exactly so," replied Chowles. "My business is daily—hourly on the increase. My men are incessantly employed, and my only fear is that an order will be issued to bury the dead without coffins."

"Not unlikely," replied Mrs. Malmayns. "But there are plenty of ways of getting money in a season like this. If one fails, we must resort to another. I shall make all I can, and in the shortest manner."

"Right!" cried Chowles, with an atrocious laugh. "Right! ha! ha!"

"I have found out a means of propagating the distemper," pursued Judith, in a low tone, and with a mysterious air, "of inoculating whomsoever I please with the plague-venom. I have tried the experiment on Mr. Quatremain and that youth, and you see how well it has answered in both instances."

"I do," replied Chowles, looking askance at her. "But why destroy the poor minor-canon?"

"Because I want to get hold of the treasure discovered by the help of the mosaical rods in Saint Faith's, which by right belonged to my husband, and which is now in Mr. Quatremain's possession," replied Judith.

"I understand," nodded Chowles.

While they were thus conversing, Nizza Macascree again returned, and informed them that she could not find her father. "He has left the cathedral," she said, "and will not, probably, return till nightfall."

"I am sorry for it on your account," observed Judith, coldly.

"Why, you will not have the cruelty to neglect the poor young man till then—you will take proper precautions?" exclaimed Nizza.

" Why should I exert myself for one about whose
recovery I am indifferent ? " said Judith.

" Why ? " exclaimed Nizza. " But it is in vain to
argue with you. I must appeal to your avarice, since you
are deaf to the pleadings of humanity. I have just bethought me that I have an old gold coin, which was
given me years ago by my father. He told me it had been
my mother's, and charged me not to part with it. I never
should have done so, except in an emergency like the
present." As she spoke, she drew from her bosom a
broad gold piece. A hole was bored through it, and it
was suspended from her neck by a chain of twisted hair.

" Let me look at it," said Judith, taking the coin.
" Who gave you this ? " she asked, in an altered tone.

" My father," replied Nizza ; " I have just told you so.
It was my mother's."

" Impossible ! " exclaimed Judith.

Have you ever seen it before ? " inquired Nizza,
astonished at the change in the nurse's manner.

" I have," replied Judith, " and in very different hands."

" You surprise me," cried Nizza. " Explain yourself,
I beseech you."

" Not now—not now," cried Judith, hastily returning
the coin. " And this is to be mine in case I cure the
youth ? "

" I have said so," replied Nizza.

" Then make yourself easy," rejoined Judith, " he
shall be well again in less than two days."

With this, she sat a pan on the fire, and began to prepare a poultice, the materials for which she took from
a small oaken chest in one corner of the vault. Nizza
looked on anxiously, and while they were thus employed,
a knock was heard at the door, and Chowles opening it
found the piper and one of the vergers.

" Ah ! is it you, father ? " cried Nizza, rushing to him.

" I am glad I have found you," returned the piper,
" for I began to fear some misfortune must have befallen
you. Missing you in the morning, I traversed the cathedral in search of you with Bell, well knowing if you were
in the crowd she would speedily discover you."

His daughter then hastily recounted what had happened. When the piper heard that she had promised the piece of gold to the plague nurse, a cloud came over his open countenance.

" You must never part with it," he said—" never. It is an amulet, and if you lose it, or give it away, your good luck will go with it."

" Judith Malmayns says she has seen it before," rejoined Nizza.

" No such thing," cried the piper, hastily, " she knows nothing about it. But come with me. You must not stay here longer."

" But, father—dear father !—I want a small sum to pay the nurse for attending this poor young man," cried Nizza.

" I have no money," replied the piper, " and if I had, I should not throw it away in so silly a manner. Come along; I shall begin to think you are in love with the youth."

" Then you will not be far wide of the mark," observed Judith, coarsely.

The piper uttered an angry exclamation, and taking his daughter's hand, dragged her out of the vault.

" You will not get your fee," laughed Chowles, as they were left alone.

" So it appears," replied Judith, taking the pan from the fire; " there is no use in wasting a poultice."

Shortly after this, the door of the vault again opened, and Parravicin looked in. He held a handkerchief sprinkled with vinegar to his face, and had evidently, from the manner in which he spoke, some antidote against the plague in his mouth. " Nizza Macascree has been here, has she not ? " he asked.

" She has just left with her father," replied Judith.

Parravicin beckoned her to follow him, and led the way to the north aisle of Saint Faith's.

" Is the apprentice likely to recover ? " he asked.

" Humph ! " exclaimed Judith; " that depends upon circumstances. Nizza Macascree offered me a large reward to cure him."

G

" Is he any connexion of hers ? " asked the knight sharply.

" None whatever," returned Judith, with a significant smile. " But he may possibly be so."

" I thought as much," muttered the knight.

" He never *shall* recover," said Judith, halting, and speaking in a low tone, " if you make it worth my while."

" You read my wishes," replied Parravicin, in a sombre tone. " Take this purse, and free me from him."

" He will never more cross your path," replied Judith, eagerly grasping the reward.

" Enough ! " exclaimed Parravicin. " What has passed between us must be secret."

" As the grave which shall soon close over the victim," she rejoined.

Parravicin shuddered, and hurried away, while Judith returned at a slow pace, and chinking the purse as she went, to the vault.

She had scarcely passed through the door, when Nizza Macascree appeared from behind one of the massive pillars. " This dreadful crime must be prevented," she cried—" but how ? If I run to give the alarm, it may be executed, and no one will believe me. I will try to prevent it myself."

Crossing the charnel, she was about to enter the vault, when Chowles stepped forth. She shrank backwards, and allowed him to pass, and then trying the door, found it unfastened.

CHAPTER IX

How Leonard was cured of the Plague

NIZZA MACASCREE found Judith leaning over her intended victim, and examining the plague-spot on his
breast. The nurse was so occupied by her task that she
did not hear the door open, and it was not until the
piper's daughter was close beside her that she was aware
of her presence. Hastily drawing the blankets over the
apprentice, she then turned, and regarded Nizza with a
half-fearful, half-menacing look.

" What brings you here again ? " she inquired, sharply.

" Ask your own heart, and it will tell you," rejoined
Nizza, boldly. " I am come to preserve the life of this
poor youth."

" If you think you can nurse him better than I can,
you can take my place and welcome," returned Judith,
affecting not to understand her. " I have plenty of other
business to attend to, and should be glad to be released
from the trouble."

" Can she already have effected her fell purpose ? "
thought Nizza, gazing at the apprentice, whose perturbed
features proclaimed that his slumber procured him no
rest from suffering. " No—no—she has not had time.
I accept your offer," she added, aloud.

" But what will your father say to this arrangement ? "
asked Judith.

" When he knows my motive, he will not blame me,"
answered Nizza. " Here I take my place," she continued, seating herself, " and will not quit it till he is out
of danger."

" Your love for this youth borders upon insanity,"
cried Judith, angrily. " You shall not destroy yourself
thus."

" Neither shall you destroy him," retorted Nizza. " It
is to prevent the commission of the crime you meditate—

and for which you have been *paid*, that I am determined
to remain with him."

As she said this, a singular and frightful change took
place in the nurse's appearance. A slight expression of
alarm was at first visible, but it was instantly succeeded
by a look so savage and vindictive that Nizza almost repented having provoked the ire of so unscrupulous a
person. But summoning up all her resolution, she returned Judith's glance with one as stern and steady, if
not so malignant as her own. A deep silence prevailed
for a few minutes, during which each fancied she could
read the other's thoughts. In Nizza's opinion, the nurse
was revolving some desperate expedient, and she kept on
her guard, lest an attack should be made upon her life.
And some such design did, in reality, cross Judith, but
abandoning it as soon as formed, she resolved to have
recourse to more secret, but not less certain measures.

" Well," she said, breaking silence, " since you are
determined to have your own way, and catch the plague,
and most likely perish from it, I shall not try to hinder
you. Do what you please, and see what will come of it."

And she made as if about to depart, but finding Nizza
did not attempt to stop her, she halted.

" I cannot leave you thus," she continued; " if you
will remain, take this ointment," producing a small jar.
" and rub the plague-spot with it. It is a sovereign remedy
and will certainly effect a cure."

" I will not touch it," returned Nizza.

" His death then be upon your head," rejoined Judith
quitting the vault and closing the door after her.

Greatly relieved by her departure, Nizza began to consider what she should do, and whether it would be possible
to remove the apprentice to some safer place. While
occupied with these reflections, the object of her solicitude
heaved a deep sigh, and opening his eyes fixed them upon
her. It was evident, however, that he did not know her,
but, as far as could be gathered from his ravings, mistook
her for Amabel. By degrees he grew calmer, and the
throbbing anguish of the tumour in some measure sub-
siding, his faculties returned to him.

"Where am I?" he exclaimed, pressing his hand forcibly to his brow, "and what is the matter with me?"

"You are in a vault near Saint Faith's," replied Nizza, "and—I will not deceive you—the disorder you are labouring under is the plague."

"The plague!" echoed Leonard, with a look of horror. "Ah! now I recollect. I was attacked immediately after Amabel's departure with her father. Heaven be praised! she is safe. That is some consolation amid all this misery. Could my master behold me now, he would pity me, and so perhaps would his daughter."

"Heed her not," rejoined Nizza, in a slightly reproachful tone, "she does not deserve consideration. To return to yourself. You are not safe here. Judith Malmayns has been hired to take away your life. Are you able to move hence?"

"I hope so," replied Leonard, raising himself on his arm.

"Wrap a blanket round you then, and follow me," said Nizza, taking up the lamp and hastening to the door. "Ah!" she exclaimed, with a cry of anguish—"it is locked."

"This building is destined to be my prison, and that treacherous woman my gaoler," groaned Leonard, sinking backwards.

"Do not despair," cried Nizza—"I will accomplish your deliverance."

So saying, she tried, by knocking against the door and by loud outcries, to give the alarm. But no answer was returned, and she soon became convinced that Judith had fastened the door of the charnel, which, it will be remembered, lay between the vault and the body of Saint Faith's. Hence no sound could reach the outer structure. Disturbed by what had just occurred, Leonard's senses again wandered, but exerting all her powers to tranquillize him, Nizza at last succeeded so well that he sank into a slumber.

Almost regarding his situation as hopeless, she took up the lamp, and searching the vault, found the pan containing the half-made poultice. The fire smouldered

on the hearth, and replenishing it from a scanty supply
in one corner, she heated the poultice and applied it
to the tumour. This done, she continued her search.
But though she found several phials, each bearing the
name of some remedy for the pestilence, her distrust of
Judith would not allow her to use any of them. Resuming
her seat by the couch of the sufferer, and worn out with
fatigue and anxiety, she presently dropped asleep.

She was awakened after awhile by a slight noise near
her, and beheld Judith bending over the apprentice, with
a pot of ointment in her hand, which she was about to
apply to the part affected. The poultice had already been
removed. Uttering a loud cry, Nizza started to her feet,
and snatching the ointment from the nurse, threw it
away. As soon as the latter recovered from her surprise,
she seized her assailant, and forced her into the seat she
had just quitted.

" Stir not till I give you permission," she cried, fiercely,
" I wish to cure this young man, if you will let me."

" You intend to murder him," replied Nizza ; " but
while I live you shall never accomplish your atrocious
purpose. Help ! help ! " And she uttered a prolonged
piercing scream.

" Peace ! or I will strangle you," cried Judith, com-
pressing Nizza's slender throat with a powerful gripe.

And she would, in all probability, have executed her
terrible threat, if a secret door in the wall had not suddenly
opened and admitted Solomon Eagle. A torch supplied
the place of his brasier, and he held it aloft, and threw
its ruddy light upon the scene. On seeing him, Judith
relinquished her grasp, and glared at him with a mixture of
defiance and apprehension ; while Nizza, half dead
with terror, instantly rushed towards him, and throwing
herself at his feet, besought him to save her.

" No harm shall befall you," replied Solomon Eagle,
extending his arm over her. " Tell me what has happened."

Nizza hastily explained the motive of Judith's attack
upon her life. The plague nurse endeavoured to defend
herself, and, in her turn, charged her accuser with a like
attempt. But Solomon Eagle interrupted her.

" Be silent, false woman ! " he cried, " and think not to delude me with these idle fabrications. I fully believe that you would have taken the life of this poor youth, and, did I not regard you as one of the necessary agents of Heaven's vengeance, I would instantly deliver you up to justice. But the measure of your iniquities is not yet filled up. Your former crimes are not unknown to me. Neither is the last dark deed, which you imagined concealed from every human eye, hidden from me."

" I know not what you mean," returned Judith, trembling, in spite of herself.

" I will tell you, then," rejoined Solomon Eagle, catching her hand, and dragging her into the farthest corner of the vault. " Give ear to me," he continued, in a low voice, " and doubt, if you can, that I have witnessed what I relate. I saw you enter a small chamber behind the vestry, in which Thomas Quatremain, who once filled the place of minor-canon in this cathedral, was laid. No one was there beside yourself and the dying man. Your first business was to search his vestments, and take away his keys."

" Ha ! " exclaimed Judith, starting.

" While securing his keys," pursued Solomon Eagle, " the owner wakened, and uttered a low, but angry remonstrance. Better he had been silent. Dipping a napkin in an ewer of water that stood beside him, you held the wet cloth over his face, and did not remove it till life was extinct. All this I saw."

" But you will not reveal it," said Judith, tremblingly.

" I will not," replied Solomon Eagle, " for the reasons I have just stated—namely, that I look upon you as one of the scourges appointed by Heaven."

" And so I am," rejoined Judith, with impious exultation; " it is my mission to destroy and pillage, and I will fulfil it."

" Take heed you do not exceed it," replied Solomon Eagle. " Lift a finger against either of these young persons, and I will reveal all. Yes," he continued menacingly, " I will disclose such dreadful things against you,

that you will assuredly be adjudged to a gibbet higher
than the highest tower of this proud fane."

" I defy you, wretch ! " retorted Judith. " You can
prove nothing against me."

" Defy me ?—ha ! " cried Solomon Eagle, with a
terrible laugh. " First," he added, dashing her backwards against the wall—" first to prove my power.
Next," he continued, drawing from her pockets a bunch
of keys, " to show that I speak the truth. These were
taken from the vest of the murdered man. No one, as yet,
but ourselves, knows that he is dead."

" And who shall say which of the two is the
murderer ? " cried Judith. " Villain ! I charge you with
the deed."

" You are, indeed, well fitted for your appointed task,"
returned Solomon Eagle, gazing at her with astonishment. " for sometimes Heaven, for its own wise purpose
will allow the children of hell to execute its vengeance
upon earth. But think not you will always thus escape.
No, you may pursue your evil course for a while—you,
and your companion in crime—but a day of retribution
will arrive for both—a day when ye shall be devoured,
living, by flames of fire—when all your sins shall arise
before your eyes, and ye shall have no time for repentance—and when ye shall pass from one fierce fire to
another yet fiercer, and wholly unquenchable ! "

As he concluded, he again dashed her against the
wall with such violence, that she fell senseless upon the
ground.

" And now," he said, turning to Nizza Macascree,
who looked on in alarm and surprise, " what can I do
for you ? "

" Bear this youth to a place of safety," was her answer.

Solomon Eagle answered by lifting up the pallet upon
which Leonard was laid with as much ease as if it had
been an infant's cradle, and calling on Nizza to bring
the torch, passed with his burden through the secret door.
Directing her to close it after them, he took his way
along a narrow stone passage, until he came to a chink
in the wall commanding a small chamber, and desired her

to look through it. She obeyed, and beheld, stretched upon a couch, the corpse of a man.

"It is Mr. Quatremain, the minor-canon," she said, retiring.

"It is," returned Solomon Eagle, "and it will be supposed that he died of the plague. But his end was accelerated by Judith Malmayns."

Without allowing her time for reply, he pursued his course, traversing another long narrow passage.

"Where are we?" asked Nizza, as they arrived at the foot of a spiral stone staircase.

"Beneath the central tower of the cathedral," replied Solomon Eagle. "I will take you to a cell known only to myself, where this youth will be in perfect safety."

Ascending the staircase, they passed through an arched door, and entered the great northern ambulatory. Nizza gazed down for a moment into the nave, but all was buried in darkness, and no sound reached her to give her an idea that any one was below. Proceeding towards the west, Solomon Eagle arrived at a small recess in the wall opposite one of the broad-arched openings looking into the nave, and entering it, pressed against a spring at the farther extremity, and a stone door flying open, discovered a secret cell, on the floor of which his brasier was burning. Depositing his burden on the floor, he said to Nizza, "He is now safe. Go in search of proper assistance, and I will watch by him till you return."

Nizza did not require a second exhortation, but quitting the cell, and noticing its situation, swiftly descended the winding staircase, and hurrying along the northern aisle, proceeded to a small chamber beneath the tower at its western extremity, which she knew was occupied by one of the vergers. Speedily arousing him, she told him her errand, and implored him to remain on the watch till she returned with Dr. Hodges. The verger promised compliance, and opening a wicket in the great doorway, allowed her to go forth. A few seconds brought her to the doctor's dwelling, and though it was an hour after midnight, her summons was promptly answered by the old porter, who conveyed her message to his master. Doctor Hodges had just retired to rest, but, on learning in whose behalf his services were required, he sprang out of bed, and hastily slipped on his clothes.

" I would not for half I am worth that that poor youth should perish," he cried. " I take a great interest in him—a very great interest. He must not be neglected. How comes he at Saint Paul's, I wonder? But I can obtain information on that point as I go thither. No time must be lost."

Ruminating thus, he swallowed a glass of sack, and providing himself with a case of instruments, and such medicines as he thought he might require, he descended to Nizza. On the way to the cathedral, she acquainted him with what had befallen Leonard during the last four-and-twenty hours, and the only circumstance that she kept back was Judith's attempt on his life. This she intended to reveal at a more fitting opportunity. The doctor expressed somewhat emphatically his disapproval of the conduct of Mr. Bloundel, but promised to set all to rights without loss of time.

" The only difficulty I foresee," he observed, " is that the poor youth is attacked by the pestilence, and though I may succeed in curing him, his master will probably have shut up his house before I can accomplish my object, in which case all chance of his union with Amabel will be at an end."

" So much the better," rejoined Nizza, sharply; " she does not deserve him."

" There I agree with you," returned Hodges.—" But could you point out any one who does ? " he added, with a slight but significant laugh.

No answer was returned, and as they had just reached the portico of the cathedral, they entered the sacred structure in silence.

As they ascended the winding stairs, loud outcries resounding along the ambulatory, and echoed by the vaulted roof of the nave, convinced them that the sufferer was again in a state of frenzy, produced by fever and the anguish of his sore; and on reaching the cell, they found him struggling violently with Solomon Eagle, who held him down by main force.

"He is in a fearfully excited state, truly," observed Hodges, as he drew near, "and must not be left for a moment, or he will do himself a mischief. I must give him a draught to allay the fever, and compose his nerves—for in this state I dare not have recourse to the lancet."

With this he dressed the tumour, and pouring the contents of a large phial which he had brought with him in a cup, he held it to the burning lips of the apprentice, who eagerly quaffed it. It was soon apparent that the dose produced a salutary effect, and a second was administered. Still the sufferer, though calmer, continued to ramble as before—complained that his veins were filled with molten lead—entreated them to plunge him in a stream, so that he might cool his intolerable thirst, and appeared to be in great agony. Doctor Hodges watched by him till daybreak, at which time he sank into a slumber, and Solomon Eagle, who had never till then relinquished his hold of him, now ventured to resign his post. The doctor was then about to depart, but at the urgent solicitation of Nizza, who had stationed herself at the door of the cell, he agreed to remain a little longer.

Two hours after this, the doors of the cathedral were opened, and a large crowd soon assembled within the nave, as on the preceding day. The tumult of voices reached the cell and awakened the sleeper. Before he could be prevented, he started from his bed, and dashing aside the feeble opposition offered by Nizza and the doctor, ran along the ambulatory, uttering a loud and fearful cry. Finding the door of the winding staircase open, he darted through it, and in a few seconds reappeared in the aisle. Hearing the cries, several persons rushed to meet him, but on beholding his haggard looks and strange appearance,—he was merely wrapped in a blanket,—they instantly recoiled. Meantime, Doctor Hodges, who had run to one of the arched openings looking on the nave, called out to them to secure the fugitive. But all fled at his approach, and when he reached the door of the southern transept, the verger, instead of attempting to stop him, retreated with a cry of alarm. As he passed through the outlet, one man bolder than the rest caught hold of him and endeavoured to detain him. But leaving the blanket in his hands, and without other covering than his shirt, the apprentice dashed across the church-yard—next shaped his course down Saint Bennet's-hill—then crossed Thames-street,—and finally speeding along another narrow thoroughfare, reached Paul's-wharf. Gazing for a moment at the current sweeping past him,—it was high-tide,—he plunged head foremost into it from the high embankment, and on rising to the surface, being a strong and expert swimmer, struck out for the opposite shore. Those who beheld him were filled with amazement, but such was the alarm occasioned by his appearance that none ventured to interfere with him. He had not crossed more than a fourth part of the stream when Doctor Hodges arrived at the wharf; but neither promises of reward nor threats could induce any of the watermen to follow him. The humane physician would have sprung into a boat, but feeling he should be wholly unable to manage it, he most reluctantly aban-doned his purpose. Scarcely doubting what the result of this rash attempt would be, and yet unable to tear himself away, he lingered on the wharf till he saw Leonard reach the opposite bank, where an attempt was made by a party of persons to seize him. But instead of quietly surrendering himself, the apprentice instantly leapt into the river again, and began to swim back towards the point whence he had started. Amazed at what he saw, the doctor ordered his servant, who by this time had joined the group, to bring a blanket, and descending to the edge of the river, awaited the swimmer's arrival. In less than ten minutes he had reached the shore, and clambering on the bank, fell from exhaustion.

"This is a violent effort of nature, which has accom-plished more than science or skill could do," said Hodges, as he gazed on the body, and saw that the pestilential tumour had wholly disappeared—"he is completely cured of the plague." And throwing the blanket over him, he ordered him to be conveyed to his own house.

CHAPTER X

The Pest-House in Finsbury-Fields

NOT a word passed between the grocer and his daughter as he took her home from Saint Paul's. Amabel, in fact, was so overpowered by conflicting emotions that she could not speak; while her father, who could not help reproaching himself for the harshness he had displayed towards Leonard Holt, felt no disposition to break silence. They found Mrs. Bloundel at the shop-door, drowned in tears, and almost in a state of distraction. On seeing them, she rushed towards her daughter, and straining her to her bosom, gave free vent to the impulses of her affection. Allowing the first transports of joy to subside, Mr. Bloundel begged her to retire to her own room with Amabel, and not to leave it till they had both regained their composure, when he wished to have some serious conversation with them.

His request complied with, the grocer then retraced his steps to the cathedral with the intention of seeking an explanation from Leonard, and, if he saw occasion to do so, of revoking his severe mandate. But long before he reached the southern transept, the apprentice had disappeared, nor could he learn what had become of him. While anxiously pursuing his search among the crowd, and addressing inquiries to all whom he thought likely to afford him information, he perceived a man pushing his way towards him. As this person drew near, he recognised Pillichody, and would have got out of his way had it been possible.

You are looking for your apprentice, I understand, Mr. Bloundel," said the bully, raising his hat—" if you desire it, I will lead you to him."

Unwilling as he was to be obliged to one whom he knew to be leagued with the Earl of Rochester, the grocer's anxiety overcame his scruples, and signifying his acquiescence, Pillichody shouldered his way through the crowd, and did not stop till they reached the northern aisle, where they were comparatively alone.

" Your apprentice is a fortunate spark, Mr. Bloundel," he said. " No sooner does he lose one mistress than he finds another. Your daughter is already forgotten, and he is at this moment enjoying a tender *tête-à-tête* in Bishop Kempe's chapel with Nizza Macascree, the blind piper's daughter."

" It is false, sir," replied the grocer incredulously.

" Unbelieving dog ! " cried Pillichody, in a furious tone, and clapping his hand upon his sword, " it is fortunate for you that the disparity of our stations prevents me from compelling you to yield me satisfaction for the insult you have offered me. But I caution you to keep better guard upon your tongue for the future, especially when addressing one who has earned his laurels under King Charles the Martyr."

" I have no especial reverence for the monarch you served under," replied Bloundel. " But he would have blushed to own such a follower."

" You may thank my generosity that I do not crop your ears, base roundhead," rejoined Pillichody. " But I will convince you that I speak the truth, and if you have any shame in your composition it will be summoned to your cheeks."

So saying, he proceeded to Bishop Kempe's chapel, the door of which was slightly ajar, and desired the grocer to look through the chink. This occurred at the precise time that the apprentice was seized with sudden faintness, and was leaning for support upon Nizza Macascree's shoulder.

" You see how lovingly they are seated together," observed Pillichody, with a smile of triumph. " Bowers of Paphos ! I would I were as near the rich widow of Watling-street. Will you speak with him ? "

" No," replied Bloundel, turning away, " I have done with him for ever. I have been greatly deceived."

" True," chuckled Pillichody, as soon as the grocer was out of hearing; " but not by your apprentice, Mr. Bloundel. I will go and inform Parravicin and Rochester that I have discovered the girl. The knight must mind what he is about, or Leonard Holt will prove too much for him. Either I am greatly out, or the apprentice is already master of Nizza's heart."

To return to Amabel. As soon as she was alone with her mother, she threw herself on her knees before her, and imploring her forgiveness, hastily related all that had occurred.

"But for Leonard Holt," she said, "I should have been duped into a false marriage with the earl, and my peace of mind would have been for ever destroyed. As it is, I shall never be easy till he is restored to my father's favour. To have done wrong myself is reprehensible enough; but that another should suffer for my fault is utterly inexcusable."

"I lament that your father should be deceived," rejoined Mrs. Bloundel, "and I lament still more that Leonard Holt should be so unjustly treated. Nevertheless, we must act with the utmost caution. I know my husband too well to doubt for a moment that he will hesitate to fulfil his threat. And now, my dear child," she continued, "do not the repeated proofs you have received of this wicked nobleman's perfidy, and of Leonard's devotion—do they not, I say, open your eyes to the truth, and show you which of the two really loves you, and merits your regard?"

"I will hide nothing from you, mother," replied Amabel. "In spite of his perfidy—in spite of my conviction of his unworthiness, I still love the Earl of Rochester. Nor can I compel myself to feel any regard, stronger than that of friendship, for Leonard Holt."

"You distress me sadly, child," cried Mrs. Bloundel. "What will become of you! I wish my husband would shut up his house. That might put an end to the difficulty. I am not half so much afraid of the plague as I am of the Earl of Rochester. But compose yourself, as your father desired, that when he sends for us we may be ready to meet him with cheerfulness."

Mr. Bloundel, however, did *not* send for them. He

remained in the shop all day, except at meal times, when he said little, and appeared to be labouring under a great weight of anxiety. As Amabel took leave of him for the night, he dismissed her with coldness; and though he bestowed his customary blessing upon her, the look that accompanied it was not such as it used to be.

On the following day things continued in the same state. The grocer was cold and inscrutable, and his wife, fearing he was meditating some severe course against Amabel, and aware of his inflexible nature, if a resolution was once formed, shook off her habitual awe, and thus addressed him:—

" I fear you have not forgiven our daughter. Be not too hasty in your judgment. However culpable she may appear, she has been as much deceived as yourself."

" It may be so," replied Bloundel. " Still she has acted with such indiscretion that I can never place confidence in her again, and without confidence affection is as nought. Can I say to him who may seek her in marriage, and whom I may approve as a husband,—' Take her ! she has never deceived me, and will never deceive you ? ' No. She *has* deceived me, and will, therefore, deceive others. I do not know the precise truth of the story of her abduction (if such it was) by Leonard Holt, neither do I wish to know it, because I might be compelled to act with greater severity than I desire towards her. But I know enough to satisfy me she has been excessively imprudent, and has placed herself voluntarily in situations of the utmost jeopardy."

" Not voluntarily," returned Mrs. Bloundel. " She has been lured into difficulties by others."

" No more ! " interrupted the grocer, sternly. " If you wish to serve her, keep guard upon your tongue. If you have any preparations to make, they must not be delayed. I shall shut up my house to-morrow."

" Whether Leonard returns or not ? " asked Mrs. Bloundel.

" I shall wait for no one," returned her husband, peremptorily.

They then separated, and Mrs. Bloundel hastened to

her daughter to acquaint her with the result of the interview.

In the afternoon of the same day, the grocer, who began to feel extremely uneasy about Leonard, again repaired to Saint Paul's, to see whether he could obtain any tidings of him, and learnt to his great dismay, from one of the vergers, that a young man, answering to the description of the apprentice, had been attacked by the pestilence, and having been taken to the vaults of Saint Faith's had made his escape from his attendants, and, it was supposed, had perished. Horror-stricken by this intelligence, he descended to the subterranean church, where he met Judith Malmayns and Chowles, who confirmed the verger's statement.

" The poor young man, I am informed," said Chowles, " threw himself into the Thames, and was picked up by a boat, and afterwards conveyed, in a dying state, to the pest-house in Finsbury-fields, where you will probably find him, if he is still alive."

Mr. Bloundel heard no more. Quitting the cathedral, he hastened to Finsbury-fields, and sought out the building to which he had been directed. It was a solitary farm-house, of considerable size, surrounded by an extensive garden, and had only been recently converted to its present melancholy use. Near it was a barn, also fitted up with beds for the sick. On approaching the pest-house, Mr. Bloundel was greatly struck with the contrast presented by its exterior to the misery he knew to be reigning within. Its situation was charming,—in the midst, as has just been stated, of a large and, until recently, well-cultivated garden, and seen under the influence of a bright and genial May day, the whole place looked the picture of healthfulness and comfort. But a closer view speedily dispelled the illusion, and showed that it was the abode of disease and death. Horrid sounds saluted the ears; ghastly figures met the eyes; and the fragrance of the flowers was overpowered by the tainted and noisome atmosphere issuing from the open doors and windows. The grocer had scarcely entered the gate when he was arrested by an appalling shriek, followed by a succession of cries so horrifying that he felt half disposed to fly. But mustering up his resolution, and breathing at a phial of vinegar, he advanced towards the principal door, which stood wide open, and called to one of the assistants. The man, however, was too busy to attend to him, and while waiting his leisure, he saw no fewer than three corpses carried out to an outbuilding in the yard, where they were left till they could be taken away at night for interment.

Sickened by the sight, and blaming himself for entering near this contagious spot, Mr. Bloundel was about to depart, when a young chirurgeon stepped out to him, and, in reply to his inquiries after Leonard, said— " Twelve persons were brought in here last night, and five this morning, but I do not remember any of their names. You can go through the rooms and search for your apprentice, if you think proper."

Mr. Bloundel hesitated, but his humanity overcame his apprehension, and murmuring a prayer that he might be preserved from infection, he followed his conductor into the house. Prepared as he was for a dreadful spectacle, the reality far exceeded his anticipations. Along both sides of a large room, occupying nearly the whole of the ground-floor, were rows of pallets, on which were laid the sick, many of whom were tied down to their couches. Almost all seemed in a hopeless state, and the cadaverous hue of their countenances proclaimed that death was not far off. Though the doors and windows were open, and the room was filled with vapours and exhalations, arising from pans of coal and plates of hot iron, on which drugs were burning, nothing could remove the putrid and pestilential smell that pervaded the chamber. The thick vapour settled on the panes of the windows, and on the roof, and fell to the ground in heavy drops. Marching quickly past each bed, the grocer noted the features of its unfortunate occupant, but though there were many young men, Leonard was not among the number. His conductor then led him to an upper room, where he found the chirurgeons dressing the sores of their patients, most of whom uttered loud shrieks while under their hands. Here an incident occurred which deeply affected the grocer. A poor young woman, who had been brought to the pest-house with her child on the previous evening, had just expired, and the infant, unable to obtain its customary nourishment, uttered the most piteous cries. It was instantly removed by a nurse and proper food given it, but Mr. Bloundel was informed that the plague-tokens had already appeared, and that it would not probably live over the night. " I have no doubt," said the young chirurgeon, " it will be buried with its mother." And so it happened.

The grocer turned away to hide his emotion, and endeavoured through his blinded gaze to discover Leonard, but, as will be anticipated, without success. Stunned by the cries and groans that pierced, his ears, and almost stifled by the pestilential effluvia, he rushed out of the house, and gladly accepted a glass of sack offered him by his conductor, which removed the dreadful nausea that affected him.

" I now remember that the two last persons brought here were taken to the barn," observed the chirurgeon. " I will go with you thither, if you think proper."

The grocer assented, and the chirurgeon crossed the yard, and opened the door of the barn, on the floor of which upwards of twenty beds were laid. Passing between them, Mr. Bloundel narrowly scrutinized every countenance, but, to his great relief, recognised no one. One couch alone remained to be examined. The poor sufferer within it had drawn the coverings over his face, and when they were removed, he was found quite dead ! He was a young man, and the agony he had endured in the last struggle was shown by his collapsed frame and distorted features. It was not, however, Leonard, and, so far satisfied, though greatly shocked, Mr. Bloundel hurried out.

" Thank Heaven ! he is not here ! " he exclaimed, to his conductor.

" You have not seen the dead bodies, in the outhouse," returned the other. " It is possible his may be among them."

" I trust not," rejoined the grocer, shuddering. " But as I have gone thus far, I will not leave my errand un-accomplished. Suffer me to look at them."

The chirurgeon then led the way to a spacious out-building, once used for cattle, in the midst of which stood a large frame supporting six bodies, covered only with a sheet. Mr. Bloundel could not overcome his repugnance to enter this shed; but the chirurgeon, who appeared habituated to such scenes, and to regard them lightly, threw off the sheet, and raised the corpses, one by one, that he might the better view them. One peculi-arity Mr. Bloundel noticed; namely, that the limbs of these unfortunate victims of the pestilence did not stiffen as would have been the case if they had died of any other disorder, while the blotches that appeared on the livid flesh made them objects almost too horrible to look upon. In many cases the features were frightfully dis-torted—the tongues of the poor wretches swollen and protruding—the hands clenched, and the toes bent to-wards the soles of the feet. Everything denoted the dread-ful pangs that must have attended dissolution.

Greatly relieved to find that the whole of this ghastly group were strangers to him, Mr. Bloundel thanked the chirurgeon and departed. Convinced that he had been deceived by the coffin-maker, he now began to hope that the whole story was false, but he determined not to rest till he had thoroughly investigated the matter. Before doing so, however, he thought it advisable to return home, and accordingly shaped his course towards Cripple-gate, and passing through the postern, stopped at an apothecary's shop and got his apparel fumigated, and sprinkled with spirits of hartshorn and sulphur.

On reaching Wood-street, he noticed with some un-easiness a number of persons gathered together before his dwelling. His fears were speedily relieved by finding that the assemblage was collected by a preacher, who was pronouncing an exhortation to them in tones almost as loud and emphatic as those of Solomon Eagle. The preacher's appearance was very remarkable, and attracted the attention of the grocer, who joined the crowd to

listen to him. As far as could be judged, he was a middle-
aged man, with black hair floating over his shoulders,
earnest features, and a grey eye of extraordinary brilliancy.
His figure was slight and erect, and his gestures as impassioned as his looks. He spoke with great rapidity, and
his eloquence, combined with his fervent manner and
expression, completely entranced his audience. He was
habited in a cassock and bands, and had taken off his
cap, which was held by an attendant, who stood near the
stool on which he was mounted. The latter differed
materially from his master. His closely-cropped hair,
demure looks, sugar-loaf hat, and suit of rusty sable seemed
to proclaim him a Puritan; but his twinkling eye,—for
he had but one, and wore a black patch over the orifice.
—his inflamed cheeks and mulberry nose contradicted
the idea.

As soon as the preacher distinguished Mr. Bloundel,
he addressed his discourse to him; and alluding to his
religious habits and general excellence of character, held
him up as an example to others. The grocer would fain
have retreated, but the preacher besought him to stay,
and was proceeding in the same strain when a sudden
interruption took place. A slight disturbance occurring
amid the crowd, the attendant attempted to check it, and
in doing so, received a sound buffet on the ears. In endeavouring to return the blow, he struck another party,
who instantly retaliated, and a general affray commenced,
—some taking one side, some the other. In the midst of
the confusion three persons forced their way towards the
preacher, knocked him from his stool, and assailing him
with the most opprobrious epithets, dealt him several
seemingly severe blows, and would have further mal-
treated him, if Mr. Bloundel had not interposed, and,
pushing aside his assailants, gave him his hand, and led
him into his dwelling, the door of which he closed. Shortly
afterwards, the crowd dispersing, the preacher's companion entered the shop in search of his master.

"I hope you have sustained no injury during this
tumult, reverend and dear sir?" he asked, with great
apparent solicitude.

" I am not much hurt," replied the preacher; " but I
have received a blow on the head, which has stunned me.
The faintness will go off presently. You were the cause
of this disturbance, Bambolio."

" I, Doctor Maplebury?" replied Bambolio—" I endeavoured to stop it. But your reverence looks extremely ill. I am sure, sir," he added, to Mr. Bloundel,
" after the high character my master gave you in his
discourse, and which I am persuaded you deserve, you
will extend your hospitality towards him."

" Readily," replied the grocer. " Here, Blaize, assist
the reverend gentleman within, and bid your mistress
come downstairs immediately."

Doctor Maplebury was then conveyed between the
porter and Bambolio into the inner room, where he sank
into a chair in a complete state of exhaustion. The next
moment Mrs. Bloundel made her appearance with Amabel.
The latter no sooner beheld the preacher than she started
and trembled so violently, that she could scarcely support
herself; but her mother, who only saw a fainting man,
flew to his assistance, and called to Patience to bring
restoratives. These applied, Doctor Maplebury was soon
able to rouse himself sufficiently to gaze round the room,
and fix his eyes on Amabel.

" So our old friends are here again," said Patience,
in a low tone to Blaize, as they left the room together.

" Old friends !—What do you mean ? " rejoined the
porter.

" Why, the Earl of Rochester and Major Pillichody,"
replied Patience. " I knew them at a glance, and so did
Mistress Amabel. But if I hadn't discovered them, the
major would soon have let me into the secret, by the way
in which he squeezed my hand."

" Indeed ! " exclaimed Blaize, angrily. " I'll go and
acquaint my master with the trick directly."

" Do so," replied Patience, " and the house will be
shut up to-morrow. Our only chance of averting this
calamity is in the earl."

CHAPTER XI

How the Grocer shut up his House

PLACED in a warm bed, and carefully tended by the humane physician, Leonard Holt slept tranquilly for some hours, and when he awoke, though so weak as scarcely to be able to lift an arm, he was free from all ailment. Feeling ravenously hungry, he made known his wants, and provisions being set before him, he was allowed to eat and drink in moderation. Greatly revived by the meal, he arose and attired himself in habiliments provided for him by Hodges, who, finding him fully equal to conversation, questioned him as to all that had occurred prior to his seizure.

"You have acted nobly," observed the doctor, at the close of his recital, "and if Amabel had a spark of generosity in her composition, she would worthily requite you. But I do not expect it. How different is her conduct from that of the piper's pretty daughter. The latter really loves you, and I would advise you as a friend to turn your thoughts to her. She will make you happy; whereas the indulgence of your present hopeless passion—for hopeless it is—can only lead to wretchedness."

"Would I could follow your advice!" replied Leonard, "but alas! I cannot. Amabel does not love the Earl of Rochester more blindly, more constantly, than I love her; and I could as soon change my nature as transfer my affection to another."

"I am truly sorry for it," rejoined Hodges, in a tone of deep sympathy. "And you still desire to return to your master?"

"Unquestionably," replied Leonard. "If I am banished the house, I shall wander round it night and day like a ghost."

"I will accompany you there this evening," rejoined Hodges, "and trust I shall be able to arrange matters without compromising Amabel. I wish I could forward

your suit more efficiently. But I see no chance of it,
and to deal plainly with you, I do not think a marriage
with her would be for your happiness. The brilliant
qualities of your noble rival at present so dazzle her eyes,
that your own solid worth is completely overlooked. It
will be well if her father can preserve her from ruin."

" The earl shall die by my hand rather than he shall
succeed in his infamous purpose," cried Leonard, fiercely.

" No more of this ! " exclaimed Hodges. " If you
would have me take an interest in you, you will never
give utterance to such a sentiment again. Amabel has
another guardian, more powerful even than her father—
the plague. Ere long, the earl, who has a sufficient value
for his own safety, will fly the city."

" I hope the pestilence will number him among its
victims," observed Leonard, in a sombre tone.

At this juncture, the old porter entered the room,
and informed his master that the piper's daughter was
below, and had called to inquire after the apprentice.

Hodges desired she might be shown upstairs, and the
next moment Nizza was ushered into the room. On
beholding the improved appearance of Leonard, she
could not repress an exclamation of delight, while a deep
blush suffused her cheeks.

" You are surprised to find him quite well," observed
Hodges, with a smile. " Nay, you may approach him
with safety. There is no fear of contagion now."

" Having satisfied myself on that point, I will take my
leave," rejoined Nizza, in some confusion.

" Not till you have allowed me to return my thanks,
I trust," said Leonard, advancing towards her and taking
her hand. " I owe my life to you."

" Then pay the debt by devoting it to her," rejoined
Hodges. " Excuse me for a few minutes. I have business
to attend to, but will be back again directly."

Left alone together, the young couple felt so much
embarrassment that for some moments neither could
utter a word. At length, Nizza who had suffered her
hand to remain in that of Leonard, gently withdrew it.

" Circumstances have given me a claim to your confidence," she faltered, "and you will not misconstrue my motive, when I ask you whether you still retain the same affection as formerly for Amabel ? "

" Unfortunately for myself, I do," replied Leonard.

" And unfortunately for me, too," sighed Nizza. " Doctor Hodges says he can restore you to your master's favour. You will therefore return home, and we shall meet no more."

" In these precarious times, those who part, though even for a few days, can feel no certainty of meeting again," rejoined Leonard. " But I hope we shall be more fortunate."

" You mistake me," replied Nizza. " Henceforth, I shall sedulously avoid you. Till I saw you, I was happy, and indifferent to all else—my affections being centred in my father and in my dog. Now, I am restless and miserable. My former pursuits are abandoned, and I think only of you. Despise me if you will after this frank avowal. But believe that I would not have made it, if I had not resolved to see you no more."

" Despise you ! " echoed Leonard. " Oh no ! I shall ever feel the deepest gratitude towards you; but perhaps it is better we should meet no more."

" And yet you throw yourself in the way of Amabel," cried Nizza. " You have not resolution to fly from the danger which you counsel me to shun."

" It is too true," replied Leonard; " but she is beset by temptations from which I hope to preserve her."

" That excuse will not avail me," returned Nizza, bitterly. " You cannot live without her. But I have said enough—more than enough," she added, correcting herself. " I must now bid you farewell—for ever. May you be happy with Amabel, and may she love you as I love you ! "

As she said this she would have rushed out of the room, if she had not been stopped by Doctor Hodges.

" Whither so fast ? " he inquired.

" Oh ! let me go—let me go, I implore of you ! " she cried, bursting into an agony of tears.

" Not till you have composed yourself," rejoined the

doctor. "What is the matter?—But I need not ask. I wonder Leonard can be insensible to charms like yours, coupled with such devotion. Everything seems to be at cross purposes, and it requires someone more skilled in the affairs of the heart than an old bachelor like myself to set them right. Sit down. I have a few questions of importance to ask you before you depart."

And partly by entreaty, partly by compulsion, he made her take a chair, and as soon as she was sufficiently composed to answer him, questioned her as to what she knew relating to Judith Malmayns and Chowles.

"Mr. Quatremain, the minor-canon, has died of the plague in one of the vaults of Saint Faith's," he observed, "and I more than suspect, from the appearance of the body, has not met with fair play."

"Your suspicion is well founded, sir," replied Nizza. "Solomon Eagle told me that the unfortunate man's end was hastened by the plague nurse. Nor is this her sole crime. She was hired to make away with Leonard Holt in the same manner, and would have accomplished her purpose but for the intervention of Solomon Eagle."

"Neither she nor her partner in guilt, the coffin-maker, shall escape justice this time," replied Hodges. "I will instantly cause her to be arrested, and I trust she will expiate her offences at Tyburn. But, to change the subject. I am sincerely interested about you, Nizza, and wish I could make Leonard as sensible of your merits as I am myself. I still hope a change will take place in his feelings."

"My heart tells me the contrary," replied Nizza. "There is no hope for either of us. Farewell, Leonard!"

And she rushed out of the room.

Soon after this, Hodges quitted the apprentice, and going before a magistrate, detailed all that had come to his knowledge concerning the criminal practices of Judith Malmayns and Chowles. In the course of the day the accused parties were arrested, and after a long examination, conveyed to Newgate. Solomon Eagle could not be found, neither could Sir Paul Parravicin. It appeared that Mr. Quatremain's residence had been entered on that very morning, and the box of treasure discovered in Saint Faith's abstracted. But though the strongset suspicion of the robbery attached to Chowles and Judith, it could not be brought home to them.

We shall now proceed to Wood-street, and ascertain what took place there. Refreshments were placed before the supposed Doctor Maplebury by the grocer, while his attendant was sent to the kitchen, and directions given to Blaize to take every care of him; old Josyna was occupied about her own concerns, and Pillichody, perceiving from the porter's manner that his disguise was detected, laid aside concealment altogether, and endeavoured to win the other over to his patron's interests.

" If this marriage takes place," he said, " I am authorized by my noble friend to state that he will appoint you his steward with a large salary, and that will be a very different situation from the one you hold at present. A nobleman's steward ! Think of that. You will have a retinue of servants under your control, and will live quite as well as his lordship."

" I have some scruples," hesitated Blaize.

" Scruples ! Pshaw ! " cried Pillichody. " You can have no hesitation in benefiting yourself. If you remain here, the house will be shut up, and you will be kept a close prisoner for months in the very heart of an infected city, and I daresay will be buried in yonder cellar ; whereas, if you go with the Earl of Rochester, you will dwell in a magnificent country mansion—a palace, I ought to call it—enjoy every luxury, and remain there till the plague is over."

" That last reason decides me," replied Blaize. " But I suppose his lordship will provide himself with a medicine chest ? "

" He has already got one as large as this table," said Pillichody, " and you shall have the key of it."

" Enough ! " exclaimed Blaize. " I am yours."

" Pray, what am I to be ? " asked Patience, who had listened to the foregoing conversation with a smile at Blaize's credulity.

" You sweetheart!" exclaimed Pillichody. " I will take care of you. You shall be my housekeeper."

" Hold!" cried Blaize. " I cannot admit that. Patience and I are engaged."

" Since you are promoted to such an important situation, you can make a better match," observed Patience. " I release you from the engagement."

" I don't choose to be released," returned Blaize; " I will marry you on the same day that the earl weds Amabel."

" That will be to-night, or to-morrow at the latest," said Pillichody. " Consent, sweetheart," he added in a whisper to Patience; " if we can once get you and your pretty mistress out of the house, we will leave this simpleton fool in the lurch."

" No, I will never consent to any such thing." returned Patience, in the same tone.

" What's that you are saying?" inquired Blaize, suspiciously.

" Major Pillichody says he will marry me, if you won't," returned Patience.

" I have just told you I will," rejoined Blaize. " But he must not continue his attentions. I feel I shall be very jealous."

" I am glad to hear it, returned Patience, bursting into a loud laugh, " for that proves you love me."

" Well," observed Pillichody, " I won't interfere with a friend; and as there is no knowing what may occur. it will be well to prepare accordingly."

So saying, he fell to work upon the provisions loading the board, and ate and drank as if determined to lay in a stock for the next two days.

Meantime, the earl made rapid progress in the good opinion both of Mr. Bloundel and his wife. Adapting his discourse precisely to their views, and exerting his matchless conversational powers to their full extent, he so charmed them that they thought they could listen to him for ever. While thus engaged, he continued ever and anon to steal a glance at Amabel, and on these occasions his eyes were quite as eloquent and intelligible as his tongue.

Among other topics interesting to the grocer, the persecution to which his daughter had been recently subjected was brought foward. Mr. Bloundel could not reprobate the earl's conduct more strongly than his guest did; and he assailed himself with such virulence that, in spite of her uneasiness, Amabel could not repress a smile. In short, he so accommodated himself to the grocer's opinions, and so won upon his regard, that the latter offered him an asylum in his house during the continuance of the pestilence. This was eagerly accepted, and the earl, hazarding a look at Amabel at the moment, perceived her change colour and become greatly agitated. Mrs. Bloundel also noticed her confusion, but attributing it to any other than the right cause, begged her, in a low tone, to control herself.

At length, the opportunity for which the earl had been secretly sighing occurred. Mr. Bloundel called his wife out of the room for a moment, and as their eldest son, Stephen, was in the shop, and the two other children upstairs, Amabel was left alone with her lover. The door was no sooner closed than he sprang towards her and threw himself at her feet.

" Shall I avail myself of your father's offer, sweetheart ? " he cried. " Shall I remain here with you—the happiest of prisoners—or will you once more accompany me ? This time our marriage shall not be interrupted."

" Perhaps not, my lord," she replied, gravely; " but it will be a mock ceremonial, like the last. Do not attempt to deceive me. I am fully aware of your intentions, and after the awful fate of the wretched instrument of your purposed criminality, you will not readily get another person to tempt in like manner the vengeance of Heaven. I have had a severe struggle with myself. But at length I have triumphed over my irresolution. I will not disguise from you that I love you still, —and must ever, I fear, continue to love you. But I will not be yours on the terms you propose. Neither will I leave this house with you, nor suffer you to remain in it, in any other than your proper character. On my father's return I will disclose all to him. If your designs are honourable, I am sure he will no longer oppose my union with you. If not, we part for ever."

"Be prudent, sweet girl, I entreat of you," cried the earl, imploringly. "Your indiscretion will ruin all. There are a thousand reasons why your father should not be consulted on the matter."

"There are none that weigh with me," she interrupted, decidedly. "I have been bewildered—beside myself.—but, thank Heaven, I have recovered before it is too late."

"You are beside yourself at this moment," cried Rochester, unable to control his anger and mortification, "and will bitterly repent your folly. Neither your supplications nor my rank will have any weight with your father, prejudiced as he is against me. Fly with me, and I swear to make you mine, without a moment's loss of time. Will not my plighted word content you?"

"No, my lord, you have broken it already," returned Amabel. "My father shall know the truth."

A dark shade passed over Rochester's countenance, and a singular and most forbidding expression, which Amabel had once before noticed, took possesion of it. His love for her seemed changed to hate, and she tremblingly averted her gaze. At this juncture the door opened, and the grocer and his wife entered the room. The former started, on seeing Amabel and the supposed preacher in such propinquity, and a painful suspicion of the truth crossed his mind. He was not, however, kept long in suspense. Throwing off his wig, and letting his own fair ringlets fall over his shoulders, the earl tore open his cassock, and disclosed his ordinary rich attire. At the same time, his face underwent an equally striking change, —each feature resuming its original expression; and the grocer, though he witnessed the whole transformation, could scarcely believe that the same individual he had recently beheld stood before him.

"You know now who I am, Mr. Bloundel, and what brought me hither," said Rochester, and with a haughty salutation.

"I do, my lord," replied the grocer, "and I give you

full credit for your daring and ingenuity. After the manner in which I have been imposed upon myself, I can make allowance for others." He then turned to Amabel, and said, in a severe tone, " You are no longer my daughter."

" Father ! " she cried, rushing towards him and throwing herself at his feet, " do not cast me off for ever. I am not now to blame. It is owing to my determination to disclose all to you that the earl has thus revealed himself. I might have deceived you further—might have fled with him."

" Forgive her ! oh, forgive her ! " cried Mrs. Bloundel —" or, if any ill happens to her, you will be answerable for it."

" Is this the truth, my lord ? " asked the grocer.

Rochester bowed stiffly in acquiescence.

" Then you are again my child," said Bloundel, raising her, and pressing her to his bosom. " What are your intentions towards her ? " he continued, addressing the earl.

" They may be readily surmised," replied Rochester, with a scornful laugh.

" Will you wed her, if I agree to the union ? " asked Bloundel, trembling with concentrated rage.

Amabel looked at her lover as if her life hung on his answer.

Rochester affected not to hear the question, but, as it was repeated still more peremptorily, he repeated carelessly,—" I will consider of it."

" Deceived ! deceived ! " cried Amabel, falling on her mother's neck, and bursting into tears.

" This outrage shall not pass unpunished," cried Bloundel.

And before the earl could draw his sword or offer any resistance, he threw himself upon him, and hurling him to the ground, set his foot upon his bosom.

" Do not kill him," shrieked Amabel, terrified by the stern expression of her father's countenance.

" What are you about to do ? " gasped Rochester, struggling ineffectually to get free.

" Bid Stephen bring a cord," cried the grocer.

" You are not going to hang him ? " inquired Mrs. Bloundel.

" Do as I bid you," rejoined her husband, " and lose no time."

As she was about to leave the room, the door opened, and Doctor Hodges entered, followed by Leonard and Stephen.

" Mercy on us ! what's the matter ? " cried the former, in astonishment.

" You are just arrived in time to prevent mischief," replied Mrs. Bloundel. " Pray interfere between them. My husband will attend to you ! "

" Arise, my lord," said Mr. Bloundel, removing his foot from the prostrate nobleman—" you are sufficiently punished by being found in this disgraceful condition. Remember that your life has been at my disposal."

Thus liberated, Rochester sprang to his feet, and regarding the group with a menacing and disdainful look, walked up to Amabel, and saying to her, " You shall yet be mine," strode out of the room. He then marched along the passage, and called to Pillichody, who instantly answered the summons. Accompanied by Hodges, the grocer followed them to the shop, where the bully not departing so quickly as he desired, and refusing to be more expeditious, he kicked him into the street. This done, and the door fastened, he tarried only till he had received all needful explanations from the friendly physician, and then returning to the inner room, warmly greeted Leonard, and congratulated him on his extraordinary recovery from the plague.

Happiness was thus once more restored to every member of the grocer's family, except Amabel, who still continued downcast and dejected, and entreated permission to retire to her own room. A cheerful evening was then passed by the others, and the doctor did not offer to take his departure till the clock struck eleven.

" It is the last night I shall spend here for some months," he said ; " perhaps the last I shall ever spend here, and I have stayed longer than I intended, but I did not like to abridge my enjoyment." After shaking hands cordially with the whole party, he added, in an undertone, as he took leave of Leonard, " Do not forget Nizza Macascree."

On the following day the grocer nailed up the shutters, and locked and barred the doors of his house.

End of the Second Book

.

H

Book the Third

CHAPTER I

The Imprisoned Family

THE first few days of their confinement were passed by the grocer's family in a very uncomfortable manner. No one, except Mr. Bloundel, appeared reconciled to the plan, and even he found it more difficult of accomplishment than he had anticipated. The darkness of the rooms, and the want of ventilation caused by the closed windows and barred doors, gave the house the air of a prison, and occasioned a sense of oppression almost intolerable. Blaize declared it " was worse than being in Newgate, and that he must take an additional rufus a day to set right his digestion; " while Patience affirmed " that it was like being buried alive, and that she would not stand it." Mr. Bloundel paid no attention to their complaints, but addressed himself seriously to the remedy. Insisting upon the utmost attention being paid to cleanliness, he had an abundant supply of water drawn, with which the floors of every room and passage were washed down daily. By such means the house was kept cool and wholesome; and its inmates, becoming habituated to the gloom, in a great degree recovered their cheerfulness.

The daily routine of the establishment was as follows. The grocer arose at dawn, and proceeded to call up the whole of his family. They then assembled in a large room on the second story, where he offered up thanks that they had been spared during the night, and prayed for their preservation during the day. He next assigned a task to each, and took care to see it afterwards duly fulfilled; well knowing that constant employment was the best way to check repining and promote contentment. Heretofore the servants had always taken their meals in the kitchen, but now they always sat down to table with him. "I will make no distinction at this season," he said; "all shall fare as I fare, and enjoy the same comforts as myself. And I trust that my dwelling may be as sure a refuge amid this pestilential storm as the ark of the patriarch proved when Heaven's vengeance was called forth in the mighty flood."

Their devotions ended, the whole party repaired to one of the lower rooms, where a plentiful breakfast was provided, and of which they all partook. The business of the day then began, and, as has just been observed, no one was suffered to remain idle. The younger children were allowed to play and exercise themselves as much as they chose in the garret, and Blaize and Patience were occasionally invited to join them. A certain portion of the evening was also devoted to harmless recreation and amusements. The result may be anticipated. No one suffered in health, while all improved in spirits. Prayers, as usual, concluded the day, and the family retired to rest at an early hour.

This system of things may appear sufficiently monotonous, but it was precisely adapted to the exigencies of the case, and produced a most salutary effect. Regular duties and regular employments being imposed upon each, and their constant recurrence, so far from being irksome, soon became agreeable. After a while the whole family seemed to grow indifferent to the external world—to live only for each other, and to think only of each other—and to Leonard Holt, indeed, that house was all the world. Those walls contained everything dear to him, and he would have been quite content never to leave them if Amabel had been always near. He made no attempt to renew his suit—seldom or ever exchanging a word with her, and might have been supposed to have become wholly indifferent to her. But it was not so. His heart was consumed by the same flame as before. No longer, however, a prey to jealousy—no longer apprehensive of the earl—he felt so happy, in comparison with what he had been, that he almost prayed that the term of their imprisonment might be prolonged. Sometimes the image of Nizza Macascree would intrude upon him, and he thought with a feeling akin to remorse, of what she might suffer—for he was too well acquainted with the pangs of unrequited love not to sympathize deeply with her. As to Amabel, she addressed herself assiduously to the tasks enjoined by her father, and allowed her mind to dwell as little as possible on the past, but employed all her spare time in devotional exercises.

It will be remembered that the grocer had reserved a communication with the street, by means of a shutter, opening from a small room in the upper story. Hither he would now frequently repair, and though he did not as yet think it necessary to have recourse to all the precautionary measures he intended eventually to adopt—such as a flashing pistol when he looked forth—yet he never opened the shutter without holding a phial of vinegar, or a handkerchief wetted with the same liquid, to his face.

Before closing his house he had hired a porter, who occupied the hutch at his door, and held himself in readiness to execute any commission, or perform any service that might be required. Fresh vegetables, poultry, eggs, butter, and milk, were brought by a higgler from the country, and raised by means of a basket or a can attached to the pulley. Butcher's meat was fetched him from Newgate-market by the porter. This man, whose name was Ralph Dallison, had been formerly in the employ of the grocer, who, knowing his character, could place entire reliance on him. Dallison reported the progress of the pestilence daily, and acquainted him with the increasing amount of the bills of mortality. Several houses, he said, were infected in Cheapside, and two in Wood-street, one of which was but a short distance from the grocer's habitation. A watchman was stationed at the door, and the red cross marked upon it, and on the following night the grocer heard the sound of the doleful bell announcing the approach of the pest-cart.

The weather still continued as serene and beautiful as ever, but no refreshing showers fell—no soft and healthful breezes blew—and it was now found to be true, what had been prognosticated—viz., that with the heats of summer the plague would fearfully increase. The grocer was not incommoded in the same degree as his neighbours. By excluding the light he excluded the heat, and the care which he took to have his house washed down kept it cool. The middle of June had arrived, and such dismal accounts were now brought him of the havoc occasioned by the scourge, that he would no longer take in fresh provisions, but began to open his stores. Dallison told him that the alarm was worse than ever—that vast numbers were endeavouring to leave the city, but no one could now do so without a certificate, which was never granted if the slightest suspicion was attached to the party.

" If things go on in this way," said the porter, " London will soon be deserted. No business is conducted as it used to be, and everybody is viewed with distrust. The preachers, who ought to be the last to quit, have left their churches, and the Lord's day is no longer observed. Many medical men even have departed, declaring their services are no longer of any avail. All public amusements are suspended, and the taverns are only open to the profane and dissolute, who deride God's judgments, and declare they have no fear. Robberies, murders, and other crimes, have greatly increased, and the most dreadful deeds are now committed with impunity. You have done wisely, sir, in protecting yourself against them."

" I have reason to be thankful that I have done so," replied Bloundel. And he closed his shutter to meditate on what he had just heard.

And there was abundant food for reflection. Around him lay a great and populous city, hemmed in, as by a fire, by an exterminating plague, that spared neither age, condition, nor sex. No man could tell what the end of all this would be—neither at what point the wrath of the offended Deity would stop—nor whether He would relent till He had utterly destroyed a people who so contemned his word. Scarcely daring to hope for leniency, and filled with a dreadful foreboding of what would ensue, the grocer addressed a long and fervent supplication to Heaven, imploring a mitigation of its wrath.

On joining his family, his grave manner and silence showed how powerfully he had been affected. No one questioned him as to what had occurred, but all understood he had received some distressing intelligence. Amid his anxiety one circumstance gave him unalloyed satisfaction. This was the change wrought in Amabel's character. It has been stated that she had become extremely devout, and passed the whole of the time not appointed for other occupations, in the study of the Scriptures, or in prayer. Her manner was extremely sedate, and her conversation assumed a tone that gave her parents, and especially her father, inexpressible pleasure. Mrs. Bloundel would have been equally delighted with the change, if it had tended to forward her own favourite scheme of a union with Leonard; but as this was not the case, though she rejoiced in the improvement, she still was not entirely satisfied. She could not help noting also, that her daughter had become pale and thin, and though she uttered no complaint, Mrs. Bloundel began to fear her health was declining. Leonard Holt looked on in wonder and admiration, and if possible his love increased, though his hopes diminished; for though Amabel was kinder to him than before, her kindness seemed the result rather of a sense of duty than regard.

Upon one occasion they were left alone together, and instead of quitting the room, as she had been accustomed, Amabel called to Leonard, who was about to depart, and requested him to stay. The apprentice instantly obeyed; the colour forsook his cheeks, and his heart beat violently.

" You desire to speak with me, Amabel," he said:— " Have you relented?—Is there any hope for me ? "

" Alas ! no," she replied; " and it is on that very point I have now detained you. You will, I am sure, rejoice to learn that I have at length fully regained my peace of mind, and have become sensible of the weakness of which I have been guilty—of the folly, worse than folly, I have committed. My feelings are now under proper restraint, and viewing myself with other eyes, I see how culpable I have been. Oh ! Leonard, if you knew the

effort it has been to conquer the fatal passion that consumed me—if I were to tell you of the pangs it has cost
me—of the tears I have shed—of the heart-quakes endured,
you would pity me."

" I do, indeed, pity you," replied Leonard, " for my
own sufferings have been equally severe. But I have not
been as successful as you in subduing them."

" Because you have not pursued the right means,
Leonard," she rejoined. " Fix your thoughts on high;
build your hopes of happiness on Heaven; strengthen
your faith; and you will soon find the victory easy. A
short time ago, I thought only of worldly pleasures, and
was ensnared by vanity and admiration—enchained to
one whom I knew to be worthless, and who pursued me
only to destroy me. Religion has preserved me from the
snare, and religion will restore you to happiness. But
you must devote yourself to Heaven, not lightly, but with
your whole soul. You must forget me,—forget yourself,—
forget all but the grand object. And this is a season of
all others, when it is most needful to lead a life of piety,
to look upon yourself as dead to this world, and to be
ever prepared for that to come. I shudder to think what
might have been my portion had I perished in my sin."

" Yours is a most happy frame of mind," returned
Leonard, " and I would I had a chance of attaining the
same tranquillity. But if you have conquered your love
for the earl,—if your heart is disengaged,—why deny me
a hope ? "

" My heart is *not* disengaged. Leonard," she replied;
" it is engrossed by Heaven. While the plague is raging
around us thus,—while thousands are daily carried off
by that devouring scourge,—and while every hour, every
moment, may be our last, our thoughts ought always to be
fixed above. I have ceased to love the earl, but I can
never love another, and therefore it would be unjust to
you, to whom I owe so much, to hold out hopes that never
can be realized."

" Alas ! alas ! " cried Leonard, unable to control his
emotion.

" Compose yourself, dear Leonard," she cried, greatly

moved. "I would I could comply with your wishes.
But, alas! I cannot. I could only give you," she added,
in a tone so thrilling, that it froze the blood in his veins,—
" a breaking, perhaps a broken heart!"

" Gracious heaven!" exclaimed Leonard, becoming
as pale as death; "is it come to this?"

" Again, I beg you to compose yourself," she rejoined,
calmly—"and I entreat you not to let what I have told
you pass your lips. I would not alarm my father, or my
dear and anxious mother, on my account. And there
may be no reason for alarm. Promise me, therefore, you
will be silent."

Leonard reluctantly gave the required pledge.

" I have unwittingly been the cause of much affliction
to you," pursued Amabel—"and would gladly see you
happy, and there is one person, I think, who would make
you so,—I mean Nizza Macascree. From what she said
to me when we were alone together in the vaults of Saint
Faith's, I am sure she is sincerely attached to you. Could
you not requite her love?"

" No," replied Leonard. " There is no change in
affection like mine."

" Pursue the course I have advised," replied Amabel,
" and you will find all your troubles vanish. Farewell!
I depend upon your silence!"

And she quitted the room, leaving Leonard in a state
of indescribable anxiety.

Faithful, however, to his promise, he made no mention of his uneasiness to the grocer or his wife, but indulged his grief in secret. Ignorant of what was passing,
Mr. Bloundel, who was still not without apprehension
of some further attempt on the part of the earl, sent
Dallison to make inquiries after him, and learnt that he
was at Whitehall, but that the court had fixed to remove
to Hampton Court at the end of June. The porter also
informed him that the city was emptying fast,—that
the Lord Mayor's residence was literally besieged with
applications for bills of health,—that officers were
stationed at the gates,—and that, besides these, barriers
and turnpikes were erected on all the main roads, at

which the certificates were required to be exhibited,—and that such persons as escaped without them were driven back by the inhabitants of the neighbouring villages, who refused to supply them with necessaries; and as they could not return home, many had perished of want, or perhaps of the pestilence, in the open fields. Horses and coaches, he added, were not to be procured, except at exorbitant prices; and thousands had departed on foot, locking up their houses, and leaving their effects behind them.

"In consequence of this," added Dallison, "several houses have been broken open; and though the watch had been trebled, still they cannot be in all places at once; and strong as the force is, it is not adequate to the present emergency. Bands of robbers stalk the streets at night, taking vehicles with them, built to resemble pest-carts, and beating off the watch, they break open the houses, and carry off any goods they please."

This intelligence greatly alarmed the grocer, and he began to fear his plans would be defeated, in an unexpected manner. He engaged Dallison to procure another trusty companion to take his place at night, and furnished him with money to purchase arms. He no longer slept as tranquilly as before, but frequently repaired to his place of observation to see that the watchman was at his post, and that all was secure. For the last few days he had remarked with some uneasiness that a youth frequently passed the house and gazed at the barred windows, and he at first imagined he might be leagued with the nocturnal marauders he had heard of, but the prepossessing appearance of the stripling, who could not be more than sixteen, and who was singularly slightly made, soon dispelled the idea. Still, as he constantly appeared at the same spot, the grocer began to have a new apprehension, and to suspect he was an emissary of the Earl of Rochester, and he sent Dallison to inquire his business. The youth returned an evasive answer, and withdrew; but the next day he was there again. On this occasion, Mr. Bloundel pointed him out to Leonard Holt, and asked him if he had seen him before.

The youth's back being towards them, the apprentice unhesitatingly answered in the negative, but as the subject of investigation turned the next moment, and looked up, revealing features of feminine delicacy and beauty, set off by long, flowing jet-black ringlets, Leonard started, and coloured.

"I was mistaken," he said, "*I have* seen him before."

"Is he one of the Earl of Rochester's pages?" asked Mr. Bloundel.

"No," replied Leonard, "and you need not be uneasy about him. I am sure he intends no harm."

Thus satisfied, the grocer thought no more about the matter. He then arranged with Leonard that he should visit the window at certain hours on alternate nights with himself, and appointed the following night as that on which the apprentice's duties should commence.

On the same night, however, an alarming incident occurred, which kept the grocer and his apprentice for a long time on the watch. The family had just retired to rest when the report of fire-arms was heard close to the street door, and Mr. Bloundel, hastily calling up Leonard, they repaired to the room overlooking the street, and found that a desperate struggle was going on below. The moon being overclouded, and the lantern extinguished, it was too dark to discern the figures of the combatants, and in a few seconds all became silent, except the groans of a wounded man. Mr. Bloundel then called out to know what was the matter, and ascertained from the sufferer, who proved to be his own watchman, that the adjoining house, being infected, had been shut up by the authorities; and its owner, unable to bear the restraint, had burst open the door, shot the watchman stationed at it, and firing another pistol at the poor wretch who was making the statement, because he endeavoured to oppose his flight, had subsequently attacked him with his sword. It was a great grief to Mr. Bloundel not to be able to aid the unfortunate watchman, and he had almost determined to hazard a descent by the pulley, when a musical voice was heard below, and the grocer soon understood that the youth, about whom his curiosity had been excited, was raising the sufferer, and endeavouring to staunch his wounds. Finding this impossible, however, at Mr. Bloundel's request he went in search of assistance, and presently afterwards returned with a posse of men, bearing halberts and lanterns, who carried off the wounded man; and afterwards started in pursuit of the murderer.

Mr. Bloundel then entered into conversation with the youth, who informed him that his name was Flitcroft,— that he was without a home, all his relations having died of the plague,—and that he was anxious to serve as a watchman in place of the poor wretch who had just been removed. Leonard remonstrated against this arrangement, but Mr. Bloundel was so much pleased with Flitcroft's conduct that he would listen to no objection. Accordingly, provisions were lowered down in the basket to the poor youth, and he stationed himself in the hutch. Nothing material occurred during the day. Flitcroft resigned his post to Dallison, but returned in the evening.

At midnight, Leonard took his turn to watch. It was a bright moonlight night, but though he occasionally looked out into the street, and perceived Flitcroft below, he gave no intimation of his presence. All at once, however, he was alarmed by a loud cry, and opening the shutter, perceived the youth struggling with two persons whom he recognised as Sir Paul Parravicin and Pillichody.

He shouted to them to release their captive, but they laughed at his vociferations, and in spite of his resistance dragged the youth away. Maddened at the sight, Leonard lowered the rope as quickly as he could with the intention of descending by it. At this moment, Flitcroft turned an agonized look behind him, and perceiving what had been done, broke suddenly from his captors, and before he could be prevented, sprang into the basket and laid hold of the rope. Leonard, who had seen the movement, and divined its object, drew up the pulley with the quickness of thought; and so expeditiously was the whole accomplished, that ere the knight and his companion reached the spot, Flitcroft was above their heads, and the next moment was pulled through the window, and in safety by the side of Leonard.

CHAPTER II

How Fires were lighted in the Streets

NIZZA MACASCREE, for it is useless to affect further
mystery, as soon as she could find utterance, murmured
her thanks to the apprentice, whose satisfaction at her
deliverance was greatly diminished by his fears lest his
master should disapprove of what he had done. Seeing
his uneasiness, and guessing the cause, Nizza hastened to
relieve it.

"I reproach myself bitterly for having placed you in
this situation," she said; "but I could not help it, and
will free you from my presence the moment I can do so
with safety. When I bade you farewell, I meant it to be
for ever, and persuaded myself I could adhere to my
resolution. But I was deceived. You would pity me,
were I to tell you the anguish I endured. I could not
accompany my poor father in his rambles; and if I went
forth at all, my steps involuntarily led me to Wood-street.
At last, I resolved to disguise myself, and borrowed this
suit from a Jew clothesman, who has a stall in Saint
Paul's. Thus equipped, I paced backwards and forwards
before the house, in the hope of obtaining a glimpse of
you, and fortune has favoured me more than I expected,
though it has led to this unhappy result. Heaven only
knows what will become of me!" she added, bursting
into tears. "Oh! that the pestilence would select me as
one of its victims. But, like your own sex, it shuns all
those who court it."

"I can neither advise you," replied Leonard, in sombre
tone, "nor help you. Ah!" he exclaimed, as the sound
of violent blows were heard against the door below,—
"your persecutors are trying to break into the house."

Rushing to the window, and gazing downwards, he
perceived Sir Paul Parravicin and Pillichody battering
against the shop door, and endeavouring to burst it

open. It was, however, so stoutly barricaded, that it resisted all their efforts.

"What is to be done?" cried Leonard. "The noise will certainly alarm my master, and you will be discovered."

"Heed me not," rejoined Nizza, distractedly, "you shall not run any risk on my account. Let me down the pulley. Deliver me to them. Anything is better than that you should suffer by my indiscretion."

"No, no," replied Leonard; "Mr. Bloundel shall know all. His love for his own daughter will make him feel for you. But come what will, I will not abandon you."

As he spoke, a timid knock was heard at the door, and a voice without exclaimed, in accents of the utmost trepidation, "Are you there, Leonard?—Robbers are breaking into the house. We shall all be murdered."

"Come in, Blaize," returned Leonard, opening the door and admitting the porter—"you may be of some assistance to me."

"In what way?" demanded Blaize.—"Ah! who's this?" he added, perceiving Nizza—"What is this page doing here?"

"Do not concern yourself about him, but attend to me," replied Leonard. "I am about to drive away those persons from the door. You must lower me down in the basket attached to the pulley."

"And will you dare to engage them?" asked Blaize, peeping out at the shutter. "They are armed. As I live, one is Major Pillichody, the rascal who dared to make love to Patience. I have half a mind to go down with you, and give him a sound drubbing."

"You shall not encounter this danger for me," interposed Nizza, endeavouring to stay Leonard, who, having thrust a sword into his girdle, was about to pass through the window.'

"Do not hinder me," replied the apprentice, breaking from her. "Take hold of the rope, Blaize, and mind it does not run down too quickly."

With this, he got into the basket, and as the porter

carefully obeyed his instructions, he reached the ground in safety. On seeing him, Pillichody bolted across the street, and flourishing his sword, and uttering tremendous imprecations, held himself in readiness to beat an immediate retreat. Not so Parravicin. Instantly assailing the apprentice, he slightly wounded him in the arm. Seeing how matters stood, and that victory was pretty certain to declare itself for his patron, Pillichody returned, and, attacking the apprentice, by their combined efforts he was speedily disarmed. Pillichody would have passed his sword through his body, but the knight stayed his hand.

"The fool has placed himself in our power," he said, "and he shall pay for his temerity; "nevertheless, I will spare his life provided he assist us to get into the house, or will deliver up Nizza Macascree."

"I will do neither," replied Leonard, fiercely.

Parravicin raised his sword, and was about to strike, when, at the moment, the basket was again quickly lowered to the ground. It bore Nizza Macascree, who, rushing between them, arrested the stroke.

"Oh! why have you done this?" cried Leonard, in a tone of reproach.

"I will tell you why," rejoined Parravicin, triumphantly; "because she saw you were unable to defend her, and, like a true woman, surrendered herself to the victor. Take care of him, Pillichody, while I secure the girl. Spit him, if he attempts to stir."

And twining his arms round Nizza, notwithstanding her shrieks and resistance, he bore her away. Infuriated by the sight, Leonard Holt threw himself upon Pillichody, and a desperate struggle took place between them, which terminated this time successfully for the apprentice. Wresting his long rapier from the bully, Leonard rushed after Parravicin, and reached the end of Wood-street, just in time to see him spring into a coach and drive off with his prize. Speeding after them along Blowbladder-street, and Middle-row, as Newgate-street was then termed, the apprentice shouted to the coachman to stop, but no attention being paid to his vociferations, and finding pursuit unavailing, he came to a halt. He then more slowly retraced his steps, and on arriving at the grocer's residence, found the basket drawn up. Almost afraid to call out, he at length mustered courage enough to shout to Blaize to lower it, and was answered by Mr. Bloundel, who, putting his head through the window, demanded in a stern tone why he had left the house?

Leonard briefly explained.

" I deeply regret your imprudence," replied his master; " because I can now no more admit you. It is my fixed determination, as you well know, not to suffer any member of my family who may quit my house to enter it again."

" I shall not attempt to remonstrate with you, sir," replied Leonard. " All I pray of you is to allow me to occupy this hutch, and to act as your porter."

" Willingly," rejoined Mr. Bloundel; " and as you have had the plague, you will run no risk of infection. You shall know all that passes within doors, and I only lament that you should have banished yourself from the asylum which I hoped to afford you."

After some further conversation between them a bundle was lowered by the grocer, containing a change of clothes and a couple of blankets. On receiving these, Leonard retired to the hutch, and tying a handkerchief round his wounded arm, wrapped himself in a nightrail, and stretching himself on the ground, in spite of his anxiety, soon sank asleep. He awoke about four o'clock in the morning, with a painful consciousness of what had taken place during the night. It was just beginning to grow light, and he walked across the street to gaze at the house from which he was exiled. Its melancholy, uninhabited look did not serve to cheer him. It seemed totally altered since he knew it first. The sign, which then invited the passers-by to enter the shop and deal with its honest owner, now appeared no longer significant, unless—and it will be remembered it was the Noah's Ark—it could be supposed to have reference to those shut up within. The apprentice looked at the habitation with misgiving, and, instead of regarding it as a sanctuary from the pestilence, could not help picturing it as a living tomb. The last

conversation he had had with Amabel also arose forcibly
to his recollection, and the little likelihood there appeared
of seeing her again gave him acute agony. Oppressed by
this painful idea, and unable to exclude from his thoughts
the unhappy situation of Nizza Macascree, he bent his
steps, scarcely knowing whither he was going, towards
Saint Paul's.

Having passed so much of his time of late in the cathedral, Leonard began to regard it as a sort of home, and
it now appeared like a place of refuge to him. Proceeding
to the great western entrance, he seated himself on one
of the large blocks of stone left there by the masons
occupied in repairing the exterior of the fane. His eye
rested upon the mighty edifice before him, and the clear
sparkling light revealed numberless points of architectural
grandeur and beauty which he had never before noticed.
The enormous buttresses and lofty pinnacles of the central
tower were tinged with the beams of the rising sun, and
glowed as if built of porphyry. While gazing at the
summit of this tower, and calling to mind the magnificent
view he had recently witnessed from it at the same hour,
if a wish could have transported him thither at that
moment, he would have enjoyed it again. But as this
could not be, he tried to summon before his mental vision
the whole glorious prospect,—the broad and shining
river, with its moving or motionless craft,—the gardens,
the noble mansions, the warehouses, and mighty wharves
on its banks,—London Bridge, with its enormous pile
of habitations,—the old and picturesque city, with its
innumerable towers and spires and girdle of grey walls,—
the green fields and winding lanes leading to the lovely
hills around it:—all these objects arose obedient to his
fancy, and came arrayed in colouring as fresh as that
wherein they had before appeared to him. While thus
occupied, his gaze remained riveted on the summit of
the central tower, and he fancied he perceived someone
leaning over the balustrade, but as little beyond the
upper part of the figure could be discerned, and as it
appeared perfectly motionless, he could not be quite
sure that his eyes did not deceive him. Having gazed at

the object for some minutes, during which it maintained the same attitude, he continued his survey of the pile, and became so excited by the sublime emotions inspired by the contemplation, as to be insensible to aught else.

After a while, he arose, and was about to proceed towards the portico, when chancing to look at the top of the tower, he remarked that the figure had disappeared, and while wondering who it could be, he perceived a person emerge from one of the tall windows in the lower part of the tower. It was Solomon Eagle, and he no longer wondered at what he had seen. The enthusiast was without his brazier, but carried a long stout staff. He ran along the pointed roof of the nave with inconceivable swiftness, till reaching the vast stone cross, upwards of twelve feet in height, ornamenting the western extremity, he climbed its base, and clasping the transverse bar of the sacred symbol of his faith with his left arm, extended his staff with his right, and described a circle, as if pointing out the walls of the city. He then raised his staff towards Heaven to invoke its vengeance, and anon pointed it menacingly downwards. After this, he broke into loud denunciations; but though the apprentice could not hear the words, he gathered their purport from his gestures.

By this time, a few masons had assembled, and, producing their implements, commenced working at the blocks of stone. Glancing at the enthusiast, one of them observed with a smile to his companion, " There is Solomon Eagle pronouncing his morning curse upon the city. I wonder whether the judgments he utters against it will come to pass ? "

" Assuredly, Phil Gatford," replied the other mason, gravely; " and I look upon all the work we are now doing as labour thrown away. Was he not right about the plague ? Did he not foretell the devouring scourge by which we are visited ? And he will be right also about the fire. Since he has doomed it, this cathedral will be consumed by flames, and one stone will not be left standing on another."

" It is strange, Ned Turgis," observed Gatford, " that, though Solomon Eagle may always be seen at daybreak

at the top of the tower, or on the roof of the cathedral—
sometimes at one point, and sometimes at another—no
one can tell where he hides himself at other times. He
no longer roams the streets at night, but you may remember when the officers of justice were in search of him,
to give evidence against Mother Malmayns and Chowles,
he was not to be found."

"I remember it," replied Turgis; "but I have no
doubt he was hidden in some out-of-the-way corner of
the cathedral—perhaps among the immense wooden
beams of the clerestory."

"Or in some of the secret passages or cells contrived
in the thickness of the walls," rejoined the first speaker.
—"I say, Ned Turgis, if the plague increases, as there
is every likelihood it will, Solomon Eagle will be the only
preacher left in Saint Paul's. Neither deans, prebends,
minor-canons, nor vicars will attend. As it is, they have
almost abandoned it."

"Shame on them!" exclaimed Leonard Holt, who,
being much interested in the conversation of the masons,
had silently approached them. "At this season, more
than ever, they are bound to attend to their duty."

"Why, so I think," rejoined Gatford; "but I suppose
they consider self-preservation their first duty. They
aver that all assemblages, whether called together for
religious purposes or not, are dangerous, and likely to
extend the pestilence."

"And yet crowds are permitted to assemble for purposes of amusement, if not for worship, in those holy
walls," returned Leonard.

"Not so," replied Gatford. "Very few persons now
come there, and none for amusement. Paul's-walk is
completely deserted. The shops and stalls have been
removed, and the pillars to which they were attached are
restored to their former appearance."

"I am glad to hear it," rejoined Leonard. "I would
far rather the sacred edifice were altogether abandoned
than be what it has been of late,—a den of thieves."

"It was a stable and a magazine of arms in the time of
the Commonwealth," remarked Gatford.

"And if Solomon Eagle's foreboding come to pass, it will be a heap of ruins in our own time," rejoined Turgis. "But I see the prophet of ill has quitted his post, and retired to his hiding-place."

Looking up as this was said, Leonard saw that the enthusiast had disappeared. At this moment the great door of the cathedral was thrown open, and, quitting the masons, he ascended the broad steps under the portico, and entered the fane, where he found that the information he had received was correct, and that the stalls and other disfigurements to the pillars had been removed. After pacing the solitary aisles for some time, he made inquiries from the verger concerning Solomon Eagle.

"I know nothing about him," replied the man, reluctantly. "I believe he always appears at daybreak on some part of the roof, but I am as ignorant as yourself where he hides himself. The door of the winding staircase leading to the central tower is open. You can ascend it, and search for him, if you think proper."

Acting upon the suggestion, Leonard mounted to the belfry, and from thence to the summit of the tower. Having indulged himself with a brief survey of the glorious view around, he descended, and glanced into every cell and chamber as he passed, in the hopes of meeting with the enthusiast, but he was disappointed. At length, as he got about half-way down, he felt his arm forcibly grasped, and instantly conjecturing who it was, offered no resistance. Without uttering a word, the person who had seized him, dragged him up a few steps, pushed aside a secret door, which closed behind them with a hollow clangour, and leading him along a dark narrow passage, opened another door, and they emerged upon the roof. He then found that his suspicion was correct, and that his mysterious guide was no other than Solomon Eagle.

"I am glad to find you have recovered from the pestilence," said the enthusiast, regarding him with a friendly glance,—" it proves you are favoured by Heaven. I saw you in the open space before the cathedral this morning, and instantly recognised you. I was in the belfry when you descended, but you did not perceive me,

and I wished to be"certain you were alone before I discovered myself."

"You have ceased to roam the streets at night, and
rouse the slumbering citizens to repentance?" asked
Leonard.

"For the present, I have," returned Solomon Eagle.
"But I shall appear again when I am required. But you
shall now learn why I have brought you hither. Look
along those streets," he added, pointing to the thoroughfares opening in different directions. "What see you?"

"I see men piling heaps of wood and coals at certain
distances, as if they were preparing bonfires," replied
Leonard. "And yet it cannot be. This is no season for
rejoicing."

"It has been supposed that the lighting of many thous-
and fires at once will purify the air," replied Solomon
Eagle, "and therefore the Lord Mayor has given orders
that heaps of fuel shall be placed before every house in
every street in the city, and that all these heaps shall be
kindled at a certain hour. But it will be of no avail. The
weather is now fine and settled, and the sky cloudless. But
the offended Deity will cause the heaviest rain to descend,
and extinguish the fires. No; the way to avert the pestilence is not by fire, but by prayer and penitence, by humili-
ation and fasting. Let this sinful people put on sackcloth
and ashes. Let them beseech God, by constant prayer, to
forgive them, and they may prevail, but not otherwise."

"And when are these fires to be lighted?" asked the
apprentice.

"To-night, at midnight," replied Solomon Eagle.

He then took Leonard by the hand, and led him back
the same way he had brought him. On reaching the spiral
staircase, he said, "If you desire to behold a sight such
as a man has seldom witnessed, ascend to the summit of
this tower an hour after midnight, when all these fires are
lighted. A small door on the left of the northern entrance shall be left open. It will conduct you to the back
of the choir, and you must then find your way hither as
well as you can."

Murmuring his thanks, Leonard hurried down the

spiral staircase, and quitting the cathedral, proceeded in the direction of Wood-street. Preparations were everywhere being made for carrying the Lord Mayor's orders into effect; and such was the beneficial result anticipated, that a general liveliness prevailed. On reaching his master's residence, he found him at the shutter, curious to know what was going forward; and having informed him, the grocer immediately threw him down money to procure wood and coal.

"I have but little faith in the experiment," he said, "but the Lord Mayor's injunctions must be obeyed."

With the help of Dallison, who had now arrived, Leonard Holt soon procured a large heap of fuel, and placed it in the middle of the street. The day was passed in executing other commissions for the grocer, and he took his meals in the hutch with the porter. Time appeared to pass with unusual slowness, and not he alone, but anxious thousands, awaited the signal to kindle their fires. The night was profoundly dark and sultry, and Leonard could not help thinking that the enthusiast's prediction would be verified, and that rain would fall. But these gloomy anticipations vanished as the hour of midnight was tolled forth by the neighbouring clocks of Saint Michael's and Saint Alban's. Scarcely had the strokes died away, when Leonard seized a light and set fire to the pile. Ten thousand other piles were kindled at the same moment, and in an instant the pitchy darkness was converted into light as bright as that of noonday.

Anxious to behold this prodigious illumination at its best, Leonard Holt committed the replenishing of the pile and the custody of the house to Dallison, and hastened to Saint Paul's. A great fire was burning at each angle of the cathedral, but without pausing to notice the effect of the flames upon the walls of the building, he passed through the door to which he had been directed, and hastening to the spiral staircase beyond the choir, ascended it with swift steps. He did not pause till he reached the summit of the tower, and there, indeed, a wondrous spectacle awaited him. The whole city seemed on fire, and girded with a flaming belt—for piles were lighted at certain

distances along the whole line of walls. The groups of
dark figures collected round the fires added to their
picturesque effect; and the course of every street could
be traced by the reflection of the flames on the walls
and gables of the houses. London Bridge was discernible
from the fires burning upon it—and even upon the river
braziers were lighted on all the larger craft, which cast a
ruddy glow upon the stream.

After gazing at this extraordinary sight for some time,
Leonard began to descend. As yet he had seen nothing
of Solomon Eagle, and searching for him in vain in the
belfry, he quitted the cathedral. From a knot of persons
gathered round one of the fires he learnt that the enthusiast
was addressing the crowd at the west side of the building,
and proceeding thither he perceived him standing on the
edge of the balustrade of the south-western tower, sur-
mounting the little church of Saint Gregory. His brazier
was placed on one of the buttresses, and threw its light on
the mighty central tower of the fabric, and on a large
clock-face immediately beneath. Solomon Eagle was
evidently denouncing the city, but his words were lost
in the distance. As he proceeded, a loud clap of thunder
pealed overhead.

" It comes—it comes ! " cried the enthusiast, in a voice
that could be distinctly heard in the death-like stillness
that followed the thunder. " The wrath of Heaven is at
hand."

As he spoke, a bright flash cut the air, and a bolt struck
down one of the pinnacles of the great tower. Flash
after flash followed in quick succession, and the enthusiast,
who seemed wrapped in flame, extended his arms towards
Heaven, as if beseeching a further display of its vengeance.
Suddenly the lightning ceased to flash and the thunder to
roll. A few heavy drops of rain fell. These were succeeded
by a deluging shower of such violence, that in less than
a quarter of an hour every fire within the city was extinguished, and all was darkness and despair.

The deepest gloom and despondency prevailed that
night throughout London. The sudden storm was regarded as a manifestation of the displeasure of Heaven,

and as an intimation that the arrows of its wrath were not to be turned aside by any human efforts. So impressed were all with this feeling, that when, in less than half an hour, the rain entirely ceased, the clouds cleared off, and the stars again poured down their lustre, no one attempted to re-light the quenched embers, fearing to provoke the Divine vengeance. Nor was a monitor wanting to enforce the awful lesson. Solomon Eagle, with his brazier on his head, ran through the streets, calling on the inhabitants to take to heart what had happened, to repent, and prepare for their doom.

" The Lord will not spare you," he cried, as he stationed himself in the open space before Saint Stephen's, Walbrook. " He will visit your sins upon you. Pray, therefore, that ye may not be destroyed, both body and soul. Little time is allowed you for repentance. Many that hear me shall not live till to-morrow : few shall survive the year ! "

" Thou, thyself, shalt not survive the night, false prophet," cried a voice from a neighbouring window. And immediately afterwards the barrel of a gun was thrust forth and a shot fired at the enthusiast. But though Solomon Eagle never altered his position, he was wholly uninjured—the ball striking a bystander, who fell to the ground mortally wounded.

" You have shot your own son, Mr. Westwood," cried one of the spectators, rushing up to the fallen man. " Who will henceforth doubt that Solomon Eagle is under the care of a special Providence ? "

" Not I," replied another spectator. " I shall never disregard his words in future."

Setting down his brazier, the enthusiast bent over the dead man—for dead he was—and noted the placid smile upon his features. By this time the unfortunate father had joined the group, and, on seeing the body of his son, wrung his hands in a pitiable manner, and gave utterance to the wildest expression of despair. No one attempted to seize him, till at length Solomon Eagle, rising from his kneeling posture, laid his hand upon his arm, and regarding him sternly, said, " What wrong have I done you, that you should seek to slay me ? "

"What wrong?" rejoined Westwood—"such wrong as can never be repaired. Your fearful prophecies and denunciations so terrified my daughter, that she died distracted. My broken-hearted wife was not long in following her; and now you have made me the murderer of my son. Complete the tragedy, and take my life."

"I have no desire to do so," replied Solomon Eagle, in a tone of commiseration. "My wish is to save your soul, and the souls of all who listen to me. I wonder not that your anger was at first stirred against me; but if your heart had been properly directed, indignation would have soon given way to better feelings. My mission is not to terrify, but to warn. Why will ye thus continue impenitent when ye are spoken to, not by my voice alone, but by a thousand others?—by the thunder—by the rain— by the pestilence !—and ye shall be spoken to, if ye continue senseless, by fire and by famine. Look at these quenched embers—at these flooded streets—they are types of your vain struggle with a superior power. Now, mark me what you must do to free the city from contagion. You must utterly and for ever abandon your evil courses. You must pray incessantly for remission of your sins. You must resign yourselves without repining to such chastisement as you have provoked, and must put your whole trust and confidence in God. Do this, and do it heartily; it is possible that his wrath may be averted."

"I feel the force of your words," faltered Westwood— "would I had felt it sooner ! "

"Repentance never comes too late," rejoined the enthusiast. "Let this be an example to you all."

And snatching up his brazier, he continued his course at the same lightning speed as before. The unfortunate father was taken into his own dwelling, whither likewise the body of his son was conveyed. A strict watch was kept over him during the night, and in the morning he was removed to Newgate, where he perished, in less than a week, of the distemper.

The aspect of the streets on the following day was deplorable enough. Not that the weather was unfavourable. On the contrary, it was bright and sunny, while the heated atmosphere, cooled by the showers, felt no longer oppressive. But the sight of the half-burnt fires struck a chill into every bosom, and it was not until the heaps were removed that the more timorous ventured forth at all. The result, too, of the experiment was singularly unfortunate. Whether it was from the extraordinary heat occasioned by the lighting of so many fires, or that the smoke did not ascend, and so kept down the pestilential effluvia, or that the number of persons who met together spread the contagion, certain it was that the pestilence was more widely extended than before, and the mortality fearfully increased.

On the commencement of the storm, Leonard Holt hurried back to Wood-street, and reached his master's dwelling just as the rain began to descend in torrents. Mr. Bloundel was at the window, and a few words only passed between him and the apprentice when the latter was compelled to take refuge in the hutch. Here he found Dallison the watchman, and they listened in awestruck silence to the heavy showers, and to the hissing of the blazing embers in their struggle against the hostile element. By-and-by the latter sound ceased. Not a light could be seen throughout the whole length of the street, nor was there any red reflection of the innumerable fires as heretofore in the sky. It was evident all were extinguished; and the pitiless pelting of the rain, the roar of the water-spouts, and the rush of the over-filled kennels, now converted into rivulets, could alone be heard. After awhile the storm cleared off, and Leonard and his companion issued from their retreat, and gazed in silence at the drenched heap before them. While thus occupied, the window above them opened, and the grocer appeared at it.

" This is, indeed, a sad and striking lesson," he said, " and I hope will not be lost upon those who have witnessed it. It shows the utter impotency of a struggle against the Divine will, and that when man relies upon himself for preservation, he depends upon a broken reed. If I did not place myself under Heaven's protection, I should be sure that all my own precautions were unavailing. I am now about to call up my family to prayer. You can join us in our supplications, and I trust they will not be unheard."

Closing the window, the grocer retired, and Leonard returned to the hutch, where he fell upon his knees, and as soon as he supposed the family were gathered together, commenced his own prayers. He pictured the whole group assembled—the fervour of the grocer excited to an unwonted pitch by what had just occurred—the earnest countenances of his wife and the younger children—and the exalted looks of Amabel. He could not see her—neither could he hear her voice—but he fancied how she looked, and in what terms she prayed—and it was no slight satisfaction to him to think that his own voice ascended to Heaven coupled with hers.

On quitting the hutch, he found Dallison conversing with Doctor Hodges. The physician expressed great surprise at seeing him, and inquired how he came to have left his master's house. Leonard related all that had happened, and besought his assistance in Nizza's behalf.

" I will do all I can for her," replied Hodges, " for I feel greatly interested about her. But who is this Sir Paul Parravicin ? I never heard of him."

" I know nothing more of him that what I have told you, sir," replied Leonard. " He is a friend of the Earl of Rochester."

" It must be a feigned name," rejoined Hodges; " but I will speedily find him out. You must lodge at my house to-night. It will be better for you than sleeping in that damp shed. But first, I must have a word or two with your master. I have been abroad all night, and came hither to ascertain what he thought of this plan of the fires, and what he had done. How do you give the signal to him ? "

" There is a cord within the hutch by which you can sound a bell within his chamber," returned Leonard; " I will ring it."

Accordingly he did so, and the summons was almost instantly answered by the grocer. A kindly greeting passed between the latter and Hodges, who inquired whether all was going on satisfactorily within, and whether anything could be done for the family.

" I would not have disturbed you at this unseasonable hour," he said, " but chancing to be in your neighbourhood, and thinking it likely you would be on the watch, I called to have a word with you. Though I could not foresee what would happens, I entirely disapproved of these fires as likely to increase rather than check the pestilence."

" The hand of Heaven has extinguished them, because they were lighted in opposition to its decrees," replied Bloundel; " but you have asked me whether all is going on well within. I should answer readily in the affirmative, but that my wife expresses much anxiety respecting Amabel. We have no longer any apprehension of misconduct. She is all we could desire—serious and devout. But we have fears for her health. The confinement may be too much for her. What would you recommend ? "

" I must see her to be able to speak confidently," replied Hodges.

" I know not how that can be accomplished, unless you choose to ascend by a basket attached to the pulley," replied the grocer, with some hesitation, " and it is against my plan to admit you."

" But your daughter's life, my good friend," rejoined Hodges; " think of that. If I choose to risk life and limb to visit her, you may surely risk the chance of contagion to admit me. But you need have no fear. Sprinkle your room with spirits of sulphur, and place a phial of vinegar so that I can use it on my first entrance into the house, and I will answer for the safety of your family."

These preparations made, Mr. Bloundel lowered the basket, into which Hodges got, and grasping the rope, not without some misgiving on his part, he was drawn up. Leonard witnessed his ascent with a beating heart, and could scarcely repress a feeling of envy when he saw him pass through the window, and knew that he would soon be in the presence of Amabel. But this feeling quickly changed into one of deep anxiety concerning her. Her father's account of her had increased the uneasiness he previously felt, and he was as anxious to know the doctor's opinion of her, as if his own fate had depended upon it. He was kept in this painful state of suspense for nearly an hour, when voices were heard at the window, and presently afterwards Hodges was carefully let down. Bidding the grocer farewell, he desired Leonard to follow him, and led the way towards Cheapside. They proceeded a short distance in silence, when the latter ventured to remark, " You say nothing about Amabel, sir ? I fear you found her seriously indisposed."

" Do not question me about her just now," rejoined the doctor, in a subdued emotion. " I would rather not discuss the subject."

Nothing more was said, for though the apprentice would willingly have continued the conversation, his companion's evident disinclination to pursue it compelled him to desist. In this way, they reached the doctor's residence, where Leonard was immediately shown to a comfortable bed.

It was late when he awoke next day, and as the doctor was gone forth, he partook of a plentiful breakfast which was placed before him, and repaired to Wood-street, but his master having no commissions for him to execute, he went back again. By this time, Doctor Hodges had returned, and calling him into his library, told him he wished to speak with him.

" You were right last night," he said, " in construing my silence into alarm for Amabel. In truth, I fear she is rapidly sinking into a decline, and nothing will arrest the progress of the insidious disease but instant removal to the country. To this she will not consent, neither do I know how it could be accomplished. It is pitiable to see so lovely a creature dying, as I fear she is, of a broken heart."

Leonard covered his face with his hands, and wept aloud.

" We have not yet spoken of Nizza Macascree," said Hodges, after a pause, tapping him kindly on the shoulder. " I think I have discovered a trace of her."

" I am glad to hear it," replied Leonard, rousing him-

self. " She is another victim of these profligates. But I
will be revenged upon them all."

" I have before enjoined you to restrain your indignation. just though it be," returned Hodges. " I have not
yet found out whither she has been taken. But I have a
clue which. unless I am mistaken, will lead me to it. But
I must now dismiss you. I have other affairs to attend to,
and must give a dangerous and difficult case on which I
have been consulted. undisturbed consideration. Make
my house your home as long as you think proper."

Warmly thanking the doctor, Leonard then withdrew.
Shortly after this, he walked forth, and ascertaining that
he was not required by his master, determined to satisfy
himself by actual observation of the extent of the ravages
of the plague.

With this view he shaped his course along Lad-lane,
and traversing Cateaton-street, entered Lothbury. The
number of houses which he here found closed, with red
crosses on the doors, and the fatal inscription above them,
convinced him that the deplorable accounts he had heard
were not exaggerated. In passing some of these habitations
he saw such ghastly faces at the windows, and heard such
lamentable cries, that he was glad to hurry on and get out
of sight and hearing. In Throgmorton-street, nearly opposite Drapers'-hall, a poor wretch suddenly opened a casement, and before his attendants could force him back,
threw himself from a great height to the ground, and
broke his neck. Another incident, of an equally distressing
nature, occurred. A young and richly-dressed young man
issued from a tavern in Broad-street, and with a wild and
inflamed countenance staggered along. He addressed
some insulting language to Leonard, but the latter, who
desired no quarrel, disregarded his remarks and let him
pass. The next person encountered by the drunken man
was a young female. Suddenly catching her in his arms,
he imprinted a kiss upon her lips, and then, with a frightful
laugh, shouted, " I have given you the plague ! Look
here ! " and tearing aside the collar of his shirt, he exhibited a large tumour. The young woman uttered a shriek
of terror and fainted, while her ruthless assailant took to

his heels, and running as long as his strength lasted, fell down, and was taken to the pest-house, where he was joined that same night by his victim. And this was by no means an uncommon occurrence. The distemper acted differently on different temperaments. Some of it inflamed to an ungovernable pitch of madness—others it reduced to the depths of despair—while in many cases it brought out and aggravated the worst parts of the character. Wives conveyed the infection intentionally to their husbands—husbands to their wives—parents to their children—lovers to the object of their affection—while, as in the case above mentioned, many persons ran about like rabid hounds, striving to communicate it to all they met. Greatly shocked at what had occurred, and yet not altogether surprised at it, for his mind had become familiarised with horrors, Leonard struck down Finch-lane, and proceeded towards Cornhill. On the way, he noticed two dead bodies lying at the mouth of a small alley, and hastening past was stopped at the entrance to Cornhill by a butcher's apprentice, who was wheeling away the body of an old man, who had just died while purchasing meat at a stall at Stocks' Market. Filled with unutterable loathing at this miserable spectacle, Leonard was fain to procure a glass of canary to recruit his spirits.

Accordingly he proceeded to the Globe tavern at the corner of Birchin-lane. As he entered the house, a lively strain of music caught his ear, and glancing in the direction of the sound, he found it proceeded from the blind piper, Mike Macascree, who was playing to some half-dozen roystering youths. Bell lay at her master's feet, and as Leonard approached the party, she pricked up her ears, and being called by name, instantly sprang towards him, and manifested the strongest delight. The piper stopped playing to listen to what was going forward, but the young men urged him to proceed, and again filled his glass.

" Don't drink any more, Mike," said Leonard, " but step aside with me. I've something to say to you—something about your daughter."

" My daughter ! " exclaimed the piper, in a half-angry, half-sorrowful voice, while a slight moisture forced itself through his orbless lids—" I don't want to hear anything about her, except that she is dead. She has deserted me, and disgraced herself."

" You are mistaken," rejoined Leonard; " and if you will come with me, I will explain the truth to you."

" I will listen to no explanation," rejoined the piper, furiously—" she has given me pain enough already. I'm engaged with this jovial company. Fill my glass, my masters—there, fill it again," he added, draining it eagerly, and with the evident wish to drown all thought. "There, now you shall have such a tune, as was never listened to by mortal ears."

A loud laugh from the young men followed this proposition, and the piper played away so furiously that it added to their merriment. Touched with compassion, Leonard walked aside, hoping, when the party broke up, to be able to have a word with the poor man. But the piper's excitement increased. He played faster and drank harder, until it was evident he was no longer in a condition to speak rationally. Leonard, therefore, addressed himself to the drawer, and desired him to look after the piper, engaging to return before midnight to see how he went on. The drawer promising compliance, Leonard departed; and not feeling disposed to continue his walk, returned to Wood-street.

Nothing particular occurred during the evening. Leonard did not see Doctor Hodges, who was engaged in his professional duties; and after keeping watch before the grocer's till nearly midnight, he again retraced his steps to the Globe. The drawer was at the door, and about to close the house.

" You will be sorry to learn the fate of the poor piper," he said.

" Why, what has happened to him ? " cried Leonard.

" He is dead of the plague," was the reply.

" What, so suddenly ! " exclaimed the apprentice. " You are jesting with me."

" Alas ! it is no jest," rejoined the drawer, in a tone that convinced the apprentice of his sincerity. " His entertainers quitted him about two hours ago, and in spite of my efforts to detain him, he left the house, and sat down on those steps. Concluding he would fall asleep, I did not disturb him, and his dog kept careful watch over him. I forgot all about him till a short time ago, when hearing the pest-cart pass, I went forth, and learnt that the drivers having found him dead, as they supposed, of the pestilence, had placed their forks under his belt and thrown him upon the other dead bodies."

" And where is the dog ? " cried Leonard.

" She would not quit her master," replied the drawer, " so the men threw her into the cart with him, saying, they would bury her in the plague-pit as all dogs were ordered to be destroyed."

" This must be prevented," cried Leonard. " Which way did the dead-cart go ? "

" Towards Moorgate," replied the drawer.

Leonard heard no more, but dashing through a narrow passage opposite the Conduit, passed Bartholomew-lane, and traversing Lothbury, soon reached Coleman-street and the old city gate, to which he had been directed. Here he learnt that the dead-cart had passed through it about five minutes before, and he hurried on towards Finsbury-fields. He had not proceeded far when he heard a sound as of a pipe at a distance, furiously played, and accompanied by the barking of a dog. These sounds were followed by cries of alarm, and he presently perceived two persons running towards him, with a swiftness which could only be occasioned by terror. One of them carried a lantern, and grasping his arm, the apprentice detained him.

" What is the matter ? " he asked.

" The devil's the matter," replied the man—" the piper's ghost has appeared in that cart, and is playing his old tunes again."

" Ay, it's either his spirit, or he is come to life again," observed the other man, stopping likewise. " I tossed him into the cart myself, and will swear he was dead enough then."

" You have committed a dreadful mistake," cried Leonard. " You have tossed a living man into the cart

instead of a dead one. Do you not hear those sounds?"
And as he spoke, the notes of the pipe swelled to a louder
strain than ever.

"I tell you it is the devil—or a ghost," replied the
driver;—"I will stay here no longer."

"Lend me your lantern, and I will go to the cart,"
rejoined Leonard.

"Take it," replied the man; "but I caution you to
stay where you are. You may receive a shock you will
never survive."

Paying no attention to what was said, Leonard ran towards the cart, and found the piper seated upon a pile of
dead bodies, most of them stripped of their covering,
with Bell by his side, and playing away at a prodigious
rate.

CHAPTER III

The Dance of Death

THE condition of the prisons at this season was really
frightful. In Newgate, in particular, where the distemper
broke out at the beginning of June, it raged with such
violence that in less than a week more than half the
prisoners were swept off, and it appeared probable that,
unless its fury abated, not a soul would be left alive within
it. At all times, this crowded and ill-kept prison was
infested by the gaol-fever and other pestilential disorders,
but these were mild in comparison with the present terrible
visitation. The atmosphere was noisome and malignant;
the wards were never cleansed; and many poor wretches
who died in their cells, were left there till the attendants on
the dead cart chose to drag them forth. No restraint
being placed upon the sick, and the rules of the prison
allowing them the free use of any strong liquors they
could purchase, the scenes that occurred were too dreadful
and revolting for description, and could only be paralleled
by the orgies of a pandemonium. Many reckless beings,
conscious that they were attacked by a fatal disorder,

I

drank as long as they could raise the cup to their lips, and after committing the wildest and most shocking extravagancies, died in a state of frenzy.

Newgate became thus, as it were, the very focus of infection, where the plague assumed its worst aspect, and where its victims perished far more expeditiously than elsewhere. Two of the turnkeys had already died of the distemper, and such was the alarm entertained, that no persons could be found to supply their places. To penetrate the recesses of the prison was almost to ensure destruction, and none but the attendants of the dead-cart and the nurses attempted it. Among the latter was Judith. Employed as a nurse on the first outbreak of the plague, she willingly and fearlessly undertook the office. The worse the disease became, the better pleased she appeared ; and she was so utterly without apprehension, that when no one would approach the cell where some wretched sufferer lay expiring, she unhesitatingly entered it. But it was not to render aid, but to plunder, that she thus exercised her functions. She administered no medicine, dressed no tumours, and did not contribute in the slightest degree to the comfort of the miserable wretches committed to her charge. All she desired was to obtain whatever valuables they possessed, or to wring from them any secret that might afterwards be turned to account. Foreseeing that Newgate must ere long be depopulated, and having no fears for herself, she knew that she must then be liberated, and be able once more to renew her mischievous practices upon mankind. Her marvellous preservation throughout all the dangers to which she was exposed, seemed almost to warrant the supposition that she had entered into a compact with the pestilence, to extend its ravages by every means in her power, on the condition of being spared herself.

Soon after the outbreak of the plague in Newgate, all the debtors were liberated, and if the keepers had had their own way, the common felons would have been likewise released. But this could not be, and they were kept to perish as before described. Matters, however, grew so serious, that it became a question whether the few miserable wretches left alive ought to be longer detained, and at last the turnkeys refusing to act any longer, and delivering their keys to the governor, the whole of the prisoners were set free.

On the night of their liberation, Chowles and Judith proceeded to the vaults of Saint Faith's, to deposit within them the plunder they had obtained in the prison. They found them entirely deserted. Neither verger, sexton, nor any other person, was to be seen, and they took up their quarters in the crypt. Having brought a basket of provisions and a few bottles of wine with them, they determined to pass the night in revelry; and, accordingly, having lighted a fire with the fragments of old coffins brought from the charnel, they sat down to their meal. Having done full justice to it, and disposed of the first flask, they were about to abandon themselves to unrestrained enjoyment, when their glee was all at once interrupted by a strange and unaccountable noise in the adjoining church. Chowles, who had just commenced chanting one of his wild melodies, suddenly stopped, and Judith set down the glass she had raised to her lips untasted. What could it mean? Neither of them could tell. It seemed like strains of unearthly music, mixed with shrieks and groans as of tortured spirits, accompanied by peals of such laughter as might be supposed to proceed from demons.

"The dead are burst forth from their tombs," cried Chowles, in a quavering voice, "and are attended by a legion of evil spirits."

"It would seem so," replied Judith, rising. "I should like to behold the sight. Come with me."

"Not for the world!" rejoined Chowles, shuddering, "and I would recommend you to stay where you are. You may behold your dead husband among them."

"Do you think so?" rejoined Judith, halting.

"I am sure of it," cried Chowles, eagerly. "Stay where you are—stay where you are."

As he spoke, there was another peal of infernal laughter, and the strains of music grew louder each moment.

"Come what may, I will see what it is," said Judith,

emptying her glass, as if seeking courage from the draught.
" Surely," she added, in a taunting tone, " you will come
with me ? "

" I am afraid of nothing earthly," rejoined Chowles—
" but I do not like to face beings of another world."

" Then I will go alone," rejoined Judith.

" Nay, that shall never be," replied Chowles, tottering
after her.

As they opened the door and crossed the charnel, such
an extraordinary combination of sounds burst upon their
ears that they again paused, and looked anxiously at each
other. Chowles laid his hand on his companion's arm,
and strove to detain her, but she would not be stayed, and
he was forced to proceed. Setting down the lamp on the
stone floor, Judith passed into the subterranean church,
where she beheld a sight that almost petrified her. In the
midst of the nave, which was illumined by a blue glimmering light, whence proceeding it was impossible to
determine, stood a number of grotesque figures, apparelled
in fantastic garbs, and each attended by a skeleton. Some
of the latter grisly shapes were playing on tambours,
others on psalteries, others on rebecs—every instrument
producing the strangest sound imaginable. Viewed
through the massive pillars, beneath that dark and ponderous roof, and by the mystic light before described,
this strange company had a supernatural appearance, and
neither Chowles nor Judith doubted for a moment that
they beheld before them a congregation of phantoms. An
irresistible feeling of curiosity prompted them to advance.
On drawing nearer, they found the assemblage compre-
hended all ranks of society. There was a pope in his tiara
and pontifical dress; a cardinal in his cap and robes; a
monarch with a sceptre in his hand, and arrayed in the
habiliments of royalty; a crowned queen; a bishop
wearing his mitre, and carrying his crosier; an abbot
likewise in his mitre, and bearing a crosier; a duke in his
robes of state; a grave canon of the church; a knight
sheathed in armour; a judge, an advocate, and a magistrate, all in their robes; a mendicant friar and a nun; and
the list was completed by a physician, an astrologer, a

miser, a merchant, a duchess, a pedlar, a soldier, a games-
ter, an idiot, a robber, a blind man, and a beggar—each
distinguishable by his apparel.

By-and-by, with a wild and gibbering laugh that chilled
the beholders' blood, one of the tallest and grisliest of the
skeletons sprang forward, and beating his drum, the
whole ghostly company formed, two and two, into a line—
a skeleton placing itself on the right of every mortal. In
this order, the fantastic procession marched between the
pillars, the unearthly music playing all the while, and disappeared at the further extremity of the church. With the
last of the group, the mysterious light vanished, and
Chowles and his companion were left in profound darkness.

"What can it mean?" cried Judith, as soon as she
recovered her speech. "Are they human, or spirits?"

"Human beings don't generally amuse themselves in
this way," returned Chowles. "But hark!—I still hear
the music.—They are above—in Saint Paul's."

"Then I will join them," said Judith. "I am resolved
to see the end of it."

"Don't leave me behind," returned Chowles, following
her. "I would rather keep company with Beelzebub and
all his imps than be alone."

Both were too well acquainted with the way to need
any light. Ascending the broad stone steps, they presently emerged into the cathedral, which they found
illumined by the same glimmering light as the lower
church, and they perceived the ghostly assemblage
gathered into an immense ring, and dancing round the
tall skeleton, who continued beating his drum, and uttering a strange gibbering sound, which was echoed by the
others. Each moment the dancers increased the swiftness
of their pace, until at last it grew to a giddy whirl, and
then, all at once, with a shriek of laughter, the whole
company fell to the ground.

Chowles and Judith, then, for the first time, understood, from the confusion that ensued, and the exclamations uttered, that they were no spirits they had to deal
with, but beings of the same mould as themselves. Accord-

ingly, they approached the party of masquers, for such
they proved, and found on inquiry that they were a party
of young gallants, who, headed by the Earl of Rochester—
the representative of the tall skeleton—had determined
to realise the Dance of Death, as once depicted on the
walls of an ancient cloister at the north of the cathedral,
called Pardon-churchyard, on the walls of which, says
Stowe, were " artificially and richly painted the Dance of
Macabre, or Dance of Death, commonly called the Dance
of Paul's, the like whereof was painted about Saint
Innocent's, at Paris. The metres, or poesy of this dance,"
proceeds the same authority, " were translated out of
French into English by John Lydgate, monk of Bury;
and with the picture of Death leading all estates, painted
about the cloister, at the special request and expense of
Jenkin Carpenter, in the reign of Henry the Sixth."
Pardon-churchyard was pulled down by the Protector
Somerset, in the reign of Edward the Sixth, and the
materials employed in the erection of his own palace in the
Strand. It was the discussion of these singular paintings,
and of the designs on the same subject ascribed to Holbein,
that led the Earl of Rochester and his companions to propose the fantastic spectacle above described. With the
disposition which this reckless nobleman possessed to
turn the most solemn and appalling subjects to jest, he
thought no season so fitting for such an entertainment
as the present—just as in our own time the lively Parisians
made the cholera, while raging in their city, the subject of
a carnival pastime. The exhibition witnessed by Chowles
and Judith was a rehearsal of the masque intended to be
represented in the cathedral on the following night.

Again marshalling his band, the Earl of Rochester beat
his drum, and skipping before them, led the way towards
the south door of the cathedral, which was thrown open
by an unseen hand, and the procession glided through it
like a troop of spectres. Chowles, whose appearance was
not unlike that of an animated skeleton, was seized with
a strange desire to join in what was going forward, and
taking off his doublet, and baring his bony arms and
legs, he followed the others, dancing round Judith in the

same manner that the other skeletons danced round their partners.

On reaching the Convocation House, a door was opened, and the procession entered the cloisters; and here Chowles dragging Judith into the area between him and the beautiful structure they surrounded, began a dance of so extraordinary a character that the whole troop collected round to witness it. Rochester beat his drum, and the other representatives of mortality who were provided with musical instruments struck up a wild kind of accompaniment, to which Chowles executed the most grotesque flourishes. So wildly excited did he become, and such extravagances did he commit, that even Judith stared aghast at him, and began to think his wits were fled. Now he whirled round her—now sprang high into the air —now twined his lean arms round her waist—now peeped over one shoulder, now over the other—and at last gripped her neck so forcibly, that he might perhaps have strangled her, if she had not broken from him, and dealt him a severe blow that brought him senseless to the ground. On recovering he found himself in the arched entrance of a large octagonal chamber, lighted at each side by a long pointed window filled with stained glass. Round this chamber ran a wide stone bench, with a richly-carved back of the same material, on which the masquers were seated, and opposite the entrance was a raised seat, ordinarily allotted to the dean, but now occupied by the Earl of Rochester. A circular oak table stood in the midst of the chamber, covered with magnificent silver dishes heaped with the choicest viands, which were handed to the guests by the earl's servants, all of whom represented skeletons, and it had a strange effect, to behold these ghastly objects filling the cups of the revellers, bending obsequiously before some blooming dame, or crowding round their spectral-looking lord.

At first, Chowles was so confused, that he thought he must have awakened in another world, but by degrees he called to mind what occurred, and ascertained from Judith that he was in the Convocation House. Getting up, he joined the train of grisly attendants, and acquitted

himself so well that the earl engaged him as performer in
the masque. He was furthermore informed that, in all
probability, the king himself, with many of his favourite
nobles, and the chief court beauties, would be present to
witness the spectacle.

The banquet over, word was brought that chairs and
coaches were without, and the company departed, leaving
behind only a few attendants, who remained to put
matters in order.

While they were thus occupied, Judith, who had fixed
her greedy eyes upon the plate, observed, in an undertone
to Chowles, " There will be fine plunder for us. We must
manage to carry off all that plate while they are engaged
in the masque."

" You must do it yourself, then," returned Chowles,
in the same tone—" for I shall have to play a principal
part in the entertainment, and as the king himself will
be present, I cannot give up such an opportunity of dis-
tinguishing myself."

" You can have no share in the prize, if you lend no
assistance, replied Judith, with a dissatisfied look.

" Of course not," rejoined Chowles; " on this occasion
it is all yours. The Dance of Death is too much to my
taste to be given up."

Perceiving they were noticed, Chowles and Judith then
left the Convocation House, and returned to the vault
in Saint Faith's, nor did they emerge from it until late
on the following day.

Some rumour of the masque having gone abroad, towards evening a crowd, chiefly composed of the most
worthless order of society, collected under the portico
at the western entrance, and the great doors being opened
by Chowles, they entered the cathedral. Thus was this
sacred building once more invaded—once again a scene
of noise, riot, and confusion—its vaulted roofs, instead
of echoing the voice of prayer, or the choral hymn,
resounded with loud laughter, imprecations, and licentious discourse. This disorder, however, was kept in
some bounds by a strong body of the royal guard, who
soon afterwards arrived, and stationing themselves in

parties of three or four at each of the massive columns
flanking the aisles, maintained some show of decorum.
Besides these, there were others of the royal attendants
bearing torches who walked from place to place, and
compelled all loiterers in dark corners to proceed to the
nave.

A little before midnight, the great doors were again
thrown open, and a large troop of richly-attired personages,
all wearing masks, were admitted. For a short time they
paced to and fro between its shafted pillars, gazing at the
spectators grouped around, and evidently from their jests
and laughter not a little entertained by the scene. As the
clock struck twelve, however, all sounds were hushed, and
the courtly party stationed themselves on the steps leading
to the choir. At the same moment, also, the torches were
extinguished, and the whole of the building buried in
profound darkness. Presently after, a sound was heard
of footsteps approaching the nave, but nothing could be
discerned. Expectation was kept on the rack for some
minutes, during which many a stifled cry was heard from
those whose courage failed them at this trying juncture.
All at once, a blue light illumined the nave, and partially
revealed the lofty pillars by which it was surrounded.
By this light the whole of the ghostly company could be
seen drawn up near the western door. They were arranged
two and two, a skeleton standing as before on the right of
each character. The procession next marched slowly
and silently towards the choir, and drew up at the foot of
the steps, to give the royal party an opportunity of examining them. After pausing there for a few minutes,
Rochester, in the dress of the larger skeleton, started off
and, beating his drum, was followed by the pope and his
attendant skeleton. This couple having danced together
for some minutes, to the infinite diversion of the spectators, disappeared behind a pillar, and were succeeded
by the monarch and a second skeleton. These, in their
turn, gave way to the cardinal and his companion, and so
on till the whole of the masquers had exhibited themselves,
when at a signal from the earl the party reappeared, and
formed a ring round him. The dance was executed with

great spirit, and elicited tumultuous applause from all the beholders. The earl now retired, and Chowles took his place. He was clothed in an elastic dress painted of a leaden and cadaverous colour, which fitted closely to his fleshless figure, and defined all his angularities. He carried an hour-glass in one hand, and a dart in the other, and in the course of the dance kept continually pointing the latter at those who moved around him. His feats of the previous evening were nothing to his present achievements. His joints creaked, and his eyes flamed like burning coals. As he continued, his excitement increased. He bounded higher, and his countenance assumed so hideous an expression, that those near him recoiled in terror, crying, " Death himself had broke loose among them." The consternation soon became general. The masquers fled in dismay, and scampered along the aisles scarcely knowing whither they were going. Delighted with the alarm he occasioned, Chowles chased a large party along the northern aisle, and was pursuing them across the transept upon which it opened, when he was arrested in his turn by another equally formidable figure, who suddenly placed himself in his path.

" Hold ! " exclaimed Solomon Eagle—for it was the enthusiast—in a voice of thunder, " it is time this scandalous exhibition should cease. Know all ye who make a mockery of death that His power will be speedily and fearfully approved upon you. Think not to escape the vengeance of the Great Being whose temple you have profaned. And you, O king ! who have sanctioned these evil doings by your presence, and who by your own dissolute life set a pernicious example to all your subjects, know that your city shall be utterly laid waste, first by plague and then by fire. Tremble ! my warning is as terrible and true as the handwriting on the wall."

" Who art thou who holdest this language towards me ? " demanded Charles.

" I am called Solomon Eagle," replied the enthusiast, " and am charged with a mission from on high to warn your doomed people of their fate. Be warned yourself, sire. Your end will be sudden. You will be snatched away in the midst of your guilty pleasure, and with little time for repentance. Be warned, I say again."

With this he turned to depart.

" Secure the knave," cried Charles, angrily. " He shall be soundly scourged for his insolence."

But bursting through the guard, Solomon Eagle ran swiftly up the choir and disappeared, nor could his pursuers discover any traces of him.

" Strange ! " exclaimed the king, when he was told of the enthusiast's escape. " Let us go to supper. This masque has given me the vapours."

" Pray Heaven it has not given us the plague," observed the fair Stewart, who stood beside him, taking his arm.

" It is to be hoped not," rejoined Charles; " but, odds fish ! it is a most dismal affair."

" It is so, in more ways than one," replied Rochester, " for I have just learnt that all my best plate has been carried off from the Convocation House. I shall only be able to offer your Majesty and your fair partner a sorry supper."

CHAPTER IV

The Plague-pit

ON being made acquainted by Leonard, who helped him out of the pest-cart, with the danger he had run, the piper uttered a cry of terror, and swooned away. The buriers seeing how matters stood, and that their superstitious fears were altogether groundless, now returned, and one of them producing a phial of vinegar, sprinkled the fainting man with it, and speedily brought him to himself. But though so far recovered, his terror had by no means abated, and he declared his firm conviction that he was infected by the pestilence.

" I have been carried towards the plague-pit by mistake," he said. " I shall soon be conveyed thither in right earnest, and not have the power of frightening away my conductors on the road."

" Pooh ! pooh ! " cried one of the buriers, jestingly.
" I hope you will often ride with us, and play us many a
merry tune as you go. You shall always be welcome to a
seat in the cart."

" Be of good cheer," added Leonard, " and all will
be well. Come with me to an apothecary's shop, and
I will procure a cordial for you, which shall speedily
dispel your qualms."

The piper shook his head, and replied, with a deep
groan, that he was certain all was over with him.

" However, I will not reject your kindness," he added,
" though I feel I am past the help of medicine."

With this, he whistled to Bell, who was skipping about
Leonard, having recognised him on his first approach,
and they proceeded towards the second postern in London-
wall, between Moorgate and Cripplegate; while the
buriers, laughing heartily at the adventure, took their way
towards the plague-pit, and discharged their dreadful
load within it. Arrived in Basinghall-street, and looking
round, Leonard soon discovered by the links at the door,
as well as by the crowd collected before it,—for day and
night the apothecaries' dwellings were besieged by the
sick,—the shop of which he was in search. It was long
before they could obtain admittance, and during this
time the piper said he felt himself getting rapidly worse;
but, imagining he was merely labouring under the effect
of fright, Leonard paid little attention to his complaints.
The apothecary, however, no sooner set eyes upon him
than he pronounced him infected, and, on examination,
it proved that the fatal tokens had already appeared.

" I knew it was so," cried the piper. " Take me to the
pest-house—take me to the pest-house ! "

" His desire had better be complied with," observed the
apothecary. " He is able to walk thither now, but I will
not answer for his being able to do so two hours hence.
It is a bad case," he added in an undertone to Leonard.

Feeing the apothecary, Leonard set out with the piper,
and passing through Cripplegate, they entered the open
fields. Here they paused for a moment, and the little dog
ran round and round them, barking gleefully.

"Poor Bell!" cried the piper; "what will become of thee when I am gone?"

"If you will intrust her to me, I will take care of her," replied Leonard.

"She is yours," rejoined the piper, in a voice hoarse with emotion. "Be kind to her for my sake, and for the sake of her unfortunate mistress."

"Since you have alluded to your daughter," returned Leonard, "I must tell you what has become of her. I have not hitherto mentioned the subject, fearing it might distress you."

"Have no further consideration, but speak out," rejoined the piper. "Be it what it may, I will bear it like a man."

Leonard then briefly recounted all that had occurred, describing Nizza's disguise as a page, and her forcible abduction by Parravicin. He was frequently interrupted by the groans of his hearer, who at last gave vent to his rage and anguish in words.

"Heaven's direst curse upon her ravisher!" he cried. "May he endure worse misery than I now endure! She is lost for ever."

"She may yet be preserved," rejoined Leonard. "Doctor Hodges thinks he has discovered her retreat, and I will not rest till I find her."

"No—no, you will never find her," replied the piper, bitterly; "or if you do, it will be only to bewail her ruin."

His rage then gave way to such an access of grief, that, letting his head fall on Leonard's shoulder, he wept aloud.

"There is a secret connected with that poor girl," he said, at length, controlling his emotion by a powerful effort, "which must now go to the grave with me. The knowledge of it would only add to her distress."

"You view the matter too unfavourably," replied Leonard; "and if the secret is of any moment, I entreat you to confide it to me. If your worst apprehensions should prove well founded, I promise you it shall never be revealed to her."

"On that condition only, I will confide it to you,"

replied the piper ; " but not now—not now—to-morrow morning, if I am alive."

" It may be out of your power then," returned Leonard. " For your daughter's sake, I urge you not to delay."

" It is for her sake I am silent," rejoined the piper. " Come along—come along ! " he added, hurrying forward. " Are we far from the pest-house ? My strength is failing me."

On arriving at their destination, they were readily admitted to the asylum, but a slight difficulty arose, which, however, was speedily obviated. All the couches were filled, but on examining them, it was found that one of the sick persons had just been released from his sufferings, and the body being removed, the piper was allowed to take its place. Leonard remained by him for a short time, but, overpowered by the pestilential effluvia, and the sight of so many miserable objects, he was compelled to seek the open air. Returning, however, shortly afterwards, he found the piper in a very perturbed state. On hearing Leonard's voice he appeared greatly relieved, and, taking his gown from beneath his pillow, gave it to him, and desired him to unrip a part of the garment, in which it was evident something was sewn. The apprentice complied, and a small packet dropped forth.

" Take it," said the piper ; " and if I die, and Nizza should happily be preserved from her ravisher, give it her. But not otherwise,—not otherwise. Implore her to forgive me—to pity me."

" Forgive you—her father ? " cried Leonard, in astonishment.

" That packet will explain all," replied the piper in a troubled tone. " You promised to take charge of poor Bell," he added, drawing forth the little animal, who had crept to the foot of the bed,—" here she is. Farewell ! my faithful friend." he added, pressing his rough lips to her forehead, while she whined piteously, as if beseeching him to allow her to remain; " farewell for ever."

" Not for ever. I trust," replied Leonard. taking her gently from him.

" And now you had better go." said the piper. " Return
if you can to-morrow."

" I will,—I will," replied Leonard. And he hurried out
of the room.

He was followed to the door by the young chirurgeon—
the same who had accompanied Mr. Bloundel during his
inspection of the pest-house,—and he inquired of him
if he thought the piper's case utterly hopeless.

" Not utterly so," replied the young man. " I shall be
able to speak more positively in a few hours. At present,
I think, with care and attention, there *is* a chance of his
recovery."

Much comforted by this assurance, Leonard departed,
and afraid to put Bell to the ground lest she should run
back to her master, he continued to carry her, and endeavoured to attach her to him by caresses and endear-
ments. The little animal showed her sense of his kindness
by licking his hands, but she still remained inconsolable,
and ever and anon struggled to get free. Making the best
of his way to Wood-street, he entered the hutch, and
placing a little straw in one corner for Bell, threw himself
on a bench and dropped asleep. At six o'clock he was
awakened by the barking of the dog, and opening the door
beheld Dallison. The grocer was at the window above,
and about to let down a basket of provisions to
them. To Leonard's eager inquiries after Amabel, Mr.
Bloundel replied by a melancholy shake of the head,
and soon afterwards withdrew. With a sad heart, the
apprentice then broke his fast,—not forgetting at the
same time the wants of his little companion,—and
finding he was not required by his master, he proceeded
to Doctor Hodges' residence. He was fortunate enough
to find the friendly physician at home; and, after
relating to him what had occurred, committed the packet
to his custody.

" It will be safer in your keeping than mine," he said;
" and if anything should happen to me, you will, I am
sure, observe the wishes of the poor piper."

" Rely upon it, I will," replied Hodges. " I am sorry
to tell you I have been misled as to the clue I fancied I

had obtained to Nizza's retreat. We are as far from the mark as ever."

" Might not the real name of the villain who has assumed the name of Sir Paul Parravicin be ascertained from the Earl of Rochester ? " rejoined Leonard.

" So I thought," replied Hodges; " and I made the attempt yesterday, but it failed. I was at Whitehall, and finding the earl in the king's presence, suddenly asked him where I could find his friend Sir Paul Parravicin. He looked surprised at the question, glanced significantly at the monarch, and then carelessly answered that he knew no such person."

" A strange idea crosses me," cried Leonard. " Can it be the king who has assumed this disguise ? "

" At one time I suspected as much," rejoined Hodges; " but setting aside your description of the person, which does not tally with that of Charles, I am satisfied from other circumstances it is not so. After all, I should not wonder if poor Bell," smoothing her long silky ears as she lay in the apprentice's arms. " should help us to discover her mistress. And now," he added, " I shall go to Wood-street to inquire after Amabel, and will then accompany you to the pest-house. From what you tell me the young chirurgeon said of the piper, I do not despair of his recovery."

" Poor as his chance may appear, it is better, I fear, than Amabel's," sighed the apprentice.

" Ah ! " exclaimed Hodges, in a sorrowful tone. " hers is slight indeed."

And perceiving that the apprentice was greatly moved, he waited for a moment till he had recovered himself, and then, motioning him to follow him, they quitted the house together.

On reaching Mr. Bloundel's habitation, Leonard pulled the cord in the hutch, and the grocer appeared at the window.

" My daughter has not left her bed this morning," he said, in answer to the doctor's inquiries, " and I fear she is much worse. My wife is with her. It would be a great satisfaction to me if you would see her again."

After some little hesitation, Hodges assented, and was drawn up as before. He returned in about half an hour, and his grave countenance convinced Leonard that his worst anticipations were correct. He therefore forebore to question him, and they walked towards Cripplegate in silence.

On emerging into the fields, Hodges observed to his companion, " It is strange that I who daily witness such dreadful suffering should be pained by the gradual and easy decline of Amabel. But so it is. Her case touches me more than the worst I have seen of the plague."

" I can easily account for the feeling," groaned Leonard.

" I am happy to say I have prevailed on her, if she does not improve in a short time,—and there is not the slightest chance of it,—to try the effect of a removal to the country. Her father, also, consents to the plan."

" I am glad to hear it," replied Leonard. " But whither will she go, and who will watch over her ? "

" That is not yet settled," rejoined Hodges.

" Oh ! that I might be permitted to undertake the office ! " cried Leonard, passionately.

" Restrain yourself," said Hodges, in a tone of slight rebuke. " Fitting attendance will be found, if needed."

The conversation then dropped, and they walked briskly forward. They were now within a short distance of the pest-house, and Leonard, hearing footsteps behind him, turned and beheld a closed litter, borne by two stout porters, and evidently containing a plague patient. He stepped aside to let it pass, when Bell suddenly pricking her ears, uttered a singular cry, and bursting from him, flew after the litter, leaping against it and barking joyfully. The porters, who were proceeding at a quick pace, tried to drive her away, but without effect, and she continued her cries until they reached the gates of the pest-house. In vain Leonard whistled to her, and called her back. She paid no attention whatever to him.

" I almost begin to fear," said Hodges, unable to repress a shudder, " that the poor animal will, indeed, be the means of discovering for us the object of our search."

"I understand what you mean," rejoined Leonard, "and am of the same opinion as yourself. Heaven grant we may be mistaken!"

And as he spoke, he ran forward, and followed by Hodges reached the pest-house just as the litter was taken into it.

"Silence that accursed dog," cried one of the porters, "and bid a nurse attend us. We have a patient for the women's ward.

"Let me see her," cried Hodges. "I am a physician."

"Readily, sir," replied the porter. "It is almost over with her, poor soul! It would have saved time and trouble to take her to the plague-pit at once. She cannot last many hours. Curse the dog! Will it never cease howling?"

Leonard here seized Bell, fearing she might do some mischief, and with a sad foreboding beheld the man draw back the curtains of the litter. His fears proved well founded. There, stretched upon the couch, with her dark hair unbound, and flowing in wild disorder over her neck, lay Nizza Macascree. The ghastly paleness of her face could not, however, entirely rob it of its beauty, and her dark eyes were glazed and lustreless. At the sight of her mistress, poor Bell uttered so piteous a cry, that Leonard, moved by compassion, placed her on the pillow beside her, and the sagacious animal did not attempt to approach nearer, but merely licked her cheek. Roused by the touch, Nizza turned to see what was near her, and recognising the animal, made a movement to strain her to her bosom, but the pain she endured was so intense that she sank back with a deep groan.

"From whom did you receive this young woman?" demanded Hodges of one of the porters.

"She was brought to us by two richly-attired lacqueys," replied the man, "in this very litter. They paid us to carry her here without loss of time."

"You have an idea whose servants they were?" pursued Hodges.

"Not the least," replied the fellow; "but I should judge, from the richness of their dress, that they belonged to some nobleman."

"Did they belong to the royal household?" inquired Leonard.

"No, no," rejoined the man. "I am certain as to that."

"The poor girl shall not remain here," observed Hodges, to the apprentice. "You must convey her to my residence in Great Knightrider-street," he added, to the porters.

"We will convey her wherever you please," replied the men, "if we are paid for our trouble."

And they were about to close the curtains, when Nizza, having caught sight of the apprentice, slightly raised herself, and cried, in a voice of the utmost anxiety, "Is that you, Leonard?"

"It is," he replied, approaching her.

"Then I shall die happy, since I have seen you once more," she said. "Oh, do not stay near me You may catch the infection."

"Nizza," said Leonard, disregarding the caution, and breathing the words in her ear; "allay my fears by a word. You have not fallen a victim to the villain who carried you away?"

"I have not, Leonard," she replied, solemnly. "I resisted his importunities, his threats, his violence, and would have slain myself rather than have yielded to him. The plague, at length, came to my rescue, and I have reason to be grateful to it; for it has not only delivered me from him, but has brought me to you."

"I must now impose silence upon you," interposed Hodges, laying his finger on his lips: "further conversation will be hurtful."

"One question more and I have done," replied Nizza. "How came Bell with you—and where is my father? Nothing has happened to him?" she continued, observing Leonard's countenance change. "Speak! do not keep me in suspense. Your silence fills me with apprehension. Speak, I implore you. He is dead?"

"No," replied Leonard, "he is not dead—but he is an inmate of this place."

"Ah!" exclaimed Nizza, falling back senseless upon the pillow.

And in this state she was conveyed with the greatest
expedition to the doctor's residence.

Leonard only tarried to visit the piper, whom he found
slightly delirious, and unable to hold any conversation
with him, and promising to return in the evening, he set
out after the litter. Nizza was placed in the best apartment of the doctor's house, and attended by an experienced
and trustworthy nurse. But Hodges positively refused
to let Leonard see her again, affirming that the excitement was too much for her, and might militate against the
chance of her recovery.

" I am not without hopes of bringing her through," he
said, " and though it will be a severe struggle, yet as she
has youth and a good constitution on her side, I do not
despair. If she herself would second me, I should be yet
more confident."

" How mean you ? " inquired Leonard.

" I think if she thought life worth a struggle—if, in
short, she believed you would return her attachment, she
would rally," answered Hodges.

" I cannot consent to deceive her thus," rejoined
Leonard, sadly. " My heart is fixed elsewhere."

" Your heart is fixed upon one who will soon be in her
grave," replied the doctor.

" And with her my affections will be buried," rejoined
Leonard, turning away to hide his tears.

So well was the doctor's solicitude rewarded, that three
days after Nizza had come under his care, he pronounced
her out of danger. But the violence of the attack left her
so weak and exhausted, that he still would not allow an
interview to take place between her and Leonard. During
all this time Bell never left her side, and her presence was
an inexpressible comfort to her. The piper, too, was
slowly recovering, and Leonard, who daily visited him,
was glad to learn from the young chirurgeon that he
would be able to leave the pest-house shortly. Having
ascertained from Leonard that his daughter was under
the care of Doctor Hodges, and likely to do well, the piper
begged so earnestly that the packet might not be delivered
to her, that after some consultation with Hodges, Leonard

restored it to him. He was delighted to get it back, felt it carefully over to ascertain that the seals were unbroken, and satisfied that all was safe, had it again sewn up in his gown, which he placed under his pillow.

" I would rather disclose the secret to her by word of mouth than in any other way," he said.

Leonard felt doubtful whether the secret would now be disclosed at all, but he made no remark.

Night was drawing on as he quitted the pest-house, and he determined to take this opportunity of visiting the great plague-pit, which lay about a quarter of a mile distant, in a line with the church of All-hallows-in-the-wall, and he accordingly proceeded in that direction. The pit which he was about to visit was about forty feet long, twenty wide, and the like number deep. Into this tremendous chasm the dead were promiscuously thrown, without regard to sex or condition, generally stripped of their clothing, and covered with a slight layer of earth and quicklime.

The sun was setting as Leonard walked towards this dismal place, and he thought he had never witnessed so magnificent a sight. Indeed, it was remarked that at this fatal season the sunsets were unusually splendid. The glorious orb sank slowly behind Saint Paul's, which formed a prominent object in the view from the fields, and threw out its central tower, its massive roof, and the the two lesser towers flanking the portico, into strong relief. Leonard gazed at the mighty fabric, which seemed dilated to twice its size by this light, and wondered whether it was possible that it could ever be destroyed, as predicted by Solomon Eagle.

Long after the sun had set, the sky was stained with crimson, and the grey walls of the city were tinged with rosy radiance. The heat was intense, and Leonard, to cool himself, sat down in the thick grass—for though the crops were ready for the scythe, no mowers could be found,—and gazing upwards strove to mount in spirit from the tainted earth towards Heaven. After awhile he arose, and proceeded towards the plague-pit. The grass was trampled down near it, and there were marks of frequent cart-wheels upon the sod. Great heaps of soil, thrown out of the excavation, lay on either side. Holding a handkerchief steeped in vinegar to his face, Leonard ventured to the brink of the pit. But even this precaution could not conteract the horrible effluvia arising from it. It was more than half-filled with dead bodies, and through the putrid and heaving mass many disjointed limbs and ghastly faces could be discerned, the long hair of women, and the tiny arms of children, appearing on the surface. It was a horrible sight—so horrible, that it possessed a fascination peculiar to itself, and in spite of his loathing, Leonard lingered to gaze at it. Strange and fantastic thoughts possessed him. He fancied that the legs and arms moved,—that the eyes of some of the corpses opened and glared at him—and that the whole rotting mass was endowed with animation. So appalled was he by this idea that he turned away, and at that moment beheld a vehicle approaching. It was the dead-cart, charged with a heavy load to increase the already redundant heap.

The same inexplicable and irresistible feeling of curiosity that induced Leonard to continue gazing upon the loathly objects in the pit, now prompted him to stay and see what would ensue. Two persons were with the cart, and one of them, to Leonard's infinite surprise and disgust, proved to be Chowles. He had no time, however, for the expression of any sentiment, for the cart halted at a little distance from him, when its conductors, turning it round, backed it towards the edge of the pit. The horse was then taken out, and Chowles calling to Leonard, the latter involuntarily knelt down to guide its descent, while the other assistant, who had proceeded to the farther side of the chasm, threw the light of a lantern full upon the grisly load, which was thus shot into the gulf below.

Shovelling a sufficient quantity of earth and lime into the pit to cover the bodies, Chowles and his companion departed, leaving Leonard alone. He continued there a few moments longer, and was about to follow them, when a prolonged and piercing cry smote his ear, and looking in the direction of the sound, he perceived a figure running with great swiftness towards the pit. As no pursuers appeared, Leonard could scarcely doubt that this was one of the distracted persons he had heard of, who, in the frenzy produced by the intolerable anguish of their sores, would often rush to the plague-pit and bury them- selves, and he therefore resolved, if possible, to prevent the fatal attempt. Accordingly he placed himself in the way of the runner, and endeavoured with outstretched arms to stop him. But the latter dashed him aside with great violence, and hurrying to the brink of the pit, uttered a fearful cry, and exclaiming. " She is here ! she is here !— I shall find her amongst them ! " flung himself into the abyss.

As soon as he could shake off the horror inspired by this dreadful action, Leonard ran to the pit, and gazing into it, beheld him by the imperfect light struggling in the horrible mass in which he was partially immersed. The frenzied man had now, however, begun to repent his rashness, and cried out for aid. But this Leonard found it impossible to afford him; and, seeing he must speedily perish if left to himself, he ran after the dead- cart, and overtaking it just as it reached Moorgate, informed Chowles what had happened, and begged him to return.

" There will be no use in helping him out," rejoined Chowles, in a tone of indifference. " We shall have to take him back in a couple of hours. No, no; let him remain where he is. There is scarcely a night that some crazy being does not destroy himself in the same way. We never concern ourselves about such persons, except to strip them of their apparel."

" Unfeeling wretch ! " cried Leonard, unable to restrain his indignation. " Give me your fork. and I will pull him out myself."

Instead of surrendering the implement, Chowles flourished it over his head with the intention of striking the apprentice. but the latter nimbly avoided the blow, and snatching it from his grasp, ran back to the plague- pit. He was followed by Chowles and the burier, who threatened him with loud oaths. Regardless of their menaces, Leonard fixed the hook in the dress of the struggling man, and exerting all his strength, drew him out of the abyss. He had just lodged him in safety on the brink when Chowles and his companion came up.

"Keep off!" cried Leonard, brandishing the fork as he spoke, "you shall neither commit robbery nor murder here. If you will assist this unfortunate gentleman, I have no doubt you will be well rewarded. If not, get hence, or advance at your peril."

"Well," returned Chowles, who began to fancy something might be made of the matter, "if you think we should be rewarded, we would convey the gentleman back to his own home, provided we can ascertain where it is. But I am afraid he may die on the way."

"In that case you can apply to his friends," rejoined Leonard. "He must not be abandoned thus."

"First, let us know who he is," returned Chowles. "Is he able to speak?"

"I know not," answered Leonard. "Bring the lantern this way, and let us examine his countenance."

Chowles complied, and held the light over the unfortunate person. His attire was rich, but in great disorder, and sullied by the loathsome mass in which he had been plunged. He was in the flower of youth, and his features must have been remarkable for their grace and beauty, but they were now of a livid hue, and swollen and distorted by pain. Still, Leonard recognised them.

"Gracious Heaven!" he exclaimed. "It is Sir Paul Parravicin."

"Sir Paul Parravicin!" echoed Chowles. "By all that's wonderful, so it is! Here is a lucky chance! Bring the dead-cart hither, Jonas, quick—quick! I shall put him under the care of Judith Malmayns."

And the burier hurried off as fast as his legs could carry him.

"Had I known who it was," exclaimed Leonard, gazing with abhorrence at the miserable object before him, "I would have left him to die the death he so richly merits!"

A deep groan broke from the sufferer.

"Have no fear, Sir Paul," said Chowles. "You are in

good hands. Every care shall be taken of you, and you shall be cured by Judith Malmayns."

" She shall not come near me," rejoined Parravicin, faintly. " You will take care of me? " he added, in an imploring tone, to Leonard.

" You appeal in vain to me," rejoined the apprentice, sternly. " You are justly punished for your treatment of Nizza Macascree."

" I am—I am," groaned Parravicin, " but she will be speedily avenged. I shall soon join her in that pit."

" She is not there," replied Leonard, bitterly. " She is fast recovering from the plague."

" Is she not dead ? " demanded Parravicin, with frightful eagerness. " I was told she was thrown into that horrible chasm."

" You were deceived," replied Leonard. " She was taken to the pest-house by your orders, and would have perished if she had not found a friend to aid her. She is now out danger."

" Then I no longer desire to die," cried Parravicin, desperately. " I will live—live."

" Do not delude yourself," replied Leonard, coldly, " you have little chance of recovery, and should employ the short time left you in praying to Heaven for forgiveness of your sins."

" Tush ! " exclaimed Parravicin, fiercely, " I shall not weary Heaven with ineffectual supplications. I well know I am past all forgiveness. No," he added, with a fearful imprecation, " since Nizza is alive, I will not die."

" Right, Sir Paul, right," rejoined Chowles, " put a bold face on it, and I will answer for it you will get over the attack. Have no fear of Judith Malmayns," he added, in a significant tone. " However she may treat others, she will cure *you.*"

" I will make it worth her while to do so," rejoined Parravicin.

" Here is the cart," cried Chowles, seeing the vehicle approach. " I will take you in the first place to Saint Paul's. Judith must see you as soon as possible."

" Take me where you please," rejoined Parravicin,

faintly, "and remember what I have said. If I die, the nurse will get nothing:—if I am cured, she shall be proportionately rewarded."

" I will not forget it," replied Chowles. And with the help of Jonas he placed the knight carefully in the cart. " You need not trouble yourself further about him," he added to Leonard.

" Before he quits this place I must know who he is," rejoined the latter, placing himself at the horse's head.

" You know his name as well as I do," replied Chowles.

" Parravicin is not his real name," rejoined Leonard.

" Indeed ! " exclaimed Chowles, " this is news to me. But no matter who he is, he is rich enough to pay well. So stand aside, and let us go. We have no time to waste in further parleying."

" I will not move till my question is answered." replied Leonard.

" We will see that," said Jonas, approaching him behind, and dealing him so severe a blow on the head that he stretched him senseless on the ground. " Shall we throw him into the pit ? " he added to Chowles.

The latter hesitated for a moment, and then said, " No, no, it is not worth while. It may bring us into trouble. We have no time to lose." And they then put the cart in motion, and took the way to Saint Paul's.

On coming to himself, Leonard had some difficulty in recalling what had happened; and when the whole train of circumstances rushed upon his mind, he congratulated himself that he had escaped further injury. " When I think of the hands I have been placed in," he murmured, " I cannot but be grateful that they did not throw me into the pit, where no discovery could have been made as to how I came to an end. But I will not rest till I have ascertained the name and rank of Nizza's persecutor. I have no doubt they have taken him to Saint Paul's, and will proceed thither at once."

With this view, he hastened towards the nearest city gate, and passing through it, shaped his course towards the cathedral. It was a fine starlight night, and though there was no moon, the myriad lustres glowing in the deep and cloudless vault, rendered every object plainly distinguishable. At this hour, little restraint was placed upon the sick, and they wandered about the streets uttering dismal cries. Some would fling themselves upon bulks or steps, where they were not unfrequently found the next morning bereft of life. Most of those not attacked by the distemper kept close house; but there were some few reckless beings who passed the night in the wildest revelry, braving the fate awaiting them. As Leonard passed Saint Michael's church, in Basinghall-street, he perceived, to his great surprise, that it was lighted up, and at first supposed some service was going on within it, but on approaching he heard strains of lively and most irreverent music issuing from within. Pushing open the door, he entered the sacred edifice, and found it occupied by a party of twenty young men, accompanied by a like number of females, some of whom were playing at dice and cards, some drinking others singing Bacchanalian melodies, others dancing along the aisles to the notes of a theorbo and spinet. Leonard was so inexpressibly shocked by what he beheld that, unable to contain himself, he mounted the steps of the pulpit, and called to them in a loud voice to desist from their scandalous conduct, and no longer profane the house of God. But they treated his remonstrances with laughter and derision, and some of the party forming themselves into a group round the pulpit, entreated him to preach to them.

"We want a little variety," said one of the group, a good-looking young man, upon whom the wine had evidently made some impression,—"we are tired of drinking and play, and may as well listen to a sermon, especially an original one. Hold forth to us, I say."

"I would hold forth till daybreak, if I thought it would produce any impression," returned Leonard. "But I perceive you are too hardened to be aroused to repentance."

"Repentance!" cried another of the assemblage. "Do you know whom you address? These gentlemen are the Brotherhood of Saint Michael, and I am the principal.

We are determined to enjoy the few days or hours we may have left—that is all. We are not afraid of the future, and are resolved to make the most of the present."

" Ay, ay," cried the others, with a great shout of laughter, which, however, was interrupted by a cry of anguish from one of the party.

" There is another person seized," said the principal; " take him away, brothers. This is owing to listening to a sermon. Let us return to our wine."

" Will you not accept this awful warning ? " cried Leonard. " You will all share your companion's fate."

" We anticipate nothing else," returned the principal: " and are therefore resolved to banish reflection. A week ago, the Brotherhood of Saint Michael consisted of forty persons. We are already diminished to half the number, but are not the less merry on that account. On the contrary, we are more jovial than ever. We have agreed that whoever shall be seized with the distemper, shall be instantly conveyed to the pest-house, so that the hilarity of the others shall not be interrupted. The poor fellow who has just been attacked has left behind him a beautiful mistress. She is yours, if you choose to join us."

" Ay, stop with us," cried a young and very pretty woman, taking his hand, and drawing him towards the company who were dancing beneath the aisles.

But Leonard disengaged himself, and hurried away amid the laughter and hootings of the assemblage. The streets, despite their desolate appearance, were preferable to the spot he had just quitted, and he seemed to breathe more freely when he got to a little distance from the polluted fane. He had now entered Wood-street, but all was as still as death, and he paused to gaze up at his master's window, but there was no one at it. Many a lover, unable to behold the object of his affections, has in some measure satisfied the yearning of his heart by gazing at her dwelling, and feeling he was near her. Many a sad heart has been cheered by beholding a light at a window, or a shadow on its closed curtains, and such would have been Leonard's feelings if he had not been depressed by the thought of Amabel's precarious state of health.

While thus wrapt in mournful thought, he observed three figures slowly approaching from the farther end of the street, and he instinctively withdrew into a doorway. He had reason to congratulate himself upon the precaution, as, when the party drew nearer, he recognised with a pang that shot to his heart the voice of Rochester. A moment's observation from his place of concealment showed him that the earl was accompanied by Sir George Etherege and Pillichody. They paused within a short distance of him, and he could distinctly hear their conversation.

" You have not yet told us why you brought us here, my lord," said Etherege to Rochester, after the latter had gazed for a few moments in silence at the house. " Are you resolved to make another attempt to carry off the girl—and failing in it, to give her up for ever ? "

" You have guessed my purpose precisely," returned Rochester. " Doctor Hodges has informed a friend of mine that the pretty Amabel has fallen into a decline. The poor soul is, doubtless, pining for me, and it would be the height of inhumanity to let her perish."

Leonard ground his teeth with suppressed rage.

" Then you mean to make her Countess of Rochester after all," laughed Etherege. " I thought you had determined to carry off Mistress Mallett."

" Old Rowley declares he will send me to the Tower if I do," replied Rochester, " and though his threats would scarcely deter me from acting as I think proper, I have no inclination for marriage at present. What a pity, Etherege, that one cannot in these affairs have the money one's self, and give the wife to one's friend."

" That is easily accomplished," replied Etherege, laughingly; " especially where you have a friend so devoted as myself. But do you mean to carry off Amabel to-night ? "

" Ay, now we come to business," interposed Pillichody. " Bolts and barricadoes ! your lordship has only to say the word, and I will break into the house, and bear her off for you."

" Your former conduct is a good guarantee for your

present success, truly," returned Rochester, with a sneer. " No, no; I shall postpone my design for the present. I have ascertained from the source whence I obtained information of Amabel's illness, that she is to be removed into the country. This will exactly suit my purpose, and put her completely in my power."

" Then nothing is to be done to-night?" said Pillichody, secretly congratulating himself on his escape. " By my sword! I feel equal to the most desperate attempt."

" Your courage and dexterity must be reserved for some more favourable occasion," replied Rochester.

" If not to carry off the girl, I must again inquire why your lordship has come hither?" demanded Etherege.

" To be frank with you, my sole motive was to gaze at the house that contains her," replied Rochester, in a voice that bespoke his sincerity. " I have before told you, that she has a strong hold upon my heart. I have not seen her for some weeks, and during that time have endeavoured to obliterate her image by making love to a dozen others. But it will not do. She still continues absolute mistress of my affections. I sometimes think, if I can obtain her in no other way, I shall be rash enough to marry her."

" Pshaw! this must never be," said Etherege.

" Were I to lose her altogether, I should be inconsolable," cried Rochester.

" As inconsolable as I am for the rich widow of Watlingstreet, who died a fortnight ago of the plague, and left her wealth to her footman," replied Pillichody, drawing forth his handkerchief, and applying it to his eyes,— " oh! oh!"

" Silence, fool!" cried Rochester; " I am in no mood for buffoonery. If you shed tears for any one, it should be for your master."

" Truly, I am grieved for him," replied Pillichody; " but I object to the term ' master.' Sir Paul Parravicin, as he chooses to be called, is my patron, not my master. He permits me a very close familiarity, not to say friendship."

"Well, then, your patron," rejoined Rochester, scornfully. "How is he going on to-night?"

"I feared to tell your lordship," replied Pillichody, "lest it should spoil your mirth, but he broke out of his chamber a few hours ago, and has not been discovered since. Most likely, he will be found in the plague-pit or the Thames in the morning, for he was in such an infuriated state, that it is the opinion of his attendants he would certainly destroy himself. You know he was attacked two days after Nizza Macascree was seized by the pestilence, and his brain has been running upon the poor girl ever since."

"Alas!" exclaimed Rochester, "it is a sad end. I am wearied of this infected city, and shall be heartily glad to quit it. A few months in the country with Amabel will be enchanting."

"*Apropos* of melancholy subjects," said Etherege, "your masque of the Dance of Death has caused great consternation at court. Mistress Stewart declares she cannot get that strange fellow who performed such fantastic tricks in the skeleton-dance out of her head."

"You mean Chowles," replied the earl. "He is a singular being, certainly—once a coffin-maker, and now, I believe, a burier of the dead. He takes up his abode in a crypt in Saint Faith's, and leads an incomprehensible life. As we return, we shall pass the cathedral, and can see whether he is astir."

"Readily," replied Etherege. "Do you desire to tarry here longer, or shall we proceed before you, while you indulge your tender meditations undisturbed?"

"Leave me," replied Rochester, "I shall be glad to be alone for a few moments."

Etherege and Pillichody then proceeded slowly towards Cheapside, while the earl remained with his arms folded upon his breast, and his gaze fixed upon the house. Leonard watched him with intense curiosity, and had great difficulty in controlling himself. Though the earl was armed, while he had only his staff, he could have easily mastered him by assailing him unawares. But Leonard's generous nature revolted at the unworthy suggestion, and he resolved, if he attacked him at all, to give him time to stand upon his guard. A moment's reflection, however, satisfied him that his wisest course would be to remain concealed. He was now in possession of the earl's plan, and with the help of Doctor Hodges could easily defeat it; whereas if he appeared, it would be evident that he had overheard what had passed, and some other scheme, to which he could not be privy, would be necessarily adopted. Influenced by this consideration, he suffered the earl to depart unmolested, and when he had got to some distance, followed him. Rochester's companions were waiting for him in Cheapside, and joining them, they all three proceeded towards the cathedral.

They entered the great northern door, and Leonard, who was now well acquainted with all the approaches, passed through the door at the north side of the choir, to which he had been directed on a former occasion by Solomon Eagle. He found the party guided by the old verger—the only one of its former keepers who still lingered about the place,—and preparing to descend to Saint Faith's. Leonard followed as near as he could without exposing himself, and on gaining the subterranean church, easily contrived to screen himself behind the ponderous ranks of pillars.

By this time they had reached the door of the charnel. It was closed, but Rochester knocked against it, and Chowles presently appeared. He seemed greatly surprised at seeing the earl, nor was the latter less astonished when he learnt that Parravicin was within the vault. He desired to be shown to his friend, and Chowles ushered him into the crypt.

Leonard would have followed them, but as Etherege and the others declined entering the charnel, and remained at the door, he could not do so.

Shortly after this, the sick man was brought out, stretched upon a pallet, borne by Chowles and Judith, and the party proceeded slowly, and occasionally relieving each other, to the great western entrance, where a coach being procured by Pillichody, Parravicin was placed within it with Judith and Chowles, and orders being given in an undertone to the driver, he departed. The others then proceeded towards Ludgate, while Leonard, again disappointed, retraced his steps to Wood-street.

CHAPTER V

How Saint Paul's was Used as a Pest-house

THE distemper had by this time increased to such a frightful extent, that the pest-houses being found wholly inadequate to contain the number of sick persons sent to them, it was resolved by the civic authorities, who had obtained the sanction of the Dean and Chapter of Saint Paul's for that purpose, to convert the cathedral into a receptacle for the infected. Accordingly, a meeting was held in the Convocation House to make final arrangements. It was attended by Sir John Lawrence, the Lord Mayor ; by Sir George Waterman, and Sir Charles Doe, sheriffs; by Doctor Sheldon, Archbishop of Canterbury; by the Duke of Albemarle, the Earl of Craven, and a few other zealous and humane persons. Several members of the College of Physicians were likewise present, and, amongst others, Doctor Hodges; and the expediency of the measure being fully agreed upon, it was determined to carry it into immediate execution.

The cloisters surrounding the Convocation House were crowded with sick persons, drawn thither by the rumour of what was going forward; and when the meeting adjourned to the cathedral, these unfortunate beings followed them, and were with some difficulty kept aloof from the uninfected by the attendants. A very earnest and touching address was next pronounced by the archbishop. Calling upon his hearers to look upon themselves as already dead to the world,—to regard the present visitation as a just punishment of their sins, and to rejoice that their sufferings would be so soon terminated, when, if they sincerely and heartily repented, they would at once be transported from the depths of wretchedness and misery

K

to regions of unfading bliss; he concluded by stating that he, and all those around him, were prepared to devote themselves, without regard to their own safety, to the preservation of their fellow-citizens, and that they would leave nothing undone to stop the ravages of the devouring scourge.

It chanced that Leonard Holt was present on this occasion, and as he listened to the eloquent discourse of the archbishop and gazed at the group around him, all equally zealous in the good cause, and equally regardless of themselves, he could not but indulge a hope that their exertions might be crowned with success. It was indeed a touching sight to see the melancholy congregation to whom his address was delivered—many, nay, most of whom were on the verge of dissolution;—and Leonard Holt was so moved by the almost apostolic fervour of the prelate, that, but for the thought of Amabel, he might have followed the example of several of the auditors, and devoted himself altogether to the service of the sick.

His discourse concluded, the archbishop and most of his companions quitted the cathedral. Hodges, however, and three of the physicians, remained behind to superintend the necessary preparations. Shortly after, a large number of pallets were brought in, and ranged along the nave and aisles at short distances from each other; and before night the interior of the structure presented the complete appearance of an hospital. Acting under the directions of Doctor Hodges, Leonard Holt lent his assistance in arranging the pallets, in covering them with bedding and blankets, and in executing any other service required of him. A sufficient number of chirurgeons and nurses were then sent for, and such was the expedition used, that on that very night most of the pallets were occupied. Thus the cathedral underwent another afflicting change. A blight had come over it, mildewing its holy walls, and tainting and polluting its altars. Its aisles, once trodden by grave and reverend ecclesiastics and, subsequently haunted by rufflers, bullies, and other worthless characters, were now filled with miserable wretches, stricken with a loathsome and fatal distemper. Its chapels and shrines, formerly adorned with rich sculptures and costly ornaments, but stripped of them at times when they were looked upon as idolatrous and profane, were now occupied by nurses, chirurgeons, and their attendants; while every niche and corner was filled with surgical implements, phials, drugs, poultices, foul rags, and linen.

In less than a week after it had been converted into a pest-house, the cathedral was crowded to overflowing. Upwards of three hundred pallets were set up in the nave, in the aisles, in the transepts, and in the choir, and even in the chapels. But these proving insufficient, many poor wretches who were brought thither were placed on the cold flags, and protected only by a single blanket. At night, the scene was really terrific. The imperfect light borne by the attendants fell on the couches, and revealed the livid countenances of their occupants, while the vaulted roof rang with shrieks and groans so horrible and heart-piercing as to be scarcely endured, except by those whose nerves were firmly strung, or had not become blunted by their constant recurrence. At such times, too, some unhappy creature, frenzied by agony, would burst from his couch, and rend the air with his cries, until overtaken and over-powered by his attendants. On one occasion, it happened that a poor wretch, who had been thus caught, broke loose a second time, and darting through a door leading to the stone staircase in the northern transept gained the ambu-latory, and being closely followed, to escape his pursuers, sprang through one of the arched openings, and falling from a height of near sixty feet, was dashed in pieces on the flagged floor beneath.

A walk through this mighty lazar-house would have furnished a wholesome lesson to the most reckless observer. It seemed to contain all the sick of the city. And yet it was not so. Hundreds were expiring in their own dwellings, and the other pest-houses continued crowded as before. Still, as a far greater number of the infected were here congregated, and could be seen at one view, the picture was incomparably more impressive. Every part of the cathedral was occupied. Those who could not find room inside it crouched beneath the columns of the portico on rugs or blankets, and implored the chirurgeons as they passed to attend them. Want of room also drove others into Saint Faith's, and here the scene was, if possible, more hideous. In this dismal region it was found impossible to obtain a free circulation of air, and consequently the pestilential effluvia, unable to escape, acquired such a malignancy that it was almost certain destruction to inhale it. After a time, few of the nurses and attendants would venture thither; and to take a patient to Saint Faith's was considered tantamount to consigning him to the grave.

Whether Judith Malmayns had succeeded or not in curing Sir Paul Parravicin, it is not our present purpose to relate. Soon after the cathedral was converted into a lazar-house she returned thither, and, in spite of the opposition of Doctor Hodges, was appointed one of the nurses. It must not be supposed that her appointment was the result of any ill design. Such was the difficulty of obtaining attendance, that little choice was left, and the nurses being all of questionable character, it was supposed she was only a shade worse than her fellows, while she was known to be active and courageous. And this was speedily proved; for when Saint Faith's was deserted by the others, she remained at her post, and quitted it neither night nor day. A large pit was digged in the open space at the northeast corner of the cathedral, and to this great numbers of bodies were nightly conveyed by Chowles and Jonas. But it was soon filled, and they were compelled to resort, as before, to Finsbury-fields, and to another vast pit near Aldgate. When not engaged in this revolting employment, Chowles took up his quarters in the crypt, where, in spite of his propinquity to the sick, he indulged himself in his customary revelry. He and Judith had amassed, in one way or other, a vast quantity of spoil, and frequently planned how they would spend it when the pestilence ceased. Their treasure was carefully concealed in a cell in one of the secret passages with which they were acquainted, leading from Saint Faith's to the upper structure.

One night, on his return from Finsbury-fields, as Chowles was seated in the crypt, with a pipe in his mouth, and a half-finished flask of wine before him, he was startled by the sudden entrance of Judith, who, rushing up to him, seized him by the throat, and almost choked him before he could extricate himself.

" What is the matter ?—would you strangle me, you murderous harridan ? " he cried.

" Ay, that I would," replied Judith, preparing to renew the attack.

" Stand off ! " rejoined Chowles, springing back, and snatching up a spade, " or I will dash out your brains. Are you mad ? " he contiuued, gazing fearfully at her.

" I am angry enough to make me so," she replied, shaking her clenched fists at him.—" But I will be revenged —revenged, I tell you."

" Revenged ! " cried Chowles, in astonishment—" for what ! What have I done ? "

" You do well to affect ignorance," rejoined Judith, " but you cannot deceive me. No one but you can have done it."

" Done what ? " exclaimed Chowles, in increased astonishment. " Has our hoard been discovered ? "

" Ay, and been carried off—by you—you ! " screamed Judith, with a look worthy of a fury.

" By my soul, you are wrong," cried Chowles. " I have never touched it,—never even approached the hiding-place, except in your presence."

" Liar ! " returned Judith, " the whole hoard is gone ;— the plunder I obtained in Newgate,—the Earl of Rochester's plate,—all the rings, trinkets, and rich apparel I have picked up since,—everything is gone ;—and who but you can be the robber ? "

" It is difficult to say," rejoined Chowles. " But I swear to you, you suspect me wrongfully."

" Restore it," replied Judith, " or tell me where it is hidden. If not, I will be the death of you ! "

" Let us go to the hiding-place," replied Chowles, whose uneasiness was not diminished by the menace. " You may be mistaken, and I hope you are."

Though he uttered the latter part of his speech with seeming confidence, his heart misgave him. To conceal

his trepidation, he snatched up a lamp, and passing
through the secret door hurried along the narrow stone
passage. He was about to open the cell, when he perceived
near it the tall figure of the enthusiast.

" There is the robber ! " he cried to Judith. " I have
found him. It is Solomon Eagle. Villain ! you have
purloined our hoard ! "

" I have done so," replied Solomon Eagle, " and I will
carry off all other spoil you may obtain. Think not to
hide it from me. I can watch you when you see me not
and track you when you suppose me afar off."

" Indeed ! " exclaimed Chowles, trembling. " I begin
to think he is possessed of supernatural power," he added,
in an undertone to Judith.

" Go on," pursued Solomon Eagle, " continue to
plunder and destroy. Pursue your guilty career, and see
what reward you will reap."

" Restore what you have robbed us of," cried Judith,
in a menacing tone, " or dread the consequences."

" Woman, you threaten idly," returned Solomon Eagle.
" Your ill-gotten treasure is gone—whither you will never
know. Get hence ! " he added, in a terrible tone, " or I
will rid the earth of you both."

So awed were they by his voice and gestures, that they
slunk away with a discomfited air, and returned to the
crypt.

" If we are always to be robbed in this manner,"
observed Chowles, " we had better shift our quarters, and
practise elsewhere."

" He shall not repeat the offence with impunity," returned Judith. " I will speedily get rid of him."

" Beware ! " cried a voice, which they recognised as that
of Solomon Eagle, though whence proceeding they could
not precisely determine. The pair looked at each other
uneasily, but neither spoke a word.

Meanwhile, Leonard Holt did not omit to pay a daily
visit to the cathedral. It was a painful contemplation, and
yet not without deep interest, to behold the constant
succession of patients, most of whom were swept away by
the scourge in the course of a couple of days. or even in a

shorter period. Out of every hundred persons attacked, five did not recover; and whether the virulence of the distemper increased, or the summer heats rendered its victims more easily assailable, certain it is they were carried off far more expeditiously than before. Doctor Hodges was unremitting in his attentions, but his zeal and anxiety availed nothing. He had to contend with a disease over which medicine exercised little control.

One morning, as he was about to enter the cathedral, he met Leonard beneath the portico, and as soon as the latter caught sight of him, he hurried towards him.

" I have been in search of you," he said, " and was about to proceed to your residence. Mr. Bloundel wishes to see you immediately. Amabel is worse."

" I will go with you at once," replied the doctor.

And they took their way to Wood-street.

" From a few words let fall by my master, I imagine he intends sending Amabel into the country to-morrow," said Leonard, as they proceeded.

" I hope so," replied Hodges. " He has already delayed it too long. You will be glad to hear that Nizza Macascree is quite recovered. To-morrow, or the next day, she will be able to see you with safety."

" Heaven knows where I may be to-morrow," rejoined Leonard. " Wherever Amabel goes, I shall not be far off."

" Faithful to the last ! " exclaimed Hodges. " Well, I shall not oppose you. We must take care the Earl of Rochester does not get a hint of our proceeding. At this time, a chance meeting (were it nothing more) might prove fatal to the object of our solicitude."

Leonard said nothing, but the colour fled his cheek, and his lip slightly quivered. In a few seconds more they reached the grocer's house.

They found him at the window anxiously expecting them; and Doctor Hodges being drawn up in the same way as before, was conducted to Amabel's chamber. She was reclining in an easy chair, with the Bible on her knee; and though she was much wasted away, she looked more lovely than ever. A slight hectic flush increased the brilliancy of her eyes, which had now acquired that ominous lustre peculiar to persons in a decline. There were other distressing symptoms in her appearance which the skilful physician well knew how to interpret. To an inexperienced eye, however, she would have appeared charming. Nothing could exceed the delicacy of her complexion, or the lovely mould of her features, which, though they had lost much of their fullness and roundness, had gained in expression; while the pencilled brows clearly traced upon her snowy forehead, the long dark eyelashes shading her cheek, and the rich satin tresses drooping over her shoulders, completed her attractions. Her mother stood by her side, and not far from her sat little Christiana, amusing herself with some childish toy, and ever and anon stealing an anxious glance at her sister. Taking Amabel's arm, and sighing to himself to think how thin it was, the doctor placed his finger upon her pulse. Whatever might be his secret opinion, he thought fit to assume a hopeful manner, and looking smilingly at her, said, "You are better than I expected, but your departure to the country must not be deferred."

"Since it is my father's wish that I should go," replied Amabel, gently, "I am quite willing to comply. But I feel it will be of no avail, and I would rather pass the rest of my life here than with strangers. I cannot be happier than I am now."

"Perhaps not," replied Hodges; "but a few weeks spent in some salubrious spot will remove all apprehensions as to your health. You will find your strength return, and with it the desire of life."

"My life is in the hands of my Maker," replied Amabel, "and I am ready to resign it whenever it shall be required of me. At the same time, however anxious I may be to quit a world which appears a blank to me, I would make every effort for the sake of those whose happiness is dearer to me than my own, to purchase a complete restoration to health. If my father desires me to try removal to the country, and you think it will have a beneficial effect, I am ready to go. But do not urge it, unless you think there is a chance of my recovery."

"I will tell you frankly," replied the doctor, "if you remain here, you have not many weeks to live."

"But if I go, will you promise me health?" rejoined Amabel. "Do not deceive me. Is there a hope?"

"Unquestionably," replied the doctor. "Change of air will work wonders."

"I beseech you not to hesitate—for my sake do not, dearest daughter," said Mrs. Bloundel, with difficulty repressing tears.

"And for mine," added her father, more firmly, yet with deep emotion.

"I have already expressed my readiness to accede to your wishes," replied Amabel. "Whenever you have made arrangements for me, I will set out."

"And now comes the question—where is she to go?" remarked Hodges.

"I have a sister who lives as housekeeper at Lord Craven's seat, Ashdown Park," replied Mr. Bloundel. "She shall go thither, and her aunt will take every care of her. The mansion is situated amid the Berkshire hills, and the air is the purest and best in England."

"Nothing can be better," replied Hodges; "but who is to escort her thither?"

"Leonard Holt," replied Mr. Bloundel. "He will gladly undertake the office."

"No doubt," rejoined Hodges; "but cannot you go yourself?"

"Impossible," returned the grocer, a shade passing over his countenance.

"Neither do I wish it," observed Amabel. "I am content to be under the safeguard of Leonard."

"Amabel," said her father, "you know not what I shall endure in thus parting with you. I would give all I possess to be able to accompany you, but a sense of duty restrains me. I have taken the resolution to remain here with my family during the continuance of the pestilence, and I must abide by it. I little thought how severely my constancy would be tried. But hard though it be, I must submit. I shall commit you, therefore, to the care of an all-merciful Providence, who will not fail to watch over and protect you."

" Have no fear for me, father," replied Amabel; " and do not weep, dear mother," she added to Mrs. Bloundel, who, unable to restrain her grief, was now drowned in tears; " I shall be well cared for. If we meet no more in this world, our reunion is certain in that to come. I have given you much pain and uneasiness, but it will be an additional grief to me if I think you feel further anxiety on my account."

" We do not, my dear child," replied Mr. Bloundel. " I am well assured all is for the best, and if it pleases Heaven to spare you, I shall rejoice beyond measure in your return. If not, I shall feel a firm reliance that you will continue in the same happy frame, as at present, to the last, and that we shall meet above, where there will be no further separation."

" I cannot bear to part with her," cried Mrs. Bloundel, clasping her arms round her daughter—" I cannot—I cannot ! "

" Restrain yourself, Honora," said her husband; " you will do her an injury."

" She must not be over-excited," interposed Hodges, in a low tone, and gently drawing the afflicted mother away. " The sooner," he added to Mr. Bloundel, " she now sets out the better."

" I feel it," replied the grocer. " She shall start to-morrow morning."

" I will undertake to procure horses," replied Hodges, " and Leonard will be ready at any moment."

With this he took his leave, and descending by the pulley, communicated to Leonard what had occurred.

In spite of his fears on her account, the prospect of again beholding Amabel so transported the apprentice that he could scarcely attend to what was said respecting her. When he grew calmer, it was arranged that all should be in readiness at an early hour on the following morning; that a couple of horses should be provided; and that Amabel should be let down fully equipped for the journey. This settled, Leonard at the doctor's request, accompanied him to his residence.

They were scarcely out of sight, when a man, who had been concealed behind the hutch, in such a position that not a word that had passed escaped him, issued from his hiding-place, and darting down the first alley on the right, made the best of his way to Whitehall.

Up to this time, Doctor Hodges had not judged it prudent to allow a meeting between Leonard and Nizza Macascree, but now, from reasons of his own, he resolved no longer to delay it. Accordingly, on reaching his dwelling, he took the apprentice to her chamber. She was standing in a pensive attitude, near a window which looked towards the river, and as she turned on his entrance, Leonard perceived that her eyes were filled with tears. Blushing deeply, she advanced towards him, and greeted him with all the warmth of her affectionate nature. She had quite recovered her good looks, and Leonard could not but admit that, had he seen her before his heart was plighted to another, it must have been given to her. Comparisons are ungracious, and tastes differ more perhaps as to beauty than on any other point; but if Amabel and the piper's daughter had been placed together, it would not have been difficult to determine to which of the two the palm of superior loveliness should be assigned. There was a witchery in the magnificent black eyes of the latter—in her exquisitely-formed mouth and pearly teeth— in her clear nut-brown complexion—in her dusky and luxuriant tresses, and in her light elastic figure, with which more perfect but less piquant charms could not compete. Such seemed to be the opinion of Doctor Hodges, for as he gazed at her with unaffected admiration, he exclaimed, as if to himself—" I'faith, if I had to choose between the two, I know which it would be."

This exclamation somewhat disconcerted the parties to whom it referred, and the doctor did not relieve their embarrassment by adding, " Well, I perceive I am in the way. You must have much to say to each other that can in nowise interest me. Excuse me a moment, while I see that the horses are ordered."

So saying, and disregarding Leonard's expostulating looks, he hurried out of the room, and shut the door after him.

Hitherto, the conversation had been unrestrained and agreeable on both sides, but now they were left alone together, neither appeared able to utter a word. Nizza cast her eyes timidly on the ground, while Leonard caressed little Bell, who had been vainly endeavouring by her gamesome tricks to win his attention.

" Doctor Hodges spoke of ordering horses," said Nizza, at length, breaking silence. " Are you going on a journey ? "

" I am about to take Amabel to Ashdown Park, in Berkshire, to-morrow morning," replied Leonard. " She is dangerously ill."

" Of the plague ? " asked Nizza, anxiously.

" Of a yet worse disorder," replied Leonard, heaving a deep sigh—" of a broken heart."

" Alas ! I pity her from my soul ! " replied Nizza, in a tone of the deepest commiseration. " Does her mother go with her ? "

" No," replied Leonard, " I alone shall attend her. She will be placed under the care of a near female relative at Ashdown."

" Would it not be better,—would it not be safer, if she is in the precarious state you describe, that someone of her own sex should accompany her ? " said Nizza.

" I should greatly prefer it," rejoined Leonard, " and so I am sure would Amabel. But where is such a person to be found ? "

" I will go with you, if you desire it," replied Nizza, " and will watch over her, and tend her as a sister."

" Are you equal to the journey ? " inquired Leonard, somewhat doubtfully.

" Fully," replied Nizza. " I am entirely recovered, and able to undergo far more fatigues than an invalid like Amabel."

" It will relieve me from a world of anxiety if this can be accomplished," rejoined Leonard. " I will consult Doctor Hodges on the subject on his return."

"What do you desire to consult me about?" cried the physician, who had entered the room unobserved at this juncture.

The apprentice stated Nizza's proposal to him.

"I entirely approve of the plan," observed the doctor; "it will obviate many difficulties. I have just received a message from Mr. Bloundel by Dallison the porter, to say he intends sending Blaize with you. I will therefore provide pillions for the horses, so that the whole party can be accommodated."

He then sat down and wrote out minute instructions for Amabel's treatment, and delivering the paper to Leonard, desired him to give it to the housekeeper at Ashdown Park.

"Heaven only knows what the result of all this may be!" he exclaimed. "But nothing must be neglected."

Leonard promised that his advice should be scrupulously attended to; and the discourse then turning to Nizza's father, she expressed the utmost anxiety to see him before she set out.

Hodges readily assented. "Your father has been discharged as cured from the pest-house," he said, "and is lodged at a cottage, kept by my old nurse, Dame Lucas, just without the walls, near Moorgate. I will send for him."

"On no account," replied Nizza. "I will go to him myself."

"As you please," returned Hodges. "Leonard shall accompany you. You will easily find the cottage. It is about two hundred yards beyond the gate, on the right, near the old dog-houses."

"I know the spot perfectly," rejoined Leonard.

"I would recommend you to put on a mask," observed the doctor to Nizza; "it may protect you from molestation. I will find you one below."

Leading the way to a lower room, he opened a drawer, and producing a small loo mask, gave it her. The youthful pair then quitted the house, Nizza taking Bell under her arm, as she intended leaving her with her father. The necessity of the doctor's caution was speedily manifested, for as they crossed Saint Paul's churchyard they encountered Pillichody, who, glancing inquisitively at Nizza, seemed disposed to push his inquiries further by attempting to take off her mask; but the fierce look of the apprentice, who grasped his staff in a menacing manner, induced him to abandon his purpose. He, however, followed them along Cheapside, and would have continued the pursuit along the Old Jewry, if Leonard had not come to a halt, and awaited his approach. He then took to his heels, and did not again make his appearance.

As they reached the open fields and slackened their pace, Leonard deemed it prudent to prepare his companion for her interview with her father by mentioning the circumstance of the packet, and the important secret which he had stated he had to disclose to her.

" I cannot tell what the secret can relate to, unless it is to my mother," rejoined Nizza. " She died, I believe, when I was an infant. At all events, I never remember seeing her, and I have remarked that my father is averse to talking about her. But I will now question him. I have reason to think this piece of gold," and she produced the amulet, " is in some way or other connected with the mystery."

And she then explained to Leonard all that had occurred in the vault when the coin had been shown to Judith Malmayns, describing the nurse's singular look, and her father's subsequent anger.

By this time, they had entered a narrow footpath leading across the fields in the direction of a little nest of cottages, and pursuing it, they came to a garden gate. Opening it, they beheld the piper seated beneath a little porch covered with eglantine and roses. He was playing a few notes on his pipe, but stopped on hearing their approach. Bell, who had been put to the ground by Nizza, ran barking gleefully towards him. Uttering a joyful exclamation, the piper stretched out his arms, and the next moment enfolded his daughter in a strict embrace. Leonard remained at the gate till the first transports of their meeting were over, and then advanced slowly towards them.

" Whose footsteps are those ? " inquired the piper.

Nizza explained.

"Ah, is it Leonard Holt?" exclaimed the piper, extending his hand to the apprentice. "You are heartily welcome," he added; "and I am glad to find you with Nizza. It is no secret to me that she likes you. She has been an excellent daughter, and will make an excellent wife. He who weds her will obtain a greater treasure than he expects."

"Not than he expects," said Leonard.

"Ay, than he expects," reiterated the piper. "You will one day find out that I speak the truth."

Leonard looked at Nizza, who was blushing deeply at her father's remark. She understood him.

"Father," she said, "I understand you have a secret of importance to disclose to me. I am about to make a long journey to-morrow, and may not return for some time. At this uncertain season, when those who part know not that they shall meet again, nothing of this sort ought to be withheld."

"You cannot know it while I live," replied the piper, "but I will take such precautions that, if anything happens to me, it shall be certainly revealed to you."

"I am satisfied," she rejoined, "and will only ask you one further question, and I beseech you to answer it. Does this amulet refer to the secret?"

"It does," replied her father, sullenly; "and now let the subject be dropped."

He then led the way into the cottage. The good old dame who kept it, on learning who they were, and that they were sent by Doctor Hodges, gave them a hearty welcome, and placed refreshments before them. Leonard commented upon the extreme neatness of the abode and its healthful situation, and expressed a hope that it might not be visited by the plague.

"I trust it will not," rejoined the old woman, shaking her head; "but when I hear the doleful bell at night—when I catch a glimpse of the fatal cart,—or look towards yon dreadful place," and she pointed in the direction of the plague-pit, which lay only a few hundred yards to the west of her habitation,—"I am reminded that the scourge is not far off, and that it must needs reach me ere long."

"Have no fear, Dame Lucas," said the piper; "you
see it has pleased a merciful Providence to spare the lives
of myself, my child, and this young man, and if you should
be attacked, the same beneficent Being may preserve you
in like manner."

"The Lord's will be done!" rejoined Dame Lucas.
"I know I shall be well attended to by Doctor Hodges.
I nursed him when he was an infant, and he has been
like a son to me. Bless his kind heart!" she exclaimed,
her eyes filling with tears of gratitude, "there is not his
like in London."

"Always excepting my master," observed Leonard,
with a smile at her enthusiasm.

"I except no one," rejoined Dame Lucas. "A worthier
man never lived than Doctor Hodges. If I die of the
plague," she continued, "he has promised not to let me
be thrown into that horrible pit,—ough!—but to bury me
in my garden, beneath the old apple-tree."

"And he will keep his word, dame, I am sure," replied
Leonard. "I would recommend you, however, as the
best antidote against the plague, to keep yourself constantly employed, and to indulge as few gloomy notions as
possible."

"I am seldom melancholy, and still more seldom idle,"
replied the good dame. "But despondency will steal on
me sometimes, especially when the dead-cart passes and
I think what it contains."

While the conversation was going forward, Nizza and
the piper withdrew into an inner room, where they remained closeted together for some time. On their reappearance, Nizza said she was ready to depart, and
taking an affectionate farewell of her father, and committing Bell to his charge, she quitted the cottage with the
apprentice.

Evening was now advancing, and the sun was setting
with the gorgeousness already described as peculiar to
this fatal period. Filled with the pleasing melancholy inspired by the hour, they walked on in silence. They had
not proceeded far, when they observed a man crossing the
field with a bundle in his arms. Suddenly, he staggered

and fell. Seeing he did not stir, and guessing what was the matter, Leonard ran towards him to offer him assistance. He found him lying in the grass with his left hand fixed against his heart. He groaned heavily, and his features were convulsed with pain. Near him lay the body of a beautiful little girl, with long fair hair, and finely-formed features, though now disfigured by purple blotches, proclaiming the disorder of which she had perished. She was apparently about ten years old, and was partially covered by a linen cloth. The man, whose features bore a marked resemblance to those of the child, was evidently from his attire above the middle rank. His frame was athletic, and as he was scarcely past the prime of life, the irresistible power of the disease, which could in one instant prostrate strength like his, was terribly attested.

" Alas ! " he cried, addressing the apprentice, " I was about to convey the remains of my poor child to the plague-pit. But I have been unable to accomplish my purpose. I had hoped she would have escaped the polluting touch of those loathly attendants on the dead-cart."

" She *shall* escape it," replied Leonard ; " if you wish it, I will carry her to the pit myself."

" The blessing of a dying man rest on your head," cried the sufferer ; " your charitable action will not pass unrequited."

With this, despite the agony he endured, he dragged himself to his child, kissed her cold lips, smoothed her fair tresses, and covered the body carefully with the cloth. He then delivered it to Leonard, who received it tenderly, and calling to Nizza Macascree, who had witnessed the scene at a little distance, and was deeply affected by it, to await his return, ran towards the plague-pit. Arrived there, he placed his little burden at the brink of the excavation, and kneeling beside it, uttered a short prayer inspired by the occasion. He then tore his handkerchief into strips, and tying them together, lowered the body gently down. Throwing a little earth over it, he hastened to the sick man, and told him what he had done. A smile of satisfaction illumined the sufferer's countenance, and holding out his hand, on which a valuable ring glistened, he said, "Take it—it is but a poor reward for the service you have rendered me;—nay, take it," he added, seeing that the apprentice hesitated, "others will not be so scrupulous."

Unable to gainsay the remark, Leonard took the ring from his finger, and placed it on his own. At this moment, the sick man's gaze fell upon Nizza, who stood at a little distance from him. He started, and made an effort to clear his vision.

"Do my eyes deceive me?" he cried; "or is a female standing there?"

"You are not deceived," replied Leonard.

"Let her come near me, in Heaven's name!" cried the sick man, staring at her as if his eyes would start from their sockets. "Who are you?" he continued, as Nizza approached.

"I am called Nizza Macascree, and am the daughter of a poor piper," she replied.

"Ah!" exclaimed the sick man, with a look of deep disappointment. "The resemblance is wonderful! And yet it cannot be. My brain is bewildered."

"Whom does she resemble?" asked Leonard, eagerly.

"One very dear to me," replied the sick man, with an expression of remorse and anguish, "one I would not think of now." And he buried his face in the grass.

"Is there aught more I can do for you?" inquired Leonard, after a pause.

"No," replied the sick man; "I have done with the world. With that child, the last tie that bound me to it was snapped. I now only wish to die."

"Do not give way thus," replied Leonard; "a short time ago my condition was as apparently hopeless as your own, and you see I am now perfectly recovered."

"You had something to live for—something to love," groaned the sick man. "All I lived for, all I loved, are gone."

"Be comforted, sir," said Nizza, in a commiserating tone. "Much happiness may yet be in store for you."

"That voice!" exclaimed the sick man, with a look denoting the approach of delirium. "It must be my

Isabella. Oh! forgive me! sweet injured saint, forgive me!"

" Your presence evidently distresses him," said Leonard. " Let us hasten for assistance. Your name, sir?" he added, to the sick man.

" Why should you seek to know it?" replied the other. " No tombstone will be placed over the plague-pit."

" Not a moment must be lost if you would save him," cried Nizza.

" You are right," replied Leonard. " Let us fly to the nearest apothecary's."

Accordingly, they set off at a quick pace towards Moorgate. Just as they reached it, they heard the bell ring, and saw the dead-cart approaching. Shrinking back while it passed, they ran on till they came to an apothecary's shop, where Leonard, describing the state of the sick man, by his entreaties induced the master of the establishment and one of his assistants to accompany him. Leaving Nizza in the shop, he then retraced his steps with his companions. The sick man was lying where he had left him, but perfectly insensible. On searching his pockets, a purse of money was found, but neither letter nor tablet to tell who he was. Leonard offered the purse to the apothecary, but the latter declined it, and desired his assistant, who had brought a barrow with him, to place the sick man within it, and convey him to the pest-house.

" He will be better cared for there than if I were to take charge of him," he observed. " As to the money, you can return it if he recovers. If not, it of right belongs to you."

Seeing that remonstrance would be useless, Leonard did not attempt it, and while the assistant wheeled away the sick man, he returned with the apothecary to his dwelling. Thanking him for his kindness, he then hastened with Nizza Macascree to Great Knightrider-street. He related to the doctor all that had occurred, and showed him the ring. Hodges listened to the recital with great attention, and at its close said, " This is a very singular affair, and excites my curiosity greatly. I will go to the pest-house and see the sick man to-morrow. And now we will proceed to supper; and then you had better retire to rest, for you will have to be astir before daybreak. All is in readiness for the journey."

The last night (for such she considered it) spent by Amabel in her father's dwelling, was passed in the kindliest interchanges of affection. Mr. Bloundel had much ado to maintain his firmness, and ever and anon, in spite of his efforts, his labouring bosom and faltering tones proclaimed the struggle within. He sat beside his daughter, with her thin fingers clasped in his, and spoke to her on every consolatory topic that suggested itself. Their discourse, however, insensibly took a serious turn, and the grocer became fully convinced that his daughter was not merely reconciled to the early death that to all appearances awaited her, but wishful for it. He found, too, to his inexpressible grief, that the sense of the Earl of Rochester's treachery, combined with her own indiscretion, and the consequences that might have attended it, had sunk deep in her heart, and produced the present sad result.

Mrs. Bloundel it will scarcely be supposed could support herself so well as her husband, but when any paroxysm of grief approached, she rushed out of the room, and gave vent to her affliction alone. All the rest of the family were present, and were equally distressed. But what most strongly affected Amabel was a simple, natural remark of little Christiana, who, fixing her tearful gaze on her, entreated her " to come back soon."

Weak as she was, Amabel took the child upon her knee, and said to her, " I am going a long journey, Christiana, and, perhaps, may never come back. But if you attend to what your father says to you, if you never omit, morning and evening, to implore the blessing of Heaven, we shall meet again."

" I understand what you mean, sister," said Christiana, " The place you are going to is the grave."

" You have guessed rightly, Christiana," rejoined Amabel, solemnly. " Do not forget my last words to you, and when you are grown into a woman, think upon the poor sister who loved you tenderly."

" I shall always think of you," said Christiana, clasping

her arms round her sister's neck. " Oh ! I wish I could go to the grave instead of you ! "

Amabel pressed her to her bosom, and in a broken voice murmured a blessing over her.

Mr. Bloundel here thought it necessary to interfere, and taking the weeping child in his arms, carried her into the adjoining apartment.

Soon after this, the household were summoned to prayers, and as the grocer poured forth an address to Heaven for the preservation of his daughter, all earnestly joined in the supplication. Their devotions ended, Amabel took leave of her brothers, and the parting might have been painfully prolonged, but for the interposition of her father. The last and severest trial was at hand. She had now to part from her mother, from whom—except on the occasion of her flight with the Earl of Rochester—she had never yet been separated. She had now to part with her, in all probability, for ever. It was a heart-breaking reflection to both. Knowing it would only renew their affliction, and perhaps unfit Amabel for the journey, Mr. Bloundel had prevailed upon his wife not to see her in the morning. The moment had, therefore, arrived when they were to bid each other farewell. The anguish displayed in his wife's countenance was too much for the grocer, and he covered his face with his hands. He heard her approach Amabel— he listened to their mutual sobs—to their last embrace. It was succeeded by a stifled cry, and uncovering his face at the sound, he sprang to his feet just in time to receive his swooning wife in his arms.

CHAPTER VI

The Departure

IT struck four by Saint Paul's as Doctor Hodges, accompanied by Leonard and Nizza Macascree, issued from his dwelling, and proceeded towards Wood-street. The party was followed by a man leading a couple of horses, equipped with pillions, and furnished with saddle-bags, partly filled with the scanty luggage which the apprentice and the piper's daughter took with them. A slight haze, indicative of the intense heat about to follow, hung around the lower part of the cathedral, but its topmost pinnacles glittered in the beams of the newly-risen sun. As Leonard gazed at the central tower, he descried Solomon Eagle on its summit, and pointed him out to Hodges. Motioning the apprentice, in a manner that could not be misunderstood, to halt, the enthusiast vanished, and in another moment appeared upon the roof, and descended to the battlements, overlooking the spot where the little party stood. This was at the north-west corner of the cathedral, at a short distance from the portico. The enthusiast had a small sack in his hand, and calling to Nizza Macascree to take it, flung it to the ground. The ringing sound which it made on its fall proved that it contained gold or silver, while its size showed that the amount must be considerable. Nizza looked at it in astonishment, but did not offer to touch it.

"Take it!" thundered Solomon Eagle; "it is your dowry." And perceiving she hesitated to comply with the injunction, he shouted to Leonard, "Give it her. I have no use for gold. May it make you and her happy!"

"I know not where he can have obtained this money," observed Hodges; "but I am sure in no unlawful manner, and I, therefore, counsel Nizza to accept the boon. It may be of the greatest use to her at some future time."

His scruples being thus overcome, Leonard took the sack, and placed it in one of the saddle-bags.

"You can examine it at your leisure," remarked Hodges to Nizza. "We have no more time to lose."

Solomon Eagle, meanwhile, expressed his satisfaction at the apprentice's compliance by his gestures, and waving his staff round his head, pointed towards the west of the city, as if inquiring whether that was the route they meant to take. Leonard nodded an affirmative; and the enthusiast, spreading out his arms and pronouncing an audible benediction over them, they resumed their course.

The streets were silent and deserted, except by the watchmen, stationed at the infected dwellings, and a few sick persons stretched on the steps of some of the better habitations. In order to avoid coming in contact with these miserable creatures, the party, with the exception of Doctor Hodges, kept in the middle of the road. Attracted by the piteous exclamations of the sufferers, Doctor Hodges, ever and anon, humanely paused to speak to them; and he promised one poor woman, who was suckling an infant, to visit her on his return.

"I have no hopes of saving her," he observed to Leonard, "but I may preserve her child. There is an establishment in Aldgate for infants whose mothers have died of the plague, where more than a hundred little creatures are suckled by she-goats, and it is wonderful how well they thrive under their nurses. If I can induce this poor woman to part with her child, I will send it thither."

Just then, their attention was arrested by the sudden opening of a casement, and a middle-aged woman, wringing her hands, cried, with a look of unutterable anguish and despair,—"Pray for us, good people! pray for us!"

"We do pray for you, my poor soul!" rejoined Hodges, "as well as for all who are similarly afflicted. What sick have you within?"

"There were ten yesterday," replied the woman. "Two have died in the night—my husband and my eldest son,—and there are eight others whose recovery is hopeless. Pray for us! As you hope to be spared yourselves, pray for us!" And with a lamentable cry, she closed the casement.

Familiarized as all who heard her were with spectacles
of horror and tales of woe, they could not listen to this
sad recital, nor look upon her distracted countenance,
without the deepest commiseration. Other sights had
previously affected them, but not in the same degree.
Around the little conduit standing in front of the Old
'Change, at the western extremity of Cheapside, were three
lazars laving their sores in the water; while, in the short
space between this spot and Wood-street, Leonard counted
upwards of twenty doors marked with the fatal red cross,
and bearing upon them the sad inscription, " Lord have
mercy upon us ! "

A few minutes' walking brought them to the grocer's
habitation, and on reaching it, they found that Blaize had
already descended. He was capering about the street with
joy at his restoration to freedom.

" Mistress Amabel will make her appearance in a few
minutes," he said to Leonard.—" Our master is with her,
and is getting all ready for her departure. I have not come
unprovided with medicine," he added to Doctor Hodges.
" I have got a bottle of plague-water in one pocket and a
phial of vinegar in the other. Besides these, I have a small
pot of Mayerne's electuary in my bag, another of the grand
anti-pestilential confection, and a fourth of the infallible
antidote which I bought of the celebrated Greek physician,
Doctor Constantine Rhodocanaceis, at his shop near the
Three Kings' Inn, in Southampton-buildings. I dare say
you have heard of him ? "

" I *have* heard of the quack," replied Hodges. " His
end was a just retribution for the tricks he practised on his
dupes. In spite of his infallible antidote, he was carried off
by the scourge. But what else have you got ? "

" Only a few trifles," replied Blaize, with a chop-fallen
look. " Patience has made me a pomander-ball composed
of angelica, rue, zedoary, camphor, wax, and laudanum,
which I have hung round my neck with a string. Then I
have got a good-sized box of rufuses, and have swallowed
three of them preparatory to the journey."

" A proper precaution," observed Hodges, with a smile.

" This is not all," replied Blaize. " By my mother's

advice, I have eaten twenty leaves of rue, two roasted figs, and two pickled walnuts for breakfast, washing them down with an ale posset, with pimpernel seethed in it."

" Indeed ! " exclaimed Hodges. " You must be in a pretty condition for a journey. But how could you bear to part with your mother and Patience ? "

" The parting from Patience *was* heart-breaking," replied Blaize, taking out his handkerchief and applying it to his eyes. " We sat up half the night together, and I felt so much overcome that I began to waver in my resolution of departing. I am glad I did not give way now," he added, in a more sprightly tone. " Fresh air and bright sunshine are very different things from the close rooms in that dark house."

" You must not forget that you were free there from the contagion," rejoined Hodges; " while you are here exposed to its assaults."

" True," replied Blaize; " that makes a vast difference. I almost wish I was back again."

" It is too late to think of returning," said Hodges. " Mount your horse, and I will assist Nizza into the pillion."

By the time that Blaize, who was but an indifferent horseman, had got into the saddle, and Nizza had taken her place behind him, the window opened, and Mr. Bloundel appeared at it.

Amabel had only retired to rest for a few hours during the night. When left to herself in her chamber, she continued to pray till exhaustion compelled her to seek some repose. Arising about two o'clock, she employed herself for more than an hour in further devotion, and then took a last survey of every object in the room. She had occupied it from her childhood, and as she opened drawer after drawer, and cupboard after cupboard, and examined their contents, each article recalled some circumstance connected with the past, and brought back a train of long-forgotten emotions. While she was thus engaged, Patience tapped at the door, and was instantly admitted. The tender-hearted kitchen-maid assisted her to dress, and to put together some few articles omitted to be packed by her mother. During this employment, she shed abundance of tears, and Amabel's efforts to console her only made matters worse. Poor Patience was forced, at last, to sit down and indulge a hearty fit of crying, after which she felt considerably relieved.

As soon as she was sufficiently recovered to be able to speak, she observed to Amabel—" Pardon what I am about to say to you, my dear young mistress, but I cannot help thinking that the real seat of your disease is in the heart."

A slight blush overspread Amabel's pale features, but she made no answer.

" I see I am right," continued Patience, " and indeed I have long suspected it. Let me entreat you, therefore, dear young lady, not to sacrifice yourself. Only say the word, and I will find means of making your retreat known to the Earl of Rochester. Blaize is devoted to you, and will do anything you bid him. I cannot wonder you fret after so handsome—so captivating a man as the earl, especially when you are worried to death to marry a common apprentice like Leonard Holt, who is not fit to hold a candle to your noble admirer. Ah! we women can never blind ourselves to the advantages of rank and appearance. We are too good judges for that. I hope you will soon be restored to your lover, and that the happiness you will enjoy will make amends for all the misery you have endured."

" Patience," said Amabel, whose cheek, as the other spoke, had returned to its original paleness—" Patience," she said, gravely, but kindly, " I have suffered you to proceed too far without interruption, and must correct the very serious error into which you have fallen. I am so far from pining for an interview with the Earl of Rochester, that nothing in the world should induce me to see him again. I have loved him deeply," she continued in a tremulous tone, " nay, I will not attempt to disguise that I feel strongly towards him still, while I will also freely confess that his conduct towards me has so preyed upon my spirits that it has impaired, perhaps destroyed my health. In spite of this, I cannot sufficiently rejoice that I have escaped the earl's snares,—I cannot be sufficiently thankful to the merciful Being, who, while he has thought fit to chastise me, has preserved me from utter ruin."

" Since you are of this mind," returned Patience, in a tone of incredulity, " you are more to be rejoiced with than pitied. But we are not overheard," she added, almost in a whisper, and glancing towards the door. " You may entirely confide in me. The time is arrived when you can escape to your lover."

" No more of this," rejoined Amabel, severely, " or I shall command you to leave the room."

" This is nothing more than pique," thought Patience. " We women are all hypocrites, even to ourselves. I will serve her whether she will or not. She *shall* see the earl.— I hope there is no harm in wishing you may be happy with Leonard Holt," she added aloud. " *He* will make you a capital husband."

" That subject is equally disagreeable—equally painful to me," said Amabel.

" I had better hold my tongue altogether," rejoined Patience, somewhat pertly. " Whatever I say seems to be wrong. It won't prevent me from doing as I would be done by," she added to herself.

Amabel's preparations finished, she dismissed Patience, to whom she gave some few slight remembrances, and was soon afterwards joined by her father. They passed half an hour together, as on the former night, in serious and devout conversation, after which, Mr. Bloundel left her for a few minutes to let down Blaize. On his return, he tenderly embraced her, and led her into the passage. They had not advanced many steps, when Mrs. Bloundel rushed forth to meet them. She was in her night-dress, and seemed overwhelmed with affliction.

" How is this, Honora ? " cried her husband, in a severe tone. " You promised me you would see Amabel no more. You will only distress her."

" I could not let her go thus," cried Mrs. Bloundel. " I was listening at my chamber-door to hear her depart, and when I caught the sound of her footsteps, I could no longer

control myself." So saying, she rushed to her daughter
and clasped her in her arms.

Affectionately returning her mother's embrace, Amabel
gave her hand to her father, who conducted her to the
little room overlooking the street. Nothing more, except
a deep and passionate look, was exchanged between them.
Both repressed their emotion, and though the heart of
each was bursting, neither shed a tear. At that moment,
and for the first time, they greatly resembled each other,
and this was not surprising, for intense emotion, whether
of grief or joy, will bring out lines in the features that lie
hidden at other times. Without a word, Mr. Bloundel
busied himself in arranging the pulley, and calling to those
below to prepare for Amabel's descent, again embraced
her, kissed her pale brow, and placing her carefully in the
basket, lowered her slowly to the ground. She was
received in safety by Leonard, who carried her in his arms,
and placed her on the pillion. The pulley was then drawn
up, and her luggage lowered by Mr. Bloundel, and placed
in the saddle-bags by the apprentice. Every one saw the
necessity for terminating this painful scene. A kindly
farewell was taken of Hodges. Amabel waved her hand
to her father, when at this moment Patience appeared at
the window, and calling to Blaize, threw a little package
tied in a handkerchief to him. Doctor Hodges took up
the parcel and gave it to the porter, who, untying the
handkerchief, glanced at a note it enclosed, and striking
his horse with his stick, dashed off towards Cheapside.

" Pursue him," cried Amabel to Leonard, " he is flying
to the Earl of Rochester."

The intimation was sufficient for the apprentice. Urging
his horse into a quick pace, he came up with the fugitive
just as he reached Cheapside. Blaize's mad career had been
checked by Nizza Macascree, who seizing the bridle,
stopped the steed. Leonard, who was armed with a heavy
riding-whip, applied it unsparingly to Blaize's shoulders.

" Entreat him to hold his hand, dear, good Mistress
Amabel," cried the porter ; " it was for your sake alone
I made this rash attempt. Patience told me you were dying
to see the Earl of Rochester, and made me promise I

would ride to Whitehall to acquaint his lordship whither
you were going. Here is her letter which I was about to
deliver." And as he spoke, he handed her the note, which
was tied with a piece of packthread, and directed in
strange and almost illegible characters.

" Do not hurt him more," said Amabel; " he was not
aware of the mischief he was about to commit. And learn
from me, Blaize, that, so far from desiring to see the Earl
of Rochester, all my anxiety is to avoid him."

" If I had known that," returned the porter, " I would
not have stirred a step. But Patience assured me the
contrary."

By this time, Doctor Hodges had come up, and an
explanation ensued. It was agreed, however, that it would
be better not to alarm Mr. Bloundel, but to attribute the
porter's sudden flight to mismanagement of his steed.
Accordingly, they returned to the residence of the grocer,
who was anxiously looking out for them ; and after a brief
delay, during which the saddle-bags were again examined
and secured, they departed. Mr. Bloundel looked wistfully after his daughter, and she returned his gaze as long
as her blinding eyes would permit her. So unwonted was
the sound of horses' feet at this period, that many a
melancholy face appeared at the window to gaze at them
as they rode by, and Nizza Macascree shuddered as she
witnessed the envious glances cast after them by these
poor captives. As to Blaize, when they got into Cheapside,
he was so terrified by the dismal evidences of the pestilence
that met him at every turn, that he could scarcely keep his
seat, and it was not until he had drenched himself and
his companion with vinegar and stuffed his mouth with
myrrh and zedoary that he felt anything like composure.

On approaching Newgate Market, they found it entirely
deserted. Most of the stalls were removed, the shops
closed, and the window-shutters nailed up. It was never,
in fact, used at all, except by a few countrymen and
higglers, who ventured thither on certain days of the
week to sell fresh eggs, butter, poultry, and such com-
modities. The manner of sale was this. The article disposed of was placed on a flag on one side of the market,

near which stood a pump and a trough of water. The vendor then retired, while the purchaser approached, took the article, and put its price into the water, whence it was removed when supposed to be sufficiently purified.

As the party passed Grey Friars, the tramp of their horses was mistaken for the dead-cart, and a door was suddenly opened and a corpse brought forth. Leonard would have avoided the spectacle, had it been possible, but they were now close to Newgate, where they were detained for a few minutes at the gate, while their bills of health were examined and countersigned by the officer stationed there. During this pause, Leonard glanced at the grated windows of the prison, the debtors' side of which fronted the street. But not a single face was to be seen. In fact, as has already been stated, the prison was shut up.

The gate was now opened to them, and descending Snow-hill, they entered a region completely devastated by the pestilence. So saddening was the sight, that Leonard involuntarily quickened his horse's pace, resolved to get out of this forlorn district as speedily as possible. He was, however, stopped by an unexpected and fearful impediment. When within a short distance of Holborn-bridge, he observed on the further side of it a large black vehicle, and, unable to make out what it was, though a fearful suspicion crossed him, slackened his pace. A nearer approach showed him that it was the pest-cart, filled with its charnel load. The horse was in the shafts, and was standing quite still. Rising in his stirrups to obtain a better view, Leonard perceived that the driver was lying on the ground at a little distance from the cart, in an attitude that proclaimed he had been suddenly seized by the pestilence, and had probably just expired.

Not choosing to incur the risk of passing this contagious load, Leonard retraced his course as far as Holborn-conduit, then turning into Seacoal-lane, and making the best of his way to Fleet-bridge, crossed it, and entered the great thoroughfare with which it communicated. He had not proceeded far when he encountered a small party of the watch, to whom he showed his certificate, and recounted the fate of the driver of the dead-cart. At Temple Bar, he was again obliged to exhibit his passports, and, while there detained, he observed three other horsemen riding towards them from the further end of Fleet-street.

Though much alarmed by the sight, Leonard did not communicate his apprehensions to his companions, but as soon as the guard allowed him to pass, called out to Blaize to follow him, and urging his horse to a quick pace, dashed up Drury-lane. A few minutes' hard riding, during which nothing occurred to give the apprentice further uneasiness, brought them to a road skirting the open fields, in which a pest-house had just been built by the chivalrous nobleman whose habitation, in Berkshire, they were about to visit. With a courage and devotion that redound more to his honour than the brilliant qualities that won him so high a reputation in the court and in the field, Lord Craven not merely provided the present receptacle for the sick, but remained in London during the whole continuance of the dreadful visitation; " braving," says Pennant, " the fury of the pestilence with the same coolness that he fought the battles of his beloved mistress, Elizabeth, titular Queen of Bohemia, or mounted the tremendous breach of Creutznach." The spot where this asylum was built, and which is the present site of Golden-square, retained nearly half a century afterwards the name of the Pest-house Fields. Leonard had already been made acquainted by Dr. Hodges with the earl's generous devotion to the public welfare, and warmly commenting upon it, he pointed out the structure to Amabel. But the speed at which she was borne along did not allow her time to bestow more than a hasty glance at it. On gaining Hyde-park-corner, the apprentice cast a look backwards, and his apprehensions were revived by perceiving the three horsemen again in view, and evidently using their utmost exertions to come up with them.

While Leonard was hesitating whether he should make known their danger to Amabel, he perceived Solomon Eagle dart from behind a wall on the left of the road, and plant himself in the direct course of their pursuers, and he involuntarily drew in the rein to see what would ensue.

In another moment, the horsemen, who were advancing at full gallop,—and whom Leonard now recognised as the Earl of Rochester, Pillichody, and Sir Paul Parravicin, —had approached within a few yards of the enthusiast, and threatened to ride over him if he did not get out of the way. Seeing, however, that he did not offer to move, they opened on either side of him, and were passing swiftly by, when with infinite dexterity, he caught hold of the bridle of Rochester's steed, and checking him, seized the earl by the leg and threw him to the ground.

Sir Paul Parravicin pulled up as soon as he could, and drawing his sword, rode back to assist his friend and punish the aggressor, but the enthusiast, nothing daunted, met him in full career, and, suddenly lifting up his arms, uttered a loud cry, which so startled the knight's high-spirited horse, that it reared and flung him. All this was the work of a few seconds. Pillichody had been borne forward by the impetuosity of his steed to within a short distance of the apprentice, and seeing the fate of his companions, and not liking Leonard's menacing gestures, he clapped spurs into his horse, and rode up Park-lane.

Overjoyed at his unexpected deliverance, Leonard, whose attention had been completely engrossed by what was passing, now ventured to look at Amabel, and became greatly alarmed at her appearance. She was as pale as death, except a small scarlet patch on either cheek, which contrasted powerfully with the death-like hue of the rest of her countenance. Her hands convulsively clasped the back of the pillion; her lips were slightly apart; and her eyes fixed upon the prostrate form of the Earl of Rochester. On finding they were pursued, and by whom, her first impulse had been to fling herself from the horse, and to seek safety in flight, but controlling herself, she awaited the result with forced composure, and was now sinking from the exhaustion of the effort.

"Thank Heaven! we are safe," cried the apprentice; "but I fear the shock has been too much for you."

"It has," gasped Amabel, falling against his shoulder. "Let us fly—oh! let us fly."

Inexpressibly shocked and alarmed, Leonard twined

his left arm round her waist so as to hold her on the steed, for she was utterly unable to support herself, and glancing anxiously at Nizza Macascree, struck off on the right into the road skirting the Park, and in the direction of Tyburn, where there was a small inn, at which he hoped to procure assistance. Before reaching this place, he was beyond description relieved to find that Amabel had so far recovered as to be able to raise her head.

"The deadly faintness has passed," she murmured, "I shall be better soon. But I fear I am too weak to pursue the journey at present."

Leonard spurred on his steed, and in another instant reached Tyburn, and drew up at the little inn. But no assistance could be obtained there. The house was closed; there was a red cross on the door; and a watchman, stationed in front of it, informed him that all the family had died of the plague except the landlord,—"and he will be buried beside them in Paddington churchyard before to-morrow morning," added the man; "for his nurse tells me it is impossible he can survive many hours."

As he spoke, an upper window was opened, and a woman thrusting forth her head, cried, "Poor Master Sandys has just breathed his last. Come in, Philip, and help me to prepare the body for the dead-cart."

"I will be with you in a minute," rejoined the watchman. "You may possibly procure accommodation at the Wheatsheaf at Paddington," he added to Leonard; "It is but a short distance up the road."

Thanking him for the information, Leonard took the course indicated. He had not proceeded far, when he was alarmed by hearing a piteous cry of "Stop! stop!" proceeding from Blaize; and halting, found that the porter had been so greatly terrified by the watchman's account of the frightful mortality in the poor innkeeper's family, that he had applied to his phial of plague-water, and in pulling it out had dropped his box of rufuses, and the jar of anti-pestilential confection. He had just ascertained his loss, and wished to go back, but this Nizza Macascree would not permit. Enraged at the delay, Leonard peremtorily ordered the porter to come

L

on; and Blaize, casting a rueful glance at his treasures, which he perceived at a little distance in the middle of the road, was compelled to obey.

At Paddington another disappointment awaited them. The Wheatsheaf was occupied by two large families, who were flying from the infected city, and no accommodation could be obtained. Leonard looked wistfully at Nizza Macascree, as if to ascertain what to do, and she was equally perplexed; but the difficulty was relieved by Amabel herself, who said she felt much better, and able to proceed a little further. "Do not return to London," she continued, with great earnestness. "I would rather die on the road than go home again. Some cottage will receive us. If not, I can rest for a short time in the fields."

Thinking it best to comply, Leonard proceeded along the Harrow-road. Soon after crossing Paddington-green, he overtook a little train of fugitives driving a cart filled with children, and laden with luggage. Further on, as he surveyed the beautiful meadows, stretching out on either side of him, he perceived a line of small tents, resembling a gipsy encampment, pitched at a certain distance from each other, and evidently occupied by families who had fled from their homes from fear of infection. This gave a singular character to the prospect. But there were other and far more painful sights on the road, which could not fail to attract attention. For the first half-mile, almost at every hundred yards, might be seen some sick man, who, unable to proceed further, had fallen against the hedge-side, and exhibited his sores to move the pity of the passers-by. But these supplications were wholly unheeded. Self-preservation was the first object with all, and the travellers, holding handkerchiefs steeped in vinegar to their faces, and averting their heads, passed by on the other side of the way.

The pestilence, it may be remarked, had visited with extraordinary rigour the whole of the higher country at the west and north-west of the metropolis. The charmingly-situated, and, at other seasons, healthful villages

of Hampstead and Highgate suffered severely from
the scourge; and it even extended its ravages as
far as Harrow-on-the-Hill, which it half depopulated.
This will account for the circumstance of a large
pest-house being erected in the neighbourhood of Westbourne-green, which the party now approached. Two
litters were seen crossing the fields in the direction
of the hospital, and the circumstance called Leonard's
attention to it. Shudderingly averting his gaze, he
quickened his pace, and soon reached a small farm-
house, on the summit of the hill rising from Kensal-
green. Determined to seek a temporary asylum here
for Amabel, he opened a gate, and riding into the yard,
fortunately met with the owner of the house, a worthy
farmer, named Wingfield, to whom he explained her
situation. The man at first hesitated, but, on receiving
Leonard's solemn assurance that she was free from the
plague, consented to receive the whole party.

Assisting Amabel to dismount, Wingfield conveyed
her in his arms into the house, and delivered her to his
wife, bidding her take care of her. The injunction was
scarcely needed. The good dame, who was a middle-
aged woman, with pleasing features, which lost none of
their interest from being stamped with profound melancholy, gazed at her for a moment fixedly, and then observed, in an undertone, but with much emotion, to
her husband, " Ah! Robert, how much this sweet creature resembles our poor Sarah!"

" Hush! hush! dame," rejoined her husband, hastily
brushing away the moisture that sprang to his eyes;
" take her to your chamber, and see that she wants
nothing. There is another young woman outside, whom
I will send to you."

So saying he returned to the yard. Meantime, the
others had dismounted, and Wingfield, bidding Nizza
Macascree go in, led the way to the barn, where the
horses were tied up, and fodder placed before them.
This done, he conducted his guests to the house, and
placing cold meat, bread, and a jug of ale before them,
desired them to fall to,—an injunction which Blaize.

notwithstanding his previous repast of roasted figs and pickled walnuts, very readily complied with. While they were thus employed, Dame Wingfield made her appearance. She said that the poor creature (meaning Amabel) was too ill to proceed on her journey that day, and begged her husband to allow her to stop till the next morning, when she hoped she would be able to undertake it.

"To-morrow morning, say you, dame?" cried Wingfield; "she may stop till the day after, and the day after that, if you desire it, or she wishes it. Go tell her so."

And as his wife withdrew, well pleased at having obtained her request, Wingfield addressed himself to Leonard, and inquired the cause of Amabel's illness; and as the apprentice saw no necessity for secrecy, and felt exceedingly grateful for the kind treatment he had experienced, he acquainted him with the chief particulars of her history. The farmer appeared greatly moved by the recital.

"She resembles my poor Sarah very strongly," he said. "My daughter was hurried into an early grave by a villain who won her affections and betrayed her. She now lies in Willesden Churchyard, but her seducer is one of the chief favourites of our profligate monarch."

"Do you mean the Earl of Rochester?" cried Leonard.

"No, no," replied the farmer, whose good-natured countenance had assumed a stern expression. "The villain I mean is worse, if possible, than the earl. He is called Sir Paul Parravicin."

"Gracious heaven!" exclaimed Leonard, in astonishment; "what a strange coincidence is this!"

And he then proceeded to relate to Wingfield the persecution which Nizza Macascree had endured from the profligate knight. The farmer listened to his recital with breathless interest, and when it was ended, arose, and taking a hasty turn round the room, halted at the table and struck it forcibly with his clenched hand.

"I hope that man will never cross my path," he said, all the blood mounting to his face, and his eye kindling

with fury. " As God shall judge me, I will kill him if I
meet him."

" Then I hope you never will meet him," observed
Leonard. " He has injured you enough already, without putting you out of the pale of Divine mercy."

" These rascals have done us all an injury," observed
Blaize. " Patience has never been like herself since
Major Pillichody entered my master's dwelling, and
made love to her. I feel quite uneasy to think how the
little hussy will go on during my absence. She can't get
out of the house, that's one comfort."

" You have mentioned another wretch, who was constantly with Sir Paul," cried Wingfield. " Perdition seize
them!"

" Ay, perdition seize them!" echoed Blaize, striking
the table in his turn—" especially Major Pillichody."

" Did you ever suspect Sir Paul to be of a higher rank
than he pretends?" asked Leonard.

" No," rejoined Wingfield; " what motive have you
for the question?"

Leonard then told him of the inquiries instituted by
Doctor Hodges relative to Nizza's retreat, and how they
had been baffled. " It is strange," he continued, " that
Nizza herself never heard the real name of her persecutor, neither can she tell where the house to which she
was conveyed, when in a fainting condition, and from
which she was removed when attacked with the plague,
is situated."

" It is strange, indeed," observed the farmer,
musingly.

Soon after this, Nizza Macascree made her appearance, and informed them that Amabel had fallen into a
tranquil slumber, which, in all probability, would completely renovate her.

" I hope it will," said Wingfield. " But I shall not part
with her to-day."

He then entered into conversation with Nizza, and
after a little time, proposed to her and Leonard to
walk across the fields with him to Willesden, to visit his
daughter's grave.

" My wife will take charge of Amabel," he said; " you may safely trust her in her hands."

Leonard could raise no objection, except the possibility that the Earl of Rochester and his companions might discover their retreat, and carry off Amabel in his absence; but, after a little reflection, considering this altogether unlikely, he assented, and they set out. A pleasant walk across the fields brought them to the pretty little village of Willesden and its old and beautiful church. They proceeded to the grave of poor Sarah Wingfield, which lay at the east of the church beneath one of the tall elms, and Nizza, as she stood by the rounded sod covering the remains of the unfortunate girl, could not restrain her tears.

" This might have been my own fate," she said. " What an escape I have had!"

" I did not bring you here to read you a lesson," said Wingfield, in a tone of deep emotion, " but because you, who know the temptation to which the poor creature who lies there was exposed, will pity her. Not alone did remorse for her conduct prey upon her spirits,—not alone did she suffer from self-reproach,—but the scoffs and jeers of her sex, who never forgive an erring sister, broke her heart. She is now, however, beyond the reach of human malice, and, I trust, at peace."

As he said this, he walked away to hide his emotion, and presently afterwards rejoining them, they quitted the churchyard together.

As they recrossed the fields, Wingfield observed two men digging a hole in the gronnd, and guessing their object, paused for a few minutes to watch them. Having thrown out the earth to the depth of a couple of feet, one of them took a long hooked pole, and attaching it to the body of a victim of the pestilence, who had wandered into the fields and died there, dragged it towards the pit. As soon as the corpse was pushed into its narrow receptacle, the clay was shovelled over it, and trodden down.

" This is a sad mode of burial for a Christian," observed Wingfield. " But it would not do to leave an infected body to rot in the fields, and spread the contagion."

"Such a grave is better than the plague-pit," rejoined Leonard, recalling the frightful scenes he had witnessed there.

On reaching Wingfield's dwelling, they found from the good dame that Amabel had awakened from her slumber greatly refreshed; but she gave it as her opinion that she had better remain undisturbed. Accordingly, no one went into the room to her except Nizza Macascree. A substantial dinner was provided for his guests by the hospitable farmer; and Blaize, who had been for some time confined to salt provisions at his master's house, did ample justice to the fresh meat and vegetables.

The meal over, Leonard, who felt exceedingly curious to learn what had become of the mysterious stranger whose child he had carried to the plague-pit, and who had appeared so strangely interested in Nizza Macascree, determined to walk to the pest-house in Finsbury-fields, and inquire after him. On communicating his intention to his host, Wingfield would have dissuaded him, but as Leonard affirmed he had no fear of infection, he desisted from the attempt. Just as the apprentice was starting, Blaize came up to him, and said,—" Leonard, I have a great curiosity to see a pest-house, and should like to go with you, if you will let me."

The apprentice stared at him in astonishment.

" You will never dare to enter it," he said.

" I will go wherever you go," replied the porter, with a confidence mainly inspired by the hospitable farmer's strong ale.

" We shall see," replied Leonard. " I shall keep you to your word."

In less than an hour they reached Marylebone-fields (now the Regent's-park), and crossing them, entered a lane, running in pretty nearly the same direction as the present New-road. It brought them to Clerkenwell, when they proceeded to Finsbury-fields, and soon came in sight of the pest-house. When Blaize found himself so near this dreaded asylum, all his courage vanished.

"I would certainly enter the pest-house with you," he said to Leonard, "but I have used up all my vinegar, and you know I lost my box of rufuses, and the pot of anti-pestilential confection this morning."

"That excuse shall not serve your turn," replied Leonard. "You can get plenty of vinegar and plague medicine in the pest-house.'

"But I have not money to pay for them," rejoined Blaize.

"I will lend you some," said Leonard, placing a few pieces in his hand. "Now, come along."

Blaize would fain have run away, but afraid of incurring the apprentice's anger, he walked tremblingly after him. They entered the garden-gate, and soon reached the principal door, which, as usual, stood open. Scarcely able to support himself, the porter tottered into the large room; but as he cast his eyes around, and beheld the miserable occupants of the pallets, and heard their cries and groans, he was so scared that he could not move another step, but stood like one transfixed with terror. Paying little attention to him, Leonard walked forward, and at the further extremity of the chamber found the young chirurgeon whom he had formerly seen, and describing the stranger, inquired where he was placed.

"The person you allude to has been removed," returned the chirurgeon. "Doctor Hodges visited him this morning, and had him conveyed to his own dwelling."

"Was he sensible at the time?" asked the apprentice.

"I think not," replied the chirurgeon; "but the doctor appeared to recognise in him an old friend. though I did not hear him mention his name; and it was on, that account, I conclude, that he had him removed."

"Is he he likely to recover?" asked Leonard, whose curiosity was aroused by what he heard.

"That is impossible to say," replied the young man.

" But he cannot be in better hands than those of Doctor Hodges."

Leonard perfectly concurred with him, and after a few minutes' further conversation, turned to depart. Not seeing Blaize, he concluded he had gone forth, and expected to find him in the garden, or, at all events, in the field adjoining. But he was nowhere to be seen. While wondering what had become of him, Leonard heard a loud cry, in the voice of the porter, issuing from the barn, which, as has already been stated, had been converted into a receptacle for the sick; and hurrying thither, he found Blaize in the hands of two stout assistants, who had stripped him of his clothes, and were tying him down to a pallet. On seeing Leonard, Blaize implored him to deliver him from the hands of his persecutors; and the apprentice assuring the assistants that the poor fellow was perfectly free from infection, they liberated him.

It appeared, on inquiry, that Blaize had fallen against one of the pallets in a state almost of insensibility, and the two assistants, chancing to pass at the time, and taking him for a plague patient, had conveyed him to the barn. On reaching it, he recovered, and besought them to set him free, but they paid no attention to his cries, and proceeded to strip him, and bind him to the bed, as before related.

Thus released, the porter lost no time in dressing himself; and Leonard, to allay his terrors, had a strong dose of anti-pestilential elixer administered to him. After which, having procured him a box of rufuses, and a phial of plague-water, Blaize shook off his apprehension, and they set out at a brisk pace for Kensal-green.

CHAPTER VII

The Journey

BLAIZE was destined to experience a second fright. It has been mentioned that the infected were sometimes seized with a rabid desire of communicating the disorder to such as had not been attacked by it; and as the pair were making the best of their way along the Harrow-road, a poor lazar who was lying against the hedge-side, and had vainly implored their assistance, suddenly started up, and with furious cries and gestures, made towards the porter. Guessing his intention, Blaize took to his heels, and finding himself closely pressed, broke through the hedge on the right, and speeded across the field. In spite of the alarming nature of the occurrence, the apprentice could not help laughing at the unwonted agility displayed by the fat little porter, who ran so swiftly that it appeared probable he would distance his pursuer. To prevent mischief, however, Leonard set off after him, and was fast gaining upon the lazar, whose strength was evidently failing, when the poor wretch uttered a loud cry, and fell to the ground. On coming up, Leonard found him lying with his face in the grass, and convulsed by the agonies of death, and perceiving that all was over, hurried after the porter, whom he found seated on a gate, at the further end of the field, solacing himself with a draught of plague-water.

"Oh, Leonard!" groaned the latter, "how little do we know what is for our good! I was delighted to quit my master's house this morning, but I now wish with all my heart I was back again. I am afraid I shall die of the plague after all. Pray what are the first symptoms?"

"Pooh! pooh! don't think about it, and you will take no harm," rejoined Leonard. "Put by your phial, and let us made the best of our way to Farmer Wingfield's dwelling."

Being now in sight of the farm, which, from its

elevated situation, could be distinguished at a distance
of two miles in this direction, they easily shaped their
course towards it across the fields. When about half
way up the hill, Leonard paused to look behind him.
The view was exquisite, and it was precisely the hour
(just before sunset) at which it could be seen to the
greatest advantage. On the right, his gaze wandered
to the beautiful and well-wooded heights of Richmond
and Wimbledon, beyond which he could trace the long
line of the Surrey hills, while nearer he perceived Not-
ting-hill, now covered with habitations, but then a ver-
dant knoll, crowned by a few trees, but without so much
as a cottage upon it. On the left stood Hampstead: at
that time a collection of pretty cottages, but wanting its
present chief ornament, the church. At the foot of
the hill rich meadows, bordered with fine hedges, inter-
spersed with well-grown timber, spread out as far as the
eye could reach. Nothing destroyed the rural character
of the prospect; nor was there any indication of the
neighbourhood of a great city, except the lofty tower
and massive body of Saint Paul's, which appeared above
the tops of the intervening trees in the distance.

As on former occasions, when contemplating the
surrounding country from the summit of the cathedral,
Leonard could not help contrasting the beauty of the
scene before him with the horrible scourge by which it
was ravaged. Never had the country looked so beautiful—never, therefore, was the contrast so forcible; and
it appeared to him like a lovely mask hiding the hideous
and ghastly features of death. Tinged by the sombre
hue of his thoughts, the whole scene changed its complexion. The smiling landscape seemed to darken, and
the cool air of evening to become hot and noisome, as
if laden with the deadly exhalations of the pestilence.
Nor did the workings of his imagination stop here. He
fancied even at this distance,—nearly seven miles,—that
he could discern Solomon Eagle on the summit of Saint
Paul's. At first, the figure looked like a small black
speck; but it gradually dilated, until it became twice
the size of the cathedral, upon the central tower of

which its feet rested, while its arms were spread abroad over the city. In its right hand the gigantic figure held a blazing torch, and in the left a phial, from the mouth of which a stream of dark liquid descended. So vividly did this phantasm present itself to Leonard, that, almost convinced of its reality, he placed his hands before his eyes for a few moments, and on withdrawing them, was glad to find that the delusion was occasioned by a black cloud over the cathedral, which his distempered fancy had converted into the colossal figure of the enthusiast.

Blaize, who had taken the opportunity of his companion's abstraction to sip a little more plague-water, now approached, and told him that Wingfield was descending the hill to meet them. Rousing himself, Leonard ran towards the farmer, who appeared delighted to see them back again, and conducted them to his dwelling. Owing to the tender and truly maternal attention of Dame Wingfield, Amabel was so much better that she was able to join the party at supper, though she took no share in the meal. Wingfield listened to the soft tones of her voice as she conversed with his wife, and at last, unable to control his emotion, laid down his knife and fork, and quitted the table.

" What is the matter with your husband?" inquired Amabel, of her hostess. " I hope he is not unwell."

" Oh! no," replied the good dame; " your voice reminds him of our daughter, whose history I have related to you,—that is all."

" Alas!" exclaimed Amabel, with a sympathizing look, " I will be silent, if it pains him to hear me speak."

" On no account," rejoined Dame Wingfield. " The tears he has shed will relieve him. He could not weep when poor Sarah died, and I feared his heart would break. Talk to him as you have talked to me, and you will do him a world of good."

Shortly afterwards, the farmer returned to the table, and the meal proceeded to its close without further interruption. As soon as the board was cleared, Wing-

OLD ST. PAUL'S   333

field took a chair by Amabel, who, in compliance with his wife's request, spoke to him about his daughter, and in terms calculated to afford him consolation. Leonard was enraptured by her discourse, and put so little constraint upon his admiration, that Nizza Macascree could not repress a pang of jealousy. As to Blaize, who had eaten as much as he could cram, and emptied a large jug of the farmer's stout ale, he took his chair to a corner, and speedily fell asleep; his hoarse but tranquil breathing proving that the alarms he had undergone during the day did not haunt his slumbers. Before separating for the night, Amabel entreated that prayers might be said, and her request being readily granted, she was about to retire with Nizza, when Wingfield detained them.

"I have been thinking that I might offer you a safe asylum here," he said. "If you like it, you shall remain with us till your health is fully reinstated."

"I thank you most kindly for the offer," returned Amabel, gratefully; "and if I do not accept it, it is neither because I should not esteem myself safe here, nor because I am unwilling to be indebted to your hospitality, but that I have been specially advised, as my last chance of recovery, to try the air of Berkshire. I have little hope myself, but I owe it to those who love me, to make the experiment."

"If such is the case," returned the farmer, "I will not attempt to persuade you further. But if, at any future time, you should need change of air, my house shall be entirely at your service."

Dame Wingfield warmly seconded her husband's wish, and with renewed thanks, Amabel and her companion withdrew. As there was not sufficient room for their accommodation within the house, Leonard and the porter took up their quarters in the barn, and throwing themselves upon a heap of straw, slept soundly till three o'clock, when they arose, and began to prepare for their journey. Wingfield was likewise astir, and after assisting them to feed and dress their horses, took them into the house, where a plentiful breakfast awaited them. At the close of the meal, Amabel and Nizza, who had breakfasted in their own room, made their appearance. All being in readiness for their departure, Dame Wingfield took leave of her guests with tears in her eyes, and the honest farmer was little less affected. Both gazed after them as long as they continued in sight.

Having ascertained from Wingfield the route they ought to pursue, Leonard proceeded about a quarter of a mile along the Harrow-road, and then turned off on the left into a common, which brought them to Acton, from whence they threaded a devious lane to Brentford. Here they encountered several fugitives from the great city, and as they approached Hounslow, learnt from other wayfarers that a band of highwaymen, by whom the heath was infested, had become more than usually daring since the outbreak of the pestilence, and claimed a heavy tax from all travellers. This was bad news to Leonard, who became apprehensive for the safety of the bag of gold given to Nizza by the enthusiast, and he would have taken another road if it had been practicable; but as there was no alternative except to proceed, he put all the money he had about him into a leathern purse, trusting that the highwaymen, if they attacked them, would be content with this booty.

When about half way across the vast heath, which spread around them, in a wild but not unpicturesque expanse, for many miles on either side, Leonard perceived a band of horsemen, amounting perhaps to a dozen, galloping towards them, and not doubting they were the robbers in question, communicated his suspicions to his companions. Neither Amabel not Nizza Macascree appeared much alarmed, but Blaize was so terrified that he could scarcely keep his seat, and was with difficulty prevented from turning his horse's head and riding off in the opposite direction.

By this time the highwaymen had come up. With loud oaths, two of their number held pistols to the heads of Leonard and Blaize, and demanded their money. The apprentice replied by drawing forth his purse, and besought the fellow to whom he gave it not to maltreat his companion. The man rejoined with a savage imprecation

that he "would maltreat them both if they did not instantly dismount and let him search the saddle-bags;"
and he was proceeding to drag Amabel from the saddle,
when Leonard struck him a violent blow with his heavy
riding-whip, which brought him to the ground. He was
up again, however, in an instant, and would have fired
his pistol at the apprentice, if a masked individual, who
was evidently, from the richness of his attire and the
deference paid him by the others, the captain of the band,
had not interfered.

"You are rightly served, Dick Dosset," said the person,
"for your rudeness to a lady. I will have none of my
band guilty of incivility, and if this young man had not
punished you, I would have done so myself. Pass free,
my pretty damsel," he added, bowing gallantly to
Amabel; "you shall not be further molested."

Meanwhile, Blaize exhibited the contents of his
pockets to the other highwayman, who, having opened
the box of rufuses and smelt at the phial of plague-
water, returned them to him with a look of disgust, and
bade him follow his companions. As Leonard was departing, the captain of the band rode after him, and
inquired whether he had heard at what hour the king
meant to leave Whitehall.

"The court is about to adjourn to Oxford," he added,
"and the king and some of his courtiers will cross the
heath to-day, when I propose to levy the same tax from
his Majesty that I do from his subjects."

Leonard replied that he was utterly ignorant of the
king's movements; and explaining whence he came, the
captain left him. The intelligence he had thus accidentally obtained was far from satisfactory to the apprentice.
For some distance their road would be the same as that
about to be taken by the monarch and his attendants,
amongst whom it was not improbable Rochester might
be numbered; and the possibility that the earl might over-
take them and discover Amabel filled him with uneasiness. Concealing his alarm, however, he urged his steed
to a quicker pace, and proceeded briskly on his way,
glad, at least, that he had not lost Solomon Eagle's gift

to Nizza. Amabel's weakly condition compelled them to
rest at frequent intervals, and it was not until evening was
drawing in that they descended the steep hill leading to
the beautiful village of Henley-upon-Thames, where they
proposed to halt for the night.

Crossing the bridge, they found a considerable number
of the inhabitants assembled in the main street and in
the market-place, in expectation of the king's passing
through the town on his way to Oxford, intimation of
his approach having been conveyed by avant-couriers.
Leonard proceeded to the principal inn, and was fortunate enough to procure accommodation. Having
conducted Amabel and Nizza to their room, he was
repairing to the stable with Blaize to see after their
steeds, when a loud blowing of horns was heard on the
bridge, succeeded by the tramp of horses and the rattling
of wheels, and the next moment, four valets in splendid
livery rode up, followed by a magnificent coach The
shouts of the assemblage proclaimed that it was the king.
The cavalcade stopped before the inn, from the yard of
which six fine horses were brought and attached to the
royal carriage, in place of others which were removed.
Charles was laughing heartily, and desired his attendants,
who were neither numerous nor well-armed, to take care
they were not robbed again between this place and
Oxford; " though," added the monarch, " it is now of
little consequence, since we have nothing to lose."

" Is it possible your Majesty can have been robbed?"
asked the landlord, who stood cap in hand at the door
of the carriage.

" I'faith, man, it *is* possible," rejoined the king. " We
were stopped on Hounslow Heath by a band of highwaymen, who carried off two large coffers filled with gold,
and would have eased us of our swords and snuff-boxes,
but for the interposition of their captain, who, as we live,
is one of the politest men breathing,—is he not,
Rochester?"

Leonard Holt, who was among the crowd of spectators, started at the mention of this name, and he
trembled as the earl leaned forward, in answer to the

king's question. The eyes of the rivals met at this moment, for both were within a few yards of each other, and Rochester, whose cheek was flushed with anger, solicited the king's permission to alight, but Charles, affirming it was getting late, would not permit him, and as the horses were harnessed, and the drivers mounted, he ordered them to proceed without delay.

Inexpressibly relieved by his rival's departure, Leonard returned to the house, and acquainted Amabel with what had occurred. Quitting Henley betimes on the following morning, they arrived in about three hours at Wallingford, where they halted for some time, and then pursuing their journey, reached Wantage at four o'clock, where they tarried for an hour. Up to this hour Leonard had doubted the possibility of reaching their destination that night; but Amabel assuring him she felt no fatigue, he determined to push on. Accordingly, having refreshed their steeds, they set forward, and soon began to mount the beautiful downs lying on the west of this ancient town.

Crossing these heights, whence they obtained the most magnificent and extensive views of the surrounding country, they reached in about three-quarters of an hour the pretty little hamlet of Kingston Lisle. Here they again paused at a small inn at the foot of a lofty hill, denominated, from a curious relic kept there, the Blowing Stone. This rocky fragment, which is still in existence, is perforated by a number of holes, which emit, if blown into, a strange bellowing sound. Unaware of this circumstance, Leonard entered the house with the others, and had just seated himself, when they were astounded by a strange unearthly roar. Rushing forth, Leonard found Blaize with his cheeks puffed out and his mouth applied to the stone, into which he was blowing with all his force, and producing the above-mentioned extraordinary noise.

Shortly after this the party quitted the Blowing Stone, and having toiled up the steep sides of the hill, they were amply repaid on reaching its summit by one of the finest views they had ever beheld. In fact, the

hill on which they stood commanded the whole of the
extensive and beautiful vale of the White Horse, which
was spread out before them as far as the eye could
reach, like a vast panorama, disclosing a thousand fields
covered with abundant, though as yet immature crops.
It was a goodly prospect, and seemed to promise plenty
and prosperity to the country. Almost beneath them
stood the reverend church of Uffington over-topping
the ancient village clustering around it. Numerous other
towers and spires could be seen peeping out of groves
of trees, which, together with the scattered mansions
and farmhouses surrounded by granges and stacks of
hay and beans, gave interest and diversity to the prospect.
The two most prominent objects in the view were the
wooded heights of Farringdon, on the one hand, and
those of Abingdon on the other.

Proceeding along the old Roman road, still distinctly
marked out, and running along the ridge of this beautiful chain of hills, they arrived at an immense Roman
encampment, vulgarly called Uffingham Castle, occupying the crown of a hill. A shepherd, who was tending
a flock of sheep which were browsing on the delicious
herbage to be found within the vast circular space
enclosed by the inner vallum of the camp, explained its
purpose, and they could not but regard it with interest.
He informed them that they were in the neighbourhood
of the famous White Horse, a figure cut out of the turf
on the hillside by the Saxons, and visible for many
miles. Conducting them to a point whence they could
survey this curious work, their guide next directed them
to Ashdown Lodge, which lay, he told them, at about
four miles' distance. They had wandered a little out of
their course, but he accompanied them for a mile, until
they came in sight of a thick grove of trees clothing a
beautiful valley, above which could be seen the lofty
cupola of the mansion.

Cheered by the sight, and invigorated by the fresh
breeze blowing in this healthful region, they pressed forward, and soon drew near the mansion, which they found
was approached by four noble avenues. They had not

advanced far, when a stalwart personage, six feet two high, and proportionately stoutly made, issued from the covert. He had a gun over his shoulder, and was attended by a couple of fine dogs. Telling them he was called John Lutcombe, and was the Earl of Craven's gamekeeper, he inquired their business; and on being informed of it, changed his surly manner to one of grea cordiality, and informed them that Mrs. Buscot—such was the name of Amabel's aunt,—was at home, and would be heartily glad to see them.

" I have often heard her speak of her brother, Mr. Bloundel," he said, " and am well aware that he is an excellent man. Poor soul! she has been very uneasy about him and his family during this awful dispensation, though she had received a letter to say that he was about to close his house, and hoped, under the blessing of Providence, to escape the pestilence. His daughter will be welcome, and she cannot come to a healthier spot than Ashdown, nor to a better nurse than Mrs. Buscot."

With this, he led the way to the court-yard, and entering the dwelling, presently returned with a middle-aged woman, whom Amabel instantly knew, from the likeness to her father, must be her aunt. Mrs. Buscot caught her in her arms and most smothered her with kisses. As soon as the first transports of surprise and joy had subsided, the good housekeeper took her niece and Nizza Macascree into the house, and desired John Lutcombe to attend to the others.

CHAPTER VIII

Ashdown Lodge

ERECTED by Inigo Jones, and still continuing in precisely the same state as at the period of this history, Ashdown Lodge is a large square edifice, built in the formal French taste of the seventeenth century, with immense casements, giving it the appearance of being all glass, a high roof lighted by dormer windows, terminated at each angle by a tall and not very ornamental chimney, and surmounted by a lofty and lantern-like belvedere, crowned in its turn by a glass cupola. The belvedere opens upon a square gallery defended by a broad balustrade, and overlooking the umbrageous masses and lovely hills around it. The house, as has been stated, is approached by four noble avenues, the timber constituting which is of course much finer now than at the period under consideration, and possesses a delightful old-fashioned garden, and stately terrace. The rooms are lofty but small, and there is a magnificent staircase, occupying nearly half the interior of the building. Among other portraits decorating the walls, is one of Elizabeth Stuart, daughter of James the First, and Queen of Bohemia, for whom the first Earl of Craven entertained so romantic an attachment, and to whom he was supposed to be privately united. Nothing can be more secluded than the situation of the mansion, lying as it does in the midst of a gentle valley, surrounded by a thick wood, and without having a single habitation in view. Its chief interest, however, must always be derived from its connexion with the memory of the chivalrous and high-souled nobleman by whom it was erected, and who made it occasionally his retreat after the death of his presumed royal consort, which occurred about four years previous to the date of this history.

Amabel was delighted with her new abode, and she experienced the kindness of a parent from her aunt, with whom, owing to circumstances, she had not hitherto been personally acquainted, having only seen her when too young to retain any recollection of the event. The widow of a farmer, who had resided on Lord Craven's estate near Kingston Lisle, Mrs. Buscot, after her husband's death, had been engaged as housekeeper at Ashdown Lodge, and had filled the situation for many years to the entire satisfaction of her employer. She was two or three years older than her brother, Mr. Bloundel; but the perfect health she enjoyed, and which she attributed to the salubrious air of the downs, combined with her natural cheerfulness of disposition, made her look much the younger of the two. Her features, besides their kindly and benevolent expression, were extremely pleasing, and must, some years ago, have been beautiful. Even now, what with her fresh complexion, her white teeth, and plump figure, she made no slight pretensions to comeliness. She possessed the same good sense and integrity of character as her brother, together with his strong religious feeling, but entirely unaccompanied by austerity.

Having no children, she was able to bestow her entire affections upon Amabel, whose sad story, when she became acquainted with it, painfully affected her; nor was she less concerned at her precarious state of health. For the first day or two after their arrival, Amabel suffered greatly from the effects of the journey, but after that time she gained strength so rapidly that Mrs. Buscot, who, at first, had well-nigh despaired of her recovery, began to indulge a hope. The gentle sufferer would sit throughout the day with her aunt and Nizza Macascree in the gallery near the belvedere, inhaling the pure breeze blowing from the surrounding hills, and stirring the tree-tops beneath her.

" I never expected so much happiness," she observed, on one occasion, to Mrs. Buscot," and begin to experience the truth of Doctor Hodges' assertion, that with returning health the desire of life would return. I now wish to live."

" I am heartily glad to hear you say so," replied Mrs.

Buscot, " and hold it a certain sign of your speedy restoration to health. Before you have been a month with me,
I expect to bring back the roses to those pale cheeks."

" You are too sanguine, I fear, dear aunt," rejoined
Amabel, " but the change that has taken place in my
feelings may operate beneficially upon my constitution."

" No doubt of it, my dear," replied Mrs. Buscot; " no
doubt."

The good dame felt a strong inclination at this
moment to introduce a subject very near her heart,
but feeling doubtful as to its reception, she checked
herself. The devoted attachment of the apprentice to
her niece had entirely won her regard, and she fondly
hoped she would be able to wean Amabel from all
thought of the Earl of Rochester, and induce her to give
her hand to her faithful lover. With this view, she
often spoke to her of Leonard—of his devotion and
constancy—his good looks and excellent qualities, and
though Amabel assented to all she said, Mrs. Buscot
was sorry to perceive that the impression she desired
was not produced. It was not so with Nizza Macascree.
Whenever Leonard's name was mentioned, her eye
sparkled, her cheeks glowed, and she responded so
warmly to all that was said in his praise, that Mrs. Buscot
soon found out the state of her heart. The discovery
occasioned her some little disquietude, for the worthy
creature could not bear the idea of making even her
niece happy at the expense of another.

As to the object of all this tender interest, he felt
far happier than he had done for some time. He saw
Amabel every day, and noted with unspeakable delight
the gradual improvement which appeared to be taking
place in her health. The greater part of his time,
however, was not passed in her society, but in threading the intricacies of the wood, or in rambling over the
neighbouring downs; and he not only derived pleasure
from these rambles, but his health and spirits, which
had been not a little shaken by the awful scenes he had
recently witnessed, were materially improved. Here, at
last, he seemed to have got rid of the grim spectre

which, for two months, had constantly haunted him.
No greater contrast can be conceived than his present
quiet life offered to the fearful excitement he had recently undergone. For hot and narrow thoroughfares
reeking with pestilential effluva, resounding with frightful shrieks or piteous cries, and bearing on every side
marks of the destructive progress of the scourge—for
these terrible sights and sounds—for the charnel horrors
of the plague-pit—the scarcely less revolting scenes at
the pest-house—the dismal bell announcing the dead-
cart—the doleful cries of the buriers—for graves sur-
feited with corruption, and streets filled with the dying
and the dead—and, above all, for the ever-haunting
expectation that a like fate might be his own,—he had
exchanged green hills, fresh breezes, spreading views,
the song of the lark, and a thousand other delights, and
assurances of health and contentment. Often, as he
gazed from the ridge of the downs into the wide-
spread vale beneath, he wondered whether the destroying angel had smitten any of its peaceful habitations,
and breathed a prayer for their preservation.

But the satisfaction he derived from having quitted
the infected city was trifling compared with that of
Blaize, whose sole anxiety was lest he should be sent
back to London. Seldom straying further than the
gates of the mansion, though often invited by John Lutcombe to accompany him to some of the neighbouring
villages; having little to do, and less to think of,
unless to calculate how much he could consume at the
next meal,—for he had banished all idea of the plague,—
he conceived himself at the summit of happiness, and
waxed so sleek and round that his face shone like a full
moon, while his doublet would scarcely meet around
his waist.

One day, about a fortnight after their arrival, and
when things were in this happy state, Amabel, who was
seated as usual in the gallery at the summit of the house,
observed a troop of horsemen, very gallantly equipped,
appear at the further end of the northern avenue. An

inexpressible terror seized her, and she would have fled
into the house, but her limbs refused their office.

"Look there!" she cried to Nizza, who, at that
moment, presented herself at the glass door. "Look
there!" she said, pointing to the cavalcade; "what I
dreaded has come to pass. The Earl of Rochester has
found me out, and is coming hither to carry me off. But
I will die rather than accompany him."

"You may be mistaken," replied Nizza, expressing a
hopefulness which her looks belied; "it may be the
Earl of Craven."

"You give me new life," rejoined Amabel; "but
no—no—my aunt has told me that the good earl will
not quit the city during the continuance of the plague.
And see! some of the horsemen have distinguished us,
and are waving their hats. My heart tells me the Earl
of Rochester is amongst them. Give me your arm, Nizza,
and I will try to gain some place of concealment."

"Ay, let us fly," replied the other, assisting her towards the door; "I am in equal danger with yourself,
for Sir Paul Parravicin is doubtless with them. Oh!
where—where is Leonard?"

"He must be below," cried Amabel. "But he could
not aid us at this juncture; we must depend upon
ourselves."

Descending a short staircase, they entered Amabel's
chamber, and fastening the door, awaited with breathless anxiety the arrival of the horsemen. Through the
room whither they had retreated was in the upper part
of the house, they could distinctly hear what was going
on below, and shortly afterwards the sound of footsteps
on the stairs, blended with merry voices and loud
laughter—amid which Amabel could distinguish the
tones of the Earl of Rochester—reached them.

While both were palpitating with fright, the handle
of the door was tried, and a voice announced that the
apprentice was without.

"All is lost!" he cried, speaking through the keyhole;
"the king is here, and is accompanied by the Earl of
Rochester and other profligates."

"The king!" exclaimed Amabel, joyfully; "then I am no longer apprehensive."

"As yet, no inquiries have been made after you," continued Leonard, unconscious of the effect produced by his intelligence, "but it is evident they know you are here. Be prepared, therefore."

"I *am* prepared," rejoined Amabel. And as she spoke, she threw open the door and admitted Leonard. "Do not stay with us," she added to him. "In case of need, I will throw myself on his Majesty's protection."

"It will avail you little," rejoined Leonard, distrustfully.

"I do not think so," said Amabel, confidently. "I have faith in his acknowledged kindness of heart."

"Perhaps you are right," returned Leonard. "Mrs. Buscot is at present with his Majesty in the receiving-room. Will you not make fast your door?"

"No," replied Amabel, firmly; "if the king will not defend me, I will defend myself."

Leonard glanced at her with admiration, but he said nothing.

"Is Sir Paul Parravicin here?" asked Nizza Macascree, with great anxiety.

"I have not seen him," replied Leonard; "and I have carefully examined the countenances of all the king's attendants."

"Heaven be praised!" exclaimed Nizza.

At this juncture, Mrs. Buscot entered the room. Her looks bespoke great agitation, and she trembled violently.

"You have no doubt heard from Leonard that the king and his courtiers are below," she said. "His Majesty inquired whether you were here, and I did not dare to deceive him. He desires to see you, and has sent me for you. What is to be done?" she added, with a look of distraction. "I suppose you must obey."

"There is no alternative," replied Amabel; "I will obey his Majesty's commands as soon as I can collect myself. Take back that answer, dear aunt."

"Has Leonard told you that the Earl of Rochester is here?" pursued Mrs. Buscot.

Amabel replied in the affirmative.

" God grant that good may come of it!" cried Mrs.
Buscot, clasping her hands together, as she quitted the
room; " but I am sorely afraid."

A half-suppressed groan from the apprentice told that
he shared in her apprehensions.

" Leave us, Leonard," said Amabel; " I would prepare
myself for the interview."

The apprentice obeyed, and closing the door after
him, stationed himself at the foot of the staircase. Left
alone with Nizza, Amabel threw herself on her knees,
and besought the support of Heaven on this trying
occasion. She then arose, and giving her hand to
Nizza, they went downstairs together. Leonard followed them at a little distance, and with a beating heart.
Two gentlemen-ushers were posted at the door of the
chamber occupied by the King. Not far from them
stood Mrs. Buscot, who, having made known her niece
to the officials, they instantly admitted her, but ordered
Nizza to remain outside.

On entering the room, Amabel at once discovered the
king. He was habited in a magnificent riding-dress,
and was seated on a rich fauteuil, around which were
grouped a dozen gaily-attired courtiers. Among these
were the Earl of Rochester and Sir George Etherege.
As Amabel advanced, glances of insolent curiosity were
directed towards her, and Rochester, stepping forward,
offered to lead her to the king. She, however, declined
the attention. Greatly mortified, the earl would have
seized her hand; but there was so much dignity in her
deportment, so much coldness in her looks, that in spite
of his effrontery, he felt abashed. Charles smiled at his
favourite's rebuff, but, in common with the others, he
could not help being struck by Amabel's extraordinary
beauty and natural dignity, and he observed, in an undertone, to Etherege, " Is it possible this can be a grocer's
daughter?"

" She passes for such, my liege," replied Etherege,
with a smile. " But I cannot swear to her parentage."

" Since I have seen her, I do not wonder at Rochester's

extravagant passion," rejoined the monarch. " But, odds fish! she seems to care little for him."

Having approached within a short distance of the king, Amabel would have prostrated herself before him, but he prevented her.

" Nay, do not kneel, sweetheart," he said, " I am fully satisfied of your loyalty, and never exact homage from one of your sex, but, on the contrary, am ever ready to pay it. I have heard much of your attractions, and, what is seldom the case in such matters, find they have not been overrated. The brightest of our court beauties cannot compare with you."

" A moment ago the fair Amabel might be said to lack bloom," observed Etherege; " but your Majesty's praises have called a glowing colour to her cheek."

" Would you deign to grant me a moment's hearing, my liege?" said Amabel, looking steadfastly at the king.

" Not a moment's hearing merely, sweetheart," returned Charles; " but an hour's, if you list. I could dwell on the music of your tones for ever."

" I thank your Majesty for your condescension," she replied; " but I will not long trespass on your patience. What I have to say concerns the Earl of Rochester."

" Stand forward, my lord!" said Charles to the earl, " and let us hear what complaint is to be made against you."

Rochester advanced, and threw a passionate and half-reproachful glance at Amabel.

" It may be improper for me to trouble your Majesty on so light a matter," said Amabel; " but your kindness emboldens me to speak unreservedly. You may be aware that this nobleman once entertained, or feigned to entertain, an ardent attachment to me."

" I need scarcely assure you, my liege," interposed Rochester, " that it was no feigned passion. And it is needless to add, that however ardently I felt towards my fair accuser then, my passion has in nowise abated."

" I should wonder if it had," rejoined Charles, gallantly.

" I will not contradict you, my lord," said Amabel;

"it *is* possible you may have loved me, though I find it difficult to reconcile your professions of regard with your conduct—but this is not to the purpose. Whether you loved me or not, I loved *you*—deeply and devotedly. There is no sacrifice I would not have made for him," she continued, turning to the king, "and influenced by these feelings, and deluded by false promises, I forgot my duty, and was rash enough to quit my home with him."

"All this I have heard, sweetheart," replied Charles. "There is nothing very remarkable in it. It is the ordinary course of such affairs. I am happy to be the means of restoring your lover to you, and, in fact, came hither for that very purpose."

"You mistake me, my liege," replied Amabel. "I do not desire to have him restored to me. Fortunately for myself, I have succeeded in mastering my love for him. The struggle has well-nigh cost me my life—but I *have* conquered."

"I have yet to learn, sweetheart," observed Charles, with an incredulous look, "that woman's love, if deeply fixed, *can* be subdued."

"If I had not been supported by religion, my liege, I could *not* have subdued it," rejoined Amabel. "Night and day I have passed in supplicating the Great Power that implanted this fatal passion in my breast, and, at length, my prayers have prevailed."

"Aha! we have a devotee here!" thought Charles. "Am I to understand, fair saint, that you would reject the earl, if he were to offer you his hand?" he asked.

"Unquestionably," replied Amabel, firmly.

"This is strange," muttered Charles. "The girl is evidently in earnest. What say your lordship?" he added to Rochester.

"That she shall be mine, whether she loves me or not," replied the earl. "My pride is piqued to the conquest."

"No wonder!—the resistless Rochester flouted by a grocer's daughter. Ha! ha!" observed Charles, laughing, while the rest of the courtiers joined in his merriment.

"Oh! sire," exclaimed Amabel, throwing herself at the king's feet, and bursting into tears, "do not abandon me, I beseech you. I cannot requite the earl's attachment—and shall die if he continues his pursuit. Command him—oh! command him to desist."

"I fear you have not dealt fairly with me, sweetheart," said the king. "There is a well-favoured youth without, whom the earl pointed out as your father's apprentice. Have you transferred your affections to him?"

"Your Majesty has solved the enigma," observed Rochester, bitterly.

"You wrong me, my lord," replied Amabel. "Leonard Holt is without. Let him be brought into the royal presence and interrogated; and if he will affirm that I have given him the slightest encouragement by look or word, or even state that he himself indulges a hope of holding a place in my regards, I will admit there is some foundation for the charge. I pray your Majesty to send for him."

"It is needless," replied Charles, coldly. "I do not doubt your assertion. But you will do the earl an injustice as well as yourself, if you do not allow him a fair hearing."

"If you will allow me five minutes alone with you, Amabel, or will take a single turn with me on the terrace, I will engage to remove every doubt," insinuated Rochester.

"You would fail to do so, my lord," replied Amabel. "The time is gone by when those accents, once so winning in my ear, can move me."

"At least give me the opportunity," implored the earl.

"No," replied Amabel, decidedly, "I will never willingly meet you more ; for though I am firm in my purpose, I do not think it right to expose myself to temptation And now that I have put your Majesty in full possession of my sentiments," she added, to the king; "now that I have told you with what bitter tears I have striven to wash out my error,—I implore you to extend your protecting hand towards me, and to save me from further persecution on the part of the earl."

"I shall remain at this place to-night," returned Charles. "Take till to-morrow to consider of it, and if you continue in the same mind, your request shall be granted."

"At least, enjoin the earl to leave me unmolested till then," cried Amabel.

"Hum!" exclaimed the king, exchanging a look with Rochester.

"For pity, sire, do not hesitate," cried Amabel, in a tone of such agony that the good-natured monarch could not resist it.

"Well, well," he rejoined; "it shall be as you desire. Rochester, you have heard our promise, and will act in conformity with it."

The earl bowed carelessly.

"Nay, nay, my lord," pursued Charles, authoritatively, "my commands *shall* be obeyed, and if you purpose otherwise, I will place you under restraint."

"Your Majesty's wishes are sufficient restraint," rejoined Rochester; "I am all obedience."

"It is well," replied Charles. "Are you satisfied, fair damsel?"

"Perfectly," replied Amabel. And making a profound and grateful reverence to the king, she retired.

Nizza Macascree met her at the door, and it was fortunate she did so, or Amabel, whose strength began to fail her, would otherwise have fallen. While she was thus engaged, Charles caught sight of the piper's daughter, and being greatly struck by her beauty, inquired her name.

"Odds fish!" he exclaimed, when informed of it by Rochester, "a piper's daughter! She is far more beautiful than your mistress."

"If I procure her for your Majesty, will you withdraw your interdiction from me?" rejoined the earl.

"No—no—that is impossible, after the pledge I have given," replied Charles. "But you must bring this lovely creature to me anon. I am enchanted with her, and do not regret this long ride, since it has brought her under my notice."

"Your Majesty's wishes shall be obeyed," said Rochester. "I will not wait till to-morrow for an interview with Amabel," he added to himself.

Supported by Nizza Macascree and her aunt, and followed by Leonard, Amabel contrived to reach her own chamber, and as soon as she was sufficiently recovered from the agitation she had experienced, detailed to them all that had passed in her interview with the king. While the party were consulting together as to the course to be pursued in this emergency, the tap of a wand was heard at the door, and the summons being answered by Mrs. Buscot, she found one of the ushers without who informed her it was the king's pleasure that no one should leave the house till the following day, without his permission.

"To ensure obedience to his orders," continued the usher, "his Majesty requires that the keys of the stables be delivered to the keeping of his chief page, Mr. Chiffinch, who has orders, together with myself, to keep watch during the night."

So saying he bowed and retired, while Mrs. Buscot returned with this new and alarming piece of intelligence to the others.

"Why should the mandate be respected?" cried Leonard, indignantly. "We have committed no crime, and ought not to be detained prisoners. Trust to me, and I will find some means of eluding their vigilance. If you remain here till to-morrow," he added to Amabel, "you are lost."

"Do not expect any rational advice from me, my dear niece," observed Mrs. Bruscot, "for I am fairly bewildered."

"Shall I not forfeit the king's protection by disobeying his injunctions?" replied Amabel. "I am safer here than if I were to seek a new asylum, which would be speedily discovered."

"Heaven grant you may not have cause to repent your decision!" cried Leonard, despondingly.

"I must now, perforce, quit you, my dear niece," said Mrs. Buscot, "though it breaks my heart to do so. His Majesty's arrival has thrown everything into confusion, and if I do not look after the supper, which is commanded at an early hour, it will never be ready. As it is, there will be nothing fit to set before him. What with my distress about you, and my anxiety about the royal repast, I am well-nigh beside myself."

With this, she quitted the room, and Amabel signifying to Leonard that she desired to be left alone with Nizza Macascree, he departed at the same time.

As Mrs. Buscot had stated, the utmost confusion prevailed below. The royal purveyor, and cook, who formed part of the king's suite, were busily employed in the kitchen, and though they had the whole household at their command, they made rather slow progress at first, owing to the want of materials. In a short time, however, this difficulty was remedied. Ducks were slaughtered by the dozen; fowls by the score, and a couple of fat geese shared the same fate. The store-ponds were visited for fish by John Lutcombe; and as the country abounded with game, a large supply of pheasants, partridges and rabbits were speedily procured by the keeper and his assistants. Amongst others, Blaize lent a helping hand in this devastation of the poultry-yard, and he had just returned to the kitchen, and commenced plucking one of the geese, when he was aroused by a slap on the shoulder, and looking up beheld Pillichody.

"What ho! my little Blaize, my physic-taking porter," cried the bully; "how wags the world with you? And how is my pretty Patience? How is that peerless kitchen-maid? By the god of love! I am dying to behold her again."

"Patience is well enough, for aught I know," replied Blaize, in a surly tone. "But it is useless for you to think of her. She is betrothed to me."

"I know it," replied Pillichody; "but do not suppose you are the sole master of her affections. The little charmer has too good taste for that. 'Blaize,' said she to me, 'will do very well for a husband, but he cannot expect me to continue faithful to him.'"

"Cannot I?" exclaimed the porter, reddening. "Fiends take her! but I do! When did she say this?"

"When I last visited your master's house," replied Pillichody. "Sweet soul! I shall never forget her tender looks, nor the kisses she allowed me to snatch from her honeyed lips when your back was turned. The very recollection of them is enchanting."

"Zounds and fury!" cried Blaize, transported with rage. "If I am only a porter, while you pretend to be a major, I will let you see I am the better man of the two." And taking the goose by the neck, he swung it round his head like a flail, and began to batter Phillichody about the face with it.

"S'death!" cried the bully, endeavouring to draw his sword, "if you do not instantly desist, I will treat you like that accursed bird—cut your throat, pluck, stuff, roast, and eat you afterwards." He was, however, so confounded by the attack that he could offer no resistance, and in retreating caught his foot against the leg of a table, and fell backwards on the floor. Being now completely at the porter's mercy, and seeing that the latter was preparing to pursue his advantage with a rolling-pin which he had snatched from the dresser, he besought him piteously to spare him.

"Recant all you have said," cried Blaize, brandishing the rolling-pin over him. "Confess that you have calumniated Patience. Confess that she rejected your advances, if you ever dared to make any to her. Confess that she is a model of purity and constancy. Confess all this, villain, or I will break every bone in your body."

"I do confess it," replied Pillichody, abjectly. "She is all you described. She never allowed me greater freedom than a squeeze of the hand."

"That was too much," replied the porter, belabouring him with the rolling-pin. "Swear that you will never attempt such a liberty again, or I will pummel you to death. Swear it."

M

" I swear," replied Pillichody.

" Before I allow you to rise, I must disarm you to prevent mischief," cried Blaize. And kneeling down upon the prostrate bully, who groaned aloud, he drew his long blade from his side. " There, now, you may get up," he added.

So elated was Blaize with his conquest, that he could do nothing for some time but strut up and down the kitchen with the sword over his shoulder, to the infinite diversion of the other domestics, and especially of John Lutcombe, who chanced to make his appearance at the time, laden with a fresh supply of game.

" Why, Blaize, man," cried the keeper, approvingly, " I did not give you credit for half so much spirit."

" No man's courage is duly appreciated until it has been tried," rejoined Blaize. " I would combat with you, gigantic John, if Patience's fidelity were called in question."

Pillichody, meanwhile, had retired with a discomfited air into a corner, where he seated himself on a stool, and eyed the porter askance, as if meditating some terrible retaliation. Secretly apprehensive of this, and thinking it becoming to act with generosity towards his foe, Blaize marched up to him, and extended his hand in token of reconciliation. To the surprise of all, Pillichody did not reject his overtures.

" I have a great regard for you, friend Blaize," he said, " otherwise I should never rest till I had been repaid, with terrible interest, for the indignities I have endured."

" Nay, heed them not," replied Blaize. " You must make allowances for the jealous feelings you excited. I love Patience better than my life."

" Since you put it in that light," rejoined Pillichody, " I am willing to overlook the offence. Snakes and scorpions ! no man can be a greater martyr to jealousy than myself. I killed three of my most intimate friends for merely presuming to ogle the widow of Watling-street, who would have been mine, if she had not died of the plague."

" Don't talk of the plague, I beseech you," replied Blaize, with a shudder. " It is a subject never mentioned here."

"I am sorry I alluded to it, then," rejoined Pillichody. "Give me back my sword. Nay, fear nothing. I entirely forgive you, and am willing to drown the remembrance of our quarrel in a bottle of sack."

Readily assenting to the proposition, Blaize obtained the key of the cellar from the butler, and adjourning thither with Pillichody, they seated themselves on a cask with a bottle of sack and a couple of large glasses on a stool between them.

"I suppose you know why I am come hither?" observed the major, smacking his lips after his second bumper.

"Not precisely," replied Blaize. "But I presume your visit has some reference to Mistress Amabel."

"A shrewd guess," rejoined Pillichody. "And this reminds me that we have omitted to drink her health."

"Her better health," returned Blaize, emptying his glass. "Heaven be praised! she has plucked up a little since we came here."

"She would soon be herself again if she were united to the Earl of Rochester," said Pillichody.

"There you are wrong," replied Blaize. "She declares she has no longer any regard for him."

"Mere caprice, believe me," rejoined Pillichody. "She loves him better than ever."

"It may be so," returned Blaize, "for Patience, who ought to know something of the matter, assured me she was dying for the earl. And if she had not told me the contrary herself, I should not have believed it."

"Did she tell you so in the presence of Leonard?" asked Pillichody.

"Why, now I bethink me, he *was* present," replied Blaize, involuntarily putting his hand to his shoulder, as he recalled the horsewhipping he had received on that occasion.

"I knew it!" cried Pillichody. "She is afraid to confess her attachment to the earl. Is Leonard as much devoted to her as ever?"

"I fancy so," replied Blaize; "but she certainly gives *him* no encouragement."

"Confirmation!" exclaimed Pillichody. "But fill your

glass. We will drink to the earl's speedy union with Amabel."

" Not so loud," cried Blaize, looking uneasily round the cellar. " I should not like Leonard to overhear us."

" Neither should I," returned Pillichody, " for I have something to say to you respecting him."

" You need not propose any more plans for carrying off Amabel," cried Blaize, " for I won't take any part in them."

" I have no such intention," rejoined Pillichody. " The truth is," he added mysteriously, " I am inclined to side with you and Leonard. But as we have finished our bottle, suppose we take a turn in the court-yard."

" With all my heart," replied Blaize.

Immediately after Amabel's departure, Charles proceeded with his courtiers to the garden, and continued to saunter up and down the terrace for some time, during which he engaged Rochester in conversation, so as to give him no pretext for absenting himself. The king next ascended to the belvedere, and having surveyed the prospect from it, was about to descend when he caught a glimpse of Nizza Macascree on the great staircase, and instantly flew towards her.

" I must have a word with you, sweetheart," he cried, taking her hand, which she did not dare withdraw.

Ready to sink with confusion, Nizza suffered herself to be led towards the receiving-room. Motioning to the courtiers to remain without, Charles entered it with his blushing companion, and after putting several questions to her, which she answered with great timidity and modesty, inquired into the state of her heart.

" Answer me frankly," he said. " Are your affections engaged ? "

" Since your Majesty deigns to interest yourself so much about me," replied Nizza, " I will use no disguise. They are."

" To whom ? " demanded the king.

" To Leonard Holt," was the answer.

" What ! the apprentice who brought Amabel hither ? " cried the king. " Why, the Earl of Rochester seemed to intimate that he was in love with Amabel. Is it so ? "

" I cannot deny it," replied Nizza, hanging down her head.

" If this is the case, it is incumbent on me to provide you with a new lover," replied Charles. " What will you say, sweetheart, if I tell you you have made a royal conquest ? "

" I should tremble to hear it," replied Nizza. " But your Majesty is jesting with me."

" On my soul, no ! " rejoined the king, passionately. " I have never seen beauty equal to yours, sweetheart,— never have been so suddenly—so completely captivated before."

" Oh ! do not use this language towards me, my liege," replied Nizza, dropping on her knee before him. " I am unworthy your notice. My heart is entirely given to Leonard Holt."

" You will speedily forget him in the brilliant destiny which awaits you, child," returned Charles, raising her. " Do not bestow another thought on the senseless dolt who can prefer Amabel's sickly charms to your piquant attractions. By Heaven ! you shall be mine."

" Never ! " exclaimed Nizza, extricating herself from his grasp, and rushing towards the door.

" You fly in vain," cried the king, laughingly pursuing her.

As he spoke, the door opened, and Sir Paul Parravicin entered the room. The knight started on seeing how matters stood, and the king looked surprised and angry. Taking advantage of their embarassment, Nizza made good her retreat, and hurrying to Amabel's chamber, closed and bolted the door.

" What is the matter ? " cried Amabel, startled by her agitated appearance.

" Sir Paul Parravicin is here," replied Nizza. " I have seen him. But that is not all. I am unlucky enough to have attracted the king's fancy. He has terrified me with his proposals."

" Our persecution is never to end," rejoined Amabel; " you are as unfortunate as myself."

" And there is no possibility of escape," returned Nizza,

bursting into tears; " we are snared like birds in the nets
of the fowler."

" You can fly with Leonard, if you choose," replied
Amabel.

" And leave you—impossible ! " rejoined Nizza.

" There is nothing for it, then, but resignation," returned
Amabel. " Let us put a firm trust in Heaven, and no ill
can befal us."

After passing several hours of the greatest disquietude,
they were about to retire to rest, when Mrs. Buscot tapped
at the door, and making herself known, was instantly
admitted.

" Alas ! " she cried, clasping her niece round the neck,
" I tremble to tell you what I have heard. Despite the
king's injunctions, the wicked Earl of Rochester is determined to see you before morning, and to force you to
compliance with his wishes. You must fly as soon as it is
dark."

" But how am I to fly, dear aunt ? " rejoined Amabel.
" You yourself know that the keys of the stable are taken
away, and that two of the king's attendants will remain on
the watch all night. How will it be possible to elude their
vigilance ? "

" Leave Leonard to manage it," replied Mrs. Buscot.
" Only prepare to set out. John Lutcombe will guide you
across the downs to Kingston Lisle, where good Mrs.
Compton will take care of you, and when the danger is
over you can return to me."

" It is a hazardous expedient," rejoined Amabel, " and
I would rather run all risks, and remain here. If the earl
should resort to violence, I can appeal to the king for
protection."

" If you have any regard for me, fly," cried Nizza
Macascree. " I am lost if I remain here till to-morrow."

" For *your* sake I will go, then," returned Amabel.
" But I have a foreboding that I am running into the teeth
of danger."

" Oh ! say not so," rejoined Mrs. Buscot. " I am persuaded it is for the best. I must leave you now, but I will
send Leonard to you."

" It is needless," replied Amabel. " Let him come to us at the proper time. We will be ready."

To explain the cause of Mrs. Buscot's alarm, it will be necessary to return to the receiving-room, and ascertain what occurred after Nizza's flight. Charles, who at first had been greatly annoyed by Parravicin's abrupt entrance, speedily recovered his temper, and laughed at the other's forced apologies.

" I find I have a rival in your Majesty," observed the knight. " It is unlucky for me that you have encountered Nizza. Her charms were certain to inflame you. But when I tell you I am desperately enamoured of her, I am persuaded you will not interfere with me."

" I will tell you what I will do," replied the good-humoured monarch, after a moment's reflection. " I remember your mentioning that you once played with a Captain Disbrowe for his wife, and won her from him. We will play for this girl in the same manner."

" But your Majesty is a far more skilful player than Disbrowe," replied Parravicin, reluctantly.

" It matters not," rejoined the monarch; " the chances will be more equal—or rather the advantage will be greatly on your side, for you are allowed to be the luckiest and best player at my court. If I win, she is mine. If, on the contrary, fortune favours you, I resign her."

" Since there is no avoiding it, I accept the challenge," replied Parravicin.

" The decision shall not be delayed an instant," cried Charles. " What, ho !—dice !—dice ! "

An attendant answering the summons, he desired that the other courtiers should be admitted, and dice brought. The latter order could not be so easily obeyed, there being no such articles at Ashdown; and the attendants were driven to their wits' ends, when Pillichody chancing to overhear what was going forward, produced a box and dice, which were instantly conveyed to the king, and the play commenced. Charles, to his inexpressible delight and Parravicin's chagrin, came off the winner, and the mortification of the latter was increased by the laughter and taunts of the spectators.

" You are not in your usual luck to-day," observed Rochester to him, as they walked aside.

" For all this, do not think I will surrender Nizza," replied Parravicin, in a low tone, " I love her too well for that."

" I cannot blame you," replied Rochester. " Step this way," he added, drawing him to the farther end of the room. " It is my intention to carry off Amabel to-night, notwithstanding old Rowley's injunctions to the contrary, and I propose to accomplish my purpose in the following manner. I will frighten her into flying with Leonard Holt, and will then secretly follow her. Nizza Macascree is sure to accompany her, and will, therefore, be in your power."

" I see ! " cried Parravicin. " A capital project ! "

" Pillichody has contrived to ingratiate himself with Blaize," pursued the earl, " and through him the matter can be easily managed. The keys of the stables, which are now intrusted to Chiffinch, shall be stolen—the horses set free—and the two damsels caught in the trap prepared for them, while the only person blamed in the matter will be Leonard."

" Bravo ! " exclaimed Parravicin. " I am impatient for the scheme to be put into execution."

" I will set about it at once," returned Rochester.

And separating from Parravicin, he formed some excuse for quitting the royal presence.

About an hour afterwards, Pillichody sought out Blaize, and told him, with a very mysterious air, that he had something to confide to him.

" You know my regard for the Earl of Rochester and Sir Paul Parravicin," he said, " and that I would do anything an honourable man ought to do to assist them. But there are certain bounds which even friendship cannot induce me to pass. They meditate the worst designs against Amabel and Nizza Macascree, and intend to accomplish their base purpose before daybreak. I therefore give you notice, that you may acquaint Leonard Holt with the dangerous situation of the poor girls, and contrive their escape in the early part of the night. I will steal the keys of the stable for you from Chiffinch, and will render you every assistance in my power. But if you are discovered, you must not betray me."

" Not for the world ! " replied Blaize. " I am sure we are infinitely obliged to you. It is a horrible design, and must be prevented. I wish all this flying and escaping was over. I desire to be quiet, and am quite sorry to leave this charming place."

" There is no alternative now," rejoined Pillichody.

" So it appears," groaned Blaize.

The substance of Pillichody's communication was immediately conveyed to Leonard, who told Blaize to acquaint his informer that he should have two pieces of gold if he brought them the keys. To obtain them was not very difficult, and the bully was aided in accomplishing the task by the Earl of Rochester in the following manner. Chiffinch was an inordinate drinker, and satisfied he could turn this failing to account, the earl went into the hall where he was stationed and after a little conversation, called for a flask of wine. It was brought, and while they were quaffing bumpers, Pillichody, who had entered unperceived, contrived to open a table-drawer in which the keys were placed, and slip them noiselessly into his doublet. He then stole away, and delivered his prize to Blaize, receiving in return the promised reward, and chuckling to himself at the success of his roguery. The keys were conveyed by the porter to Leonard, and the latter handed them in his turn to John Lutcombe, who engaged to have the horses at the lower end of the south avenue an hour before midnight.

CHAPTER IX

King ton Lisle

ABOUT half-past ten, and when it was supposed that the
king and his courtiers had retired to rest (for early hours
were kept in those days), Mrs. Buscot and Leonard repaired to Amabel's chamber. The good house-keeper
noticed with great uneasiness that her niece looked excessively pale and agitated, and she would have persuaded
her to abandon all idea of flight, if she had not feared that
her stay might be attended with still worse consequences.

Before the party set out, Mrs. Buscot crept downstairs
to see that all was safe, and returned almost instantly,
with the very satisfactory intelligence that Chiffinch was
snoring in a chair in the hall, and that the usher had probably retired to rest, as he was nowhere to be seen. Not a
moment, therefore, was to be lost, and they descended
the great staircase as noiselessly as possible. So far all had
gone well; but on gaining the hall, Amabel's strength
completely deserted her, and if Leonard had not caught
her in his arms, she must have fallen. He was hurrying
forward with his burden towards a passage on the right,
when Chiffinch, who had been disturbed by the noise,
suddenly started to his feet, and commanded him to stop.
At this moment, a figure enveloped in a cloak darted from
behind the door, and extinguishing the lamp which Chaf-
finch had taken from the table, seized him with a powerful
grasp. All was now buried in darkness, and while Leonard
Holt was hesitating what to do, he heard a voice, which he
knew to be that of Pillichody, whisper in his ear, " Come
with me—I will secure your retreat. Quick ! quick ! "

Suffering himself to be drawn along, and closely followed by Nizza Macascree and Mrs. Buscot, Leonard
crossed the dining-chamber, not without stumbling against
some of the furniture by the way, and through an open
window into the court, where he found Blaize awaiting

him. Without waiting for thanks, Pillichody then disappeared, and Mrs. Buscot, having pointed out the course he ought to pursue, bade them farewell.

Hurrying across the court, he reached the south avenue, but had not proceeded far when it became evident, from the lights at the windows, as well as from the shouts and other noises proceeding from the court, that their flight was discovered. Encumbered as he was by his lovely burden, Leonard ran on so swiftly that Nizza Macascree and Blaize could scarcely keep up with him. They found John Lutcombe at the end of the avenue with the horses, and mounting them, set off along the downs, accompanied by the keeper, who acted as their guide. Striking off on the right, they came to a spot covered over with immense grey stones, resembling those rocky fragments used by the Druids in the construction of a cromlech, and, as it was quite dark, it required some caution in passing through them. Guided by the keeper, who here took hold of the bridle of his horse, Leonard threaded the pass with safety; but Blaize was not equally fortunate. Alarmed by the sounds in the rear, and not attending to the keeper's caution, he urged his horse on, and the animal coming in contact with a stone, stumbled, and precipitated him and Nizza Macascree to the ground. Luckily, neither of them fell against the stone, or the consequences might have been fatal. John Lutcombe instantly flew to their aid, but before he reached them, Nizza Macascree had regained her feet. Blaize, however, who was considerably shaken and bruised by the fall, was not quite so expeditious, and his dilatoriness so provoked the keeper, that, seizing him in his arms, he lifted him into the saddle. Just as Nizza Macascree was placed on the pillion behind him, the tramp of horses was heard rapidly approaching. In another moment their pursuers came up, and the foremost, whose tones proclaimed him the Earl of Rochester, commanded them to stop. Inexpressibly alarmed, Amabel could not repress a scream, and guided by the sound, the earl dashed to her side and seized the bridle of her steed.

A short struggle took place between him and Leonard,

in which the latter strove to break away; but the earl, drawing his sword, held it to his throat.

"Deliver up your mistress instantly," he cried, in a menacing tone, "or you are a dead man."

Leonard returned a peremptory refusal.

"Hold!" exclaimed Amabel, springing from the horse. "I will not be the cause of bloodshed. I implore you, my lord, to desist from this outrage. You will gain nothing by it but my death."

"Let him touch you at his peril," cried John Lutcombe, rushing towards them, and interposing his stalwart person between her and the earl.

"Stand aside, dog!" cried Rochester, furiously, "or I will trample you beneath my horse's hoofs."

"You must first get near me to do it," rejoined the keeper. And as he spoke, he struck the horse so violent a blow with a stout oaken cudgel with which he was provided, that the animal became unmanageable, and dashed across the downs to some distance with his rider.

Meanwhile, Parracivin having ridden up with Pillichody (for they proved to be the earl's companions), assailed Blaize, and commanded him to deliver up Nizza Macascree. Scared almost out of his senses, the porter would have instantly complied, if the piper's daughter had not kept fast hold of him, and reproaching him with his cowardice, screamed loudly for help. Heedless of her cries, Parravicin seized her, and strove to drag her from the horse; but she only clung the closer to Blaize, and the other, expecting every moment to pay another visit to the ground, added his vociferations for assistance to hers.

"Leave go your hold," he cried, to Pillichody, who had seized him on the other side by the collar. "Leave go, I say, or you will rend my jerkin asunder. What are you doing here? I thought you were to help us to escape."

"So I have done," rejoined Pillichody, bursting into a loud laugh; "and I am now helping to catch you again. What a blind buzzard you must be not to perceive the net spread for you! Deliver up Nizza Macascree without more ado, or, by all the fiends, I will pay you off for your dastardly assault upon me this morning."

" I cannot deliver her up," cried Blaize; " she sticks to me as fast as a burr. I shall be torn asunder between you. Help ! help ! "

Parravicin having dismounted, now tore away Nizza Macascree, and was just about to transfer her to his own steed, when John Lutcombe, having driven away the earl in the manner before described, came to the rescue. One blow from his cudgel stretched the knight on the sod, and liberated Nizza Macascree, who instantly flew to her preserver. Finding how matters stood, and that he was likely to be well backed, Blaize plucked up his courage, and grappled with Pillichody. In the struggle they both tumbled to the ground. The keeper rushed towards them, and seizing Pillichody, began to belabour him soundly. In vain the bully implored mercy. He underwent a severe chastisement, and Blaize added a few kicks to the shower of blows proceeding from the keeper, crying, as he dealt them, " Who is the buzzard now, I should like to know ? "

By this time, Parravicin had regained his legs, and the Earl of Rochester, having forced back his steed, both drew their swords, and burning for vengeance, prepared to renew the charge. The affair might have assumed a serious aspect, if it had not chanced that at this juncture lights were seen hurrying along the avenue, and the next moment a large party issued from it.

" It is the king ! " cried Rochester. " What is to be done ? "

" Our prey must be abandoned," rejoined Parravicin. " It will never do to be caught here."

With this he sprang upon his steed, and disappeared across the downs with the earl.

John Lutcombe, on perceiving the approach of the torch-bearers, instantly abandoned Pillichody, and assisting Blaize to the saddle, placed Nizza behind him. Leonard, likewise, who had dismounted to support Amabel, replaced her in the pillion, and in a few seconds the party were in motion. Pillichody, who was the only person now left, did not care to wait for the king's arrival, but snatching the bridle of his steed, which was quietly grazing at a little distance, mounted him, and galloped off in the direction which he fancied had been taken by the earl and his companion.

Guided by the keeper, who ran beside them, the fugitives proceeded for a couple of miles at a rapid pace over the downs, when, it not appearing that they were followed, John Lutcombe halted for a moment to recover breath. The fresh air had in some degree revived Amabel, and the circumstance of their providential deliverance raised the spirits of the whole party. Soon after this, they reached the ridge of the downs, the magnificent view from which was completely hidden by the shades of night, and tracking the old Roman road for about a mile, descended the steep hill in the direction of the Blowing Stone. Skirting a thick grove of trees, they presently came to a gate, which the keeper opened, and led them through an orchard towar what appeared to be in the gloom a moderately-sized and comfortable habitation.

" The owner of this house, Mrs. Compton,'' observed John Lutcombe, to Amabel, " is a widow, and the kindest lady in Berkshire. A message has been sent by your aunt to beg her to afford you an asylum for a few days, and I will answer for it you will be hospitably received."

As he spoke, the loud barking of a dog was heard, and old grey-headed butler was seen advancing towards them with a lantern in his hand. At the same time, a groom issued from the stable on the right, accompanied by the dog in question, and hastening towards them, assisted them to dismount. The dog seemed to recognise the keeper, and leapt upon him, licked his hand, and exhibited other symptoms of delight.

" What, Ringwood," cried the keeper, patting his head, " dost thou know thy old master again ? I see you have taken good care of him, Sam," he added to the groom. " I knew I was placing him in good hands when I gave him to Mrs. Compton."

" Ay, ay, he can't find a better home, I fancy," said the groom.

" Will it please you to walk this way, ladies ? " interposed the butler. " My mistress has been expecting you for some time, and had become quite uneasy about you."

So saying, he led the way through a garden, filled with the odours of a hundred unseen flowers, and ushered them into the house. Mrs. Compton, an elderly lady, of very pleasing exterior, received them with great kindness, and conducted them to a comfortable apartment, surrounded with book-shelves and old family portraits, where refreshments were spread out for them. The good old lady seemed particularly interested in Amabel, and pressed her, but in vain, to partake of the refreshments. With extreme delicacy, she refrained from inquiring into the cause of their visit, and seeing that they appeared much fatigued, rang for a female attendant, and conducted them to a sleeping-chamber, where she took leave of them for the night. Amabel was delighted with her kind hostess, and contrary to her expectations and to those of Nizza Macascree, enjoyed undisturbed repose. She awoke in the morning greatly refreshed, and after attiring herself, gazed through her chamber window. It looked upon a trim and beautiful garden, with a green and mossy plot carved out into quaintly-fashioned beds, filled with the choicest flowers, and surrounded by fine timber, amid which a tall fir-tree appeared proudly conspicuous. Mrs. Compton, who, it appeared, always arose with the sun, was busied in tending her flowers, and as Amabel watched her interesting pursuits, she could scarcely help envying her.

" What a delightful life your mistress must lead," she obeserved to a female attendant who was present. " I cannot imagine greater happiness than hers."

" My mistress ought to be happy," said the attendant; " for there is no one living who does more good. Not a cottage nor a farm-house in the neighbourhood but she visits to inquire whether she can be of any service to its inmates, and wherever her services are required, they are always rendered. Mrs. Compton's name will never be forgotten in Kingston Lisle."

At this moment, Amabel caught sight of the benevolent countenance of the good old lady looking up at the window, and a kindly greeting passed between them. Ringwood, who was a privileged intruder, was careering round the garden, and though his mistress watched his gambols round her favourite flower-beds with some anxiety, she did not check him. Amabel and Nizza now went downstairs, and Mrs. Compton returning from the garden, all the household, including Leonard and Blaize, assembled in the breakfast-room for morning prayers.

Breakfast over, Mrs. Compton entered into conversation with Amabel, and ascertained all the particulars of her history. She was greatly interested in it, but did not affect to conceal the anxiety it gave her.

"Yours is really a very dangerous position," she said, "and I should be acting unfairly towards you, if I told you otherwise. However, I will give you all the protection in my power, and I trust your retreat may not be discovered."

Mrs. Compton's remark did not tend to dispel Amabel's uneasiness, and both she and Nizza Macascree passed a day of great disquietude.

In the meantime, Leonard and Blaize were treated with great hospitality by the old butler in the servants' hall; and though the former was not without apprehension that their retreat might be discovered, he trusted, if it were so, to some fortunate chance to effect their escape. He did not dare to confide his apprehensions to the butler, nor did the other make any inquiries, but it being understood that their visit was to be secret, every precaution was taken to keep it so. John Lutcombe had tarried no longer than enabled him to discuss a jug of ale, and then set out for Ashdown, promising to return on the following day; but he had not yet made his appearance. Evening arrived, and nothing alarming having occurred, all became comparatively easy; and Mrs. Compton herself who had looked unusually grave throughout the day, now recovered her wonted cheerfulness.

Their satisfaction, however, was not long afterwards disturbed by the arrival of a large train of horsemen at the gate, and a stately personage alighted, and walked, at the head of a gallant train, towards the house. At the sight of the new-comers, whom they instantly knew were the king and his suite, Amabel and Nizza Macascree flew up-

stairs, and shutting themselves in their chamber, awaited
the result in the utmost trepidation. They were not kept
long in suspense. Shortly after the king's arrival, Mrs.
Compton herself knocked at the door, and in a tone of
deep commiseration, informed Amabel that his Majesty
desired to see her. Knowing that refusal was impossible,
Amabel complied, and descended to a room looking upon
the garden, in which she found the king. He was attended
only by Chiffinch, and received her with a somewhat severe
aspect, and demanded why she had left Ashdown contrary
to his express injunctions ?

Amabel stated her motives.

" What you tell me is by no means satisfactory," rejoined the king; " but since you have chosen to trust
yourself, you can no longer look for protection from me."

" I beseech your Majesty to consider the strait into which
I was driven," returned Amabel, imploringly.

" Summon the Earl of Rochester to the presence," said
the king, turning from her to Chiffinch.

" In pity, sire," cried Amabel, throwing herself at his
feet.

" Let the injunction be obeyed," rejoined Charles,
peremptorily.

And the chief page departed.

Amabel instantly arose, and drew herself proudly up.
Soon afterwards, Rochester made his appearance, and on
seeing Amabel, a flush of triumphant joy overspread his
features.

" I withdraw my interdiction, my lord," said the king
to him. " You are at liberty to renew your suit to this
girl."

" Hear me, Lord Rochester," said Amabel, addressing
the earl; " I have conquered the passion I once felt for
you, and regard you only as one who has sought my ruin,
and from whom I have fortunately escaped. When you
learn from my own lips that my heart is dead to you, that
I never can love you more, and that I only desire to be
freed from your addresses, I cannot doubt but you will
discontinue them."

" Your declaration only inflames me the more, lovely

Amabel," replied the earl, passionately. " You must, and shall be mine."

" Then my death will rest at your door," she rejoined.

" I will take my chance of that," rejoined the earl, carelessly.

Amabel then quitted the king's presence, and returned to her own chamber, where she found Nizza Macascree in a state of indescribable agitation.

" All has happened that I anticipated," said she to Nizza Macascree. " The king will no longer protect me, and I am exposed to the persecutions of the Earl of Rochester, who is here."

As she spoke an usher entered, and informed Nizza Macascree that the king commanded her presence. The piper's daughter looked at Amabel with a glance of unutterable anguish.

" I fear you must go," said Amabel, " but Heaven will protect you ! "

They then tenderly embraced each other, and Nizza Macascree departed with the usher.

Some time having elapsed, and Nizza not returning, Amabel became seriously uneasy. Hearing a noise below, she looked forth from the window, and perceived the king and all his train departing. A terrible foreboding shot through her heart. She gazed anxiously after them, but could not perceive Nizza Macascree. Overcome at last by her anxiety, she rushed downstairs, and had just reached the last step when she was seized by two persons. A shawl was passed over her head, and she was forced out of the house.

End of the Third Book.

Book the Fourth

The Plague at its Height

AMABEL'S departure for Berkshire caused no change in her father's mode of life. Everthing proceeded as before within his quiet dwelling; and, except that the family were diminished in number, all appeared the same. It is true they wanted the interest, and indeed the occupation afforded them by the gentle invalid, but in other respects no difference was observable. Devotional exercises, meals, the various duties of the house, and cheerful discourse, filled up the day, which never proved wearisome. The result proved the correctness of Mr. Bloundel's judgment. While the scourge continued weekly to extend its ravages throughout the city, it never crossed his threshold; and, except suffering in a slight degree from scorbutic affections, occasioned by the salt meats to which they were now confined, and for which the lemon and lime-juice, provided against such a contingency, proved an efficacious remedy, all the family enjoyed perfect health. For some weeks after her separation from her daughter, Mrs. Bloundel continued in a desponding state, but after that time she became more reconciled to the deprivation, and partially recovered her spirits. Mr. Bloundel did not dare to indulge a hope that Amabel would ever return, but though he suffered much in secret, he never allowed his grief to manifest itself. The circumstance that he had not received any intelligence of her did not weigh much with him, because the difficulty of communication became greater and greater, as each week the scourge increased in violence, and he was inclined to take no news as good news. It was not so in the present case, but of this he was happily ignorant.

In this way, a month passed on. And now every other consideration was merged in the alarm occasioned by the daily increasing fury of the pestilence. Throughout July, the excessive heat of the weather underwent no abatement, but in place of the clear atmosphere that had prevailed during the preceeding month, unwholesome blights filled the air, and, confining the pestilential effluvia, spread the contagion far and wide with extraordinary rapidity. Not only was the city suffocated with heat, but filled with noisome smells, arising from the carcases with which the close alleys and other out-of-the-way places were crowded, and which were so far decomposed as not to be capable of removal. The aspect of the river was as much changed as that of the city. Numbers of bodies were thrown into it, and floating up with the tides, were left to taint the air on its banks, while strange ill-omened fowl, attracted thither by their instinct, preyed upon them. Below the bridge, all captains of ships moored in the Pool or off Wapping, held as little communication as possible with those on shore, and only received fresh provisions with the greatest precaution. As the plague increased, most of these removed lower down the river, and many of them put out entirely to sea. Above the bridge, most of the wherries and other smaller craft had disappeared, their owners having taken them up the river, and moored them against its banks at different spots, where they lived in them under tilts. Many hundreds of persons remained upon the river in this way during the whole continuance of the visitation.

August had now arrived, but the distemper knew no cessation. On the contrary, it manifestly increased in violence and malignity. The deaths rose a thousand in each week, and in the last week in this fatal month amounted to upwards of six thousand !

But terrible as this was, the pestilence had not yet reached its height. Hopes were entertained that when the weather became cooler, its fury would abate; but these anticipations were fearfully disappointed. The bills of mortality rose the first week in September to seven thousand and though they slightly decreased during the second week, —awakening a momentary hope,—on the third they advanced to twelve thousand ! In less than ten days, upwards of two thousand persons perished in the parish of

Aldgate alone; while Whitechapel suffered equally severely. Out of the hundred parishes in and about the city, one only, that of Saint John the Evangelist in Watling-street, remained uninfected, and this merely because there was scarcely a soul left within it, the greater part of the inhabitants having quitted their houses, and fled into the country.

The deepest despair now seized upon all the survivors. Scarcely a family but had lost half of its number,—many more than half,—while those who were left felt assured that their turn would speedily arrive. Even the reckless were appalled, and abandoned their evil courses. Not only were the dead lying in the passages and alleys, but even in the main throughfares, and none would remove them. The awful prediction of Solomon Eagle that " grass would grow in the streets, and that the living should not be able to bury the dead," had come to pass. London had become one vast lazar-house, and seemed in a fair way of becoming a mighty sepulchre.

During all this time, Saint Paul's continued to be used as a pest-house, but it was not so crowded as heretofore, because, as not one in fifty of the infected recovered when placed under medical care, it was not thought worth while to remove them from their own abodes. The number of attendants, too, had diminished. Some had died, but the greater part had abandoned their offices from a fear of sharing the fate of their patients. In consequence of these changes, Judith Malmayns had been advanced to the post of chief nurse at the cathedral. Both she and Chowles had been attacked by the plague, and both had recovered. Judith attended the coffin-maker, and it was mainly owing to her that he got through the attack. She never left him for a moment, and would never suffer any one to approach him—a necessary precaution, as he was so much alarmed by his situation that he would infallibly have made some awkward revelations. When Judith, in her turn, was seized, Chowles exhibited no such consideration for her, and scarcely affected to conceal his disappointment at her recovery. This want of feeling on his part greatly incensed her against him, and though he contrived in some degree to appease her, it was long before she entirely forgave him. Far from being amended by her sufferings, she seemed to have grown more obdurate, and instantly commenced a fresh career of crime. It was not, however, necessary now to hasten the end of the sick. The distemper had acquired such force and malignity that it did its work quickly enough—often too quickly;—and all she sought was to obtain possession of the poor patients' attire, or any valuables they might possess worth appropriating. To turn to the brighter side of the picture, it must not be omitted, that when the pestilence was at its height, and no offers could induce the timorous to venture forth, or render assistance to the sufferers, Sir John Lawrence the Lord Mayor, the Duke of Albemarle, the Earl of Craven, and the Archbishop of Canterbury devoted themselves to the care of the infected, and supplied them with every necessary they required. Among the physicians no one deserves more honourable mention than Doctor Hodges, who was unremitting in his attentions to the sufferers.

To return to the grocer. While the plague was thus raging around him, and while every house in Wood-street, except one or two, from which the inmates had fled, was attacked by the pestilence, he and his family had remained untouched. About the middle of August, he experienced a great alarm. His second son, Hubert, fell sick, and he removed him to one of the upper rooms, which he had set aside as a hospital, and attended upon him himself. In a few days, however, his fears were removed, and he found, to his great satisfaction, that the youth had not been attacked by the plague, but was only suffering from a slight fever, which quickly yielded to the remedies applied. About the same time, too, he lost his porter, Dallison. The poor fellow did not make his appearance as usual for two days, and intelligence of his fate was brought on the following day by his wife, who came to state that her husband was dead, and had been thrown into the plague-pit at Aldgate. The same night, however, she brought another man, named Allestry, who took the place of the late porter, and acquainted his employer with the deplorable state of the city.

Two days afterwards, Allestry himself died, and Mr. Bloundel had no one to replace him. He thus lost all means of ascertaining what was going forward; but the death-like stillness around him, broken only by the hoarse tolling of a bell, by a wild shriek or other appalling cry, proclaimed too surely the terrible state of things. Sometimes, too, a passenger would go by, and would tell him the dreadful height to which the bills of mortality had risen, assuring him that ere another month had expired, not a soul would be left alive in London.

One night, as Solomon Eagle, who had likewise been miraculously preserved, pursued his course through the streets, he paused before Mr. Bloundel's house, and looking up at the window at which the latter had chanced to be stationed, cried in a loud voice, " Be of good cheer. You have served God faithfully, and there shall no evil befall you, neither shall the plague come nigh your dwelling." And raising his arms, as if invoking a blessing upon the habitation, he departed.

It was now the second week in September, and as yet Mr. Bloundel had received no tidings of his daughter. At any other season he would have been seriously uneasy, but now, as has been already stated, all private grief was swallowed up in the horror of the general calamity. Satisfied that she was in a healthful situation, and that her chance of preservation from the pestilence was better than that of any other member of his family, he turned his thoughts entirely to them. Redoubling his precautions, he tried by every means to keep up the failing spirits of his household, and but rarely ventured to open his shutter, and look forth on the external world.

On the tenth of September, which was afterwards accounted the most fatal day of this fatal month, a young man of a very dejected appearance, and wearing the traces of severe suffering in his countenance, entered the west end of London, and took his way slowly towards the city. He had passed St. Giles without seeing a single living creature, or the sign of one in any of the houses. The broad thoroughfare was completely grown over with grass, and the habitations had the most melancholy and deserted air imaginable. Some doors and windows were wide open, discovering rooms with goods and furniture scattered about, having been left in this state by their inmates; but most part of them were closely fastened up.

As he proceeded along Holborn, the ravages of the scourge were yet more apparent. Every house, on either side of the way, had a red cross, with the fatal inscription above it, upon the door. Here and there, a watchman might be seen, looking more like a phantom than a living thing. Formerly, the dead were conveyed away at night, but now the carts went about in the day-time. On reaching Saint Andrew's, Holborn, several persons were seen wheeling hand-barrows filled with corpses, scarcely covered with clothing, and revealing the blue and white stripes of the pestilence, towards a cart which was standing near the church gates. The driver of the vehicle, a tall, cadaverous-looking man, was ringing his bell, and jesting with another person, whom the young man recognised, with a shudder, as Chowles. The coffin-maker also recognised him at the same moment, and called to him, but the other paid no attention to the summons and passed on.

Crossing Holborn-bridge, he toiled faintly up the opposite hill, for he was evidently suffering from extreme debility, and on gaining the summit was obliged to support himself against a wall, for a few minutes, before he could proceed. The same frightful evidences of the ravages of the pestilence were observable here as elsewhere. The houses were all marked with the fatal cross, and shut up. Another dead-cart was heard rumbling along, accompanied by the harsh cries of the driver, and the doleful ringing of the bell. The next moment the loathly vehicle was seen coming along the Old Bailey. It paused before a house, from which four bodies were brought, and then passed on towards Smithfield. Watching its progress with fearful curiosity, the young man noted how often it paused to increase its load. His thoughts, coloured by the scene, were of the saddest and dreariest complexion. All around wore the aspect of death. The few figures in sight seemed staggering towards the grave, and the houses appeared to be plague-stricken like the inhabitants. The heat was intolerably oppressive, and the air tainted with noisome exhalations. Ever and anon, a window would be opened, and a ghastly face thrust from it, while a piercing shriek or lamentable cry was uttered. No business seemed going on—there were no passengers—no vehicles in the streets. The mighty city was completely laid prostrate.

After a short rest, the young man shaped his course towards Saint Paul's, and on reaching its western precincts, gazed for some time at the reverend structure, as if its contemplation called up many and painful recollections. Tears started to his eyes, and he was about to turn away, when he perceived the figure of Solomon Eagle stationed near the cross at the western extremity of the roof. The enthusiast caught sight of him at the same moment, and motioned him to come nearer.

" What has happened ? " he demanded, as the other approached the steps of the portico.

The young man shook his head mournfully.

" It is a sad tale," he said, " and cannot be told now."

" I can conjecture what it is," replied Solomon Eagle. " But come to the small door near the northern entrance of the cathedral at midnight. I will meet you there."

" I will not fail," replied the young man.

" One of the terrible judgments which I predicted would befall this devoted city has come to pass," cried Solomon Eagle. " Another yet remains—the judgment by fire, and if its surviving inhabitants repent not, of which there is as yet no sign, it will assuredly follow."

" Heaven avert it ! " groaned the other, turning away.

Proceeding along Cheapside, he entered Wood-street, and took his way towards the grocer's dwelling. When at a little distance from it, he paused, and some minutes elapsed before he could muster strength to go forward. Here, as elsewhere, there were abundant indications of the havoc occasioned by the fell disease. Not far from the grocer's shop, and in the middle of the street, lay the body of a man, with the face turned upwards, while crouching in an angle of the wall sat a young woman watching it. As the young man drew nearer, he recognised in the dead man the principal of the Brotherhood of Saint Michael and in the poor mourner one of his profligate female associates.

" What has become of your unhappy companions ? " he demanded of the woman.

" The last of them lies there," she rejoined, mournfully. " All the rest died long ago. My lover was true to his vow, and instead of deploring their fate, lived with me and three other women in mirth and revelry till yesterday, when the three women died, and he fell sick. He did not, however, give in, but continued carousing until an hour before his death."

Too much shocked to make any reply, the young man proceeded towards the hutch. Beneath a doorway, at a little distance from it, sat a watchman with a halbert on his shoulder, guarding the house; but it was evident he would be of little further use. His face was covered with his hands, and his groans proclaimed that he himself was attacked by the pestilence. Entering the hutch, the young man pulled the cord of the bell, and the summons was soon afterwards answered by the grocer, who appeared at the window.

" What, Leonard Holt ! " he exclaimed, in surprise, on seeing the young man,—" is it you ?—what ails you ?— you look frightfully ill."

" I have been attacked a second time by the plague," replied the apprentice, " and am only just recovered from it."

" What of my child ? " cried the grocer eagerly,—" what of her ? "

" Alas ! alas ! " exclaimed the apprentice.

" Do not keep me in suspense," rejoined the grocer. " Is she dead ? "

" No, not dead," replied the apprentice, " but——"

" But what ? " ejaculated the grocer—" in Heaven's name, speak ! "

" These letters will tell you all," replied the apprentice, producing a packet. " I had prepared them to send you in case of my death. I am not equal to further explanation now."

With trembling eagerness the grocer lowered the rope,

and Leonard, having tied the packet to it, it was instantly drawn up.

Notwithstanding his anxiety to ascertain the fate of Amabel, Mr. Bloundel would not touch the packet until he had guarded against the possibility of being infected by it. Seizing it with a pair of tongs, he plunged it into a pan containing a strong solution of vinegar and sulphur, which he had always in readiness in the chamber, and when thoroughly saturated, laid it in the sun to dry. On first opening the shutter to answer Leonard's summons, he had flashed off a pistol, and he now thought to expel the external air by setting fire to a ball, composed of quick-brimstone, saltpetre, and yellow amber, which being placed on an iron plate, speedily filled the room with a thick vapour, and prevented the entrance of any obnoxious particles. These precautions taken, he again addressed himself, while the packet was drying, to Leonard, whom he found gazing anxiously at the window, and informed him that all his family had hitherto escaped contagion.

" A special Providence must have watched over you, sir," replied the apprentice; " and I believe yours is the only family in the whole city that has been so spared. I have reason to be grateful for my own extraordinary preservation, and yet I would rather it had pleased Heaven to take me away than leave me to my present misery."

" You keep me in a frightful state of suspense, Leonard," rejoined the grocer, regarding the packet wistfully, " for I dare not open your letters till they are thoroughly fumigated. You assure me my child is living. Has she been attacked by the plague ? "

" Would she had ! " groaned Leonard.

" Is she still at Ashdown ? " pursued the grocer. " Ah ! you shake your head. I see !—I must be beside myself not to have thought of it before. She is in the power of the Earl of Rochester."

" She is," cried Leonard, catching at the angle of the shed for support.

" And I am here ! " exclaimed Mr. Bloundel, forgetting his caution, and thrusting himself far out of the window,

as if with the intention of letting himself down by the rope,
—" I am here, when I ought to be near her ! "

" Calm yourself, I beseech you, sir," cried Leonard.
" A moment's rashness will undo all you have done."

" True ! " replied the grocer, checking himself. " I must
think of the others as well as of her. But where is she ?
Hide nothing from me."

" I have reason to believe she is in London," replied the
apprentice. " I traced her hither, and should not have desisted from my search if I had not been checked by the
plague, which attacked me on the night of my arrival. I
was taken to the pest-house near Westbourne-green, where
I have been for the last three weeks."

" If she was brought to London, as you state," rejoined
the grocer, " I cannot doubt but she has fallen a victim to
the scourge."

" It may be," replied Leonard, moodily, " and I would
almost hope it is so. When you peruse my letters you will
learn that she was carried off by the earl from the residence
of a lady at Kingston Lisle, whither she had been removed
for safety, and after being taken from place to place, was
at last conveyed to an old hall in the neighbourhood of
Oxford, where she was concealed for nearly a month."

" Answer me, Leonard," cried the grocer, " and do not
attempt to deceive me. Has she preserved her honour ? "

" Up to the time of quitting Oxford, she had preserved
it," replied the apprentice. " She herself assured me she
had resisted all the earl's importunities, and would die
rather than yield to him. But I will tell you how I obtained
an interview with her. After a long search, I discovered
the place of her concealment, the old hall I have just
mentioned, and climbed in the night, and at the hazard of
my life, to the window of the chamber where she was confined. I saw and spoke with her; and having arranged a
plan by which I hoped to accomplish her deliverance on
the following night, descended. Whether our brief conference was overheard, and communicated to the earl, I
know not; but it would seem so, for he secretly departed
with her the next morning, taking the road, as I subsequently learnt, to London. I instantly started in pursuit,

and had reached Paddington, when I fell ill, as I have related."

"What you tell me in some measure eases my mind," replied Mr. Bloundel, after a pause; "for I feel that my daughter, if alive, will be able to resist her persecutor. What has become of your companions?"

"Nizza Macascree has met with the same fate as Amabel," replied Leonard. "She was unfortunate enough to attract the king's attention, when he visited Ashdown Lodge in company of the Earl of Rochester, and was conveyed to Oxford, where the court is now held, and must speedily have fallen a victim to her royal lover if she had not disappeared, having been carried off, it was supposed, by Sir Paul Parravicin. But the villain was frustrated in his infamous design. The king's suspicion falling upon him, he was instantly arrested, and though he denied all knowledge of Nizza's retreat, and was afterwards liberated, his movements were so strictly watched, that he had no opportunity of visiting her."

"You do not mention Blaize," said Mr. Bloundel. "No ill, I trust, has befallen him?"

"I grieve to say he has been attacked by the distemper he so much dreaded," replied Leonard. "He accompanied me to London, but quitted me when I fell sick, and took refuge with a farmer named Wingfield, residing near Kensal-green. I accidentally met Wingfield this morning, and he informed me that Blaize was taken ill the day before yesterday, and removed to the pest-house in Finsbury-fields. I will go thither presently, and see what has become of him. Is Dr. Hodges still among the living?"

"I trust so," replied Mr. Bloundel, "though I have not seen him for the last ten days."

He then disappeared for a few minutes, and on his return lowered a small basket containing a flask of canary, a loaf which he himself had baked, and a piece of cold boiled beef. The apprentice thankfully received the provisions, and retiring to the hutch, began to discuss them, fortifying himself with a copious draught of canary. Having concluded his repast, he issued forth, and acquainting Mr. Bloundel, who had at length ventured to commence reading the contents of the packet by the aid of powerful glasses, that he was about to proceed to Dr. Hodges' residence, to inquire after him, set off in that direction.

Arrived in Great Knightrider-street, he was greatly shocked at finding the door of the doctor's habitation fastened, nor could he make any one hear, though he knocked loudly and repeatedly against it. The shutters of the lower windows were closed, and the place looked completely deserted. All the adjoining houses were shut up, and not a living being could be discerned in the street from whom information could be obtained relative to the physician. Here, as elsewhere, the pavement was overgrown with grass, and the very houses had a strange and melancholy look, as if sharing in the general desolation. On looking down a narrow street leading to the river, Leonard perceived a flock of poultry scratching among the staves in search of food, and instinctively calling them, they flew towards him, as if delighted at the unwonted sound of a human voice. These, and a half-starved cat, were the only things living that he could perceive. At the farther end of the street, he caught sight of the river, speeding in its course towards the bridge, and scarcely knowing whither he was going, sauntered to its edge. The tide had just turned, and the stream was sparkling in the sunshine, but no craft could be discovered upon its bosom, and except a few barges moored to its sides, all vestiges of the numberless vessels with which it was once crowded were gone. Its quays were completely deserted. Boxes and bales of goods lay untouched on the wharves; the cheering cries with which the workmen formerly animated their labour were hushed. There was no sound of creaking cords, no rattle of heavy chains;—none of the busy hum ordinarily attending the discharge of freight from a vessel, or the packing of goods and stores on board. All traffic was at an end; and this scene, usually one of the liveliest possible, was now forlorn and desolate. On the opposite shore of the river it appeared to be the same,—indeed, the borough of Southwark was now suffering the utmost rigour of the scourge;—and except for the rows of houses on its banks, and the noble bridge by which it was spanned, the Thames appeared as undisturbed as it must have been before the great city was built upon its banks.

The apprentice viewed this scene with a singular kind of interest. He had become so accustomed to melancholy sights that his feelings had lost their acuteness, and the contemplation of the deserted buildings and neglected wharves around him harmonized with his own gloomy thoughts. Pursuing his walk along the side of the river, he was checked by a horrible smell, and looking downward, he perceived a carcase in the last stage of decomposition lying in the mud. It had been washed ashore by the tide, and a large bird of prey was contending for the possession of it with a legion of water-rats. Sickened by the sight, he turned up a narrow thoroughfare near Baynard's Castle, and crossing Thames-street, was about to ascend Addle-hill, when he perceived a man wheeling a handbarrow, containing a couple of corpses, in the direction of the river, with the intention, doubtless, of throwing them into it, as the readiest means of disposing of them. Both bodies were stripped of their clothing, and the blue tint of the nails, as well as the blotches with which they were covered, left no doubt as to the disease of which they had died. Averting his gaze from the spectacle, Leonard turned off on the right along Carter-lane, and threading a short passage, approached the southern boundary of the cathedral; and proceeding towards the great door opposite him, passed through it. The mighty lazar-house was less crowded than he expected to find it, but its terrible condition far exceeded his worst conceptions. Not more than half the pallets were occupied, but as the sick were in a great measure left to themselves, the utmost disorder prevailed. A troop of lazars, with sheets folded around them, glided, like phantoms, along Paul's-walk, and mimicked in a ghastly manner the air and deportment of the gallants who had formerly thronged the place. No attempt being made to maintain silence, the noise was perfectly stunning; some of the sick were shrieking,—some laughing in a wild unearthly manner,—some praying,—some uttering loud execrations,—others groaning and lamenting. The holy building seemed to have become the abode of evil and tormented spirits. Many dead were lying in the beds,—the few attendants who were present not caring to remove them; and Leonard had little doubt that before another sun went down the whole of the ghastly assemblage before him would share their fate. If the habitations he had recently gazed upon had appeared plague-stricken, the sacred structure in which he was now standing seemed yet more horribly contaminated. Ill-kept, and ill-ventilated, the air was loaded with noxious effluvia, while the various abominations that met the eye at every turn would have been sufficient to produce the distemper in any one who had come in contact with them. They were, however, utterly disregarded by the miserable sufferers and their attendants. The magnificent painted windows were dimmed by a thick clammy steam, which could scarcely be washed off;—while the carved oak screens, the sculptured tombs, the pillars, the walls, and the flagged floors were covered with impurities.

Satisfied with a brief survey of this frightful scene, Leonard turned to depart, and was passing the entrance to Saint Faith's, which stood open, when he caught sight of Judith standing at the foot of the broad stone steps, and holding a lamp in her hand. She was conversing with a tall, richly-dressed man, whose features he fancied he had seen before, though he could not at the moment call them to mind. After a brief conversation, they moved off into the depths of the vault, and he lost sight of them. All at once, it occured to Leonard that Judith's companion was the unfortunate stranger whose child he had interred, and who had been so strangely affected at the sight of Nizza Macascree. Determined to ascertain the point, he hurried down the steps, and plunged into the vault. It was buried in profound darkness, and he had not proceeded far when he stumbled over something lying in his path, and found from the groan that followed that it was a plague-patient. Before he could regain his feet, the unfortunate sufferer whom he had thus disturbed, implored him in piteous accents, which, with a shudder, he recognised as those of Blaize, to remove him. Leonard immediately gave the poor porter to understand that he was near him, and would render him every aid in his power.

" Your assistance comes too late, Leonard," groaned Blaize,—" it's all over with me now, but I don't like to breathe my last in this dismal vault, without medicine or food, both of which I am denied by that infernal hag, Mother Malmayns, who calls herself a nurse, but who is in reality a robber and murderess. Oh ! the frightful scenes I have witnessed since I have been brought here ! I told you I should not escape the plague. I shall die of it—I am sure I shall."

" I thought you were in the pest-house in Finsbury-fields," said Leonard.

" I was taken there," replied Blaize; " but the place was full, and they would not admit me, so I was sent to Saint Paul's, where there was plenty of room. Yesterday I did pretty well, for I was in the great ward above, and one of the attendants obeyed my directions implicitly, and I am certain if they had been fully carried out, I should have got well. I will tell you what I did. As soon as I was placed on a pallet, and covered with blankets, I ordered a drink to be prepared of the inner bark of an ash tree, green walnuts, scabious vervain, and saffron, boiled in two quarts of the strongest vinegar. Of this mixture I drank plentifully, and it soon produced a plentiful perspiration. I next had a hen,—a live one of course,—stripped of the feathers, and brought to me. Its bill was held to the large blotch under my arm, and kept there till the fowl died from the noxious matter it drew forth. I next repeated the experiment with a pigeon, and derived the greatest benefit from it. The tumour had nearly subsided, and if I had been properly treated afterwards, I should now be in a fair way of recovery. But instead of nice strengthening chicken broth, flavoured with succory and marigolds; or water-gruel, mixed with rosemary and winter-savoury; or a panado, seasoned with verjuice or wood-sorrel; instead of swallowing large draughts of warm beer, or water boiled with carduus seeds; or a posset drink, made with sorrel, bugloss, and borage;—instead of these remedies, or any other, I was carried to this horrible place when I was

N

asleep, and strapped to my pallet as you perceive. Unloose me, if you can do nothing else."

"That I will readily do," replied Leonard; "but I must first procure a light."

With this, he groped his way among the close ranks of ponderous pillars, but though he proceeded with the utmost caution, he could not avoid coming in contact with the beds of some of the other patients, and disturbing them. At length, he descried a glimmer of light issuing from a door which he knew to be that of the vestry, and which was standing slightly ajar. Opening it, he perceived a lamp burning on the table, and without stopping to look around him, seized it, and hurried back to the porter. Poor Blaize presented a lamentable, and yet grotesque appearance. His plump person was greatly reduced in bulk, and his round cheeks had become hollow and cadaverous. He was strapped, as he had stated, to the pallet, which in its turn was fastened to the adjoining pillar. A blanket was tightly swathed around him, and a large cloth was bound round his head in lieu of a night-cap. Leonard instantly set about releasing him, and had just unfastened the straps when he heard footsteps approaching, and looking up, perceived the stranger and Judith Malmayns advancing towards him.

CHAPTER II

The Second Plague-Pit

JUDITH, being a little in advance of her companion, took Leonard in the first instance for a chirurgeon's assistant, and called to him in a harsh and menacing voice to let her charge alone. On drawing near, however, she perceived her mistake, and, recognising the apprentice, halted with a disconcerted look. By this time, the stranger had come up, and remarking her embarassment, inquired the cause of it.

"Look there," cried Judith, pointing towards the apprentice. "Yonder stands the very man you seek."

"What! Leonard Holt," cried the other, in astonishment.

"Ay, Leonard Holt," rejoined Judith. "You can now put any questions to him you think proper."

The stranger did not require the suggestion to be repeated, but instantly hastened to the apprentice.

"Do you remember me?" he asked.

Leonard answered in the affirmative.

"I owe you a large debt of obligation," continued the stranger, "and you shall not find me slow in paying it. But let it pass for the moment. Do you know aught of Nizza Macascree? I know she was taken to Oxford by the king, and subsequently disappeared."

"Then you know as much as I do of her, sir," rejoined Leonard.

"I was right, you see, Mr. Thirlby," interposed Judith, with a malicious grin. "I told you this youth would be utterly ignorant of her retreat."

"My firm conviction is, that she is in the power of Sir Paul Parravicin," observed Leonard. "But it is impossible to say where she is concealed."

"Then my last hope of finding her has fallen to the ground," replied Thirlby, with a look of great distress. "Ever since my recovery from the plague, I have been in search of her. I traced her from Ashdown Park to Oxford, but she was gone before my arrival at the latter place; and though I made every possible inquiry after her, and kept strict and secret watch upon the villain whom I suspected, as you do, of carrying her off, I could gain no clue to her retreat. Having ascertained, however, that you were seen in the neighbourhood of Oxford about the time of her disappearance, I had persuaded myself you must have aided her escape. But now," he added, with a groan, "I find I was mistaken."

"You were so," replied Leonard, mournfully. "I was in search of my master's daughter, Amabel, who was carried off at the same time by the Earl of Rochester, and my anxiety about her made me neglectful of Nizza."

"I am not ignorant of your devoted attachment to her," remarked the stranger.

"You will never find Amabel again," observed Judith, bitterly.

"What mean you, woman?" asked Leonard.

"I mean what I say," rejoined Judith. "I repeat, you will never see her again."

"You would not speak thus positively without some motive," returned Leonard, seizing her arm. "Where is she? What has happened to her?"

"That you shall never learn from me," returned Judith, with a triumphant glance.

"Speak, or I will force you to do so," cried Leonard, furiously.

"Force me!" cried Judith, laughing derisively; "you know not whom you threaten."

"But *I* do," interposed Thirlby. "*This* young man *shall* have an answer to this question," he continued, addressing her in an authoritative tone. "Do you know anything of the girl?"

"No," replied Judith; "I was merely jesting with him."

"Shame on you, to trifle with his feelings thus," rejoined Thirlby. "Step with me this way, young man, I wish to speak with you."

"Do not leave me here, Leonard," cried Blaize, "or I shall die before you come back."

"I have no intention of leaving you," rejoined Leonard. "Are you aware whether Doctor Hodges is still alive, sir?" he added, to Thirlby. "I have just been to his residence in Great Knightrider-street, and found it shut up."

"He has removed to Watling-street," replied the other; "but I have not seen him since my return to London. If you wish it, I will go to his house at once, and send him to look after your poor friend."

Leonard was about to return thanks for the offer, when the design was frustrated by Blaize himself, who was so terrified by Judith's looks, that he could pay no attention to what was going forward; and fearing, notwithstanding Leonard's assurance to the contrary, that he should be left behind, he started to his feet, and wrapping the blanket about him, ran up the steps leading to the cathedral.

Leonard and Thirlby followed, and seeing him dart into the southern aisle, would have pursued him along it, but were afraid of coming in contact with the many sick persons by whom it was thronged. They contented themselves, therefore, with watching his course, and were not a little surprised and alarmed to find the whole troop of lazars set off after him, making the sacred walls ring with their cries. Frightened by the clamour, Blaize redoubled his speed, and, with this ghastly train at his heels, crossed the lower part of the mid aisle, and darting through the pillars, took refuge within Bishop Kempe's Chapel, the door of which stood open, and which she instantly closed after him. Judith, who had followed the party from the subterranean church, laughed heartily at the chase of the poor porter, and uttered an exclamation of regret at its sudden conclusion. Leonard, however, being apprehensive of mischief from the crowd of sick persons collected before the door, some of whom were knocking against it and trying to force it open, addressed himself to a couple of the attendants, and prevailed on them to accompany him to the chapel. The assemblage was speedily dispersed, and Blaize hearing Leonard's voice, instantly opened the door and admitted him; and, as soon as his fears were allayed, he was placed on a pallet within the chapel, and wrapped up in blankets, while such remedies as were deemed proper were administered to him. Committing him to the care of the attendants, and promising to reward them well for their trouble, Leonard told Blaize he should go and bring Doctor Hodges to him. Accordingly, he departed, and finding Thirlby waiting for him at the south door, they went forth together.

" I am almost afraid of leaving the poor fellow," said Leonard, hesitating, as he was about to descend the steps. " Judith Malmayns is so cunning and unscrupulous that she may find some means of doing him an injury."

" Have no fear," replied Thirlby. " She has promised me not to molest him further."

" You appear to have a strange influence over her, then," obeserved Leonard. " May I ask how you have attained it ? "

" No matter," replied the other. " It must suffice that I am willing to exercise it in your behalf."

" And you are not disposed to tell me the nature of the interest you feel in Nizza Macascree ? " pursued Leonard.

" Not as yet," replied Thirlby, with a look and tone calculated to put a stop to further inquiries.

Passing through Saint Austin's-gate, they approached Watling-street, at the corner of which stood the house where Doctor Hodges had taken up his temporary abode, that he might visit the sick in the cathedral with greater convenience, and be more readily summoned whenever his attendance might be required. Thirlby's knock at the door was answered to Leonard's great satisfaction by the old porter, who was equally delighted to see him. It did not escape Leonard that the porter treated the stranger with great respect, and he inferred from this that he was a person of some consideration, as indeed his deportment bespoke him. The old man informed them that his master had been summoned on a case of urgency early in the morning, and had not yet returned, neither was he aware whither he was gone. He promised, however, to acquaint him with Blaize's condition immediately on his return— " and I need not assure you," he added to Leonard, " that he will instantly go to him."

Thirlby then inquired of the porter whether Mike Macascree, the blind piper, was still at Dame Lucas's cottage, in Finsbury-fields, and was answered in the affirmative by the old man, who added, however, in a voice of much emotion, that the good dame herself was no more.

" She died about a fortnight ago of the plague," he said, " and is buried where she desired to be, beneath an old apple-tree in her garden."

" Alas ! " exclaimed Leonard, brushing away a tear, " her own foreboding is too truly realized."

" I am about to visit the old piper," observed Thirlby to the apprentice. " Will you go with me ? "

The other readily acquiesced, only stipulating that they should call in Wood-street on the way, that he might inquire whether his master wanted him. Thirlby agreeing to this, and the old porter repeating his assurance that

Leonard might make himself quite easy as to Blaize, for
he would send his master to him the instant he returned,
they set out. On reaching Wood-street, the apprentice
gave the customary signal, and the grocer answering it, he
informed him of his unexpected meeting with Blaize, and
of the state in which he had left him. Mr. Bloundel was
much distressed by the intelligence, and telling Leonard
that he should not require him again that night, besought
him to observe the utmost caution. This the apprentice
promised, and joining Thirlby, who had walked forward
to a little distance, they struck into a narrow street on the
right, and proceeding along Aldermanbury, soon arrived
at the first postern in the city walls beyond Cripplegate.

Hitherto, Thirlby had maintained a profound silence,
and appeared lost in melancholy reflection. Except now
and then casting a commiserating glance at the wretched
objects they encountered on the road, he kept his eyes
steadily fixed upon the ground, and walked at a brisk
pace, as if desirous of getting out of the city as quickly as
possible. Notwithstanding his weakness, Leonard managed
to keep up with him, and his curiosity being greatly
aroused by what had just occurred, he began to study his
appearance and features attentively. Thirlby was full six
feet in height, and possessed a powerful and well-proportioned figure, and would have been considered extremely
handsome but for a certain sinister expression about the
eyes, which were large and dark, but lighted by a fierce
and peculiar fire. His complexion was dark, and his
countenance still bore the impress of the dreadful disease
from which he had recently recovered. A gloomy shade
sat about his brow, and it seemed to Leonard as if he had
been led by his passions into the commission of crimes of
which he had afterwards bitterly repented. His deportment was proud and commanding, and though he exhibited no haughtiness towards the apprentice, but on the
contrary treated him with great familiarity, it was plain
he did so merely from a sense of gratitude. His age was
under forty, and his habiliments were rich, though of a
sombre colour.

Passing through the postern, which stood wide open,

the watchman having disappeared, they entered a narrow lane, skirted by a few detached houses, all of which were shut up, and marked with the fatal cross. As they passed one of these habitations, they were arrested by loud and continued shrieks of the most heart-rendering nature, and questioning a watchman who stood at an adjoining door, as to the cause of them, he said they proceeded from a poor lady who had just lost the last of her family by the plague.

" Her husband and all her children, except one daughter, died last week," said the man, " and though she seemed deeply afflicted, yet she bore her loss with resignation. Yesterday, her daughter was taken ill, and she died about two hours ago, since when the poor mother has done nothing but shriek in the way you hear. Poor soul ! she will die of grief, as many have done before her at this awful time."

" Something must be done to pacify her," returned Thirlby, in a voice of much emotion,—" she must be removed from her child."

" Where can she be removed to ? " rejoined the watchman. " Who will receive her ? "

" At all events, we can remove the object that occasions her affliction," rejoined Thirlby. " My heart bleeds for her. I never heard shrieks so dreadful."

" The dead-cart will pass by in an hour," said the watchman ; " and then the body can be taken away."

" An hour will be too late," rejoined Thirlby. " If she continues in this frantic state, she will be dead before that time. You have a hand-barrow there. Take the body to the plague-pit at once, and I will reward you for your trouble."

" We shall find some difficulty in getting into the house," said the watchman, who evidently felt some repugnance to the task.

" Not so," replied Thirlby. And pushing forcibly against the door, he burst it open, and, directed by the cries, entered a room on the right. The watchman's statement proved correct. Stretched upon a bed in one corner lay the body of a beautiful girl, while the poor mother was bending over it in a state bordering on distraction. On seeing Thirlby, she fled to the further end of the room, but did not desist from her cries. In fact she was unable to do so, being under the dominion of the wildest hysterical passion. In vain Thirlby endeavoured to make her comprehend by signs the nature of his errand. Waving him off, she continued shrieking more loudly than ever. Half-stunned by the cries, and greatly agitated by the sight of the child, whose appearance reminded him of his own daughter, Thirlby motioned the watchman, who had followed him into the room, to bring away the body, and rushed forth. His injunctions were obeyed. The remains of the unfortunate girl were wrapped in a sheet, and deposited in the hand-barrow. The miserable mother followed the watchman to the door, but did not attempt to interfere with him, and having seen the body of her child disposed of in the manner above described, turned back. The next moment a heavy sound proclaimed that she had fallen to the ground, and her shrieks were hushed. Thirlby and Leonard exchanged sad and significant looks, but neither of them went back to see what had happened to her. The watchman shook his head, and setting the barrow in motion, proceeded along a narrow foot-path across the fields. Remarking that he did not take the direct road to the plague-pit, Leonard called to him, and pointed out the corner in which it lay.

" I know where the old plague-pit is, as well as you," replied the watchman, " but it has been filled these three weeks. The new pit lies in this direction."

So saying, he pursued his course, and they presently entered a field, in the middle of which lay the plague-pit, as was evident from the immense mound of clay thrown out of the excavation.

" That pit is neither so deep nor so wide as the old one," said the watchman, " and if the plague goes on at this rate, they will soon have to dig another,—that is, if any one should be left alive to undertake the job."

And chuckling as if he had said a good thing, he impelled his barrow forward more quickly. A few seconds brought them near the horrible chasm. It was more than half full, and in all respects resembled the other pit, except that it was somewhat smaller. There was the same heaving and putrefying mass,—the same ghastly objects of every kind, —the grey-headed old man, the dark-haired maiden, the tender infant,—all huddled together.

Wheeling the barrow to the edge of the pit, the watchman cast his load into it; and without even tarrying to throw a handful of soil over it, turned back, and rejoined Thirlby, who had halted at some distance from the excavation.

While the latter was searching for his purse to reward the watchman, they heard wild shrieks in the adjoining field, and the next moment perceived the wretched mother running towards them. Guessing her purpose from his former experience, Leonard called to the others to stop her, and stretching out his arms placed himself in her path. But all their efforts were in vain. She darted past them, and though Leonard caught hold of her, she broke from him, and leaving a fragment of her dress in his grasp, flung herself into the chasm.

Well knowing that all help was in vain, Thirlby placed a few pieces of money in the watchman's hand, and hurried away. He was followed by Leonard, who was equally eager to quit the spot. It so chanced that the path they had taken led them near the site of the old plague-pit, and Leonard pointed it out to his companion. The latter stopped for a moment, and then, without saying a word, ran quickly towards it. On reaching the spot, they found that the pit was completely filled up. The vast cake of clay with which it was covered had swollen and cracked in an extraordinary manner, and emitted such a horrible effluvium that they both instantly retreated.

" And that is the grave of my poor child," cried Thirlby, halting, and bursting into a passionate flood of tears. " It would have been a fitting resting-place for a guilty wretch like me; but for her it is horrible."

Allowing time for the violence of his grief to subside, Leonard addressed a few words of consolation to him, and then tried to turn the current of his thoughts by introducing a different subject. With this view, he proceeded to detail the piper's mysterious conduct as to the packet, and concluded by mentioning the piece of gold which Nizza wore as an amulet, and which she fancied must have some connexion with her early history.

"I have heard of the packet and amulet from Doctor Hodges," said Thirlby; "and should have visited the piper on my recovery from the plague, but I was all impatience to behold Nizza, and could not brook an instant's delay. But you know his cottage. We cannot be far from it."

"Yonder it is," replied Leonard, pointing to the little habitation which lay at a field's distance from them— "and we are certain to meet with him, for I hear the notes of his pipe."

Nor was he deceived, for as they crossed the field, and approached the cottage, the sounds of a melancholy air played on the pipe became each instant more distinct. Before entering the gate, they paused for a moment to listen to the music, and Leonard could not help contrasting the present neglected appearance of the garden with the neatness it exhibited when he last saw it. It was overgrown with weeds, while the drooping flowers seemed to bemoan the loss of their mistress. Leonard's gaze involuntarily wandered in search of the old apple-tree, and he presently discovered it. It was loaded with fruit, and the rounded sod beneath it proclaimed the grave of the ill-fated Dame Lucas.

Satisfied with this survey, Leonard opened the gate, but had no sooner set foot in the garden than the loud barking of a dog was heard, and Bell rushed forward. Leonard instantly called to her, and on hearing his voice, the little animal instantly changed her angry tones to a gladsome whine, and skipping towards him fawned at his feet.

While he stooped to caress her, the piper, who had been alarmed by the barking, appeared by the door, and called out to know who was there? At the sight of him, Thirlby, who was close behind Leonard, uttered a cry of surprise, and exclaiming, "It is he!" rushed towards him.

The cry of recognition uttered by the stranger caused the piper to start as if he had received a sudden and violent shock. The ruddy tint instantly deserted his cheek, and was succeeded by a deadly paleness; his limbs trembled, and he bent forward with a countenance of the utmost anxiety, as if awaiting a confirmation of his fears. When within a couple of yards of him, Thirlby paused, and having narrowly scrutinized his features, as if to satisfy himself he was not mistaken, again exclaimed, though in a lower and deeper tone than before, " It is he ! " and seizing his arm, pushed him into the house, banging the door to after him in such a manner as to leave no doubt in the apprentice's mind that his presence was not desired. Accordingly, though extremely anxious to hear what passed between them, certain their conversation must relate to Nizza Macascree, Leonard did not attempt to follow, but accompanied by Bell, who continued to gambol round him, directed his steps towards the grave of Dame Lucas. Here he endeavoured to beguile the time in meditation, but in spite of his efforts to turn his thoughts into a different channel, they perpetually recurred to what he supposed to be taking place inside the house. The extraordinary effect produced by Nizza Macascree on Thirlby—the resemblance he had discovered between her and some person dear to him—the anxiety he appeared to feel for her, as evinced by his recent search for her—the mysterious connexion which clearly subsisted between him and the piper—all these circumstances convinced Leonard that Thirlby was, or imagined himself, connected by ties of the closest relationship with the supposed piper's daughter.

Leonard had never been able to discern the slighest resemblance either in manner or feature, or in those indescribably slight personal pecularities that constitute a family likeness, between Nizza and her reputed father,—neither could he now recall any particular resemblance between her and Thirlby; still he could not help thinking her beauty and high-bred looks savoured more of the latter than the former. He came, therefore, to the conclusion that she must be the offspring of some early and unfortunate attachment on the part of Thirlby, whose remorse might naturally be the consequence of his culpable conduct at that time. His sole perplexity was the piper's connexion with the affair; but he got over this difficulty by supposing that Nizza's mother, whoever she was, must have committed her to Macascree's care when an infant, probably with strict injunctions, which circumstances might render necessary, to conceal her even from her father. Such was Leonard's solution of the mystery; and feeling convinced that he had made himself master of the stranger's secret, he resolved to give him to understand as much as soon as he beheld him again.

More than half an hour having elapsed, and Thirlby not coming forth, Leonard began to think sufficient time had been allowed him for private conference with the piper, and he therefore walked towards the door, and coughing to announce his approach, raised the latch and entered the house. He found the pair seated close together, and conversing in a low and earnest tone. The piper had completely recovered from his alarm, and seemed perfectly at ease with his companion, while all traces of anger had disappeared from the countenance of the other. Before them on the table lay several letters, taken from a packet, the cover of which Leonard recognised as the one that had been formerly intrusted to him. Amidst them was the miniature of a lady,—at least, it appeared so to Leonard, in the hasty glance he caught of it; but he could not be quite sure, for, on seeing him, Thirlby closed the case, and placing his hand on the piper's mouth, to check his further speech, arose.

"Forgive my rudeness," he said to the apprentice, "but I have been so deeply interested in what I have just heard, that I quite forgot you were waiting without. I shall remain here for some hours longer, but will not detain you, especially as I am unable to admit you to our conference. I will meet you at Doctor Hodges' in the evening, and shall have much to say to you."

"I can anticipate some part of your communication," replied Leonard. "You will tell me you have a daughter still living."

"You are inquisitive, young man," rejoined Thirlby, sternly.

"You do me wrong, sir," replied Leonard. "I have no

curiosity as regards yourself; and if I had, would never lower myself in my own estimation to gratify it. Feeling a strong interest in Nizza Macascree, I am naturally anxious to know whether my suspicions that a near relationship subsists between yourself and her is correct."

" I cannot enter into further explanation now," returned Thirlby. " Meet me at Doctor Hodges' this evening, and you shall know more. And now, farewell. I am in the midst of a deeply-interesting conversation, which your presence interrupts. Do not think me rude,—do not think me ungrateful. My anxiety must plead my excuse."

" None is necessary, sir," replied Leonard; " I will no longer place any restraint upon you."

So saying, and taking care not to let Bell out, he passed through the door, and closed it after him. Having walked to some distance across the fields, musing on what had just occurred, and scarcely conscious whither he was going, he threw himself down on the grass, and fell asleep. He awoke after some time much refreshed, and finding he was considerably nearer Bishopsgate than any other entrance into the city, determined to make for it. A few minutes brought him to a row of houses without the walls, none of which appeared to have escaped infection, and passing them, he entered the city gate. As he proceeded along the once-crowded but now utterly-deserted thoroughfare that opened upon him, he could scarcely believe he was in a spot which had once been the busiest of the busy haunts of men,—so silent, so desolate did it appear ! On reaching Cornhill, he found it equally deserted. The Exchange was closed, and as Leonard looked at its barred gates, a saddening train of reflection passed through his mind. His head declined upon his breast, and he continued lost in a mournful reverie until he was roused by a hand laid on his shoulder, and starting—for such a salutation at this season was alarming—he looked round, and beheld Solomon Eagle.

" You are looking upon that structure," said the enthusiast, " and are thinking how much it is changed. Men who possess boundless riches imagine their power above that of their Maker, and suppose they may neglect and defy him. But they are mistaken. Where are now the wealthy merchants who used to haunt those courts and chambers ?—why do they not come here as of old ?—why do they not buy and sell, and send their messengers and ships to the farthest parts of the world ? Because the Lord hath smitten them and driven them forth—' From the least of them even to the greatest of them,' as the prophet Jeremiah saith, ' every one has been given to covetousness.' The balances of deceit have been in their hands. They have cozened their neighbours, and greedily gained from them, and will find it true what the prophet Ezekiel hath written, that ' the Lord will pour out of his indignation upon them, and consume them with the fire of his wrath.' Yea, I tell you, unless they turn from their evil ways,—unless they cast aside the golden idol they now worship, and set up the Holy One of Israel in its stead, a fire will be sent to consume them, and that pile which they have erected as a temple to their god, shall be burnt to the ground."

Leonard's heart was too full to make any answer, and the enthusiast, after a brief pause, again addressed him.

" Have you seen Doctor Hodges pass this way ? I am in search of him."

" On what account ? " asked Leonard, anxiously. " His advice, I trust, is not needed on behalf of any one in whom I am interested."

" No matter," replied Solomon Eagle, in a sombre tone. " Have you seen him ? "

" I have not," rejoined the apprentice; " but he is probably at Saint Paul's."

" I have just left the cathedral, and was told he had proceeded to some house near Cornhill," rejoined the enthusiast.

" If you have been there, you can perhaps tell me how my master's porter, Blaize Shotterel, is getting on," said Leonard.

" I can," replied the enthusiast. " I heard one of the chirurgeons say that Doctor Hodges had pronounced him in a fair way of recovery. But I must either find the doctor, or go elsewhere. Farewell ! "

" I will go with you in search of him," said Leonard.

"No, no,—you must not—shall not," cried Solomon Eagle.

"Wherefore not?" asked the apprentice.

"Do not question me,—but leave me," rejoined the enthusiast.

"Do you know aught of Amabel—of her retreat?" persisted Leonard, who had a strange misgiving that the enthusiast's errand in some way referred to her.

"I do," replied Solomon Eagle, gloomily; "but I again advise you not to press me further."

"Answer me one question, at least," cried Leonard. "Is she with the Earl of Rochester?"

"She is," replied Solomon Eagle; "but I shall allay your fears in that respect when I tell you she is sick of the plague."

Leonard heard nothing more, for, uttering a wild shriek, he fell to the ground insensible. He was aroused to consciousness by a sudden sense of strangulation, and opening his eyes, beheld two dark figures bending over him, one of whom was kneeling on his chest. A glance showed him that this person was Chowles; and instantly comprehending what was the matter, and aware that the coffin-maker was stripping him previously to throwing him into the dead-cart, which was standing hard-by, he cried aloud, and struggled desperately to set himself free. Little opposition was offered; for, on hearing the cry, Chowles quitted his hold, and retreating to a short distance, exclaimed, with a look of surprise, "Why, the fellow is not dead, after all!"

"I am neither dead, nor likely to die, as you shall find to your cost, rascal, if you do not restore me the clothes you have robbed me of," cried Leonard, furiously.

And chancing to perceive a fork, dropped by Chowles in his hasty retreat, he snatched it up, and brandishing it over his head, advanced towards him. Thus threatened, Chowles tossed him a rich suit of livery.

"These are not mine," said the apprentice, gazing at the habiliments.

"They are better than your own," replied Chowles, "and therefore you ought to be glad of the exchange. But give me them back again. I have no intention of making you a present."

"This is the livery of the Earl of Rochester," cried Leonard.

"To be sure it is," replied Chowles, with a ghastly smile. "One of his servants is just dead."

"Where is the profligate noble?" cried Leonard, eagerly.

"There is the person who owned these clothes," replied Chowles, pointing to the dead-cart. "You had better ask him."

"Where is the Earl of Rochester, I say, villain?" cried Leonard, menacingly.

"How should I know?" rejoined Chowles. "Here are your clothes," he added, pushing them towards him.

"I will have an answer," cried Leonard.

"Not from me," replied Chowles.

And hastily snatching up the livery, he put the cart in motion, and proceeded on his road.

Leonard would have followed him, but the state of his attire did not permit him to do so. Having dressed himself, he hastened to the cathedral, where he soon found the attendant who had charge of Blaize.

"Doctor Hodges has been with him," said the man, in reply to his inquiries after the porter, "and has good hopes of him. But the patient is not entirely satisfied with the treatment he has received, and wishes to try some remedies of his own. Were his request granted, all would soon be over with him."

"That I am sure of," replied Leonard. "But let us go to him."

"You must not heed his complaints," returned the attendant. "I assure you he is doing as well as possible; but he is so dreadfully frightened at a trifling operation which Doctor Hodges finds it necessary to perform upon him, that we have been obliged to fasten him to the bed."

"Indeed!" exclaimed Leonard, suspiciously. "Has Judith Malmayns had no hand in this arrangement?"

"Judith Malmayns has been absent during the whole of

the afternoon," said the man, "and another nurse has
taken her place in Saint Faith's. She has never been near
Blaize since I have had charge of him."

By this time they had reached the pallet on which the
porter was laid. His eyes and a small portion of his snub-
nose were alone visible, his head being still enveloped by
the linen cloth, while his mouth was covered by blankets.
He looked so anxiously at the apprentice, that the latter
removed the covering from his mouth, and enabled him to
speak.

"I am glad to find you are getting on so well," said
Leonard, in a cheerful tone. "Doctor Hodges has been
with you, I understand?"

"He has," groaned Blaize; "but he has done me no
good,—none whatever. I would doctor myself much better,
if I might be allowed; for I knew every remedy that has
been prescribed for the plague, but he would adopt none
that I mentioned to him. I wanted him to place a hot loaf,
fresh from the oven, to the tumour, to draw it; but he
would not consent. Then I asked for a cataplasm, composed of radish-roots, mustard-seed, onions and garlic
roasted, mithridate, salt, and soot from a chimney where
wood only has been burnt. This he liked no better than
the first. Next, I begged for an ale posset with pimpernel
soaked in it, assuring him that by frequently drinking such
a mixture, Secretary Naunton drew the infection from his
very heart. But the doctor would have none of it, and
seemed to doubt the fact."

"What did he do?" inquired Leonard.

"He applied oil of St. John's wort to the tumour," replied Blaize, with a dismal groan, "and said if the scar did
not fall off, he must cauterize it. Oh! I shall never be able
to bear the pain of the operation."

"Recollect your life is at stake," rejoined Leonard.
"You must either submit to it or die."

"I know I must," replied Blaize, with a prolonged groan;
"but it is a terrible alternative."

"You will not find the operation so painful as you
imagine," rejoined Leonard; "and you know I speak
from personal experience."

"You give me great comfort," said Blaize. "And so you really think I shall get better?"

"I have no doubt of it, if you keep up your spirits," replied Leonard. "The worst is evidently over. Behave like a man."

"I will try to do so," rejoined Blaize. "I have been told that if a circle is drawn with a blue sapphire round a plague-blotch, it will fall off. Couldn't we just try the experiment?"

"It will not do to rely upon it," observed the attendant, with a smile. "You will find a small nob of red-hot iron, which we call ' the button,' much more efficacious."

"Oh, dear! oh, dear!" exclaimed Blaize, "I already feel that dreadful button burning into my flesh."

"On the contrary, you won't feel it at all," replied the attendant. "The iron only touches the point of the tumour, in which there is no sensibility."

"In that case, I don't care how soon the operation is performed," replied Blaize.

"Doctor Hodges will choose his own time for it," said the attendant. "In the meantime, here is a cup of barley-broth for you. You will find it do you good."

While the man applied the cup to the poor porter's lips, —for he would not unloose the straps, for fear of mischief, —Leonard, who was sickened by the terrible scene around him, took his departure, and quitted the cathedral by the great western entrance. Seating himself on one of the great blocks of stone left there by the workmen employed in repairing the cathedral, but who had long since abandoned their task, he thought over all that had recently occurred. Raising his eyes at length, he looked toward the cathedral. The oblique rays of the sun had quitted the columns of the portico, which looked cold and grey, while the roof and towers were glittering in light. In ten minutes more only the summit of the central tower caught the last reflection of the declining orb. Leonard watched the rosy gleam till it disappeared, and then steadfastly regarded the reverend pile as its hue changed from grey to black, until at length each pinnacle and buttress, each battlement and tower, was lost in one vast indistinct mass. Night had fallen upon the city,—a night destined to be more fatal than any that had preceded it. And yet it was so calm, so beautiful, so clear, that it was scarcely possible to imagine that it was unhealthy. The destroying angel was, however, fearfully at work. Hundreds were falling beneath his touch; and as Leonard wondered how many miserable wretches were at that moment released from suffering, it crossed him like an icy chill that among the number might be Amabel. So forcibly was he impressed by this idea, that he fell on his knees and prayed aloud.

He was aroused by hearing the ringing of a bell, which announced the approach of the dead-cart, and presently afterwards the gloomy vehicle approached from Ludgate-hill, and moved slowly towards the portico of the cathedral, where it halted. A great number of the dead were placed within it, and the driver, ringing his bell, proceeded in the direction of Cheapside. A very heavy dew had fallen, for as Leonard put his hand to his clothes they felt damp, and his long hair was filled with moisture. Reproaching himself with having needlessly exposed himself to risk, he was about to walk away, when he heard footsteps at a little distance, and looking in the direction of the sound, perceived the tall figure of Thirlby. Calling to him, the other, who appeared to be in haste, halted for a moment, and telling the apprentice he was going to Doctor Hodges', desired him to accompany him thither, and went on.

CHAPTER III

The House in Nicholas-Lane

ON reaching Watling-street, Leonard and his companion found Doctor Hodges was from home. This did not much surprise the apprentice, after the information he had received from Solomon Eagle, but Thirlby was greatly disappointed, and eagerly questioned the porter as to the probable time of his master's return. The man replied that it was quite uncertain, adding, " He has been in since you were last here, and has seen Blaize. He had not been gone to the cathedral many minutes when a gentleman arrived, desiring his instant attendance upon a young woman who was sick of the plague."

" Did you hear her name ? " asked Leonard and Thirlby, in a breath.

" No," replied the porter, " neither did I obtain any information respecting her from the gentleman, who appeared in great distress. But I observed that my master, on his return, looked much surprised at seeing him, and treated him with a sort of cold respect."

" Was the gentleman young or old ? " demanded Leonard, hastily.

" As far as I noticed," replied the porter, " for he kept his face covered with a handkerchief, I should say he was young—very young."

" You are sure it was not Lord Rochester ? " pursued Leonard.

" How should I be sure of it," rejoined the porter, " since I have never seen his lordship that I am aware of ? But I will tell you all that happened, and you can judge for yourselves. My master, as I have just said, on seeing the stranger, looked surprised and angry, and bowing gravely, conducted him to his study, taking care to close the door after him. I did not, of course, hear what passed, but the interview was brief enough, and the gentleman, issuing forth, said, as he quitted the room, ' You will not

fail to come ? ' To which my master replied, ' Certainly
not, on the terms I have mentioned.' With this, the gentleman hurried out of the house. Shortly afterwards the
doctor came out, and said to me, ' I am going to attend a
young woman who is sick of the plague, and may be absent
for some time. If Mr. Thirlby or Leonard Holt should call,
detain them till my return.' "

" My heart tells me that the young woman he is gone to
visit is no other than Amabel," said Leonard Holt,
sorrowfully.

" I suspect it is Nizza Macascree," cried Thirlby.
" Which way did your master take ? "

" I did not observe," replied the porter, " but he told me
he should cross London-bridge."

" I will go into Southwark in quest of him," said Thirlby.
" Every moment is of consequence now."

" You had better stay where you are," replied the old
porter. " It is the surest way to meet with him."

Thirlby, however, was too full of anxiety to listen to
reason, and his impatience producing a corresponding effect
upon Leonard, though from a different motive, they set
forth together.

" If I fail to find him, you may expect me back ere long,"
were Thirlby's last words to the porter. Hurrying along
Watling-street, and taking the first turning on the right, he
descended to Thames-street, and made the best of his way
towards the bridge. Leonard followed him closely, and
they pursued their rapid course in silence. By the time
they reached the north gate of the bridge, Leonard found
his strength failing him, and halting at one of the openings
between the tall houses overlooking the river, where there
was a wooden bench for the accommodation of passengers,
he sank upon it, and begged Thirlby to go on, saying he
would return to Watling-street as soon as he recovered
from his exhaustion. Thirlby did not attempt to dissuade
him from his purpose, but instantly disappeared.

The night, it has before been remarked, was singularly
beautiful. It was almost as light as day, for the full harvest
moon (alas ! there was no harvest for it to smile upon !)
having just risen, revealed every object with perfect distinct-

ness. The bench on which Leonard was seated lay on the right side of the bridge, and commanded a magnificent reach of the river, that flowed beneath like a sheet of molten silver. The apprentice gazed along its banks, and noted the tall spectral-looking houses on the right, until his eye finally settled on the massive fabric of Saint Paul's, the roof and towers of which rose high above the lesser structures. His meditations were suddenly interrupted by the opening of a window in the house near him, while a loud splash in the water told that a body had been thrown into it. He turned away with a shudder, and at the same moment perceived a watchman, with a halbert upon his shoulder, advancing slowly towards him from the Southwark side of the bridge. Pausing as he drew near the apprentice, the watchman compassionately inquired whether he was sick, and being answered in the negative, was about to pass on, when Leonard, fancying he recognised his voice, stopped him.

"We have met somewhere before, friend," he said, "though where, or under what circumstances, I cannot at this moment call to mind."

"Not unlikely," returned the other, roughly; "but the chances are against our meeting again."

Leonard heaved a sigh at the remark.

"I now recollect where I met you, friend," he remarked. "It was at Saint Paul's, when I was in search of my master's daughter, who had been carried off by the Earl of Rochester. But you were then in the garb of a smith."

"I recollect the circumstance, too, now you remind me of it," replied the other. "Your name is Leonard Holt as surely as mine is Robert Rainbird. I recollect, also, that you offended me about a dog belonging to the piper's pretty daughter, Nizza Macascree, which I was about to destroy in obedience to the Lord Mayor's commands. However, I bear no malice, and if I did, this is not the time to rip up old quarrels."

"You are right, friend," returned Leonard. "The few of us left ought to be in charity with each other."

"Truly, ought we," rejoined Rainbird. "For my own part, I have seen so much misery within the last few weeks,

that my disposition is wholly changed. I was obliged to
abandon my old occupation of a smith, because my master
died of the plague, and there was no one else to employ me.
I have therefore served as a watchman, and in twenty days
have stood at the doors of more than twenty houses. It
wonld freeze your blood were I to relate the scenes I have
witnessed."

" It might have done formerly," replied Leonard; " but
my feelings are as much changed as your own. I have had
the plague twice myself."

" Then, indeed, you *can* speak," replied Rainbird.
" Thank God, I have hitherto escaped it ! Ah ! these are
terrible times—terrible times ! The worst that ever London
knew. Although I have been hitherto miraculously preserved myself, I am firmly persuaded no one will escape."

" I am almost inclined to agree with you," replied
Leonard.

" For the last week the distemper has raged fearfully—
fearfully, indeed," said Rainbird; " but yesterday and to-
day have far exceeded all that have gone before. The distempered have died quicker than cattle of the murrain. I
visited upwards of a hundred houses in the Borough this
morning, and only found ten persons alive; and out of
those ten, not one, I will venture to say, is alive now. It
will, in truth, be a mercy if they are gone. There were distracted mothers raving over their children—a young husband lamenting his wife,—two little children weeping over
their dead parents, with none to attend them, none to feed
them,—an old man mourning over his son cut off in his
prime. In short, misery and distress in their worst form,
—the streets ringing with shrieks and groans, and the
numbers of dead so great that it was impossible to carry
them off. You remember Solomon Eagle's prophecy ? "

" Perfectly," replied Leonard; " and I lament to see its
fulfilment."

" ' The streets shall be covered with grass, and the living
shall not be able to bury their dead,'—so it ran," said
Rainbird. " And it has come to pass. Not a carriage of
any description, save the dead-cart, is to be seen in the
broadest streets of London, which are now as green as the

fields without her walls, and as silent as the grave itself. Terrible times, as I said before—terrible times ! The dead are rotting in heaps in the courts, in the alleys, in the very houses, and no one to remove them. What will be the end of it all ? What will become of this great city ? "

" It is not difficult to foresee what will become of it," replied Leonard, " unless it pleases the Lord to stay his vengeful arm. And something whispers in my ear that we are now at the worst. The scourge cannot exceed its present violence without working our ruin; and deeply as we have sinned, little as we repent, I cannot bring myself to believe that God will sweep his people entirely from the face of the earth."

" I dare not hope otherwise," rejoined Rainbird, " though I would fain to do so. I discern no symptoms of abatement of the distemper, but, on the contrary, an evident increase of malignity, and such is the opinion of all I have spoken with on the subject. Chowles told me he buried two hundred more yesterday than he had ever done before, and yet he did not carry one third of the dead to the plague-pit. He is a strange fellow, that Chowles. But for his passion for his horrible calling there is no necessity for him to follow it, for he is now one of the richest men in London."

" He must have amassed his riches by robbery, then," remarked Leonard.

" True," returned Rainbird. " He helps himself without scruple to the clothes, goods, and other property of all who die of the pestilence, and after ransacking their houses, conveys his plunder in the dead-cart to his own dwelling."

" In Saint Paul's," asked Leonard.

" No, a large house in Nicholas-lane, once belonging to a wealthy merchant, who perished with his family of the plague," replied Rainbird. " He has filled it from cellar to garret with the spoil he has obtained."

" And how has he preserved it ? " inquired the apprentice.

" The plague has preserved it for him," replied Rainbird. " The few authorities who now act have, perhaps, no know-ledge of his proceedings; or if they have, have not cared to interfere, awaiting a more favourable season, if it should

ever arrive, to dispossess him of his hoard, and punish him
for his delinquencies; while in the meantime they are glad,
on any terms, to avail themselves of his services as a burier.
Other people do not care to meddle with him, and the most
daring robber would be afraid to touch infected money or
clothes."

" If you are going towards Nicholas-lane," said Leonard,
as if struck with a sudden idea, " and will point out to me
the house in question, you will do me a favour."

Rainbird nodded assent, and they walked on together
towards Fish-street-hill. Ascending it, and turning off on
the right, they entered Great Eastcheap, but had not proceeded far when they were obliged to turn back, the street
being literally choked up with a pile of carcases deposited
there by the burier's assistants. Shaping their course along
Gracechurch-street, they turned off into Lombard-street,
and as Leonard gazed at the goldsmiths' houses on either
side, which were all shut up, with the fatal red cross on the
doors, he could not help remarking to his companion,
" The plague has not spared any of these on account of
their riches."

" True," replied the other, " and of the thousands who
used formerly to throng this street not one is left. Woe to
London !—woe !—woe ! "

Leonard echoed the sentiment, and fell into a melancholy train of reflection. It has been more than once remarked that the particular day now under consideration
was the one in which the plague exercised its fiercest
dominion over the city; and though at first its decline was
as imperceptible as the gradual diminution of the day after
the longest has passed, yet still the alteration began. On
that day, as if Death had known that his power was to be
speedily arrested, he sharpened his fellest arrows, and discharged them with unerring aim. To pursue the course of
the Destroyer from house to house—to show with what
unrelenting fury he assailed his victims—to describe their
sufferings—to number the dead left within their beds,
thrown into the streets, or conveyed to the plague-pits—
would be to present a narrative as painful as revolting.
On this terrible night it was as hot as if it had been the

middle of June. No air was stirring, and the silence was
so profound that a slight noise was audible at a great distance. Hushed in the seemingly placid repose lay the great
city, while hundreds of its inhabitants were groaning in
agony, or breathing their last sigh.

On reaching the upper end of Nicholas-lane, Rainbird
stood still for a moment, and pointed out a large house on
the right, just below the old church dedicated to the saint
from which the thoroughfare took its name. They were
about to proceed towards it, when the smith again paused,
and called Leonard's attention to two figures quickly advancing from the lower end of the street. As the apprentice
and his companion stood in the shade, they could not be
seen, while the two persons, being in the moonlight, were
fully revealed. One of them, it was easy to perceive, was
Chowles. He stopped before the door of his dwelling and
unfastened it, and while he was thus occupied, the other
person turned his face so as to catch the full radiance of
the moon, disclosing the features of Sir Paul Parravicin.
Before Leonard recovered from the surprise into which he
was thrown by the unexpected discovery, they had entered
the house.

He then hurried forward, but, to his great disappointment, found the door locked. Anxious to get into the
house without alarming those who had preceded him, he
glanced at the windows; but the shutters were closed and
strongly barred. While hesitating what to do, Rainbird
came up, and guessing his wishes, told him there was a
door at the back of the house by which he might probably
gain admittance. Accordingly they hastened down a passage skirting the churchyard, which brought them to a
narrow alley lying between Nicholas-lane and Abchurch-
lane. Tracking it for about twenty yards, Rainbird paused
before a small yard door, and trying the latch, found it
yielded to his touch.

Crossing the yard, they came to another door. It was
locked, and though they could have easily burst it open,
they preferred having recourse to an adjoining window,
the shutter of which, being carelessly fastened, was removed without noise or difficulty. In another moment

they gained a small dark room on the ground-floor, whence they issued into a passage, where, to their great joy, they found a lighted lantern placed on a chair. Leonard hastily possessed himself of it, and was about to enter a room on the left when his companion arrested him.

" Before we proceed further," he said, in a low voice, " I must know what you are about to do."

" My purpose will be explained in a word," replied the apprentice in the same tone. " I suspect that Nizza Macascree is confined here by Sir Paul Parravicin and Chowles, and if it turns out I am right in my conjecture, I propose to liberate her. Will you help me ? "

" Humph ! " exclaimed Rainbird, " I don't much fancy the job. However, since I am here, I'll not go back. I am curious to see the coffin-maker's hoards. Look at yon heap of clothes. There are velvet doublets and silken hose enow to furnish the wardrobes for a dozen court gallants. And yet, rich as the stuffs are, I would not put the best of them on for all the wealth of London."

" Nor I," replied Leonard. " I shall make free, however, with a sword," he added, selecting one from the heap. " I may need a weapon."

" I require nothing more than my halbert," observed the smith; " and I would advise you to throw away that velvet scabbard. It is a certain harbour for infection."

Leonard did not neglect the caution, and pushing open the door, they entered a large room which resembled an upholsterer's shop, being literally crammed with chairs, tables, cabinets, movable cupboards, bedsteads, curtains, and hangings, all of the richest description.

" What I heard is true," observed Rainbird, gazing around in astonishment. " Chowles must have carried off everything he could lay hands upon. What can he do with all that furniture ? "

"What the miser does with his store," replied Leonard; " feast his eyes with it, but never use it."

They then proceeded to the next room. It was crowded with books, looking-glasses, and pictures; many of them originally of great value, but greatly damaged by the care-less manner in which they were piled one upon another.

A third apartment was filled with flasks of wine, with casks probably containing spirits, and boxes, the contents of which they did not pause to examine. A fourth contained male and female habiliments, spread out like the dresses in a theatrical wardrobe. Most of these garments were of the gayest and costliest description, and of the latest fashion, and Leonard sighed as he looked upon them and thought of the fate of those they had so lately adorned.

" There is contagion enough in those clothes to infect a whole city," said Rainbird, who regarded them with different feelings. " I have half a mind to set fire to them."

" It were a good deed to do so," returned Leonard; " but it must not be done now. Let us go upstairs. These are the only rooms below."

Accordingly, they ascended the staircase, and entered chamber after chamber, all of which were as full of spoil as those they had just visited; but they could find no one, nor was there any symptom that the house was tenanted. They next stood still within the gallery, and listened intently for some sound to reveal those they sought, but all was still and silent as the grave.

" We cannot be mistaken," observed Leonard. " It is clear this house is the receptacle for Chowles' plunder. Besides, we should not have found the lantern burning if they had gone forth again. No, no; they must be hidden somewhere, and I will not quit the place till I find them."

Their search, however, was fruitless. They mounted to the garrets, opened every door, and glanced into every corner. Still, no one was to be seen.

" I begin to think Nizza cannot be here," said the apprentice; " but I am resolved not to depart without questioning Chowles on the subject."

" You must find him first," rejoined Rainbird. " If he is anywhere, he must be in the cellar, for we have been into every room in this part of the house. For my own part, I think you had better abandon the search altogether. No good will come of it."

Leonard, however, was not to be dissuaded, and they went downstairs. A short flight of stone steps brought them to a spacious kitchen, but it was quite empty, and

seemed to have been long disused. They then peeped into
the scullery adjoining, and were about to retrace their
steps, when Rainbird plucked Leonard's sleeve to call attention to a gleam of light issuing from a door which stood
partly ajar, in a long narrow passage leading apparently to
the cellars.

" They are there," he said, in a whisper.

" So I see," replied Leonard, in the same tone. And
raising his finger to his lips in token of silence, he stole forward on the points of his feet and cautiously opened the
door.

At the further end of the cellar—for such it was—knelt
Chowles, examining with greedy eyes the contents of a
large chest, which, from the hasty glance that Leonard
caught of it, appeared to be filled with gold and silver plate.
A link stuck against the wall threw a strong light over the
scene, and showed that the coffin-maker was alone. As
Leonard advanced, the sound of his footsteps caught
Chowles' ear, and uttering a cry of surprise and alarm, he
let fall the lid of the chest, and sprang to his feet.

" What do you want ? " he cried, looking uneasily
round, as if in search of some weapon. " Are you come
to rob me ? "

" No," replied Leonard; " neither are we come to reclaim the plunder you have taken from others. We are
come in search of Nizza Macascree."

" Then you have come on a fool's errand," replied
Chowles, regaining his courage, " for she is not here. I
know nothing of her."

" That is false," rejoined Leonard. " You have just conducted Sir Paul Parravicin to her."

This assertion on the part of the apprentice, which he
thought himself justified under the circumstances in making, produced a strong effect on Chowles. He appeared
startled and confounded.

" What right have you to play the spy upon me thus ? "
he faltered.

" The right that every honest man possesses to check the
designs of the wicked," replied Leonard. " You admit she
is here. Lead me to her hiding-place without more ado."

" If you know where it is," rejoined Chowles, who now perceived the trick that had been practised upon him, " you will not want me to conduct you to it. Neither Nizza nor Sir Paul Parravicin are here."

" That is false, prevaricating scoundrel," cried Leonard. " My companion and I saw you enter the house with your profligate employer. And as we gained admittance a few minutes after you, it is certain no one can have left it. Lead me to Nizza's retreat instantly, or I will cut your throat."

And seizing Chowles by the collar, he held the point of his sword to his breast.

" Use no violence," cried Chowles, struggling to free himself, " and I will take you wherever you please. This way—this way."

And he motioned as if he would take them upstairs.

" Do not think to mislead me, villain," cried Leonard, tightening his grasp. " We have searched every room in the upper part of the house, and though we have discovered the whole of your ill-gotten hoards, we have found nothing else. No one is there."

" Well, then," rejoined Chowles, " since the truth must out, Sir Paul is in the next house. But it is his own abode. I have nothing to do with it, nothing whatever. He is accountable for his own actions, and you will be accountable to *him* if you intrude upon his privacy. Release me, and I swear to conduct you to him. But you will take the consequences of your rashness upon yourself. I only go upon compulsion."

" I am ready to take any consequences," replied Leonard, resolutely.

" Come along, then," said Chowles, pointing down the passage.

" You mean us no mischief ? " cried Leonard, suspiciously, " If you do, the attempt will cost you your life."

Chowles made no answer, but moved along the passage as quickly as Leonard, who kept fast hold of him and walked by his side, would permit. Presently they reached a door, which neither the apprentice nor Rainbird had observed before, and which admitted them into an extensive vault, with a short staircase at the further end, communicating with a passage that Leonard did not require to be informed was in another house.

Here Chowles paused.

" I think it right to warn you you are running into a danger from which ere long you will be glad to draw back, young man," he said, to the apprentice. " As a friend, I advise you to proceed no further in the matter."

" Waste no more time in talking," cried Leonard, fiercely, and forcing him forward, as he spoke; " where is Nizza ? Lead me to hear without an instant's delay."

" A wilful man must have his way," returned Chowles, hurrying up the main staircase. " It is not my fault if any harm befalls you."

They had just gained the landing when a door on the right was suddenly thrown open, and Sir Paul Parravicin stood before them. He looked surprised and startled at the sight of the apprentice, and angrily demanded his business.

" I am come for Nizza Macascree," replied Leonard, " whom you and Chowles have detained against her will."

Parravicin glanced sternly and inquiringly at the coffin-maker.

" I have protested to him that she is not here, Sir Paul," said the latter, " but he will not believe me, and has compelled me by threats of taking my life, to bring him and his companion to you."

" Then take them back again," rejoined Parravicin, turning haughtily upon his heel.

" That answer will not suffice, Sir Paul," cried Leonard —" I will not depart without her."

" How ! " exclaimed the knight, drawing his sword. " Do you dare to intrude upon my presence ? Begone, or I will punish your presumption." And he prepared to attack the apprentice.

" Advance a footstep," rejoined Leonard, who had never relinquished his grasp of Chowles, " and I pass my sword through this man's body. Speak, villain," he continued, in a tone so formidable that the coffin-maker shook with apprehension,—" is she here or not ? "

Chowles gazed from him to the knight, whose deportment was equally menacing, and appeared bewildered with terror.

" It is needless," said Leonard, " your looks answer for you. She *is*."

" Yes, yes, I confess she is," replied Chowles.

" You hear what he says, Sir Paul," remarked Leonard.

" His fears would make him assert anything," rejoined Parravicin, disdainfully. " If you do not depart instantly, I will drive you forth."

" Sir Paul Parravicin," rejoined Leonard, in an authoritative tone, " I command you, in the king's name, to deliver up this girl."

Parravicin laughed scornfully.

" The king has no authority here," he said.

" Pardon me, Sir Paul," rejoined Chowles, who began to be seriously alarmed at his own situation, and eagerly grasped at the opportunity that offered of extricating himself from it,—" pardon me. If it is the king's pleasure she should be removed, it materially alters the case, and I can be no party to her detention."

" Both you and your employer will incur his Majesty's severest displeasure by detaining her after this notice," remarked Leonard.

" Before I listen to the young man's request, let him declare that it is his intention to deliver her up to the king," rejoined Parravicin, coldly.

" It is my intention to deliver her up to one who has the best right to take charge of her," returned Leonard.

" You mean her father," sneered Parravicin.

" Ay, but not the person you suppose to be her father," replied Leonard. " An important discovery has been made respecting her parentage."

" Indeed ! " exclaimed Parravicin, with a look of surprise. " Who has the honour to be her father ? "

" A gentleman named Thirlby," replied Leonard.

" What ! " cried Parravicin, starting, and turning pale. " Did you say Thirlby ? "

The apprentice reiterated his assertion.

Parravicin uttered a deep groan, and pressed his hand forcibly against his brow for some moments, during which

O

the apprentice watched him narrowly. He then controlled himself by a powerful effort, and returned his sword to its scabbard.

" Come into this room, young man," he said to the apprentice, " and let your companion remain outside with Chowles. Fear nothing. I intend you no injury."

" I do not distrust you," replied Leonard, " and if I did, should have no apprehension."

And motioning Rainbird to remain where he was, he entered the room with the knight, who instantly closed the door.

Parravicin's first proceeding was to question him as to his reasons for supposing Nizza to be Thirlby's daughter, and clearly perceiving the deep interest his interrogator took in the matter, and the favourable change that, from some unknown cause, had been wrought in his sentiments, the apprentice did not think fit to hide anything from him. Parravicin's agitation increased as he listened to the recital; and at last, overcome by emotion, he sank into a chair, and covered his face with his hands. Recovering himself in a short time, he arose, and began to pace the chamber to and fro.

" What I have told you seems to have disturbed you, Sir Paul," remarked Leonard. " May I ask the cause of your agitation ? "

" No, man, you may not," replied Parravicin, angrily. And then suddenly checking himself, he added, with forced calmness, " And so you parted with Mr. Thirlby on London-bridge, and you think he will return to Doctor Hodges' residence in Watling-street ? "

" I am sure of it," replied Leonard.

" I must see him without delay," rejoined Parravicin.

" I will take you to him," remarked Leonard; " but first I must see Nizza."

Parravicin walked to a table, on which stood a small silver bell, and ringing it, the summons was immediately answered by an old woman. He was about to deliver a message to her, when the disturbed expression of her countenance struck him, and he hastily inquired the cause of it.

" You must not see the young lady to-night, Sir Paul," said the old woman.

" Why not ? " demanded the knight, hastily. " Why not ? "

" Because,—but you frighten me so that I dare not speak," was the answer.

" I will frighten you still more if you keep me in this state of suspense," rejoined Parravicin, furiously. " Is she ill ? "

" I fear she has got the plague," returned the old woman. " Now you can see her if you think proper."

" *I* will see her," said Leonard. " I have no fear of infection."

The old woman looked hard at Parravicin, as if awaiting his orders.

" Yes, yes, you can take him to her room," said the knight, who seemed completely overpowered by the intelligence, " if he chooses to go thither. But why do you suppose it is the plague ? "

" One cannot well be deceived in a seizure of that kind," replied the old woman, shaking her head.

" I thought the disorder never attacked the same person twice," said Parravicin.

" I myself am an instance to the contrary," replied Leonard.

" And, as you have twice recovered, there may be a chance for Nizza," said Parravicin. " This old woman will take you to her. I will hasten to Doctor Hodges' residence, and if I should fail in meeting him, will not rest till I procure assistance elsewhere. Do not leave her till I return."

Leonard readily gave a promise to the desired effect, and accompanying him to the door, told Rainbird what had happened. The latter agreed to wait below to render any assistance that might be required, and went downstairs with Parravicin and Chowles. The two latter instantly quitted the house together, and hastened to Watling-street.

With a beating heart, Leonard then followed the old woman to Nizza's chamber. They had to pass through a small ante-room, the door of which was carefully locked. The suite of apartments occupied by the captive girl were

exquisitely and luxuriously furnished, and formed a striking contrast to the rest of the house. The air was loaded
with perfumes; choice pictures adorned the walls; and
the tables were covered with books and china ornaments.
The windows, however, were strictly barred, and every
precaution appeared to be taken to prevent an attempt at
escape. Leonard cast an anxious look round as he entered
the ante-room, and its luxurious air filled him with anxiety.
His conductress, however, did not allow him time for reflection, but led him into another room, still more richly
furnished than the first, and lighted by a large coloured
lamp, that shed a warm glow around it. An old dwarfed
African, in a fantastic dress and with a large scimitar stuck
in his girdle, stepped forward on their approach, and shook
his head significantly.

" He is dumb," said the old woman, " but his gestures
are easy to be understood. He means that Nizza is worse."

Leonard heaved a deep sigh.

Passing into a third room, they perceived the poor girl
stretched on a couch placed in a recess at one side. She
heard their footsteps, and without raising her head, or
looking towards them, said, in a weak but determined
voice—" Tell your master I will see him no more. The
plague has again attacked me, and I am glad of it, for it
will deliver me from him. It will be useless to offer me
any remedies, for I will not take them."

" It is not Sir Paul Parravicin," replied the old woman.
" I have brought a stranger, with whose name I am unacquainted, to see you."

" Then you have done very wrong," replied Nizza. " I
will see no one."

" Not even me, Nizza ? " asked Leonard, advancing.

The poor girl started at the sound of his voice, and raising herself on one arm, looked wildly towards him. As
soon as she was satisfied that her fancy did not deceive her,
she uttered a cry of delight, and falling backwards on the
couch, became insensible.

Leonard and the old woman instantly flew to the poor
girl's assistance, and restoratives being applied, she speedily opened her eyes, and fixed them tenderly and inquiringly

on the apprentice. Before replying to her mute inter-
rogatories, Leonard requested the old woman to leave
them—an order very reluctantly obeyed,—and as soon as
they were left alone, proceeded to explain, as briefly as he
could, the manner in which he had discovered her place of
captivity. Nizza listened to his recital with the greatest
interest, and though evidently suffering acute pain, uttered
no complaint, but endeavoured to assume an appearance
of composure and tranquillity.

"I must now tell you all that has befallen me since we
last met," she said, as he concluded. "I will not dwell
upon the persecution I endured from the king, whose
passion increased in proportion to my resistance,—I will
not dwell upon the arts, the infamous arts, used to induce
me to comply with his wishes,—neither will I dwell upon
the desperate measure I had determined to resort to, if
driven to the last strait,—nor would I mention the subject
at all, except to assure you I escaped contamination, where
few escaped it."

"You need not give me any such assurance," remarked
Leonard.

"While I was thus almost driven to despair," pursued
Nizza, "a young female, who attended me, and affected
to deplore my situation, offered to help me to escape. I
eagerly embraced the offer; and one night, having
purloined, as she stated, the key of the chamber in which
I was lodged, she conducted me by a back staircase into
the palace gardens. Thinking myself free, I warmly thanked
my supposed deliverer, who hurried me towards a gate, at
which she informed me a man was waiting to guide me to
a cottage about a mile from the city, where I should be in
perfect safety."

"I see the device," cried Leonard. "But why—why did
you trust her?"

"What could I do?" rejoined Nizza. "To stay was as
bad as to fly, and might have been worse. At all events, I
had no distrust. My companion opened the gate, and
called to some person without. It was profoundly dark;
but I could perceive a carriage, or some other vehicle, at a
little distance. Alarmed at the sight, I whispered my fears

to my companion, and would have retreated; but she laid
hold of my hand, and detained me. The next moment, I
felt a rude grasp upon my arm. Before I could cry out, a
hand was placed over my mouth so closely as almost to
stifle me; and I was forced into the carriage by two
persons, who seated themselves on either side of me,
threatening to put me to death if I made the slightest noise.
The carriage was then driven off at a furious pace. For
some miles it pursued the high road, and then struck into
a lane, where, in consequence of the deep and dangerous
ruts, the driver was obliged to relax his speed. But in
spite of all his caution, one of the wheels sunk into a hole,
and in the efforts to extricate it, the carriage was over-
turned. No injury was sustained either by me or the
others inside, and the door being forced open without
much difficulty, we were let out. One of my captors kept
near me, while the other lent his assistance to the coachman to set the carriage to rights. It proved, however, to
be so much damaged that it could not proceed; and after
considerable delay, my conductors ordered the coachman
to remain with it till further assistance could be sent; and,
taking the horses, one of them, notwithstanding my resistance, placed me beside him, and galloped off. Having
ridden about five miles, we crossed an extensive common,
and passed an avenue of trees, which brought us to the
entrance of an old house. Our arrival seemed to be expected; for the instant we appeared, the gate was opened,
and the old woman you have just seen, and who is called
Mrs. Carteret, together with a dumb African, named
Hassan, appeared at it. Some muttered discourse passed
between my conductors and these persons, which ended
in my being committed to the care of Mrs. Carteret, who
led me upstairs to a richly-furnished chamber, and urged
me to take some refreshment before I retired to rest, which,
however, I declined."

"Still you saw nothing of Sir Paul Parravicin?" asked
Leonard.

"On going downstairs next morning, he was the first
person I beheld," replied Nizza. "Falling upon his knees,
he implored my pardon for the artifice he had practised,

and said he had been compelled to have recourse to it in order to save me from the king. He then began to plead his own suit; but finding his protestations of passion of no effect, he became yet more importunate; when, at this juncture, one of the men who had acted as my conductors on the previous night, suddenly entered the room, and told him he must return to Oxford without an instant's delay, as the king's attendants were in search of him. Casting a look at me that made me tremble, he then departed; and though I remained more than two months in that house, I saw nothing more of him."

" Did you not attempt to escape during that time? " asked Leonard.

" I was so carefully watched by Mrs. Carteret and Hassan, that it would have been vain to attempt it," she replied. " About a week ago, the two men who had conducted me to my place of captivity, again made their appearance, and told me I must accompany them to London. I attempted no resistance, well aware it would be useless; and as the journey was made by by-roads, three days elapsed before we reached the capital. We arrived at night, and I almost forgot my own alarm in the terrible sights I beheld at every turn. It would have been useless to call out for assistance, for there was no one to afford it. I asked my conductors if they had brought me there to die, and they answered sternly, it depended on myself. At Ludgate we met Chowles, the coffin-maker, and he brought us to this house. Yesterday, Sir Paul Parravicin made his appearance, and told me he had brought me hither to be out of the king's way. He then renewed his odious solicitations. I resisted him as firmly as before; but he was more determined, and I might have been reduced to the last extremity but for your arrival, or for the terrible disorder that has seized me. But I have spoken enough of myself. Tell me what has become of Amabel."

" She, too, has got the plague," replied Leonard, mournfully.

" Alas ! alas ! " cried Nizza, bursting into tears—" she is so dear to you, that I grieve for her far more than for myself."

"I have not seen her since I last beheld you," said Leonard, greatly touched by the poor girl's devotion. "She was carried off by the Earl of Rochester on the same night that you were taken from Kingston Lisle by the king."

"And she has been in his power ever since?" demanded Nizza, eagerly.

"Ever since," repeated Leonard.

"The same power that has watched over me, I trust has protected her," cried Nizza, fervently.

"I cannot doubt it," replied Leonard. "She would not now be alive were it otherwise. But I have now something of importance to disclose to you. You remember the stranger we met near the plague-pit in Finsbury-fields, and whose child I buried?"

"Perfectly," replied Nizza.

"What if I tell you he is your father?" said Leonard.

"What!" cried Nizza, in the utmost surprise. "Have I then been mistaken all these years in supposing the piper to be my father?"

"You have," replied Leonard. "I cannot explain more to you at present, but a few hours will reveal all. Thirlby is the name of your father. Have you ever heard it before?"

"Never," returned Nizza. "It is strange what you tell me. I have often reproached myself for not feeling a stronger affection for the piper, who always treated me with the kindness of a parent. But it now seems the true instinct was wanting. Tell me your reasons for supposing this person to be my father."

As Leonard was about to reply, the door was opened by Mrs. Carteret, who said that Sir Paul Parravicin had just returned with Doctor Hodges and another gentleman. The words were scarcely uttered, when Thirlby rushed into the room, and flinging himself on his knees before the couch, cried—"At last I have found you,—my child! my child!"

The surprise which Nizza must have experienced at such an address was materially lessened by what Leonard had just told her, and after earnestly regarding the stranger for some time, she exclaimed in a gentle voice, "My father!"

Thirlby sprang to his feet, and would have folded her in his arms, if Doctor Hodges, who by this time had reached the couch, had not prevented him.

" Touch her not, or you destroy yourself," he cried.

" I care not if I do," rejoined Thirlby. " The gratification would be cheaply purchased at the price of my life, and if I could preserve hers by the sacrifice, I would gladly make it."

" No more of this," cried Hodges, impatiently, " or you will defeat any attempt I may make to cure her. You had better not remain here. Your presence agitates her."

Gazing -wistfully at his daughter, and scarcely able to tear himself away, Thirlby yielded at last to the doctor's advice, and quitted the room. He was followed by Leonard, who received a hint to the same effect. On reaching the adjoining room, they found Sir Paul Parravicin walking to and fro in an agitated manner. He immediately came up to Thirlby, and in an anxious but deferential tone, inquired how he had found Nizza. The latter shook his head, and sternly declining any further conversation, passed on with the apprentice to an outer room. He then flung himself into a chair, and appeared lost in deep and bitter reflection. Leonard was unwilling to disturb him, but at last his own anxieties compelled him to break silence.

" Can you tell me aught of Amabel ? " he asked.

" Alas ! no," replied Thirlby, rousing himself. " I have had no time to inquire about her, as you shall hear. After leaving you on the bridge, I went into Southwark, and hurrying through all the principal streets, inquired from every watchman I met whether he had seen any person answering to Doctor Hodges' description, but could hear nothing of him. At last, I gave up the quest, and retracing my steps, was proceeding along Cannon-street, when I descried a person a little in advance of me whom I thought must be the doctor, and calling out to him, found I was not mistaken. I had just reached him, when two other persons turned the corner of Nicholas-lane. On seeing us one of them ran up to the doctor, exclaiming, ' By Heaven, the very person I want ! ' It was Sir Paul Parravicin, and he instantly explained his errand. Imagine the feelings with

which I heard his account of the illness of my daughter·
Imagine, also, the horror I must have experienced in recognising in her persecutor my——"

The sentence was not completed, for at that moment the
door was opened by Sir Paul Parravicin, who, advancing
towards Thirlby, begged, in the same deferential tone as
before, to have a few words with him.

"I might well refuse you," replied Thirlby, sternly, "but
it is necessary we should have some explanation of what
has occurred."

"It is," rejoined Parravicin, "and, therefore, I have
sought you."

Thirlby arose, and accompanied the knight into the
outer room, closing the door after him. More than a
quarter of an hour,—it seemed an age to Leonard,—
elapsed, and still no one came. Listening intently, he heard
voices in the next room. They were loud and angry, as if
in quarrel. Then all was quiet, and at last Thirlby reappeared, and took his seat beside him.

"Have you seen Doctor Hodges?" inquired the apprentice, eagerly.

"I have," replied Thirlby, "and he speaks favourably
of my poor child. He has administered all needful remedies,
but as it is necessary to watch their effect, he will remain
with her some time longer."

"And, meanwhile, I shall know nothing of Amabel,"
cried Leonard, in a tone of bitter disappointment.

"Your anxiety is natural," returned Thirlby, "but you
may rest satisfied, if Doctor Hodges has seen her, he has
done all that human aid can affect. But as you must perforce wait his coming forth, I will endeavour to beguile
the tedious interval by relating to you so much of my
history as refers to Nizza Macascree."—

After a brief pause, he commenced:—

"You must know, then, that in my youth I became
desperately enamoured of a lady named Isabella Morley.
She was most beautiful—but I need not enlarge upon her
attractions, since you have beheld her very image in Nizza.
When I first met her, she was attached to another, but I
soon rid myself of my rival. I quarrelled with him, and

slew him in a duel. After a long and urgent suit, for the successful issue of which I was mainly indebted to my rank and wealth, which gave great influence with her parents, Isabella became mine. But I soon found out she did not love me. In consequence of this discovery, I became madly jealous, and embittered her life and my own by constant and, now I know too well, groundless suspicions. She had borne me a son, and in the excess of my jealous fury, fancying the child was not my own, I threatened to put it to death. This violence led to the unhappy result I am about to relate. Another child was born, a daughter—need I say Nizza, or, to give her her proper name, Isabella, for she was so christened after her mother —and one night—one luckless night, maddened by some causeless doubt, I snatched the innocent babe from her mother's arms, and if I had not been prevented by the attendants, who rushed into the room on hearing their mistress's shrieks, should have destroyed her. After awhile I became pacified, and on reviewing my conduct more calmly on the morrow, bitterly reproached myself, and hastened to express my penitence to my wife. ' You will never have an opportunity of repeating your violence,' she said; ' the object of your cruel and unfounded suspicions is gone.' ' Gone ! ' I exclaimed; ' whither ? ' And as I spoke I looked around the chamber. But the babe was nowhere to be seen. In answer to my inquiries, my wife admitted that she had caused her to be removed to a place of safety, but refused, even on my most urgent entreaties accompanied by promises of amended conduct, to tell me where. I next interrogated the servants, but they professed entire ignorance of the matter. For three whole days I made ineffectual search for the child, and offered large rewards to any one who could bring her to me. But they failed to produce her; and repairing to my wife's chamber, I threatened her with the most terrible consequences if she persisted in her vindictive project. She defied me, and, transported with rage, I passed my sword through her body, exclaiming, as I dealt the murderous blow, ' You have sent the brat to her father—to your lover, madam.' Horror and remorse seized me the moment I had committed

the ruthless act, and I should have turned my sword against
myself, if I had not been stayed by the cry of my poor
victim, who implored me to hold my hand. ' Do not add
crime to crime,' she cried; 'you have done me grievous
wrong. I have not, indeed, loved you, because my affections
were not under my control, but I have been ever true to
you, and this I declare with my latest breath. I freely forgive you, and pray God to turn your heart.' And with
these words she expired. I was roused from the stupefaction into which I was thrown by the appearance of the
servants. Heaping execrations upon me, they strove to
seize me; but I broke through them, and gained a garden
at the back of my mansion, which was situated on the
bank of the Thames, not far from Chelsea. This garden
ran down to the river-side, and was defended by a low
wall, which I leapt, and plunged into the stream. A boat
was instantly sent in pursuit of me, and a number of
persons ran along the banks, all eager for my capture.
But being an excellent swimmer, I tried to elude them,
and as I never appeared again, it was supposed I was
drowned."

"And Nizza, or as I ought now to call her, Isabella,
was confided, I suppose, to the piper?" inquired
Leonard.

"She was confided to his helpmate," replied Thirlby,
"who had been nurse to my wife. Mike Macascree was
one of my father's servants, and was in his younger days
a merry, worthless fellow. The heavy calamity under which
he now labours had not then befallen him. On taking
charge of my daughter, his wife received certain papers
substantiating the child's origin, together with a miniature,
and a small golden amulet. The papers and miniature
were delivered by her on her death-bed to the piper, who
showed them to me to-night."

"And the amulet I myself have seen," remarked
Leonard.

"To resume my own history," said Thirlby—"after the
dreadful catastrophe I have related, I remained concealed
in London for some months, and was glad to find the
report of my death generally believed. I then passed over

into Holland, where I resided for several years, in the course of which time I married the widow of a rich merchant, who died soon after our union, leaving me one child."

And he covered his face with his hands to hide his emotion. After awhile, he proceeded:—

" Having passed many years, as peacefully as one whose conscience was so heavily burdened as mine could hope to pass them, in Amsterdam, I last summer brought my daughter, around whom my affections were closely twined, to London, and took up my abode in the eastern environs of the city. There again I was happy—too happy!—until at last the plague came—but why should I relate the rest of my sad story?" he added, in a voice suffocated with emotion—" you know it as well as I do."

" You said you had a son," observed Leonard, after a pause—" is he yet living?"

" He is," replied Thirlby, a shade passing over his countenance. " On my return to England I communicated to him through Judith Malmayns, who is my foster-sister, that I was still alive, telling him the name I had adopted, and adding, I should never disturb him in the possession of his title and estates."

" Title!" exclaimed Leonard.

" Ay, title!" echoed Thirlby. " The title I once bore was that of Lord Argentine."

" I am glad to hear it," said Leonard, " for I began to fear Sir Paul Parravicin was your son."

" Sir Paul Parravicin, or, rather, the Lord Argentine, for such is his rightful title, is my son," returned Thirlby; " and I lament to own I am his father. When among his worthless associates,—nay, even with the king,—he drops the higher title, and assumes that by which you have known him; and it is well he does so, for his actions are sufficient to tarnish a far nobler name than that he bears. Owing to this disguise I knew not he was the person who carried off my daughter. But, thank Heaven! more another, and fouler crime, has been spared us. All these things have been strangely explained to me to-night. And thus, you see,

young man, the poor piper's daughter turns out to be the
Lady Isabella Argentine."

Before an answer could be returned, the door was
opened by Hodges, and both starting to their feet, hurried
towards him.

CHAPTER IV

The Trials of Amabel

IT will now be necessary to return to the period of Amabel's
abduction from Kingston Lisle. The shawl thrown over
her head prevented her cries from being heard; and, notwithstanding her struggles, she was placed on horseback
before a powerful man, who galloped off with her along
the Wantage road. After proceeding at a rapid pace for
about two miles, her conductor came to a halt, and she
could distinguish the sound of other horsemen approaching. At first she hoped it might prove a rescue; but she
was quickly undeceived. The shawl was removed, and she
beheld the Earl of Rochester, accompanied by Pillichody,
and some half-dozen mounted attendants. The earl would
have transferred her to his own steed, but she offered such
determined resistance to the arrangement, that he was compelled to content himself with riding by her side. All his
efforts to engage her in conversation were equally unsuccessful. She made no reply to his remarks, but averted her
gaze from him; and, whenever he approached, shrank
from him with abhorrence. The earl, however, was not
easily repulsed, but continued his attentions and discourse,
as if both had been favourably received.

In this way they proceeded for some miles, one of the
earl's attendants, who was well acquainted with the
country, being, in fact, a native of it, serving as their guide.
They had quitted the Wantage road, and leaving that
ancient town, renowned as the birthplace of the great
Alfred, on the right, had taken the direction of Abingdon
and Oxford. It was a lovely evening, and their course led
them through many charming places. But the dreariest

waste would have been as agreeable as the richest prospect to Amabel. She noted neither the broad meadows, yet white from the the scythe, nor the cornfields waving with their deep and abundant, though yet immature crops; nor did she cast even a passing glance at any one of those green spots which every lane offers, and upon which the eye of the traveller ordinarily delights to linger. She rode beneath a natural avenue of trees, whose branches met overhead like the arches of a cathedral, and was scarcely conscious of their pleasant shade. She heard neither the song of the wooing thrush, nor the cry of the startled blackbird, nor the evening hymn of the soaring lark. Alike to her was the gorse-covered common, along which they swiftly speeded, and the steep hill-side up which they more swiftly mounted. She breathed not the delicious fragrance of the new-mown hay, nor listened to the distant lowing herds, the bleating sheep, or the cawing rooks. She thought of nothing but her perilous situation,—heard nothing but the voice of Rochester,—felt nothing but the terror inspired by his presence.

As the earl did not desire to pass through any village, if he could help it, his guide led him along the most unfrequented roads; but, in spite of his caution, an interruption occurred which had nearly resulted in Amabel's deliverance. While threading a narrow lane, they came suddenly upon a troop of haymakers, in a field on the right, who, up to that moment, had been hidden from view by the high hedges. On seeing them, Amabel screamed loudly for assistance, and was instantly answered by their shouts. Rochester ordered his men to gallop forward, but the road winding round the meadow, the haymakers were enabled to take a shorter cut and intercept them. Leaping the hedge, a stout fellow rushed towards Amabel's conductor, and seized the bridle of his steed. He was followed by two others, who would have instantly liberated the captive girl, if the earl had not, with great presence of mind, cried out, " Touch her not, as you value your lives ! She is ill of the plague ! "

At this formidable announcement, which operated like magic upon Amabel's defenders, and made them fall back more quickly than the weapons of the earl's attendants could have done, they retreated, and communicating their fears to their comrades, who were breaking through the hedge in all directions, and hurrying to their aid, the whole band took to their heels, and regardless of Amabel's continued shrieks, never stopped till they supposed themselves out of the reach of infection. The earl was thus at liberty to pursue his way unmolested, and laughing heartily at the success of his stratagem and at the consternation he had created among the haymakers, pressed forward.

Nothing further occurred till, in crossing the little river Ock, near Lyford, the horse ridden by Amabel's conductor missed its footing, and precipitated them both into the water. No ill consequences followed the accident. Throwing himself into the shallow stream, Rochester seized Amabel, and placed her beside him on his own steed. A deathly paleness overspread her countenance, and a convulsion shook her frame as she was thus brought into contact with the earl, who fearing the immersion might prove dangerous in her present delicate state of health, quickened his pace to procure assistance. Before he had proceeded a hundred yards, Amabel fainted. Gazing at her with admiration, and pressing her inanimate frame to his breast, Rochester imprinted a passionate kiss on her cheek.

" By my soul ! " he mentally ejaculated, " I never thought I could be so desperately enamoured. I would not part with her for the crown of these realms."

While considering whither he should take her, and much alarmed at her situation, the man who acted as guide came to his relief. Halting till the earl came up, he said, " If you want assistance for the young lady, my lord, I can take you to a good country inn, not far from this, where she will be attended to, and where, as it is kept by my father, I can answer that no questions will be asked."

" Precisely what I wish, Sherborne," replied Rochester. " We will halt there for the night. Ride on as fast as you can."

Sherborne struck spurs into his steed, and passing Kingston Bagpuze, reached the high road between Abingdon and Faringdon, at the corner of which stood the inn in question,—a good-sized habitation, with large stables and a barn attached to it. Here he halted, and calling out in a loud and authoritative voice, the landlord instantly answered the summons; and, on being informed by his son of the rank of his guest, doffed his cap, and hastened to assist the earl to dismount. But Rochester declined his services, and bidding him summon his wife, she shortly afterwards made her appearance in the shape of a stout middle-aged dame. Committing Amabel to her care, the earl then alighted, and followed them into the house.

The Plough, for so the inn was denominated, was thrown into the utmost confusion by the arrival of the earl and his suite. All the ordinary frequenters of the inn were ejected, while the best parlour was instantly prepared for the accommodation of his lordship and Pillochody. But Rochester was far more anxious for Amabel than himself, and could not rest for a moment till assured by Dame Sherborne that she was restored to sensibility, and about to retire to rest. He then became easy, and sat down to supper with Pillichody. So elated was he by his success, that, yielding to his natural inclination for hard drinking, he continued to revel so freely and so long with his follower, that day-break found them over their wine, the one toasting the grocer's daughter, and the other Patience, when they both staggered off to bed.

A couple of hours sufficed Rochester to sleep off the effects of his carouse. At six o'clock he arose, and ordered his attendants to prepare to set out without delay. When all was ready, he sent for Amabel, but she refused to come downstairs, and finding his repeated messages of no avail, he rushed into her room, and bore her, shrieking, to his steed.

In an hour after this, they arrived at an old hall, belonging to the earl, in the neighbourhood of Oxford. Amabel was entrusted to the care of a female attendant, named Prudence, and towards evening Rochester, who was burning with impatience for an interview, learnt to his infinite disappointment that she was so seriously unwell that if he forced himself into her presence her life might be placed in jeopardy. She continued in the same state for several days, at the end of which time the chirurgeon who attended her, and who was a creature of the earl's, pronounced her out of danger. Rochester then sent her word by Prudence that he must see her in the course of that day, and a few hours after the delivery of the message, he sought her room. She was much enfeebled by illness, but received him with great self-possession.

" I cannot believe, my lord," she said, " that you desire to destroy me, and when I assure you—solemnly assure you, that if you continue to persecute me thus, my death will be the consequence, I am persuaded you will desist and suffer me to depart."

" Amabel," rejoined the earl, passionately, " is it possible you can be so changed towards me ? Nothing now interferes to prevent our union."

" Except my own determination to the contrary, my lord," she replied. " I can never be yours."

" Wherefore not ? " asked the earl, half angrily, half reproachfully.

" Because I know and feel that I should condemn myself to wretchedness," she replied. " Because—for since your lordship will force the truth from me, I must speak out,— I have learnt to regard your character in its true light,— and because my heart is wedded to heaven."

" Pshaw ! " exclaimed the earl, contemptuously; " you have been listening so long to your saintly father's discourses, that you fancy them applicable to yourself. But you are mistaken in me," he added, altering his tone; " I see where the main difficulty lies. You think I am about to delude you, as before, into a mock marriage. But I swear to you you are mistaken. I love you so well that I would risk my temporal and eternal happiness for you. It will rejoice me to raise you to my own rank—to place you among the radiant beauties of our sovereign's court, the brightest of whom you will outshine, and to devote my whole life to your happiness."

" It is too late," sighed Amabel.

" Why too late ? " cried the earl, imploringly. " We have gone through severe trials, it is true. I have been constantly baffled in my pursuit of you, but disappointment has only made me love you more devotedly. Why too late? What is to prevent our nuptials from taking place to-day—to-morrow—when you will? The king himself shall be present at the ceremony, and shall give you away. Will this satisfy your scruples? I know I have offended you. I know I deserve your anger. But the love that prompted me to act thus, must also plead my pardon."

"Strengthen me!" she murmured, looking supplicatingly upwards. "Strengthen me, for my trial is very severe."

"Be not deceived, Amabel," continued Rochester, yet more ardently; "that you love me I am well assured, however strongly you may at this moment persuade yourself to the contrary. Be not governed by your father's strait-laced and puritanical opinions. Men, such as he is, cannot judge of fiery natures like mine. I myself have had to conquer a stubborn and rebellious spirit, the demon pride. But I have conquered. Love has achieved the victory,—love for you. I offer you my heart, my hand, my title. A haughty noble makes this offer to a grocer's daughter. Can you, will you refuse me?"

"I can and do, my lord," she replied. "I have achieved a yet harder victory. With me, principle has conquered love. I no longer respect you, no longer love you—and, therefore, cannot wed you."

"Rash and obstinate girl," cried the earl, unable to conceal his mortification; "you will bitterly repent your inconsiderate conduct. I offer you devotion such as no other person could offer you, and rank such as no other is likely to offer you. You are now in my power, and you *shall* be mine,—in what way rests with yourself. You shall have a week to consider the matter. At the end of that time, I will again renew my proposal. If you accept it, well and good. If not, you know the alternative."

And without waiting for a reply, he quitted the room.

He was as good as his word. During the whole of the week allowed Amabel for consideration, he never intruded upon her, nor was his name at any time mentioned by her attendants. If she had been, indeed, Countess of Rochester, she could not have been treated with greater respect than was shown her. The apartment allotted her opened upon a large garden, surrounded by high walls, and she walked within it daily. Her serenity of mind remained undisturbed; her health visibly improved; and, what was yet more surprising, she entirely recovered her beauty. The whole of her time not devoted to exercise, was spent in reading, or in prayer.

On the appointed day, Rochester presented himself. She received him with the most perfect composure, and with a bland look, from which he augured favourably. He waved his hand to the attendants, and they were alone.

"I came for your answer, Amabel," he said; "but I scarcely require it, being convinced from your looks that I have nothing to fear. Oh! why did you not abridge this tedious interval? Why not inform me you had altered your mind? But I will not reproach you. I am too happy to complain of the delay."

"I must undeceive you, my lord," returned Amabel, gravely. "No change has taken place in my feelings. I still adhere to the resolution I had come to when we last parted."

"How!" exclaimed the earl, his countenance darkening, and the evil look which Amabel had before noticed taking possession of it. "One moment lured on, and next rebuffed. But no—no!" he added, constraining himself, "you cannot mean it. It is not in woman's nature to act thus. You have loved me—you love me still. Make me happy—make yourself happy."

"My lord," she replied, "strange and unnatural as my conduct may appear, you will find it consistent. You have lost the sway you had once over me, and, for the reasons I have already given you, I can never be yours."

"Oh, recall your words, Amabel," he cried in the most moving tones he could command; "if you have no regard for me—at least have compassion. I will quit the court, if you desire it; will abandon title, rank, wealth; and live in the humblest station with you. You know not what I am capable of when under the dominion of passion. I am capable of the darkest crimes, or of the brightest virtues.

The woman who has a man's heart in her power may mould it to her own purposes, be they good or ill. Reject me, and you drive me to despair, and plunge me into guilt. Accept me, and you may lead me into any course you please."

" Were I assured of this——" cried Amabel.

" Rest assured of it," returned the earl, passionately. " Oh, yield to impulses of natural affection, and do not suffer a cold and calculating creed to chill your better feelings. How many a warm and loving heart has been so frozen ! Do not let yours be one of them. Be mine ! be mine ! "

Amabel looked at him earnestly for a moment; while he, assured that he had gained his point, could not conceal a slightly triumphant smile.

" Now, your answer ! " he cried. " My life hangs upon it."

" I am still unmoved," she replied, coldly and firmly.

" Ah ! " exclaimed the earl with a terrible imprecation, and starting to his feet. " You refuse me. Be it so. But think not that you shall escape me. No, you are in my power, and I will use it. You shall be mine, and without the priest's interference. I will not degrade myself by an alliance with one so lowly born. The strongest love is nearest allied to hatred, and mine has become hatred— bitter hatred. You shall be mine, I tell you, and when I am indifferent to you, I will cast you off. Then, when you are neglected, despised, shunned, you will regret—deeply but unavailingly—your rejection of my proposals."

" No, my lord, I shall never regret it," replied Amabel, " and I cannot sufficiently rejoice that I did not yield to the momentary weakness that inclined me to accept them. I thank you for the insight you have afforded me into your character."

" You have formed an erroneous opinion of me, Amabel," cried the earl, seeing his error, and trying to correct it. " I am well-nigh distracted by conflicting emotions. Oh, forgive my violence;—forget it."

" Readily," she replied; " but think not I attach the least credit to your professions."

"Away, then, with further disguise," returned the earl,
relapsing into his furious mood, "and recognise in me the
person I am,—or rather the person you would have me be.
You say you are immovable. So am I; nor will I further
delay my purpose."

Amabel, who had watched him uneasily during this
speech, retreated a step, and taking a small dagger from
a handkerchief in which she kept it concealed, placed its
point against her breast.

"I well know whom I have to deal with, my lord," she
said, "and am, therefore, provided against the last extremity. Attempt to touch me, and I plunge this dagger
into my heart."

"Your sense of religion will not allow you to commit
so desperate a deed," replied the earl, derisively.

"My blood be upon your head, my lord," she rejoined;
"for it is your hand that strikes the blow, and not my own.
My honour is dearer to me than life, and I will unhesitatingly sacrifice the one to preserve the other. I have no
fear but that the action, wrongful though it be, will be
forgiven me."

"Hold!" exclaimed the earl, seeing from her determined look and manner that she would unquestionably
execute her purpose. "I have no desire to drive you to
destruction. Think over what I have said to you—and we
will renew the subject to-morrow."

"Renew it when you please, my lord, my answer will
still be the same," she replied. "I have but one refuge
from you—the grave, and thither, if need be, I will fly."

And as she spoke, she moved slowly towards the adjoining chamber, the door of which she fastened after her.

"I thought I had some experience of her sex," said
Rochester to himself, "but I find I was mistaken. To-
morrow's mood, however, may be unlike to-day's. At all
events, I must take my measures differently."

CHAPTER V

The Marriage and its Consequences

UNWILLING to believe he had become an object of aversion to Amabel, Rochester renewed his solicitations on the following day, and calling into play his utmost fascination of manner, endeavoured to remove any ill impression produced by his previous violence. She was proof, however, against his arts; and though he never lost his mastery over himself, he had some difficulty in concealing his chagrin at the result of the interview. He now began to adopt a different course, and entering into long discussions with Amabel, strove by every effort of wit and ridicule to shake and subvert her moral and religious principles. But here again he failed, and once more shifting his ground, affected to be convinced by her arguments. He entirely altered his demeanour, and though Amabel could not put much faith in the change, it was a subject of real rejoicing to her. Though scarcely conscious of it herself, he sensibly won upon her regards, and she passed many hours of each day in his society without finding it irksome. Seeing the advantage he had gained, and well aware that he should lose it by the slightest indescretion, Rochester acted with the greatest caution. The more at ease she felt with him, the more deferential did he become; and before she was conscious of her danger, the poor girl was once more on the brink of the precipice.

It was about this time that Leonard Holt, as has been previously intimated, discovered her retreat, and contrived by clambering up a pear-tree, which was nailed against the wall of the house, to reach her chamber window. Having received her assurance that she had resisted all Rochester's importunities, the apprentice promised to return on the following night with means to effect her liberation, and departed. Fully persuaded that she could now repose confidence in the earl, Amabel acquainted him, the next morning, with Leonard's visit, adding that he would now

have an opportunity of proving the sincerity of his professions by delivering her up to her friends.

" Since you desire it," replied the earl, who heard her
with an unmoved countenance, though internally torn with
passion, " I will convey you to your father myself. I had
hoped," he added, with a sigh, " that we should never part
again."

" I fear I have been mistaken in you, my lord," rejoined
Amabel, half repenting her frankness.

" Not so," he replied. " I will do anything you require,
except deliver you to this hateful apprentice. If it is your
pleasure, I repeat, I will take you back to your father."

" Promise me this, my lord, and I shall be quite easy,"
cried Amabel, joyfully.

" I do promise it," he returned. " But oh ! why not stay
with me, and complete the good work you have begun ? "

Amabel averted her head, and Rochester, sighing deeply,
quitted the room. An attendant shortly afterwards came
to inform her that the earl intended to start for London
without delay, and begged her to prepare for the journey.
In an hour's time, a carriage drove to the door, and
Rochester having placed her and Prudence in it, mounted
his horse, and set forth. Late on the second day they arrived in London, and passing through the silent and deserted streets, the aspect of which struck terror into all the
party, shaped their course towards the city. Presently
they reached Ludgate, but instead of proceeding to Wood-
street, the carriage turned off on the right, and traversing
Thames-street, crossed London-bridge. Amabel could obtain no explanation of this change from Prudence, and her
uneasiness was not diminished when the vehicle, which
was driven down a narrow street on the left immediately
after quitting the bridge, stopped at the entrance of a large
court-yard. Rochester, who had already dismounted, assisted her to alight, and in answer to her hasty inquiries
why he had brought her thither, told her he thought it
better to defer taking her to her father till the morrow.
Obliged to be content with this excuse, she was led into
the house, severely reproaching herself for her indiscretion.
Nothing, however, occurred to alarm her that night. The

earl was even more deferential than before, and assuring
her he would fulfil his promise in the morning, confided
her to Prudence.

The house whither she had been brought was large and
old-fashioned. The rooms had once been magnificently
fitted up, but the hangings and furniture were much faded,
and had a gloomy and neglected air. This was especially
observable in the sleeping-chamber appointed for her reception. It was large and lofty, panelled with black and
shining oak, with a highly-polished floor of the same
material, and was filled with cumbrous chests and cabinets,
and antique high-backed chairs. But the most noticeable
object was a large state-bed, with a heavy square canopy,
covered with the richest damask, woven with gold, and
hung with curtains of the same stuff, though now decayed
and tarnished. A chill crept over Amabel as she gazed
around.

" I cannot help thinking," she observed to Prudence,
" that I shall breathe my last in this room, and in that bed."

" I hope not, madam," returned the attendant, unable
to repress a shudder.

Nothing more was said, and Amabel retired to rest.
But not being able to sleep, and having vainly tried to
compose herself, she arose and opened the window. It was
a serene and beautiful night, and she could see the smooth
river sparkling in the starlight, and flowing at a hundred
yards' distance at the foot of the garden. Beyond, she
could indistinctly perceive the outline of the mighty city,
while nearer, on the left, lay the bridge. Solemnly across
the water came the sound of innumerable bells, tolling for
those who had died of the plague, and were now being
borne to their last home. While listening to these sad
sounds, another, but more doleful and appalling noise,
caught her ears. It was the rumbling of cart-wheels in the
adjoining street, accompanied by the ringing of a hand-
bell, while a hoarse voice cried, " Bring out your dead !
bring out your dead ! " On hearing this cry, she closed
the window and retired. Morning broke before sleep
visited her weary eyelids, and then, overcome by fatigue,
she dropped into a slumber, from which she did not awake

until the day was far advanced. She found Prudence sitting by her bedside, and alarmed by the expression of her countenance, anxiously inquired what was the matter.

" Alas ! madam," replied the attendant, " the earl has been taken suddenly ill. He set out for Wood-street the first thing this morning, and has seen your father, who refuses to receive you. On his return, he complained of a slight sickness, which has gradually increased in violence, and there can be little doubt it is the plague. Advice has been sent for. He prays you not to disturb yourself on his account, but to consider yourself sole mistress of this house, whatever may befall him."

Amabel passed a miserably anxious day. A fresh interest had been awakened in her heart on behalf of the earl, and the precarious state in which she conceived him placed did not tend to diminish it. She made many inquiries after him, and learned that he was worse, while the fearful nature of the attack could not be questioned. On the following day, Prudence reported that the distemper had made such rapid and terrible progress, that his recovery was considered almost hopeless.

" He raves continually of you, madam," said the attendant, " and I have no doubt he will expire with your name on his lips."

Amabel was moved to tears by the information, and withdrawing into a corner of the room, prayed fervently for the supposed sufferer. Prudence gazed at her earnestly and compassionately, and muttering something to herself, quitted the room. The next day was the critical one (so it was said) for the earl, and Amabel awaited, in tearful anxiety, the moment that was to decide his fate. It came, and he was pronounced out of danger. When the news was brought the anxious girl, she fainted.

A week passed, and the earl continued to improve, and all danger of infection—if any such existed—being at an end, he sent a message to Amabel, beseeching her to grant him an interview in his own room. She willingly assented, and, following the attendant, found him stretched upon a couch. In spite of his paleness and apparent debility, however, his good looks were but little impaired, and his attire, though negligent, was studiously arranged for effect. On Amabel's appearance, he made an effort to rise, but she hastened to prevent him. After thanking her for her kind inquiries, he entered into a long conversation with her, in the course of which he displayed sentiments so exactly coinciding with her own, that the good opinion she had already begun to entertain for him was soon heightened into the liveliest interest. They parted, to meet again on the following day—and on the day following that. The bloom returned to the earl's countenance, and he looked handsomer than ever. A week thus passed, and at the end of it, he said—" To-morrow I shall be well enough to venture forth again, and my first business shall be to proceed to your father, and see whether he is now able to receive you."

" The plague has not yet abated, my lord," she observed, blushingly.

" True," he replied, looking passionately at her. " Oh, forgive me, Amabel," he added, taking her hand, which she did not attempt to withdraw. " Forgive me, if I am wrong. But I now think your feelings are altered towards me, and that I may venture to hope you will be mine ? "

Amabel's bosom heaved with emotion. She tried to speak, but could not. Her head declined upon his shoulder, and her tears flowed fast.

" I am answered," he cried, scarcely able to contain his rapture, and straining her to his bosom.

" I know not whether I am doing rightly," she murmured, gazing at him through her tears, " but I believe you mean me truly. God forgive you if you do not."

" Have no more doubts," cried the earl. " You have wrought an entire change in me. Our union shall not be delayed an hour. It shall take place in Saint Saviour's to-night."

" Not to-night," cried Amabel, trembling at his eagerness—" to-morrow."

" To-night, to-night ! " reiterated the earl, victoriously. And he rushed out of the room.

Amabel was no sooner left to herself than she repented what she had done. " I fear I have made a false step," she mused; " but it is now too late to retreat, and I will hope for the best. He cannot mean to deceive me."

Her meditations were interrupted by the entrance of Prudence, who came towards her with a face full of glee.

" My lord has informed me of the good news," she said. " You are to be wedded to him to-day. I have expected it all along, but it is somewhat sudden at last. He is gone in search of the priest, and in the meantime has ordered me to attire you for the ceremony. I have several rich dresses for your ladyship—for so I must now call you—to choose from."

" The simplest will suit me best," replied Amabel, " and do not call me ladyship till I have a right to that title."

" That will be so soon that I am sure there can be no harm in using it now," returned Prudence. " But pray let me show you the dresses."

Amabel suffered herself to be led into another room, where she saw several sumptuous female habiliments, and selecting the least showy of them, was soon arrayed in it by the officious attendant.

More than two hours elapsed before Rochester returned, when he entered Amabel's chamber, accompanied by Sir George Etherege and Pillichody. A feeling of misgiving crossed Amabel, as she beheld his companions.

" I have had some difficulty in finding a clergyman," said the earl, " for the rector of Saint Saviour's has fled from the plague. His curate, however, will officiate for him, and is now in the church."

Amabel fixed a searching look upon him.

" Why are these gentlemen here ? " she asked.

" I have brought them with me," rejoined Rochester, " because, as they were aware of the injury I once intended you, I wish them to be present at its reparation."

" I am satisfied," she replied.

Taking her hand, the earl then led her to a carriage, which conveyed them to Saint Saviour's. Just as they alighted, the dead-cart passed, and several bodies were brought towards it. Eager to withdraw her attention from the spectacle, Rochester hurried her into the old and beautiful church. In another moment, they were joined by Etherege and Pillichody, and they proceeded to the altar, where the priest, a young man, was standing. The ceremony was then performed, and the earl led his bride back to the carriage. On their return, they had to undergo another ill-omened interruption. The dead-cart was stationed near the gateway, and some delay occurred before it could be moved forward.

Amabel, however, suffered no further misgiving to take possession of her. Dreaming herself wedded to the earl, she put no constraint on her affection for him, and her happiness, though short-lived, was deep and full.

A month passed away like a dream of delight. Nothing occurred in the slightest degree to mar her felicity. Rochester seemed only to live for her—to think only of her. At the end of this time, some indifference began to manifest itself in his deportment to her, and he evinced a disposition to return to the court and to its pleasures.

" I thought you had for ever abandoned them, my dear lord," said Amabel, reproachfully.

" For awhile I have," he replied, carelessly.

" You must leave me, if you return to them," she rejoined.

" If I must, I must," said the earl.

" You cannot mean this, my lord," she cried, bursting into tears. " You cannot be so changed."

" I have never changed since you first knew me," replied Rochester.

" Impossible ! " she cried, in a tone of anguish, " you have not the faults—the vices, you once had."

" I know not what you call faults and vices, madam," replied the earl, sharply, " but I have the same qualities as heretofore."

" Am I to understand, then," cried Amabel, a fearful suspicion of the truth breaking upon her, " that you never sincerely repented your former actions ? "

" You are to understand it," replied Rochester.

" And you deceived me when you affirmed the contrary ? "

" I deceived you," he replied.

" I begin to suspect," she cried, with a look of horror and doubt, " that the attack of the plague was feigned."

" You are not far wide of the truth," was the reply.

" And our marriage ? " she cried, " our marriage ? Was that feigned likewise ? "

" It was," replied Rochester, calmly.

Amabel looked at him fixedly for a few minutes, as if she could not credit his assertion, and then receiving no contradiction, uttered a wild scream, and rushed out of the room. Rochester followed, and saw her dart with lightning swiftness across the court-yard. On gaining the street, he perceived her flying figure already at some distance, and greatly alarmed, started in pursuit. The unfortunate girl was not allowed to proceed far. Two persons who were approaching, and who proved to be Etherege and Pillichody, caught hold of her, and detained her till Rochester came up. When the latter attempted to touch her, she uttered such fearful shrieks, that Etherege entreated him to desist. With some difficulty she was taken back to the house. But it was evident that the shock had unsettled her reason. She alternately uttered wild, piercing screams, or broke into hysterical laughter. The earl's presence so much increased her frenzy, that he gladly withdrew.

" This is a melancholy business, my lord," observed Etherege, as they quitted the room together, " and I am sorry for my share in it. We have both much to answer for."

" Do you think her life in danger ? " rejoined Rochester.

" It would be well if it were so," returned the other; " but I fear she will live to be a perpetual memento to you of the crime you have committed."

Amabel's delirium produced a high fever, which continued for three days. Her screams were at times so dreadful, that her betrayer shut himself up in the furthest part of the house, that he might not hear them. When at last she sank into a sleep like that of death, produced by powerful opiates, he stole into the room, and gazed at her with feelings which those who watched his countenance did not envy.

It was hoped by the chirurgeon in attendance, that when the violence of the fever abated, Amabel's reason would be restored. But it was not so. Her faculties were completely shaken, and the cause of her affliction being effaced from her memory, she now spoke of the Earl of Rochester with her former affection.

Her betrayer once ventured into her presence, but he did not repeat the visit. Her looks and her tenderness were more than even *his* firmness could bear, and he hurried away to hide his emotion from the attendants. Several days passed on, and as no improvement took place, the earl, who began to find the stings of conscience too sharp for further endurance, resolved to try to deaden the pangs by again plunging into the dissipation of the court. Prudence had been seized by the plague, and removed to the pest-house, and not knowing to whom to intrust Amabel, it at last occurred to him that Judith Malmayns would be a fitting person, and he accordingly sent for her from Saint Paul's, and communicated his wishes to her, offering her a considerable reward for the service. Judith readily undertook the office, and the earl delayed his departure for two days, to see how all went on, and finding the arrangements, to all appearances, answer perfectly, he departed with Etherege and Pillichody.

Ever since the communication of the fatal truth had been made to her by the earl, his unfortunate victim had occupied the large oak-panelled chamber, on entering which so sad a presentiment had seized her; and she had never quitted the bed where she thought she would breathe her last. On the night of Rochester's departure, she made many inquiries concerning him from Judith Malmayns, who was seated in an old broad-cushioned, velvet-covered chair beside her, and was told that the king required his attendance at Oxford, but that he would soon return. At this answer, the tears gathered thickly in Amabel's dark eyelashes, and she remained silent. By-and-by, she resumed the conversation.

" Do you know, nurse," she said, with a look of extreme anxiety, " I have forgotten my prayers. Repeat them to me, and I will say them after you."

" My memory is as bad as your ladyship's," replied Judith, contemptuously. " It is so long since I said mine, that I have quite forgotten them."

" That is wrong in you," returned Amabel, " very wrong. When I lived with my dear father, we had prayers morning and evening, and I was never so happy as then. I feel it would do me good if I could pray as I used to do."

" Well, well, all in good time," replied Judith. " As soon as you are better, you shall go back to your father, and then you can do as you please."

" No, no, I cannot go back to him," returned Amabel. " I am the Earl of Rochester's wife—his wedded wife. Am I not Countess of Rochester ? "

" To be sure you are," replied Judith. " To be sure."

" I sometimes think otherwise," rejoined Amabel, mournfully. " And so my dear lord is gone to Oxford ? "

" He is," returned Judith, " but he will be back soon. And now," she added, with some impatience, " you have talked quite long enough. You must take your composing draught, and go to sleep."

With this, she arose, and stepping to the table which stood by the side of the bed, filled a wine-glass with the contents of a silver flagon, and gave it to her.

Amabel drank the mixture, and complaining of its nauseous taste, Judith handed her a plate of fruit from the table to remove it. Soon after this, she dropt asleep, when the nurse arose, and talking a light from the table, cautiously possessed herself of a bunch of keys which were placed in a small pocket over Amabel's head, and proceeded to unlock a large chest that stood near the foot of the bed. She found it filled with valuables; with chains of gold, necklaces of precious stones, loops of pearl, diamond crosses, and other ornaments. Besides these, there were shawls and stuffs of the richest description. While contemplating these treasures, and considering how she could carry them off without alarming the household, she was startled by a profound sigh, and looking towards the bed, perceived, to her great alarm, that Amabel had opened her eyes, and was watching her.

" What are you doing there, nurse ? " she cried.

" Only looking at these pretty things, your ladyship,"
replied Judith, in an embarrassed tone.

" I hope you are not going to steal them ? " said Amabel.

" Steal them ! " echoed Judith, alarmed. " Oh, no !
What should make your ladyship think so ? "

" I don't know," said Amabel; " but put them by, and
bring the keys to me."

Judith feigned compliance, but long before she had restored the things to the chest, Amabel had again fallen
asleep. Apprised by her tranquil breathing of this circumstance, Judith arose, and shading the candle with her hand,
crept noiselessly towards the bed. Dark thoughts crossed
her as she gazed at the unfortunate sleeper, and moving
with the utmost caution, she set the light on the table behind
the curtains, and had just grasped the pillow, with the intention of plucking it from under Amabel's head, and of
smothering her with it, when she felt herself restrained by
a powerful grasp, and turning in utmost alarm, beheld the
Earl of Rochester.

CHAPTER VI

The Certificate

" WRETCH ! " cried the earl. " An instinctive dread that
you would do your poor charge some injury brought me
back, and I thank Heaven I have arrived in time to prevent
your atrocious purpose."

" Your lordship would have acted more discreetly in
staying away," replied Judith, recovering her resolution;
" and I would recommend you not to meddle in the matter,
but to leave it to me. No suspicion shall alight on you,
nor shall it even be known that her end was hastened.
Leave the house as secretly as you came, and proceed on
your journey with a light heart. She will never trouble
you further."

" What ! " exclaimed Rochester, who was struck dumb

P

for the moment by surprise and indignation, "you do imagine I would listen to such a proposal? Do you think I would sanction her murder?"

"I am sure you would, if you knew as much as I do," replied Judith, calmly. "Hear me, my lord," she continued, drawing him to a little distance from the bed, and speaking in a deep low tone. "You cannot marry Mistress Mallet while this girl lives."

Rochester looked sternly and inquiringly at her.

"You think your marriage was feigned," pursued Judith; "that he was no priest who performed the ceremony; and that no other witnesses were present except Sir George Etherege and Pillichody. But you are mistaken. I and Chowles were present; and he who officiated *was* a priest. The marriage was a lawful one; and yon sleeping girl, who, but for your ill-timed interference, would, ere this, have breathed her last, is to all intents and purposes Countess of Rochester."

"A lie!" cried the earl, furiously.

"I will soon prove it to be truth," rejoined Judith. "Your retainer and unscrupulous agent, Major Pillichody, applied to Chowles to find some one to personate a clergyman in a mock marriage, which your lordship wished to have performed, and promised a handsome reward for the service. Chowles mentioned the subject to me, and we speedily contrived a plan to outwit your lordship, and turn the affair to our own advantage.

"Being acquainted with one of the minor-canons of Saint Paul's, a worthy and pious young man, named Vincent," pursued Judith, utterly unmoved by Rochester's anger, "who resided hard by the cathedral, we hastened to him, and acquainted him with the design, representing ourselves as anxious to serve the poor girl, and defeat your lordship's wicked design,—for such we termed it. With a little persuasion, Mr. Vincent consented to the scheme. Pillichody was easily duped by Chowles' statement, and the ceremony was fully performed."

"The whole story is a fabrication," cried the earl, with affected incredulity.

"I have a certificate of the marriage," replied Judith,

" signed by Mr. Vincent, and attested by Chowles and my-self. If ever woman was wedded to man, Amabel is wedded to your lordship."

" If this is the case, why seek to destroy her ? " demanded the earl. " Her life must be of more consequence to you than her removal."

" I will deal frankly with you," replied Judith. " She discovered me in the act of emptying that chest, and an irresistible impulse prompted me to make away with her. But your lordship is in the right. Her life *is* valuable to me, and she *shall* live. But, I repeat, you cannot marry the rich heiress, Mistress Mallett."

" Temptress ! " cried the earl, " you put frightful thoughts into my head."

" Go your ways," replied Judith, " and think no more about her. All shall be done that you require. I claim as my reward the contents of that chest."

" Your reward shall be the gallows," rejoined the earl, indignantly. " I reject your proposal at once. Begone, wretch ! or I shall forget you are a woman, and sacrifice you to my fury. Begone ! "

" As your lordship pleases," she replied ; " but first, the Countess of Rochester shall be made acquainted with her rights." So saying, she broke from him, and rushed to the bed.

" What are you about to do ? " he cried.

" Waken her," rejoined Judith, slightly shaking the sleeper.

" Ah ! " exclaimed Amabel, opening her eyes, and gaz-ing at her with a terrified and bewildered look.

" His lordship is returned," said Judith.

" Indeed ! " exclaimed Amabel, raising herself in the bed. " Where is he ?—Ah, I see him.—Come to me, my dear lord," she added, stretching out her arms to him, " Come to me."

But evil thoughts kept Rochester motionless.

" Oh ! come to me, my lord," cried Amabel, in a troubled tone, " or I shall begin to think what I have dreamed is true, and that I am not wedded to you."

" It *was* merely a dream, your ladyship," observed

Judith. "I will bear witness you are wedded to his lordship, for I was present at the ceremony."

"I did not see you," remarked Amabel.

"I was there, nevertheless," replied Judith.

"I am sorry to hear it," replied Amabel.

"Your ladyship would rejoice if you knew all," returned Judith, significantly.

"Why so?" inquired the other, curiously.

"Because the clergyman who married you is dead of the plague," was the answer; "and it may chance in these terrible times that the two gentlemen who were present at the ceremony may die of the same distemper, and then there will be no one left but me and another person to prove that your marriage was lawful."

"But its lawfulness will never be questioned, my dear lord, will it?" asked Amabel, looking beseechingly at Rochester.

"Never," replied Judith, producing a small piece of parchment, "while I hold this certificate."

"Give me that document," said the earl, in an undertone to her.

Judith directed her eyes towards the chest.

"It is yours," said the earl, in the same tone as before.

"What are you whispering, my lord," inquired Amabel, uneasily.

"I am merely telling her to remove that chest, sweetheart," he replied.

"Do not send it away," cried Amabel. "It contains all the ornaments and trinkets you have given me. Do you know," she added in a whisper, "I caught her looking into it just now, and I suspect she was about to steal something."

"Pshaw!" cried the earl,—"she acted by my directions. Take the chest away," he added to Judith.

"Has your lordship no further orders?" she rejoined, significantly.

"None whatever," he replied with a frown.

"Before you go, give me the certificate," cried Amabel. "I must have it."

Judith pretended not to hear her.

"Give it her," whispered the earl, "I will remove it when she falls asleep."

Nodding acquiescence, Judith took the parchment from her bosom, and returned with it to the bed. While this was passing, the earl walked towards the chest, and cast his eye over such of its contents as were scattered upon the floor. Judith watched him carefully, and when his back was turned, drew a small lancet, and affecting to arrange her dress, slightly punctured Amabel's neck. The pain was trifling, but the poor girl uttered a cry.

"What is the matter?" cried the earl, turning suddenly round.

"Nothing—nothing," replied Judith; "a pin in my sleeve pricked her as I was fastening her cap, that was all. Her death is certain," she added to herself, "she is inoculated with the plague-venom."

She then went to the chest, and replacing everything within it, removed it by the help of the Earl of Rochester into the adjoining room.

"I will send for it at midnight," she said.

"It shall be delivered to your messenger," rejoined the earl; "but you will answer for Chowles' secrecy?"

"I will," returned Judith, with a meaning smile. "But you may take my word for it you will not be troubled long with your wife. If I have any judgment respecting the plague, she is already infected."

"Indeed!" cried Rochester,—"then—" but he checked himself, and added, "I do not believe it. Begone."

"He *does* believe it for all that," muttered Judith, as she slunk away.

Rochester returned to Amabel, and sat by her until she fell asleep, when he took the parchment from beneath the pillow where she had placed it. Examining it, he found it, as Judith had stated, a certificate of his marriage, signed by Mark Vincent, the clergyman who had officiated, and duly attested. Having carefully perused it, he held it towards the taper, with the intention of destroying it.

As he was about to perpetrate this unworthy action, he

looked towards the bed. The soft sweet smile that played
upon the sleeper's features turned him from his purpose.
Placing the parchment in his doublet, he left the room, and
summoning a female attendant, alleged some reason for
his unexpected return, and ordered her to watch by the
bedside of her mistress. Giving some further directions,
he threw himself upon a couch and sought a few hours'
repose.

At daybreak, he repaired to Amabel's chamber, and finding her wrapped in a peaceful slumber, he commended her
to the attendant, and departed.

On awaking, Amabel complained of an uneasy sensation
on her neck, and the attendant examining the spot, found,
to her great alarm, a small red pustule. Without making
a single observation, she left the room, and despatched a
messenger after the Earl of Rochester to acquaint him that
the countess was attacked by the plague. Such was the
terror inspired by this dread disorder, that the moment it
was known that Amabel was attacked by it, the whole
household, except an old woman, fled. This old woman,
whose name was Batley, and who acted as the earl's housekeeper, took upon herself the office of nurse. Before
evening, the poor sufferer, who had endured great agony
during the whole of the day, became so much worse, that
Mrs. Batley ran out in search of assistance. She met with
a watchman, who told her that a famous apothecary, from
Clerkenwell, named Sibbald, who was celebrated for the
cures he had effected, had just entered a neighbouring
house, and offered to await his coming forth, and send
him to her. Thanking him, Mrs. Batley returned to the
house, and presently afterwards, Sibbald made his appearance. His looks and person had become even more
repulsive than formerly. He desired to be led to the
patient, and on seeing her, shook his head. He examined
the pustule, which had greatly increased in size, and turning away, muttered, " I can do nothing for her."

" At least make the attempt," implored Mrs. Batley.
" She is the Countess of Rochester. You shall be well
rewarded—and if you cure her, the earl will make your
fortune."

" If his lordship would change stations with me, I could not cure her," replied Sibbald. " Let me look at her again," he added, examining the pustule. " There is a strange appearance about this tumour. Has Judith Malmayns attended her ? "

" She was here yesterday," replied Mrs. Batley.

" I thought so," he muttered. " I repeat, it is all over with her."

And he turned to depart.

" Do not leave her thus, in pity do not," cried the old woman, detaining him. " Make some effort to save her. My lord loves her to distraction, and will abundantly reward you."

" All I can do is to give her something to allay the pain," returned Sibbald.

And drawing a small phial from his doublet, he poured its contents into a glass, and administered it to the patient.

" That will throw her into a slumber," he said, " and when she wakes, she will be without pain. But her end will not be far off."

Mrs. Batley took a purse from a drawer in one of the cabinets, and gave it to the apothecary, who bowed, and retired. As he had foretold, Amabel fell into a heavy lethargy, which continued during the whole of the night. Mrs. Batley, who had never left her, noticed that an extraordinary and fearful change had taken place in her countenance, and she could not doubt that the apothecary's prediction would be realized. The tumour had increased in size, and was surrounded by a dusky brown circle, which she knew to be a bad sign. The sufferer's eyes, when she opened them and gazed around, had a dim and glazed look. But she was perfectly calm and composed, and as had been prognosticated, free from pain. She had, also, fully regained her faculties, and seemed quite aware of her dangerous situation.

But the return of reason brought with it no solace. On the contrary, the earl's treachery rushed upon her recollection, and gave her infinitely more anguish than the bodily pain she had recently endured. She bedewed the

pillow with her tears, and fervently prayed for forgiveness
for her involuntary fault. Mrs. Batley was deeply moved
by her affliction, and offered her every consolation in her
power.

" I would the plague had selected me for a victim instead
of your ladyship," she said. " It is hard to leave the world
at your age, possessed of beauty, honours, and wealth. At
mine, it would not signify."

" You mistake the cause of my grief," returned Amabel;
" I do not lament that my hour is at hand, but——" and
her emotion so overpowered her that she could not
proceed.

" Do not disturb yourself further, dear lady," rejoined
the old woman. " Let the worst happen, I am sure you are
well prepared to meet your Maker."

" I once was," replied Amabel in a voice of despair,
" but now—Oh, Heaven forgive me ! "

" Shall I fetch some holy minister to pray beside you, my
lady ? " said Mrs. Batley; " one to whom you can pour
forth the sorrows of your heart ? "

" Do so ! oh, do ! " cried Amabel, " and do not call me
lady. I am not worthy to be placed in the same rank as
yourself."

" Her wits are clean gone," muttered Mrs. Batley, looking at her compassionately.

" Heed me not," cried Amabel; " but if you have any
pity for the unfortunate, do as you have promised."

" I will,—I will," said Mrs. Batley, departing.

Half an hour, which scarcely seemed a moment to the
poor sufferer, who was employed in fervent prayer,
elapsed before Mrs. Batley returned. She was accompanied by a tall man, whom Amabel recognised as
Solomon Eagle.

" I have not been able to find a clergyman," said the
old woman, " but I have brought a devout man who is
willing to pray with you."

" Ah ! " exclaimed the enthusiast, starting as he beheld
Amabel. " Can it be Mr. Bloundel's daughter ?."

" It is," returned Amabel, with a groan. " Leave us, my
good woman," she added to Mrs. Batley, " I have some-

thing to impart to Solomon Eagle which is for his ear alone."

The old woman instantly retired, and Amabel briefly related her hapless story to the enthusiast.

" May I hope for forgiveness ? " she inquired, as she concluded.

" Assuredly," replied Solomon Eagle, " assuredly ! You have not erred wilfully, but through ignorance, and, therefore, have committed no offence. *You* will be forgiven— but woe to your deceiver, here and hereafter."

" Oh ! say not so," she cried. " May Heaven pardon him as I do. While I have strength left, I will pray for him."

And she poured forth her supplications for the earl in terms so earnest and pathetic, that the tears flowed down Solomon Eagle's rough cheek. At this juncture, hasty steps were heard in the adjoining passage, and the door opening, admitted the Earl of Rochester, who rushed towards the bed.

" Back ! " cried Solomon Eagle, pushing him forcibly aside. " Back ! "

" What do you here ? " cried Rochester, fiercely.

" I am watching over the death-bed of your victim," returned Solomon Eagle. " Retire, my lord. You disturb her."

" Oh, no," returned Amabel, meekly. " Let him come near me." And as Solomon Eagle drew a little aside, and allowed the earl to approach, she added, " With my latest breath I forgive you, my lord, for the wrong you have done me, and bless you."

The earl tried to speak, but his voice was suffocated by emotion. As soon as he could find words, he said, " Your goodness completely overpowers me, dearest Amabel. Heaven is my witness, that even now I would make you all reparation in my power, were it needful. But it is not so. The wrong I intended you was never committed. I myself was deceived. I intended a feigned marriage, but it was rightfully performed. Time will not allow me to enter into further particulars of the unhappy transaction, but you may credit my assertion

when I tell you you are indeed my wife, and Countess of
Rochester."

" If I thought so, I should die happy," replied Amabel.

" Behold this proof ! " said Rochester, producing the
certificate.

" I cannot read it," replied Amabel. " But you could
not have the heart to deceive me now."

" I will read it, and you well know *I* would not deceive
you," cried Solomon Eagle, casting his eye over it. " His
lordship has avouched the truth," he continued. " It is a
certificate of your marriage with him, duly signed and
attested."

" God be thanked," ejaculated Amabel, fervently.
" God be thanked ! You have been spared that guilt,
and I shall die content."

" I trust your life will long be spared," rejoined the
earl.

Amabel shook her head.

" There is but one man in this city who could save her,"
whispered Solomon Eagle, " and I doubt even his power
to do so."

" Who do you mean ? " cried Rochester, eagerly.

" Doctor Hodges," replied the enthusiast.

" I know him well," cried the earl. " I will fly to him
instantly. Remain with her till I return."

" My lord—my dear lord," interposed Amabel, faintly,
" you trouble yourself needlessly. I am past all human
aid."

" Do not despair," replied the earl. " Many years of
happiness are, I trust, in store for us. Do not detain me.
I go to save you. Farewell for a short time."

" Farewell for ever, my lord," she said, gently pressing
his hand. " We shall not meet again. Your name will be
coupled with my latest breath."

" I shall be completely unmanned if I stay here a moment
longer," cried the earl, breaking from her, and rushing out
of the room.

As soon as he was gone, Amabel addressed herself once
more to prayer with Solomon Eagle, and in this way an
hour passed by. The earl not returning at the end of that

time, Solomon Eagle became extremely uneasy, every moment being of the utmost consequence, and summoning Mrs. Batley, committed the patient to her care, and set off in search of Hodges. He hastened to the doctor's house—he was absent—to Saint Paul's—he was not there, but he learnt that a person answering to the earl's description had been making similar inquiries after him. At last, one of the chirurgeon's assistants told him that he thought the doctor was gone towards Cornhill, and hoping accidentally to meet with him, the enthusiast set off in that direction. While passing near the Exchange, he encountered Leonard, as before related, but did not think fit to acquaint him with more than Amabel's dangerous situation; and he had reason to regret making the communication at all, on finding its effect upon the poor youth. There was, however, no help for it, and placing him in what appeared a situation of safety, he left him.

Rochester, meanwhile, had been equally unsuccessful in his search for Hodges. Hurrying first in one direction and then in another, at the suggestion of the chirurgeon's assistant, he at last repaired to the doctor's residence, determined to await his return. In half an hour he came, and received the earl, as the old porter stated to Thirlby and Leonard, with angry astonishment. As soon as they were alone, the earl told him all that had occurred, and besought him to accompany him to the poor sufferer.

" I will go to her," said Hodges, who had listened to the recital with mixed feelings of sorrow and indignation, " on one condition—and one only—namely, that your lordship does not see her again without my permission."

" Why do you impose this restriction upon me, sir ? " demanded Rochester.

" I do not think it necessary to give my reasons, my lord," returned Hodges; " but I will only go upon such terms."

" Then I must perforce submit," replied the earl; " but I entreat you to set forth without a moment's delay, or you will be too late."

" I will follow you instantly," rejoined Hodges. " Your lordship can wait for me at the Southwark side of the bridge." He then opened the door, reiterating the terms upon which alone he would attend, and the earl departed.

Shortly afterwards he set out, and making the best of his way, found Rochester at the appointed place. The latter conducted him to the entrance of the habitation, and indicating a spot where he would remain till his return, left him.

Hodges soon found his way to the chamber of the sufferer, and at once perceived that all human aid was vain. She exhibited much pleasure at seeing him, and looked round, as if in search of the earl. Guessing her meaning, the physician, who now began to regret the interdiction he had placed upon him, told her that he was the cause of his absence.

" It is well," she murmured,—" well."

She then made some inquiries after her relatives, and receiving a satisfactory answer, said, " I am glad you are come. You will be able to tell my father how I died."

" It will be a great comfort to him to learn the tranquil frame in which I have found you," replied Hodges.

" How long have I to live ? " asked Amabel, somewhat quickly. " Do not deceive me."

" You had better make your preparations without delay," returned Hodges.

" I understand," she replied. And joining her hands upon her breast, she began to murmur a prayer.

Hodges, who up to this moment had had some difficulty in repressing his emotion, withdrew to a short distance to hide his fast-falling tears. He was roused shortly after, by a sudden and startling cry from the old woman.

" Oh, sir, she is going ! she is going ! " ejaculated Mrs. Batley.

He found the exclamation true. The eyes of the dying girl were closed. There was a slight quiver of the lips, as if she murmured some name—probably Rochester's—and then all was over.

Hodges gazed at her sorrowfully for some time. He then roused himself, and giving some necessary directions to the old woman respecting the body, quitted the house. Not finding the earl at the place he had appointed to meet him, after waiting for a short time, he proceeded towards his own house. On the way he was met by Thirlby and Parravicin, as previously related, and conducted to the house in Nicholas-lane. It will not be necessary to re-capitulate what subsequently occurred. We shall, there-fore, proceed to the point of time when he quitted his new patient, and entered the room where Thirlby and Leonard were waiting for him. Both, as has been stated, rushed towards him, and the former eagerly asked his opinion respecting his daughter.

"My opinion is positive," replied Hodges. "With care, she will undoubtedly recover."

"Heaven be thanked!" cried Thirlby, dropping on his knees.

"And now, one word to me, sir," cried Leonard. "What of Amabel?"

"Alas!" exclaimed the doctor, "her troubles are ended."

"Dead!" shrieked Leonard.

"Ay, dead!" repeated the doctor. "She died of the plague to-night."

He then proceeded to detail briefly all that had occurred. Leonard listened like one stupefied, till he brought his recital to a close, and then asking where the house in which she had died was situated, rushed out of the room, and made his way, he knew not how, into the street. His brain seemed on fire, and he ran so quickly that his feet appeared scarcely to touch the ground. A few seconds brought him to London-bridge. He crossed it, and turning down the street on the left, had nearly reached the house to which he had been directed, when his career was suddenly checked. The gate of the court-yard was opened, and two men, evidently, from their apparel, buriers of the dead, issued from it. They carried a long narrow board between them, with a body wrapped in a white sheet placed upon it. A freezing horror rooted Leonard to the spot where he stood. He could neither move nor utter a cry.

The men proceeded with their burden towards the adjoining habitation, which was marked with the fatal red cross and inscription. Before it stood the dead-cart, partly filled with corpses. The foremost burier carried a lantern, but he held it so low that its light did not fall upon his burden. Leonard, however, did not require to see the body to know whose it was. The moon was at its full, and shed a ghastly light over the group, and a large bat wheeled in narrow circles round the dead-cart.

On reaching the door of the house, the burier set down the lantern near the body of a young man which had just been thrust forth. At the same moment, Chowles, with a lantern in his hand, stepped out upon the threshold.

" Who have you got, Jonas ? " he asked.

" I know not," replied the hindmost burier. " We entered yon large house, the door of which stood open, and in one of the rooms found an old woman in a fainting state, and the body of this young girl, wrapped in a sheet, and ready for the cart. So we clapped it on the board, and brought it away with us."

" You did right," replied Chowles. " I wonder whose body it is."

As he spoke, he held up his lantern, and unfastening it, threw the light full upon the face. The features were pale as marble ; calm in their expression, and like those of one wrapped in placid slumber. The long fair hair hung over the side of the board. It was a sad and touching sight.

" Why, as I am a living man, it is the grocer's daughter, Amabel,—somewhile Countess of Rochester ! " exclaimed Chowles.

" It is, it is ! " cried the earl, suddenly rushing from behind a building where he had hitherto remained concealed. " Whither are you about to take her ? Set her down—set her down."

" Hinder them not, my lord," vociferated another person, also appearing on the scene with equal suddenness. " Place her in the cart," cried Solomon Eagle—for he it was—to the bearers. " This is a just punishment upon you, my lord," he added to Rochester, as his injunctions were obeyed—" oppose them not in their duty."

It was not in the earl's power to do so. Like Leonard, he was transfixed with horror. The other bodies were soon placed in the cart, and it was put in motion.

At this juncture, the apprentice's suspended faculties were for an instant—and an instant only—restored to him. He uttered a piercing cry, and staggering forward, fell senseless on the ground.

End of the Fourth Book

Book the Fifth

CHAPTER I

The Decline of the Plague

MORE than two months must be passed over in silence. During that time, the pestilence had so greatly abated as no longer to occasion alarm to those who had escaped its ravages. It has been mentioned that the distemper arrived at its height about the 10th of September, and though for the two following weeks the decline was scarcely perceptible, yet it had already commenced. On the last week in that fatal month, when all hope had been abandoned, the Bills of Mortality suddenly decreased in number to one thousand eight hundred and thirty-four. And this fortunate change could not be attributed to the want of materials to act upon, for the sick continued as numerous as before, while the deaths were less frequent. In the next week there was a further decrease of six hundred; in the next after that of six hundred; and so on till the end of October, when the cold weather setting in, the amount was reduced to nearly one thousand.

At first, when the distemper began to lose somewhat of its malignancy, a few scared individuals appeared in the streets, but carefully shunned each other. In a few days, however, considerable numbers joined them, and for the first time for nearly three months, there was something like life abroad. It is astonishing how soon hope and confidence are revived. Now that it could no longer be doubted that the plague was on the decline, it seemed as if a miracle had been performed in favour of the city. Houses were opened—shopkeepers resumed their business —and it was a marvel to every one that so many persons were left alive. Dejection and despair of the darkest kind were succeeded by frenzied delight, and no bound was put to the public satisfaction. Strangers stopped each other in the streets, and conversed together like old friends. The bells that had grown hoarse with tolling funerals, were now cracked with joyous peals. The general joy extended even to the sick, and many, buoyed up by hope, recovered, when in the former season of despondency, they would inevitably have perished. All fear of the plague seemed to vanish with the flying disorder. Those who were scarcely out of danger joined in the throng, and it was no uncommon sight to see men with bandages round their necks, or supported by staves and crutches, shaking hands with their friends, and even embracing them.

The consequence of this incautious conduct may be easily foreseen. The plague had received too severe a check to burst forth anew, but it spread further than it otherwise would have done, and attacked many persons, who, but for their own imprudence, would have escaped. Amongst others, a barber in Saint Martin's-le-Grand, who had fled into the country in August, returned to his shop in the middle of October, and catching the disorder from one of his customers, perished with the whole of his family.

But these, and several other equally fatal instances, produced no effect on the multitude. Fully persuaded that the virulence of the disorder was exhausted, as, indeed, appeared to be the case, they gave free scope to their satisfaction, which was greater than was ever experienced by the inhabitants of a besieged city reduced by famine to the last strait of despair, and suddenly restored to freedom and plenty. The more pious part of the community thronged to the churches, from which they had been so long absent, and returned thanks for their unexpected deliverance. Others, who had been terrified into seriousness and devotion, speedily forgot their former terrors, and resumed their old habits. Profaneness and debauchery again prevailed, and the taverns were as well filled as the churches. Solomon Eagle continued his midnight courses through the streets, but he could no longer find an audience as before. Those who listened to him only laughed at his denunciations of a new judgment, and told him his preachings and prophesyings were now completely out of date.

By this time, numbers of those who had quitted London

having returned to it, the streets began to resume their wonted appearance. The utmost care was taken by the authorities to cleanse and purify the houses, in order to remove all chance of keeping alive the infection. Every room in every habitation where a person had died of the plague—and there were few that had escaped the visitation —was ordered to be whitewashed, and the strongest fumigations were employed to remove the pestilential effluvia. Brimstone, resin, and pitch were burnt in the houses of the poor; benjamin, myrrh, and other more expensive perfumes in those of the rich; while vast quantities of powder were consumed in creating blasts to carry off the foul air. Large and constant fires were kept in all the houses, and several were burnt down in consequence of the negligence of their owners.

All goods, clothes, and bedding capable of harbouring infection, were condemned to be publicly burned, and vast bonfires were lighted in Finsbury-fields and elsewhere, into which many hundred cartloads of such articles were thrown. The whole of Chowles' hoard, except the plate, which he managed, with Judith's aid, to carry off and conceal in certain hiding-places in the vaults of Saint Faith's, was taken from the house in Nicholas-lane and cast into the fire.

The cathedral was one of the first places ordered to be purified. The pallets of the sick were removed and burned, and all the stains and impurities with which its floor and columns were polluted were cleansed. Nothing was left untried to free it from infection. It was washed throughout with vinegar, fumigated with the strongest scents, and several large barrels of pitch were set fire to in the aisles.

" It shall undergo another species of purification," said Solomon Eagle, who was present during these proceedings; " one that shall search every nook within it—shall embrace all those columns, and pierce every crack and crevice in those sculptured ornaments,—and then, and not till then, will it be thoroughly cleansed."

During all this time the grocer had not opened his dwelling. The wisdom of his plan was now made fully apparent.

The plague was declining fast, and not an inmate of his house had been attacked by it. Soon after the melancholy occurrence, he had been informed by Doctor Hodges of Amabel's death, but the humane physician concealed from him the painful circumstances under which it occurred. It required all Mr. Bloundel's fortitude to support him under the shock of this intelligence, and he did not communicate the afflicting tidings to his wife until he had prepared her for their reception. But she bore them better than he had anticipated, and though she mourned her daughter deeply and truly, she appeared completely resigned to the loss. Sorrow pervaded the whole household for some weeks, and the grocer, who never relaxed his system, shrouded his sufferings under the appearance of additional austerity of manner. It would have been a great consolation to him to see Leonard Holt, but the apprentice had disappeared, and even Doctor Hodges could give no account of him.

One night, in the middle of November, Mr. Bloundel signified to his wife his intention of going forth early on the following morning to satisfy himself that the plague was really abating. Accordingly, after he had finished his devotions, and broken his fast, he put his design into execution. His first act, after locking the door behind him, which he did as a measure of precaution, was to fall on his knees and offer up prayers to Heaven for his signal preservation. He then arose, and stepping into the middle of the street, gazed at the habitation which had formed his prison and refuge for nearly six months. There it was, with its shutters closed and barred—a secure asylum, with all alive within it, while every other dwelling in the street was desolate.

The grocer's sensations were novel and extraordinary. His first impulse was to enjoy his newly-recovered freedom, and to put himself into active motion. But he checked the feeling as sinful, and proceeded along the street at a slow pace. He did not meet a single person until he reached Cheapside, where he found matters completely changed. Several shops were already opened, and there were a few carts and other vehicles tracking the way through the broad and yet grass-grown street. It was a clear, frosty morning, and there was a healthful feeling in the bracing atmosphere that produced an exhilarating effect on the spirits. The grocer pursued his course through the middle of the street, carefully avoiding all contact with such persons as he encountered, though he cordially returned their greetings, and wandered on, scarcely knowing whither he was going, but deeply interested in all he beheld.

The aspect of the city was indeed most curious. The houses were for the most part unoccupied—the streets overgrown with grass—while every object, animate and inanimate, bore some marks of the recent visitation. Still, all looked hopeful, and the grocer could not doubt that the worst was past. The different demeanour of the various individuals he met struck him. Now he passed a young man whistling cheerily, who saluted him, and said—" I have lost my sweetheart by the plague, but I shall soon get another." The next was a grave man, who muttered, " I have lost all," and walked pensively on. Then came others in different moods, but all concurred in thinking that the plague was at an end; and the grocer derived additional confirmation of the fact from meeting numerous carts and other vehicles bringing families back to their houses from the country.

After roaming about for several hours, and pondering on all he saw, he found himself before the great western entrance of St. Paul's. It chanced to be the morning on which the pallets and bedding were brought forth, and he watched the proceeding at a distance. All had been removed, and he was about to depart, when he perceived a person seated on a block of stone, not far from him, whom he instantly recognised.

" Leonard," he cried, " Leonard Holt, is it you ? "

Thus addressed, and in these familiar tones, the apprentice looked up, and Mr. Bloundel started at the change that had taken place in him. Profound grief was written in every line of his thin and haggard countenance; his eyes were hollow, and had the most melancholy expression imaginable; and his flesh was wasted away to the bone. He looked the very image of hopeless affliction.

" I am sorry to find you in this state, Leonard," said the

grocer, in a tone of deep commiseration; "but I am well aware of the cause. I myself have suffered severely, but I deem it my duty to control my affliction."

"I *would* control it if it were possible, Mr. Bloundel," replied Leonard. "But hope is dead in my breast. I shall never be happy again."

"I trust otherwise," replied the grocer, kindly. "Your trials have been very great, and so were those of the poor creature we both of us deplore. But she is at peace, and therefore we need not lament her."

"Alas!" exclaimed Leonard, mournfully, "I am now only anxious to rejoin her."

"It is selfish, if not sinful, to grieve in this way," rejoined Mr. Bloundel, somewhat sternly. "You must bear your sorrows like a man. Come home with me. I will be a father to you. Nay, do not hesitate. I will have no refusal."

So saying, he took Leonard's arm, and led him in the direction of Wood-street. Nothing passed between them on the way, nor did Leonard evince any further emotion until he entered the door of the grocer's dwelling, when he uttered a deep groan. Mrs. Bloundel was greatly affected at seeing him, as were the rest of the family, and abundance of tears were shed by all, except Mr. Bloundel, who maintained his customary stoical demeanour throughout the meeting.

Satisfied that the pestilence had not declined sufficiently to warrant him in opening his house, the grocer determined to await the result of a few weeks. Indeed, that very night, he had reason to think he had defeated his plans by precipitancy. While sitting after prayers with his family, he was seized with a sudden shivering and sickness, which he could not doubt were the precursors of the plague. He was greatly alarmed, but did not lose his command over himself.

"I have been most imprudent," he said, "in thus exposing myself to infection. I have symptoms of the plague about me, and will instantly repair to one of the upper rooms which I have laid aside as a hospital, in case of any emergency like the present. None of you must attend me. Leonard will fetch Doctor Hodges and a nurse. I shall then do very well. Farewell, dear wife and children ! God bless you all, and watch over you. Remember me in your prayers."

So saying, he arose and walked towards the door. His wife and eldest son would have assisted him, but he motioned them away.

" Let me go with you, sir," cried Leonard, who had arisen with the others. " I will nurse you; my life is of little consequence; and I cannot be more satisfactorily employed."

The grocer reluctantly assented, and the apprentice assisted him upstairs, and helped to place him in bed. No plague-token could be found about his person, but as the same alarming symptoms still continued, Leonard administered such remedies as he thought needful, and then went in search of Doctor Hodges.

On reaching Watling-street, he found Doctor Hodges about to retire to rest. The worthy physician was greatly distressed by the apprentice's account of his master's illness; but was somewhat reassured when the symptoms were more minutely described to him.

While preparing certain medicines, and arming himself with his surgical implements, he questioned Leonard as to the cause of his long disappearance.

" Having seen nothing of you," he said, " since the fatal night when our poor Amabel's sorrows were ended, I began to feel very apprehensive on your account. Where have you been ? "

" You shall hear," replied Leonard, " though the relation will be like opening my wounds afresh. On recovering from the terrible shock I had received, I found myself stretched upon a bed in a house whither I had been conveyed by Rainbird the watchman, who had discovered me lying in a state of insensibility in the street. For nearly a week I continued delirious, and should probably have lost my senses altogether but for the attentions of the watchman. As soon as I was able to move, I wandered to the lesser plague-pit, in Finsbury-fields; you will guess with what intent. My heart seemed breaking, and I thought I should pour forth my very soul in grief, as I gazed into that dreadful gulf, and thought she was there interred. Still my tears were a relief. Every evening for a month I went to that sad spot, and remained there till daybreak admonished me to return to Rainbird's dwelling. At last, he was seized by the distemper; but though I nursed him, voluntarily exposing myself to infection, and praying to be carried off, I remained untouched. Poor Rainbird died; and having seen his body thrown into the pit, I set off into Berkshire, and after three days' toilsome travel on foot, reached Ashdown-park. It was a melancholy pleasure to behold the abode where she I had loved passed her last few days of happiness, and where I had been near her. Her aunt, good Mrs. Buscot, though overwhelmed by affliction at the sad tidings I brought her, received me with the utmost kindness, and tried to console me. My sorrow, however, was too deeply seated to be removed. Wandering over the downs, I visited Mrs. Compton at Kingston Lisle, from whose house Amabel was carried off by the perfidious earl. She, also, received me with kindness, and strove, like Mrs. Buscot, to comfort me, and, like her, ineffectually. Finding my strength declining, and persuaded that my days were drawing to a close, I retraced my steps to London, hoping to find a final resting-place near her I had loved."

"You are, indeed, faithful to the grave, Leonard," said the physician, brushing away a tear; "and I never heard or read of affection stronger than yours. Sorrow is a great purifier, and you will come out all the better for your trial. You are yet young, and though you never can love as you *have* loved a second time, your heart is not utterly seared."

"Utterly, sir," echoed Leonard, "utterly."

"You think so now," rejoined the physician, "but you will find it otherwise hereafter. I can tell you of one person who has suffered almost as much from your absence as you have done for the loss of Amabel. The Lady Isabella Argentine has made constant inquiries after you; and though I should be the last person to try to rouse you from your present state of despondency, by awakening hopes of alliance with the sister of a proud noble, yet it may afford you consolation to know that she still cherishes the warmest regard for you."

" I am grateful to her," replied Leonard, sadly, but without exhibiting any other emotion. " She was dear to Amabel, and therefore will be ever dear to me. I would fain know," he added, his brow suddenly contracting, and his lip quivering, " what has become of the Earl of Rochester ? "

" He has married a wealthy heiress, the fair Mistress Mallett," replied Hodges.

" Married, and so soon ! " cried Leonard. " And he has quite forgotten his victim ? "

" Apparently so," replied the doctor, with an expression of disgust.

" And it was for one who so lightly regarded her that she sacrified herself," groaned Leonard, his head dropping upon his breast.

" Come," cried Hodges, taking his arm, and leading him out of the room. " We must go and look after your master."

With this they made the best of their way to Wood-street. Arrived at the grocer's house, they went upstairs, and Hodges immediately pronounced Mr. Bloundel to be suffering from a slight feverish attack, which a sudorific powder would remove. Having administered the remedy, he descended to the lower room to allay the fears of the family.

Mrs. Bloundel received the happy tidings with tears of joy, and the doctor remained a short time to condole with her on the loss she had sustained. The good dame wept bitterly on hearing the whole particulars, with which she had been hitherto unacquainted, attending her daughter's untimely death, but she soon regained her composure. They then spoke of Leonard, who had remained above with his master,—of his blighted hopes, and seemingly incurable affliction.

" His is true love, indeed, doctor," sighed Mrs. Bloundel. " Pity it is that it could not be requited."

" I know not how it is," rejoined Hodges, " and will not question the decrees of our All-Wise Ruler, but the strongest affection seldom, if ever, meets a return. Leonard himself was insensible to the devotion of one, of whom I may say, without disparagement to our poor Amabel, that she was in my opinion her superior in beauty."

" And does this person love him still ? " inquired Mrs. Bloundel, eagerly. " I ask, because I regard him as a son, and earnestly desire to restore him to happiness."

" Alas ! " exclaimed Hodges, " there are obstacles in the way that cannot be removed. We must endeavour to cure him of his grief in some other way."

The conversation then dropped, and Hodges took his leave, promising to return on the morrow, and assuring Mrs. Bloundel that she need be under no further apprehension about her husband.

And so it proved. The powders removed all the grocer's feverish symptoms, and when Doctor Hodges made his appearance the next day, he found him dressed, and ready to go downstairs. Having received the physician's congratulations on his entire recovery, Mr. Bloundel inquired from him when he thought he might with entire safety open his shop. Hodges considered for a moment, and then replied, " I do not see any great risk in doing so now, but I would advise you to defer the step for a fortnight. I would, also, recommend you to take the whole of your family for a short time into the country. Pure air and change of scene are absolutely necessary after their long confinement."

" Farmer Wingfield, of Kensal-green, who sheltered us on our way to Ashdown-park, will, I am sure, receive you," observed Leonard.

" If so, you cannot go to a better place," rejoined the physician.

" I will think of it," returned Mr. Bloundel. And leading the way downstairs, he was welcomed by his wife and children with the warmest demonstrations of delight.

" My fears, you perceive, were groundless," he remarked to Mrs. Bloundel.

" Heaven be praised they were so ! " she rejoined. " But I entreat you not to go forth again till all danger is at an end."

" Rest assured I will not," he answered.

Soon after this, Doctor Hodges took his leave, and had

already reached the street door, when he was arrested by Patience, who inquired with much anxiety whether he knew anything of Blaize.

" Make yourself easy about him, child," replied the doctor, " I am pretty sure he is safe and sound. He has had the plague, certainly; but he left the hospital at Saint Paul's cured."

" Oh, then, I *shall* see him again," cried Patience, joyfully. " Poor dear little fellow, it would break my heart to lose him."

" I will make inquiries about him," rejoined Hodges, " and if I can find him, will send him home."

And without waiting to receive the kitchen-maid's thanks, he departed.

For some days the grocer continued to pursue pretty nearly the same line of conduct that he had adopted during the height of the pestilence. But he did not neglect to make preparations for resuming his business; and here Leonard was of material assistance to him. They often spoke of Amabel, and Mr. Bloundel strove, by every argument he was master of, to remove the weight of affliction under which his apprentice laboured. He so far succeeded that Leonard's health improved, though he still seemed a prey to secret sorrow. Things were in this state, when one day a knock was heard at the street door, and the summons being answered by the grocer's eldest son, Stephen, he returned with the intelligence that a person was without who desired to see Patience. After some consideration, Mr. Bloundel summoned the kitchen-maid, and told her she might admit the stranger into the passage, and hear what he had to say. Patience hastened with a beating heart to the door, expecting to learn some tidings of Blaize, and opening it, admitted a man wrapped in a large cloak, and having a broad-leaved hat pulled over his brows. Stepping into the passage, he threw aside the cloak and raised his hat, discovering the figure and features of Pillichody.

" What brings you here, sir ? " demanded Patience, in alarm, and glancing over her shoulder to see whether any one observed them. " What do you want ? "

" I have brought you news of Blaize," returned the bully.
" But how charmingly you look. By the coral lips of
Venus ! your long confinement has added to your attrac-
tions."

" Never mind my attractions, sir," rejoined Patience,
impatiently. " Where is Blaize ? Why did he not come
with you ? "

" Alas ! " replied Pillichody, shaking his head in a
melancholy manner, " he could not."

" Could not ! " half screamed Patience. " Why not ? "

" Do not question me," replied Pillichody, feigning to
brush away a tear. " He was my friend, and I would rather
banish him from my memory. The sight of your beauty
transports me so, that, by the treasures of Croesus ! I
would rather have you without a crown than the wealthiest
widow in the country."

" Don't talk nonsense to me in this way," sobbed
Patience. " I'm not in the humour for it."

" Nonsense ! " echoed Pillichody. " I swear to you I
am in earnest. By Cupid ! I am ravished with your
charms." And he would have seized her hand, but
Patience hastily withdrew it ; and, provoked at his im-
pertinence, dealt him a sound box on the ear. As she did
this, she thought she heard a suppressed laugh near her,
and looked round, but could see no one. The sound
certainly did not proceed from Pillichody, for he looked
very red and very angry.

" Do not repeat this affront, mistress," he said to her.
" I can bear anything but a blow from your sex."

" Then tell me what has become of Blaize ? " she
cried.

" I will no longer spare your feelings," he rejoined.
" He is defunct."

" Defunct ! " echoed Patience, with a scream. " Oh,
dear me !—I shall never survive it,—I shall die."

" Not while I am left to supply his place," cried Pillichody, catching her in his arms.

" You ! " cried Patience, contemptuously ; " I would
not have you for the world. Where is he buried ? "

" In the plague-pit," replied Pillichody. " I attended

him during his illness. It was his second attack of the disorder. He spoke of you."

"Did he?—dear little fellow," she exclaimed. "Oh,
what did he say?"

"'Tell her,' he cried," rejoined Pillichody, "'that my
last thoughts were of her.'"

"Oh, dear! oh, dear!" cried Patience, hysterically.

"'Tell her also,' he added," pursued Pillichody, "'that
I trust she will fulfil my last injunction.'"

"That I will," replied Patience. "Name it."

"He conjured you to marry me," replied Pillichody.
"I am sure you will not hesitate to comply with the
request."

"I don't believe a word of this," cried Patience. "Blaize
was a great deal too jealous to bequeath me to another."

"Right, sweetheart, right," cried the individual in
question, pushing open the door. "This has all been done
to try your fidelity. I am now fully satisfied of your attachment; and am ready to marry you whenever you please."

"So this was all a trick," cried Patience, pettishly; "I
wish I had known it; I would have retaliated upon you
nicely. You ought to be ashamed of yourself, Major
Pillichody, to lend a helping hand in such a ridiculous
affair."

"I did it to oblige my friend Blaize," replied Pillichody.
"It was agreed between us that if you showed any inconstancy, you were to be mine."

"Indeed!" exclaimed Patience. "I would not advise
you to repeat the experiment, Mr. Blaize."

"I never intend to do so, my angel," replied the porter.
"I esteem myself the happiest and most fortunate of men."

"You have great reason to do so," observed Pillichody.
"I do not despair of supplanting him yet," he muttered to
himself. "And, now, farewell!" he added, aloud. "I am
only in the way, and, besides, I have no particular desire
to encounter Mr. Bloundel or his apprentice." And wink-
ing his solitary orb significantly at Patience, he strutted
away. It was well he took that opportunity of departing,
for the lovers' raptures were instantly afterwards interrupted by the appearance of Mr. Bloundel, who was

greatly delighted to see the porter, and gave him a hearty welcome.

"Ah, sir, I have had a narrow escape," cried Blaize, "and never more expected to see you, or my mother, or Patience. I *have* had the plague, sir, and a terrible disorder it is."

"I heard of your seizure from Leonard Holt," replied Mr. Bloundel. "But where have you been since you left the hospital at Saint Paul's?"

"In the country, sir," rejoined Blaize; "sometimes at one farm-house, and sometimes at another. I only returned to London yesterday, and met an old friend, whom I begged to go before me, and see that all was right before I ventured in."

"We all have been providentially spared," observed Mr. Bloundel, "and you will find your mother as well as when you last quitted her. You had better go to her."

Blaize obeyed, and was received by old Josyna with a scream of delight. Having embraced him, and sobbed over him, she ran for a bottle of sack, and poured its contents down his throat so hastily as nearly to choke him. She then spread abundance of eatables before him, and after he had eaten and drank his full, offered him as a treat a little of the plague-medicine, which she had in reserve.

"No, thank you, mother," replied Blaize. "I have had enough of *that*. But if there should be a box of rufuses amongst the store, you can bring it, as I think a couple might do me good."

Three days after this event, the apprentice was sent forth to ascertain the precise state of the city, as, if all proved favourable, the grocer proposed to open his house on the following day. Leonard set out betimes, and was speedily convinced that all danger was at an end. A severe frost set in, and had completely purified the air. For the last few days, there had been no deaths of the plague, and but little mortality of any kind. Leonard traversed several of the main streets, and some narrow thoroughfares, and found evidences of restored health and confidence everywhere. It is true there were many houses in which whole families had been swept off still left untenanted. But these

were only memorials of the past calamity, and could not
be referred to any existing danger. Before returning to
Wood-street, an irresistible impulse led him to Finsbury-
fields. He passed through the postern east of Cripplegate,
and shaped his way towards the lesser plague-pit. The sun,
which had been bright all the morning, was now partially
obscured; the air had grown thick, and a little snow fell.
The ground was blackened up and bound by the hard
frost, and the stiffened grass felt crisp beneath his feet.
Insensible to all external circumstances, he hurried forward,
taking the most direct course, and leaping every impediment in his path. Having crossed several fields, he at
length stood before a swollen heap of clay, round which a
wooden railing was placed. Springing over the enclosure,
and uttering a wild cry that evinced the uncontrollable
anguish of his breast, he flung himself upon the mound.
He remained for some time in the deepest affliction, and
was at last roused by a hand laid upon his shoulder, and
raising himself, beheld Thirlby.

"I thought it must be you," said the new-comer, in
accents of the deepest commiseration. "I have been visiting yonder plague-pit for the same melancholy purpose as
yourself,—to mourn over my lost child. I have been in
search of you, and have much to say to you. Will you
meet me in this place at midnight to-morrow?"

Leonard signified his assent.

"I am in danger," pursued Thirlby, "for, by some
means, the secret of my existence has been made known,
and the officers of justice are in pursuit of me. I suspect
that Judith Malmayns is my betrayer. You will not fail
me?"

"I will not," returned Leonard.

Upon this, Thirlby hurried away, and leaping a hedge,
disappeared from view.

Leonard slowly and sorrowfully returned to Wood-
street. On arriving there, he assured his master that he
might with entire safety open his house, as he proposed,
on the morrow; and Doctor Hodges, who visited the
grocer the same evening, confirmed the opinion. Early,
therefore, the next morning, Mr. Bloundel summoned his

family to prayers; and after pouring forth his supplications with peculiar fervour and solemnity, he went, accompanied by them all, and threw open the street door. Again kneeling down at the threshold, he prayed fervently, as before. He then proceeded to remove the bars and shutters from the windows. The transition from gloom and darkness to bright daylight was almost overpowering. For the first time for six months, the imprisoned family looked forth on the external world, and were dazzled and bewildered by the sight. The grocer himself, despite his sober judgment, could scarcely believe he had not been in a trance during the whole period. The shop was scarcely opened before it was filled with customers, and Leonard and Stephen were instantly employed. But the grocer would sell nothing. To those who asked for any article he possessed, he presented them with it, but would receive no payment.

He next despatched Blaize to bring together all the poor he could find; and distributed among them the remainder of his store,—his casks of flour, his salted meat, his cheeses, his biscuits, his wine,—in short, all that was left.

"This I give," he said, "as a thanksgiving to the Lord, and as a humble testimony of gratitude for my signal deliverance."

CHAPTER II

The Midnight Meeting

THE first day of his deliverance being spent by the grocer in the praiseworthy manner before related, he laid his head upon his pillow with a feeling of satisfaction such as he had not for months experienced. A very remarkable dream occurred to him that night, and its recollection afterwards afforded him the greatest consolation. While thinking of Amabel, and of the delight her presence would have afforded him, slumber stole upon him, and his dreams were naturally influenced by his previous meditations. It appeared to him that he was alone within his house, and while visiting one of the upper rooms, which had formerly been appropriated to his lost daughter, he noticed a small door in the wall that had never before attracted his attention. He immediately pushed against it, and, yielding to the touch, it admitted him to an apartment with which he seemed acquainted, though he could not recall the time when he had seen it. It was large and gloomy, panelled with dark and lustrous oak, and filled with rich but decayed furniture. At the further end stood a large antique bed, hung round with tarnished brocade curtains. The grocer shuddered at the sight, for he remembered to have heard Doctor Hodges assert, that in such a bed, and in such a room as this, his daughter had breathed her last. Some one appeared to be within the bed, and rushing forward with a throbbing heart, and a foreboding of what was to follow, he beheld the form of Amabel. Yes, there she was, with features like those she wore on earth, but clothed with such celestial beauty, and bearing the impress of such serene happiness, that the grocer felt awe-struck as he gazed at her !

" Approach, my father," said the visionary form, in a voice so musical that it thrilled through his frame— " approach, and let what you now hear be for ever graven upon your heart. Do not lament me more, but rather rejoice that I am removed from trouble, and in the enjoyment of supreme felicity. Such a state you will yourself attain. You have run the good race, and will assuredly reap your reward. Comfort my dear mother, my brothers, my little sister, with the assurance of what I tell you, and bid them dry their tears. I can now read the secrets of all hearts, and know how true was Leonard Holt's love for me, and how deep and sincere is his present sorrow. But I am not permitted to appear to him as I now appear to you. Often have I heard him invoke me in accents of the wildest despair, and have floated past him on the midnight breeze, but could neither impart consolation to him nor make him sensible of my presence, because his grief was sinful. Bid him be comforted. Bid him put a due control on his feelings. Bid him open his heart anew, and he shall yet be happy, yet love again, and have his love requited. Farewell, dear father ! "

And with these words, the curtains of the bed closed. The grocer stretched out his arm to draw them aside, and in the effort awoke. He slept no more that night, but dwelt with unutterable delight on the words he had heard. On rising, his first object was to seek out Leonard, and relate his vision to him. The apprentice listened in speechless wonder, and remained for some time lost in reflection.

" From any other person than yourself, sir," he said, at length, " I might have doubted this singular story, but coming from you, I attach implicit credence to it. I *will* obey your sainted daughter's injunctions. I *will* struggle against the grief that overwhelms me, and will try to hope that her words may be fulfilled."

" You will do wisely," rejoined Mr. Bloundel. " After breakfast, we will walk together to the farmhouse you spoke of at Kensal-green, and if its owner should prove willing to receive my family for a few weeks, I will remove them thither at once."

Leonard applauded his master's resolution, expressing his firm conviction that Farmer Wingfield would readily accede to the proposal, and the rest of the family having by this time assembled, they sat down to breakfast. As soon as the meal was over, Mr. Bloundel intrusted the care of the shop to Stephen and Blaize, and accompanied by Leonard, set forth. On the way to the west end of the town, the grocer met one or two of his old friends, and they welcomed each other like men risen from the grave. Their course took them through Saint Giles's, where the plague had raged with the greatest severity, and where many houses were still without tenants.

" If all had acted as I have done," sighed the grocer, as he gazed at these desolate habitations, " how many lives, under God's providence, would have been saved ! "

" In my opinion, sir," replied Leonard, " you owe your preservation as much to your piety as to your prudence."

" I have placed my trust on high," rejoined the grocer, " and have not been forsaken. And yet many evildoers have escaped. Amongst others——"

" I know whom you mean, sir," interrupted Leonard,

Q

with some fierceness, " but a day of retribution will arrive for him."

" No more of this." rejoined the grocer, severely. " Remember the solemn injunction you have received."

At this moment they observed a horseman, richly attired, and followed by a couple of attendants, riding rapidly towards them. Both instantly recognised him. The apprentice's cheek and brow flushed with anger, and Mr. Bloundel had much ado to control his emotion. It was the Earl of Rochester, and on seeing them he instantly dismounted, and flinging his bridle to one of the attendants, advanced towards them. Noticing the fury that gleamed in Leonard's eyes, and apprehending some violence on his part, the grocer laid his hand upon his arm, and sternly enjoined him to calm himself.

By this time, the Earl had reached them. " Mr. Bloundel," he said, in a tone of much emotion, and with a look that seemed to bespeak contrition, " I heard that you had opened your house yesterday, and was about to call upon you. I have a few words to say to you on a subject painful to both of us, but doubly painful to me— your daughter."

" I must decline to hear them, my lord," replied the grocer, coldly; " nor shall you ever cross my threshold again with my consent. My poor child is now at peace. You can do no further injury, and must settle your own account with your Maker."

" Do not refuse me your forgiveness," implored the earl. " I will make every reparation in my power."

" You *can* make none," replied the grocer, repelling him : " and as to my forgiveness, I neither refuse it nor accord it. I pray your lordship to let me pass. The sole favour I ask of you is to come near me no more."

" I obey you," replied the earl. " Stay," he added to Leonard, who stood by, regarding him with a look of deadly animosity. " I would give you a piece of caution Your life is in danger."

" I can easily guess from whom," replied the apprentice, scornfully.

" You mistake," rejoined Rochester; " you have

nothing to apprehend from me. You have promised to meet some one to-night," he added, in so low a tone as to be inaudible to the grocer. " Do not go."

" Your lordship's warning will not deter me," rejoined the apprentice.

" As you will," rejoined Rochester, turning away.

And springing upon his horse, and striking his spurs into his side, he, dashed off, while Leonard and the grocer took the opposite direction. In less than half an hour they reached the little village of Paddington, then consisting of a few houses, but now one of the most populous and important parishes of the metropolis, and speedily gained the open country. Even at this dreary season, the country had charms, which Mr. Bloundel, after his long confinement, could fully appreciate. His eye roamed over the wide prospect; and the leafless trees, the bare hedges, and the frost-bound fields seemed pleasant in his sight.

He quickened his pace, and being wholly indifferent to the cold, greatly enjoyed the exercise. Leonard pointed out to him the spots where the fugitives from the plague had pitched their tents, and also the pest-house near Westbourne-green, where he himself had been received during his second attack of the distemper, and which was now altogether abandoned.

Soon after this, they mounted the hill beyond Kensalgreen, and approached the farm-house. Leonard descried Wingfield near one of the barns, and hailing him, he immediately came forward. On being informed of Mr. Bloundel's desire, he at once assented, and taking them into the house, mentioned the matter to his dame, who was quite of the same opinion as himself.

" The only difference between us," he said to Mr. Bloundel, " is as to the payment you propose. Now I will take none—not a farthing. Come when you please, bring whom you please, and stay as long as you please. But don't offer me anything if you would not offend me. Recollect," he added, the moisture forcing itself into his eyes, and his strong clear voice becoming husky with emotion, " that I loved your daughter for her resemblance to my poor child. She, too, is gone. I do this for her sake."

Mr. Bloundel shook the worthy man warmly by the hand, but he made no further objection, resolved in his own mind to find some other means of requiting his hospitality. It was then agreed that the grocer should bring his family on the following day, and remain there for a month, and every other arrangement being made, and a hearty meal partaken of, he cordially thanked his host, and returned with Leonard to Wood-street.

In spite of his efforts to resist the impression produced by the earl's warning, Leonard could not banish it from his mind; and though he did not for a moment think of abandoning his purpose, he resolved to attend the meeting armed. He told Mr. Bloundel he should go out that night, but did not state his object, and the grocer did not inquire it. Blaize sat up with him, and displayed much anxiety to know whither he was going, but, as may be supposed, his curiosity was not gratified. As the clock struck eleven, Leonard thrust a sword into his girdle, and arming himself furthermore with his staff, proceeded towards the door, and bade Blaize lock it after him.

" I shall probably be back in a couple of hours," he said, as he went forth. " You must sit up for me."

" I wonder where he is going ! " thought Blaize. " From his gloomy looks, and the weapon he has taken with him, I should judge he is about to murder someone—perhaps the Earl of Rochester. It must be prevented."

With this view, though perhaps rather more influenced by curiosity than any better feeling, the porter waited a few seconds to allow the apprentice to get out of sight, and then locking the door outside, put the key in his pocket, and followed him. The night was profoundly dark, but he had noticed the direction taken by Leonard, and running noiselessly along the street, soon perceived him a little in advance. Regulating his pace by that of the apprentice, and keeping about fifty yards behind him, he tracked his course along several streets, until he saw him pass through the second postern in the city wall, near Moorgate. Here he debated with himself whether to proceed further or turn back; but at length curiosity got the better of his fears, and he went on. A few steps brought him into the open fields, and fancying he saw Leonard at a little distance before him, he hurried on in that direction. But he soon found he had been deceived by the stump of a tree, and began to fear he must have taken the wrong course. He looked around in vain for some object to guide him. The darkness was so profound that he could see nothing, and he set off again at random, and not without much self-reproach and misgiving. At last, he reached a hedge, and continued to skirt it, until he perceived through the bushes the light of a lantern in the adjoining field. He immediately called out, but at a cry the light disappeared. This did not prevent him from making towards the spot where he had seen it; but he had not proceeded far when he was forcibly seized by some unseen person, thrown on the ground, and a drawn sword—for he felt the point—placed at his throat.

" Utter a cry, and it is your last," cried a stern voice. " Where is he ? "

" Who—who ? " demanded Blaize, half dead with terror.

" He whom you appointed to meet," replied the unknown.

" I appointed to meet no one," rejoined Blaize.

" Liar ! " exclaimed the other; " if you do not instantly lead me to him, I will cut your throat."

" I will lead you wherever you please, if you will only let me get up," rejoined Blaize, with difficulty repressing a cry.

" By the daughters of Nox and Acheron ! " exclaimed a voice which sounded like music in the porter's ears, " I think you are mistaken in your man, my lord. It does not sound like the apprentice's voice."

" It is *not* the apprentice's voice, good Major Pilli-chody," rejoined the porter. " It is mine, your friend—Blaize's."

" Blaize ! " exclaimed Pillichody, unmasking a dark lantern, and revealing the terror-stricken countenance of the porter; " so it is. In the devil's name, what are you doing here ? "

" The devil himself, who put it into my head to come,

only knows," replied Blaize; " but I followed Leonard
Holt."

" Which way did he take ? " asked the person who had
assailed him.

" I cannot exactly say," replied Blaize, " but he seemed
to go straight into the fields."

" He is no doubt gone to the plague-pit," replied the
other. " You are now at liberty," he added to Blaize,
" and I counsel you to make the best of your way home.
Say nothing to your master of what has occurred. The
city walls lie in that direction."

Overjoyed to be released, Blaize ran off as fast as his
legs could carry him, and never stopped till he reached
Moorgate.

Meanwhile Leonard had reached the place of meeting.
As he stood by the rail surrounding the plague-pit, he
thought of Mr. Bloundel's singular dream, and almost hoping to be similarly favoured, flung himself on his knees,
and besought Amabel, if it were possible, to appear to him.
But his entreaties produced no result. The chill blast
whistled past him, and mindful of what had been told him,
he was fain to interpret this into an answer to his request.
The night was bitterly cold, and Leonard, whose limbs
were almost stiffened by long kneeling, walked round and
round the enclosure at a quick pace to put his blood into
circulation. As the hour of midnight was tolled forth by
the neighbouring churches, he heard footsteps, and could
just detect a figure advancing towards him.

" Are you there ? " was asked in the voice of Thirlby.

Leonard replied in the affirmative, and the other instantly
joined him.

" Have you mentioned our meeting to any one ? " inquired Leonard. " I ask because I was warned by the
Earl of Rochester not to attend it."

" Strange ! " exclaimed Thirlby, musingly. " However,
do not let us waste time. I am about to leave London,
perhaps the country,—for ever. But I could not depart
without an interview with you. You are aware of my
strong attachment to my poor lost child. My daughter
Isabella now supplies her place in my heart. She is the

only being I love on earth, for my son has alienated himself from my affections. All I desire is to see her happy. This I find can only be accomplished in one way."

Here he paused for a moment, but as Leonard made no remark, he proceeded.

" Why should I hesitate to declare it ? " he said, " since it was for that object I brought you hither. She loves you —devotedly loves you, and if her wishes were opposed, I should tremble for the consequences. Now, listen to me. Situated as you are, you never can wed her. I will, however, point out a means by which you can raise yourself to distinction in a short time, and so entitle yourself to claim her hand. I will supply you with money—more than you can require—will place you at court—near the king's person—and if you act under my direction, your rise is certain. I have extorted a promise to this effect from my own son. I told him my object, and that if he did not make your fortune, I could ruin him by revealing myself. I may, perhaps, pay the penalty of my crime on the scaffold ; but I may also escape. In the latter case, my reappearance would be fatal to him. He has consented to co-operate with me—to watch over your fortunes—and as soon as you have attained sufficient eminence, to bestow his sister upon you. Now do you understand ? "

" I do," replied Leonard ; " and I understand also against whom the Earl of Rochester warned me."

" And you consent ? " demanded Thirlby.

Leonard was about to answer, when he felt a light and trembling hand placed upon his own.

" Do not answer inconsiderately, Leonard," said a low, sweet voice, which he recognised as that of the Lady Isabella ; " I am here to receive your determination."

" I am glad of it," replied the apprentice. " The deep devotion you have displayed towards me deserves to be requited. I will strive to render myself worthy of you, and I feel that by doing so I shall best fulfil the injunctions of her who lies beside us. Henceforth, Lady Isabella, I wholly devote myself to you."

A murmur of delight escaped her.

" My blessings on you both ! " exclaimed her father. " Give me your hand, Isabella," he added, taking it and placing it in that of the apprentice. " Here, beside the grave of her whom you both loved, I affiance you. Pursue the course I point out to you, Leonard, and she will soon be yours."

As he spoke, the light of a lantern was suddenly thrown upon them, disclosing two persons who had noiselessly approached. They were Lord Argentine and Pillichody.

" You affirm more than you have warrant for, my lord," said the former. " I will never consent to this ill-assorted and dishonourable union; and so far from permitting it, will oppose it to the utmost of my power. If this presumptuous apprentice dares to raise his views towards my sister, let him look to himself. Your safety lies in instant flight. The officers are in search of you."

" They shall find me," replied Thirlby, sternly.

" As you please," rejoined Argentine. " Come with me, Isabella," he added to his sister.

But she flew with a cry towards Leonard.

" Ah ! " exclaimed her brother, drawing his sword. " Do you dare to detain her ? Deliver her to me, villain, instantly ! "

" Not when thus menaced, my lord," rejoined Leonard, likewise drawing his sword, and standing upon the defensive.

" Then look to yourself," replied Argentine, assaulting him.

Isabella uttered a wild shriek, and Thirlby tried to rush between them. But before they could be separated, Lord Argentine's fury had exposed him to his adversary, whose sword passed through his body. He fell to the ground, weltering in his blood.

While Leonard stood stupefied and confounded at what had occurred, and Isabella, uttering a loud cry, threw herself upon the body and tried to stanch the wound, two men, with halberts in their hands, rushed forward, and seizing Thirlby, cried, " We arrest you as a murderer ! "

Thirlby, who seemed utterly overcome by surprise and horror, offered no resistance.

At this juncture Leonard felt his arm seized by a bystander—he did not know whom—and scarcely conscious of what was taking place, suffered himself to be dragged from the scene.

End of the Fifth Book

Book the Sixth

SEPTEMBER, 1666

CHAPTER I

The Fire-Ball

About nine o'clock on the night of Saturday, the second of September, 1666—and rather more than nine months after the incidents last related,—three men took their way from Smithfield to Islington. They proceeded at a swift pace and in silence, until, having mounted the steep hill on which the suburb in question is situated, they halted at a short distance from the high walls surrounding the great water-works, formed by the New River-head. The night was dark, but free from cloud, in consequence of a strong easterly wind which prevailed at the time.

" It is dark in London now," observed one of the three persons to his companions as he cast his eye in the direction of the great city, that lay buried in gloom beneath them; " but there will be light enough soon."

" A second dawn, and brighter than the first, shall arise upon it," replied one of his companions, a tall, gaunt man, whose sole covering was a sheepskin, girded round his loins. " Such a flame shall be kindled within it, as hath not been seen since showers of brimstone and fire descended upon the sinful cities of the plain. ' The Lord shall come with flames of fire,' " he added, pointing his long staff towards the city. " ' He shall make them like a fiery oven, in the time of his wrath. They shall be utterly consumed.' "

" Amen ! " exclaimed the third person, who stood near him, in a deep voice, and with something of a foreign accent.

" Not so loud, friends," rejoined the first speaker. " Let us set about the task. I will ascertain that no one is on the watch."

With this he moved towards the water-works, and skirting the circular walls, to satisfy himself that all was secure, he returned to his companions, and they proceeded to the principal entrance to the place. Noiselessly unlocking the gates, the leader of the party admitted the others into an open space of some extent, in the midst of which was a large reservoir of water. He then gave each of them a small key, and bidding them use despatch, they began to turn the cocks of the leaden pipes connected with the reservoir, while he hastened to the further end of the enclosure, and employed himself in a similar manner. In this way, and in less than a quarter of an hour, the whole of the cocks were stopped.

" And now give me the keys," said the leader.

Taking them as they were offered, he added his own to the number, and flung them as far as he could into the reservoir, laughing slightly as the noise of the splash occasioned by their fall into the water reached his ears.

" They will not be found till this pool is drained," he observed to his companions. " And now let us go. Our business here is done."

" Stay yet a moment," cried Solomon Eagle, who was standing at the brink of the reservoir, with his eyes fixed upon it. " Stay ! " he cried, arresting him. " A vision rises before me. I see in this watery mirror a representation of the burning city. And what are those fearful forms that feed the flames ? Fiends, in our likeness—fiends ! And see how wide and far the conflagration spreads. The whole city is swallowed up by an earthquake. It sinks to the bottomless pit—down—down ! "

" No more of this," cried the leader, impatiently. " Come along."

And followed by the others, he rushed to the gates, and locking them after him, flung the key away.

" A hundred pounds were paid to the servant of the chief officer of the works to bring those keys to me," he said, " and he executed his commission faithfully and well. Water will be vainly sought for to quench the conflagration."

" I like not the vision I have just beheld," said Solomon

Eagle, in a troubled tone. "It seems to portend mischief."

" Think of it no more," rejoined the leader, " or regard it as it was,—a phantom created by your overheated imagination. Yon city has sinned so deeply that it is the will of Heaven it should be destroyed; and it has been put into our hearts by the Supreme Power to undertake the terrible task. We are the chosen instruments of the divine displeasure. Everything favours the design,—the long-continued dry weather,—the strong easterly wind, which will bear the flames into the heart of the city,—the want of water, occasioned by the stopping of these pipes, the emptying of the various aqueducts, and the destruction of the Thames water-tower, which we have accomplished. Everything favours it, I say, and proves that the hand of Heaven directs us. Yes, London shall fall. We have received our commission from on high, and must execute it, regardless of the consequences. For my own part, I feel as little compunction to the task, as the thunder-bolt launched from on high does for the tree it shivers."

" Philip Grant has uttered my sentiments exactly," said the man who it has been mentioned spoke with a slight foreign accent. " I have neither misgiving nor compunction. You appear to have forgotten your own denunciations, brother."

" Not so, Brother Hubert," rejoined the enthusiast, " and now I recognise in the vision a delusion of the Evil One to turn me from my holy purpose. But it has failed. The impious and impenitent city is doomed, and nothing can save it. And yet I would fain see it once more as I beheld it this morn when day arose upon it for the last time, from the summit of Saint Paul's. It looked so beautiful that my heart smote me, and tears started to my eyes, to think that those goodly habitations, those towers, temples, halls, and palaces, should so soon be levelled with the dust."

" Hear what the prophet saith," rejoined Hubert. " ' Thou hast defiled thy sanctuaries by the multitude of thine iniquities, by the iniquity of thy traffic. Therefore will I bring forth a fire from the midst of thee, and will

bring thee to ashes upon the earth, in the sight of all those
that behold thee.' "

Solomon Eagle flung himself upon his knees, and his
example was imitated by the others. Having recited a
prayer in a low deep tone, he arose, and stretching out his
arms, solemnly denounced the city. As he pronounced
the words, a red and fiery star shot from the dark vault of
the sky, and seemed to fall in the midst of the city.

"Did you not see that sign?" cried Grant, eagerly.
"It heralds us to our task."

So saying, he ran swiftly down the hill, and, followed
by the others, did not slacken his pace till they reached
the city. They then shaped their course more slowly towards Saint Paul's, and having gained the precincts of the
cathedral, Solomon Eagle, who now assumed the place of
leader, conducted them to a small door on the left of the
great northern entrance, and unlocking it, ushered them
into a narrow passage behind the rich carved work of the
choir. Traversing it, they crossed the mid aisle, and soon
reached the steps leading to Saint Faith's. It was profoundly dark, but they were all well acquainted with the
road, and did not miss their footing. It required, however,
some caution to thread the ranks of the mighty pillars
filling the subterranean church. But at last this was accomplished, and they entered the vault beyond the charnel,
where they found Chowles and Judith Malmayns. The
former was wrapped in a long black cloak, and was pacing
to and fro within the narrow chamber. When Solomon
Eagle appeared, he sprang towards him, and regarding
him inquiringly, cried, "Have you done it?—have you
done it?"

The enthusiast replied in the affirmative.

"Heaven be praised!" exclaimed Chowles. And he
skipped about with the wildest expressions of delight. A
gleam of satisfaction, too, darted from Judith's savage eyes.
She had neither risen nor altered her position on the arrival
of the party, but she now got up, and addressed the
enthusiast. A small iron lamp, suspended by a chain from
the vaulted roof, lighted the chamber. The most noticeable
figure amidst the group was that of Solomon Eagle, who,

with his blazing eyes, long jet-black locks, giant frame, and tawny skin, looked like a supernatural being. Near him stood the person designated as Robert Hubert. He was a young man, and appeared to have lived a life of great austerity. His features were thin; his large black eyes set in deep caverns; his limbs seemed almost destitute of flesh; and his looks wild and uncertain, like those of an insane person. His tattered and threadbare garb resembled that of a French ecclesiastic. The third person, who went by the name of Philip Grant, had a powerful frame, though somewhat bent, and a haughty deportment and look, greatly at variance with his miserable attire and haggard looks. His beard was long and grizzled, and his features, though sharpened by care, retained some traces of a noble expression.

A few minutes having passed in conversation, Grant observed to the enthusiast, " I must now leave you for a short time. Give me the key that I may let myself out."

" You are not going to betray us ? " cried Chowles, suspiciously.

" Why should I betray you ? " rejoined Grant, sternly. " I am too anxious for the event to disclose it."

" True, true," replied Chowles.

" *I* do not distrust you, brother," observed Solomon Eagle, giving him the key.

" I know whither you are going," observed Judith Malmayns. " You are about to warn Mr. Bloundel and his partner,—apprentice no longer,—Leonard Holt, of the approaching conflagration. But your care will be thrown away."

" Does she speak the truth, brother ? " demanded Hubert, raising his eyes from the Bible which he was reading in the corner of the vault.

" I will do nothing to endanger the design," rejoined Grant. " Of that rest assured."

With this, he strode forth, traversed Saint Faith's, and, notwithstanding the gloom, reached, without difficulty, the little door by which he had entered the cathedral. Issuing from it, he took the way, as Judith had surmised, to Wood-street, and pausing before the grocer's door, knocked against it.

The summons was presently answered by Blaize; and to Grant's inquiries whether his master was within, he replied, "Which of my masters do you mean? I have two."

"The younger," replied Grant,—"Leonard Holt."

"So far you are fortunate," rejoined Blaize. "Mr. Bloundel had retired to rest, but Mr. Holt is still downstairs. Pray what may be your business with him at this hour? It should be important."

"It *is* important," rejoined Grant, "and does not admit of a moment's delay. Tell him so."

Eyeing the stranger with a look of suspicion, the porter was about to enter into a parley with him, when Leonard himself cut it short, and learning the nature of the application, desired Grant to follow him into the adjoining room. The nine months which had passed over Leonard's head since he was last brought under notice, had wrought a material change in his appearance. He had a grave and thoughtful air, somewhat inclining to melancholy, but in other respects he was greatly improved. His health was completely restored, and the thoughtful expression added character to his handsome physiognomy, and harmonised well with his manly and determined bearing. He was habited plainly, but with some degree of taste. As Judith Malmayns had intimated, he was now Mr. Bloundel's partner, and his whole appearance denoted his improved circumstances. The alteration did not escape the notice of the stranger, who regarded him with much curiosity, and closed the door behind him as he entered the room.

"You are looking much better than when we last met, Leonard Holt," he said, in tones that made his hearer start, "and I am glad to perceive it. Prosperity seems to attend your path, and you deserve it; whereas misery and every other ill—and I deserve them—dog mine."

"I did not recognise you at first, Mr. Thirlby," replied Leonard; "for, in truth, you are much changed. But you desire to speak with me on a matter of importance. Can I aid you? You may need money. Here is my purse."

"I do not want it," replied the other, scornfully rejecting the offer. "I have a proposal to make to you."

"I shall be glad to hear it," replied Leonard. "But first tell me how you effected your escape after your arrest on that disastrous night when, in self-defence, and unintentionally, I wounded your son, Lord Argentine."

"Would you had killed him ! " cried the other, fiercely. "I have lost all feelings of a father for him. He it was who contrived my arrest, and he would have gladly seen me borne to the scaffold, certain it would have freed him from me for ever. I was hurried away by the officers from the scene of strife, and conveyed to the Tun at Cornhill, which you know has been converted into a round-house, and where I was locked up for the night. But while I was lying on the floor of my prison, driven well-nigh frantic by what had occurred, there were two persons without labouring to effect my deliverance,—nor did they labour in vain. These were Chowles and Judith, my foster-sister, and whom, you may remember, I suspected,—and most unfairly,—of intending my betrayal. By means of a heavy bribe, they prevailed on one of the officers to connive at my escape. An iron bar was removed from the window of my prison, and I got through the aperture. Judith concealed me for some days in the vaults of Saint Faith's, after which I fled into the country, where I wandered about for several months under the name of Philip Grant. Having learnt that my son, though severely hurt by you, had recovered from his wound, and that his sister, the Lady Isabella, had accompanied him to his seat in Staffordshire. I proceeded thither, and saw her, unknown to him. I found her heart still true to you. She told me you had disappeared immediately after the termination of the conflict, and had not been heard of till her brother was out of danger, when you returned to Woodstreet."

"The information was correct," replied Leonard. "I was dragged away by a person whom I did not recognise at the time, but who proved to be the Earl of Rochester. He conducted me to a place of safety, thrust a purse into my hand, and left me. As soon as I could do so with safety, I returned to my master's house. But how long have you been in London ? "

" Nearly a month," replied Grant. " And now, let me ask you one question. Do you ever think of Isabella ? "

" Often, very often." replied Leonard. " But as I dare not indulge the hope of a union with her, I have striven to banish her image from my mind."

" She cannot forget *you*, Leonard," rejoined Grant. " And now to my proposal. I have another plan for your aggrandisement that cannot fail. I am in possession of a monstrous design, the revelation of which will procure you whatever you desire. Ask a title from the king, and he will give it; and when in possession of that title, demand the hand of the Lady Isabella, and her proud brother will not refuse you. Call in your porter—seize me. I will offer a feigned resistance. Convey me before the king. Make your own terms with him. He will accede to them. Will you do it ? '

" No," replied Leonard, " I will not purchase the daughter at the price of the father's life."

" Heed me not," replied Grant, supplicatingly, " I am wholly indifferent to life. And what matters it whether I am dragged to the scaffold for one crime or another ? "

" You plead in vain," returned Leonard, firmly.

" Reflect," cried Grant, in an agonized tone. " A word from you will not only win you Isabella, but save the city from destruction."

" Save the city ! " exclaimed Leonard. " What mean you ? "

" Swear to comply with my request, and you shall know. But not otherwise," replied Grant.

" I cannot—I cannot," rejoined Leonard; " and unfortunately you have said too much for your own safety. I must, though most reluctantly, detain you."

" Hear me, Leonard, and consider well what you do," cried Grant, planting himself before the door. " I love you next to my daughter, and chiefly because she loves you. I have told you I have a design to discover, to which I am a party,—a hellish, horrible design,—which threatens this whole city with destruction. It is your duty, having told you thus much, to arrest me, and I will offer no resistance. Will you not turn this to your advantage? Will you not make a bargain with the king?"

"I have said I will not," rejoined Leonard.

"Then be warned by me," rejoined Grant. "Arouse your partner. Pack up all your goods and make preparations for instant flight, for the danger will invade you before you are aware of it."

"Is it fire?" demanded Leonard, upon whose mind the denunciations of Solomon Eagle now rushed.

"You will see," replied Grant, with a terrible laugh. "You will repent your determination when it is too late. Farewell."

"Hold!" cried Leonard, advancing towards him, and trying to lay hands upon him, "I arrest you in the king's name."

"Off!" exclaimed Grant, dashing him forcibly backwards.

And striking down Blaize, who tried to stop him in the passage, he threw open the street door, and disappeared.

Fearful of pursuit, Grant took a circuitous route to Saint Paul's, and it was full half an hour after the interview above related before he reached the cathedral. Just as he passed through the small door, the clock tolled forth the hour of midnight, and when he gained the mid aisle, he heard footsteps approaching, and encountered his friends.

"We have given you up," said Chowles, "and fearing you intended us some treachery, were about to do the job without you."

"I have been unavoidably detained," replied Grant. "Let us about it at once."

"I have got the fire-balls with me," observed Hubert.

"It is well," returned Grant.

Quitting the cathedral, they proceeded to Thames-street, and tracking it to Fish-street-hill, struck off on the right into an alley that brought them to Pudding-lane.

"This is the house," said Chowles, halting before a two-storied wooden habitation, over the door of which was

suspended the sign of the Wheat Sheaf, with the name
THOMAS FARRYNER, BAKER, inscribed beneath it.

" And here," said Hubert, " shall begin the Great Fire
of London."

As he said this, he gave a fire-ball to Solomon Eagle,
who lighted the fuze at Chowles' lantern. The enthusiast
then approached a window of the baker's shop, and breaking a small pane of glass within it, threw the fire-ball into
the room. It alighted upon a heap of chips and fagots
lying near a large stack of wood used for the oven, and in
a few minutes the whole pile had caught and burst into a
flame, which, quickly mounting to the ceiling, set fire to
the old, dry, half-decayed timber that composed it.

CHAPTER II

The First Night of the Fire

HAVING seen the stack of wood kindled, and the flames
attack the building in such a manner as to leave no doubt
they would destroy it, the incendiaries separated, previously
agreeing to meet together in half an hour at the foot of
London-bridge; and while the others started off in different
directions, Chowles and Judith retreated to a neighbouring
alley commanding a view of the burning habitation.

" At last the great design is executed," observed Chowles,
rubbing his hands gleefully. " The fire burns right merrily,
and will not soon be extinguished. Who would have
thought we should have found such famous assistants as
the two madmen, Solomon Eagle and Robert Hubert—
and your scarcely less mad foster-brother, Philip Grant?
I can understand the motives that influenced the two first
to the deed, but not those of the other."

" Nor I," replied Judith, " unless he wishes in some way
or other to benefit Leonard Holt by it. For my part, I
shall enjoy this fire quite as much on its own account as
for the plunder it will bring us. I should like to see every
house in this great city destroyed."

" You are in a fair way of obtaining your wish," replied

Chowles,—" but provided I have the sacking of them, I don't care how many are saved. Not but that such a fire will be a grand sight, which I should be sorry to miss. You forgot, too, that if Saint Paul's should be burnt down, we shall lose our hoards. However, there's no chance of that."

" Not much," replied Judith, interrupting him. " But see ! the baker has at last discovered that his dwelling is on fire. He bursts open the window, and, as I live, is about to throw himself out of it."

As she spoke, one of the upper windows in the burning habitation was burst open, and a poor terrified wretch appeared at it in his night-dress, vociferating in tones of the wildest alarm,·" Fire ! fire !—help, help ! "

" Shall we go forward ? " said Chowles.

Judith hesitated for a moment, and then assenting, they hurried towards the spot.

" Can we give you any help, friend ? " cried Chowles.

" Take care of this," rejoined the baker, flinging a bag of money to the ground, " and I will endeavour to let down my wife and children. The staircase is on fire, and we are almost stifled with smoke. God help us ! "

And the exclamation was followed by fearful shrieks from within, followed by the appearance of a woman, holding two little children in her arms, at the window.

" This must be money," said Judith, utterly heedless of the fearful scene occurring above, and taking up the bag and chinking it. " Silver, by the sound. Shall we make off with it ? "

" No, no," replied Chowles, " we must not run any risk for such a paltry booty. Let us bide our time."

At this juncture, the baker, who had disappeared for a few seconds from the window, again presented himself at it, and, with some difficulty, forced a feather bed through it, which was instantly placed by Chowles in such a position beneath as to break the fall of the descending parties. Tying a couple of sheets together, and fastening one end round his wife's waist, the baker lowered her and the children to the ground. They alighted in safety; but just as he was about to follow their example, the floor of the room gave way, and though he succeeded in springing through the window, he missed the feather bed, and broke his leg in the fall. He was picked up by Chowles and Judith, and placed upon the bed in a state of insensibility, and was soon afterwards conveyed with his family to the house of a neighbour.

Meanwhile, the fire had spread to the houses on either side of the unfortunate man's habitation, and both of them being built entirely of wood, they were almost instantly in flames. The alarm, too, had become general,—the inhabitants of the adjoining houses were filled with indescribable terror, and the narrow street was speedily crowded with persons of both sexes, who had rushed from their beds to ascertain the extent of the danger. All was terror and confusion. The fire-bells of Saint Margaret's, Saint George's, and Saint Andrew's, in Botolph-lane, began to toll, and shouts were heard on every side, proving that the whole neighbourhood was roused.

To add to the general distress, a report was raised that a house in Fish-street-hill was on fire, and it was soon found to be true, as an immense volume of flames burst forth in that quarter. While the rest of the spectators, distracted by this calamity, and hardly knowing what to do, hurried in the direction of the new fire, Chowles and Judith eyed each other askance, and the former whispered to his companion, " This is another piece of Hubert's handiwork."

The two wretches now thought it time to bestir themselves. So much confusion prevailed, that they were wholly unobserved, and under the plea of rendering assistance, they entered houses and carried off whatever excited their cupidity, or was sufficiently portable. No wealthy house had been attacked as yet, and therefore their spoil was but trifling. The poor baker seemed to be the bearer of ill-luck, for he had not been many minutes in his new asylum before it likewise caught fire. Another house, too, in Fish-street-hill, and lower down than the first, was observed to be burning, and as this was out of the current of the wind, and consequently could not have been occasioned by the showers of sparks that marked its course, a cry was instantly raised that incendiaries were abroad, and several suspicious looking persons were seized in consequence.

Meantime no efforts had been made to stop the progress of the original conflagration in Pudding-lane, which continued to rage with the greatest fury, spreading from house to house with astonishing rapidity. All the buildings in this neighbourhood being old, and of wood which was as dry as tinder, a spark alighting upon them would have sufficed to set them on fire. It may be conceived, therefore, what must have been the effect of a vast volume of flame, fanned by a powerful wind. House after house caught, as if constructed of touchwood, and the fire roared and raged to such a dregree, that those who stood by were too much terrified to render any effectual assistance. Indeed, the sole thought that now seemed to influence all was the preservation of a portion of their property. No one regarded his neighbour, or the safety of the city. The narrow street was instantly filled with goods and furniture of all kinds, thrown out of the windows or pushed out of the doors, but such was the fierceness of the fire, and the extraordinary rapidity with which it advanced, that the very articles attempted to be saved were seized by it, and thus formed a means of conveying it to the opposite houses.

In this way a number of persons were inclosed for a short time between two fires, and seemed in imminent danger of being burned to death. The perilous nature of their situation was, moreover, increased by a sudden and violent gust of wind, which, blowing the flames right across the street, seemed to envelop all within them. The shrieks that burst from the poor creatures thus involved were most appalling. Fortunately, they sustained no greater damage than was occasioned by the fright and a slight scorching, for the next moment the wind shifted, and, sweeping back the flames, they were enabled to effect their retreat. Chowles and Judith were among the sufferers, and in the alarm of the moment lost all the booty they had obtained.

Soon after this the whole street was on fire. All idea of preserving their property was therefore abandoned by the inhabitants, and they thought only of saving themselves.

Hundreds of half-naked persons of both sexes rushed towards Thames-street in search of a place of refuge. The scene was wholly without parallel for terror. Many fires had occurred in London, but none that raged with such fierceness as the present conflagration, or promised to be so generally destructive. It gathered strength and fury each moment, now rising high into the air in a towering sheet of flame, now shooting forward like an enormous dragon vomiting streams of fire upon its foes.

All at once the flames changed colour, and were partially obscured by a thick black smoke. A large warehouse filled with resin, tar, and other combustible matters, had caught fire, and the dense vapour proceeded from the burning pitch. But it cleared off in a few minutes, and the flames burnt more brightly and fiercely than ever.

Up to this time, none of the civic authorities having arrived, several persons set off to give information of the calamity to the Lord Mayor (Sir Thomas Bludworth), and the other magistrates. A small party of the watch were on the spot, but they were unable to render any effectual assistance. As the conflagration advanced, those occupying houses in its track quitted them, and left their goods a prey to the numerous plunderers, who were now gathered together pursuing their vocation like unhallowed beings amid the raging element. The whole presented a scene of the wildest alarm, confusion, and licence. Vociferations, oaths, shrieks, and outcries of every description stunned the ear. Night was turned into day. The awful roaring of the flames was ever and anon broken by the thundering fall of some heavy roof. Flakes of fire were scattered far and wide by the driving wind, carrying destruction wherever they alighted, and spreading the conflagration on all sides, till it seemed like a vast wedge of fire driven into the heart of the city. And thus it went on, swallowing up all before it, like an insatiate monster, and roaring for very joy.

Meanwhile, the incendiaries had met, as concerted, near the foot of the bridge, and all except Philip Grant seemed to rejoice in the progress of the conflagration. Chowles made some comment upon his moody looks and silence,

and whispered in his ear, " You have now an opportunity
of retrieving your fortune, and may make yourself
richer than your son. Take my advice, and do not let it
pass."

" Away, tempter ! " cried Grant—" I have lighted a fire
within my breast which never will be quenched."

" Poh, poh ! " rejoined Judith—" do not turn faint-
hearted now."

" The fire rages fiercely," cried Solomon Eagle, gazing
at the vast sheet of flame overtopping the buildings near
them, " but we must keep it alive. Take the remainder of
the fire-balls, Hubert, and cast them into some of the old
houses in Crooked-lane."

Hubert prepared to obey.

" I will go with you and point out the best spots," said
Chowles. " Our next place of rendezvous must be the
vaults beneath Saint Faith's."

" Agreed ! " exclaimed the others. And they again
separated,—Hubert and Chowles to kindle fresh fires, and
Grant to watch the conflagration at a distance. As to
Solomon Eagle, he rushed towards the scene of destruction,
and forcing himself into the midst of the crowd, mounted
a post, crying in a loud voice:—

" I told you a second judgment would come upon you
on account of your iniquities, and you now find that I
avouched the truth. The Lord himself hath come to preach
to you, as he did in the fiery mount of Sinai, and a terrible
exhortation it shall be, and one ye shall not easily forget.
This fire shall not be quenched till the whole city is laid
prostrate. Ye doubted my words when I told you of the
plague ; ye laughed at me and scoffed me ; but ye became
believers in the end, and now conviction is forced upon
you a second time. You will vainly attempt to save your
dwellings. It is the Lord's will they should be destroyed,
and a man's effort to avert the judgment will be
ineffectual ! "

While the majority listened to him with fear and trembling, and regarded him as a prophet, a few took the
opposite view of the question, and coupling his appearance
with the sudden outbreak of the fire, were disposed to

regard him as an incendiary. They therefore cried out—
" He has set fire to our houses. Down with him ! down
with him ! "

Other voices joined in the outcry, and an attempt was
made to carry the menace into effect; but a strong party
rallied round the enthusiast, who derided the attempts of
his opponents. Planting himself on the steps of Saint
Margaret's church, he continued to pour forth exhortations
to the crowd, until he was driven into the interior of the
pile by the fast-approaching flames. The whole body of
the church was filled with poor wretches who had sought
refuge within it, having brought with them such of their
goods as they were able to carry off. But it soon became
evident that the sacred structure would be destroyed, and
their screams and cries on quitting it were truly heart-
rending. Solomon Eagle was the last to go forth, and he
delayed his departure till the flames burst through the
windows. Another great storehouse of oil, tar, cordage,
hemp, flax, and other highly inflammable articles, adjoining the church, had caught fire, and the flames speedily
reached the sacred fabric. The glass within the windows
was shivered; the stone bars split asunder; and the seats
and other wood-work withinside catching fire, the flames
ascended to the roof, and kindled its massive rafters.

Great efforts were now made to check the fire. A few
of the cumbrous and unmanageable engines of the day were
brought to the spot, but no water could be obtained. All
the aqueducts, pipes, and sluices were dry, and the Thames
Water Tower was found to be out of order, and the pipes
connected with it empty. To add to the calamity, the tide
was out, and it was not only difficult, but dangerous, to
obtain water from the river. The scanty supply served
rather to increase than check the flames.

All sorts of rumours prevailed among the crowd. It
could no longer be doubted that the fire, which kept
continually breaking out in fresh places, was the work of
incendiaries, and it was now supposed that it must have
been caused by the French or the Dutch, with both of
which nations the country was then at war, and the most
fearful anticipations that it was only the prelude of a sudden

invasion were entertained. Some conjectured it might be the work of the Papists; and it chancing that a professor of that religion was discovered among the mob, he was with difficulty rescued from their fury by the watch, and conveyed to Newgate. Other persons, who were likewise suspected of being incendiaries, were conveyed with him.

This, though it satisfied the multitude, did not check the progress of the fire, nor put a stop to the terror and tumult that prevailed. Every moment a fresh family were turned into the street, and by their cries added to the confusion. The plunderers had formed themselves into bands. pillaging everything they could lay hands on—carrying off boxes, goods, and coffers, breaking into cellars, broaching casks of spirits and ale, and emptying flasks of wine. Hundreds of persons who did not join in the pillage made free with the contents of the cellars, and a large portion of the concourse was soon in a state of intoxication.

Thus, wild laughter and exclamations of frenzied mirth were heard amid the wailings of women and the piteous cries of children. It was indeed dreadful to see the old and bed-ridden forced into the street to seek a home where they could; nor yet less dreadful to behold others roused from a bed of sickness at dead of night, and by such a fearful summons. Still, fanned by the wind, and fed by a thousand combustible matters, the fire pressed fearfully on, devouring all before it, and increasing in fury and power each instant; while the drunken mob laughed, roared, shouted, and rejoiced, beside it, as if in emulation of the raging flames.

To proceed for a moment to Wood-street. When Philip Grant quitted Leonard in the manner before related, the latter followed him to the door, and saw him disappear in the gloom. But he did not attempt pursuit, because he could not persuade himself that any danger was really to be apprehended. He thought it, however, advisable to consult with Mr. Bloundel on the subject, and accordingly proceeded to his room and roused him.

After hearing what had occurred, the grocer looked very grave, and said, " I am not disposed to treat this matter so lightly as you do, Leonard. I fear this unhappy man has

some desperate design in view. What it is I cannot—dare
not—conjecture. But I confess I am full of apprehension.
I shall not retire to rest to-night, but shall hold myself in
readiness to act in whatever way may be necessary. You
had better go forth, and if anything occurs, give notice to
the proper authorities. We have not now such a lord
mayor as we had during the season of the plague. The
firm and courageous Sir John Lawrence is but ill succeeded
by the weak and vacillating Sir Thomas Bludworth. Still,
the latter may be equal to this emergency, and if anything
happens, you must apply to him."

"I will follow your advice implicitly," rejoined Leonard.
" At the same time, I think there is nothing to apprehend."

" It is better to err on the safe side," observed the grocer.
" You cannot then reproach yourself with want of caution."

Shortly after this, Leonard sallied forth, and having determined what course to pursue in the first instance, proceeded to Saint Paul's. He found every door in the sacred
structure fast closed. Not satisfied with this, he knocked
at the great northern entrance till the summons was
answered by a verger, and stating his object, demanded to
be admitted, and to search the cathedral, as well as Saint
Faith's. The verger offered no objection, and having
examined the old building throughout, without discovering
any traces of the person he was in quest of, Leonard
quitted it.

More than ever convinced that he was right in his supposition, and that no danger was to be apprehended, he
was about to return home, when the idea occurred to him
that he might perhaps find Grant at the plague-pit in
Finsbury-fields, and he accordingly shaped his course
thither. A long period had elapsed since he had last visited
the melancholy spot, and it was not without much painful
emotion that he draw near the vast mound covering the
victims of the great pestilence. But Grant was not there,
and though he paced round and round the dreary enclosure
for some time, no one came. He then proceeded to the
lesser plague-pit, and kneeling beside the grave of Amabel
bedewed it with his tears.

As he arose, with the intention of returning to Wood-street, he observed an extraordinary light in the sky a little to the left, evidently produced by the reflection of a great fire in that direction. On beholding this light, he said to himself, " Mr. Bloundel was right. This is the danger with which the city is threatened. It is now too late to avert it." Determined, however, to ascertain the extent of the calamity, without an instant's loss of time, he set off at a swift pace, and in less than half an hour reached Fish-street-hill, and stood beside the conflagration. It was then nearly three o'clock, and a vast chasm of blackening ruins proclaimed the devastation that had been committed. Just as he arrived, the roof of Saint Margaret's fell in with a tremendous crash, and for a few minutes the fire was subdued. It then arose with greater fury than ever; burst out on both sides of the sacred structure, and caught the line of houses leading towards London-bridge. The first house was that of a vintner; and the lower part of the premises —the cellars and vaults—were filled with wine and spirits. These instantly blazed up, and burnt with such intensity that the adjoining habitation was presently in flames.

" I know who hath done all this ! " exclaimed Leonard, half involuntarily, as he gazed on the work of destruction.

" Indeed ! " exclaimed a bystander, gazing at him. " Who is it ?—the Dutchman or the Frenchman ? "

" Neither," replied Leonard, who at that moment discovered Grant among the group opposite him. " Yonder stands the incendiary ! "

CHAPTER III

Progress of the Fire

INSTANTLY surrounded and seized by the mob, Grant offered no resistance, but demanded to be led with his accuser before a magistrate. Almost as the words were uttered, a cry was raised that the lord mayor and the sheriffs were coming along Eastcheap, and the prisoner and Leonard were immediately hurried off in that direction. They met the civic authorities at the corner of Saint Clement's-lane; but instead of paying any attention to them, the lord mayor, who appeared to be in a state of great agitation and excitement, ordered the javelin-men, by whom he was attended, to push the mob aside.

" I will not delay your worship an instant" cried Leonard —" but this dreadful fire is the work of incendiaries, of whom that man," pointing to Grant, " is the principal. I pray your worship to question him. He may have important revelations to make."

" Eh, what ? " cried the lord mayor, addressing Grant. " Is it true you are an incendiary ? Who are your accomplices ? Where are they ? "

" I have none," replied Grant, boldly,—" I deny the charge altogether. Let my accuser prove it if he can."

" You hear what he says, young man," said the mayor. " Did you see him set fire to any house ? Did you find any fire-balls on his person ? "

" I did not," replied Leonard.

" I searched him, your worship," cried Chowles, who was among the bystanders, " the moment he was seized, and found nothing upon him. It is a false and malicious charge."

" It looks like it, I must say," replied the mayor. On what grounds do you accuse him ? " he added, angrily, to Leonard.

" On these," replied Leonard. " He came to me three hours ago, and confessed that he had a desperate design

against the safety of the city, and made certain proposals
to me, to which I would not listen. This is not the season
for a full explanation of the matter. But I pray your worship, as you value the welfare of the city, to have him
secured."

"There can be no harm in that," replied the lord mayor.
" His appearance is decidedly against him. Let him be
taken care of till the morrow, when I will examine further
into the matter. Your name and place of abode, young
man ? "

" I am called Leonard Holt, and my business is that of
a grocer, in Wood-street," was the reply.

" Enough," rejoined the mayor. " Take away the
prisoner. I will hear nothing further now. Lord ! Lord !
how the fire rages, to be sure. We shall have the whole
city burnt down, if we do not take care."

" That we shall, indeed," replied Sir Robert Viner, one
of the sheriffs, " unless the most prompt and decisive
measures are immediately adopted."

" What would you recommend ? " cried the lord mayor,
despairingly.

Sir Robert looked perplexed by the question.

" If I might offer an opinion," interposed Leonard, " I
would advise your worship to pull down all the houses in
the way of the fire, as the only means of checking it."

" Pull down the houses ! " cried the lord mayor. " Who
ever heard of such an idea ? Why, that would be worse
than the fire. No, no; that will never do."

" The young man is in the right," observed Sir Joseph
Sheldon, the other sheriff.

" Well, well—we shall see," replied the mayor. " But
we are losing time here. Forward ! forward ! "

And while Grant was borne off to Newgate by a guard
of javelin-men, the lord mayor and his company proceeded
to Fish-street-hill, where the whole conflagration burst
upon them. The moment the lord mayor appeared, he was
beset on all sides by hundreds of families soliciting his protection. Others came to give him the alarming intelligence
that a very scanty supply of water only could be obtained,
and that already two engines had been destroyed, while the

firemen who worked them had narrowly escaped with life. Others again pressed him for instructions how to act,—some suggesting one plan,—some another,—and being of a weak and irresolute character, and utterly unequal to a fearful emergency like the present, he was completely bewildered. Bidding the houseless families take refuge in the churches, he ordered certain officers to attend them, and affecting to doubt the statement of those who affirmed there was no water, advised them to go to the river, where they would find plenty. In vain they assured him the tide was out, the Thames Water Tower empty, the pipes and conduits dry. He would not believe anything of the sort, but, upbraiding his informants with neglect, bade them try again. As to instructions, he could give none.

At last, a reluctant assent being wrung from him by Sir Joseph Sheldon, that a house should be pulled down, as suggested by Leonard, preparations were instantly made for putting the design into execution. The house selected was about four doors from the top of Fish-street-hill, and belonged to a birdcage-maker. But they encountered an unexpected opposition. Having ascertained their purpose, the owner fastened his doors, and refused to admit them. He harangued the mob from one of the upper windows, and producing a pistol, threatened to fire upon them if they attempted to gain a forcible entrance. The officers, however, having received their orders, were not to be intimidated, and commenced breaking down the door. The birdcage-maker then fired, but without effect; and before he had time to reload, the door had yielded to the combined efforts of the multitude, who were greatly enraged at his strange conduct. They rushed upstairs, but finding he had locked himself in the room, left him there, supposing him secure, and commenced the work of demolition. More than a hundred men were engaged in the task, but though they used the utmost exertion, they had little more than unroofed the building, when a cry was raised by those in the street that the house was on fire. Alarmed by the shout, they descended, and found the report true. Flames were issuing from the room lately occupied by the birdcage-maker. The wretch had set fire to his dwelling, and then made his escape with his family by a back staircase. Thus defeated, the workmen, with bitter imprecations on the fugitive, withdrew, and Leonard, who had lent his best assistance to the task, repaired to the lord mayor. He found him in greater consternation than ever.

" We must go further off, if we would do any good," said Leonard; " and as the present plan is evidently too slow, we must have recourse to gunpowder."

" Gunpowder ! " exclaimed the lord mayor. " Would you blow up the city, like a second Guy Fawkes ? I begin to suspect you are one of the incendiaries yourself, young man. Lord, Lord ! what will become of us ? "

" If your worship disapproves of my suggestion, at least give orders what is to be done," rejoined Leonard.

" I have done all I can," replied the mayor. " Who are you that talk to me thus ? "

" I have told your worship I am a simple tradesman," replied Leonard. " But I have the welfare of the city at heart, and I cannot stand by and see it burnt to the ground without an effort to save it."

" Well, well, I dare say you mean very well, young man," rejoined the lord mayor, somewhat pacified. " But don't you perceive it's impossible to stop such a fire as this without water, or engines. I'm sure I would willingly lay down my life to preserve the city. But what can I do ?—what can any man do ? "

" Much may be done if there is resolution to attempt it," returned Leonard. " I would recommend your worship to proceed, in the first place, to the wharves on the banks of the Thames, and cause the removal of the wood, coal, and other combustible matter, with which they are crowded."

" Well thought of," cried the lord mayor. " I will go thither at once. Do you stay here. Your advice will be useful. I will examine you touching the incendiary to-morrow—that is, if we are any of us left alive, which I don't expect. Lord, Lord ! what will become of us ? "

And with many similar ejaculations, he hurried off with the sheriffs, and the greater part of his attendants, and taking his way down Saint Michael's-lane, soon reached the river-side.

By this time, the fire had approached the summit of Fish-street-hill, and here the overhanging stories of the houses coming so close together as almost to meet at the top, the flames speedily caught the other side, and spread the conflagration in that direction. Two other houses were likewise discovered to be on fire in Crooked-lane, and in an incredibly short space the whole dense mass of habitations lying at the west side of Fish-street-hill, and between Crooked-lane and Eastcheap, were in flames, and threatening the venerable church of Saint Michael, which stood in the midst of them, with instant destruction. To the astonishment of all who witnessed it, the conflagration seemed to proceed as rapidly against the wind as with it, and to be approaching Thames-street, both by Pudding-lane and Saint Michael's-lane. A large stable, filled with straw and hay, at the back of the Star Inn, in Little East-cheap, caught fire, and carrying the conflagration eastward, had already conveyed it as far as Botolph-lane.

It chanced that a poor Catholic priest, travelling from Douay to England, had landed that night, and taken up his quarters at the hotel above mentioned. The landlord, who had been roused by the cries of fire, and alarmed by the rumours of incendiaries, immediately called to mind his guest, and dragging him from his room, thrust him, half-naked, into the street. Announcing his conviction that the poor priest was an incendiary to the mob without, they seized him, and in spite of his protestations and explanations, which, being uttered in a foreign tongue, they could not comprehend, they were about to exercise summary punishment upon him, by hanging him to the sign-post before the landlord's door, when they were diverted from their dreadful purpose by Solomon Eagle, who prevailed upon them to carry him to Newgate.

The conflagration had now assumed so terrific a character that it appalled even the stoutest spectator. It had been mentioned that for many weeks previous to the direful calamity, the weather had been remarkably dry and warm, a circumstance which had prepared the old wooden houses, abounding in this part of the city, for almost instantaneous ignition. Added to this, if the incendiaries themselves had

R

deposited combustible materials at certain spots to extend
the conflagration, they could not have selected better places
than accident had arranged. All sorts of inflammable
goods were contained in the shops and warehouses, oil,
hemp, flax, pitch, tar, cordage, sugar, wine, and spirits;
and when any magazine of this sort caught fire it spread
the conflagration with tenfold rapidity.

The heat of the flames had now become almost insuffer-
able, and the sparks and flakes of fire fell so fast and thick,
that the spectators were compelled to retreat to a considerable distance from the burning buildings. The noise occasioned by the cracking of the timbers, and the falling of
walls and roofs, was awful in the extreme. All the avenues
and thoroughfares near the fire were now choked up by
carts, coaches, and other vehicles, which had been hastily
brought thither to remove the goods of the inhabitants,
and the hurry of the poor people to save a wreck of their
property, and the attempts made by the gangs of plunderers
to deprive them of it, constituted a scene of unparalleled
tumult and confusion. As yet, no troops had appeared to
maintain order, and seeing that as much mischief was
almost done by the plunderers as by the fire, Leonard determined to go in search of the lord mayor, and acquaint
him with the mischief that was occurring. Having heard
that the fire had already reached London-bridge, he resolved to ascertain whether the report was true. As he
proceeded down Saint Michael's-lane, he found the
venerable church from which it was designated on fire,
and with some difficulty forcing his way through the crowd,
reached Thames-street, where he discovered that the conflagration had even made more fearful progress than he had
anticipated. Fishmongers'-hall, a large square structure,
was on fire, and burning swiftly,—the flames encircling its
high roof and the turret by which it was surmounted.
Streams of fire, too, had darted down the numerous narrow
alleys leading to the river-side, and reaching the wharves,
had kindled the heaps of wood and coal with which they
were filled. The party under the command of the lord
mayor had used their utmost exertions to get rid of these
combustible materials by flinging them into the Thames;

but they came too late, and were driven away by the approach of the fire. Most of the barges and heavy craft were aground, and they, too, caught fire, and were burned, with their contents.

Finding he could neither render any assistance, nor obtain speech with the lord mayor, and anxious to behold the terrible, yet sublime spectacle from the river, Leonard hastened to Old Swan-stairs, and springing into a boat, ordered the waterman to row into the middle of the Thames. He could then discern the full extent of the conflagration, and trace the progress it was making. All the houses between Fishmongers'-hall and the bridge were on fire, and behind them rose a vast sheet of flame. Saint Magnus' Church, at the foot of the bridge, was next seized by the flames, and Leonard watched its destruction. An ancient gateway followed, and soon afterwards a large stack of houses erected upon the bridge burst into flames.

The inhabitants of the houses on the bridge, having now become thoroughly alarmed, flung bedding, boxes, and articles of furniture, out of their windows into the river. A crowd of boats surrounded the starlings, and the terrified occupants of the structure above descending to them by the staircases in the interior of the piers, embarked with every article they could carry off. The river presented a most extraordinary scene. Lighted by the red and fierce reflection of the fire, and covered with boats, filled with families who had just quitted their habitations either on the bridge or in some other street adjoining it, its whole surface was speckled with pieces of furniture, or goods, that had been cast into it, and which were now floating up with the tide. Great crowds were collected on the Southwark shore to watch the conflagration, while in the opposite side the wharves and quays were thronged with persons removing their goods, and embarking them in boats. One circumstance noted by Pepys, and which also struck Leonard, was the singular attachment displayed by the pigeons, kept by the owners of several houses on the bridge, to the spots they had been accustomed to. Even when the flames attacked the buildings to which the dovecots were attached, the birds wheeled round and round

them, until, their pinions being scorched by the fire, they
dropped into the water.

Leonard remained on the river nearly two hours. He
could not in fact, tear himself away from the spectacle,
which possessed a strange fascination in his eyes. He began
to think that all the efforts of men were unavailing to arrest
the progress of destruction, and he was for a while content
to regard it as a mere spectacle. And never had he beheld
a more impressive—a more terrible sight. There lay the
vast and populous city before him, which he had once
before known to be invaded by an invisible, but exterminating foe, now attacked by a furious and far seen enemy. The
fire seemed to form a vast arch—many-coloured as a rain-
bow,—reflected in the sky, and re-reflected in all its horrible
splendour in the river.

Nor was the aspect of the city less striking. The innumerable towers and spires of the churches rose tall and
dark through the wavering sheet of flame, and every now
and then one of them would topple down or disappear, as
if swallowed up by the devouring element. For a short
space, the fire seemed to observe a regular progressive
movement, but when it fell upon better material, it reared
its blazing crest aloft, changed its hues, and burnt with redoubled intensity. Leonard watched it thread narrow
alleys, and firing every lesser habitation in its course, kindle
some great hall or other structure, whose remoteness
seemed to secure it from immediate danger. At this
distance, the roaring of the flames resembled that of a
thousand furnaces. Ever and anon, it was broken by a
sound like thunder, occasioned by the fall of some mighty
edifice. Then there would come a quick succession of
reports like the discharge of artillery, followed by a shower
of fiery flakes and sparks blown aloft, like the explosion
of some stupendous firework. Mixed with the roaring of
the flames, the thunder of falling roofs, the cracking of
timber, was a wild hubbub of human voices, that sounded
afar off like a dismal wail. In spite of its terror, the appearance of the fire was at that time beautiful beyond
description. Its varying colours—its fanciful forms—now
shooting out in a hundred different directions, like lightning

flashes,—now drawing itself up, as it were, and soaring aloft,—now splitting into a million tongues of flame,— these aspects so riveted the attention of Leonard, that he almost forgot in the sight the dreadful devastation going forward. His eyes ached with gazing at the fiery spectacle, and he was glad to rest them on the black masses of building that stood in stern relief against it, and which there could be little doubt would soon become its prey.

It was now broad daylight, except for the mighty cloud of smoke, which o'er canopied the city, creating an artificial gloom. Leonard's troubled gaze wandered from the scene of destruction to Saint Paul's—an edifice, which, from the many events connected with his fortunes that had occurred there, had always a singular interest in his eyes. Calling to mind the denunciations poured forth by Solomon Eagle against this fane, he could not help fearing they would now be fulfilled. What added to his misgivings was, that it was now almost entirely surrounded by poles and scaffolding. Ever since the cessation of the plague, the repairs, suspended during that awful season, had been recommenced under the superintendence of Doctor Christopher Wren, and were now proceeding with renewed activity. The whole of the building was under repair, and a vast number of masons were employed upon it, and it was their scaffolding that impressed Leonard with a dread of what afterwards actually occurred. Accustomed to connect the figure of Solomon Eagle with the sacred structure, he could not help fancying that he discovered a speck resembling a human figure on the central tower. If it were the enthusiast, what must his feelings be at finding his predictions so fatally fulfilled ? Little did Leonard think how the prophecy had been accomplished !

But his attention was speedily called to the progress of the conflagration. From the increased tumult in the city, it was evident the inhabitants were now thoroughly roused, and actively bestirring themselves to save their property. This was apparent, even on the river, from the multitude of boats deeply laden with goods of all kinds, which were now seen shaping their course towards Westminster. The fire, also, had made rapid progress on all sides. The vast pile of habitations at the north side of the bridge was now entirely in flames. The effect of this was awfully fine. Not only did the flames mount to a greater height, and appear singularly conspicuous from the situation of the houses, but every instant some blazing fragment fell with a tremendous splash into the water, where it hissed for a moment, and then was for ever quenched, a floating black mass upon the surface. From the foot of the bridge to Coal Harbour-stairs, extended what Dryden finely calls " a quay of fire." All the wharves and warehouses were in flames, and burning with astonishing rapidity, while this part of Thames-street, " the lodge of all combustibles," had likewise become a prey to the devouring element. The fire, too, had spread in an easterly direction, and consuming three churches, namely, Saint Andrew's, in Botolph-lane, Saint Mary's, in Love-lane, and Saint Dunstan's in the East, had invaded Tower-street, and seemed fast approaching the ancient fortress.

So fascinated was Leonard with the sight, that he could have been well content to remain all day gazing at it, but he now recollected that he had other duties to perform, and directing the waterman to land him at Queenhithe, ascended Bread-street-hill, and betook himself to Wood-street.

CHAPTER IV

Leonard's Interview with the King

SOME rumours of the conflagration, as will be supposed had ere this reached Mr. Bloundel, but he had no idea of the extent of the direful calamity, and when informed of it by Leonard, lifted up his hands despairingly, exclaiming, in accents of the deepest affliction—" Another judgment, then, has fallen upon this sinful city,—another judgment yet more terrible than the first. Man may have kindled this great fire, but the hand of God is apparent in it. ' Alas ! alas ! for thee, thou great city, Babylon ! Alas for thee, thou mighty city ! for in one hour is thy judgment come.

The kings of the earth shall bewail thee, and lament for thee, when they see the smoke of thy burning.' "

"Your dwelling was spared in the last visitation, sir," observed Leonard, after a pause, "and you were able to shut yourself up, as in a strong castle, against the all-exterminating foe. But I fear you will not be able to ward off the assaults of the present enemy, and recommend you to remove your family and goods without delay to some place of security far from this doomed city."

"This is the Lord's-day, Leonard, and must be kept holy," replied the grocer. "To-morrow, if I am spared so long, I will endeavour to find some place of shelter."

"If the conflagration continues to spread as rapidly as it is now doing, to-morrow will be too late," rejoined Leonard.

"It may be so," returned the grocer, "but I will not violate the Sabbath. If the safety of my family is threatened, that is another matter, but I will not attempt to preserve my goods. Do not, however, let me influence you. Take such portion of our stock as belongs to you, and you know that a third of the whole is yours, and convey it where you please."

"On no account, sir," interrupted Leonard. "I should never think of acting in opposition to your wishes. This will be a sad Sunday for London."

"The saddest she has ever seen," replied the grocer; "for though the voice of prayer was silenced in her churches during the awful season of the plague, yet the men's minds had been gradually prepared for the calamity, and though filled with terror, they were not taken by surprise, as must now be the case. But let us to prayers, and may our earnest supplications avail in turning aside the Divine displeasure."

And summoning his family and household, all of whom were by this time stirring, and in the utmost consternation at what they had heard of the fire, he commenced a prayer adapted to the occasion in a strain of the utmost fervour; and as Leonard gazed at his austere countenance, now lighted up with holy zeal, and listened to his earnest intercessions in behalf of the devoted city, he was reminded of the prophet Jeremiah weeping for Jerusalem before the throne of grace.

Prayers over, the whole party sat down to their morning repast, after which, the grocer and his eldest son, accompanied by Leonard and Blaize, mounted to the roof of the house, and gazing in the direction of the conflagration, they could plainly distinguish the vast cloud of yellow smoke commingled with flame, that marked the scene of its ravages. As the wind blew from this quarter, charged, as has been stated, with a cloud of sparks, many of the fire-drops were dashed in their faces, and compelled them to shade their eyes. The same awful roar which Leonard had heard on the river, likewise broke upon their ears, while from all the adjoining streets arose a wild clamour of human voices, the burden of whose cries was " Fire ! Fire ! " The church bells, which should have been tolling to early devotion, were now loudly ringing the alarm, while their towers were crowded, as were the roofs of most of the houses, with persons gazing towards the scene of devastation. Nothing could be more opposite to the stillness and quiet of a Sabbath morn, and as the grocer listened to the noise and tumult prevailing around him, he could not repress a groan.

" I never thought my ears would be so much offended on this day," he said. " Let us go down. I have seen and heard enough."

They then descended, and Stephen Bloundel, who was greatly alarmed by what he had just witnessed, stronglv urged his father to remove immediately.

" There are seasons," said the young man, " when even our duty to Heaven becomes a secondary consideration, and I should be sorry if the fruit of your industry were sacrificed to your religious scruples."

" There are no such seasons," replied the grocer, severely, " and I grieve that a son of mine should think so. If the inhabitants of this sinful city had not broken the Sabbath, and neglected God's commandments, this heavy judgment would not have fallen upon them. I shall neglect no precaution for the personal safety of my family, but I place my worldly goods in the hands of Him from whom I derived them, and to whom I am ready to restore them, whenever it shall please Him to take them."

"I am rebuked, father," replied Stephen, humbly; "and retreat your pardon for having ventured to differ with you. I am now fully sensible of the propriety of your conduct."

"And I have ever acquiesced in your wishes, be they what they may," said Mrs. Bloundel to her husband, "but I confess I am dreadfully frightened. I hope you will remove the first thing to-morrow."

"When midnight has struck, and the Sabbath is past, I shall commence my preparations," replied the grocer. "You must rest content till then."

Mrs. Bloundel heaved a sigh, but said no more, and the grocer, retiring to a side table, opened the Bible, and sat down calmly to its perusal. But though no further remonstrances reached his ears, there was great murmuring in the kitchen on the part of Blaize and Patience.

"Goodness knows what will become of us!" cried the latter. "I expect we shall all be burnt alive, owing to our master's obstinacy. What harm can there be in moving on a Sunday, I should like to know? I'm sure I'm too much hurried and flurried to say my prayers as I ought to do."

"And so am I," replied Blaize. "Mr. Bloundel is a great deal too particular. What a dreadful thing it would be if the house should be burnt down, and all my mother's savings, which were to form a provision for our marriage, lost."

"That would be terrible, indeed," cried Patience, with a look of dismay. "I think the wedding had better take place as soon as the fire is over. It can't last many days if it goes on at this rate."

"You are right," returned Blaize. "I have no objection. I'll speak to my mother at once." And stepping into the scullery, where old Josyna was washing some dishes, he addressed her—"Mother, I'm sadly afraid this great fire will reach us before our master will allow us to move. Hadn't you better let me take care of the money you intended giving me on my marriage with Patience?"

"No, no, myn goed zoon," replied Josyna, shaking her head—"I must zee you married virsd."

" But I can't be married to-day," cried Blaize—" and there's no time to lose. The fire will be upon us directly."

" I cand help dat," returned his mother. " We musd place our drusd in God."

" There I quite agree with you, mother," replied Blaize —" but we must also take care of ourselves. If you won't give me the money, at least put it in a box to carry off at a moment's notice."

" Don't be afraid, myn zoon," replied Josyna. " I won'd forged id."

" I'm sadly afraid you will though," muttered Blaize, as he walked away. " There's no doing any good with her," he added to Patience. " She's as obstinate as Mr. Bloundel. I should like to see the fire of all things, but I suppose I mustn't leave the house."

" Of course not," replied Patience, pettishly ; " at such a time it would be highly improper. *I* forbid that."

" Then I must need submit," groaned Blaize,—" I can't even have my own way before marriage."

When the proper time arrived, the grocer, accompanied by all his family and household, except old Josyna, who was left in charge of the house, repaired to the neighbouring church of Saint Alban's, but finding the doors closed, and that no service was to be performed, he returned home with a sorrowful heart.

Soon after this, Leonard took Mr. Bloundel apart, and observed to him, " I have a strong conviction that I could be useful in arresting the progress of the conflagration, and as I cannot attend church service, I will, with your permission, devote myself to that object. It is my intention to proceed to Whitehall, and if possible, obtain an audience of the king, and if I succeed in doing so, to lay a plan before him, which I think would prove efficacious."

" I will not ask what the plan is," rejoined the grocer, " because I doubt its success. Neither will I oppose your design, which is praiseworthy. Go, and may it prosper. Return in the evening, for I may need your assistance,— perhaps, protection."

Leonard then prepared to set forth. Blaize begged hard to accompany him, but was refused. Forcing his way through the host of carts, coaches, drays, and other vehicles thronging the streets, Leonard made the best of his way to Whitehall, where he speedily arrived. A large body of mounted troopers were stationed before the gates of the palace, and a regiment of the footguards were drawn up in the court. Drums were beating to arms, and other martial sounds were heard, showing the alarm that was felt. Leonard was stopped at the gate by a sentinel, and refused admittance, and he would in all probability have been turned back, if at that moment the Lords Argentine and Rochester had not come up. On seeing him, the former frowned, and passed quickly on, but the latter halted.

"You seem to be in some difficulty," remarked Rochester. "Can I help you?"

Leonard was about to turn away, but he checked himself.

"I will not suffer my resentful feelings to operate injuriously to others," he muttered. "I desire to see the king, my lord," he added, to the earl. "I have a proposal to make to him, which I think would be a means of checking the conflagration."

"Say you so?" cried Rochester. "Come along, then. Heaven grant your plan may prove successful, in which case, I promise you, you shall be nobly rewarded."

"I seek no reward, my lord," replied Leonard. "All I desire is to save the city."

"Well, well," rejoined Rochester, "it will be time enough to refuse his Majesty's bounty when offered."

Upon this, he ordered the sentinel to withdraw, and Leonard followed him into the palace. They found the entrance-hall filled with groups of officers and attendants, all conversing together, it was evident from their looks and manner, on the one engrossing topic,—the conflagration.

Ascending a magnificent staircase, and traversing part of a grand gallery, they entered an ante-room, in which a number of courtiers and pages—amongst the latter of whom was Chiffinch—were assembled. At the door of the inner chamber stood a couple of ushers, and as the earl approached, it was instantly thrown open. As Leonard, who followed close behind his leader, passed Chiffinch, the

latter caught hold of his arm and detained him. Hearing
the movement, Rochester turned, and said quickly to the
page, " Let him pass, he is going with me."

" Old Rowley is in no humour for a jest to-day, my
lord," replied Chiffinch, familiarly. " He is more serious
than I have ever before seen him, and takes this terrible fire
sadly to heart, as well as he may. Mr. Secretary Pepys, of
the Admiralty, is with him, and is detailing all particulars
of the calamity to him, I believe."

" It is in reference to the fire that I have brought this
young man with me," returned the earl. " Let him pass, I
say. State your plan boldly," he added, as they entered the
audience-chamber.

At the further end of the long apartment, on a chair of
state, and beneath a canopy, sat Charles. He was evidently
much disturbed, and looked eagerly at the new-comers,
especially at Leonard, expecting to find him the bearer of
some important intelligence. On the right of the king, and
near an open window, which, looking towards the river,
commanded a view of the fire on the bridge, as well as of
part of the burning city, stood the Duke of York. The
duke did not appear much concerned at the calamity, but
was laughing with Lord Argentine, who stood close beside
him. The smile fled from the lips of the latter as he beheld
Leonard, and he looked angrily at Rochester, who did not,
however, appear to notice his displeasure. On the left of
the royal chair was Mr. Pepys, engaged, as Chiffinch had
intimated, in detailing to the king the progress of the conflagration; and next to the secretary stood the Earl of
Craven,—a handsome, commanding, and martial-looking
personage, though somewhat stricken in years. Three
other noblemen—namely, the Lords Hollis, Arlington, and
Ashley,—were likewise present.

" Who have you with you, Rochester ? " demanded
Charles, as the earl and his companion approached him.

" A young man, my liege, who desires to make known
to you a plan for checking this conflagration," replied the
earl.

" Ah ! " exclaimed the king. " Let him accomplish that
for us, and he shall ask what he will in return."

"I ventured to promise him as much," observed Rochester.

"Mine is a very simple and a very obvious plan, sire," said Leonard, "but I will engage, on the peril of my life, if you will give me sufficient authority, and means to work withal. to stop the further progress of this fire."

"In what way?" asked Charles, impatiently. "In what way?"

"By demolishing the houses around the conflagration with gunpowder, so as to form a wide gap between those left and the flames," replied Leonard.

"A short and summary process, truly," replied the king. "But it would occasion great waste of property, and might be attended with other serious consequences."

"Not half so much property will be destroyed as if the slower and seemingly safer course of pulling down the houses is pursued," rejoined Leonard. "That experiment had been tried and failed."

"I am of the young man's opinion," observed the Earl of Craven.

"And I," added Pepys. "Better lose half the city than the whole. As it is, your Majesty is not safe in your palace."

"Why, you do not think it can reach Whitehall?" cried the king, rising, and walking to the window. "How say you, brother?" he added, to the Duke of York—"shall we act upon this young man's suggestion, and order the wholesale demolition of the houses which he recommends?"

"I would not advise your Majesty to do so,—at least, not without consideration," answered the duke. "This is a terrible fire, no doubt, but the danger may be greatly exaggerated, and if any ill consequences should result from the proposed scheme, the blame will be entirely laid upon your Majesty."

"I care not for that," replied the king, "provided I feel assured it is for the best."

"The plan would do incalculably more mischief than the fire itself," observed Lord Argentine, "and would be met by the most determined opposition on the part of the

owners of the habitations condemned to destruction.
Whole streets will have to be blown up, and your Majesty
will easily comprehend the confusion and damage that
will ensue."

" Lord Argentine has expressed my sentiments exactly,"
said the Duke of York.

" There is nothing for it, then, but for your Majesty to
call for a fiddle, and amuse yourself like Nero, while your
city is burning," remarked Rochester, sarcastically.

" Another such jest, my lord," rejoined the king, sternly,
" and it shall cost you your liberty. I will go upon the
river instantly, and view the fire myself, and then decide
what course shall be adopted."

" There are rumours that incendiaries are abroad, your
Majesty," remarked Argentine, glancing maliciously at
Leonard,—" it is not unlikely that he who lighted the fire
should know how to extinguish it."

" His lordship says truly," rejoined Leonard. " There
are incendiaries abroad, and the chief of them was taken
by my hand, and lodged in Newgate, where he lies for
examination."

" Ah ! " exclaimed the king, eagerly. " Did you catch
the miscreant in the act ? "

" No, my liege," replied Leonard; " but he came to
me a few hours before the outbreak of the fire, intimating
that he was in possession of a plot against the city,—a design so monstrous, that your Majesty would give any reward to the discloser of it. He proposed to reveal this plot
to me on certain terms."

" And you accepted them ? " cried the king.

" No, my liege," replied Leonard. " I refused them, and
would have secured him, but he escaped me at that time.
I afterwards discovered him among the spectators near the
fire, and caused his arrest."

" And who is this villain ? " cried the king.

" I must refer your Majesty to Lord Argentine," replied
Leonard.

" Do you know anything of the transaction, my lord ? "
said Charles, appealing to him.

" Not I, your Majesty," said Argentine, vainly endeavouring to conceal his anger and confusion. "The knave has spoken falsely."

"He shall rue it, if he has done so," rejoined the monarch. "What has the man you speak of to do with Lord Argentine?" he added, to Leonard.

"He is his father," was the reply.

Charles looked at Lord Argentine, and became convinced from the altered expression of his countenance that the truth had been spoken. He, therefore, arose, and motioning him to follow him, led him into the recess of a window, where they remained in conversation for some minutes.

While this was passing, the Earl of Rochester observed, in an undertone, to Leonard, "You have made a mortal foe of Lord Argentine, but I will protect you."

"I require no other protection than I can afford myself, my lord," rejoined Leonard, coldly.

Shortly after this, Charles stepped forward with a graver aspect than before, and said, "Before proceeding to view this conflagration, I must give some directions in reference to it. To you, my Lord Craven, whose intrepidity I well know, I intrust the most important post. You will station yourself at the east of the conflagration, and if you find it making its way to the Tower, as I hear is the case, check it at all hazards. The old fortress must be preserved at any risk. But do not resort to gunpowder unless you receive an order from me accompanied by my signet ring. My Lords Hollis and Ashley, you will have the care of the northwest of the city. Station yourselves near Newgate-market. Rochester and Arlington, your posts will be at Saint Paul's. Watch over the august cathedral. I would not have it injured for half my kingdom. Brother," he added to the Duke of York, "you will accompany me in my barge,—and you, Mr. Pepys. You, young man," to Leonard, "can follow in my train."

"Has your Majesty no post for me?" asked Argentine.

"No," replied Charles, turning coldly from him.

"Had not your Majesty better let him have the custody of your gaol of Newgate?" remarked Rochester, sarcastically; "he has an interest in its safe keeping."

Lord Argentine turned deadly pale, but he made no answer.

Attended by the Duke of York and Mr. Pepys, and followed at a respectful distance by Leonard, the king then passed through the ante-room, and, descending the grand staircase, traversed a variety of passages, until he reached the private stairs communicating with the river. At the foot lay the royal barge, in which he embarked with his train.

Charles appeared greatly moved by the sight of the thousands of his houseless subjects, whom he encountered in his passage down the Thames, and whenever a feeble shout was raised for him, he returned it with a blessing. When nearly opposite Queenhithe, he commanded the rowers to pause. The conflagration had made formidable progress since Leonard beheld it a few hours back, and had, advanced nearly as far as the Stillyard on the river-side, while it was burning upwards through thick ranks of houses, almost as far as Cannon-street. The roaring of the flames was louder than ever—and the crash of falling habitations, and the tumult and cries of the affrighted populace, yet more terrific.

Charles gazed at the appalling spectacle like one who could not believe his senses, and it was some time before the overwhelming truth could force itself upon him. Tears then started to his eyes, and uttering an ejaculation of despair, he commanded the rowers to make instantly for the shore.

CHAPTER V

How Leonard Saved the King's Life

THE royal barge landed at Queenhithe, and Charles instantly disembarking, proceeded on foot, and at a pace that compelled his attendants to move quickly to keep up with him, to Thames-street. Here, however, the confusion was so great, owing to the rush of people, and the number of vehicles employed in the removal of goods, that he was obliged to come to a halt. Fortunately, at this moment, a company of the train-bands rode up, and their leader dismounting, offered his horse to the king, who instantly sprang into the saddle, and scarcely waiting till the Duke of York could be similarly accommodated, forced his way through the crowd as far as Brewer-lane, where his progress was stopped by the intense heat. A little more than a hundred yards from this point, the whole street was on fire, and the flames bursting from the windows and roofs of the houses, with a roar like that which might be supposed to be produced by the forges of the Cyclops, united in a vast blazing arch overhead. It chanced, too, that in some places cellars filled with combustible materials extended under the street, and here the ground would crack and jets of fire shoot forth like the eruption of a volcano. The walls and timbers of the houses at some distance from the conflagration were scorched and blistered with the heat, and completely prepared for ignition. Overhead being a vast and momentarily increasing cloud of flame-coloured smoke, which spread all over the city, filling it with a thick mist, while the glowing vault above looked, as Evelyn expresses it, "like the top of a burning oven."

Two churches, namely, Allhallows the Great and Allhallows the Less, were burnt down in the king's sight, and the lofty spire of a third, Saint Lawrence Poulteney, had just caught fire, and looked like a flame-tipped spear. After contemplating this spectacle for some time, Charles roused himself from the state of stupefaction into which he was thrown, and determined, if possible, to arrest the further progress of the devouring element along the riverside, commanded all the houses on the west of Dowgate Dock to be instantly demolished. A large body of men were, therefore, set upon this difficult and dangerous, and as it proved futile task. Another party were ordered to the same duty on Dowgate-hill; and the crash of tumbling walls and beams was soon added to the general uproar, while clouds of dust darkened the air. It was with some difficulty that a sufficient space could be kept clear for carrying these operations into effect; and long before they were half completed, Charles had the mortification of finding the fire gaining ground so rapidly, that they must prove ineffectual. Word was brought at this juncture that a fresh fire had broken out in Elbow-lane, and while the monarch was listening to this dreary intelligence, a fearful cry was heard near the river, followed, the next moment, by a tumultuous rush of persons from that quarter. The fire, as if in scorn, had leapt across Dowgate Dock, and seizing upon the half-demolished houses, instantly made them its prey. The rapidity with which the conflagration proceeded was astounding, and completely baffled all attempts to check it. The wind continued blowing as furiously as ever, nor was there the slightest prospect of its abatement. All the king's better qualities were called into play by the present terrible crisis. With a courage and devotion that he seldom displayed, he exposed himself to the greatest risk, personally assisting at all the operations he commanded; while his humane attention to the sufferers by the calamity almost reconciled them to their deplorable situation. His movements were almost as rapid as those of the fire itself. Riding up Cannon-street, and from thence by Sweeting's-lane to Lombard-street, and so on by Fenchurch-street to Tower-street, he issued directions all the way, checking every disturbance, and causing a band of depredators, who had broken into the house of a wealthy goldsmith, to be carried off to Newgate. Arrived in Tower-street, he found the Earl of Craven and his party stationed a little beyond Saint Dunstan's in the East.

All immediate apprehensions in this quarter appeared at

an end. The church had been destroyed, as before mentioned, but several houses in its vicinity having been demolished, the fire had not extended eastward. Satisfied that the Tower was in no immediate danger, the king retraced his course, and encountering the lord mayor in Lombard-street, sharply reproved him for his want of zeal and discretion.

"I do not deserve your Majesty's reproaches," replied the lord mayor. "Ever since the fire broke out I have not rested an instant, and am almost worn to death with anxiety and fatigue. I am just returned from Guildhall, where a vast quantity of plate belonging to the city companies has been deposited. Lord! Lord! what a fire this is!"

"You are chiefly to blame for its getting so much ahead," replied the king, angrily. "Had you adopted vigorous measures at the outset, it might have easily been got under. I hear no water was to be obtained. How was that?"

"It is a damnable plot, your Majesty, designed by the Papists, or the Dutch, or the French,—I don't know which —perhaps all three," rejoined the lord mayor; "and it appears that the cocks of all the pipes at the water-works at Islington were turned, while the pipes and conduits in the city were empty. This is no accidental fire, your Majesty."

"So I find," replied the king; "but it will be time enough to inquire into its origin hereafter. Meantime, we must act, and energetically, or we shall be equally as much to blame as the incendiaries. Let a proclamation be made, enjoining all those persons who have been driven from their homes by the fire to proceed with such effects as they have preserved, to Moorfields, where their wants shall be cared for."

"It shall be made instantly, your Majesty," replied the lord mayor.

"Your next business will be to see to the removal of all the wealth from the goldsmiths' houses in this street, all in Gracechurch-street, to some places of security,—Guildhall, or the Royal Exchange, for instance," continued the king.

" Your Majesty's directions shall be implicitly obeyed,"
replied the lord mayor.

" You will then pull down all the houses to the east of
the fire," pursued the king. " Get all the men you can
muster—and never relax your exertions till you have made
a wide and clear breach between the flames and their prey."

" I will—I will, your Majesty," groaned the lord mayor

" About it, then," rejoined the king. And striking spurs
into his horse, he rode off with his train.

He now penetrated one of the narrow alleys leading to
the Three Cranes in the Vintry, where he ascended to the
roof of the habitation that he might view the fire. He saw
that it was making such rapid advances towards him that
it must very soon reach the building on which he stood,
and, half suffocated with the smoke, and scorched with the
fire-drops, he descended.

Not long after this Waterman's Hall was discovered to
be on fire, and stirred by the sight, Charles made fresh
efforts to check the progress of the conflagration, by demolishing more houses. So eagerly did he occupy himself
in the task, that his life had well-nigh fallen a sacrifice to
his zeal. He was standing below a building which the
workmen were unroofing, when all at once the whole of
the upper part of the wall gave way, dragging several heavy
beams with it, and would have infallibly crushed him, if
Leonard, who was stationed behind him, had not noticed
the circumstance, and rushing forward with the greatest
promptitude, dragged him out of harm's way. An engineer,
with whom the king was conversing at the time of the accident, was buried in the ruins, and when taken out was
found fearfully mutilated, and quite dead. Both Charles
and his preserver were covered with dust and rubbish, and
Leonard received a severe blow on the shoulder from a
falling brick.

On recovering from the shock which for some moments
deprived him of the power of speech, Charles inquired for
his deliverer, and on being shown him, said, with a look
of surprise and pleasure : " What, is it you, young man ?
I am glad of it. Depend upon it, I shall not forget the
important service you have rendered me."

" If he remembers it, it will be the first time he has ever so exercised his memory," observed Chiffinch, in a loud whisper, to Leonard. " I advise you, as a friend, not to let his gratitude cool."

Undeterred by this late narrow escape, Charles ordered fresh houses to be demolished, and stimulated the workmen to exertion by his personal superintendence of their operations. He commanded Leonard to keep constantly near him, laughingly observing, " I shall feel safe while you are by. You have a better eye for a falling house than any of my attendants."

Worn out, at length, with fatigue, Charles proceeded with the Duke of York and his immediate attendants to Painters' Hall, in Little Trinity-lane, in quest of refreshment, where a repast was hastily prepared for him, and he sat down to it with an appetite such as the most magnificent banquet could not, under other circumstances, have provoked. His hunger satisfied, he despatched messengers to command the immediate attendance of the lord mayor, the sheriffs, and aldermen, and when they arrived, he thus addressed them,—" My lord mayor and gentlemen, it has been recommended to me by this young man," pointing to Leonard, " that the sole way of checking the further progress of this disastrous conflagration, which threatens the total destruction of our city, will be by blowing up the houses with gunpowder, so as to form a wide gap between the flames and the habitations yet remaining unseized. This plan will necessarily involve great destruction of property, and may, notwithstanding all the care that can be adopted, be attended with some loss of life, but I conceive it will be effectual. Before ordering it, however, to be put into execution, I desire to learn your opinion of it. How say you, my lord mayor and gentlemen? Does the plan meet with your approbation?"

" I pray your Majesty to allow me to confer for a moment with my brethren," replied the lord mayor, cautiously, " before I return an answer. It is too serious a matter to decide upon at once."

" Be it so," replied the king.

And the civic authorities withdrew from the king.

Leonard heard, though he did not dare to remark upon it, that the Duke of York leaned forward as the lord mayor passed him, and whispered in his ear, " Take heed what you do. He only desires to shift the responsibility of the act from his own shoulders to yours."

" If they assent," said the king to Leonard, " I will place you at the head of a party of engineers."

" I beseech your Majesty neither to regard me nor them," replied Leonard. " Use the authority it has pleased Heaven to bestow upon you for the preservation of the city, and think and act for yourself, or you will assuredly regret your want of decision. It has been my fortune, with the assistance of God, to be the humble instrument of accomplishing your Majesty's deliverance from peril, and I have your royal word that you will not forget it."

" Nor will I," cried the king, hastily.

" Then suffer the petition I now make to you to prevail," cried Leonard, falling on his knees. • " Be not influenced by the opinion of the lord mayor and his brethren, whose own interests may lead them to oppose the plan, but if you think well of it, instantly adopt it."

Charles looked irresolute, but might have yielded, if the Duke of York had not stepped forward.

" Your Majesty had better not act too precipitately," said the duke. " A false step in such a case will be irretrievable."

" Nay, brother," rejoined the king, " I see no particular risk in it, after all, and I incline towards the young man's opinion."

" At least hear what they have got to say," rejoined the duke. " And here they come. They have not been long in deliberation."

" The result of it may be easily predicted," said Leonard, rising.

As Leonard had foreseen, the civic authorities were averse to the plan. The lord mayor, in the name of himself and his brethren, earnestly solicited the king to postpone the execution of his order till all other means of checking the progress of the conflagration had been tried, and till such time, at least, as the property of the owners of the

houses to be destroyed could be removed. He further
added, that it was the unanimous opinion of himself and
his brethren, that the plan was fraught with great peril to
the safety of the citizens, and that they could not bring
themselves to assent to it. If, therefore, his Majesty chose
to adopt it, they must leave the responsibility with him.

"I told your Majesty how it would be," observed the
Duke of York, triumphantly.

"I am sorry to find you are right, brother," replied the
king, frowning. "We are overruled, you see, friend," he
added to Leonard.

"Your Majesty has signed the doom of your city," rejoined Leonard, mournfully.

"I trust not—I trust not," replied Charles, hastly, and
with an uneasy shrug of the shoulder. "Fail not to remind
me when all is over of the obligation I am under to you."

"Your Majesty has refused the sole boon I desired to
have granted," rejoined Leonard.

"And do you not see the reason, friend?" returned the
king. "These worthy and wealthy citizens desire to remove their property. Their arguments are unanswerable.
I *must* give them time to do it. But we waste time here,"
he added, rising. "Remenber," to Leonard, "my debt is
not discharged. And I command you, on pain of my
sovereign displeasure, not to omit to claim its payment."

"I will enter it in my memorandum-book, and will put
your Majesty in mind of it at a fitting season," observed
Chiffinch, who had taken a great fancy to Leonard.

The king smiled good-humouredly, and quitting the hall
with his attendants, proceeded to superintend the further
demolition of houses. He next visited all the posts, saw
that the different noblemen were at their appointed stations,
and by his unremitting exertions contrived to restore something like order to the tumultuous streets. Thousands of
men were now employed in different quarters in pulling
down houses, and the most powerful engines of war were
employed in the work. The confusion that attended these
proceedings is indescribable. The engineers and workmen
wrought in clouds of dust and smoke, and the crash of
falling timber and walls was deafening. In a short time,

the upper part of Cornhill was rendered wholly impassable, owing to heaps of rubbish, and directions were given to the engineers to proceed to the Poultry, and demolish the houses as far as the conduit in Cheapside, by which means it was hoped that the Royal Exchange would be saved.

Meanwhile all the wealthy goldsmiths and merchants in Lombard-street and Gracechurch-street had been actively employed in removing all their money, plate, and goods to places of security. A vast quantity was conveyed to Guildhall, as has been stated, and the rest to different churches and halls remote from the scene of conflagration. But in spite of all their caution, much property was carried off by the depredators, and amongst others by Chowles and Judith, who contrived to secure a mass of plate, gold, and jewels, that satisfied even their rapacious souls.

While this was passing in the heart of the burning city, vast crowds were streaming out of its gates, and encamping themselves, in pursuance of the royal injunction, in Fins-bury-fields and Spital-fields. Others crossed the water to Southwark, and took refuge in Saint George's-field—and it was a sad and touching sight to see all these families collected without shelter or food, most of whom a few hours before were in possession of all the comforts of life, but were now reduced to the condition of beggars.

To return to the conflagration. While one party continued to labour incessantly at the work of demolition, and ineffectually sought to quench the flames, by bringing a few engines to play upon them,—a scanty supply of water having now been obtained,—the fire, disdaining such puny opposition, and determined to show its giant strength, leaped over all the breaches, drove the water-carriers back, compelled them to relinquish their buckets, and to abandon their engines, which it made its prey, and seizing upon the heaps of timber and other fragments occasioned by the demolition, consumed them, and marched onwards with furious exultation.

It was now proceeding up Gracechurch-street, Saint Clement's-lane, Nicholas-lane, and Abchurch-lane at the same time, destroying all in its course. The whole of Lombard-street was choked up with the ruins and rubbish of demolished houses, through which thousands of persons were toiling to carry off goods, either for the purpose of assistance or of plunder. The king was at the west end of the street, near the church of Saint Mary Woolnoth, and the fearful havoc and destruction going forward drew tears from his eyes. A scene of greater confusion cannot be imagined. Leonard was in the midst of it, and careless of his own safety, toiled amid the tumbling fragments of the houses to rescue some article of value for its unfortunate owner. While he was thus employed, he observed a man leap out of a window of a partly-demolished house, disclosing in the action that he had a casket concealed under his cloak.

A second glance showed him that this individual was Pillichody, and satisfied that he had been plundering the house, he instantly seized him. The bully struggled violently, but at last, dropping the casket, made his escape, vowing to be revenged. Leonard laughed at his threats, and the next moment had the satisfaction of restoring the casket to its rightful owner, an old merchant who issued from the house, and who, after thanking him, told him it contained jewels of immense value.

Not half an hour after this, the flames poured upon Lombard-street from the four avenues before mentioned, and the whole neighbourhood was on fire. With inconceivable rapidity, they then ran up Birchin-lane, and reaching Cornhill, spread to the right and left in that great thoroughfare. The conflagration had now reached the highest point of the city, and presented the grandest and most terrific aspect it had yet assumed from the river. Thus viewed, it appeared, as Pepys describes it, " as an entire arch of fire from the Three Cranes to the other side of the bridge, and in a bow up the hill, for an arch of above a mile long; *it made me weep to see it.*" Vincent also likens its appearance at this juncture to that of a bow. " A dreadful bow it was," writes this eloquent Nonconformist preacher, " such as mine eyes have never before seen; a bow which had God's arrow in it with a flaming point; a shining bow, not like that in the cloud which brings water with it, and withal signifieth God's covenant not to destroy

the world any more with water, but a bow having fire in it,
and signifying God's anger, and his intention to destroy
London with fire."

As the day drew to a close, and it became darker, the
spectacle increased in terror and sublimity. The tall black
towers of the churches assumed ghastly forms, and to some
eyes appeared like infernal spirits plunging in a lake of
flame, while even to the most reckless the conflagration
seemed to present a picture of the terrors of the Last Day.

Never before had such a night as that which ensued
fallen upon London. None of its inhabitants thought of
retiring to rest, or if they sought repose after the excessive
fatigue they had undergone, it was only in such manner as
would best enable them to rise and renew their exertions
to check the flames, which were continued throughout the
night, but wholly without success. The conflagration appeared to proceed at the same appalling rapidity. Halls,
towers, churches, public and private buildings, were burning to the number of more than ten thousand, while clouds
of smoke covered the vast expanse of more than fifty miles.
Travellers approaching London from the north-east were
enveloped in it ten miles off. and the fiery reflection in the
sky could be discerned at an equal distance. The " hideous
storm," as Evelyn terms the fearful and astounding noise
produced by the roaring of the flames and the falling of
the numerous fabrics, continued without intermission
during the whole of that fatal night.

CHAPTER VI

How the Grocer's House was burnt

IT was full ten o'clock before Leonard could obtain permission to quit the king's party, and he immediately hurried
to Wood-street. He had scarcely entered it, when the cry
of " Fire ! " smote his ears, and rushing forward in an
agony of apprehension. he beheld Mr. Bloundel's dwelling
in flames. A large crowd was collected before the burning

habitation, keeping guard over a vast heap of goods and furniture that had been removed from it.

So much beloved was Mr. Bloundel, and in such high estimation was his character held, that all his neighbours, on learning that his house was on fire, flew to his assistance, and bestirred themselves so actively, that in an extraordinary short space of time they had emptied the house of every article of value, and placed it out of danger in the street. In vain the grocer urged them to desist: his entreaties were disregarded by his zealous friends; and when he told them they were profaning the Sabbath, they replied that the responsibility of their conduct would rest entirely on themselves, and they hoped they might never have anything worse to answer for. In spite of his disapproval of what was done, the grocer could not but be sensibly touched by their devotion, and as to his wife, she said, with tears in her eyes, that "it was almost worth while having a fire to prove what good friends they had."

It was at this juncture that Leonard arrived. Way was instantly made for him, and leaping over the piles of chests and goods that blocked up the thoroughfare, he flew to Mr. Bloundel, who was standing in front of his flaming habitation with as calm and unmoved an expression of countenance as if nothing was happening, and presently ascertained from him in what manner the fire had originated.

It appeared that while the whole of the family were assembled at prayers, in the room ordinarily used for that purpose, they were alarmed at supper by a strong smell of smoke, which seemed to arise from the lower part of the house, and that as soon as their devotions were ended, for Mr. Bloundel would not allow them to stir before, Stephen and Blaize had proceeded to ascertain the cause, and on going down to the kitchen, found a dense smoke issuing from the adjoining cellar, the door of which stood ajar. Hearing a noise in the yard, they darted up the back steps, communicating with the cellar, and discovered a man trying to make his escape over the wall by a rope-ladder. Stephen instantly seized him, and the man drawing his sword, tried to free himself from his captor. In the struggle, he dropped a pistol, which Blaize snatching up, discharged with fatal effect against the wretch, who, on examination, proved to be Pillichody.

Efforts were made to check the fire, but in vain. The villain had accomplished his diabolical purpose too well. Acquainted with the premises, and with the habits of the family, he had got into the yard by means of a rope-ladder, and hiding himself till the servants were summoned to prayers, stole into the cellar, and placing a fire-ball amid a heap of fagots and coals, and near several large casks of oil, and other inflammable matters, struck a light, and set fire to it.

" I shall ever reproach myself that I was away when this calamity occurred," observed Leonard, as the grocer brought his relation to an end.

" Then you will do so without reason," replied Mr. Bloundel, " for you could have rendered no assistance, and you see my good neighbours have taken the matter entirely out of my hands."

"Whither do you intend removing, sir?" rejoined Leonard. " If I might suggest, I would advise you to go to Farmer Wingfield's at Kensal-green."

" You have anticipated my intention," replied the grocer; " but we must now obtain some vehicles to transport these goods thither."

" Be that my part," replied Leonard. And in a short space of time he had procured half-a-dozen large carts, into which the whole of the goods were speedily packed, and a coach having been likewise fetched by Blaize, Mrs. Bloundel and the three younger children, together with old Josyna and Patience, were placed in it.

" I hope your mother has taken care of her money," whispered the latter to the porter, as he assisted her into the vehicle.

" Never mind whether she has or not," rejoined Blaize, in the same tone; " we sha'n't want it. I am now as rich as my master,—perhaps richer. On stripping that rascal Pillichody, I found a large bag of gold, besides several caskets of jewels, upon him, all of which I consider lawful spoil, as he fell by my hand."

" To be sure," rejoined Patience. " I dare say he did not come very honestly by the treasures, but you can't help that, you know."

Blaize made no reply, but pushing her into the coach, shut the door.

All being now in readiness, directions were given to the drivers of the carts whither to proceed, and they were put in motion. At this moment the grocer's firmness deserted him. Gazing at the old habitation, which was now wrapped in a sheet of flame, he cried, in a voice broken with emotion, " In that house I have dwelt nearly thirty years—in that house all my children were born—in that house I found a safe refuge from the devouring pestilence. It is hard to quit it thus."

Controlling his emotion, however, the next moment, he turned away. But his feelings were destined to another trial. His neighbours flocked round him to bid him farewell, in tones of such sympathy and regard, that his constancy again deserted him.

" Thank you, thank you," he cried, pressing in turn each hand that was offered him. " Your kindness will never be effaced from my memory. God bless you all, and may he watch over you and protect you ! " And with these words he broke from them.

So great was the crowd and confusion in Cheapside, that nearly two hours elapsed before they reached Newgate ; and indeed, if it had not been for the interference of the Earl of Rochester, they would not, in all probability, have got out of the city at all. The earl was stationed near the Old 'Change, at the entrance to Saint Paul's churchyard, and learning their distress, ordered a party of the guard by whom he was attended to force a passage for them. Both Mr. Bloundel and Leonard would have declined this assistance if they had had the power of doing so, but there was no help in the present case.

They encountered no further difficulties, but were necessarily compelled to proceed at a slow pace, and did not reach Paddington for nearly two hours, being frequently stopped by persons eagerly asking as to the progress of the fire. One circumstance struck the whole party as remarkable. Such was the tremendous glare of the conflagration, that even at this distance the fire seemed close beside them, and if they had not known the contrary, they would have thought it could not be further off than Saint Giles's. The whole eastern sky in that direction seemed on fire, and glowed through the clouds of yellow smoke with which the air was filled with fearful splendour. After halting for a short time at the Wheat Sheaf, which they found open, —for, indeed, no house was closed that night,—to obtain some refreshment, and allay the intolerable thirst by which they were tormented, the party pursued their journey along the Harrow road, and in due time approached Wingfield's residence.

The honest farmer, who, with his wife and two of his men, was standing in a field at the top of the hill, gazing at the conflagration, hearing the noise occasioned by the carts, ran to the road-side to see what was coming, and encountered Mr. Bloundel and Leonard, who had walked up the ascent a little more quickly than the others.

" I have been thinking of you," he said, after a cordial greeting had passed between them, " and wondering what would become of you in this dreadful fire. Nay, I had just told my good dame I should go and look after you, and see whether I could be of any service to you. Well, I should be better pleased to see you in any way but this, though you could not be welcomer. I have room in the barn and outhouses for all you have brought, and hope and trust you have not lost much."

" I have lost nothing except the old house," replied the grocer, heaving a sigh.

" Another will soon be built," rejoined Wingfield, " and till that is done you shall not quit mine."

The coach having by this time arrived, Wingfield hastened towards it, and assisted its occupants to alight. Mrs. Bloundel was warmly welcomed by Dame Wingfield, and being taken with her children to the house, was truly happy to find herself under the shelter of its hospitable roof. The rest of the party, assisted by Wingfield and his men, exerting themselves to the utmost, the carts were speedily unloaded, and the goods deposited in the barns and outhouses. This done, the drivers were liberally re-warded for their trouble by Mr. Bloundel, and after drain-ing several large jugs of ale brought them by the farmer, made the best of their way back, certain of obtaining further employment during the night.

Fatigued as he was, Leonard, before retiring to rest, could not help lingering on the brow of the hill to gaze at the burning city. The same effect was observable here as at Paddington, and the conflagration appeared little more than a mile off. The whole heavens seemed on fire, and a distant roar was heard like the rush of a high wind through a mighty forest. Westminster Abbey and Saint Paul's could be distinctly seen in black relief against the sheet of flame, together with innumerable towers, spires, and other buildings, the whole constituting a picture unsur-passed for terrific grandeur since the world began, and only to be equalled by its final destruction.

Having gazed at the conflagration for some time, and fancied that he could even at this distance discern the fear-ful progress it made, Leonard retired to the barn, and throwing himself upon a heap of straw, instantly fell asleep. He was awakened the next morning by Farmer Wingfield, who came to tell him breakfast was ready, and having per-formed his ablutions, they adjourned to the house. Finding Mr. Bloundel comfortably established in his new quarters, Leonard proposed as soon as breakfast was over to proceed to town, and Wingfield volunteered to accompany him. Blaize, also, having placed his treasures, except a few pieces of gold, in the custody of Patience, begged to make one of the party, and his request being acceded to, the trio set out on foot, and gleaning fresh particulars of the fearful progress of the fire, as they advanced, passed along Oxford-road, and crossing Holborn-bridge, on the western side of which they were now demolishing the houses, mounted Snow-hill, and passed through the portal of Newgate.

Here they learned that the whole of Wood-street was consumed, that the fire had spread eastward as far as Gutter-lane, and that Saint Michael's church, adjoining Wood-street, Goldsmiths' Hall, and the church of Saint John Zachary were in flames. They were also told that the greater part of Cheapside was on fire, and wholly impassable —while the destructive element was invading at one and the same time Guildhall and the Royal Exchange. They furthermore learnt that the conflagration had spread fearfully along the side of the river, had passed Queenhithe, consuming all the wharves and warehouses in its way, and having just destroyed Paul's-wharf, was at that time assailing Baynard's-castle. This intelligence determined them not to attempt to proceed further into the city, which they saw was wholly impracticable; and they accordingly turned down Ivy-lane, and approached the cathedral with the intention, if possible, of ascending the central tower. They found a swarm of booksellers' porters and assistants at the northern entrance, engaged in transporting immense bales of books and paper to the vaults in Saint Faith's, where it was supposed the stock would be in safety, permission to that effect having been obtained from the dean and chapter.

Forcing their way through this crowd, Leonard and his companions crossed the transept, and proceeded towards the door of the spiral staircase leading to the central tower. It was open, and they passed through it. On reaching the summit of the tower, which they found occupied by some dozen or twenty persons, a spectacle that far exceeded the utmost stretch of their imaginations burst upon them. Through clouds of tawny smoke scarcely distinguishable from flame, so thickly were they charged with sparks and fire-flakes, they beheld a line of fire spreading along Cheapside and Cornhill, as far as the Royal Exchange, which was now in flames, and branching upwards in another line through Lawrence-lane to Guildhall, which was likewise burning. Nearer to them, on the north, the fire kindled by the wretched Pillichody, who only, perhaps, anticipated the work of destruction by a few hours, had, as they had heard, proceeded to Goldsmiths' Hall, and was rapidly advancing down Saint Anne's-lane to Aldersgate. But it was on the right, and to the south-east, that the conflagration assumed its most terrific aspect. There, from Bow church to the river-side, beyond the bridge as far as Billingsgate, and from thence up Mincing-lane, crossing

Fenchurch-street and Lime-street to Gracechurch and Cornhill, describing a space of more than two miles in length and one in depth, every habitation was on fire. The appearance of this bed of flame was like an ocean of fire agitated by a tempest, in which a number of barks were struggling, some of them being each moment ingulphed. The stunning and unearthly roar of the flames aided this appearance, which was further heightened by the enormous billows of flame that ever and anon rolled tumultuously onward as they were caught by some gust of wind of more than usual violence. The spire of the churches looked like the spears of " tall ammirals," that had foundered, while the blackening ruins of the halls and larger buildings well represented the ribs and beams of mighty hulks.

Leaving Leonard and his companions to the contemplation of this tremendous spectacle, we shall proceed to take a nearer view of its ravages.

Every effort had been used to preserve the Royal Exchange by the city authorities, and by the engineers headed by the king in person. All the buildings in its vicinity were demolished. But in vain. The irresistible and unrelenting foe drove the defenders back as before, seized upon their barricades, and used them, like a skilful besieger, against the fortress they sought to protect. Solomon Eagle, who was mounted upon a heap of ruins, witnessed this scene of destruction, and uttered a laugh of exultation as the flames seized upon their prey.

" I told you," he cried, " that the extortioners and usurers who resorted to that building, and made gold their god, would be driven forth, and their temple destroyed. And my words have come to pass. It burns—it burns—and so shall they, if they turn not from their ways."

Hearing this wild speech, and beholding the extraordinary figure of the enthusiast, whose scorched locks and smoke-begrimed limbs gave him almost the appearance of an infernal spirit, the king inquired with some trepidation from his attendants who, or what he was, and being informed, ordered them to seize him. But the enthusiast set their attempts at nought. Springing with wonderful agility

S

from fragment to fragment of the ruins, and continuing his
vociferations, he at last plunged through the flame into the
Exchange itself, rendering further pursuit, of course, impossible, unless those who desired to capture him were determined to share his fate, which now seemed inevitable.
To the astonishment of all, however, he appeared a few
minutes afterwards on the roof of the blazing pile, and
continued his denunciations till driven away by the flames.
He seemed, indeed, to bear a charmed life, for it was
rumoured—though the report was scarcely credited—that
he had escaped from the burning building, and made good
his retreat to Saint Paul's. Soon after this, the Exchange
was one mass of flame. Having gained an entrance to the
galleries, the fire ran round them with inconceivable swiftness, as was the case in the conflagration of this later
structure, and filling every chamber, gushed out of the
windows, and poured down upon the courts and walks
below. Fearful and prodigious was the ruin that ensued.
The stone walls cracked with the intense heat—tottered and
fell—the pillars shivered and broke asunder, the statues
dropped from their niches, and were destroyed, one only
surviving the wreck—that of the illustrious founder, Sir
Thomas Gresham.

Deploring the fate of the Royal Exchange, the king and
his attendants proceeded to Guildhall. But here they were
too late, nor could they even rescue a tithe of the plate and
valuables lodged within it for security. The effects of the
fire as displayed in this structure, were singularly grand and
surprising. The greater part of the ancient fabric being
composed of oak of the hardest kind, it emitted little flame,
but became after a time red-hot, and remained in this glowing state till night, when it resembled, as an eye-witness
describes, " a mighty palace of gold, or a great building of
burnished brass."

The greatest fury of the conflagration was displayed at
the Poultry, where five distinct fires met, and united their
forces,—one which came roaring down Cornhill from the
Royal Exchange—a second down Threadneedle-street—a
third up Walbrook—a fourth along Bucklersbury, and the
fifth that marched against the wind up Cheapside, all these

uniting, as at a focus, a whirl of flame, an intensity of heat, and a thundering roar were produced, such as were nowhere else experienced.

To return to the party on the central tower of the cathedral. Stunned and half stifled by the roar and smoke, Leonard and his companions descended from their lofty post, and returned to the body of the fane. They were about to issue forth, when Leonard, glancing down the northern aisle, perceived the Earl of Rochester and Lord Argentine standing together at the lower end of it. Their gestures showed that it was not an amicable meeting, and mindful of what had passed at Whitehall, Leonard resolved to abide the result. Presently, he saw Lord Argentine turn sharply round, and strike his companion in the face with his glove. The clash of swords instantly succeeded, and Leonard and Wingfield started forward to separate the combatants. Blaize followed, but more cautiously, contenting himself with screaming at the top of his voice, " Murder ! murder ! sacrilege ! a duel ! a duel ! "

Wingfield was the first to arrive at the scene of strife, but just as he reached the combatants, who were too much blinded by passion to notice his approach, Lord Argentine struck his adversary's weapon from his grasp, and would have followed up the advantage if the farmer had not withheld his arm. Enraged at the interference, Argentine turned his fury against the newcomer, and strove to use his sword against him,—but in the terrible struggle that ensued, and at the close of which they fell together, the weapon, as if directed by the hand of an avenging fate, passed through his own breast, inflicting a mortal wound.

" Susan Wingfield is avenged ! " said the farmer, as he arose, drenched in the blood of his opponent.

" Susan Wingfield ! " exclaimed the wounded man,— " what was she to you ? "

" Much," said the farmer, " She was my daughter."

" Ah ! " exclaimed Argentine, with an expression of unutterable anguish. " Let me have your forgiveness," he groaned.

" You have it," replied Wingfield, kneeling beside him, " and may God pardon us both, you for the wrong you did my daughter, me for being the cause of your death. But I trust you are not mortally hurt ? "

" I have not many minutes to live," replied Argentine. " But is not that Leonard Holt ? "

" It is," said Rochester, stepping forward.

" I can then do one rightful act before I die," he said, raising himself on one hand, and holding the other forcibly to his side, so as to stanch in some degree the effusion of blood. "Leonard Holt," he continued, "my sister Isabella loves you—deeply, devotedly. I have tried to conquer the passion, but in vain. You have my consent to wed her."

" I am a witness to your words, my lord," said Rochester, " and I call upon all present to be so likewise."

" Rochester, you were once my friend," groaned Argentine, " and may yet be a friend to the dead. Remember the king sells titles. Teach this young man how to purchase one. My sister must not wed one of his degree."

" Make yourself easy on that score," replied Rochester ; " he has already sufficient claim upon the king. He saved his life yesterday."

" He will trust to a broken reed if he trusts to Charles's gratitude," replied Argentine. " Buy the title—*buy* it, I say. My sister left me yesterday. I visited my anger on her head, and she fled. I believe she took refuge with Doctor Hodges, but I am sure he can tell you where she is. One thing more," continued the dying man, fixing his glazing eyes on Leonard. " Go to Newgate—to—to a prisoner there—an incendiary—and obtain a document of him. Tell him, with my dying breath I charged you to do this. It will enable you to act as I have directed. Promise me you will go. Promise me you will fulfil my injunctions."

" I do," replied Leonard.

" Enough," rejoined Argentine. " May you be happy with Isabella." And removing his hand from his side, a copious effusion of blood followed, and sinking backwards, he expired.

CHAPTER VII

The Burning of Saint Paul's

SEVERAL other persons having by this time come up, the body of Lord Argentine was conveyed to Bishop Kempe's chapel, and left there till a fitting season should arrive for its removal. Confounded by the tragical event that had taken place, Leonard remained with his eyes fixed upon the blood-stained pavement, until he was roused by an arm which gently drew him away, while the voice of the Earl of Rochester breathed in his ear, " This is a sad occurrence, Leonard, and yet it is most fortunate for you, for it removes the only obstacle to your union with the Lady Isabella. You see how fleeting life is, and how easily we may be deprived of it. I tried to reason Lord Argentine into calmness, but nothing would satisfy him except my blood, and there he lies, though not by my hand. Let his fate be a lesson to us, and teach us to live in charity with each other. I have wronged you—deeply wronged you— but I will make all the atonement in my power, and let me think I am forgiven."

The blood rushed tumultuously to Leonard's heart, as he listened to what the earl said, but overcoming his feelings of aversion by a powerful effort, he took the proffered hand.

" I do forgive you, my lord," he said.

" Those words have removed a heavy weight from my soul," replied Rochester, " and if Death should trip up my heels as suddenly as he did his who perished on this spot, I shall be better prepared to meet him. And now let me advise you to repair to Newgate without delay, and see the wretched man, and obtain the document from him. The fire will reach the goal ere long, and the prisoners must of necessity be removed. Amid the confusion his escape might be easily accomplished."

" Recollect, my lord, that the direful conflagration now

prevailing without is owing to him," replied Leonard. "I will never accessory to his escape."

"And yet his death by the public executioner," urged Rochester. "Think of its effect on his daughter."

"Justice must take its course," rejoined Leonard. "I would not aid him to escape if he were my own father."

"In that case, nothing more is to be said," replied Rochester. "But at all events see him as quickly as you can. I would accompany you, but my duty detains me here. When you return from your errand you will find me at my post near the entrance of the churchyard in front of Saint Michael's le Quern—that is, if I am not beaten from it. Having seen the father, your next business must be to seek out the daughter, and remove her from this dangerous neighbourhood. You have heard where she is to be found."

Upon this, they separated,—Leonard and his companions quitting the cathedral by the great western entrance, and proceeding towards Paul's-alley, and the earl betaking himself to the north-east corner of the churchyard. The former got as far as Ivy-lane, but found it wholly impassable, in consequence of the goods and furniture with which it was blocked up. They were, therefore, obliged to return to the precincts of the cathedral, where Blaize, who was greatly terrified by what he had seen, expressed his determination of quitting them, and hurried back to the sacred pile. Leonard and the farmer next essayed to get up Ave-Maria-lane, but finding that also impassable, they made for Ludgate, and after a long delay and severe struggle, got through the portal. The Old Bailey was entirely filled with persons removing their goods, and they were here informed, to their great dismay, that the conflagration had already reached Newgate Market, which was burning with the greatest fury, and was at that moment seizing upon the gaol. No one, however, in answer to Leonard's inquiries, could tell him what had become of the prisoners.

"I suppose they have left them to burn," observed a bystander, who heard the question, with a malicious look; "and it is the best way of getting rid of them."

Paying no attention to the remark, nor the brutal laugh accompanying it, Leonard, assisted by Wingfield, fought

his way through the crowd till he reached the prison. The
flames were bursting through its grated windows, and both
wings, as well as the massive gate connecting them, were
on fire. Regardless of the risk he ran, Leonard forced his
way to the lodge door, where two turnkeys were standing,
removing their goods.

" What has become of the prisoners ? " he asked.

" The debtors are set free," replied the turnkey addressed, " and all but one or two of the common felons
are removed."

" And where are those poor creatures ? " cried Leonard,
horror-stricken.

" In the Stone Hold," replied the turnkey.

" And have you left them to perish there ? " demanded
Leonard.

" We couldn't help it," rejoined the turnkey. " It would
have been risking our lives to venture near them. One is
a murderer taken in the fact ; and the other is quite as bad,
for he set the city on fire ; so it's right and fair he should
perish by his own contrivance."

" Where does the Stone Hold lie ? " cried Leonard, in a
tone that startled the turnkey. " I must get these prisoners
out."

" You can't, I tell you," rejoined the turnkey, doggedly.
" They're burnt to a cinder by this time."

" Give me your keys, and show me the way to the cell,"
cried Leonard, authoritatively. " I will at least attempt to
save them."

" Well, if you're determined to put an end to yourself,
you may try," replied the turnkey ; " but I've warned you
as to what you may expect. This way," he added, opening
a door, from which a thick volume of smoke issued ; " if
any of 'em's alive you'll soon know by the cries."

And, as if in answer to his remark, a most terrific shriek
at that moment burst on their ears.

" Here are the keys," cried the turnkey, delivering them
to Leonard. " You are not going too ? " he added, as
Wingfield pushed past him. " A couple of madmen ! I
shouldn't wonder if they were incendiaries."

Directed by the cries, Leonard pressed forward through

the blinding and stifling smoke. After proceeding about twenty yards, he arrived at a cross passage where the smoke was not quite so dense, as it found an escape through a small grated aperture in the wall. And here a horrible sight was presented to him. At the further extremity of this passage was a small cell, from which the cries he had heard issued. Not far from it the stone roof had fallen in, and from the chasm thus caused the flames were pouring into the passage.. Regardless of the risk he ran, Leonard dashed forward, and reaching the cell, beheld Grant, still living, but in such a dreadful state, that it was evident his sufferings must soon be ended. His hair and beard were singed close to his head and face, and his flesh was blistered, blackened, and scorched to the bone. On seeing Leonard, he uttered a hoarse cry, and attempted to speak, but the words rattled in his throat. He then staggered forward, and to Leonard's inexpressible horror, thrust his arms through the bars of the cage, which were literally red-hot. Seeing he had something in one hand, though he could not unclose his fingers, Leonard took it from him, and the wretched man fell backwards. At this moment a loud crack was heard in the wall behind. Several ponderous stones dropped from their places, admitting a volume of flame that filled the whole cell, and disclosing another body on the floor, near which lay that of Grant. Horrified by the spectacle, Leonard staggered off, and catching Wingfield's arm, sought to retrace his steps. This was no easy matter, the smoke being so dense that they could not see a foot before them, and were obliged to feel their way along the wall. On arriving at the cross passage Wingfield would fain have turned off to the right, but Leonard drew him forcibly in the opposite direction; and most fortunate was it that he did so, or the worthy farmer would inevitably have perished. At last they reached the lodge, and sank down on a bench from exhaustion.

"So, my masters," observed the turnkey, with a grim smile, "you were not able to rescue them, I perceive?" But receiving no answer, he added, "Well, and what did you see?"

"A sight that would have moved even your stony heart

to compassion," returned Leonard, getting up and quitting the lodge. Followed by Wingfield, and scarcely knowing where he was going, he forced his way through the crowd, and dashing down Snow-hill, did not stop till he reached Holborn-conduit, where, seizing a leathern bucket, he filled it with water, and plunged his head into it. Refreshed by the immersion, he now glanced at the document committed to him by Grant. It was a piece of parchment, and showed by its shrivelled and scorched appearance the agony which its late possessor must have endured. Leonard did not open it, but thrust it with a shudder into his doublet.

Meditating on the strange and terrible events that had just occurred, Leonard's thoughts involuntarily wandered to the Lady Isabella, whose image appeared to him like a bright star shining on troubled waters, and for the first time venturing to indulge in a hope that she might indeed be his, he determined immediately to proceed in search of her.

It was now high noon, but the midday sun was scarcely visible, or visible at all; as it struggled through the masses of yellow vapour it looked red as blood. Bands of workmen were demolishing houses on the western side of Fleet-ditch, and casting the rubbish into the muddy sluice before them, by which means it was confidently but vainly hoped that the progress of the fire would be checked. Shaping their course along the opposite side of the ditch, and crossing to Fleet-bridge, Leonard and his companion passed through Salisbury-court to Whitefriars, and taking a boat, directed the waterman to land them at Puddle-dock. The river was still covered with craft of every description laden with goods, and Baynard's-castle, an embattled stone built at the beginning of the fifteenth century on the site of another castle as old as the Conquest, being now wrapped in flames from foundation to turret, offered a magnificent spectacle.

From this point the four ascents leading to the cathedral, namely, Addle-hill, Saint Bennet's-hill, Saint Peter's-hill, and Lambert-hill, with all their throng of habitations, were burning—the black lines of ruined walls standing in bold relief against the white sheet of flame.

Billows of fire rolled upwards every moment towards Saint
Paul's and threatened it with destruction.

Landing at the appointed place, Leonard and his companion ascended Saint Andrew's-hill, and, proceeding along
Carter-lane, soon gained the precincts of the cathedral.
Here the whole mass of habitations on the summit of Saint
Bennet's-hill, extending from the eastern end of Carter-
lane to Distaff-lane, was on fire, and the flames were dashed
by the fierce wind against the south-east corner of the
cathedral. A large crowd was collected at this point, and
great efforts were made to save the venerable pile, but
Leonard saw that its destruction was inevitable. Forcing
a way through the throng with his companion, they reached
Doctor Hodges' residence at the corner of Watling-street,
and Leonard, without waiting to knock, tried the door,
which yielded to his touch. The habitation was empty, and
from the various articles scattered about, it was evident
its inmates must have fled with the greatest precipitation.
Alarmed at this discovery, Leonard rushed forth with
Wingfield, and sought to ascertain from the crowd without
whither Doctor Hodges was gone, but could learn nothing
more than that he had departed with his whole household
a few hours before. At last it occurred to him that he
might obtain some information from the Earl of Rochester,
and he was about to cross to the other side of the churchyard, when he was arrested by a simultaneous cry of horror
from the assemblage. Looking upwards, for there he saw
the general gaze directed, he perceived that the scaffolding
around the roof and tower of the cathedral had kindled,
and was enveloping the whole upper part of the fabric in
a network of fire. Flames were likewise bursting from the
belfry, and from the lofty pointed windows below it, flicker-
ing and playing round the hoary buttresses, and disturbing
the numerous jackdaws that built in their time-worn
crevices, and now flew screaming forth. As Leonard gazed
at the summit of the tower, he discerned through the circ-
ling eddies of smoke that enveloped it the figure of Solomon
Eagle standing on the top of the battlements and waving
his staff, and almost fancied he could hear his voice.
After remaining in this perilous situation for some minutes,

as if to raise anxiety for his safety to the highest pitch, the
enthusiast sprang upon a portion of the scaffolding that
was only partly consumed, and descended from pole to
pole, regardless whether burning or not, with marvellous
swiftness, and apparently without injury. Alighting on
the roof, he speeded to the eastern extremity of the
fane, and there commenced his exhortations to the crowd
below.

It now became evident also, from the strange roaring
noise proceeding from the tower, that the flames were descending the spiral staircase, and forcing their way through
some secret doors or passages to the roof. Determined to
take one last survey of the interior of the cathedral before
its destruction, which he now saw was inevitable, Leonard
motioned to Wingfield, and forcing his way through the
crowd which was now considerably thinned, entered the
southern door. He had scarcely gained the middle of the
transept when the door opened behind him, and two persons, whom, even in the brief glimpse he caught of them,
he knew to be Chowles and Judith, darted towards the
steps leading to Saint Faith's. They appeared to be carrying a large chest, but Leonard was too much interested in
what was occurring to pay much attention to them. There
were but few persons besides himself and his companion
within the cathedral, and these few were chiefly booksellers' porters, who were hurrying out of Saint Faith's in
the utmost trepidation. By-and-by, these were gone, and
they were alone,—alone within that vast structure, and at
such a moment. Their situation, though perilous, was one
that awakened thrilling and sublime emotions. The cries
of the multitude, coupled with the roaring of the conflagration, resounded from without, while the fierce glare of the
flames lighted up the painted windows at the head of the
choir with unwonted splendour. Overhead was heard a
hollow rumbling noise like that of distant thunder, which
continued for a short time, while fluid streams of smoke
crept through the mighty rafters of the roof, and gradually
filled the whole interior of the fabric with vapour. Suddenly
a tremendous cracking was heard, as if the whole pile were
tumbling in pieces. So appalling was this sound, that

Leonard and his companions would have fled, but they were completely transfixed by terror.

While they were in this state, the flames, which had long been burning in secret, burst through the roof at the other end of the choir, and instantaneously spread over its whole expanse. At this juncture, a cry of wild exultation was heard in the great northern gallery, and looking up, Leonard beheld Solomon Eagle, hurrying with lightning swiftness around it; and shouting in tones of exultation, " My words have come to pass—it burns—it burns—and will be utterly consumed ! "

The vociferations of the enthusiast were answered by a piercing cry from below, proceeding from Blaize, who at that moment rushed from the entrance of Saint Faith's. On seeing the porter, Leonard shouted to him, and the poor fellow hurried towards him. At this juncture, a strange hissing sound was heard, as if a heavy shower of rain was descending upon the roof, and through the yawning gap over the choir there poured a stream of molten lead of silvery brightness. Nothing can be conceived more beautiful than this shining yet terrible cascade, which descended with momentarily increasing fury, sparkling, flashing, hissing, and consuming all before it. All the elaborately carved woodwork and stalls upon which it fell were presently in flames. Leonard and his companions now turned to fly, but they had scarcely moved a few paces when another fiery cascade burst through the roof near the great western entrance, for which they were making, flooding the aisles and plashing against the massive columns. At the same moment, too, a third stream began to fall over the northern transept, not far from where Blaize stood, and a few drops of the burning metal reaching him, caused him to utter the most fearful outcries. Seriously alarmed, Leonard and Wingfield now rushed to one of the monuments in the northern aisle, and hastily clambering it, reached a window, which they burst open. Blaize followed them, but not without receiving a few accidental plashes from the fiery torrents, which elicited from him the most astounding yells. Having helped him to climb the monument, Leonard pushed him through the window after Wingfield, and then cast his eye round the building before he himself descended. The sight was magnificent in the extreme. From the flaming roof three silvery cascades descended. The choir was in flame, and a glowing stream like lava was spreading over the floor, and slowly trickling down the steps leading to the body of the church. The transepts and the greater part of the nave were similarly flooded. Above the roar of the flames and the hissing plash of the descending torrents, was heard the wild laughter of Solomon Eagle. Perceiving him in one of the arcades of the southern gallery, Leonard shouted to him to descend and make good his escape while there was yet time, adding that in a few moments it would be too late.

"I shall never quit it more," rejoined the enthusiast, in a voice of thunder, "but shall perish with the fire I have kindled. No monarch on earth ever lighted a nobler funeral pyre."

And as Leonard passed through the window, he disappeared along the gallery. Breaking through the crowd collected round Wingfield and Blaize, and calling to them to follow him, Leonard made his way to the north-east of the churchyard, where he found a large assemblage of persons, in the midst of which were the king, the Duke of York, Rochester, Arlington, and many others. As Leonard advanced, Charles discerned him amid the crowd, and motioned him to come forward. A passage was then cleared for him, through which Wingfield and Blaize, who kept close beside him, were permitted to pass.

"I am glad to find no harm has happened to you, friend," said Charles, as he approached. "Rochester informed me you were gone to Newgate, and as the gaol had been burnt down, I feared you might have met with the same mishap. I now regret that I did not adopt your plan, but it may not be yet too late."

"It is not too late to save a portion of your city, sire," replied Leonard; "but, alas! how much is gone!"

"It is so," replied the king, mournfully.

Further conversation was here interrupted by the sudden breaking out of the fire from the magnificent rose window of the cathedral, the effect of which, being extraordinarily

fine, attracted the monarch's attention. By this time
Solomon Eagle had again ascended the roof, and making
his way to the eastern extremity, clasped the great stone
cross that terminated it with his left hand, while with his
right he menaced the king and his party, uttering denunciations that were lost in the terrible roar prevailing around
him. The flames now raged with a fierceness wholly inconceivable, considering the material they had to work upon.
The molten lead poured down in torrents, and not merely
flooded the whole interior of the fabric, but ran down in
a wide and boiling stream almost as far as the Thames,
consuming everything in its way, and rendering the very
pavements red-hot. Every stone, spout, and gutter in the
sacred pile, of which there were some hundreds, added to
this fatal shower, and scattered destruction far and wide;
nor will this be wondered at when it is considered that the
quantity of lead thus melted covered a space of no less
than six acres. Having burned with incredible fury and
fierceness for some time, the whole roof of the sacred
structure fell in at once, with a crash heard at an amazing
distance. After an instant's pause, the flames burst forth
from every window in the fabric, producing such an intensity of heat, that the stone pinnacles, transom beams,
and mullions split and cracked with a sound like volleys
of artillery, shivering and flying in every direction. The
whole interior of the pile was now one vast sheet of flame,
which soared upwards, and consumed even the very stones.
Not a vestige of the reverend structure was left untouched,
—its bells—its plate—its woodwork—its monuments—its
mighty pillars—its galleries—its chapels—all, all were destroyed. The fire raged throughout all that night and the
next day, till it had consumed all but the mere shell, and
rendered the venerable cathedral, " one of the most ancient
pieces of piety in the Christian world," to use the words
of Evelyn, a heap of ruin and ashes.

CHAPTER VIII

How Leonard Rescued the Lady Isabella

THE course of events having been somewhat anticipated in the last chapter, it will now be necessary to return to an earlier stage in the destruction of the cathedral, namely, soon after the furious bursting forth of the flames from the great eastern windows. While Leonard, in common with the rest of the assemblage, was gazing at this magnificent spectacle, he heard a loud cry of distress behind him, and turning at the sound, beheld Doctor Hodges rush forth from an adjoining house, the upper part of which was on fire, almost in a state of distraction. An elderly man and woman, and two or three female servants, all of whom were crying as loud as himself, followed him. But their screams fell on indifferent ears, for the crowd had become by this time too much accustomed to such appeals to pay any particular attention to them. Leonard, however, instantly rushed towards the doctor, and anxiously inquired what was the matter; the latter was so bewildered that he did not recognise the voice of the speaker, but gazing up at the house with an indescribable anguish, cried, " Merciful God ! the flames have by this time reached her room—she will be burned—horror ! "

" Who will be burned ? " cried Leonard, seizing his arm, and gazing at him with a look of apprehension and anguish equal to his own—" Not the Lady Isabella ? "

" Yes, Isabella," replied Hodges, regarding the speaker, and for the first time perceiving by whom he was addressed. " Not a moment is to be lost if you would save her from a terrible death. She was left in a fainting state in one of the upper rooms by a female attendant, who deserted her mistress to save herself. The staircase is on fire, or I myself would have saved her."

" A ladder ! a ladder ! " cried Leonard.

" Here is one," cried Wingfield, pointing to one propped against an adjoining house.

And in another moment, by the combined efforts of the crowd, the ladder was brought and placed against the burning building.

" Which is the window ? " cried Leonard.

" That on the right, on the second floor," replied Hodges. " Gracious Heaven ! the flames are bursting from it."

But Leonard's foot was now on the ladder, and rushing up with inconceivable swiftness, he plunged through the window regardless of the flame. All those who witnessed this daring deed, regarded his destruction as certain, and even Hodges gave him up for lost. But the next moment he appeared at the window, bearing the fainting female form in his arms, and with extraordinary dexterity obtaining a firm footing and hold of the ladder, descended in safety. The shout that burst from such part of the assemblage as had witnessed this achievement, and its successful termination, attracted the king's attention, and he inquired the cause of the clamour.

" I will ascertain it for your Majesty," replied Rochester, and proceeding to the group, he learnt, to his great satisfaction, what had occurred.

Having gained this intelligence, he flew back to the king, and briefly explained the situation of the parties. Doctor Hodges, it appeared, had just removed to the house in question, which belonged to one of his patients, as a temporary asylum, and the Lady Isabella had accompanied him. She was in the upper part of the house when the fire broke out, and was so much terrified that she swooned away, in which condition her attendant left her ; nor was the latter so much to blame as might appear, for the stairs were burning at the time, and a moment's delay would have endangered her own safety.

" Fate, indeed, seems to have brought these young persons together," replied Charles, as he listened to Rochester's recital, who took this opportunity of acquainting him with Lord Argentine's dying injunctions, " and it would be a pity to separate them."

" I am sure your Majesty has no such intention," said Rochester.

" You will see," rejoined the monarch.

And as he spoke, he turned his horse's head, and moved towards the spot where Leonard was kneeling beside Isabella, and supporting her. Some restoratives having been applied by Doctor Hodges, she had regained her sensibility, and was murmuring her thanks to her deliverer.

" She has not lost her beauty, I perceive," cried Charles, gazing at her with admiration, and feeling something of his former passion revive within his breast.

" Your Majesty, I trust, will not mar their happiness," said Rochester, noticing the monarch's libertine look with uneasiness. " Remember, you owe your life to that young man."

" And I will pay the debt royally," replied Charles; " I will give him permission to marry her."

" Your Majesty's permission is scarcely needed," muttered Rochester.

" There you are wrong, my lord," replied the king. " She is now my ward, and I can dispose of her in marriage as I please; nor will I so dispose of her, except to her equal in rank."

" I discern your Majesty's gracious intentions," replied Rochester, gratefully inclining his head.

" I almost forget my deliverer's name," whispered Charles, with a smile, " but it is of no consequence, since he will so speedily change it."

" His name is Leonard Holt," replied Rochester, in the same tone.

" Ah !—true," returned the king. " What ho ! good master Leonard Holt," he added, addressing the young man, " commit the Lady Isabella Argentine to the care of our worthy friend Doctor Hodges for a moment, and stand up before me." His injunctions being complied with, he continued, " The Lady Isabella Argentine and I owe our lives to you, and we must both evince our gratitude—she by devoting that life, which, if I am not misinformed, she will be right willing to do, to you, and I by putting you in a position to unite yourself to her. The title of Argentine has been this day extinguished by most unhappy circumstances; I therefore confer the title on you, and here in this presence create you Baron Argentine, of Argentine, in Staffordshire. Your patent shall be made out with all convenient despatch, and with it you shall receive the hand of the sole representative of that ancient and noble house."

" Your Majesty overwhelms me," replied Leonard, falling on his knee, and pressing the king's hand, which was kindly extended towards him, to his lips. " I can scarcely persuade myself I am not in a dream."

" You will soon awaken to the sense of the joyful reality," returned the king. " Have I not now discharged my debt ? " he added to Rochester.

" Right royally, indeed, my liege," replied the earl, in a tone of unaffected emotion. " My lord," he added, grasping Leonard's hand, " I sincerely congratulate you on your newly-acquired dignities, nor less in the happiness that awaits you there."

" If I do not answer you fittingly, my lord," replied the new-made peer, " it is not because I do not feel your kindness. But my brain reels. Pray Heaven my senses may not desert me."

" You must not forget the document you obtained this morning, my lord," replied Rochester, endeavouring to divert his thoughts into a new channel. " The proper moment for consulting it may have arrived."

Lord Argentine, for we shall henceforth give him his title, thrust his hand into his doublet, and drew forth the parchment. He opened it, and endeavoured to read it, but a mist swam before his eyes.

" Let me look at it," said Rochester, taking it from him. " It is a deed of gift," he said, after glancing at it for a moment, " from the late Lord Argentine—I mean the elder baron—of a large estate in Yorkshire, which he possessed in right of his wife, to you, my lord, here described as Leonard Holt, provided you shall marry the Lady Isabella Argentine. Another piece of good fortune. Again and again, I congratulate you."

" And now," said Charles, " other and less pleasing matters claim our attention. Let the Lady Isabella be removed, under the charge of Doctor Hodges, to Whitehall, where apartments shall be provided for her at once, together with fitting attendants, and where she can remain till this terrible conflagration is over, which, I trust, soon will be, when I will no longer delay her happiness, but give her away in person. Chiffinch," he added to the chief page, " see all this carried into effect."

" I will, my liege, and right willingly," replied Chiffinch.

" I would send you with her, my lord," pursued Charles to Argentine, " but I have other duties for you to fulfil. The plan you proposed of demolishing the houses with gunpowder shall be immediately put into operation, under your own superintendence."

A chair was now brought, and Lady Isabella, after a tender parting with her lover, being placed within it, she was thus transported, under the charge of Hodges and Chiffinch, to Whitehall, where she arrived in safety, though not without having sustained some hindrance and inconvenience.

She had not been gone many minutes, when the conflagration of the cathedral assumed its most terrific character; the whole of the mighty roof falling in, and the flames soaring upwards, as before related. Up to this time, Solomon Eagle had maintained his position at the eastern end of the roof, and still grasped the stone cross. His situation now attracted universal attention, and it was evident he must speedily perish.

" Poor wretch ! " exclaimed the king, shuddering, " I fear there is no way of saving him."

" None whatever, my liege," replied Rochester, " nor do I believe he would consent to it if there was. But he is again menacing your Majesty."

As Rochester spoke, Solomon Eagle shook his arm menacingly at the royal party, raising it aloft, as if invoking the vengeance of Heaven. He then knelt down upon the sloping ridge of the roof, as if in prayer, and his figure, thus seen relieved against the mighty sheet of flame, might have been taken for an image of Saint John the Baptist carved in stone. Not an eye in the vast crowd below but was fixed on him. In a few moments, he rose again, and tossing his arms aloft, and shrieking, in a voice distinctly heard above the awful roar around him, the single word,

" *Resurgam!* " flung himself headlong into the flaming abyss. A simultaneous cry of horror rose from the whole assemblage on beholding this desperate action.

" The last exclamation of the poor wretch may apply to the cathedral as well as to himself," remarked the monarch, to a middle-aged personage, with a pleasing and highly intellectual countenance, standing near him : " for the old building shall rise again, like the phœnix from its fires, with renewed beauty, and under your superintendence, Doctor Christopher Wren."

The great architect bowed.

" I cannot hope to erect such another structure," he said, modestly; " but I will endeavour to design an edifice that shall not disgrace your Majesty's city."

" You must build me another city at the same time, Doctor Wren," sighed the king. " Ah ! " he added, " is not that Mr. Lilly, the almanack-maker, whom I see among the crowd ? "

" It is," replied Rochester.

" Bid him come to me," replied the king. And the order being obeyed, he said to the astrologer, " Well, Mr. Lilly your second prediction has come to pass. We have had the Plague, and now we have the Fire. You may thank my clemency that I do not order you to be cast into the flames, like the poor wretch who has just perished before our eyes, as a wizard and professor of the black art. How did you obtain information of these fatal events ? "

" By a careful study of the heavenly bodies, sire," replied Lilly, " and by long and patient calculations, which, if your Majesty or any of your attendants had had leisure or inclination to make, would have afforded you the same information. *I* make no pretence to the gift of prophecy, but this calamity was predicted in the last century."

" Indeed ! by whom ? " asked the king.

" By Michael Nostradamus," replied Lilly, " his prediction runs thus :—

La sang du juste à Londres fera faute
Bruslez par feu, le vingt et trois, les Six;

La Dame antique cherra de place haute.
De même secte plusieurs seront occis.*

And thus I venture to explain it. The ' blood of the just '
refers to the impious and execrable murder of your
Majesty's royal father of blessed memory. ' Three-and-
twenty and six ' gives the exact year of the calamity; and
it may likewise give us, as will be seen by computation
hereafter, the amount of habitations to be destroyed. The
' Ancient Dame ' undoubtedly refers to the venerable pile
now burning before us, which, as it stands in the most
eminent spot in the city, clearly ' falls from its high place.'
The expression ' of the same sect,' refers not to men, but
churches, of which a large number, I grieve to say it, are
already destroyed."

"The prophecy is a singular one," remarked Charles,
musingly, " and you have given it a plausible interpreta-
tion." And for some moments he appeared lost in reflection. Suddenly rousing himself, he took forth his tablets,
and hastily tracing a few lines upon a leaf, tore it out, and
delivered it with his signet ring to Lord Argentine. " Take
this, my lord," he said, " to Lord Craven. You will find
him at his post in Tower-street. A band of my attendants
shall go with you. Embark at the nearest stairs you can
—those at Blackfriars I should conceive the most accessible.
Bid the men row for their lives. As soon as you join Lord
Craven, commence operations. The Tower must be preserved at all hazards. Mark me !—at all hazards."

" I understand your Majesty," replied Argentine—
" your commands shall be implicitly obeyed. And if the
conflagration has not gone too far, I will answer with my
life that I preserve the fortress."

And he departed on his mission.

* The blood of the just shall be wanting in London,
Burnt by fire of three-and-twenty, the Six;
The ancient Dame shall fall from her high plrce,
Of the same sect many shall be killed.

CHAPTER IX

*What befel Chowles and Judith in the Vaults of Saint
Faith's*

HAVING now seen what occurred outside Saint Paul's we
shall proceed to the vaults beneath it. Chowles and Judith,
it has been mentioned, were descried by Leonard, just
before the outbreak of the fire, stealing into Saint Faith's,
and carrying a heavy chest between them. This chest contained some of the altar-plate, which they had pillaged
from the Convocation House. As they traversed the aisles
of Saint Faith's, which were now filled with books and
paper, they could distinctly hear the raging of the fire without, and Judith, who was far less intimidated than her companion, observed, " Let it roar on. It cannot injure us."
    " I am not so sure of that," replied Chowles, doubtfully,
" I wish we had taken our hoards elsewhere."
    " There is no use in wishing that now," rejoined Judith.
" And it would have been wholly impossible to get them
out of the city. But have no fear. The fire, I tell you, cannot reach us. It could as soon burn into the solid earth as
into this place."
    " It comforts me to hear you say so," replied Chowles.
" And when I think of those mighty stone floors above us,
I feel we are quite safe. No, no, it can never make its way
through them."
    Thus discoursing, they reached the charnel at the further
end of the church, where Chowles struck a light, and producing a flask of strong waters, took a copious draught
himself and handed the flask to Judith, who imitated his
example. Their courage being thus stimulated, they opened
the chest, and Chowles was so enraptured with its glittering
contents that he commenced capering round the vault.
Recalled to quietude by a stern reproof from Judith, he
opened a secret door in the wall, and pushed the chest into
a narrow passage beyond it. Fearful of being discovered
in their retreat, they took a basket of provisions and liquor

with them, and then closed the door. For some time, they proceeded along the passage, pushing the chest before them, until they came to a descent of a few steps, which brought them to a large vault, half-filled with bags of gold, chests of plate, caskets, and other plunder. At the further end of this vault was a strong wooden door. Pushing the chest into the middle of the chamber, Chowles seated himself upon it, and opening the basket of provisions, took out the bottle of spirits, and again had recourse to it.

"How comfortable and secure we feel in this quiet place," he said; "while all above us is burning. I declare I feel quite merry—ha! ha!" And he forced a harsh and discordant laugh.

"Give me the bottle," rejoined Judith, sternly, "and don't grin like a death's head. I don't like to see the frightful face you make."

"It's the first time you ever thought my face frightful," replied Chowles, "and I begin to think you are afraid."

"Afraid!" echoed Judith, forcing a derisive laugh in her turn; "afraid—of what?"

"Nay, I don't know," replied Chowles; "only I feel a little uncomfortable. What if we should not be able to breathe here? The very idea gives me a tightness across the chest."

"Silence," cried Judith, with a fierceness that effectually ensured obedience to her command.

Chowles again had recourse to the bottle, and deriving a false courage from it, as before, commenced skipping about the chamber in his usual fantastical manner. Judith did not attempt to check him, but remained with her chin resting upon her hand gazing at him.

"Do you remember the Dance of Death, Judith?" he cried, executing some of the wildest flourishes he had then performed, "and how I surprised the Earl of Rochester and his crew?"

"I do," replied Judith, "and I hope we may not soon have to perform that dance together in reality."

"It was a merry night," rejoined Chowles, who did not hear what she said, "a right merry night—and so to-night shall be, in spite of what is occurring overhead—ha! ha!"

And he took another long pull at the flask. "I breathe freely now." And he continued his wild flourishes until he was completely exhausted. He then sat down by Judith, and would have twined his bony arms round her neck, but she strongly repulsed him.

With a growl of displeasure, he then proceeded to open and examine the various bags, chests, and caskets piled upon the floor, and the sight of their contents so excited Judith, that, shaking off her misgivings, she joined him, and they continued opening case after case, glutting their greedy eyes, until Chowles became aware that the vault was filled with smoke. As soon as he perceived this, he started to his feet in terror.

"We are lost !—we shall be suffocated ! " he cried.

Judith likewise arose, and her looks showed that she shared in his apprehensions.

"We must not stay here," cried Chowles; "and yet," he added, with an agonised look at the rich store before him, "the treasure ! the treasure ! "

"Ay, let us, at least, take something with us," rejoined Judith, snatching up two or three of the most valuable caskets. While Chowles gazed at the heap before him, hesitating what to select, the smoke grew so dense around them, that Judith seized his arm and dragged him away.

"I come—I come ! " he cried, snatching up a bag of gold.

They then threaded the narrow passage, Judith leading the way and bearing the light. The smoke grew thicker and thicker as they advanced, but regardless of this, they hurried to the secret door leading to the charnel. Judith touched the spring, but as she did so, a sheet of flame burst in and drove her back. Chowles dashed past her, and with great presence of mind shut the door, excluding the flame. They then hastily retraced their steps, feeling that not a moment was to be lost if they would escape. The air in the vault, thickened by the smoke, had become so hot that they could scarcely breathe; added to which, to increase their terror, they heard the most awful cracking of the walls overhead, as if the whole fabric was breaking asunder to its foundation.

" The cathedral is tumbling upon us ! We shall be buried alive ! " exclaimed Chowles, as he listened with indescribable terror to the noise overhead.

" I owe my death to you, wretch ! " cried Judith, fiercely. " You persuaded me to come hither."

" I ! " cried Chowles. " It is a lie ! You were the person who proposed it. But for you I should have left our hoards here, and come for them after the fire was over."

" It is you who lie," returned Judith, with increased fury, " that was my proposal."

" Hold your tongue, you she-devil," cried Chowles, " it is you who have brought me into this strait—and if you do not cease taunting me, I will silence you for ever."

" Coward and fool ! " cried Judith, " I will at least have the satisfaction of seeing you die before me."

And as she spoke, she rushed towards him, and a desperate struggle commenced. And thus while the walls were cracking overhead, threatening them with instant destruction, the two wretches continued their strife, uttering the most horrible blasphemies and execrations. Judith, being the stronger of the two, had the advantage, and she had seized her opponent by the throat with the intention of strangling him, when a most terrific crash was heard, causing her to loose her grip. The air instantly became as hot as the breath of a furnace, and both started to their feet.

" What has happened ? " gasped Chowles.

" I know not," replied Judith, " and I dare not look down the passage."

" Then I will," replied Chowles, and he advanced a few paces up it, and then hastily returned, shrieking: " It is filled with boiling lead, and the stream is flowing towards us."

Scarcely able to credit the extent of the danger, Judith gazed down the passage, and there beheld a glowing silvery stream trickling slowly onwards. She saw too well, that if they could not effect their retreat instantly, their fate was sealed.

" The door of the vault ! " she cried, pointing towards it, " where is the key ? where is the key ? "

"I have not got it," replied Chowles, distractedly, "I cannot tell where to find it."

"Then we are lost!" cried Judith, with a terrible execration.

"Not so," replied Chowles, snatching up a pickaxe, "if I cannot unlock the door, I can break it open."

With this, he commenced furiously striking against it, while Judith, who was completely horror-stricken, and filled with the conviction that her last moments were at hand, fell on her knees beside him, and gazing down the passage, along which she could see the stream of molten lead, now nearly a foot in depth, gradually advancing, and hissing as it came, shrieked to Chowles to increase his exertions. He needed no incitement to do so, but nerved by fear, continued to deal blow after blow against the door, until at last he effected a small breach just above the lock. But this only showed him how vain were his hopes, for a stream of fire and smoke poured through the aperture. Notwithstanding this, he continued his exertions, Judith shrieking all the time, until the lock at last yielded. He then threw open the door, but finding the whole passage involved in flame, was obliged to close it. Judith had now risen, and their looks at each other at this fearful moment were terrible in the extreme. Retreating to either side of the cell, they glared at each other like wild beasts. Suddenly Judith casting her eyes to the entrance of the vault, uttered a yell of terror, that caused her companion to look in that direction, and he perceived that the stream of molten lead had gained it, and was descending the steps. He made a rush towards the door at the same time with Judith, and another struggle ensued, in which he succeeded in dashing her upon the floor. He again opened the door, but was again driven backwards by the terrific flame, and perceived that the fiery current had reached Judith, who was writhing and shrieking in its embrace. Before Chowles could again stir it was upon him. With a yell of anguish, he fell forward, and was instantly stifled in the glowing torrent, which in a short time flooded the whole chamber, burying the two partners in iniquity, and the whole of their ill-gotten gains, in its burning waves.

CHAPTER X

Conclusion

LORD ARGENTINE proceeded, as directed by the king, to
the eastern end of Tower-street, where he found Lord
Craven, and having delivered him the king's missive, and
shown him the signet, they proceeded to the western side
of the Tower-dock, and having procured a sufficient number
of miners and engineers, together with a supply of powder
from the fortress, commenced undermining the whole of
the row of habitations called Tower-bank, on the edge of
the dock, having first, it is scarcely necessary to state, taken
care to clear them of their inhabitants. The powder deposited, the trains were fired, and the buildings blown into
the air. At this time the whole of the western side of the
tower moat was covered with low wooden houses and sheds,
and mindful of the king's instructions, Lord Argentine suggested to Lord Craven that they should be destroyed.
The latter acquiescing, they proceeded to their task, and
in a short time the whole of the buildings of whatever description, from the bulwark-gate to the city postern, at the
north of the Tower, and nearly opposite the Bowyer
Tower, were destroyed. Long before this was accomplished they were joined by the Duke of York, who lent his
utmost assistance to the task, and when night came on,
a clear space of at least a hundred yards in depth, had been
formed between the ancient fortress and the danger with
which it was threatened.

Meantime the conflagration continued to rage with un-
abated fury. It burnt throughout the whole of Monday
night, and having destroyed Saint Paul's, as before related,
poured down Ludgate-hill, consuming all in its way, and
crossing Fleet-bridge, commenced its ravages upon the
great thoroughfare adjoining it.

On Tuesday an immense tract was on fire. All Fleet-
street, as far as the Inner Temple, Ludgate-hill, and the
whole of the city eastwards, along the banks of the Thames,

up to the Tower-dock, where the devastation was checked
by the vast gap of houses demolished, were in flames.
From thence the boundary of the fire extented to the end
of Mark-lane, Lime-street, and Leadenhall, the strong
walls of which resisted its fury. Ascending again by the
Standard on Cornhill, Thread-needle-street, and Austin-
friars, it embraced Drapers' Hall, and the whole mass of
buildings to the west of Throgmorton-street. It next proceeded to the then new buildings behind Saint Margaret's,
Lothbury, and so on westward to the upper end of
Cateaton-street, whence it spread to the second postern in
London-wall, and destroying the ramparts and suburbs as
far as Cripplegate, consumed Little Wood-street, Mungwell-
street, and the whole of the city wall on the west as far as
Aldersgate. Passing a little to the north of Saint Sepulchre's,
which it destroyed, it crossed Holborn-bridge, and ascending Saint Andrew's-hill, passed the end of Shoe-lane, and
so on to the end of Fetter-lane. The whole of the buildings
contained within this boundary were now on fire, and burning with terrific fury. And so they continued till the middle
of Wednesday, when the wind abating, and an immense
quantity of houses being demolished according to Lord
Argentine's plan, the conflagration was got under; and
though it broke out in several places after that time, little
mischief was done, and it may be said to have ceased on
the middle of that day.

On Saturday morning in that week, soon after daybreak,
a young man, plainly yet richly attired in the habiliments
then worn by persons of high rank, took his way over the
smouldering heaps of rubbish, and along the ranks of
ruined and blackened walls denoting the habitations that
had once constituted Fleet-street. It was with no little
risk, and some difficulty, that he could force his way, now
clambering over heaps of smouldering ashes, now passing
by some toppling wall, which fell with a terrific crash after
he had just passed it—now creeping under an immense
pile of blackened rafters—but he at length reached Fleet-
bridge, where he paused to gaze at the scene of devastation
around him. It was indeed a melancholy sight, and drew
tears to his eyes. The ravages of the fire were almost incon-

ceivable. Great beams were burnt to charcoal—stones
calcined, and as white as snow, and such walls and towers
as were left standing were so damaged, that their instant
fall was to be expected. The very water in the wells and
fountains was boiling, and even the muddy Fleet sent forth
a hot steam. The fire still lingered in the lower parts of
many habitations, especially where wine, spirits, or inflammable goods had been kept; and these " voragos of
subterranean cellars," as Evelyn terms them, still emitted
flames, together with a prodigious smoke and stench.
Undismayed by the dangers of the path he had to traverse,
the young man ascended Ludgate-hill, still encountering
the same devastation, and passing through the ruined gateway, the end of which remained perfect, approached what
had once been Saint Paul's Cathedral. Mounting a heap
of rubbish at the end of Ludgate-street, he gazed at the
mighty ruin, which looked more like the remains of a city
than those of a single edifice.

The solid walls and buttresses were split and rent
asunder; enormous stones were splintered and calcined
by the heat; and vast flakes having scaled from off the
pillars, gave them a hoary and almost ghostly appearance.
Its enormous extent was now for the first time clearly seen,
and strange to say, it looked twice as large in ruins as when
entire. The central tower was still standing—but chipped,
broken, and calcined, like the rest of the structure, by the
vehement heat of the flames. Part of the roof in its fall
broke through the solid floor of the choir, which was of
immense thickness, into Saint Faith's, and destroyed the
magazine of books and paper deposited there by the booksellers. The portico, erected by Inigo Jones, and which
found so much favour in Evelyn's eyes, that he describes
it as " comparable to any in Europe," and particularly de-
plores its loss, shared the fate of the rest of the building,
—the only part left uninjured being the architrave, the inscription on which was undefaced.

Having satiated himself with this sad but striking prospect, the young man, with some toil and trouble, crossed
the churchyard, and gained Cheapside, where a yet more
terrific scene of devastation than that which he had previ-

ously witnessed burst upon him. On the right to London-bridge, which he could discern through the chasms of the houses, and almost to the Tower, were nothing but ruins, while a similar waste lay on the left. Such was the terrible change that had been wrought in the aspect of the ruined city, that if the young man had not had some marks to guide him, he would not have known where he was. The tower and ruined walls of Saint Peter's church pointed out to him the entrance to Wood-street, and entering it, he traversed it with considerable difficulty,—for the narrow thoroughfares were much fuller of rubbish, and much less freed from smoke and fiery vapour, than the wider,—until he reached a part of it with which he had once been well acquainted. But, alas! how changed was that familiar spot. The house he sought was a mere heap of ruins. While gazing at them, he heard a voice behind him, and turning, beheld Mr. Bloundel and his son Stephen, forcing their way through what once had been Maiden-lane. A warm greeting passed between them, and Mr. Bloundel gazed for some time in silence upon the wreck of his dwelling. Tears forced themselves into his eyes, and his companions were no less moved. As he turned to depart, he observed to the young man, with some severity, " How is it, Leonard, that I see you in this gay apparel? Surely, the present is not a fitting season for such idle display."

Lord Argentine, for such it was, now explained to the wonder-stricken grocer all that had occurred to him, adding that he had intended coming to him that very day, if he had not been thus anticipated, to give him the present explanation.

" And where are Farmer Wingfield and Blaize? " asked Mr. Bloundel. " We have been extremely uneasy at your prolonged absence."

" They are both at the palace," replied Lord Argentine, " and have both been laid up with slight injuries received during the conflagration, but I believe—nay, I am sure, they will get out to-day."

" That is well," replied Mr. Bloundel—" and now let me congratulate you, Leonard—that is, my lord—how strange such a title sounds!—on your new dignity."

" And accept my congratulations, too, my lord," said Stephen.

" Oh ! do not style me thus," said Argentine. " With you, at least, let me be ever Leonard Holt."

" You are still my old apprentice, I see," cried the grocer, warmly grasping his hand.

" And such I shall ever continue in feeling," returned the other, cordially returning the pressure.

Three days after this, Lord Argentine was united to the Lady Isabella—the king, as he had promised, giving away the bride. The Earl of Rochester was present, together with the grocer and his wife, and the whole of their family. Another marriage also took place on the same day between Blaize and Patience. Both unions, it is satisfactory to be able to state, were extremely happy, though it would be uncandid not to mention, that in the latter case, to use a homely but expressive phrase, " the grey mare proved the better horse." Blaize, however, was exceedingly content under his government. He settled at Willesden with his wife, where they lived to a good old age, and where some of his descendants may still be found.

Mr. Bloundel sustained only a trifling loss by the fire. Another house was erected on the site of the old habitation, where he carried on his business as respectably and as profitably as before, until, in the course of nature, he was gathered to his fathers, and succeeded by his son Stephen, leaving an unblemished character behind him as a legacy to his family. Nor was it his only legacy, in a worldly sense, for his time had not been misspent, and he had well husbanded his money. All his family turned out well, and were successful in the world. Stephen rose to the highest civic dignities, and the younger obtained great distinction. Their daughter Christiana became Lady Argentine, being wedded to the eldest son of the baron and baroness.

Mike Macascree, the piper, and Bell, found a happy asylum with the same noble family.

As to Lord and Lady Argentine, theirs was a life of uninterrupted happiness. Devotedly attached to her lord, the Lady Isabella seemed only to live for him, and he well repaid her affection. By sedulously cultivating his talents and powers, which were considerable, he was enabled to reflect credit upon the high rank to which it had pleased a grateful sovereign to elevate him. He lived to see the new cathedral completed by Sir Christopher Wren, and often visited it with feelings of admiration, but never with the same sentiments of veneration and awe that he had experienced, when, in times long gone by, he had repaired to OLD SAINT PAUL'S.

Lightning Source UK Ltd.
Milton Keynes UK
UKOW051709100812

197350UK00001B/36/A